CLANCY'S
CROSSING

CLANCY'S
CROSSING

EVAN GREEN

MACMILLAN

Pan Macmillan Australia

First published 1995 in Macmillan by Pan Macmillan Australia Pty Limited
St Martins Tower, 31 Market Street, Sydney

National Library of Australia
cataloguing-in-publication data:

Green, Evan.
Clancy's crossing.
ISBN 0 7329 0834 5.
I. Title.
A823.3

Typeset in 12/14pt Garamond by Post Typesetters, Brisbane
Printed in Australia by Australian Print Group

*For Yolanta as always
and our children, Mitieli and Ellia*

ACKNOWLEDGEMENTS

With special thanks to two people for their help in guiding this work towards historical accuracy.

First, my aunt, Lesley Harwin, for many years secretary, curator and historical researcher of the Parramatta Historical Society and encyclopaedic in her knowledge of the era and much of the area covered in this story. Her invaluable assistance was given with love and enthusiasm.

Second, to Captain Stan Brown, former commander of the Fijian Navy—now a historian specialising in military and naval matters—whose contributions regarding the extraordinary career of Lord Thomas Cochrane were particularly valuable.

Part One

ONE

On the Hawkesbury River in the Colony of New South Wales February 1798

I T WAS A hot night and the mosquitoes were fierce and Clancy Fitzgerald's ankle hurt. The cut was festering and the sharp edge of the leg iron was digging into it. Old Jenkins had done the damage. He hadn't meant to, but Jenkins was always doing things he didn't mean to do. He had been staggering under the weight of a sandstone block that only Macaulay should have tried to lift and he'd tripped and dragged his chain around Clancy's leg, setting its links snapping for blood as viciously as one of the hounds. A shackle's jagged edge had laid the ankle open to the bone. Not the old man's fault. He was too doddery to be carrying those weights but everyone had to work in this gang, even if you were over fifty, like Jenkins, and your fingers were bent from arthritis and mangled from dropping too many stones.

Clancy reached down to ease the metal band away from the cut. He hated the chains. He reckoned he could put up with the work and the food but the chains would drive him mad long before these last four years were up. It was not merely that they were heavy and they hurt; they offended his dignity. They made him feel like a tethered animal, to be moved only at the whim of its master.

The guard was asleep. The man was supposed to be watching them but Clancy could see him slumped against a tree trunk with his gun propped between his knees. The others were in the

3

bark hut. Earlier in the night the soldiers had drunk rum while carousing with the women they'd dragged from the compound. Some of the women had laughed. Some screamed. Now the men were snoring loudly, making the hut drone like a sawmill.

A mosquito bit the back of Clancy's hand and he slapped at it, setting the metal links jangling. Macaulay, lying next to him, nudged him in the ribs. 'Don't make too much noise, now,' the big man whispered.

'Sorry. Mosquito.' Both stared at the guard under the tree but the man didn't move.

Macaulay squirmed forward, nursing his chain as if it were a sleeping baby, and peered up at the clouds scudding across the moon. 'I reckon in another hour. The moon'll be gone by then.'

'I'm ready.'

'Good lad. It's a perfect night for it.'

'Yes.'

'Still game?'

'Yes.' And he'd see it through, even if it meant being shot on the run. He'd sworn that he'd die rather than be put back in chains—but he was only twenty-six, an age when men make themselves rash promises.

One of the men coughed and rolled over and a few bodies moved in the straw and the chain linking them made a tinkling sound.

Macaulay gazed towards the hills, which glowed a ghostly violet in the last of the moonlight. 'You're sure you know the way?'

'No one knows the way,' Clancy said, his voice as sharp as a whisper would allow.

'But you went with Tench.'

'That was a long time ago. And we didn't find the way over.'

'But you went further than anyone else.'

They'd had this discussion before. Macaulay dreamed of a paradise beyond the mountains. 'At least you can find the way you went with Tench,' he persisted.

4

'I think so.' What did it matter? They'd go as far as they could. The country was wild with plenty of hiding places. He'd seen caves in the sandstone cliffs.

Macaulay made a low, rumbling noise, as if trying to restructure a forgotten melody. Clancy recognised the sound. The big man was fantasising again, thinking of the country they would find once they'd crossed the mountains.

Before them, some men had escaped and tried to find a way through the maze of valleys and cliffs that lay to the west of the river. Most had been caught or had staggered back, scratched and starving and glad to exchange a bowl of gruel for the lash, but some hadn't returned and their disappearance had started the rumours. Over the mountains, where no soldier had been, was a paradise on earth. That's what the lads said. Some reckoned it was the way to China.

Clancy didn't believe the stories because, like death, no one had ever come back to tell.

Macaulay believed. It was what kept him alive and sane. Almost sane, Clancy corrected himself. All the men in the gang were a little crazy.

'We're all mad and we're already dead,' was how Noxious Watts put it. He reckoned this camp was a stop on the road to hell. He called the Nepean the Styx and Johnson, the head guard, the Devil's apprentice. Watts read a lot, or had in the days when he had access to books, and said the more he learned, the more he believed in nothing. Well, nothing good. He was the sort of man who would wake to a brilliant dawn and curse God for trying to deceive him about the forthcoming horrors of the day.

Clancy eased the iron band away from the cut and lay back to rest. They had an hour to wait. He closed his eyes.

He might have been a thief but Clancy Fitzgerald thought of himself as a fair man, honest in his opinions about things. For instance, about this country: he despised it. His feelings, he liked to assure himself, weren't because of the cruelty or the hardship he'd known from the moment when, as a youth, he'd climbed down the ladder into a longboat in Sydney Cove and got a cuff across the ear for putting his foot in the wrong place, but because this wretched land was so wrong. So different to England. For one thing, absurdly, the seasons were reversed. December was blisteringly hot and June was not the balmy month it should have been but a time of cold winds and bleak nights.

He missed the green, rolling hills of Somerset.

From Sydney Town to the Hawkesbury River the land was worn and dry and dusty. Good rain hadn't fallen for a couple of years with the result that the crops had failed, the grass was the colour of sand and the leaves of the trees—such strange trees—hung limp in the heat. Every step on the eight-hour march to the river had stirred up dust. Old Jenkins, who walked at the back, had coughed all the way. And it was so unbearably hot—much hotter than he'd ever experienced except for those terrible days when they were sailing down the African coast—that he understood what Noxious Watts's oft-repeated version of hell would be like.

It would be like New South Wales.

The blacks who lived here were the most miserable people he had seen. They were skinny, with legs that looked like finely whittled sticks, and they had rotund paunches that seemed gross on such thin bodies. Their hair was matted and they had beetle brows that squeezed their eyes into dark slits. And some of the men stood with one leg up, like a stork, and they'd stay like that, watching you for hours. Some people said they stank but no black stank worse than his fellow convicts so Clancy couldn't criticise them for that. But they were sub-human. Everyone said so.

Clancy liked birds and used to keep birds back home when he was a boy, but here, the birds were different. They didn't sing the melodic, trilling songs of English birds, but made sharp, aggressive noises. Some had wonderful colours but they squawked. And the one they called the Hawkesbury Clock, the one that looked like a kingfisher and roused everyone before dawn with its raucous cry, laughed. Not a friendly laugh but a mocking sound.

He missed his beautiful birds. He wondered if his sister had fed them or opened the cage and let them go. Not that it mattered. Either way, they'd be long dead.

His stomach ached from hunger and he laid his arms across his belly. Everyone was hungry, even the soldiers and the free settlers who were trying to grow crops along the river. What they needed were some farmers. The crops were failing, not just because of the drought and the reversed seasons but because there was almost no one in the colony who knew how to grow things. The few 'farmers' were usually military men who'd been given land grants and they knew as much about farming as he knew about watchmaking. Which was nothing. He'd been good at stealing watches, not making them.

He opened his eyes. A wash of pale moonlight illuminated the walls of the granary they were building. The site was surrounded by trees. Such alien trees. They turned grey in summer and shed their bark in great coils. They were not stout trees, swathed in green like the English oak, but gaunt and emaciated things, like the men chained together in the crude shelter made from the trees' cast-off bark.

He thought of his sister.

She was all he had. She would be twenty-two now but he hadn't seen her since she was twelve. Married? Maybe, and with children. There'd been no suitor when he was around but he'd frightened boys away. He'd been a wild one, feared by the youngsters in the village. He was trying to protect his sister, that was all. Keep the undesirables away. He laughed at that. He'd been the most undesirable youth in the district.

Charlotte could be dead. People died young, even when they weren't in chains. Plenty of young ones had died when the plague swept through the village. He hadn't heard from Charlotte, not in ten years. That was the hardest thing: the sense of being so isolated. She was in England, if she were still alive, and he might just as well be on the moon.

He twisted around, taking care to cradle the long chain in his arms. The moon was slipping behind the hills.

She crawled around the inside of the hut, searching for the scattered pieces of her clothing, taking care not to wake one of the soldiers or trip over one of the whores who were sleeping with their skirts still raised and their legs obscenely bent among the tangle of boots and lowered trousers.

One lantern was still burning and, aided by its faint light, she found everything, even the boots which the red-haired man had thrown against the wall. The blouse was torn but she could mend that. She would like to kill the man who had done this to her but what was the point? Others had done it before, one on only her third night ashore, and other men would do it again. That was to be her life from now on. She was the plaything of the soldiers, to be used by day and abused by night.

As she buttoned up her skirt, she thought it would be easier, better, to kill herself. It wasn't a new thought and it didn't last long because she'd been brought up by a religious aunt who had terrified her with stories of fire and brimstone and eternal damnation, and the frightful images of what happened to suicides were still vivid. Besides, taking one of the soldiers' bayonets and stabbing herself through the heart or cutting her throat would be both painful and disgustingly messy. And she was afraid of dying. She didn't like this life but she was terrified of what might lie beyond.

She was almost dressed when a thought struck her. She was free to leave. No one had taken her back to the compound. When he'd discarded her, the red-haired man had gone after that dreadful slut Sal Tully but, within minutes, had collapsed in a drunken stupor. The other guards were all snoring and farting and dead to the world. She could walk out, go where she pleased.

Until daylight. They'd find her in daylight and whip her and maybe send her down to Van Diemen's Land or off to Norfolk Island. She was terrified of those places which, in her mind, were as vivid as her images of hell.

Eliza Phillips crept towards the door, stepping over bodies, pausing when someone moved and having time to reflect that life offered her few choices and that none of them was good. She was twenty-two but felt old. She hadn't seen herself in a mirror for months, not since the time she was working for Lieutenant Moore's wife at Rose Hill and had glanced in the bedroom mirror and not recognised the worn creature who stared back. Sunken eyes, lined face, terrible colour. Like her aunt had looked before she died.

Eliza felt sure she would die young. Some of the guards, especially the brutes out here on the limits of the colony, had a habit of bashing their women after they'd had enough and there were a couple of sadists who'd killed. One had been hanged but that didn't bring the poor girl back from her grave.

No, if she stayed she'd be raped every other night and, one night, some drunken brute would bash her brains in. She'd leave now and take her chances.

As she reached the door, Eliza remembered there would be a guard outside. The moon was dipping below the hills but there was enough light to see him near the shelter where the male convicts were kept for the night. It was the young, thin one with the terrible pockmarks on his face. He was sitting down, leaning against a tree and not moving. She watched him for a full minute. He was asleep.

Treading with great care she circled around the hut, past the pile of cut sandstone, and headed for the river. She didn't want to cross it. She couldn't swim and, in any case, there was nothing on the other side but wild unexplored country where the blacks lived.

She felt sinfully unclean. She would go to the river and bathe and decide what to do.

TWO

MACAULAY'S BREATH STANK of rotten food and bad teeth. 'Lad,' he whispered once more, so close his beard brushed Clancy's cheek, 'it's time.' Clancy had been asleep. Reeling from the ghastly smell, he jerked his hands away from the other man. The shackles rattled.

Macaulay grabbed his wrist and pulled him close. 'Don't move.' He waited until Clancy was fully awake and as motionless as he was. 'We don't want you rousing that young lad over there now, do we?' Faces pressed together, both men stared towards the tree where the guard slept. With the moon gone, the man was hard to distinguish; one low shadow in a jumble of dark and indistinct shapes.

'He's sleeping like a baby,' Macaulay said eventually and belched. Clancy almost fainted. The big man raised both his legs, to indicate he was off the chain. 'I'll have you clear in just a moment. Don't make a noise.'

Macaulay was the last man on the line. He'd slept in that position for four nights, having nearly broken tough little Ned Corcoran's arm. Corcoran had sworn and scratched and spat at him before being persuaded to change places. Now Macaulay began to pull the short end of the chain across his lap.

'Give me your feet. Quiet as you can.'

Clancy edged his legs towards Macaulay. The man was a

marvel. No one else in the gang had the strength to uproot the metal stake that anchored the line. Or to have done it in silence. 'I can't believe it,' Clancy whispered. 'You got it loose.'

'Perseverance, lad. Just perseverance.' Clancy couldn't see Macaulay's face, but he was sure he winked. Macaulay had a twitch in one eye and was always winking. He'd taken a few beatings until the guards realised it was a nervous mannerism and no more insolent than a hiccup. 'I've been working on it every night. Little by little. My old dad used to say that was the way to get big jobs done. Little by little.'

With a delicacy that was surprising in such a massively built man, Macaulay began to pass the chain through the coupling that secured Clancy's ankles, fondling each link like a miser lovingly counting his gold. Like Macaulay, Clancy was still manacled, hand to hand and foot to foot, and as the other man worked at removing the chain that bound them to the others, doubt began to spread within him. 'How are we going to move like this?' he said, rattling the manacles around his wrists. The question needed an urgent reply. Not only did he not know the answer, he hadn't bothered with the question until this moment.

Clancy had gone along with Macaulay's plan to escape for two reasons: to impress the big man with his boldness, for Clancy liked to impress people, and because he didn't believe the naive Macaulay could make his scheme work. It was a wild dream, good for passing otherwise miserable hours with fantasies about the land on the other side of the mountains and good for exchanging tight-lipped whispers about the rivers and valleys he'd seen with Watkin Tench, but no more than that.

And now they were off the chain.

Clancy began to sweat. He'd thought only of where they might go, not of how they would accomplish the life-or-death journey that faced them. They must move silently, cross the river without drowning—neither man could swim—and make their way through thick, virtually unexplored bush with no food and with heavy bands of iron linking their wrists and ankles. Then find a path no one had ever discovered and keep ahead of the soldiers and their baying pack of hounds. Impossible.

'Macaulay,' he said in a voice made fragile by fear, 'how are we going to get away, hobbled like this? They've got dogs. They'll catch us.'

Having pulled the last link through, Macaulay grasped the metal stake with both hands. He winked, slowly and deliberately. 'You leave that to me,' he said and crawled from beneath the shelter's low roof. Slowly, like a bear emerging from hibernation, he stood up.

At the other end of the line, Noxious Watts raised his head. He spoke in the urgent, furtive hiss of convicts. 'What are you up to?'

Brandishing the stake like a gun with bayonet attached, Macaulay shuffled up to Watts. He bent low. 'None of your business.'

'You won't get away.'

'You make one noise and I'll do you in.'

Having long ago decided he was as good as dead, Watts was not intimidated. 'Who are you taking with you?'

Macaulay let the tip of the stake touch Watts's bald skull. 'Not you.'

'They'll catch you.'

Macaulay tapped Watts on the head. 'Not if you keep your mouth shut.' He tapped again, with sufficient force to make Watts bare his teeth in a defiant snarl, and turned away to rejoin Clancy.

'They'll have you back here by noon and strung up at dawn.' Watts lay down, as if no longer interested. 'You couldn't talk me into going with you, not if you tried.'

Over his shoulder, Macaulay shoved a derogatory finger in the air. He shuffled back to the waiting Clancy.

'Is everything all right?'

'Good as gold. Old Noxious was just being his usual happy self. It's a shame he wasn't able to talk when his mother gave birth or he could have told her she'd made a terrible mistake.' He gripped Clancy's elbow. 'You go down to the river. You know the place. I'll meet you there.'

'What are you going to do?'

Macaulay winked and raised his manacles. 'I know where the keys are.'

Eliza Phillips had found a place where the water was shallow and calm, being protected from the rush of the current by the trunk of a fallen tree. She removed all her clothes, arranged them neatly on the bank—first the bonnet and the boots, then the chemise, the dress of coarse Indian cotton, the slip, singlet, pants and white stockings—and stepped warily into the river. She sat down.

The great eucalypts lining the bank formed monstrous shapes and she imagined fearful creatures in every gnarled trunk and grasping limb. The river made urgent, gurgling noises. At first she thought they were the sounds of soldiers and the ravenous hounds they used to hunt escapees, but after a while, when the noises were constant and the shapes around her became more distinct, she relaxed and lowered herself into the water. She lay back, little by little until her shoulders touched the pebbly bottom.

She was afraid of water. When she was only seven, she'd seen her young sister drown in a millrace and that was a nightmare that haunted her, but on this summer's night, with cool water lapping her body and with lacy clouds flitting across the stars and with the chirp of insects making the air throb, Eliza was feeling light-headed. Even daring. She had actually run away from that vile camp. She leaned back and put her hair in the water. Then she immersed the back of her head until only her face was exposed.

Like all the convict women, her hair was cut short because of lice and she scratched her scalp vigorously. She sat up and shook her head. Amazed at her new-found courage, she lay back and put her whole head under the water. With one hand clasping her nose and the other raking her scalp, she stayed underwater for a full three seconds. It was a delicious sensation.

She sat up, spluttering but feeling wonderfully clean. It was as though the river had washed away all filth and sin. Like a Catholic after confession, she supposed. She'd only heard about confession a few weeks ago and was fascinated by it. Sheilagh Donaghy had rambled on about confession when she was tossing and delirious, before dying of the fever. Such a strange concept. You told someone of your every bad deed and thought and that someone, a priest, a mortal man dressed in fancy robes, took upon himself the powers of God to forgive you.

How could that be? A priest was just a man and, as her aunt had constantly reminded her, a particularly wicked one, being an agent of the Pope and the Devil, which was the same thing. If her aunt saw a priest coming towards her she would hurriedly cross to the other side of the road. She'd talked a lot about the evils of priests and the Catholic Church but she'd never told Eliza about confession.

Eliza was frightened of priests and suspicious of Catholics but she'd liked Sheilagh Donaghy. Sheilagh spoke in a funny voice and believed in some weird things but that was understandable because she was Irish. She was good-hearted, though, and always kind to Eliza, which made her a rare person. Sheilagh had left two children behind in whatever town it was she'd come from. She'd stolen food for them, or so she said. You could never be sure what the convicts had done. They were always making excuses for being transported. Most were liars.

On outstretched arms and legs, Eliza slithered crablike to a deeper hole where the bottom was sandy and the water flowed at a gentle pace. There, she crouched low, allowing the current to curl over her shoulders. She rubbed her arms gently, relishing the sensuous, soothing touch of the river.

She hurt in a few places. The red-haired guard had bruised her ribs and her legs and put long scratches across her back. She was massaging the bruise on one leg when she heard a noise. It was a stick snapping. Then another. Someone was coming. They're searching for me already, she thought, and sat up, covering her mouth to stifle the grunts of panic rising in her throat. Another noise, a scraping sound. It came from the bank, near where she had left her clothes, and with that new sound she became conscious of her nakedness. If she stayed where she was and didn't move she might not be seen, but if they found her she'd be in a shameful state of undress. Yet if she tried to get her clothes she'd make so much noise, splashing and scrambling through the shallows, they'd almost certainly hear her.

Her years of puritanical upbringing triumphed and she rushed for the bank and her clothes.

Clancy thought it was a dog charging through the water and, unable to control himself, yelped in fright. He had been bent low, carrying the leg chain to ease his way through the bush, but now he dropped it and stood up. He could make out a dark shape splashing towards him. He wouldn't run. He'd stand and fight, use the chain to strangle the first dog, lash out with the manacles when the other dogs dragged him down . . .

The noise stopped. There were no dogs. He could see a figure, someone bending low at the river bank, frantically picking up things.

He crept forward, still holding his hands wide apart so that the chain between them was both a barrier and a weapon. 'Macaulay?' It was a whisper, made coarse by hope.

The other person stopped moving. Each peered into the darkness, trying to distinguish the other. Neither made a sound.

16

Clancy moved closer. 'Who is it?'

'You're not a soldier?' It was a woman's voice.

'Not me.' He sat down, exhausted now the fear had gone, and felt his ankle. It was bleeding again. 'What are you doing here?'

'Don't come any closer.'

'You shouldn't be here.'

'Neither should you.'

'Don't be saucy. What are you up to?'

'Turn your back. Please.'

He could see now that she was standing in the water and holding things against her chest. He felt like laughing.

'Were you washing yourself?'

'And why not?'

He did laugh, so softly the sound scarcely reached her. 'It's after midnight and you shouldn't be here.'

'And you should, I suppose?'

'What are you doing?'

'That's none of your business. Please turn around. I have to get dressed.'

No dogs. No guards. Just a woman who, somehow, had sneaked out of the camp to bathe. It was ridiculous. She was risking so much to clean herself when, tomorrow, she'd be as dirty as ever. He sat and covered his eyes. 'Go ahead. Put your clothes on. And take care when you go sneaking back. I don't want you raising the alarm.'

'I'm not sneaking back.'

He became agitated. 'You're running away?'

'I'm not going back.'

How like a woman, or what he remembered of their ways. 'That's the same thing,' he said, irritated now. The guard at the female compound might notice her missing and raise the alarm before Macaulay and he could cross the river. They'd search for her and find them all.

17

'Where are you making for?'

She didn't answer. She was getting dressed. He could see her in vague silhouette, bending and lifting one leg after another. He hadn't seen a woman dress for a long time, even in shadows, and old memories stirred within him. Gruffly, he said, 'Don't tell me you don't know where you're heading for?'

'I'm just going away.'

He grunted in disgust. She couldn't have done this tomorrow night. No, it had to be the same night he and Macaulay made their break. She'd even come to their chosen place at the river where the water was no more than shoulder deep and a bold man might walk across. 'And you have no destination in mind?'

'I wouldn't be telling you if I did.' She was not bending any more but seemed to be adjusting her blouse. 'Have you escaped?'

'No. I do this every night. I like it down here.'

She believed him. 'You're mad. If they found you . . .'

He was growing impatient. 'Look, if you're all dressed and a decent woman again, why don't you just go somewhere, very quiet like, and hide until morning?'

'So they'll find me?'

'You could say you walked in your sleep. That's if you don't go too far from the camp.'

From somewhere in the distance, a man called out. It was a cry of distress.

'What was that?' she said.

Wild fears coursed through him. 'I have a friend . . .'

'There are two of you? Where's you friend?'

'I'm not sure. We were to meet . . .'

From farther away came a cry which generated a chorus of faint shouts.

They could hear another noise now. Close to them, someone was crashing through the bush, running clumsily, unevenly. The sounds advanced: the snap of timber, the crunch of bushes

18

being flattened, the raucous panting of someone desperately short of breath.

'Who's that?' she said.

Clancy knew. Only one person would be bolting for the river.

The running noises stopped with a sickening thud, followed by a rattle of branches and a loud, male groan.

'Clancy, where are you?' Macaulay's voice was a wail of misery.

'Here.' Clancy was shaking now.

Macaulay staggered into the clearing. One hand was pressed against his forehead. From the other, he jangled a set of keys. 'They're after us. Quick, give me your legs.'

Clancy sat down. There were more distant shouts and a volley of barking while Macaulay fumbled to find the right key. Blood dripped from his forehead and he kept wiping his eyes.

'You're hurt.'

'I think I knocked a tree down. By the Holy Jesus it hurt.' He wiped his face. 'I can't see proper.'

'What happened? What's all the noise?'

'They must have found Johnson.'

Found Johnson? Clancy had difficulty drawing his next breath. What had this great ox done?

With a clunking sound, one metal band opened its jaws.

'Take your leg out, man.'

Clancy shook his ankle free. All he could say was, 'Johnson?'

Macaulay winked. 'That's one son of a poxy whorehouse bitch that won't be whipping no one else.' He saw Eliza and jumped up. 'Who's that?'

'Did you kill Johnson?'

Macaulay brandished the big key like a knife. 'I said who's over there?'

Clancy tugged at the torn cuff of the other man's trousers. 'A woman. Forget her. Sit down and finish the job.'

Macaulay wiped his face. 'What's she doing here?'

'Washing herself.'

Eliza made a shooshing sound and said, 'They're coming,' and they listened. There was more shouting. High-pitched, angry voices. Dogs barking.

'They're getting the pack.' Macaulay made a whimpering noise.

Clancy rattled the leg iron. 'Get this off me.'

Macaulay was dancing a dithery, indecisive hop, glancing first towards the river, then back into the bush.

'The keys, Macaulay, the keys.'

There was another shout. 'This way,' a strong voice commanded. The barking of the dogs rose a pitch.

'They're letting them loose,' Macaulay said.

'Over here.' It was another, closer voice and the dogs seemed to bark in unison.

Macaulay threw the keys which bounced off Clancy's chest. 'Do it yourself,' he said and ran for the river. He pushed aside the girl, sending her spinning to the grass, and waded into the water.

On his hands and knees, frantically searching for the keys, Clancy called out to Macaulay, 'You bastard, what did you do to Johnson?'

The question seemed to calm Macaulay who, knee-deep in the water, stopped and turned. 'I put the stake through his throat. It was a pretty sight.' With a laugh and with his arms pumping the air, he set off again to wade to the far bank.

Eliza was beside Clancy. She gripped his arm. 'If I help you, will you take me with you?'

'I can't find the keys.'

The dogs were closer and Clancy, in a frenzy of lunging and grasping, scratched at weeds and sticks and stones but couldn't find the keys.

She found them. 'Give me your leg.' She had the iron band

off in seconds. 'Now, you promised to take me with you.'

He pushed her away and, awkwardly, got to his feet. 'I never did.'

She dangled the keys. 'Would you like your hands to be free or not?'

A man shouted and they could see the glow from a lantern. Clancy found it hard to walk without chains and he limped into the shallows. Macaulay was almost halfway across. Only the man's head and shoulders showed, rippling shadows in the flow of water.

Some guards, straining to hold hounds on the leash, became entangled in the bushes or fell over logs and there was a flood of oaths.

'You're going to need free hands,' she said, speaking only a little faster than normal. Keeping up with him, she held the keys high. 'You won't get far like that.'

'Give me the keys.'

'No.' She splashed out of range.

'I can't wait and play your silly games.' Head ringing with the baying of the pack, Clancy waded into deeper water. 'You keep up with me. I'm not waiting for you.'

She put the keys down her blouse and followed him.

THREE

BEING UNABLE TO sleep, Lieutenant Quinton de Lacey had been reading for several hours. At first he'd read from his leather-bound, illuminated edition of Homer's *Odyssey*—in Greek, of course—and then from the simple wood-and-leather-covered Bible his mother had given him, with its loving, pious inscription. He was only twenty-eight but already needed a magnifying glass to read, even with two candles close to the pillow. The flames sent long shadows across the roof and walls of the tent and when he grew tired of reading he would watch the dark, wavering shapes, and think.

The lieutenant was a rarity among the members of the New South Wales Corps in that he'd wanted to sail to Port Jackson. Blinded by patriotism and cocooned by xenophobia, de Lacey had another attribute much admired in an officer: he was impelled by a sense of duty. Although he thought most physical punishment barbaric, he'd have men flogged if that's what the rules required. Only the week before in Sydney Town, he'd ordered a hundred strokes for a convict who'd sworn at an officer. He'd watched the administration of the first seventy-three, which was when the man collapsed, and been back two days later to see the final twenty-seven lashes delivered. He hated the whole business, but duty was paramount.

As a boy, he had been shamed when England lost its

American colonies. Defeated in a badly run war against rene-
gade Englishmen! And not even by soldiers but by traitorous
civilians! Well, England would lose no more wars. He and his
friends had made that vow although his friends, coming from
wealthier and more influential families, had eventually bought
commissions in elite military regiments and stayed home.

He had been prepared to travel to the ends of the earth and,
having made the journey, was now acting as caretaker to Mother
England's overflow of scum.

Never mind. Men were judged by the way they did difficult,
unsavoury tasks. He would serve his time, have an unblemished
record, win praise, gain seniority. And possibly do great things,
because there were great things to be done here. New South
Wales and New Holland—surely two halves that formed one
island, although this was yet to be proved—were virgin lands,
huge in size yet unexplored. No one—English, Dutch, Spanish
or Portuguese—knew what lay beyond the daunting coastline.
He dreamed of making great journeys of discovery and was
excited; just as Ulysses had been when he set sail from Troy.

He closed his Bible and, in the shadows flickering across the
canvas, the lieutenant imagined the ripple of unknown streams,
the peaks of mysterious mountains, the faces of an unseen race of
people. Perhaps he would discover as much gold as Pizarro found
in Peru or return with the manifold riches that the Venetian,
Marco Polo, had brought from Cathay. Who knew what lay
beyond the mountains? The country was ready for exploration
and ripe for exploitation—which, in his eyes, made it a preferable
possession to a land peopled by white traitors and feathered savages. Let the rebels keep the Atlantic colonies and consort with
their allies, the damned French and the heathen redskins.
England was on its way to possessing the greatest, richest, most
far-flung empire the world had ever known and he would play a
part in its wondrous growth. A significant part, he hoped.

23

He was about to extinguish the candles when he heard the commotion. At first he ignored it, hoping it was just some drunken brawl, but when the dogs began barking and he could hear a babble of shouted orders, he got out of bed and began dressing. He was pulling on his boots when the corporal pulled back the flap of the tent.

'What is it, Williamson?' The man had lost part of one nostril in a knife fight in Cape Town and always seemed about to sneeze. He was nervous and stood scratching the back of his hand. 'Speak up.'

'It's Johnson, sir.'

De Lacey stood, to help force his foot into the second boot. 'What about Johnson?'

'Dead, sir. With an iron stake through his throat.'

De Lacey wiped dust from the cap of one boot. There were so many drunken brawls. The men were as degraded as the convicts. He sighed. 'Who did it?'

'We don't know, sir. One of the prisoners was seen running away.'

De Lacey frowned. 'He was killed by one of the convicts?'

'Yes, sir. Seen heading towards the river. They're getting up a party to follow him.'

'How did he get away?' De Lacey began buttoning his shirt. He was a slimly built man but finely muscled.

'I don't know, sir. They'll have him back in a couple of minutes, sir.'

De Lacey grunted in doubt. He'd been here only a few days on his tour of the outer camps and this was a bad one, run in a slovenly fashion and with unnecessarily harsh discipline. The men would be drunk. He doubted their ability to catch anyone.

'They've got the dogs on the trail, sir.'

That was different. He said, 'Who's our talkative friend? That ruffian Watts?'

'Yes, sir.'

'Get him. Be a little rough with him. You know what to do.'

The lieutenant was fully dressed when Williamson returned with Noxious Watts, who was rubbing his ear and glancing venomously at the corporal.

'All right, Watts, what happened?'

'It was Macaulay, sir. The big man.' He touched his ear and searched his fingers for blood.

'Get on with it.'

'Macaulay and another man were making a break for it.'

'Who was the other man?'

'Fitzgerald, sir.'

De Lacey looked at the corporal. 'Fitzgerald's a young man, sir. Quiet. Doesn't cause trouble normally.'

'Irish?'

Williamson's misshapen nose twitched. 'I don't think so, sir.'

'Nonsense. With a name like Fitzgerald, the man's Irish.' He smoothed his hair and turned back to Watts. 'How did they get away?'

'I don't know, sir. They got off the line, somehow.'

'And why didn't the guard see them leaving?'

Watts hesitated. 'He was asleep, I think.'

'And where is the guard now?' Again de Lacey turned to the corporal. His face was absolutely without expression, which frightened the man.

'Oh, he's wide awake, sir, and involved in the hunt.' Williamson glared at Watts.

'Did anyone know about this escape attempt?'

Watts said, 'No, sir. Not a word.'

'We'll see. Corporal, take him back and bring me someone else. We might as well continue with the charade.'

'Yes, sir. How many do you want this time, sir?'

'Two. Treat them exactly as you treated Watts.' With a

dampened finger, he slicked his moustache. 'I'll be outside. Hurry.'

As the men left, de Lacey heard the baying of the pack, more distant now as the dogs raced for the river and, for a moment, he felt sorry for the two convicts. The dogs hadn't been fed for a few days. The men would be torn apart.

Then he thought: a sergeant had been murdered while he'd been at the camp. Although he was not in charge, he was the most senior officer present. He would be disgraced if the men were not apprehended. It was essential they be caught, and quickly.

Lieutenant Quinton de Lacey hurried out, to take charge of the search.

The river bottom was rough, being formed of large, rounded stones, and several times Clancy slipped and thought he would be swept downstream. At the deepest part of the crossing, with his chained wrists crossed above his head, he stopped to get his breath. The current was swift and water curled around his shoulders. Eliza had been trying desperately to keep up with him and lunged for his raised arms.

'Let go.' He tried to push her away.

She swallowed water and sounded as if she were choking but she had caught the chain and held on tight. She pulled herself closer and grabbed his hair. 'Don't let me drown.'

She was smaller than he and the water was up to her chin but she was pulling him under and he fought to free himself.

While they struggled, slipping, spluttering, fighting for air and each entangled in the chain, he heard a shout. A man had reached the place where Eliza had bathed and was waving a lantern to guide the others. Then a dozen dogs burst from the bush, satanic shapes that writhed and jumped and darted first one way then the other along the bank.

Clancy managed to seize both her wrists. 'Let go my hair. Get on my back. I'll carry you.' He bent to help her up. She grabbed him around the throat, he lost his footing and they were swept away.

Down the Hawkesbury they went, he pulled under by the weight of his manacles, she encumbered by her long skirt and shoes. But they clung to each other, rising, sinking in the swirling current, breaching the surface to gasp for air, tumbling feet up, tail up, head up as they were swept along.

The flow grew stronger. Choking for air, Clancy went under, spinning upside-down, hitting his head, then his hip as he bumped along the river bed. She was with him, her skirt over her head, the chain tangled around her arm, her legs thrashing, kicking him, kicking the water, kicking the air. Still turning, they rose to the surface. For a few seconds Clancy's face was clear of the water but he had time only to exhale, not to breathe in, before being sucked down again. But now his boots were dragging through something. Pebbles. His boots were on the bottom. He lunged with his legs and somehow he was above the water and gulping in air and he felt his feet sinking into the loose river bed. He managed to stand erect because the water was only waist-deep, then fell because Eliza was still caught in the chain and she was ahead of him and the drag of her body and clothes pulled him off his feet. He stood again, bracing himself to haul her towards him. She came feet first, with her legs exposed and her head under water and covered by layers of cotton garments. He grabbed her by the waist, dragged her to her feet, pulled the clothing from her face. She coughed violently and sprayed him with water.

Retching and gasping, hugging each other for support, leaning against the flow, they staggered to the shore.

There, they fell on their knees. They were on a strip of sand. She vomited. He was gulping in air and coughing out water and he was sore from scraping against rocks and being kicked and he had a violent, burning pain behind the eyes.

They stayed on the beach, heaving, gasping, for more than a minute. When she could speak, she sat up, wiped her mouth and said, 'It's a miracle. We should pray.'

'We were saved,' he said and coughed again, 'because the river's shallow.' The pain in his head was terrible but he felt the need to be rational, to be dismissive. 'There's been no rain. The water level's low. We were lucky. That's all.'

Nevertheless, she prayed. He retched a few times.

They had been swept around a bend in the river. Above the rush of water, they could hear the faint yapping and howling of the dogs.

'No one's coming,' she said hopefully.

'Not yet.' He drew in a deep breath.

'Did your friend kill a man?'

'Yes. The sergeant.'

'Will they blame us?'

'Of course. And hang us if they catch us.'

'But we didn't do it.'

He laughed bitterly.

She clasped her hands as though still in prayer. 'What do we do?'

Clancy crawled to a log which had been left on the sand by a past flood, and sat against it. 'The men are drunk. It'll take time for them to get organised. We should go, making good ground while we can.' He held out his hands. 'Take these damned chains off first.'

The keys had slipped down among her inner garments but she retrieved them and, hands shaking, freed his wrists. She said, 'I'll not have you swearing in front of me like that.'

'I'll do whatever I like. Here, give me those.' He reached for the manacles and slung the chain across his shoulder. 'It's the

28

only weapon I've got in case the dogs catch up. I'll brain at least one of the bastard mongrels before they get us.'

'Please, I asked you not to swear.'

He pushed himself to his feet. 'Oh, you're a real lady, aren't you. Come on, your highness, before the hounds start sniffing at your petticoat.'

She didn't have a petticoat. She'd forgotten to put it on when dressing by the river bank but she would not tell a man a thing like that.

Faint sounds were drifting down with the current: men uttering oaths and shouting in distress. And the dogs were howling and moaning.

'They're crossing the river.' He pulled at the log and it moved. 'Help me. I've got an idea.'

They dragged the log into the water. It floated.

'I'm not going any further,' she said, already up to her knees in water.

'Yes you are. Or you can stay here.' He pushed the log into deeper water. 'The dogs will sniff us out on land. We'll leave no scent if we stay in the river.'

She hadn't moved.

'Look, we just hold on to the log and float with it.'

She couldn't see his face distinctly but said, 'No.'

'We can walk where it's shallow, float where it's deep.'

She shook her head.

'The dogs will tear you apart. I've seen what they do.'

So had she. She'd been there when the body of the convict Morgan was brought in on the back of a dray.

'What if I slip off the log?'

He was up to his thighs now, on the edge of the swift current. 'I can't go back. The log's drifting off and it's taking me with it. Make up your mind.'

'I'm afraid of drowning.'

29

'Would you rather hang?'

Gurgling in panic, skirt held high, she ran to join him. She slipped and almost went under. He grabbed her. He'd wrapped the chain around the log and gave her one iron manacle to hold. 'Don't let go. Do what I'm doing.' He lay with his outstretched arms over the log. She did the same and he kicked hard to propel them into deeper water.

Legs trailing, their faces barely above the surface, they began drifting downstream, with the log turning lazily in the current.

'Don't talk,' he whispered. 'They might have sent someone on ahead, along the river bank.' But she was too frightened to speak. She was thinking of her sister and the millrace.

Once he'd crossed the river, Macaulay couldn't remember which way he was supposed to go. Clancy had told him about the Tench expedition but he'd been relying on Clancy to lead the way and had forgotten whether they were to turn left or right. It wasn't straight ahead; he remembered that. Panicking at the sound of the dogs, Macaulay had run to the left, keeping close to the river, but now, after ten minutes of picking his way through bush, he encountered a barrier of dense scrub. It was dark and he could find no way through.

He turned around and headed north. His forehead was still bleeding and he felt dizzy. Once he had to stop when he blundered into a branch and, clinging to the tree, listened to the shouting and yapping to determine where he was in relation to the crossing.

When the dizziness eased, he walked away from the sounds. That meant he should be heading west. By now he had no idea whether he was travelling in the right direction or not. Nor did he care. All he wanted to do was get away from the dogs.

More clouds had drifted across the sky, blotting out the faint light from the stars, and he had to feel his way from one bush or tree to the next. He began to climb a hill. The going was too rough, too slow, so he turned to the right and worked his way around the base of the slope. He heard the trickle of running water, then came to a creek. The water was only inches deep. He recalled that Clancy, who boasted of his prowess as a poacher, had said dogs weren't able to follow a scent through water so he waded up the stream, bent forward with his arms outstretched, guided by touch and the slosh and crunch of boots in the creek bed.

From somewhere behind him—a long way back but with a surprising clarity—came the cry of a man who'd discovered something. His tracks? Frightened, unthinking, Macaulay rushed forward. He trod on a loose stone and twisted his ankle.

Mumbling oaths, he sat hip-deep in the water, nursing the leg. They were going to catch him now and they'd hang him. His pursuers were crude men, given to quick revenge. They'd string him to the nearest tree, then give his body to the dogs so no one would know what they'd done.

A tree? He was in a thick grove. He could climb up, hide from the dogs and rest his leg. He glanced up at the lattice of shadows above the creek. He could make out the shape of one big tree with gnarled, low branches that overhung the water. Macaulay got up and, hopping on one foot, splashed his way to the tree. Without letting his feet touch dry land, he hauled himself into the tree's shadowy embrace.

When he reached the river, de Lacey was appalled at what he found. Several men had lost their dogs, which had bolted after some wild animal. One man had collapsed in a drunken stupor and was lying face up in the shallows. Others were sitting on the bank with their heads in their hands. Three men with dogs had tried to cross the river but two had come back, sick with the mix of river water and grog. No one knew whether the third man had got across or drowned.

31

One man, who'd carried a lantern and been the first to the river, thought he had seen the two fugitives swept away. He was more sober than the rest. 'They was out there.' He pointed. 'A big man and a small man. They were together, a bit more than halfway across.'

'It's very hard to make out anything.'

'Yes, sir, but I seen them washed that way.' He swung the lantern downstream. 'They'd be drownded by now.'

Maybe. But it was his reputation at risk and de Lacey wanted to see the bodies before he'd call off the search. He walked along the bank, kicking men to their feet, finding the few who were clear-headed enough to understand his orders. He sent a man back to the camp to get a length of rope. Then he ordered the twelve fittest men to cross the river. Six had dogs. All the men were linked by the rope and all got across. Once on the far side, they split up, half the party turning left, the others right.

He sent the man with the lantern and three others, who could walk and hold their guns, to search downstream, in case the escapees had made their way back to this bank.

Williamson arrived with a convict in tow. He had a rope around the man's neck. The corporal was out of breath. 'He don't know nothing, sir.'

'Well why did you bring him?' De Lacey knew why and immediately raised his hand to stifle the response. He was in no mood for idiotic conversations. 'Take him back. I'll talk to him later.'

Williamson jerked the rope savagely.

'No need to decapitate the poor wretch, corporal.'

'No, sir,' he said in the voice of one who hadn't understood the admonishment.

'Who's guarding the convicts?'

'I don't know, sir.'

'Well, as from now, you are. Watch them until I get back. We

32

don't want any more of them getting away, do we, corporal?'

Williamson made a low, growling noise and led the man back through the bush.

De Lacey broke off a stick and used it to tap his boot. Just his luck. He had command of a camp full of drunkards. At least the dogs were sober so if the two convicts had managed to cross the river, the animals should pick up their trail. The fugitives were chained so they'd make slow progress through the bush. The dogs should catch them before dawn.

He found a corporal who was standing but perilously close to being asleep.

'Leave me six men. Take the rest back to camp. I want them ready to move out at dawn, armed and with provisions for two days.'

The corporal saluted and staggered off to find his men.

De Lacey looked up at the sky. Sun-up, he estimated, was still four hours away. He walked to the river's edge, put down his lantern and scooped up water to wash his face. His foot caught in something hard. He kicked and it jangled. He bent and retrieved a set of leg irons. He frowned, then saw another object, crumpled and pale, lying partly in the water. He picked it up and let it hang from his fingers. It was a woman's petticoat.

FOUR

THE THIRD SOLDIER of the original group to enter the river *had* succeeded in reaching the far side. He couldn't swim but he'd kept erect, holding his musket and powder horn clear of the water with one hand, grasping the dog's collar with the other. He was fortunate to have a dog that was smaller than most and a good swimmer. A savage beast, it was part bull terrier, part native dog, and loved nothing more than attacking strangers. It seemed to know the chase would begin on the far bank and therefore swam furiously to get there, with the man in tow.

After five minutes of slipping and cursing and struggling to hold on to the animal, the soldier had scrambled up the far bank. There, he'd tied the dog to a tree and loaded his musket. It was too dark to see the gun but, feeling for the distinctive Tower of London stamp on the barrel—just as he'd done many times in blindfold drill—he'd worked quickly, pouring in the powder, dropping the ball and ramming home the soft wad to keep the round in place. By now the dog was leaping and howling in its anxiety to begin the hunt.

The soldier's name was Paterson. He was twenty, he was strong and he wasn't drunk. He was determined to catch the escapees and bring them back, to show what one good man could do. He would parade his captives in front of that new lieutenant, the one who socialised with the Governor and therefore had influence, and reveal the other men as drunken incompetents. Maybe earn a transfer back to Sydney Town or, better still, to Parramatta where even the convicts had huts and plots of land to grow vegetables. He hated this camp. The men were lazy, cruel and degenerate; worse than the convicts.

At first Paterson had followed the dog on a long but fruitless loop to the south but now he was definitely on the trail, with the animal pulling him through unseen bushes so that his hands and cheeks were constantly being scratched. He shouted for the others to follow but there was no answer. Had no one else crossed the river?

Paterson came to a creek, slid down its bank, stumbled on rocks and fell. The dog pulled hard and was gone. Up the creek it raced, or so Paterson thought, but, sprawled on all fours, face pressed against the oozing softness of a muddy bank, he couldn't see. He could hear the animal barking frenziedly as it crashed through bushes. The convicts must be close. Still in chains, they would be blundering through the scrub and falling constantly. The dog would soon have them on the ground, bleeding from a dozen bites and screaming for help.

Paterson scrambled to his feet, took the musket in both hands and followed as rapidly as he dared. He wanted to reach the men before the dog tore them apart.

From somewhere in the darkness ahead of him the animal began howling mournfully, as though it had lost the trail. Then it barked a few times; savage, snapping sounds. It had someone! Paterson began to run.

The snarling and snapping became a hideous, high-pitched yelp. Paterson stopped. After a flurry of splashing and crunching the dog began making whimpering, choking sounds. Then silence. Breathing heavily, more from fright than exertion, Paterson crouched low, listening. He heard a scraping noise and possibly a groan, a human sound, a muffled cry of pain.

He strained to hear more but heard only the rustle of running water.

Still bending low, moving slowly now, he felt his way around bushes and past the grasping limbs of trees. When the banks became too rough for walking he went along the creek's rocky bed, ankle-deep in running water, musket at the ready. He paused frequently, listening for the clank of chains, the sounds of sticks breaking, of men moaning in pain or breathing heavily, but there was nothing.

His foot touched something soft and he bent down to feel it. Partly submerged in the water, unmoving, not breathing, was the dog.

While he was touching the animal's warm, breathless flanks and at the instant he discovered the chain wrapped around its neck, the great body of Macaulay, hands outstretched for the throat, fell on him.

They were drifting slowly now. The water was deeper and its pace sluggish, with confusing eddies that turned the log in slow circles and seemed intent on taking them back upriver. Once they heard a furious flapping, splashing sound, so close they thought something was charging from the bank and Eliza, cold and stiff and with her waterlogged clothes dragging her down, almost let go of the log in fright.

The sounds disappeared in a hiss of feathery landings.

'Ducks,' Clancy said. He'd trapped plenty of ducks. Usually at night because they were always someone else's ducks.

After several minutes she said, 'I can't hold on much longer.'

He was so cold he had difficulty speaking. 'We'll have to land soon.' How, he didn't know because they had been spinning lazily in the middle of the river for the past hour. He doubted whether they'd covered more than a quarter of a mile in that time. The river was wider, too. Maybe three hundred yards across, judging by the vague shadows. He peered at the sky. 'It'll be dawn in an hour. Must be out of sight by then.'

'I couldn't last another . . .' she began but he clapped a hand across her mouth.

'Something up ahead.'

She saw it too. A dark shape rising from the river. Not moving, but in their path. They drifted closer.

'A boat,' he said. It must be one of the cargo vessels that took wheat and maize from the local farms to Port Jackson. He'd seen a couple of sloops moored in the river. They were handsome sailing vessels, weighing as much as 20 tons.

They must have drifted to The Green Hills, centre of the Hawkesbury settlement. He looked to the right and thought he saw the silhouettes of buildings near the river bank.

The boat grew larger. It had a single mast and rigging that filled the night sky with shadowy webs.

'We're going to hit it,' she whispered, but then the log spun in a slow arc and she could no longer see the boat. She heard a shiver of spray hit the water. He cursed softly.

'What happened?'

'Made a noise. Didn't mean to.'

'But we turned around.'

'I've grabbed the mooring rope.'

She looked back at the looming shape. 'What are you going to do?'

'Hang on to the rope.'

She seemed to gain strength and pulled herself closer to him. 'Could we get on the boat?'

'And do what?'

'Sail somewhere.'

'Just be quiet.'

'Can't you sail?'

He lowered his face until it touched the water. 'If I'd been a sailor I wouldn't have had to steal watches, would I? Then I wouldn't be here, listening to your foolish questions.' Even whispering exhausted him and they were silent for a long time.

A new current, curling around the stern of the sloop, began tugging at them. 'We're going the other way,' he said and let go of the rope.

'Why did you do that?'

'Because I couldn't hold on any longer. And because we have to get to the bank, away from those buildings.' The settlement was clearly visible now as the first hint of dawn flushed the sky.

'Why are we going the other way?'

'Ask the river.'

Quietly, she began to sob. 'It's God's will. We're going back to be punished.'

'It's the tide, you silly woman.' He began paddling with his free hand. 'Help me. We have to get to the far shore before the sun rises.'

De Lacey had a small rowing boat brought to the site and, fifteen minutes before sunrise, he crossed the Hawkesbury with ten men. The boat made two crossings. The lieutenant went with six men on the first trip. The remaining four, with two dogs, crossed next. Questioning the men who'd been marched down to the river revealed that only two knew how to handle dogs. That set the limit: two dogs. He wasn't going to waste time with incompetents who would become entangled in the scrub or lose the leash at the first excited tug. He had sufficient for the task: two dogs to follow the trail, eight armed soldiers to recapture the escapees.

It now seemed they were following three convicts. A young female named Eliza Phillips was missing. Presumably, it was her petticoat he'd found by the river bank. She was, he'd been told, a mild woman, given to frequent bouts of melancholy and prayer. She seemed the most unlikely person to attempt escape and, as far as anyone knew, had had no contact with either Macaulay or Fitzgerald. No matter. Sergeant Johnson was dead and if she was caught with the men, they'd all hang.

Johnson's keys were missing and de Lacey assumed the male convicts were free of their chains and thus would be able to travel quickly. But where would they go? Patches of cultivated land could be found on the far side of the river, where some of the original twenty-two Hawkesbury settlers—all ex-convicts—were attempting to grow crops in the fertile alluvial soil but, generally, the land beyond the river was covered in scrub and forest and was a maze of uncharted rivers, unscaleable cliffs and impenetrable valleys. It was home only to blackfellows and snakes.

He could leave the men and the Phillips woman to die but a quick recapture and rapid hanging would end the matter decisively. It would be good for his career. No, it would be vital.

On the far bank the dogs became confused. One wanted to go left along the river, the other straight ahead.

De Lacey decided to follow the instincts of the second dog and strike to the west. Soon, both animals were barking excitedly and straining to go faster. The newly risen sun was streaking the land with long shadows when the squad reached the creek where Paterson had followed Macaulay's trail. Within minutes, the dogs were clawing at the trunk of a tree.

High up in its branches hung two shapes, dappled by leafy shadows.

De Lacey stepped back and, involuntarily, put a hand to his mouth to stifle a cry. The lower form was a dog with a broken neck. It was hanging from a chain. The other was the body of young Paterson, purple-faced and grotesque in the contortion of violent death. He was hooked by his collar to the end of a broken branch.

39

Wiping a sweaty palm on the handle of his sword, de Lacey looked around at the encircling bush. The three convicts could be anywhere. Even watching them now. The thought alarmed him and, with sword drawn, he hurried to the tree where the dogs were still frantically pawing at the trunk. Their handlers pulled them back as he approached. Not looking up, de Lacey scoured the ground beneath the tree. Damn. The dead soldier's musket, powder horn, balls of ammunition and bayonet were missing.

The armed soldiers were standing back, their eyes raised to the ghastly sight in the branches.

'You men,' de Lacey said, indicating six soldiers, 'form a circle around the tree.' He spun the tip of his sword in the air to make sure they understood. 'Each man move out ten paces. Face outwards. Keep watch. There are three of them. They now have a gun. If you see something, shoot.'

He pointed to the men with the dogs. 'Get those blasted creatures away from the tree and try to pick up a trail.' One on either bank, the men moved up the creek with the dogs sniffing and dithering in distress.

'Nothing, sir,' one man called. He'd travelled no more than five yards and was looking around him nervously.

'Keep going.' He was about to say 'you'll be safe with the dog' but remembered what was hanging above him.

The lieutenant had the remaining two men unhook Paterson. They had great difficulty climbing the tree and freeing the body.

'Who could have done this, sir?' one of the men asked, panting with exertion when they had lowered the dead man to the bank. 'It's hard enough getting the poor blighter down. How could they have got him up there?'

De Lacey had been pondering the same question. 'Fear gives men great strength, soldier.'

The soldier shook his head. 'They weren't too frightened by this poor lad.'

'Or the hound neither,' the other man said.

'That'll be enough of that. You two take the body back to the river. Carry it in turns but one man must be armed and ready at all times.'

'Yes, sir,' the first man said. He seemed glad to be leaving.

'Tell the sergeant what's happened. Have him put armed patrols along the banks in case they try to cross back.'

Before the soldier could acknowledge the order, the dogs, hidden from sight in a dense patch of bushes, began barking furiously. 'They've found the scent,' one of the handlers called out.

'Wait for us.' Sheathing his sword, de Lacey led the others up the creek.

FIVE

CARRIED UPSTREAM ON the turning tide, Clancy and Eliza had rounded a long, sweeping bend in the river and beached the log on a sandy spit. They landed at dawn, during the moments when the sun's first rays began flickering through the highest branches of the trees. Breathless from paddling, cold and stiff from their hours in the water, they clambered up the sloping embankment to collapse in the dewy embrace of long grass. They were out of sight of the settlement and the moored sloop and for several minutes they lay there, letting water drain from their clothes, rubbing chilled hands, regaining strength, until they were stirred by the sound of voices coming from the other side of the river. Two men were talking. The voices were far away and the words indistinct, fragments of sound carried on a faint breeze, but they revealed that people from the settlement were awake and moving. Before long, someone would come down to the water. And see them.

Slowly, painfully, they rose from the grass and crawled until they were beyond the ribbon of trees lining the bank. Once shielded by the dense growth, they stood and walked away from the river.

They were in a region of marshes. Clancy led the way, choosing a meandering path along low ridges of dry land. Then he stopped. The river was behind them but they were walking towards the rising sun.

The wrong way. They were walking east. They should be heading west, towards the mountains.

He turned, scratched his scalp and looked around him.

'What's wrong?' she asked, touching his hand lightly to help speed a reassuring answer.

'There's something very strange happening.' He was never one to confess mistakes and rarely expressed misgivings. But he was tired and let his doubts escape. 'Everything's back to front.'

'Are we on the wrong side of the river?' In despair, she sat down. 'Do we have to cross the river again? I don't think . . .'

'Don't talk so loud.' He squatted beside her. 'If we can hear people talking, they can hear us.'

She lay on the ground. She was so tired she could sleep where she was, on a patch of bristling, spiky grass with the flies already astir and picking maddening paths across her forehead and cheeks. She closed her eyes. In the distance, the birds were sounding their regular overture to a new day. Such strange sounds. Cries, gobbling noises, mocking laughter. The ones she liked best were the birds that sounded as if they were gargling. They were black and white and brazen, coming boldly to the camp every morning in search of scraps, and gobbling and gurgling to each other.

The birds seemed pleased to be greeting a new day. She was thinking she might have done better to have drowned in the river. So far, they had eluded the soldiers but that had been in the dark and now it was bright and hot and they were exposed for anyone to see on this vast stretch of flat marshland and the thought of being hanged in front of a jeering mob was tormenting her. Drowning would have been a private way to die. She was also tired and hungry and had no idea where they were going. Obviously, neither did the man.

Man? If she were to hang on the same gallows as he, she should know who he was.

'I don't know your name,' she whispered.

'I don't think it matters.' He was sitting with his head held in his hands, trying to picture the river and the points of the compass.

'My name's Eliza Phillips.' She didn't extend her hand.

He didn't look up. 'Clancy Fitzgerald.'

'I like Clancy for a name.'

'So did my mother. Shhh. I'm trying to think.'

His mother had done more than give Clancy his first name; she'd taught him to read and write and to tackle problems logically. Not always honestly, although that was more a matter of his inclination than of her intention, but he was able to consider a problem from the beginning and work his way through it. With a finger, he began drawing in the dirt. If the river was behind them, as it certainly was, and they were heading east, as they must be, then the river was flowing north and south. Which was the way it should flow. And yet they were walking in the wrong direction. He drew a circle for the sun and a line for the river. They had run aground on the river's far bank, the one opposite The Green Hills—he was certain of that—and yet they were heading towards the rising sun. Even in this country, the sun rose in the east. So what was happening?

He drew a few squiggles.

'What are you doing?'

He hushed her into silence, because he wasn't sure. He drew curves, bends that a river might make. They made no sense. He smoothed the dirt and started again, drawing the points of the compass and a single vertical line for the river. He pondered the drawing, then drew a half loop at the top of the line, so that the river turned south. Then he drew a U at the bottom of the line, so that the river swung north again. That was it. The river had turned through several big bends. Rivers did that. They never ran in straight lines but wandered all over the place. He peered

44

into the sun. On the horizon, he could see a thick line of trees. It was the river again, running south to north. They must be at the bottom of a sweeping bend and there must be another bend, curving the other way, upstream.

'We have to turn left,' he said and pointed to the north. 'Follow the line of the river. We're in the middle of a big bend. Up there, the river should turn left and go back down to the south.'

'I don't understand.'

'Just follow me and keep quiet.' He fingered the cut on his ankle. It was clean but white-edged from the hours of immersion.

'What's that?' she asked, trying to penetrate his rudeness.

'A reminder of why I'm doing this. Come on.'

They walked for more than an hour, keeping the river on their left. Clancy wore a perpetual frown because they were travelling almost north-east, but he said nothing. He had no idea which way they had drifted in the dark. They could have gone in circles for all he knew. He was certain, however, that they were now following the river upstream and that was what they must do, to get off this marshy plain and be near the mountains. Despite his cut ankle, he walked faster than Eliza until she trailed him by 100 yards.

Only when they neared a thick grove of trees did he slow and allow her to catch up. He could see hills ahead. He led the way into the grove. 'We'll rest for a while,' he said, when they reached a grassy patch. She fell to the ground and was asleep before he could speak again.

He'd been thinking about their chances. Not just of escape but of survival. Where would they get food? If they were to cross the mountains, how were they to carry water? He needed clothes other than the wretched yellow prison garb he was wearing. He needed an axe, a knife, a flint. Canvas to lie on or to protect them from rain. So many things.

They were heading away from civilisation, for God's sake, and never returning.

Eliza should go back. She would slow his progress, not be able to run or climb hills, or she'd faint when stressed, like women did. They wouldn't hang her, not if she went back voluntarily. She could pretend she hadn't seen the men. She might get a flogging but they wouldn't string her up.

She would certainly die if she stayed with him.

He thought about Macaulay. They could both go back if it hadn't been for Macaulay.

The big man had walked until the pain from his twisted ankle was too great. Then he'd stopped by a small waterhole and, at dawn, had noticed a cave in the side of a nearby hill. He drank some water, took off his boot to let the water cool the pain searing his leg and then limped up to the cave. It was small, no more than a fissure in the side of the rocky hill and little longer than his own body, but he could lie out of sight. He had the soldier's gun. If they came for him, he'd spill the blood of many before one man reached him.

He put the powder horn, the pouch and the bayonet in a corner of the small cave and looked down into the valley.

One of the strange hopping creatures they called a kangaroo came to drink at the waterhole. It was smaller than the ones he'd seen and had thicker hair. He watched it go through a nervous routine of getting its morning water. It would drink, head down, tail spread along the ground, then rise to listen, with its tiny front paws scratching its chest and its ears twitching. Satisfied there was no danger, it would drink again. It was bending to drink for the fourth time when Macaulay heard the dogs.

Barking was a new sound to the animal and it rose on its hind legs, rocking backwards and forwards in a state of agitated uncertainty. Through a thicket of bush burst two dogs, snarling, fangs bared, dragging their handlers behind them. In panic, the kangaroo hopped one way, then turned and came up the hill towards Macaulay's cave.

Now Macaulay could see soldiers: an officer running with his sword held high and some men following with bayonets on their extended muskets. He lay back out of sight. He heard the thud of the kangaroo as it came near the cave, heard the rattle of loose stones as it turned and followed a narrow ridge up and over the hill.

'It's a damned animal,' one man shouted—the officer, Macaulay surmised, because the same voice then shouted for the dogs to be brought back. There was a great deal of yapping and howling and yelling.

'I'm sure we were on the trail, sir.'

'Well where in damnation have they gone?'

Macaulay fondled the gun. It was loaded and ready. He risked a look. The dogs were circling the waterhole but constantly turning to face the hill and barking in frustration. The officer had sheathed his sword. Back to the cave, he had his hands on his hips. He swung around and, hurriedly, Macaulay pressed his face into the dirt. He could hear them talking.

'They want to go up the hill, sir.'

'I'm not chasing after some ridiculous animal. We go back to where they lost the scent.'

'I don't know where that is, sir.'

'Well, find out. It can't be far.' The voice was fading. 'All of you. Spread out. Look for tracks.'

Macaulay waited five minutes. In the distance, he could hear faint barking and an occasional shout. After another five minutes, he sat up and looked out. The bush was deserted. He could hear nothing, not even the dogs. He rubbed his ankle a few times, then lay back, using his bent arm as a pillow. He was soon asleep.

The sun was shining on his face. Then there was a dark shadow, and more bright light. Again the shadow. He awoke. A man was standing next to the cave. A tall man, holding a spear.

Macaulay felt for the gun.

The man was blocking the sun so that his outline was etched in a fine border of glistening light but he was naked, with skin the colour of coal. He had a mat of tangled hair, a black beard and long, wiry limbs. He seemed curious, not afraid. He took a step forward, allowing the sun to shine full on Macaulay's face. The man spoke. The words were brief and as rapid as a terrier's bark.

Macaulay had no idea what the man had said but, blinking in the bright light, smiled and nodded. He would have to sit up and turn to get a good shot. He swung his legs out of the cave and lifted the gun.

The black man pointed to one side. Macaulay bent forward and saw another man; younger than the first but holding a spear and one of the long, hooked throwing-sticks that the blacks used to bring down game. In his other hand he was carrying the body of a plump, furry animal. He had it by the tail.

The first man spoke again and the younger man held up the animal for Macaulay to admire.

Two other men, moving as silently as a languid breeze, emerged from the bushes. Both were carrying spears and throwing-sticks.

The first man had altered his grip on the spear. He could hurl it in an instant, Macaulay guessed, and put down the gun.

The man was fascinated by the musket.

Macaulay uncocked it and held it out for the man to see. The man wrinkled his brow but wouldn't come closer. Macaulay got

48

to his feet and, holding the gun by the barrel, used it as a walking-stick.

The man bent forward until a finger touched the metal barrel. He rubbed his finger and smiled.

'Magic,' Macaulay said. The second man came up. Macaulay let him touch the barrel, too. He guessed that neither had seen metal, let alone felt its cold, smooth surface. Maybe they'd never met a white man. Certainly not a man of Macaulay's size. They kept looking at him, running their eyes over him from his swollen ankle to his tousled hair. They exchanged words in sharp bursts and their eyes were wide.

'Good for blowing the heads off blackfellows,' Macaulay said and the men looked gravely at him. 'Boom, boom,' he continued, using his fingers to indicate explosions. 'Plenty noise. Plenty dead blackfellows.'

They were still staring at him They were in awe of his size and fascinated by the strange, shiny object he had brought. Good. They might help him; either hide him until his leg improved or show him the way over the mountains.

Macaulay was hungry and put his fingers to his mouth.

The first man frowned, then bent forward to examine the cave. He saw the bayonet. Macaulay picked it up and held it out, so the man could touch the blade. I could run you through right now, he thought, but the other three were well out of his reach and he'd die looking like a pincushion, with their long spears quivering in his belly.

He thrust the bayonet through the leather belt he had taken from the dead soldier and, once more brought his hand to his mouth. The man turned and, in a jabber of words, called to the men by the bushes. One disappeared, to return a few minutes later with a handful of small, yellow fruit. The man was lean and young, no more than twenty, and he moved up the hill with the easy, loping gait of a greyhound. Never taking his eyes from

49

Macaulay, he gave the fruit to the bearded man, then backed down the hill.

The older man bit into a piece of fruit, to show that it was good, then offered one to Macaulay. It had a bitter-sweet taste, like a sour apple, but it was refreshing. There were three more pieces of fruit. Macaulay ate another and pocketed the rest.

He pointed to the west. 'I want to go that way,' he said.

The men exchanged words.

'You take me over the hills.' Macaulay moved his hand to describe peaks and valleys.

The bearded man pointed to the east and said 'Deerubin.' He kept pointing and repeating the word.

'Not deerubin,' Macaulay said, shaking his head. 'West. That way.'

The younger men had withdrawn to the bottom of the hill. Macaulay, intent on his discussion with the bearded man, hadn't noticed them leave. Now the bearded man began to back away.

Macaulay hobbled after him.

The man raised his hand and pointed to the cave.

'Don't leave me or I'll blow your blasted head off.'

But the man turned and ran. Within seconds all had disappeared into the bush. Musket raised, a fuming Macaulay searched for a sign of the four men. But he saw nothing, heard nothing. No bush swayed, no stones crunched, no twig snapped.

He sat on a rock. The birds no longer sang and there was no wind to stir the trees. All across the valley and on the far hills, the bush was blanketed by an eerie silence. He had a terrible feeling of being alone.

SIX

ARK CLOUDS WERE filling the sky and the air was sweet with the taste of impending rain. De Lacey's men were near the river, boiling water for tea and resting in the shade of a large eucalypt. Despite searching all morning they had succeeded only in tracking down a four-foot-long goanna, which had sent the dogs into paroxysms of rage by scurrying up a sapling and clinging to its supple top where, visible and taunting, it swayed from side to side with the regularity of a metronome, but refused to budge.

They were a mile downstream from the crossing. The lieutenant had sent a runner back to the camp to see if there was news of the convicts. He was sitting under the tree, sweaty and yearning for sleep and using a stick to clear dirt from his boots, when the messenger returned downriver by boat. He brought with him an oarsman, the sergeant, and a quiet old Aborigine who had learned to speak some English in the four years since white settlers had moved into his territory.

The sergeant said the old man was reputed to be good at tracking. Better than any dogs, he said pointedly, because he would never mistakenly chase an animal. By footprints alone he could distinguish male from female and identify individual members of his family.

'They say he can track a bird across rocks,' the sergeant added.

'Would the bird be walking or flying?' De Lacey was in no mood for hyperbole.

The sergeant, never one to suspect irony, was slow to answer. 'I don't know, sir.'

De Lacey rolled on one hip to face the Aborigine. The man had watery eyes and a broad face eroded by age. He was wearing only a pair of old trousers that were ripped at the knees. He had rows of scars across his chest, and a big belly.

'What's your name?'

The sergeant answered. 'Jacky Jacky. At least, that's what we call him, sir.'

'Thank you, sergeant.' De Lacey, determined to look fresh in front of the men, rose to his feet with as much suggestion of boundless energy as he could muster. He dusted his pants. 'You're an expert tracker, I understand?'

Jacky Jacky looked puzzled and turned to the sergeant.

'Good tracker?' the sergeant asked.

The Aborigine grunted.

'He says "yes", sir.'

'I don't need an interpreter, thank you, sergeant. Either the man speaks English or he doesn't.' He made an impatient gesture. 'Come with me. We'll see how good you are.'

De Lacey led the squad back to the creek where they had found Paterson's body. Although much older than the lieutenant and barefooted, the Aborigine had no trouble keeping up with de Lacey's brisk pace. He moved almost silently through the bush.

De Lacey halted near the tree. The dog was still hanging from the chain. 'The men we are after did this. They also killed one of our men.' The old man ignored the tree. He was bent forward, more concerned with what was on the ground. De Lacey slapped his thigh. 'Do you understand what I'm saying?'

'Plenty feet.' He pointed to the marks around the creek banks. 'Plenty soldiers.'

'Of course. We were all here.'

'Mess up tracks,' the old man said and moved up the creek. De Lacey ordered the others to stay back. He alone followed. The Aborigine stopped near a small bush. He wiped his nose, then pointed to the ground. 'No soldier, not this one.'

De Lacey couldn't see a mark. 'What is it?'

'Big fella.'

'Not a soldier?'

He shook his head. 'Big fella.'

'So you said. Where was he heading?'

The man cocked his head to one side.

'Oh for heaven's sake . . . where did he go? Which way?'

He pointed up the creek.

'How many men? Not the soldiers. Other men. One, two, three?'

The old man held up a finger.

'Just one?'

'One fella.'

De Lacey signalled for the sergeant to join them.

'So much for your expert, sergeant. He can find the tracks of only one man.' He stroked his moustache in agitation. The old man was wasting their time. They were back where they had started and the three convicts were drawing further away by the minute. When he spoke, it was more to reassure himself than to converse. 'There are three of them. Two men and one woman. And it would have needed more than one person to string up that poor fellow Paterson. Therefore, this old villain has missed two sets of tracks.'

'Yes, sir.' The sergeant's face was creased by doubt.

'Why the look?'

'Well, one of the convicts was Macaulay and he's a huge man, sir, very strong.'

'You mean he could have done that by himself? Killed a

53

soldier and his dog with his bare hands and hanged them both?'

The sergeant shrugged. 'Macaulay's a brute of a man, sir.'

The tracker was already moving up the creek. Pleased to be leaving the tree and its grisly relic, de Lacey followed. After half a mile, the Aborigine stopped. He waited for the lieutenant. He began pointing to all the soldiers. 'Me see him, him, him.' He indicated the whole squad. 'Other fella came out of water here. Only one fella.'

'But there are three.'

The man shook his head. 'One fella. Sore.'

At first the lieutenant didn't understand and had the man repeat the last word.

'Sore. You mean hurt?'

He held his leg and simulated a limp.

'He has a sore leg?'

The old man grunted.

'How do you know?'

He pointed to the ground.

De Lacey turned to the sergeant. 'Can you see anything here?'

'Not really, sir.'

'Neither can I. Methinks your friend might be playing games with us.' De Lacey walked a few paces from the creek. Hands clasped behind his back, he said, 'What are you paying him?'

'I promised him some flour, sir.'

'The better show he provides, the more flour he gets?'

'No, sir. I think he's genuine, sir.' It was rare for the sergeant to be so forceful and de Lacey turned.

'Genuine?'

'I trust him, sir. These blackfellows can see things we can't see. They can read the ground like you and me can read a book.'

You and me. The grammar offended but the thought amused. The sergeant was barely literate.

'So you believe him?'

'Yes, sir. I think so, sir.'

'Be definite, man.'

'Yes, sir. I believe him.'

De Lacey walked away from the others until he came to some flat rocks. He climbed up and looked along a broad valley covered by thick timber and edged by ragged hills. They'd been this way hours before. They'd found nothing. Now this old blackfellow was telling him they were following only one man and the man was limping. If he was injured, how had he got away from them? And where were the other two? Had they drowned, as one of the soldiers had suggested? Or were they already hiding in one of the many valleys that scored the land to the west of the Hawkesbury?

A gust of wind brought a splattering of rain.

De Lacey grasped the handle of his sword and jumped down. He strode back to the others. 'Sergeant, go on ahead with the tracker. No more than a mile. After that, come back and tell me what he's found.' He then sent three soldiers scouting to the north and the remainder to the south, to search for tracks. They were to report back within an hour.

No sooner had the men gone than heavy rain began falling. With it came strong winds that bent the trees and filled the air with shredded leaves. De Lacey sheltered behind a large tree. In front of him a bunch of tall, reed-thin bushes were writhing in the wind, their branches bending and lashing like coachmen's whips. He pulled his cape around his shoulders and crouched against the tree trunk.

He had plenty of time to think.

It was his luck, his appalling luck which had dogged him since birth. He'd been born into a family ruled by an autocratic drunkard who'd squandered most of their money at the gaming table. Happily, his father had died of a ruined liver before he'd ruined them. Even so, his mother had been forced to sell the estate that had been in the de Lacey family for seven generations. And so number one son Quinton—good looking, aristocratic of bearing and inclination but as poor as a church mouse—had volunteered for service in the New South Wales Corps, an outfit with absolutely no tradition, to get out of England and make a name for himself. He'd done well in Sydney Town, was regarded as a bright, dependable officer, knew the Governor, was invited to all the important functions, mixed with the best people. And what happened? He'd had the wretched luck to be making a routine inspection of an outlying camp—the worst in the colony, run by a bunch of slovenly rascals—when two men had been murdered by escaping convicts. And the convicts were still at large. The news would reach the Governor that evening. Hell would erupt. There would be no use in saying he'd discovered problems at the camp. That he'd criticised the lack of discipline, drunkenness, excessive cruelty. No use pointing out he'd begun writing a report recommending changes. He should have instituted the changes immediately. That's what Hunter would say and the sycophants, who hovered around the Governor like flies, would agree.

He'd be ruined.

After an hour the soldiers returned with water cascading from caps and capes. They'd seen nothing. Ten minutes later the sergeant and the Aborigine trudged in from the west.

'Nothing, sir,' the sergeant reported, shaking his head and showering the lieutenant with spray. He shouted to be heard above the rain. 'There's a lot of rock up ahead and with all this water, Jacky Jacky can't find nothing.'

Of course not. My career is at stake and fate determines that the heavens should open to erase all tracks. De Lacey turned away. He was wondering what to do—carry on the search, blundering through the bush in this downpour, or go back, get more men and divide the search party into groups—when there was a shout. He turned to see the oarsman, who'd brought the sergeant and the black tracker in the boat, come running from the direction of the river. Ignoring the pelting rain, boots sloshing in the mud, he was waving excitedly.

'They've been seen, sir. A few miles downstream, near the settlement.'

Clancy was out of breath and had to stop. He looked back. There was no sign of anyone in pursuit. He sank into the reeds lining the marsh and waited for Eliza to catch up. She was a long way back; a pathetic figure, drenched clothes clinging to wet skin, swaying from exhaustion as she tried to follow his path through the swelling chain of ponds.

God, what rain! He squinted up at the clouds and a fury of raindrops stung his face. He covered his eyes. The rain had slowed them but its very intensity was a blessing, forming a veil that hid them from anyone standing more than a few hundred yards away.

It was several hours since they'd last seen the man. He'd been accompanied by a young boy. The man was carrying an axe and must have been seeking good timber, which is why he'd crossed the river and entered the grove where they were sleeping. They'd run. The man, a big, stout fellow in the rough but unmarked clothes of a free settler, called out for them to stop but they'd bolted for the next line of trees. He'd followed them for some time, waving the axe and shouting.

Beyond the trees, they'd entered this terrible marsh.

Eliza reached him. She stood above him, her hands still holding her skirt at shin height to keep it clear of the mud and water.

'So,' she said, but that was all she could say.

'I don't think anyone's following us.'

She nodded but didn't turn.

'Sit down.'

'If I sit down,' she gasped, 'I'll never get up again.'

Just like a woman. Offer them what they most want and they refuse. 'All right,' he said, rising slowly and wringing water from his sleeves. 'We'll go on.'

'Don't go so fast.'

'Don't go so damned slow.'

'I asked you not to . . .' She paused, needing to breathe, not waste precious energy on a reprimand. He was a crude man, who thought only of himself. He was already on his way and she followed him, skirt held high as she ploughed through ankle-deep water, head bent low to draw in air, not rain.

'I can't see the man any more,' she managed to shout, hoping to slow him.

'And I haven't seen the boy since we started running.'

'What's that mean?' She had to stop to draw breath. 'You haven't seen the boy?'

'It means the man sent the boy to tell the others. And get the soldiers. Come on.'

She was already five yards behind him. She tried to walk faster but fell twice when she stepped in submerged holes and didn't have the strength to recover her balance. She called out for him to stop and wait or go another way along the ridges of higher ground but he sloshed on, ignoring her. Had she been a coarse person she'd have sworn at him for being so stubborn, for deliberately making progress so difficult for her. She knew coarse words, having heard them since the day she was flung into prison, but she couldn't bring herself to use them. She had little idea what most of them meant—except damned which was a word her aunt had used, but in a proper, biblical sense—but guessed they were either blasphemous or disgustingly sexual so, instead, she thought wicked thoughts: wishing he'd fall and be immersed in mud so he'd look foolish, or hoping he'd hurt his leg, the one with the terrible cut on it, so he'd be compelled to slow to her pace. But as exhaustion extinguished anger, she saw sense in what he was doing: they must reach cover of some sort before the rain stopped and thus had to keep moving as rapidly as they could. And he was sticking to the shallow pools so they would leave no trail. Had he gone to higher ground, their boots would have sunk in the mud and left deep, easily distinguished tracks.

He was a clever man, she thought, reluctantly, and then changed her mind. No, he was cunning.

She put her head down and tried to keep up.

Clancy had no compunction about swearing and as he trudged through the shallows he was swearing at Eliza Phillips, muttering the worst phrases he could link together. Not because she had trouble maintaining his pace but because, now, he couldn't send her back. She'd been seen with him. If she were caught or even went back voluntarily, she'd be hanged.

De Lacey was taken down the river by rowboat. They reached The Green Hills, where the man who'd seen the convicts had a small farm. The fledgling town was on the south bank of the river, at a place where the Hawkesbury swept through a long bend. There were shacks of wattle and daub and a few small but substantial buildings, as square as dolls' houses, made of blocks hewn from the local sandstone. A small sloop was moored in midstream. A barge was alongside, stacked with sacks of grain that were covered by a large canvas sheet. On the sloop, four men who'd come to load the grain were sheltering from the rain.

De Lacey hadn't been here before but he knew a little of the settlement's history. It had good soil, something Sydney Town lacked, and men had been given land to grow wheat, maize and vegetables to prevent the colony starving. Twenty-two settlers, all freed convicts, had come here, to live and work at the outermost limits of the colony. There was a walking track back to Parramatta and Sydney Town but it was narrow and rough and unsuitable for any wheeled device like an oxen cart. Not that there were any oxen or other beasts of burden to do such work. Thus all the produce grown along the Hawkesbury had to be taken by boat to Sydney.

According to rumour, conditions were extremely hard for the small band of farmers, especially since Governor Hunter had lowered the price of grain. The people of The Green Hills, it was said, were becoming a rebellious lot.

De Lacey's boat had been seen turning the bend and a small party was waiting on the bank. A corporal brought forward Edward Wilson, the man who'd seen the couple.

Before Wilson could speak, de Lacey said, 'Couple?'

'Yes, sir.' Wilson had a northern accent with distorted vowels that roamed the far reaches of the mouth before emerging. It was the sort of voice de Lacey detested.

'There are three, Mr Wilson.'

'I saw a man and a woman.' He didn't say 'sir' again. He was a free man and not enamoured of the military.

De Lacey had been wondering how the escapees could have travelled so far through the thick bush he'd seen along the river. Now, having heard only a few words from Wilson, he was filled with doubt.

'So you saw a man and a woman. What were they doing?'

'Sleeping. They were on the other side of the river, among some trees.'

'Sleeping?'

Wilson nodded. 'Lying on the grass. They woke up when they heard me and my son.' The boy was with his father, who touched the child on the shoulder and drew him close. 'We both saw them.'

The boy nodded.

60

'How old are you, lad?'

'Eight, sir.' The boy had the foundations of the same miserable accent.

'How do you know they were convicts?' De Lacey was ignoring the father.

The boy touched his shirt. 'He had things on it.'

'Arrows,' Wilson added. 'It was convict garb. They were both wet through.'

'It's been raining very heavily, Mr Wilson,' de Lacey said, flicking water from his sleeve. 'Everyone's wet.'

'They was soaked through,' Wilson said and shrugged, like a man grown tired of talking.

De Lacey waved his hand. 'Go on, go on,' and, without interrupting, let the farmer tell his story. When Wilson had finished, he said, 'And you didn't see them again?'

'They were running across the marsh. The rain was heavy and I lost sight of them. I was worried about the boy, too. I'd sent him back to tell Higgins, who's got a farm . . .'

De Lacey waved him into silence. 'How long ago was this?'

'Since I saw them?' Wilson peered at the sky, searching for the sun's glow in the leaden clouds. 'About four hours.'

'And which way were they heading?'

Wilson pointed across the river. 'North. It's very wet in there at the moment. Marsh country.'

De Lacey had not left the boat. He turned sharply to look across the river and the boat rocked so violently he had to bend to steady himself. When he could stand again, he said, 'Mr Wilson, where would you say they were heading?'

'Nowhere in particular. They were just bolting.'

'Running in panic?'

'I'd say so.'

De Lacey turned again, taking care not to upset the boat. The rain had eased but trees lining the far bank made it difficult to see further than the river. 'What lies beyond the marsh?'

'I've never been that far. On a clear day you can see hills.'

De Lacey allowed the corporal on the bank to help him ashore. He was wet through, filthy and close to exhaustion. He thanked Wilson, then asked to be taken to the barracks.

As they walked through the settlement's wide and muddy square, he thought: the man on his own upstream must be Macaulay, who had somehow been injured but was armed with a musket and was highly dangerous, as poor Paterson had found to his cost. Some of his men were still searching for Macaulay. Almost certainly, it was Fitzgerald and the woman whom Wilson had seen and they were roaming the marshes to the north of this settlement.

He would ask the local commanding officer to send a search party into the marshes. The man and the woman should be easy to catch. Macaulay was the problem. He'd get a few hours' sleep, then work out a plan.

The Governor of New South Wales, Captain John Hunter, had travelled to Parramatta to examine the site and discuss construction of the Governor's country home. It was to be built on a hill near the water, at a reedy sweep in the river where the Aborigines could still be seen, standing one-legged in the shallows as they attempted to spear eels. This was the hill where the first Governor, Arthur Phillip, had erected a small residence for use on his visits to Rose Hill, as the town was known in the first three years of the settlement. That building was flimsy, with walls of lath and plaster and a roof that had fallen down during a storm in Hunter's time, rendering the house both unlivable and irreparable.

Hunter liked the atmosphere upriver at the farming community and the site was beautiful; rather English in character with its gently rolling hills and acres of green grass. He preferred it here to

Sydney. Certainly, there were convicts with their little cottages and vegetable gardens living all along Church Street but the atmosphere at Parramatta was of a much freer society. Sydney was becoming oppressive, with all the chain gangs and guards and drunken brawls at night, and now, even the Aborigines were coming into town to stage their ritual battles. Brickfield Hill was a favourite place for a spear fight; either a duel between two or, more common and infinitely more popular among the crowds who gathered around to watch the blood flow, a fight between groups—he could never quite work out who was who among the blacks—to settle a family or tribal difference that required someone to be hurt before they could all go home.

They chose to fight in front of the white settlers. Some warriors, like knights-errant, even travelled from down south, beyond Botany Bay, to test their skill with spear and shield, against the locals. Curious and, he thought, distasteful. Not the fighting but the spectacle of the settlers cheering them on and groaning or laughing, depending on their fancy, when a man took a spear through the ribs.

No, he preferred Parramatta.

He stayed in a tent and, on the second day of his visit, was forced to remain inside for much of the morning because of the heavy rain. Even so, he'd had an interesting time.

Early in the morning he'd been paid a visit by Silas Whittaker, the master of a visiting American brigantine, who came to offer thanks for the Governor's assistance in having repairs carried out to the vessel. His ship, the *Louise,* had lost a mast when caught in a cyclone in the South Seas. Whittaker also brought news of the war in Europe. The information was six months old but eagerly absorbed by Hunter who, as a naval officer, chafed at having to serve in an on-shore administrative post, with his prime tasks being to keep the convicts in and the French out, when others were winning glory at sea on the far side of the world.

The blockade of France continued. Horatio Nelson, the Royal Navy's brightest star, had won a series of victories against the French—usually in ship-to-ship combat, as in the great days of Drake—but had lost an arm during an engagement off Tenerife. A bullet had shattered his elbow and surgeons had been forced to take the arm. Nelson was a daring leader. Perhaps too daring, the American suggested; the poor man had lost an eye three years earlier when fighting ashore in Corsica. Hunter had spent so much time out of England in the last ten years that he'd heard only sporadic reports of the war and he was thrilled by Whittaker's accounts of the sea battles.

The American also brought news of a mutiny at the Royal Navy's base at Spithead. A mutiny! The worst in the navy's history. Whittaker knew few of the details and left Hunter eager for the arrival of the next ship from England, with more information.

At eleven o'clock the Governor was visited by Surgeon George Bass, recently returned from a voyage of exploration to the southernmost coast of New South Wales. Bass had sailed up the Parramatta River to see him and, typically, made light of the drenching rain. As he pointed out, he had just returned from a 1,200-mile voyage in a small, open boat and had known far worse weather.

Hunter knew Bass tolerably well. In 1795, both had sailed to Port Jackson on the *Reliance,* Bass as ship's surgeon, Hunter as Governor-designate. Hunter had been with Phillip on board the *Sirius* back in '88 and therefore young Bass, whose interests revolved around navigation and exploration and who was anxious to advance in status beyond mere surgeon, had plied him with questions about the colony. Bass had also shown great interest, Hunter recalled, in the Aborigine Bennelong, who'd been taken to London two years earlier and was returning to Port Jackson, dressed as and talking like an Englishman.

Bennelong was, if Hunter recalled correctly, reticent in talking to Bass about his Aboriginal ways, which was both understandable and proper. After all, the man had been exposed to the finest flourish of civilisation—he'd even been presented to George III—and must therefore have felt the shame of his humble origins.

Hunter had marked Bass as being a man of exceptional zeal and great curiosity. Also noted on that voyage as being a young man of promise was Bass's friend, the master's mate, Matthew Flinders.

Only a month after reaching the colony, Bass and Flinders had demonstrated their eagerness to explore. Bass had brought with him a tiny boat, an eight-footer he called the *Tom Thumb*. The two men, plus Bass's youthful personal servant, William Martin, sailed from Port Jackson down to Botany Bay. They had entered the bay and rowed up the Georges River, to reach a point 20 miles further than Hunter himself had gained on his first visit to the colony. On their return they'd presented a sketch of their journey and description of the newly discovered region to the Governor, who gave the site the name of Banks Town, after the great botanist who had sailed with Cook.

In March of the following year Bass and Flinders had set sail again, in a larger vessel which they also called *Tom Thumb*. This time they discovered Port Hacking. On their way down the coast, while Bass gathered fresh water from an estuary, Flinders had diverted and entertained a group of Aborigines by cutting their hair and trimming their beards. This incident greatly amused Hunter. He admired men who could control blackfellows with a pair of scissors rather than a musket.

And now Bass was back from a third, much longer, voyage. He had used an open whaleboat, constructed at Port Jackson and only 28 feet 7 inches long. He had been away ten weeks.

Hunter and Bass were drinking tea when an aide brought an

urgent report from the Hawkesbury. It had not come from The Green Hills, or Mulgrave Place as the Hawkesbury settlement was sometimes called, but from a nearby camp where convicts were erecting a log granary to store wheat and maize. The Governor put the report to one side, to be read later. He was tired of the constant problems associated with that area. It seemed the worst characters in the colony lived furthest from the sea. The settlers were always complaining, always in debt, and either suffering from drought or being attacked by the natives, some of whom were proving reluctant to share their land with the white newcomers. He'd sent a detachment of the New South Wales Corps out there to protect the settlers. What more could he do?

He turned back to his guest.

While away, Bass had turned twenty-seven but he had the bearing of an older man with his confident, unflinching gaze. Good-looking, too: thick, dark eyebrows, strong nose, rather sensuous lips.

He had returned with a theory and an important discovery.

The theory was that Van Diemen's Land was an island. While travelling westward around the southern coast, he'd noticed that the current moved with great velocity and there was a long and constant south-west swell, suggesting a strait existed between Van Diemen's Land and New South Wales. The theory needed proving and he was sure his friend Flinders—currently down at Preservation Island searching for survivors of the shipwrecked *Sydney Cove*—would be anxious to take part in such a voyage.

The discovery was of a large inlet which Bass had called Western Port, it being the westernmost port known in the colony. Bass and his crew had stayed there for thirteen days, repairing the boat and searching for water and game to replenish their almost exhausted supplies.

Bass said he had left with a crew of six and returned with eight.

The Governor smiled and cocked his head, expecting a joke.

Bass explained that on the way to Western Port they had seen seven men on a small offshore island, to the west of a deep promontory. The men were part of a convict gang who had stolen a boat in Port Jackson and sailed south, hoping to plunder the *Sydney Cove*. They'd missed the wreck, which was in the Furneaux group of islands to the south-east, and landed on this island. While the seven slept, their companions sailed away.

It being impossible to take all the men on board, Bass had left them on the island, promising to return on his way home. This he had done. He ferried five men to the mainland, giving them a musket, half of his ammunition, some hooks and lines for fishing, and directions for walking to Sydney Town.

The other two, one old and the other ill, were taken aboard the whaleboat and brought back to Sydney.

Hunter was silent for a long time. There had been a plethora of escapes. At some places more than one in ten of the convicts had tried to get away.

'You gave them a musket?'

'Yes.' Both were silent.

The Governor's aide returned. There was another message from the Hawkesbury, just delivered by a man who was close to exhaustion. He'd spoken of two brutal murders.

The Governor read both reports. He stood and walked slowly to the flap of the tent. The rain was easing. Without turning, he said, 'Men steal boats from under our noses and sail to a place where even you hadn't been.' He glanced at Bass. 'Now two of our soldiers have been murdered up near The Green Hills.' The aide was still in the tent. 'Who's in charge out there?'

'I understand Lieutenant de Lacey is there, Your Excellency.'

'What the devil is de Lacey doing out there?'

'On a tour of inspection, sir. We've had bad reports from there, sir, and he'd been sent to suggest improvements.'

'And instead of making improvements, he allows the convicts to commit mayhem.' Hunter turned to Bass. 'I wonder if de Lacey's good enough for the job.'

'I don't know him very well, Your Excellency.'

He glanced at the aide.

'I understand Lieutenant de Lacey had just arrived at the site when the first man was murdered.'

Hunter gazed up at the canvas roof. 'The second man . . . his name was Paterson?'

'Yes, sir.'

'Related to my predecessor?'

To the former lieutenant-governor? The aide shifted his feet. 'I understand he may be a nephew of Captain Paterson. It's not certain yet.'

Hunter, a tall man in the twilight of his naval career, clapped his hands behind his back. 'I have had more than enough of these outrages,' he said, his voice getting louder. 'All hell will break loose when London hears of this. These convicts must be caught and dealt with. I will not tolerate any more excuses. De Lacey has one day to catch them. One day.' He spun on Bass. 'Am I being fair, Mr Bass?'

Bass could do no more than shrug before Hunter added, 'I have been accused of being too soft, too gentle. I find that a curious condemnation. I believe I make the necessary hard decisions, even though they may cause me anguish. I believe I am fair.'

He let Bass nod his affirmation.

'Maybe now is the time to show people I can also be tough. De Lacey has one day to catch these villains and if he strings them up in the field, so much the better.'

Being curious, Bass was compelled to ask, 'And if he doesn't catch them?'

'Ah, Mr Bass,' he said, softening his tone and returning to his canvas chair, 'in that case, you wouldn't wish to be de Lacey. Now come, tell me more about this Western Port of yours.'

The rain stopped and Macaulay emerged from the cave. He was wet and stiff and his leg throbbed. Carrying the musket over his shoulder, he limped down the rocky slope, away from the flooded waterhole and towards the end of the valley where shadowy folds of deep blue cut into a range of wooded hills. He had to get further away from the river. The soldiers would be back, either this evening or in the morning and this time there'd be no animal to divert them from their quarry.

He reached the line of bushes at the bottom of the slope and stopped in surprise. The bearded Aborigine was standing there, rock still, spear in one hand, one leg tucked behind the other knee. Macaulay took a deep breath. 'By the Holy Jesus you frightened me,' he said.

The man lowered his foot and pointed to a gap through the bushes. Two men were waiting. The bearded man signalled for Macaulay to follow them.

'And what if I don't.' He lowered the musket. 'What are you devils up to?'

Frowning, the man looked towards the river. Again, he gestured for Macaulay to follow the others but, this time, he used the spear. There were other blacks in the bushes, silent figures standing on either side of the track.

The two men were moving. Macaulay followed them.

SEVEN

THE DAY WAS ending in a flourish of misty blues and, deep in the sea of leaves lapping the cliffs, the laughing jackasses were performing their evening ritual of challenge and response. Having chosen their own branches in their own trees, the birds were broadcasting their territorial claims, one raucous cry following another until the mountains rang with cackling echoes. Other birds were in the air, hurrying to their evening nests. A quartet of rosellas flew by, long-tailed and short-winged, feathers flashing brilliant hues as they caught the last rays of daylight. From out of the sunset came three flights of ducks, arrowing towards the river. Down on the flat, where long fingers of grass spread from the marsh, two kangaroos were grazing, occasionally raising their dog-like heads to twitch ears in a cautious, instinctive search for alien sounds.

Eliza watched and listened but didn't move.

'They're such beautiful creatures,' she whispered. She was lying on her side, exhausted and shivering from the embrace of sodden clothes, her eyes unblinking as she gazed at the strange scene.

They were under a jutting shelf of rock. Some animal had been there before them, having cleared the grass with long claws. Clancy opened an eye. 'I thought you were asleep.'

'No.' She sighed. 'I think I'm going to die,' she said and sighed again as if death would be a blessing.

It would be, he thought. She should go to sleep and not wake up. That would be a blessing for them both. This was hopeless. She was slowing him down. They would be caught if they stayed near the river but if he attempted to cross the mountains, as he must do, she would perish on the climb. Better for her to die now. He would say a few words over her cold, inert form, cover her body with leaves and branches, and move on.

Move on to where? He looked beyond the mountains to the crimson blaze of clouds where the sun had been. Reach a land where no other white man lived? Spend the remainder of his years among the blackfellows? Survive with nothing but the clothes he wore and a chain with manacles at each end? A sense of hopelessness joined the chill that had him twitching uncontrollably. He moved, stretching his numbed and aching legs. He would need a knife, an axe, a flint, food—God, he was hungry—seeds to plant, a spade or a hoe to dig the soil, dry clothes to wear. A dozen more things, just to live. He hadn't thought about this when talking to Macaulay. Neither had the big man. They had just wanted to get away. They had never discussed what they would do once they were out of the camp and across the river. Each had thought only of escape, not of survival.

And here he was, dragging this useless woman behind him, and Macaulay, who might have been some help—certainly, he would have been another man to talk to—was gone. Macaulay, he felt sure, was dead, caught by the soldiers and either strung up from a tree or lying in a fresh grave with a bullet in the back of his skull.

Clancy peered at the sandstone cliffs, now striped with shadows as night began claiming the sky. How was he going to climb these mountains? How long would he survive without food? And if he miraculously crossed the mountains, finding a way no one else had discovered in almost ten years of probing, where would he live? With whom? He was a solitary man who preferred his own company but that implied ignoring the presence of those nearby. What would it be like with absolutely no other man around him? Except the blackfellows, whom he feared and despised.

How was he going to live on his own?

Eliza was rubbing her shoulders. 'I'm so wet and cold.'

'So am I. We'll dry out.'

'I'll never be warm again. I think I'm going to die.'

Always talking about dying. If only it were true, he thought, but said, 'You're not.'

'How would you know?'

'If you were dying, you wouldn't be talking so much. Look, die if you want to but let me get some sleep. I'm very tired.'

'You don't think I'm tired, too?'

He laughed softly.

'I think you're a cruel, heartless man.'

'I don't care what you think. What's your name? I've forgotten.'

'Eliza Phillips and I haven't forgotten yours although I wish I could.'

'Well listen, Eliza Phillips, I'm going to get some sleep and then, before the sun comes up again, I intend to leave you and do a very foolish thing.'

'Leave me?' She lifted her head.

'Just for a while. I'll be coming back.' It would make more sense to walk away and leave her while she slept but if he left her, the soldiers would soon catch her and then she'd be hanged and while he didn't mind the thought of her dying in her sleep, he didn't like the idea of her choking on the end of a rope.

'What are you going to do?' She was trying to comb her hair with her fingers, scraping mud and weed from the tangled locks.

'I've been thinking.' He took a deep breath. Was this what he truly wanted to do? No, but it was what he must do. He said,

'I'm going back, to cross the river and try to get a few things.'

'What sort of things?'

'Things we'll need.' He'd meant 'I'll need' but he'd said 'we' without thinking. All day he had treated her with scorn as she lagged behind, stumbling, falling, but refusing to quit. Now, he realised with surprise, he felt sorry for her and was touched by the first hint of respect. She was as game as a good man. And because she'd never given up, neither had he. She'd driven him on.

'What sort of things?' she repeated.

'Food. Clothes. A few things like that.'

'And you're going back, across the river?'

'I'll go to that settlement.'

'You have to cross the river and you can't swim.'

'Our log's still there.'

'What if they catch you?'

'They'll hang me. But they won't catch me.'

She ground a worried fist into her worried face.

'Oh, I'll be back,' he said. 'This is simple.'

'It's not. It's madness.'

'Eliza Phillips,' he said, pushing himself onto one elbow, 'You forget, I'm a thief, and a good one. I'll just break into a couple of the houses on the other side of the river and get a few things we'll need if we're to cross these mountains.' He almost said damned mountains but he stopped himself.

'If you're a good thief, what are you doing here?'

He laughed softly. 'You're not going to let me sleep, are you?'

'Answer my question.'

Awkwardly, he lowered himself to the ground and swung his feet around. The movement dislodged grit from the overhanging rock and he brushed dirt from his face. 'I was unlucky.'

'Ha!'

'I was. I'd taken this gentleman's watch and got away. No one saw me.' He folded an arm behind his head. 'Well, the man who

73

owned the watch had a friend and that night the friend happened to see me, purely by chance, when I was showing the watch to someone. The friend followed me home. He brought the police. They searched my room and found other things.'

'What other things?'

He laughed. 'More watches. I'd had a very busy day.'

'Why did you steal watches?'

He raised an eyebrow in surprise. 'Because I knew a man who'd buy them from me. Did you think I wanted to tell the time?'

'You weren't unlucky. You were stupid. And a villain.'

'I still am, Eliza Phillips. And being a villain and being stupid, I'm going back tonight across that river and I'm going to rob a few houses. I might even find myself a watch.' He laughed at that. There were few clocks in all the colony, let alone pocket watches, which is why people relied on those damned laughing birds to wake them.

She gazed out, expecting to see the kangaroos but they had gone. She searched the expanse of grass where they had been grazing and all the clear spaces in the valley that stretched between the towering cliffs, but the two animals had disappeared. After a while, she turned back to him. 'When did you reach Port Jackson?'

He made a growling noise of protest. 'You'd drive a man mad, I can tell.'

'I'm curious.'

'I came with the first ships. With Phillip.' He tapped the front of his mouth. 'He had a gap in his teeth. Funny thing for a governor. Did you ever see him?'

She shook her head. 'Clancy, the first ships came ten years ago. Most people would be free by now.'

'Not me.'

'Why? What was your sentence?'

'Fourteen years.'

She shuffled into a sitting position until her shoulders touched the rock. 'Why fourteen? That's a long sentence.'

'A couple of years ago, a few of the lads tried to steal a ship and sail away. They said I knew about it.'

'Did you?'

He ignored the question. 'They gave me another seven years and fifty across the back. Want to see? I'm told it's not a pretty sight.'

He started to lift his collar and she turned away. 'No thank you.'

'Can I go to sleep now?'

'If you want to. Don't you want to know anything about me?'

'No.'

'They said I stole a kettle. Most of us were transported for trivial things. There was a man who'd only stolen a bag of carrots while another was sent out for damaging a haystack.'

'I don't want to hear.'

'I came here with the second lot of ships.'

'You were supposed to bring food.'

'We didn't have enough for ourselves. It was a nightmare. All the way from England people were dying all around me. They were either sick or starving. When we got to Port Jackson they were still throwing bodies overboard. I'm told hundreds died.'

'I've heard the stories. Can I go to sleep?'

'I don't like you, Clancy Fitzgerald.'

'Few people ever have.' He closed his eyes.

It was much darker now. No birds were flying and the jackasses were silent.

De Lacey slept until a servant woke him for dinner. His own red jacket and white trousers were drying on a rack. Other clothes were laid out for him on an adjoining bed. They were a poor fit

75

but dry and warm. He dressed and was taken to the weatherboard and shingle cottage used by the commander of the Hawkesbury detachment, a Lieutenant Atkinson. He was a small man with a large moustache and a chin that seemed bent under the weight of so much drooping hair.

'Thought you were going to sleep all day and all night, old boy.' Atkinson spoke jovially but there was an implied criticism. De Lacey had met him a few times in Sydney but didn't mix with him. He didn't like the man. He had gone to an inferior school and had little class.

'I had asked to be woken after two hours,' de Lacey said, fingering the coarse material of his jacket with distaste.

'Thought I'd let you sleep in, old boy.' Atkinson smiled. 'Sent a man to have a look. Said you were dead to the world.'

'I wanted to be up and out before the sun went down. There were things I needed to do.'

'No one's in a hurry out here, old boy.'

'I am.'

In silence, they ate a meal of salted pork, boiled potatoes and bread. When he had finished eating, Atkinson wiped his moustache with slow, loving strokes and announced casually that six of his men were still on the far side of the river, searching the marshes. So far, there'd been no sign of the man or the woman. He hurried on, not allowing de Lacey time to speak. 'I hear the man they killed—the one they strung up to the tree—might be the nephew of the former Lieutenant-Governor.' He paused to study de Lacey's face, which remained as impassive as ever. The man was a snob and as cold as a fish. He deserved to be put in his place. 'There'll be an almighty stink when the news reaches Hunter.' Atkinson spent a few moments picking meat from his teeth. 'Wouldn't like to be in your shoes, old boy.'

De Lacey pushed himself from the table. 'Nor I in yours, my dear fellow. I would have thought your men capable of finding a couple some farmer saw carousing in the woods. Apparently not.' He rose and Atkinson stood to face him. 'I trust you'll be good enough to let me have some men so I can leave at first light and do a little searching of my own.'

'I thought you were going back upriver, to join your own men.'

'They are not my men, my dear Atkinson, and I had assumed that by tonight the men under your command would have brought Fitzgerald and Phillips in here, so we could find out just what the devil has been going on. Obviously, I'll have to do that myself.'

Atkinson's face was flushed. 'I'll count on your success, sir.'

Impertinent bastard, de Lacey thought as he left. But the man was right. Unless he caught these people soon, the flames of Hell would burst forth and he was the one who would be seared.

It took Macaulay one hour to be certain the Aborigines were friendly but several more to understand what they were trying to tell him. They had taken him to their camp, which lay at the end of a gully where a small fire burned in a clearing ringed by majestic eucalypts. Several women and children were sitting around the fire when the men approached but they quickly retreated into the shadows, where only the occasional flash of reflected firelight on curious eyes revealed their presence.

The men squatted around the fire and motioned for Macaulay to join them. They ate a python. Cooking was minimal. One man threw the snake on the fire and once the diamond patterns on the python's skin began to burst and the first eruptions of sizzling fat appeared, his companions proceeded to tear it apart. They ate at the furious pace of starving men.

They laughed frequently and spoke with great animation. They knew the soldiers were hunting Macaulay. Therefore, the soldiers were the enemy of the big man. The soldiers were their enemy, too. They shook pieces of fatty meat to emphasise their words, as though the brandishing of underdone snake would make the meaning clearer. Whenever Macaulay nodded his understanding of some point, there were shouts from the men around him and a round of applause from greasy hands slapping dusty thighs.

Somehow, the blacks knew he had strung up the soldier and his dog. Macaulay was sure no one had seen him, but they mimed a man choking to death, and the dog too—they were great mimics—and they smiled approval when they told the story. They had killed white men too—three of them did a pantomime to prove it and the women hidden in the bushes laughed—and that evening, if Macaulay understood the gist of the conversation, the men were going across the river to kill more soldiers and settlers.

The white men had taken their land. If they didn't drive them away, more would come and soon they would build their houses on this side of the river—they called the Hawkesbury the Deerubin—and then they would be forced to retreat into the mountains where the nights were cold and hunting was difficult.

Macaulay was invited to join them on the raid. And bring the gun. They had seen what a musket could do—only from a distance, but they knew it could spit fire and they knew that, somehow, it killed. Three of the tribe had been shot in one raid.

Macaulay's gun was the first they had actually touched. They felt the metal barrel again as he passed it around the fire and, one by one, nodded in awe.

He couldn't come with them, Macaulay said. His injured leg was still too weak. He limped around the fire, slapping the leg and moaning and putting on such a good show of being crippled that the hidden women laughed again. He would be too slow. A handicap. They must move quickly if they were to kill the soldiers.

They agreed.

The leader, a smart man who seemed able to grasp what Macaulay was saying before the others, had an alternative plan. Macaulay should come part of the way with them. They would move slowly at first so that he could keep up. Then Macaulay would wait, with his gun, at a place the leader would choose.

Using Macaulay and his gun was an important part of the plan. That much was clear but being possessed of neither quick wits nor the cunning of a warrior waging war on invaders, Macaulay had no idea what scheme the leader had devised. However, the man was insistent, fired by an idea too good to be rejected, and Macaulay agreed to go. He was dependent on these men for his own survival and he would do whatever they wanted, even if it meant helping them wipe out the entire white settlement.

It was close to midnight when they left.

The sky being bright with the ice-blue wash of moonlight, Clancy had no trouble finding a path through the marsh. He was already well on his way to the river. He'd had little sleep and his leg ached but he hurried, driven on by the need to cross the Hawkesbury at least four hours before sun-up. His plan was simple. Float across on the log. Steal dry clothes. Raid a few more houses in the hours before dawn when people were in their deepest sleep. Hide somewhere during the day. Sleep. Wait for nightfall before returning.

The thought of stealing again, of pitting his wits and skill against the combined resources of suspicious men and Lady Luck, appealed to him. So did the challenge of the journey. If he could cover in five hours a distance that had taken the two of them nearly twelve, then he would have made a valid point about how fast he could travel on his own. And he would certainly let Eliza know when he got back. He'd mention it casually, without any suggestion of boastfulness and maybe with a laugh to suggest it really didn't matter, but he'd make the point clearly enough for her to understand how much she was holding him back.

He was a tough and wiry man, used to punishing his body and, in the days before he was put in chains, noted for his fleetness of foot and physical endurance. He could outsprint and outrun any man he'd met, a talent which had kept him out of prison for several years. Now, despite the weariness, he was relishing the freedom of being on his own, of travelling quickly through the night, unchained and unencumbered by a slow and faltering companion.

Nearing the river, he saw a light and approached slowly. It was a fire, flickering and spluttering as if the flames were struggling to gain a hold on damp wood. He could see several men, huddled in a circle, all gazing into the light. Crawling forward on his belly, he got close enough to see other men lying on the ground under canvas covers and tripods of guns stacked near the fire. It was a soldiers' camp. They must be out searching for him.

He stayed low, hiding behind a spiky clump of grass, trying to hear what they were saying but their voices were low and they mumbled, in the manner of men who were weary and displeased with their lot.

They were no longer searching; they were merely enduring the night, and he felt an insane urge to stand up, to mock their blindness. But then he realised there might be others out in the marsh, a night patrol that was continuing the search. He rolled on one side then the other, probing the dark, listening for other sounds. Nothing. He waited another five minutes then crawled away and only when he was sure he was out of sight did he stand and, walking in a wide semicircle around the camp, continue on to the river.

EIGHT

HAVING REACHED A place that was about half a mile from the river, the raiding party stopped. The moon had set and, in the intense darkness, the warriors squatted among trees, silent and bent over their spears while the leader took the white man aside. The man's name, Macaulay had discovered, was Nimboola. He led Macaulay to a mound of large rocks from which sprouted several trees. Macaulay was to wait in the rocks. Holding his hand, Nimboola took him to a tree and bade him sit beside it. He must not move. Nimboola and his companions should be back before sunrise.

All this Nimboola mimed. The black man said other things, too, but in such a rush of words and shadowy gestures that Macaulay failed to understand their meaning. But he nodded to assure Nimboola he knew what to do. All that mattered, he reasoned, was that he stay among the rocks. He would find out soon enough why Nimboola had put him there. In the meantime, he'd rest his leg and sleep for a few hours.

De Lacey had difficulty in sleeping. The hut assigned to him was crude, being roughly made of wattle and mud and so poorly sealed that a breeze which sprang up a few hours before dawn moaned and whistled as it pierced the walls. There was nothing to read and, in any case, the room had only one candle which

81

wouldn't have given him sufficient light, so he got up and stood in the doorway with a blanket wrapped around his shoulders and gazed across the settlement towards the river.

Once he thought he saw someone moving between buildings. The shape was low and moved fast, like a man bent forward as he ran, or so he imagined, but his eyes were notoriously unreliable and he'd learned to be wary of the images they conveyed when visibility was poor. He peered into the shadows for several minutes and even walked a few paces along the muddy road but saw nothing other than the angular silhouettes of the stone houses that lined the road down to the river. It could have been an animal. A native dog possibly, or even a kangaroo. Because he had overslept during the day, he presumed he was regarded as a dithering, foolish figure and had no desire to increase that perception by rousing someone to check shadows in the street. So he went back to his room, lit the candle and lay on the bed, to stare at the distorted shapes that danced across the rough walls and to think how cruelly he was being treated by perfidious fortune.

When dawn was still an hour away he got dressed with the intention of strolling down to the river.

The first place Clancy robbed was a pig farm on the outskirts of the settlement. Clothes hung from a line at the back of a shack that was the farm's only building. Feeling each garment and inspecting it in the poor light, he decided that a man, his wife and a couple of small children lived there. The man was slightly bigger than he was but he took a shirt, a vest and pair of trousers. He also pulled down a woman's dress and soiled it in a pool of water. Using the muddied tips of his fingers, he left the imprint of a dog's paw on several parts of the fabric and left the dress lying a few yards from the line.

Let some animal be blamed for the lost clothes. He smiled at that. He was proud of his cunning.

Clancy buried his sodden convict garb under a pile of pig manure. He washed his hands in a large puddle but couldn't get rid of the pig smell. No matter; he now had the ingrained animal smell of a farmer, not the sweaty, unwashed stink of a convict.

The second house, closer to town, yielded nothing. It was a poor farm with no animals and the only implement he found was a mattock with a badly chipped blade. It would have been cumbersome to carry and of doubtful use so he left it.

The third house had a small shed in which he found a short axe and a whetting stone. He also took a hammer and a handful of copper nails.

The fourth house was large, having at least four rooms and an outside kitchen. From the latter building he took a metal mug, a sharp knife and a partly eaten loaf of bread. Using the knife, he cut himself a slice of salted pork, ate it immediately, and then took all the meat from the hook on which it was hanging. He found an empty flour sack and put everything in it.

Emboldened by his success he broke into the house itself and stole a man's cotton cap, a pair of boots that were a reasonable fit, a needle, a spool of thread and a pair of scissors. Wearing the cap and boots, he was thinking of creeping into the bedroom to glimpse his benefactors but a dog began barking nearby and he left the house hurriedly.

Something was worrying the dog because its barking became frenzied. Then, quite suddenly, the barking stopped. There was no yelp, as one might have expected if the dog had been kicked or beaten, but the sudden silence was so unnatural, the dog having stopped without any whimpering or growling, that Clancy became nervous, even frightened by the sensation of threat, and crept back to the kitchen. Holding the door sufficiently ajar for him to see out, he stood there for a long time, listening for further sounds.

There were no noises but after ten minutes there was

movement. He saw some men creeping towards the farmhouse. He counted three, then three more and then from the other side of the house, another four. They were shadowy, sinister figures shuffling across the yard like spiders with one hand constantly touching the ground as they advanced. Their free hands held spears.

Blacks. A war party. Scarcely daring to breathe because his breath seemed so noisy in the overwhelming silence, Clancy took the short axe from the flour bag, gripped it in his right hand and waited by the door.

Nimboola's aim was to put such fear into the minds of the white settlers that they would leave his land and go back to where they had come from. He was not a man of savage instincts, neither cruel nor bloodthirsty, but he understood the effect fear had upon people, no matter what their colour. Thus his men would kill some white people while they slept, skewering them with their long hunting spears, then sneak away into the night. Violence, he knew, had a more shocking impact when performed in silence.

They had already speared one family, a man, his woman and a young girl who slept in a single-room shack on a hill well back from the river. The woman had made some noise but no one had heard because the house was isolated. Now they were on the edge of town, at one of the larger houses.

If things went well they might even kill a few animals, the big four-legged ones with horns and a ravenous appetite for grass or the fat, thick-skinned ones that made grunting noises. The white man didn't hunt his animals. He fed them and cared for them, as one would a human, which was exceedingly strange. For some reason, Nimboola had deduced, the settlers had come to the river because of these animals. Thus their loss would be keenly felt and be a further inducement to leave.

All his men were now in place at the back of the house. The last pair, his young nephews who were on their first raid, had reached the other side of the house. The elder brother, a sinewy lad of seventeen, slowly raised a spear to indicate they were ready.

Nimboola signalled for old Drugala, who could move with the stealth of a snake, to find a way into the house. Drugala crept to the back door and, to his surprise, found it unlocked. Quietly, he opened the door and stood aside.

Four men, spears raised for the death thrust, moved towards the opening.

From close behind them, a man's voice screamed a warning: 'Wake up! Savages! They're all around the house!'

Clancy had no idea why he'd called out. Only a crude wooden door on bent hinges was between him and a group of murderous blacks and he was screaming out a warning to a man he'd just robbed.

'Get up. You're under attack.'

In bewilderment, the blacks had turned towards the kitchen. Some bent lower, others stood erect in their confusion. One man threw a spear but it was a wild throw, prompted by panic, and Clancy heard the whistle of air as it passed the small building. Another man jabbered a command and the four who had been about to enter the house and hesitated, now raced inside with their spears held high.

Hidden by the door, Clancy took a deep breath. 'All right, men,' he yelled at the top of his voice. 'Fire!' He was a good mimic and tried to make the sound of a musket being fired. 'Bang,' he shouted, feeling foolish until he saw the effect it had on the raiding party. They backed away, some running, others looking around, one shaping up to throw a spear in his direction.

'Bang, bang.' He'd found an iron pot and each time he shouted, he struck it with the back of the axe head.

From within the house, a man called out. A woman screamed.

A spear thudded into the kitchen wall.

'All right men, fire. Bang!' Again, he hit the pot with the axe. And in another voice, 'Johnson, Jones, around the other side.' He ran on the spot, letting his feet thud on the floor. 'Bang! Bang!'

A spear rattled on the roof.

He waited. Silence. He peeped through the narrow opening. The blacks were gone.

In the house, the woman began wailing.

Another spear hit the wall but it made a twanging sound and fell to the ground. Thrown from a distance as a last defiant gesture, he thought, he hoped, but closed the door all the same. There was no inside bolt so he dragged a heavy sack across the floor and, with the urgent strength of a frightened man, wedged it in place against the door.

From somewhere near the river he heard another man's voice, an English voice. The man was shouting orders.

Axe in hand, sack held against his body like a shield, Clancy Fitzgerald crawled to the far wall and sat down because his legs would no longer support him.

Nimboola hurried his men towards the port. The river was deep and broad where the white men kept their boats but that was to his advantage. All in his party were good swimmers whereas the soldiers, he knew from much secret observation, not only didn't swim but had a strange reluctance to get their bodies wet. His warriors would cross the river with the ease of fish but the white men would wait for boats, either the broad canoes with the long paddles out each side or the bigger craft with the tall sticks that were moored in the middle of the stream.

Nimboola's men would cut loose all the canoes moored at the water's edge, keeping just one for themselves. In this, they would cross the river, not sitting within the craft and facing backwards, which was the strangers' way, but gripping its wooden planks and swimming alongside. In that manner, they would stay in a group, be out of sight, have a place to carry their spears and clubs and deny the soldiers an immediate means of pursuit. His men would be on their way to the place where they had left the big white man long before the soldiers crossed the river.

His men were hurrying but it was an orderly retreat, as he had planned in case of discovery. They moved in a bunch, jogging rather than running, spears at the ready in case of further attack. Periodically, the three men at the back stopped and turned, peering into the darkness for signs of pursuit.

Nimboola was still unsettled by the sudden attack. He'd seen no one, whereas normally the white man moved clumsily and was easily observed. And now no one was following them. This puzzled him. There had been so much noise at the house, so much firing of guns that he had expected to see soldiers on their heels, shouting and firing.

He was looking back, peering at the houses, searching for lights or signs of movement when he almost bumped into Quinton de Lacey.

De Lacey was running towards them, armed with a wooden paddle which he'd found on the jetty when he first heard the shouts and banging.

Now he stopped and swung the paddle at Nimboola who danced to one side to avoid the blow. Nimboola jabbed at de Lacey with his spear and felt the touch of flesh. He'd nicked the man. No more.

Old Drugala was beside him and he too tried to spear the white man but de Lacey was a fencer of renown, extremely

87

quick on his feet, and he dodged the thrust and whacked Drugala on the side of the head with the paddle.

It was a heavy blow. Without uttering a sound, Drugala collapsed on the road. Immediately, Nimboola grabbed his arm and dragged him away. He looked around. Where were the other soldiers and what was this man doing fighting them with a club?

The soldier was now wrestling another man. A young man; one of his nephews. Nimboola slung the unconscious body of Drugala across his shoulder. Worried about the boy but conscious of the need to get his men away from here quickly, he called out angrily for someone to spear or club the lone soldier. Then all were to hurry down to the river. He feared an ambush.

The Aborigine was young but wiry and his greased body was as slippery as an eel's. Rolling on the ground, de Lacey had his arms locked around the youth's chest and was intent on squeezing the life out of him, for he was ashamed to have been caught out of doors without a weapon and was intent on making someone pay, but then the lad kicked and wriggled and raised his arms and was gone, leaving the lieutenant with nothing but the stench of animal fat and sweat. Someone snatched at his ankle and he kicked hard. Hands seized his other leg. He still had the paddle and he swung it blindly, feeling the satisfying crunch of wood on bone. One leg was free and he kicked again and rolled to one side. He heard a spear thud into the ground, swung the paddle again but someone seized the other end. He got to his feet and pulled and kicked and the paddle came free.

Around him, figures darker than the night were running down to the river.

Where were the soldiers from the garrison? He'd heard them shouting and banging things. Now there was no one.

He was in the middle of the flight, a rock dividing a stream of rushing water. He swung wildly with the paddle, missed, was bumped by several bodies and felt a burning pain in his side.

He swung again, hit someone and heard the man groan as he fell. He leaped onto his back.

'Help,' he shouted. 'Down here.'

He heard a shout and a shot, and cheered.

'Quick. Down to the jetty!'

'Stop firing, the lieutenant's down here,' someone called but de Lacey yelled back, 'No, keep shooting.' He meant to add, 'They're getting away,' but then he was struck on the back of his head and while he couldn't shout any more, he knew he mustn't let go and had an arm locked around the Aborigine's neck, even though the man was rising and dragging him down the road, when the first soldier arrived and, using the butt of his musket, clubbed the black man to the ground.

NINE

ONLY WHEN HE heard the sound of muskets firing—
real shots, with their dull, whoofling echoes—did
Clancy emerge from the kitchen. He didn't know where to go
but he knew he couldn't stay where he was. The woman in the
house was wailing in distress. Soon she'd be at the front door,
still screaming, and people would come to help her. They'd find
the husband with a spear in his gut—he presumed the man was
dead by the noise the woman was making—and then they'd arm
themselves with meat axes and pitchforks and search around the
house, thirsting for bloody revenge.

He'd meant to hide somewhere among the buildings but that
would be impossible now. Every house would be checked, every
shed examined. Of one other thing he was certain. The search
would spread out from the settlement. Therefore, he should
head towards the centre of town. Quickly, before the settlers
organised themselves.

Dogs were barking and he could hear men shouting. He hurried between buildings until he was in the street leading down
to the river. Now he could hear what the men were shouting:
'Get the boats. Get the boats.'

A solitary voice was countering, 'The scoundrels, they've
taken the lot.' And another challenging. 'Rot, man, get a boat.
Quickly.'

90

'I tell you, they've taken all the damned boats.' Then followed a babble of words, with the occasional boom of a gun obliterating any chance of comprehension.

The blacks, it seemed, had got away and the soldiers couldn't follow.

It was almost dawn and in the ghostly light Clancy could see people emerging from houses. Some carried lanterns. A man who was adjusting the belt on his trousers hurried to catch up with Clancy.

'What happened?'

'Savages,' Clancy said, emboldened by the way the man accepted him as being a fellow resident. 'A war party. They killed a man back there.'

'Good Lord,' the man said and stopped where he was.

Alone, Clancy continued towards the river. There was less shouting now and he could hear the rumble of voices. There were no more shots. The blacks had got away. Disappeared, as was their habit.

In the faint light, he saw two men. Both soldiers. One was sitting in the middle of the road, partly disrobed. The other was bent over him, examining the man's side.

'You've been lucky,' the second man said. 'It just seems to have scraped your side.'

'Damned sore.'

Clancy stopped near them. He'd been a brazen thief, able to bluff his way out of perilous situations. Time to use the old skills.

'Are you all right?' he asked, moving closer.

De Lacey looked up. 'Perfectly, thank you, sir.' He raised a hand so the other soldier could help him to his feet. He pulled his shirt into place before turning to Clancy. 'And who are you?'

'Frank Smith. I have a farm just over the hill.' He realised he was still holding the axe. He held it up. 'I heard the noise and thought I might be able to lend a hand.'

'Very kind of you, sir,' de Lacey said. 'But I fear you're a little late. Just as we were. The birds have flown.'

'The lieutenant took them on single-handedly,' the other man said.

'Damned stupid thing to do.' De Lacey looked for the paddle but it was gone. It was probably used to hit him on the head. He took a few exploratory steps. 'Legs still function. The rest of me seems to be working satisfactorily. Come on, let's get after them.'

'You're bleeding from that wound, sir.'

'I'll have that fixed later.'

Clancy hurried after them. 'I was wondering . . .' he said.

De Lacey halted, touching the lump on his head. 'What is it, Smith?'

'I was hoping to get across the river. I have some land over there.'

'And?'

'Well, I think my boat's gone. I heard someone saying them savages cut loose all the boats. Mine would be one of them.'

'I wouldn't be venturing across the river today.'

'Oh, those blacks will be gone like the wind. Up in the hills somewhere. Miles away. They'll be no trouble to me.'

De Lacey frowned, thinking of something. 'Were you working on the other side of the river yesterday?'

Clancy shook his head. 'No, sir. Not for a couple of days. But after all that rain, there are things I got to do or I'll lose all my crop.' He lowered his voice. 'And I couldn't afford for that to happen. Things have been very hard for us here.'

De Lacey glanced towards the river where a burst of cheering had sounded. Men were bringing one of the yachts to the jetty.

'Very well, Smith,' he said. 'It's your neck. The soldier here will look after you.' He waved a finger at the private. 'You'll make the arrangements?'

'Yes, sir.'

'But do it later, when things are a little quieter. And when they've recovered some of the boats.'

'Yes, sir.'

Clancy stepped forward and held out his hand. 'I'd like to shake the hand of a brave man.'

'He fought them with a wooden paddle,' the soldier said, awe ringing in his words.

'That's enough of that,' de Lacey said. 'But what you did was highly commendable, Smith, hurrying down here to help us.' They shook hands.

'And who do I have the honour of greeting?'

'De Lacey. Lieutenant, New South Wales Corps.'

'Smith. Humble farmer. I'll remember you, sir.'

De Lacey was becoming impatient. 'Look, I'll go on alone. You take care of him, won't you, private?' he said and, buttoning his jacket, headed for the river.

'I'll get you across as soon as the soldiers are on their way,' the soldier said when de Lacey had gone. 'Do you know, he was fighting them savages on his own. Just him. And he was only visiting us, too.'

'A remarkable man. What's he doing here?'

'Searching for those escaped convicts.'

'Oh.' Clancy stroked the stubble on his chin. 'I heard about them. And has he had any luck?'

'Not yet.' He laughed. 'Won't have for a while, I'd say. He's got his hands full with all them niggers to catch.'

Clancy yawned.

'A little weary?' The soldier winked. 'Had a late night, have we?'

'I've had a lot of work to do recently. Not much sleep.'

The conspiratorial tone disappeared. 'Would you like somewhere to lie down for an hour or two?'

93

Clancy shrugged. 'I can't go home. Some of them savages might be out there now.'

The soldier gripped his arm. 'The lieutenant has a hut to himself. He won't be needing it for a while. Why don't you rest there and I'll come and fetch you when there's a boat available?'

He hurried off, flapping a hand to ward off what he presumed were Clancy's protests, but Clancy wasn't protesting. He was stammering in disbelief, choking back his surprise, not allowing himself to say what he felt. The lieutenant's bed! It would be the perfect hiding place.

The barracks were nearby. Having nodded greetings to a few soldiers who hurried past, laden with supplies and equipment needed in the pursuit of the blacks, Clancy was shown to de Lacey's hut.

'He don't belong here,' the soldier said, as if that explained the smallness of the building. 'We all thought he was a bit of a toff, but he took on those murderous savages by himself.'

'With a paddle,' Clancy prompted.

'With a damned paddle.' The soldier shook his head once more in admiration then left, promising to return when a boat was available.

Clancy had an overwhelming urge to laugh. The one place where he would be absolutely safe, the one refuge he could never have imagined, was the bedroom of the man leading the search for him.

He put down the sack and the axe and looked around the room. The bed was unmade but it had clean sheets. He'd forgotten what sheets felt like. He sat down, fingering the cotton. It was so cool, so soothing to touch. He lay down, rumpled the pillow which smelled of pomade, then sat up again. The lieutenant's other uniform, of much better quality than the one he'd been wearing, was hanging over a rack. He got up and circled the rack. The uniform needed ironing. He found a sword and took it from its scabbard. He'd never held a sword. It was heavier than he'd imagined. He swung it several times, broad sweeps that almost touched the roof timbers, then lunged at the curtains. He fingered the blade, admired the fancy engraving and put the sword back.

The lieutenant also had a pistol. It was made by a gunsmith in London and bore a coat of arms, presumably de Lacey's, as well as the maker's name. It was beautifully made, like a good watch, and Clancy handled it with reverence. He'd never held a pistol either although, he reflected, he'd had a few fired at him. He took careful aim at the hanging sword and went 'Bang', very softly and then smiled, remembering his earlier efforts at imitating gunfire.

He lay on the lieutenant's bed, giggling softly, and was soon asleep.

Having drifted upstream on the turning tide, Nimboola had his men set the boat loose and then jogged inland until, 400 yards from the river, the raiding party reached a small clump of trees. Nimboola had four men, his best runners, wait there. Still helping Drugala, who was now on his feet although weak and dizzy, he went on with the rest of his men and, fifteen minutes later, reached the rocks where Macaulay was hidden.

With daylight, Macaulay realised he had been placed at the entrance to a narrow valley, enclosed on three sides by low hills. He saw the Aborigines return and watched as Nimboola despatched six of his men to the far side of the entrance, where they hid among boulders and low scrub. The rest followed their leader to Macaulay's hiding place. Nimboola didn't speak to the white man but despatched three of the warriors, each armed with a bundle of spears, to climb a rocky hill that rose abruptly from behind the rocks.

Only when they were in place did Nimboola turn to the white man. He pointed to the musket that Macaulay was nursing in his lap. The black man mimed a gun being fired.

'All ready to go,' Macaulay said, feeling apprehensive. What on earth was the old boy up to? Warriors on both sides of the narrow valley, some up a cliff, all carrying spears and clubs. He licked his lips, not liking the scenario. They were preparing for battle and there could be only one enemy: soldiers from the settlement, in pursuit of the raiders.

The military would come with their muskets and they had two distinct advantages: the soldiers had many guns, and they knew how to use them. He had one musket and, while he knew the theory of shooting he had never fired a gun. And yet, he suspected that Nimboola expected him to wipe out a goodly part of the New South Wales Corps.

'What are you up to, you old rascal?' he asked, trying to sound jovial, but Nimboola knelt beside him and put a finger to his lips. He pointed towards the river and crouched low, as immobile as the rocks.

The sun rose as though ashamed of the new day. It peeked through a slit in the clouds lining the horizon then disappeared, leaving the sky grey and the air chilled and damp with foreboding. On the river, a ribbon of mist lay curled around the bend at The Green Hills and the water was oily and patterned by slow-moving swirls of dead leaves, left by the night's wind. Only a few jackasses were laughing and the warbling currawongs, normally so bold and entertaining in their search for food, were missing altogether. And at the jetty the soldiers who had been so garrulous only a few minutes earlier spoke in whispers.

It was because of the murders.

First had come the report that Albert Johnson, a wheat farmer who owned one of the best houses in town, had been speared through the chest while sleeping with his wife. She, poor woman, was now deranged, ripping her nightdress and pulling at her hair and screaming constantly. And then came the story, brought by a boy, red-faced from exhaustion and shock, that a family of three had been found dead in their beds on one of the outlying farms. The boy didn't know their names. Only that all had been speared, even the little girl.

On reaching the jetty de Lacey had immediately taken command of the chase. Atkinson turned up but showed no great desire to cross the river and readily handed over his sword so the visiting lieutenant might carry a weapon. A dozen men with guns were at the jetty. All had heard of de Lacey's battle with the blacks and were eager to follow him. Some extra balls and powder and a few flasks of water were brought down from the barracks and, a few minutes after sunrise, the squad crossed in one of the trading sloops, towed to the far bank by two sailors rowing the yacht's skiff.

The blacks had made no effort to hide their tracks. This was unusual, but de Lacey was a novice in bush warfare—in any sort of warfare—and was too enthused by the discovery of fresh footprints in mud to wonder why the marauding blacks would have left such clear indications of the path to be followed.

Only thirty seconds from the river one of his men shouted. There were natives up ahead. They were clearly visible: four men who had emerged from a clump of trees. Two seemed to be hurt. One held his side and ran awkwardly. Another limped and occasionally broke into a hop to keep up with his companions. They were shouting to each other. Even to an Englishman, they were clearly cries of distress.

'After 'em,' de Lacey called but the men scarcely needed urging. They broke into a run, muskets held high, whooping in their lust for blackfellows' blood.

Despite their injuries, the Aborigines covered the ground with remarkable speed. Even so, the soldiers were catching up with them and were almost within firing distance when the four men entered a small, closed valley.

'Got them,' de Lacey shouted in triumph. Breathless from the chase he stopped and, gasping for air, called to his men to spread out so that they formed a line from one side of the valley to the other. 'They can't get out. Take your time. Fire when they're in range.'

And then a curious thing happened. The four black men disappeared.

They were there one moment, one man still holding his side, another limping and hopping, the other two intact but travelling no faster than their companions and all four wailing and calling out as though in extreme fear, when they entered a region of waist-high grass. And were gone.

The grass was still. There were no sounds.

'They be vanished, sir,' one of the soldiers called out to de Lacey, who was twenty yards behind the line of men.

'They're still there. Keep advancing. Don't run. Walk.'

He needn't have added the last order. All the men had slowed.

One soldier, on the right side of the line, turned towards the nearest hillside. He had keen eyesight and although he raised one hand to shield his face from the low sun, he saw neither the thrower nor the spear that pierced the middle of his chest. The spear went through him and he toppled back, the force of the fall pinning his body to the ground.

The man nearest him, with reactions outpacing his reasoning, fired at the hill but saw only the puff of dust where the musket ball struck dirt. 'They're up that hill,' he shouted, frenziedly reloading just as a shower of spears fell on the soldiers. The spears came from both sides of the valley and had the air pulsing with the quivering of long, thin shafts.

'Trap,' a soldier at the other end of the line shouted and turned to run. A spear in the second volley pierced his thigh and he fell, screaming at the numbing impact.

For several seconds de Lacey was unable to speak. He'd

blundered into an ambush. He had thought he'd had his quarry trapped but it was he who'd been caught, outmanoeuvred by some savage as he recklessly drove his men into this deadly valley.

'Down,' he shouted when his voice returned. He dropped to one knee, furiously scanning the valley for signs of their attackers. 'Lie flat. Search for your target.'

Most men did as ordered but two were bolting, guns held low as they galloped to get beyond the range of the spears. There was a gunshot. One of the soldiers, an obese man who was slower than the other, fell.

'For God's sake, who did that?' de Lacey screamed. He stood and waved his sword at the other soldier, a red-haired youngster who'd lost his cap when he'd turned and run and whose eyes were wide in fright. 'Stop. Get down.'

The youth stopped, glancing fearfully over his shoulder.

'You'll be safer on your belly,' de Lacey said in a quiet voice. And as the youth dropped, he added, 'For heaven's sake, turn around and face the enemy.' When the soldier was in place, de Lacey knelt again.

'He's dead, sir,' one man called out.

'Who's dead?'

'Gregson. The one what got shot.'

De Lacey beat the ground with the haft of his sword. 'Who the devil fired at Gregson?'

Silence.

A voice from within the long grass said, 'None of us did, sir.'

'Nonsense. You are not to panic. There will be no more firing until I give the order.' He was counting. He'd come with a dozen men. Two had been speared, a third shot. God, how would he explain that? Nine left. They'd been chasing four natives. But there could be hundreds lining the hills, hiding behind boulders and trees.

He was halfway between the hills that formed the entrance to the valley. The men who'd been speared had been on either side. Slowly, peering from one hillside to the other, he stood up. Constantly eyeing the hills, he said, 'I want you all to come towards me.' He saw heads bob up in the grass. 'We'll be safer in the middle. They can't throw their spears this far.' He didn't know if that was true but it was important to calm the men. 'Keep down but don't take your eyes off the hills. If they show themselves, blow their bloody heads off.'

He heard the gunshot and felt his cap tugged from his head in the same instant. He was thrown forward on to his knees. His head was numb. Blood was trickling into his eyes.

'They got guns,' one of his men shouted and all rose and bolted for the river. They were farewelled by a volley of spears. Two men fell.

One soldier stopped to grab de Lacey by the arm and haul him to safety.

TEN

ELIZA SLEPT BADLY, her clothes being damp, the ground hard and her mind in turmoil. She awoke many times, hearing noises, and by dawn had convinced herself that Clancy was not coming back. He'd been caught by the soldiers. He'd drowned trying to cross the river. He'd changed his mind and set off for Parramatta or Sydney Town. Whatever had happened to him, she would never see Clancy Fitzgerald again. She was alone. Abandoned in the wilderness. And then, soon after dawn, as hunger gnawed at her and she thought for the first time she might die from starvation, not the noose, she heard gunfire.

The sounds came from far away but the reports rumbled like distant thunder through the hills. She counted three shots. They could mean only one thing. The soldiers were chasing Clancy. She thought she heard cheering. Certainly men shouting. Then silence. They'd caught him.

She sank to her knees and clasped her hands as if in prayer. It was a gesture of despair but as she knelt on the rough ground she thought of praying. Please don't let them catch me because then they will shoot me as they have shot Clancy, God rest his soul, or they will take me back and hang me and that would be even worse. And please don't let me starve to death.

What would she do if she wasn't caught and didn't starve? Where would she walk to? What would she do? She thought

101

about that and didn't know the answer. She couldn't cross the mountains on her own. She didn't know where to go (not that Clancy had known, either) but, being a woman, she couldn't survive in the bush on her own, not without food and with all those wild blackfellows around who would probably do terrible things to any white woman who fell into their hands.

She couldn't go back but she didn't know where else to go.

She was wracked by hunger pains. Please, God, show me where I can find food. If I can eat I can think clearly and then I might know what to do.

As God would not lead her to food if she stayed where she was, she rose and began walking. Her legs ached and she had no idea where she was heading but she was in her Creator's hands so she kept moving, staggering at first because she was stiff and sore but gradually getting warmth into her muscles until she was moving at a pace so brisk and determined that she would have impressed an observer as a woman striding towards some known goal, not a lost soul wandering aimlessly through the bush.

She walked with the sun behind her—not that there was much sun at first but gradually the clouds that had spilled from the night dissipated and the sky became clear and the day hot. She was thirsty and her rough clothes, drying unevenly, rubbed against her like board so that her skin chafed and every step hurt. She came to a patch of dense scrub and, seeing no way around, forced her way through and had her dress torn and her legs and arms scratched by the branches, which were low to the ground and bare of leaves and whittled to fine points.

Once through, she stopped to wipe away blood from a dozen seeping cuts and, in dismay, examined the ruin that had been her skirt. She began to cry.

I will go back. Tell them the truth. I didn't murder that man. I didn't plan to escape. I met these two men only by chance. I didn't even intend to run away.

They wouldn't believe her. With one of the guards killed they would be thirsting for revenge and would take it blindly.

She wiped her eyes and went on. She came to a small creek. There were a few pools of water filled by the recent rain and she knelt and drank. The water was muddy but good because, she told herself, mud was a natural contaminant. It was certainly better than the water at the camp on a creek near Rouse Hill where the men, convicts and soldiers alike, used to defecate no more than 50 yards upstream from the place where the women had to drink and do their washing. Why did so many men have an insatiable urge to foul things? She'd noted that most men seemed possessed by an instinct to destroy: to cut down trees no matter how beautiful, to kill animals no matter how small or harmless. Even ants. She'd never known a man who wasn't compelled to tread on any ant he saw.

Was fouling the water the same thing, a satanic urge to destroy that which was natural and beautiful?

Animals were clean. The wild animals, that was. Animals kept in pens were forced to live in filth but that was the fault of the farmers, not the pigs or the cows or whatever it was that was fenced in. But wild animals were very clean. She'd noticed that.

Near the creek was a small tree with fruit. The fruit was dark and small and little bigger than berries but she peeled and ate one and, while bitter, it seemed good so she ate some more. She sat down and felt giddy and thought she might be sick. She drank more water and then lay down and slept for an hour. When she awoke, she was hungry again and, feeling dirty, undressed and washed her clothes in the largest and clearest of the pools. By now, the heat was fierce and she spread her clothes along the limbs of the trees near the creek.

She wasn't concerned about someone seeing her. She had a feeling of comfortable isolation, of being in a part of the world where no other person existed.

Naked, warmed by the sun, she slept again.

In the afternoon, dressed in her freshly laundered clothes and still searching for food, she came to some hills that rose gently towards the west—that was where the sun was now—and began to climb. There might be food in the hills.

Clancy slept longer than he'd intended. The room was dark and he was exhausted from the exertion of the last days and he didn't wake until the private came to tell him he had a boat ready.

'I hadn't forgotten you,' the man said and circled the room while Clancy put on his farmer's boots. The soldier limped. Clancy hadn't noticed that before.

'What have you done to your leg?'

The soldier winked. 'Oh, I hurt it a week ago. Twisted me ankle.' He winked again. 'Good thing, too. Otherwise I might be over the other side of the river with a bullet in me, like the others.'

Clancy, bent over the last shoelace, straightened. 'What others?'

'Oh, it's been a terrible morning.' He stopped pacing and stood at the door, looking out. 'I think I'd be going back to the farm, not crossing the river if I were you, Mr Smith.'

'What's happened?'

'You remember the lieutenant?' Without waiting for Clancy to reply, he said, 'He led the men into a trap. They was ambushed. The blacks was waiting for them. Hundreds of the murdering devils.'

'Did you say men were shot?'

The soldier turned and nodded. 'They've got guns. Don't ask me how. The lieutenant got shot in the head.'

Clancy felt a surge of hope. This was the lieutenant leading the search for him. 'Dead?'

'No, no, no,' the man said, shaking his head with each word. 'This Lieutenant de Lacey must have divine providence looking over his shoulder. And a tough head.' He touched his skull. 'First of all he tackles these devils armed with no more than a wooden paddle and lays a few of them low and gets nothing in return but a nick in the ribs and a bang on the head. Then when they start shooting he gets hit here.' He flicked the top of his head. 'Just took some hair and a bit of skin.'

'And some men were killed?' Clancy needed to know who was left to continue the search.

'A few. I'm not sure how many. Some were shot and some were speared.'

Clancy had been standing. Now he sat on the bed again. 'How terrible. Where's the lieutenant now?'

'Out hunting for them. He's got more men, a bandage around his skull and the grandfather of all headaches.'

'So he's back out, looking for them?'

'Oh, he's a determined one, that de Lacey. Just came back, got more men and went straight back across the river.' The soldier shook his head in admiration. 'And when he's caught them niggers and shot the lot of them—and that's what he'll do, mark my words because he's angrier than a swarm of bees stuck in hell—then he'll go out and catch them convicts.'

Clancy coughed. 'Why bother with a couple of convicts? They'll either starve to death out there or come back of their own accord.' A new thought occurred and he expressed it with reluctance. 'Or they'll run into those blacks.'

'He wants to catch them and string them up because they killed two men while he was in charge of the camp.'

'Two? There was only a guard.'

The soldier opened the door. 'You haven't been keeping up with the news, Mr Smith. They murdered a soldier, a young fellow called Paterson. Hung him from a tree. Killed his dog too.'

Clancy began to shake.

'I'd go back to your farm, Mr Smith. It'd be safer there.'

Clancy folded his arms. 'No, I have to tend to my vegetables.' Was that what he'd said before? Or was he supposed to have wheat growing on the far side of the river? He couldn't remember. 'I have a few acres over there. If I don't get to them and clear the ground, they'll be ruined.' He'd never farmed in his life but what he'd said sounded logical and the soldier seemed impressed by his dedication.

'There are wild blacks and murderous convicts out there, Mr Smith.'

'I still want to go. You say the boat's ready?'

'Down at the jetty.' He held the door open and allowed Clancy to pass through.

'I'd say you were just as stubborn a man as the lieutenant,' the soldier said. 'If you don't mind me saying so, too brave for your own good.'

'Oh, I don't know about that but I'm sure the lieutenant and I would have a lot to talk about.' Had the soldier turned, he would have seen Clancy smiling broadly.

Macaulay didn't know whether to feel elated or terrified. They'd won the battle, slaughtering a couple of soldiers in Nimboola's trap and he, with his stolen musket, had shot and killed at least one man. Maybe two; he wasn't sure about the officer because one of the men had dragged him away. The blacks were delighted, even now, two hours after the battle, making chortling, bird-like sounds of delight and treating him as though he were some sort of god. But he knew the soldiers. They'd be back. Next time there'd be more of them and they wouldn't be galloping into an ambush. They now knew Nimboola was a clever and devious fighter. They'd be prepared for his tricks—and they'd bring twenty or thirty guns.

The blacks now had three guns, warriors having retrieved two muskets from the field. But they had neglected to gather any powder or lead and Macaulay had, he guessed, only enough powder for four or five shots. And, because he wasn't trained like a soldier, it would take him an inordinately long time to reload. He could have the three muskets loaded to get off three quick shots but after that he'd be at the mercy of the advancing troops.

If Nimboola thought they could stand and fight soldiers who had an overwhelming advantage in firepower, then he, his men and Macaulay with them, would be cut to pieces.

He didn't know where they were but he knew they were not going back to the camp where they had eaten last night. They were moving through thick bush, travelling slowly to ensure no tracks were left for soldiers to follow.

Macaulay tried to engage Nimboola in conversation, to tell him they should not fight again but run and hide because next time there'd be many soldiers. He was making no impression. Nimboola thought Macaulay's sign language was a retelling of the battle and smiled indulgently and, a few times, patted his shoulder.

Macaulay was trying a new approach, suggesting they travel faster, when a runner approached. Macaulay hadn't seen the man before. He was tall and wiry with a wispy beard and had a ghostly look, his face and hair being streaked with dried mud, deliberately applied in thick strokes.

Head bent forward, Nimboola listened to the man's message. He glanced at Macaulay several times as the man spoke.

When the man had finished, Nimboola approached Macaulay. He pointed to the west. He spread his hands and made an encircling motion around his knees, stretched his hair to its full length, made delicate movements with his hands and gave other signs that Macaulay didn't understand.

What was obvious was that someone had been seen to the west of where they were travelling. Not soldiers. Just one person.

Nimboola gathered his men around him and for several

minutes there was chaotic conversation, ended only by the leader raising his spear and pointing it to the west. The messenger led. All followed.

The tide was still and the river lay quiet, its surface glistening with a coating of fine dust broken only by gatherings of floating seeds that had fallen from the eucalypts lining the banks. The boat carrying Clancy moved quietly, each stroke of its oars breaking the water with the delicate splish of a bird treading the shallows. Early that afternoon the boat had been found a mile downstream and towed back, with two others, to the jetty at The Green Hills. Clancy, emboldened by his continuing luck, had persuaded the elderly oarsman to row him upstream towards the long reach in the river that lay beyond the marsh. He'd have less distance to walk that way and would be back to where he'd left Eliza well before nightfall.

He hadn't thought about Eliza for several hours. Only in the boat did he recall that he hadn't got any clothes for her. He felt a pang of guilt and was surprised. Why should he care? She wasn't his responsibility. He hadn't asked her to escape. And what did it matter? She wasn't wearing the hideously distinctive yellow garb the men were forced to wear. She would be all right wearing what she had.

If he could find her. He'd left her while it was dark and now, as he studied the landscape beyond the trees lining the Hawkesbury, he realised much of the country looked alike. He wasn't sure he would recognise the place where he'd left her. It didn't occur to him that she might have moved.

A voice within him whispered: forget her; head for the hills where you could hide and rest for a day or two; look after yourself and don't worry about anyone else. He fondled the bulging sack. He didn't have much food and it would last twice as long if he didn't have to share it.

The boatman had been staring at him for some time.

'I ain't seen you around, have I?' the man asked.

'Don't know. I haven't seen you, though. Been here long?' He made the question seem like an accusation.

'I'm always on the river,' the man said defensively. 'I know most men who work on the other side.'

'And now you know me.'

The man shook his head, dislodging a bead of sweat that had trickled to the tip of his nose. 'There are too many people coming out here. The country won't stand it.'

Clancy nodded. 'Life's hard enough without a lot of strangers pushing in.'

They glided through two more strokes and their rippling wash spread the dust and sent tiny waves to rock the islands of fallen seeds. The man looked up, 'You got your own boat they tell me?'

'Those thieving blacks stole it.' He saw the baffled look on the man's face and added, 'Little boat. Had *Mary Jane* painted on the back.'

He was guessing that the man couldn't read and might be shamed into agreeing that he'd seen the boat. But he was an honest old fellow. 'Don't recall it.'

'It mightn't be your memory that's going,' Clancy said pleasantly. 'It might be your eyes.'

That struck a chord.

'I am finding it hard to see small things.'

'The letters on the boat were very small.'

'But I'd have seen a boat.'

Clancy laughed, as if sharing a joke. They didn't talk again until the man nosed the boat into the river bank.

'How's this, friend?'

'Perfect.' Clancy scrambled ashore, bag over one shoulder, axe in the other hand. 'I'm indebted to you.'

'Want me to pick you up again?'

'Would you?'

'If I'm not doing nothing else.'

'I'm staying on my land tonight. Could you make it tomorrow evening?'

The man shrugged. 'Like I said, if I can.' As he was pulling away from the shore, he called out, 'Keep an eye out for them niggers.'

Clancy waved with the axe. 'I will.'

'And I'll keep a lookout for your boat.'

'The *Mary Jane*.'

The man swung the boat around and headed downstream.

Clancy danced a little jig. It was wonderful to be free.

ELEVEN

NONE OF THE men spoke to de Lacey, none held out a hand to help him climb the ridges of broken rock even though he staggered frequently and the bandage around his head was dark with blood, none parted the bushes to ease his way through the tangle of branches that whipped and scratched and several times brought him to his knees. They kept their distance. They knew him to be an educated gentleman, presumed he was wealthy and judged him to have considerable influence, having heard the stories of his dining with the Governor but, while each distinction was sufficient to create a chasm between common soldier and officer, there was much more to their reluctance than class barriers. In his men's eyes, the lieutenant was so driven, so abnormally determined, so indestructible, as to be superhuman. He was a man to be kept at a distance, not understood, not liked, but to be regarded with awe.

There were no new tracks to follow. De Lacey had gone to the place where the ambush had occurred and sent soldiers to scout the hills. They found nothing although, it must be said, the scouts were so anxious to return to the main body of men that they spent little time searching. The fear of a spear in the chest, flung silently by unseen hands, had become endemic.

'These are just ordinary men,' he told his squad while they rested for two minutes, squatting in a circle, all facing outwards with their muskets at the ready, which was not in the manual of warfare but was his idea. Fighting unconventional enemies demanded unconventional tactics. 'They tricked us before. That was merely good tactics on their behalf, aided by the fact,' he felt compelled to add, 'that this was their land and they knew exactly where to hide. We were at a severe disadvantage.' The men seemed not to be listening but to be searching the shadowed folds in the hills. 'They are not ghosts. They are not spirits with supernatural powers. They are primitive barbarians. Put a bullet into the belly of one of these skinny-legged blackfellows and he'll bleed and scream like anyone else.'

'Probably more,' said an older soldier who felt compelled to support the lieutenant.

'Indeed,' said de Lacey and smiled at the soldier who, embarrassed at being the odd man out, was now looking at his boots.

'They got guns,' one man mumbled, loudly enough to be heard, softly enough to be anonymous.

'So have we,' said de Lacey, not bothering to search for the speaker. 'We have more and I'm damned sure we know how to use them better than they.'

He rose, not knowing where to go but pointing to the northwest because the country over there had fewer hills and promised easier travelling. He had no idea where the blacks had gone. But in clearer country they might intercept some tracks. Even if they were the wrong tracks, he didn't care. He would slaughter whatever number of savages he found. The more the better, to balance in some measure the disaster of the morning ambush.

He led the soldiers, forcing himself to travel fast despite the dreadful weariness in his legs. He felt terrible. His head was throbbing with pain and he was suffering from fits of giddiness. His side ached where the spear had nicked him. He often stumbled on rough ground or when he had to surmount obstacles like rocky watercourses and old, fire-charred logs. The men had said nothing so they couldn't have noticed. Thank God for that. He had to put on a good show.

In the next hour, he fell several times but reacted by increasing his pace to the extent that he drew 100 yards clear of the nearest soldier, a young man of great spirit who was trying valiantly to keep up with his officer but was burdened by his heavy musket, a pouch filled with treble the normal quantity of lead and powder, a cask of water which he carried over one shoulder and one-third of the salted pork and biscuit ration for the squad, which was slung over the other. The young man, whose name was Thomas, also had keen eyesight. He noticed a footprint and called to de Lacey.

They were at the edge of a forest in the foothills of the mountains. The lieutenant hurried back while Thomas put down the cask of water and sack of food and gulped in the hot air, which was fragrant with the aromas of eucalyptus oil, wild boronia and blossoming ti-tree.

It was a single footprint in a patch of soft earth. The print was thin, with a distinct heel.

'Just one?' de Lacey asked. 'Look for more, man. We need to know which way they're heading.'

'It looks like a shoe, sir, not a bare foot,' Thomas said, which silenced de Lacey, and while the other soldiers joined them and crouched, breathless and red-faced, in the shade of the nearby trees, Thomas searched for more footprints. He found none but, gazing into the distant hills, saw something on a clear patch high on a ridge to the west.

'There's someone up there, sir.'

'Where?' De Lacey frowned. Far from being able to see distant objects, he had trouble distinguishing the young man, who was no more than fifty paces away but in front of a shadowy backdrop of trees.

Thomas had the naive arrogance of a person with perfect eye-sight. 'Why, up there on the ridge, a little more than half a mile away I'd say.' He stood with his hands on his hips. 'Just one person. On a patch of grass. A woman.'

'A woman?' De Lacey almost choked on the word. 'You can see a person who's half a mile away and you tell me it's a woman?'

'With a dress, sir. That's how I can tell.'

There could be only one woman out here. De Lacey peered in the direction the young soldier faced but saw only the fuzzy outlines of hills. 'Can you see two men?' he asked.

'Two men? No, sir.'

But they would be near. The woman must be Phillips which meant Macaulay and Fitzgerald were on that hill, too. So they'd been hiding out here, where the blackfellows lived.

'And what's the woman doing?' de Lacey asked in a slow voice.

'I don't know, sir.'

'Walking? Sitting down? Turning somersaults?'

'Standing, sir. Not moving.'

'As in waiting for someone?'

The young soldier was frightened by the sharpness of the questions and paused, to make sure his answer pleased the lieu-tenant. 'Possibly, sir,' he said. 'It is a woman and she's standing still. I'm sure.'

'Oh I'm convinced you're right.' De Lacey stroked his mous-tache and the smile was erased. 'She's someone I've been look-ing for, you see. She has two companions. I want to catch them all, very much.' For the first time de Lacey noticed the other sol-diers spread out under the trees. 'And what are you men doing?' he bellowed. 'Get up and head into those hills. There are three escaped convicts up there. They murdered two men, including one of your kind. They're only half a mile away. If you let them get away I'll have the lot of you flogged.'

'What about the blacks?' one man mumbled.

'One thing at a time, private,' said de Lacey, who was already on his way up the hill.

It was a woman. Only now could Macaulay see her, even though Nimboola and the others had been whispering about her for the last ten minutes and waving their spears in her direction for his benefit and laughing at the poor eyesight of the white man.

He didn't recognise her. She was young, or so she seemed from this distance. She was on her own, standing on a grassy hillside, sometimes gazing up the hill, at other times looking down the slope. It was as though she were trying to decide which way to go.

Nimboola pointed to her, then Macaulay, and let his fingers bind them together.

'Oh no, she's not with me,' Macaulay said, forgetting the other man needed hand signs. 'I don't know who she is.'

A bird twittered and Nimboola raised a finger to his lips. All in his party turned to the left and, without bidding, sank to the ground.

'What's going on?' Macaulay demanded as he was gently pulled down.

With a hooked finger, Nimboola pointed down the hill. Macaulay shook his head but the others were off, slithering down the slope towards the shelter of some trees.

Eliza was thinking about going back. She was hungry and frightened and, with the sun close to the horizon, she felt terrified at the prospect of another night on her own. That's when she saw the soldier. He was young and he emerged from a patch of scrub only a few hundred yards below her. He seemed grossly overladen with equipment.

'Who are you?' he called out.

She backed away.

'I'm not going to hurt you.' He put down his musket. 'See? I've even laid down my gun.'

She kept retreating, moving slowly. She stopped at a fallen tree whose trunk was partly hidden by the long grass. 'Are you on your own?'

'Yes.' Thomas slipped a bag from his shoulder. 'Would you like something to eat? I've got meat and biscuits in here.'

Food. Desperately hungry though she was, she was even more frightened and said, 'What are you doing here?'

'We were looking for some blacks. I got separated from the others. Are you on your own?'

'Where are your companions?'

'I don't know. I'm lost.'

'Do you really have food in that bag?'

'Lots of it. I've got water, too. Are you thirsty?' He drank from the cask, letting the water splash over his chin.

She took a few steps down the hill but happened to look to one side and saw two more soldiers crawling through the grass towards her.

She turned and ran. Behind her, she heard men shouting but then, strangely, the shouts thickened into an eruption of sounds: bloodcurdling screams, guns firing, men yelling and an odd whistling sound. She stumbled and fell and, from the ground, looked back.

A dozen soldiers were in sight. They were fanned out across the hill, obviously placed that way to ensnare her but none was facing her. They were looking towards the trees that edged the clearing. As she watched, one soldier fell back with a spear through his chest. She heard one gun fire and saw a puff of smoke from the trees. More muskets fired but, this time, they were the soldiers' guns and she could hear a man shouting orders in a calm but loud voice.

Another soldier fell, with a spear through his belly.

'Down,' the man was shouting. 'Fire from the ground.'

She got to her feet and turned to run up the hill. A black man grabbed her. She hadn't seen him and screamed in terror. He was almost naked and his face was daubed with white and he stank like rotten fish and when he grabbed her wrist she struggled but he lifted her from the ground and, carrying her across his shoulder, bolted for the shelter of some trees.

Clancy had not been able to find Eliza and, after a moment of disappointment—irrational, he thought later, seeing she was no more than a burden to him—he headed north, then west, threading his way through the most lightly timbered land to make quick time. Anticipating that the inquisitive boatman would talk and people would soon grow suspicious of the mysterious 'Frank Smith', he felt it wise to be as far from his imaginary plot of land as possible. Tired after so much exercise, he was resting beneath a wattle tree, eating some of his bread and salted pork and wondering where he might stop for the night, when he heard the gunfire.

De Lacey. The lieutenant must have caught up with the raiding party. The sounds came from far away and Clancy stopped chewing to listen more intently. The hills rang with so many echoes he couldn't tell which was the original sound. There were more shots, more echoes, but they were single shots rather than the crashing explosion of noise from a volley of muskets, as he might have expected. Soldiers fired in ranks. These were the sounds of individual guns, very few guns, in ragged fire.

He listened again but heard no more firing. Had de Lacey disposed of them all so easily? He felt a pang of sympathy for the Aborigines. De Lacey and his troops would be in the mood for slaughter and their muskets would cut the black people to pieces but, thinking back, he'd heard no more than a dozen shots.

All was quiet. They must be taking prisoners, he reasoned, which meant they would be marching them back to the river, the once proud warriors chained by the neck to get them used to the feel of something tight around the throat. He had no idea where they were, whether they would pass nearby or be miles away, but it was essential that he hide.

He climbed a ridge and, in the late afternoon light, thought he saw movement on another ridge to his left. So he climbed higher, stopping only when the sun had set, to burrow into some leafy bushes and pray that no one would come his way.

De Lacey moved around the field, calling softly until a voice responded, feeling his way through the long grass and over an occasional body until he reached the man who had answered. In that way he found nine men. Only nine were still alive. More correctly, who were still there. Some had bolted at the first flight of spears.

One of the men had a spear in his thigh and de Lacey used his borrowed sword to hack off its end and push the shaft right through. The man screamed and de Lacey winced, wondering if the sound would cause the blacks to return. He stayed with the man, holding his hand until the poor wretch fainted.

No one came. The blacks had gone.

Curse them. Twice now they had beaten him, humiliated him.

Intent on catching the woman, the soldiers had been caught in the open, protected by nothing but long grass. Their attackers had been hidden in the trees. De Lacey had seen a few of them, shadows that became contorted images at the moment of launching a spear, crude but lethal weapons which they hurled with a terrible accuracy. Three soldiers had fallen in the first attack. He'd charged the trees and a few men had followed, but too few. They'd been overwhelmed. He'd seen two of his men surrounded by blacks and clubbed to the ground. He didn't know what happened to the others. He'd fought hand-to-hand with a man who was too strong for him and too slippery to hold, and he'd been stunned by a blow on the back of the neck, probably by one of those damned throwing-sticks, and had fallen unconscious to the ground. Which had probably saved his life. They must have thought him dead.

Before being knocked down, he'd seen a white man among the Aborigines. A big, bearded fellow, firing a musket at the soldiers in the field. He saw just one gun. It must have been the one taken from young Paterson, so the blacks had somehow fallen into league with the escaped convicts, plotted this whole affair, and used the woman as a decoy to lead him into the trap.

He'd rushed in and half his men were dead.

TWELVE

ELIZA KICKED AND scratched at the man but didn't cry out. He was silent and so she, not knowing why, remained silent too. He was strong and as supple as a sapling and carried her to the trees at a loping run but then, instead of hiding, continued on, only stopping when they were on the far side of the ridge where the sounds of the battle were faint. He dropped her to the grass and stood above her, looking not at her but down the hill. She covered her eyes. The man was almost naked.

After a while a few warriors joined them. In the faint light she could see one was bleeding from the forehead. Another was holding his arm. All were breathless. Their eyes were unnaturally large and their faces, glistening with perspiration, wore fierce expressions of exaltation. They had won the battle; she could tell. They ignored her, answering questions flung at them by the man with the painted face.

Long after night had darkened the sky, more men came. They arrived like a faint breeze, with no more noise than a rustling of the grass. Some men were unarmed, only one carried a spear, others had the long, hooked throwing-sticks which could be used as clubs, and had been; one of the men knelt to wipe gore from his club and showed her his bloodied hand.

They had brought their dead with them. Three, she thought, but it was difficult to count in the darkness.

A white man arrived. He was clothed—that was the first thing she noticed—and he was huge. He slumped to the ground next to her.

'And who might you be?' He was breathing heavily and, when he exhaled, the stench from his breath was awful. He had two muskets strapped across his shoulders and carried one in his hand. 'I'm talking to you,' he said when she remained silent, prodding her with the barrel of the gun.

She remembered the figure she'd seen crossing the river. 'Aren't you Clancy's friend, Macaulay?'

He put down the gun and took the others from his back and sighed with relief. He rubbed his ankle, all the time looking at her.

'Are you the little wench that Clancy found at the river crossing?' She didn't answer and he laughed softly. 'Of course you are. And where is my dear friend Clancy?'

'I don't know.' She wasn't going to tell him. Instinctively, she didn't like him. And Macaulay had got them into all this trouble by killing the guard.

'Has he been caught, I wonder?'

'Who knows.' She shook her head. 'What are you doing with these people?'

'They've been looking after me. They're my friends.'

'Did they kill the soldiers back there?'

'A few. We've had a good day.'

'How could you help them kill white men?'

'Easy. Because the white men want to kill me.' He spat. 'I'm dry. Have you got any water?'

'No and I haven't eaten for a few days.'

'Oh,' he said, looking around at the warriors, 'then you've joined the right group. My friends could soon rustle up something tasty, like a lizard or a fat grub.' He reached out to lift her chin. 'So what are you doing up here? How did you get so far?'

'By walking.' She noticed some women had joined the group. 'Were they fighting too?'

Macaulay was surprised. 'I haven't seen them all day. They wasn't with us before.' He spat again and called out, 'Hey, Nimboola, where'd all these lovelies come from?'

The black chief arrived and raised a finger to his lips. He pointed towards the battle scene.

'Oh sure, there are still soldiers around. But not wanting to fight, I can guarantee, after the licking we gave them.' Even so, he spoke softly. He inclined his head towards the nearest black woman, who was using her long fingers to pick at the wound on a man's shoulder. 'What are they doing here? How did they find us?'

'Does he speak English?' Eliza said, staring up at Nimboola.

'No, but we get on just fine.'

Nimboola was waving his hands. He spoke rapidly.

'What's he saying?'

'They must have just come here,' Macaulay said. 'On their own account.'

'This was a meeting spot?'

'That must be it.' Macaulay sounded unconvinced. He'd heard that Aborigines could pass messages to each other over long distances without sending runners. People said they possessed unnatural powers. He didn't understand. Whatever it was, the women had turned up and, being needed, were now tending to the wounded.

Nimboola seemed troubled. He moved among his men, talking to the injured, touching their wounds. 'He lost a few men,' Macaulay said. 'Even so, it was a great victory. We cut them to pieces.'

'I don't know how you can talk like that. You're talking about our own people. Christians.'

'Who put us in chains and would hang us if they could catch us.'

122

'You didn't have to shoot them.'

'We could have let them catch you, eh?' He rubbed his sore leg. 'What do you think they'd have done to you? Probably hung you from the nearest tree. After the soldiers had lifted your petticoat and had their fun with you, that is.'

'You're disgusting.'

'Life's disgusting. What's your name?'

She hesitated. Her name was something she prized and was reluctant to give away.

'Come on. Mary, Elizabeth . . . what is it?'

'Eliza.'

'Just Eliza?'

'Yes.'

He scratched at something in his beard. 'And you say you've no idea where Clancy is? You haven't seen him?'

'Not for a long time.' She took a deep breath, praying hastily that God would forgive her for any lies she told this man. 'Not since we crossed the river.'

'They've got him,' Macaulay said, shaking his head sadly. 'His heart wasn't in this. He's either been caught or he's given himself up. Would have been hanged by now. With two dead men to account for, they'd be anxious to string someone up.'

'Two?'

He scratched his beard again. 'A soldier was tracking me, that first night. I broke his neck.' He demonstrated the technique. 'Only a young feller. Not very strong.'

'Oh God,' she said and covered her eyes.

'You can't get hung more than once.' He put his hand to his throat. 'We can kill as many as we like and they can't do no more to us than string us up once.'

'I haven't done anything.'

'And they won't believe you, love.' He winked. 'Best not get caught.'

Nimboola was anxious to move. The women helped the wounded to their feet. One man with a bullet in his leg had to be carried. Three of the strongest men slung the bodies of their dead companions across their shoulders.

'We're off,' Macaulay said, picking up the guns as he rose.

'What about me?' She got to her feet as dark figures began trooping past.

'Nimboola hasn't said no, so you'd better get a hurry on. They move fast and don't stop very often.'

'Where are we going?'

'Away from the soldiers. That's good enough for the time being.' Another wink. 'Just try to be friendly. If they think you're my woman, they'll let you be.'

The messenger carrying news of the first ambush reached Captain John Hunter that night. The Governor had been reading another, longer paper: a report of an experiment designed to curb the convicts' voracious appetite for escape. He had the exhausted messenger put the envelope on a table and then kept reading, for the number of recent escapes was infuriating and the report gave the results of a bizarre plan he had authorised.

Four Irish prisoners, selected for their size and fitness, had been taken to Toongabbie, just to the west of Parramatta, and released. They'd been told to walk to China, and good luck if they made it.

China was the lure that inspired many an escape, rumour suggesting that Peking was a few hundred miles up the coast or just over the Blue Mountains, depending on which story the convicts heard. There was also talk of a settlement a few hundred miles inland, to the south-west of Sydney. This was supposed to be a colony of Europeans, where no one had to work. But China was the story with the wider circulation and greater appeal.

The Governor was sick of all the escapes. There were times

when half of his men were busy searching for felons who had slipped their chains or walked off farms or had somehow gone bush. Most were recaptured or staggered back, starving and dispirited, to be rewarded with fifty lashes. Others didn't return. Hunter's theory was that they'd perished in the bush but many convicts preferred to believe the missing men had reached Peking and were now living a life of luxury and ease.

Some convicts, with either a better understanding of geography or easy access to shipping, tried to stow away on the trading vessels that were now beginning to call into Port Jackson. These ships, originally from the newly formed United States of America but increasingly from other parts of the world, came with such prized items as cured beef, pork, flour, tobacco, wine, rum, gin, pitch and tar but returned virtually empty and with plenty of room for enterprising stowaways. Some unscrupulous captains, setting off for Bombay, Batavia, Valparaiso or New Orleans, would hide convicts for a fee of five pounds per head. Therefore, a plan had been devised to smoke out—literally— any convicts hiding in the holds or in secret places. Before a ship sailed, masked constables were sent below carrying fires burning sulphur. It had become a common sight for ships at anchor to belch white fumes from the portholes and through any gaps in the decking. Spectators enjoyed the sport, lining the harbour to see how many coughing, choking convicts were flushed out. The record was thirty, discovered a few years earlier on board the *Hillsborough*.

He could understand the stowaways, being a naval man, but Hunter thought the overland escape attempts were nonsense. Walking to China indeed. It would take a good boat and a masterly sense of navigation to make the voyage, but most of the convicts were uneducated and had never seen a map or a compass. But they liked a good yarn and the more fanciful the better.

So in frustration he had authorised this radical scheme with the four Irishmen. They had been set free to prove the impossibility of the rumours. He read on.

Three had returned, starving, after ten days. Ten days! He was in charge of weak-hearted fools, not just convicts. The fourth man had stuck it out longer but, to survive, he had been reduced to trapping birds before finally staggering back to the settlement in a terrible state: gaunt, scratched and starved.

Let the Irish, great talkers that they were, now spread the truth that not China but rough bushland and impenetrable mountains lay beyond Sydney.

The Governor finished that report and re-read it with some satisfaction before turning to the message from the Hawkesbury. The soldier who had made the journey on foot in seven and a half hours had been taken elsewhere to be fed, but when Hunter read what was on the single page he had him brought back immediately.

The message was from a Lieutenant Atkinson. Hunter couldn't recall much about the man except that he was short, with a tendency to being uncouth. Which was why, he remembered, Atkinson had been sent out to The Green Hills. Let a ruffian look after his own kind was the theory because, in his mind, the settlers along the river were the least desirable, most troublesome and raucously voluble free citizens in the colony. He'd granted more than 6,000 acres of land to the blighters but they still complained.

Atkinson wrote that early that morning a raiding party of natives had entered The Green Hills and murdered several settlers. He gave names. Hunter didn't know them. Then, Atkinson continued, a detachment of soldiers under Lieutenant Quinton de Lacey had crossed the Hawkesbury in pursuit of the natives. De Lacey had led his men into an ambush and three of his soldiers had died, two on the spot and one subsequently from his injuries. De Lacey himself was injured.

That was all. There was no mention of de Lacey's lone effort to halt the raiding party in town or of the fact that he'd subsequently taken a second, larger party across the river in pursuit of the murderers.

'Why was Lieutenant de Lacey in charge?' Hunter asked the messenger. Hunter held the paper in his right hand and let it droop across his knee.

'I don't know, sir. He was keen, I think.'

'Keen.' Hunter flapped the piece of paper. 'But unqualified for this sort of thing.'

'He's brave, sir,' the soldier felt compelled to say. 'All the fellows have been talking about him.'

'Brave in what way?'

The soldier told him about de Lacey's attempt to stop the raiders from leaving town.

'Why isn't that in the report?' Hunter held the report high.

'I have no idea, sir.'

Hunter stood up. 'Is he impetuous? Inclined to do things in a rush? What would you say?'

'I wouldn't know, sir.'

The Governor turned. 'He's been hunting escaped convicts. Has he caught them, do you know?'

'I don't know, sir. I don't think so, sir.'

'He's not doing very well, is he?' he said, speaking to the tent.

'He's a brave officer, sir. All the men think so.'

'Well, that's nice to hear. When he's better, I think we might ask Lieutenant de Lacey to pay us a visit.' He turned to the soldier. 'How long will he be laid up?'

'Oh, he's not laid up, sir. He's out hunting them heathens again. Went straight out with more men and a bandage around his head.'

Hunter stretched his mouth in a gesture that could have been surprise or admiration. 'We'll have to hope he does better this time, won't we.' And then, standing in front of a small gilt-edged mirror and adjusting his collar, 'He'll damned well need to, won't he?'

Macaulay had been right. The raiding party didn't rest but walked all night, stopping only once by a small waterfall in the lower mountains to drink and bathe the wounds of the injured. At various times during the night they had been joined by other women, old men and children, until the whole tribe was present. Some of the newcomers were the dead warriors' kin and there was much soft ululating and wringing of hands, but all kept moving. How the rest of the tribe had known where to find Nimboola's party was a mystery to Macaulay but it was a puzzle that didn't bother him for long. These people did inexplicable and miraculous things and that was the way they were. He had always found it easier to accept things, rather than try to understand them.

Eliza stayed close to Macaulay. She disliked him but was frightened of the blacks, regarding them with the same suspicion and morbid dread that her aunt had reserved for Catholic priests.

One of the girls gave her food. She was as tall as Eliza but no more than sixteen, with large eyes, big teeth which she exposed in a perpetual smile and a fascination for the tattered remnants of Eliza's white stockings, which she touched constantly. She was naked but for a short length of animal skin which hung loosely from her hips. First she handed Eliza a doughy substance which she had been squeezing in the palm of her hand. She put her hand to her mouth, to indicate it should be eaten. It was cold and tasted starchy, like a bland version of sweet potato. The girl nodded frequently, to indicate it was good. Eliza held out her hand for more. There was no more of that, but later the girl gave her some meat. It was a small piece, cold and stringy with a salty taste. There was no point asking what it was and Eliza tried not to think what it might have been.

Macaulay had been hurt in the attack. The injury was not caused by any soldier but had been self-inflicted. During the frenzy of battle, while switching from one musket to another, he had run into a broken branch which had gouged a hole in his side. It wasn't bleeding but he held his side as he walked.

'Bloody thing,' he kept saying and Eliza knew better than to protest about his language. 'I must have got a piece of wood in me side. Like a splinter. It hurts like the devil.'

'Do you want me to try to get it out?' It was a begrudging offer which, happily for her, he declined. 'We'll wait till daylight. I'll get one of these black women to have a look.' He managed to laugh. 'If she can take something out of me, I might persuade her to let me put something in her.'

Eliza compressed her lips.

Macaulay, straining to be attractive, leaned towards her. 'I might ask that pretty little thing who's been touching your legs all the time.'

'She's interested in my stockings.'

Macaulay turned his head even more so she could see the wink. 'Oh no, I know these people and I know what that means. You want to be careful, love. These people have very strange habits. The women are as bad as the men.'

Eliza dropped back, to be out of range of Macaulay, but fell in with the group of men carrying the bodies of the dead and hurried forward again. Like him or not, she should stay with Macaulay.

De Lacey hadn't moved from the scene of the slaughter but had set the survivors around him in a quincuncial arrangement, with two at each corner of the square and the injured soldier and himself in the middle. No man slept, except the one who lay beside him and he, de Lacey suspected, was slowly bleeding to death. There was nothing he could do other than stuff the torn halves of his handkerchief into the wounds and bind them in place with the man's belt. Initially, he'd thought of heading back to the river but it was too dark and there was much rough ground to cover and, for all he knew, other injured men, unconscious and unable to call out, might be lying in the field. He would wait until dawn.

Every hour, he crept the ten paces from post to post, bending to touch each man's shoulder to ensure he was awake and that his musket was cocked.

'Have you seen anything?' de Lacey would whisper. The man would shake his head. 'Good man. Stay awake. Keep your eyes open. I'll have you out of here soon.' The man would nod.

They were forbidden to talk, except to shout an alarm, and while none spoke to him, he knew what each man was thinking. The blacks might return, striking in the night with their flights of softly whistling spears. That was the terrifying thing. Both attacks, the one in the valley and now the one on the hill, had come without warning. No shouted challenges, no trumpet blasts, no horses whinnying, no trample of boots or jangle of swords.

Not that he'd ever been in a battle but he'd read about these things. He'd been trained to fight the French, who fought like gentlemen, and here he was, beaten twice in one day by an enemy who hid from sight and used the world's most primitive weapons. And had won. That hurt more than the deaths. He'd been beaten by these people. Quinton de Lacey, who could trace his family back for hundreds of years, had been defeated by men who wore no pants and had runny noses.

He estimated it was four in the morning. The sun would be up in an hour and a half and then they could be moving.

Crouched on the grass and occasionally feeling for the

unconscious man's pulse to check if he were still alive, de Lacey had been wondering about the third of the escapees. He'd seen two, the woman Phillips and the man Macaulay, but he hadn't seen the other convict. Was he, too, with the Aborigines or had he been separated from the others, hurt himself, become lost, or died along the way? What was the man's name? After five minutes it came to him: Fitzgerald. He couldn't think of the man's first name, if he'd ever known it. Yes, Fitzgerald. Good. It was essential that his mind be working well, for he knew he was facing a day that would test his character and require him to be alert and clear of memory, even though he was unlikely to get any sleep.

He didn't know what the Phillips woman looked like and, with his poor eyesight, hadn't seen her clearly on the hill, but he was in no doubt it was she. Young Thomas, who had survived the attack, said it was certainly a convict woman and of the right age. Her clothing had been extremely ragged and she was ravenous and thirsty, which was to be expected after several days in this wild country. As far as de Lacey knew, there was no other female convict on the loose in this part of the colony so it must be the Phillips woman, and she had deliberately shown herself on the hill, to lead him into the trap. Damn her again. May God despatch her to hell via the slowest and most painful route.

De Lacey presumed the white man he'd seen with the musket was Macaulay. Everyone spoke of Macaulay's great size and the man with the gun, hiding in the trees and firing at the soldiers, was of enormous bulk, a veritable bull of a man. Despicable wretch. He was fighting on the side of the blacks—probably leading them—and thus following the example of the American colonists, who had used Red Indians to decimate columns of loyal and valiant English troops.

But where was Fitzgerald? He could have been involved in the attack, of course. The light had been poor and the only person

131

he'd seen with any clarity had been Macaulay. He'd been close to him, no more than ten yards away.

He despised Macaulay but didn't hate him. That feeling was reserved, with great intensity, for the Phillips woman. If his career were in ruins, she would be to blame. She had allowed herself, wilfully and probably joyfully, to be used as bait for the trap set by Macaulay and his horde of black murderers. Gripping Atkinson's sword, he swore he would devote his life to catching this trollop. He didn't like witnessing a hanging but he'd enjoy hers.

'Hanging is too good for her,' he said out loud and one of the men whispered, 'I beg your pardon, sir?'

He didn't answer and the man fell silent.

De Lacey dreaded going back. Why couldn't he have been killed, a victim of one of the first spears, stricken through the heart? Not a hero's death, because he'd be known around the colony as the fool who led his men into two ambushes in one day, but that would have been a warrior's death and a quick way to go, with no humiliating interviews with that idiot Atkinson or, far worse, having to face Hunter when he returned to Parramatta.

THIRTEEN

AT DAWN, CLANCY crawled out from under the bushes. He'd heard nothing during the night apart from the squabbling of birds in a large tree whose branches arched over his sleeping place. It was a comforting sound, assuring him that no other humans were moving through the bush, and reminding him of home. The birds seemed to be arguing over possession of a nest. Just like his own birds, which were always pecking and chirping over some tiny space in a corner of their cage. The cage was a lovely thing, six-sided and made of a honey-coloured wood, with paintings of birds in flight on the carved facia boards at the top. He'd stolen it from a farmer near Bridgwater and hung it from a rafter in a corner of the stone cottage where his family lived. The cottage was 150 years old and badly in need of repair. The shingle roof always leaked in heavy rain. Not where the cage was hung, of course. Apart from his few clothes, the birds and their cage were his only possessions and he'd made sure they were placed in the driest, warmest part of the house, close to the fireplace.

He felt lonely, without companionship, separated from his family and deprived of his most treasured possessions. For a minute or two he was depressed and almost overwhelmed by a sense of isolation, of being remote from all other beings, but then he told himself that thinking such thoughts was no more than being practical and recognising the truth. He could scarcely be further away from his home and his sister, who was the only family he had, and he was on his own. Who on earth could be more alone or more isolated than he was? Possibly some shipwrecked sailor stranded on a rocky isle off the coast of Africa might think so but he would be closer to home than Clancy Fitzgerald was, for Clancy Fitzgerald was truly at the ends of the earth.

He was a bright fellow to think like that, Clancy assured himself. Honest, too, which was a rare thing among men these days. He ate some bread.

Some ants were crawling around the cut on his ankle and he brushed them away, then squeezed and picked at the wound until he was satisfied that it was healing and his leg was not turning bad. He'd seen men with cuts that had poisoned the blood and caused a leg or arm to turn purple and swell to bursting point. They'd met terrible deaths. One man, who'd done no more than pierce the palm of his hand with a nail, had had his jaws lock tight so that, in his agony, he'd growled like a dog.

Clancy was stiff from sleeping under the bushes and sore from all the walking he'd done but he got up, took a deep breath and thought about what to do. He would not go back. Never. When in chains, he'd sworn to himself that if he ever escaped, he'd never allow himself to be caught alive. He'd rather be shot running away. That was foolish talk, he knew, an easy thing to say when you were in chains with no possibility of gaining your freedom, but now that he was out, even if he were on his own with no idea of where he was or where he should go, he would stay out. He'd starve rather than return and present himself to the hangman. He'd walk to China. Why not? Macaulay had told wonderful stories about what they would find in Peking, which he'd sworn was just a few days' march to the west beyond the mountains.

First, he had to cross the mountains.

He used the axe to cut and trim a staff, to help him on the climb. The rising sun being behind him, he knew he was facing the west so he set off, resolved to keep his face in shadow. Until afternoon, when he would need to have the sun shining in his eyes. Some convicts, he'd heard, had managed to get away but they, having no sense of direction, had walked in circles. Another had copied a drawing of a compass on to a piece of paper and used it to guide him. That man had walked in circles, too. They'd all been recaptured and whipped.

Clancy had never seen a compass and had no idea how it worked but all he needed to do was look at the sky. The sun would be his guide. Behind him in the morning, in front of him in the afternoon. And then he had a disturbing thought. What happened when he reached the west? This was something he'd never discussed with Macaulay or anyone else. Which way should he walk once he got there? He hoped he'd get to Peking before that happened, or at least find tracks. They must have tracks in China. He didn't know anything about Peking and wondered if it was as big as Sydney Town. Macaulay hadn't told him anything about Peking except it was there, over the mountains.

He drank some water from a rockhole that was perpetually shaded by ferns, then chewed another piece of bread as he walked but, within minutes, the ground began rising steeply and soon he was blocked by a sheer cliff face. It was formed of sandstone and was a couple of hundred feet high. It stretched on either side of him for as far as he could see. Some small bushes grew from the cliff, jutting out like fluff on a giant's chin, and he could see caves in a few places but it was an impossible climb. He turned left, searching for grip along the rough and rock-strewn ground at the bottom of the cliff until he was forced to turn and head downhill, to reach flatter land.

The bush was thick here and after twenty minutes of pushing

supple branches aside and ducking under the stouter limbs, he stopped and sat down. He could spend days here, use up all his food and get nowhere.

The leaves formed an opaque mat above him and he could no longer see the sun. He was thirsty, but there was no water here. The ground was covered in layers of dead leaves and was a dark, dry place. He searched for animal tracks, knowing from his poaching days that tracks led to water, but found none. He might be the first man ever to have ventured into this place, he thought, and was frightened. He tried to find his way back but couldn't remember which way he'd travelled and came to a tree that looked like one he had passed ten minutes earlier. He sat down.

When in doubt, think it out, his father had said. The old man liked rhyming phrases. So he thought it out. He was in a forest with no tracks, he couldn't see the sun and therefore had no idea where the west was, he was thirsty and tired of carrying all the things he had in the sack and . . . what else? What did it matter? He was lost and without inspiration.

He was fondling the blade of the small axe when he thought: he could use the axe to mark trees so he'd know where he'd been. He liked that idea, principally because it gave him something to do, but when he thought about it, still sitting on a soft bed of leaves with his back against the trunk of a tree, he wondered what good would it do him. If he saw a marked tree it would only confirm that he'd been walking in a circle. It might stop him walking in two circles, but nothing more. It wouldn't help him find his way. Although it could help him find his way back, if the chosen route proved a dead end.

He rose and cut a mark on the trunk of the tree that had been his backrest. He took aim for the most distant tree he could see in the tangle of timber that lay ahead of him and walked for it. On reaching it, he cut a notch and headed for another tree.

The going was slow because the forest was so dense but at least he was travelling in a straight line. The country began to rise and fall and he crossed several creek beds, but they were rocky and dry. He lifted a few rocks and found slime but no water. After a couple of hours he estimated he'd covered no more than half a mile.

He was resting on a fallen tree, hit by lightning, he reasoned, because of its split trunk, when he heard a faint sound. Running water. It was little more than a trickle but it was clearly running water and it was coming from his right. He put two marks on a tree, to indicate he'd made a turn, and headed towards the sound.

A hundred yards further on he came to a creek whose bed was solid rock, with a groove worn by the flow of water. So little water was running that he could do no more than kneel down, wet his hands and lick them. He did this several times, then swayed back on his haunches and listened. There was a stronger sound. A splashing. He got up and followed the creek upstream. After a few minutes he came to a small waterfall, no more than three feet high, but it had filled a broad rockpool that had ferns and spiky grasses and vivid clumps of mosses growing around its edges. The canopy of leaves was not as thick here and he could see patches of sky, but no sun.

He found tracks, three narrow paths that came down to the pool from the hills. He examined each one. They were narrow and well worn, tracks along which native animals came to drink at dawn and dusk.

He drank. The water was sweet and cool. He sat back and thought about eating, then he thought about trapping, using all his old skills to snare an animal or two. He could stay here for the night and get himself enough meat for the next few days. In that way he could save the salted pork for later.

He drank again, then, moving carefully along one of the

animal trails to avoid leaving his own marks on the ground, he found a jutting ledge of rock a few yards to one side of the track. Some animal had been there because there were claw marks in the ground beneath the ledge, where it had dug a bed for itself. There was room to lie down, legs curled into his body, which he did, to wait and watch.

What would he use for a trap? How big were the animals that came to the water? Maybe he should observe the traffic tonight, then act tomorrow. After all, he was in no hurry.

He had no nets or traps. What would he do? Throw the axe at a kangaroo? Use it to cut himself a spear? He'd die of starvation before he'd learned how to throw the thing accurately.

Possibly dig a pit. Put branches over the hole and cover them with leaves. Yes, that would work and he could construct a covered pit with the tools he had. But first, he needed to know how large the animals were. He'd wait for the evening and see what turned up for a drink. Hopefully, an animal would come along that was small, plump and tasty, with poor eyesight and a raging thirst.

He was feeling good. It was the clean, cool water.

He fell asleep.

The noise of crackling leaves woke him. Something was coming down the broadest track, which descended from a hill on his left. He lay still. It was moving quietly and stopping frequently, as wild creatures did when they approached a common drinking place.

He waited and when there was no more sound he began to think he had imagined the noises. But then he heard the rattle of a stone and a grunt.

It was a man. A black man, tall and willowy with a spear in one hand. His hair was plaited and covered in mud and his face was streaked with white clay. He wore a belt made from long, twisted strips of thin leather with a narrow skirt at the front. He was crouched forward, hand gripping the spear as though he were stalking game.

He was a fearsome sight and Clancy, not fully awake, sucked in his breath.

The man stopped and, very slowly, turned towards him.

De Lacey found only dead men—dead white men—on the grassy field and in the woods. Among the trees there were three, the battered and punctured bodies of the brave soldiers who had followed his charge. If all the squad had attacked they might have won the day but too few charged and, of those, only he had survived. At least none of the bodies had been mutilated, which was a relief because he had heard talk that the blacks were cannibals.

De Lacey ordered the eight walking survivors to recover all weapons and equipment, which they were to carry with them. The bodies were gathered together and left in a row at the edge of the trees. He'd send some men with a bunch of convicts to carry them home.

He had two men make a litter from saplings, to carry the wounded man down to the river. The man was alive, although still unconscious, but his breathing was weak and his skin had bleached to the colour of parchment. He'd be lucky to reach the river before death took him elsewhere.

It was a hot day and, on the long march back to the river, they stopped frequently to change litter bearers and allow men with minor wounds to rest. One man had had his ear taken off by a ball from Macaulay's musket and he was so dizzy he had to be led by the hand.

By now, de Lacey was almost fainting from exhaustion but he strode at the head of the small column, determined to lead his men back to the barracks and be the first to give an account of the ambush. He didn't want someone else spreading a garbled version. He'd been thinking. The British were proud of their defeats and he could make this episode sound like a valiant fight against overwhelming odds. Which it may well have been. He had no idea how many savages had been in the trees.

He'd have to tell his story with great precision and so he began rehearsing the words.

'We had seen no sign of the raiding party but were heading in the direction I assumed they must have taken.' Yes, he'd start like that to let them know he'd been thinking logically. He must also make them realise he was being suitably cautious, without being faint-hearted. 'We were searching for tracks, moving swiftly but keeping a watch out at all times.' In fact, he'd been setting a pace that none of the men could sustain so that they were strung out over a great distance and so exhausted they could scarcely carry their guns and equipment. Had they been attacked then, they would have been slaughtered. What did it matter? They'd been slaughtered anyhow. 'One of the men, Private Thomas who is possessed of remarkable vision, saw a white woman on a distant hill. He confirmed she was in convict garb and I knew she must be the woman escapee Phillips for whom I'd been searching for several days. I assumed, correctly as it transpired, that the male convicts Macaulay and Fitzgerald would be with her.' Never mind that he hadn't seen Fitzgerald. The more in the plot, the better. 'I then devised a plan to recapture the three convicts . . .' No, change that. Admitting that he'd devised the plan that led them into the ambush would point the finger of blame straight at him. 'We moved closer, travelling with great stealth as we ascended the hill.' That was better. There must be no suggestion of impetuosity. They lost the fight because of the trickery of the convicts who, working with the blacks, used the woman as bait; a scurrilous, treacherous thing to do. He had to make people hate this Phillips woman. She was responsible for all those men dying. The escaped convicts might even have helped the blacks in their raid on the settlement. Now, there was a thought. He'd plant it in the right place, in the mind of a gossip who would spread the supposition as fact. He himself might even recall seeing a white man running past while he was fighting—on his own, it needed to be said—in an attempt to prevent the murdering savages from reaching the jetty.

'The woman stayed on the ridge, clearly visible because she was on an extensive patch of long grass. Proceeding with great caution, we advanced up the hill, hidden first by bush then by grass, until we were within a few hundred yards of her. All my men were hidden and placed to catch her no matter which way she ran. At this stage . . .'

He stopped. He'd been picking his way down a steep slope and emerged from a thicket of ti-tree to discover a soldier sitting on a rock. The man's musket was on the ground near him. When he saw de Lacey he lurched to his feet. 'You're a fool, lieu-tenant,' he shouted. 'You rush here, there and everywhere, like one of the bloody flies that infest this damned country, and all you do is get good men killed.' He sat on the rock again.

De Lacey took a step back. The men following him had heard. All had stopped.

'Stand up, private,' de Lacey ordered.

Reluctantly, the man got to his feet. He was injured. All of one sleeve was bloodstained and his arm hung limply.

'What's your name?'

'Peterson.' He staggered.

'Sit down, Peterson.'

Surprised, the man sat on the rock again. 'I didn't know any of you was still alive,' he said.

'You deserted the battle, Peterson,' de Lacey said softly. 'You know the penalty.'

The man didn't look up. 'I never deserted. I fought. I got this.' He touched his arm. 'It was dark when I left. I thought everyone was killed.'

141

De Lacey stared up at the sky for several seconds, sighed and moved forward and put a hand on the man's shoulder. 'What happened to your arm?'

'Musket ball, sir.'

'Can you walk?'

He shook his head. 'I couldn't see them, sir. All these spears kept falling on us and I couldn't see who was throwing them. The men on either side of me got killed, just like that.' He clicked the fingers of his good hand. He began weeping. 'I was frightened, sir.'

De Lacey nodded. 'We all were, Peterson, we all were.' He bent lower. 'Let me tell you something I haven't told anyone else. I'm feeling pretty bad.' He touched the bandage on his head. 'I doubt that I can make it back to the river. Do you think you could help me?'

Peterson looked up, his eyes dazed. 'I don't know, sir.'

'Why don't we try?' He gripped the man's hand and pulled him to his feet, then picked up Peterson's musket and slung it over his own shoulder. 'Come on, we've got to get you back so they can look at that arm of yours.'

'You look pretty well knocked about yourself, sir.'

'Indeed.' He put an arm under Peterson's sound shoulder.

'Sorry about what I said, sir,' Peterson said.

'Oh, I think I'll hear a lot worse before the day's out.' He began walking. 'Tell me if I'm going too fast.'

FOURTEEN

MACAULAY WAS SQUATTING on a flat piece of ground, ignoring the view as he reloaded the second of his three muskets. A black woman knelt beside him. She was probing the wound in his side with long, supple and filthy fingers. A thin but steady stream of blood trickled over his belt. Every now and then he groaned in pain but kept working. It was a cool morning in the mountains, but he was sweating. Eyebrows compressed in concentration, he held up a small wad of cotton.

'This is the last of these beauties,' he said to Eliza, who was facing him and marvelling at the way the woman could dig into Macaulay's flesh without causing him to scream. Although, she thought, it might have been due to the man's control rather than the woman's technique.

She was pleased to look at something other than the probing fingers. 'What is it?'

'A wad. You put the gunpowder in first, which I've done, then shove in one of these things.' He picked up a long rod and rammed the lump of cotton down the barrel, tamping it several times to compact the powder and ensure the wad was firmly in place. 'I was never shown how to do this,' he said, lifting his head briefly to make sure she was watching. 'Learned it all by watching the soldiers. They used to drill near us. "Load by ball",' he shouted in a sergeant-major's voice and a group of warriors standing near him turned in alarm. He laughed and raised a hand to placate them. 'Still nervous, some of the lads,' he said, ramming the rod down the barrel once more.

'Yes, they were pretty to watch, those boys in their bright coats and starched pants. Like toy soldiers.' He winked. 'I figured out for meself that the wad's for stopping everything from spilling out.' He held up a lead ball between his thumb and forefinger. 'Now you drop down one of these, the pretty little thing that tears a lovely hole in a man's gut. Now another wad, so the ball doesn't roll out when you tip the bloody thing upside-down.' He rammed a second piece of cotton in place. 'And that's all I've got. Last wad. I've got one more lead ball and some powder, but no more wads. Unless you got a nice piece of cotton on you that I could tear up?'

She looked away. 'I need what little I have.'

'I was thinking maybe those stockings of yours would make . . .' He stopped in mid-sentence, gritting his teeth and making a low, whining noise. The Aboriginal woman had been burrowing and emerged with a large splinter.

'No wonder the bloody thing hurt.' He breathed deeply. 'Is that all?'

The woman didn't understand and he touched the wound and raised his hand in the universal signal for 'stop'.

She shook her head and held up three fingers.

'You mean there's more?' He pointed to the wound and again she showed him three fingers. She resumed her picking and pulling.

'Easy, love, or you'll come out the other side.' He winced and, despite a major effort to be quiet, gave a little yelp. 'Damned stupid, isn't it?' he said, wiping a fresh outburst of perspiration from his forehead. 'To be in a battle where men are falling like dead leaves in a wind and I get wounded by a tree.'

'It's gone all red,' Eliza said, peering around the black woman's shoulder.

'When it goes blue, you can feed me to the dogs.'

She was tired and said, 'What dogs?'

He smiled and he looked very old. 'Just a bit of humour, that's all.' He stood, swaying so much he had to spread his legs, and brushed the black woman away. 'Come back later, love. I'll get me strength back and you can have another go at me then.'

Eliza stood, too, and studied the view. The tribe had walked for two hours after dawn, climbing all the time, and had halted on a rise that gave spectacular views towards the coast on one side and across an expanse of densely wooded peaks and valleys on the other. Already, the valleys were filling with shimmering layers of eucalyptus vapour and the distant peaks were a patchwork of hazy blues.

'Why have we come here?' she asked.

'I'd say they want to get as far away from the soldiers as they can.' He held his side. 'They'll probably stay a week or two, then go back.'

Eliza faced the sea. 'You can see so far.'

'More than fifty miles.' Macaulay, who had little idea of distance, answered in a matter-of-fact voice, as though he had been up here before.

Far below them she could see a river running parallel with the mountains and surrounded by plains. 'Is that the Hawkesbury?'

Nimboola was nearby and Macaulay pointed to the river and raised his hands. He'd found this was a good way to ask a question.

'Deerubin,' said Nimboola.

'The Deerubin,' Macaulay repeated and frowned. He'd heard the word before but had forgotten its relevance.

'I wonder where the Hawkesbury is?'

Macaulay shook his head. He was too weak and his side hurt too much for him to waste energy solving this nattering woman's puzzles. 'I think I'll sit down,' he mumbled and almost fell.

Nimboola came over and bent to feel Macaulay's forehead.

'Just a bit weary, friend,' Macaulay said and, closing his eyes, sprawled on his side.

Gently, Nimboola lifted the white man's shirt to examine the wound. He called for the woman who'd tended him. Hands clasped in subservience, she approached slowly. Nimboola spoke to her, and Eliza, understanding nothing of their language, sensed the critical tone. The woman spoke rapidly, her voice high and chattery as a bird's, and spread her hands, clearly arguing she had done all she could, or was allowed to do. An old woman came up and joined in but Nimboola silenced her with a wave of his hand.

He shook his finger at the first woman and barked an order so fiercely that even Eliza jumped. The woman lowered her head and sat beside Macaulay.

And Eliza thought: if Macaulay gets sick and can't be moved, or he dies, I'll be alone with these people.

They took her to drink at a creek that ran through a stand of tall sassafras trees, and gave her meat, which some of the older women had been cooking over a small fire. It was fatty and the flesh was white and, being ravenously hungry, she ate it at once. It had a bland taste, a little like chicken. An old woman, with a thick lower lip that curled to her chin, was eating some too and kept nodding and smiling.

'It's good,' Eliza said as she removed a fragment of ash.

The old woman used her hand to describe a slithering motion.

Eliza shook her head. 'I don't want to know.'

The members of the tribe seemed friendly and were feeding her, even if they were giving her things she would normally find repugnant, but why didn't they put on clothes? She found it just as embarrassing to look at the women, with their flat, elongated breasts and wrinkled bellies, as at the men. At least most of the men were thin and muscular. If only they'd stop scratching themselves.

Nimboola returned and, seeing Macaulay asleep on the grass, prodded him with his toe. The big man didn't move. Nimboola signalled to the woman who had been assigned the role of nurse. She was sitting, unmoving, beside Macaulay and immediately began re-examining the wound. Several women came and squatted in a semicircle behind her and made 'oohing' noises with each prod of the woman's fingers. The old woman who had tried to argue with Nimboola sat beside the nurse and brought two long, thin bones whose ends were sharpened to fine points.

Fascinated, Eliza watched as the two women worked over the raw opening in Macaulay's side. One used her fingers to spread the flesh, the other the needle-like bones to dig for a second, more deeply embedded piece of wood. The rest of the women talked constantly, pointing and offering advice. They reminded Eliza of birds on a fence. They were probably used to working together. She'd heard that black women gathered most of the food, things like roots and grubs, while the men hunted. Would that be her role if she stayed with these people? Spending her days on her knees, digging up things to eat, or sitting around with the other women, gossiping and shouting advice.

And having a naked, smelly savage take her as his wife. Oh dear God, it didn't bear thinking about.

At that point in her musings, she became aware of a stirring in the people behind her. She turned and walked to a ledge where the others were standing. Below them, two men were climbing the faint track up the hill. Periodically, they would stop so the leading man could block the track behind them with a dead bush. He was the painted Aborigine who'd carried her on his shoulders. The other man was Clancy Fitzgerald.

'You've been eating snake?' Clancy was exhausted from the all-night march but he managed to laugh. 'What sort of snake?

Black, brown, green, striped, the one with the bright red belly?'
He'd seen them all. Working in the fields and even while building the log granary, he'd encountered dozens of different snakes,
especially in the dry summers when the serpents were active.
Noxious Watts said snakes had cold blood which meant they
needed a hot day to get moving. The hotter the day, the more
lively they became. A gang of twenty working out near Prospect
Hill had lost three men in one week during a heatwave. Lifting
a log and getting bitten on the hand. Simple things like that.

Clancy was still smiling.

'I can't believe you're here,' she said. 'And in those clothes.
Look at you. A real gentleman.'

He opened the flour sack, glancing around to make sure no
one else could see. He'd been surrounded by blacks, mainly children, since he'd arrived but now most had gone. They were in
the forest near the creek, sleeping. Two men were on guard at
the ledge. The women were still tending Macaulay. 'Look what
I brought you,' Clancy said.

She saw a knife, some thread, scissors, a mug, a stone for
sharpening blades.

'For me?' she said, puzzled.

'There's salted pork in there.' He and the man with the
striped face had eaten all the bread.

'Pork?' She reached for the bag but he drew it back, out of
reach.

'Not with these people around. It'll go in a flash.'

She sat back. He was right. But, she thought, these black
people have been sharing their food with me and probably
giving me all they could spare. It was the white man's way to
keep what was his and hide it away.

Clancy winked. 'We'll have some when they're not around.'

'They're always around.'

'We'll find a time.'

He was surprised at his reaction on finding her up here in the mountains. He'd been pleased to see her. Astonished at first, when the man with the painted face had delivered him to the tribe, then filled with a deep-down pleasure, as though she were family or something.

'I went back looking for you,' he said.

'I thought you weren't coming back. I thought you'd drowned or been killed by the soldiers or had just gone off on your own.'

'Not me. I said I was coming back and I'm a man of my word.' He closed the sack. 'Now, tell me, why didn't you wait? Why did you go wandering off? I might never have found you.'

'I told you why I left,' she said slowly. She was thinking of the pork and wondering what else he had. 'When I decided to leave that spot—it was very bare and exposed in daylight—I just put myself in God's hands and went where His hand led me.'

Clancy covered his mouth.

'Don't you be saying anything sacrilegious. I've had enough blasphemy and swearing from that foul-mouthed friend of yours to last me a lifetime.'

'Fancy the great ox running into a tree. It's a wonder the tree's not sick.' He hooked a thumb towards Macaulay's inert body. 'He's the strongest man I've ever known. He'll be all right.'

He could feel a sense of excitement rising within him and he stood, facing the rows of wooded hills to the west. If the blacks had come this far, they must know of a path across the mountains. 'Are they going all the way to the west?' he asked without turning.

'I don't know where they're going. Macaulay thought they might be staying here, then going home.'

'Which is where?'

'He didn't say. I don't think he knows. He can't talk their language.'

'But they could be going all the way. Or at least, know the way.'

149

She shrugged. 'I'm very tired. You must be too. I think we should sleep. Everyone else is.'

He smiled. 'I'd forgotten.'

'What?'

'You're always telling me what to do or what not to do. I'll stay up all day if I feel like it.'

'Please yourself.' She lay on the grass, cradling her head on one arm.

'I will, Eliza Phillips, I will.' He used the tip of his new boot to touch her arm. 'You see? I remembered your name.'

'You're a remarkable man.'

Remarkable? Yes, it was true, he thought. Lucky too. Supposing the man with the painted face hadn't seen him. Mind you, he'd given Clancy the scare of his life, pointing his spear at him, jabbing it at him, yabbering away. Clancy had crawled out from under the ledge and raised a hand in greeting and said, 'Hello, it's a fine day, isn't it?' and the stripes on the other man's face seemed to narrow and, for a moment, Clancy thought he was going to thrust the spear right through him.

On reflection, he'd have been better off wearing his yellow convict uniform with the arrows all over it. Then the man would have been in no doubt that he wasn't a soldier. That was the problem. He wasn't sure who Clancy was. And Clancy didn't know about the battle, not then, so he didn't know the man would have been ready to spear anyone who even frowned at him.

Luckily, he'd smiled, then given him some bread. Obviously, the man had never eaten bread. Didn't like it at first and chewed some, then spat it into his hand, looked at it, and put it back in his mouth. Clancy ate some too, just to show it wasn't poisoned or anything like that and after a long silence, maybe six or seven minutes, the Aborigine had decided the best thing he could do was bring this stranger back up the mountain, down which the poor fellow had just descended, and let the chief of the tribe decide what to do with him.

Nimboola, it seemed, had decided to keep him. He was probably waiting, Clancy reasoned, for Macaulay—who was trusted—to wake and tell him whether the man was friend or foe.

He was feeling good and, while Eliza drifted into a deep sleep, he reached down into the sack to find the knife and, making sure no one was watching, cut himself a thick piece of pork.

FIFTEEN

WHILE AN ORDERLY tended to the congealed mess that marked the line of the cut on de Lacey's head and made clucking noises about the size of the bruise at the back of his neck, Atkinson sat against the wall on the far side of the room, legs crossed and continually drumming the side of his boot with a baton. De Lacey had thought the man might be dressed at this time of the day but Atkinson had yet to put on his shirt and jacket and was wearing just a singlet under his braces. He never took his eyes from de Lacey and while his words exuded sympathy, his face wore an expression that was close to a smirk.

De Lacey hated the man. He recognised in Atkinson a species of officer—ignorant, jealous, snide and inferior—who would rejoice in the latest incident and conspire to destroy his career.

'Dashed unlucky,' Atkinson said for the third time.

'They are a clever enemy, Atkinson. We must give them that.'

'They're unwashed, uncouth, unclothed primitives, old boy.' He smiled benevolently as if, through tiredness, de Lacey had made a silly error. 'Clever is not the word. Definitely not.' He whacked his boot. 'I'm afraid a few people are going to say you rushed in. Would have done better to think about it, plan things, take your time, not go dashing headlong into another of their traps, you know?'

De Lacey lowered his head. The orderly, doing his best to imitate a graven image, began applying a new bandage. 'Had I waited for you to initiate some action,' de Lacey said, having difficulty in controlling his temper, 'we might all still be sitting around the barracks, indolent in the heat, thinking about our dinner instead of about those poor souls the Aborigines speared to death in their beds.'

'And were that so, we'd all be alive.' Atkinson rose and went to a window. He began slapping his thigh. 'Don't mean to be critical, old boy, but I can't believe you left those poor dead wretches back there.'

They'd already discussed the bodies of the slain soldiers. 'My dear Atkinson,' de Lacey said, trying to calm himself and sounding like a professor lecturing a slow student, 'had we left four men to guard the bodies, as you suggest, we'd have left four good men to be slaughtered should the blacks return.' He had to be careful what he said. Atkinson would repeat everything and magnify any slip of the tongue. 'Remember, we were vastly outnumbered in the encounter and we were considerably more than four in number.'

'Outnumbered?' Atkinson turned. 'You said you couldn't see them. How do you know they outnumbered your men?'

De Lacey hesitated. He hadn't expected this question.

'You've got to be consistent, old boy.' Atkinson waggled a finger.

An outrageous thought entered de Lacey's head. Atkinson was pleased the slaughter had occurred. He didn't give a damn about the loss of the men. He perceived de Lacey as a rival and was happy to see him embarrassed in the worst possible way. Twice already he'd alluded to the likelihood of a court martial.

It'll mean questions, of course. Mere formality. They'll hear your story, learn of your derring-do, and hang a medal on your chest.

The orderly had finished bandaging de Lacey's head. Now he

wanted to look at the spear nick on his ribs. De Lacey leaned to one side while the man, with great delicacy, lifted his torn and stained shirt.

'How do I know we were outnumbered?' de Lacey asked and waited for Atkinson's eyes to meet his before continuing. 'It's simple, old boy. Unless each of the natives could throw three spears at once with, I must say, unerring accuracy and at different targets, then we were vastly outnumbered. You see, my dear Atkinson,' he said, and paused. Why didn't the wretched man put on a shirt? 'You see, I may not have been able to see all of our assailants but I could certainly see their spears. The sky darkened.'

The last bit was a gross exaggeration but de Lacey liked it. So would his seniors. They'd much prefer to write a report of a brave defeat, in which an officer and men of the New South Wales Corps fought with valour against a horde of savages, than hear slanderous imputations of negligence and stupidity.

'I understand yesterday's raid on the settlement was not the first,' de Lacey continued, deciding it was time for him to attack.

'There have been some incidents at the outlying farms. Never in the town, of course.'

'So you've had experience in fighting these people?'

'Oh, we've shot a few of the blighters. Initially it was just some of the local blackfellows. Quite easily dealt with, really. Would you believe, they used to come armed with fishing nets and blankets to carry our corn away. They love the Indian corn the farmers grow here. Blighters used to bring the whole tribe, even women and children. Acted like they owned the place.' He grunted in amused recollection, then frowned. 'These natives from across the river are a different proposition.'

'And have you chased them back across the Hawkesbury and into the hills?'

'Chased them?' Atkinson laughed. 'The far side of the river's their territory.'

'So you haven't followed them?'

Atkinson's face was becoming flushed. 'Not me personally, no.'

'Has anyone chased them? Has anyone tried to catch them and put an end to these attacks?'

'They move like phantoms. They're gone before you know it. And they're so deucedly difficult to see, anyhow.'

'Yes, aren't they?' De Lacey gave a satisfied smile. 'But you say no one's ever given pursuit before?'

'No.' Through the window, Atkinson could see a messenger approaching. 'Too dangerous over there. And pointless. I'm not going to lose men by sending them on a wild-goose chase.'

'But you're prepared to have a few farmers and their families slaughtered every now and then.'

To Atkinson's great relief, the messenger knocked on the door and, when bidden, entered the cottage. 'For you,' he said scanning the message before handing it to de Lacey. 'You're wanted in town. By the Governor, no less.'

Clancy had been counting. There were forty-three in the tribe. Twenty-one were men, if you included the handful of boys who were about fifteen years of age and walked with the swagger of the older warriors. The rest were women and children. It seemed to him that they were better looking people than the Aborigines he'd seen in Sydney Town or near the camps along the river. They were bigger, too. Nimboola must have been almost six feet tall which made him a veritable giant among his people. Like most blacks Clancy had seen, however, they had bad teeth, either chipped and broken as if they chewed stones, or missing altogether as was common among the coastal males who often had a front tooth knocked out when they reached manhood. Many seemed to have poor eyesight and were constantly squinting

155

through half-closed lids. The blacks around Sydney Town were like that, too. He'd heard people say it was because they'd spent much of their time peering into the distance, seeking game.

Clancy wondered how long Nimboola intended staying at this camp. It was perfectly situated on the first high ridge in the mountains, being not only an extraordinarily beautiful site with panoramic views in all directions, but a secure place because, from here, they could see or hear anyone approaching them. After a while, however, it became clear that the tribesmen were using the stop to re-arm themselves. They'd found a grove of fine, straight saplings which were formed of a particularly hard wood and the men were busy cutting spears. On some, they sharpened the ends into pointed tips and then toughened the wood over the glowing coals of small fires. On other spears, they bound pieces of sharp bone to form the tip. Some weapons were short, no more than the height of a small man, while others were eight or ten feet long. Whether they intended fighting the whites again or needed the spears for hunting, Clancy had no way of knowing. Nor did he know whether they were staying or moving on. He tried questioning Nimboola a few times, using what he considered to be graphic and clear hand signals, but the chief ignored him.

Macaulay was of no use. He'd slept for hours, ever since the two women had removed more pieces of wood from his side and covered the wound with a poultice of leaves and bark. The big man was feverish and restless in his sleep, kicking the grass and filling the air with a torrent of mumbled obscenities. Eliza had moved to the other side of the camp, near the women. She said she wanted to be well clear when the Lord sent a bolt of lightning to punish Macaulay for his persistent blasphemies.

They stayed the night. Two men had gone out with their new hunting spears and returned at dusk with a small kangaroo. The dead animal was thickset, with a shorter face and more fur than the kangaroos Clancy had seen on the plains near the river. The women had also been out gathering food and had assembled a collection of roots and fat yellow grubs and tiny birds' eggs and the pith from fern trees, which grew in abundance in the forest. Some of the women had caught a large lizard, what the colonists called an iguana, and so there was a feast that night. Not that they cooked the meat of either the animal or reptile for long, in the manner of white people. Barely had the kangaroo's fur been singed from its hide, filling the air with acrid fumes, than some of the men and women began tearing at the creature's bursting entrails. The air was filled with sharp cries of pain and bursts of laughter.

Eliza and Clancy were given the same amount of food as the others. The woman who had nursed Macaulay woke him and sat with his great, shaggy head on her lap, feeding him pieces of scorched meat that she had dug from the fire.

Macaulay was quiet after he'd eaten and soon fell asleep. Eliza returned, to sit near Clancy. 'I'm frightened,' she said, using her arms to clamp her knees to her body. 'It's the women. They keep talking and looking at me. They give me such strange looks.' She'd read stories about cannibals and said, 'Do you think they intend killing us while we sleep?' She shuddered. 'And eating us?'

'If that's what they wanted, they'd have had a meal of Macaulay long before this.' He'd thought about this. 'And if they wanted to kill us, that man with the painted face would have put his spear through me, rather than bring me all the way up here, to join you two.'

'They killed the soldiers. Why don't they kill us?'

'I can only guess. Macaulay might know.'

'He helped them in the battle,' she said. 'He shot some of the soldiers.'

'Well there we are. They think we're on the same side.'

She lapsed into silence and, long after Clancy was asleep on the grass with his loose farmer's coat covering his body, she sat with her arms curled around her legs, thinking. It was a horrible thing Macaulay had done; he was an evil man who'd murdered two men with his hands and shot a few more. White men. Englishmen. Christians. She could never have done that, even if they were men who were going to hang her. But by doing what he'd done, performing deeds her aunt would have ascribed to the devil, Macaulay had saved them. If he hadn't joined the Aborigines and helped them defeat the soldiers, the blacks would have killed her, and Clancy too, on sight.

She owed her life to a murdering, blasphemous monster. It was a ghastly thought.

Clancy had said the blacks might be walking all the way across the mountains. They would know the way. They would take the three of them with them. Clancy sounded so confident. He'd been telling her China was just a few days' walk beyond the mountains but she had doubts. The man who'd lived next door to her aunt had been a sailor and he'd been to many ports in China and if he had to go by ship, how could they walk there?

Clancy was clever, like a fox is clever but, although he could read and write, he was not educated and he'd never read the Bible and didn't believe in it, so how would he know anything and how could she entrust her life to him? That's what she was doing. Putting her life in his hands. Committing herself to being with him for the rest of her life, living in isolation, never seeing white folk again. Behaving like man and wife. Unmarried. Living in sin. She hadn't thought of that but if they did get over the mountains and find somewhere to live, the only people they'd see, almost certainly, would be wild blacks, so she'd have to live with Clancy. She'd wanted to marry a good man and have babies and raise them to be educated, polite and

God-fearing but she was condemning herself to a life in the wild with only the atheistic Clancy Fitzgerald for company.

Unless Macaulay recovered and took her as his woman—but that was too awful a thought to contemplate.

She was awake for hours, long after the last baby had stopped crying and the women had doused the fires and gone to sleep with their men. And when she did sleep, she had nightmares about black men who stank and scratched themselves and looked at her with hungry eyes and there was one terrible dream of the gross Macaulay, roaming through the bush, naked but for a forest of body hair with a spear in his hand and her, tied around the neck by a rope and being dragged after him. He turned and pulled her towards him. She felt something cover her. She sat up in fright.

Clancy was bending over her. 'I didn't mean to wake you,' he said softly. He'd put his coat on her. 'I thought you might be cold.'

Her hands were shaking. 'I had a nightmare.'

'It's the cold. Lie down. I'll tuck you in.'

'You'll be cold yourself.'

'I'm used to the cold.' He moved a few paces and sat down. 'I'll be over here if you need me. Try to sleep. I've got a feeling tomorrow will be a busy day.'

SIXTEEN

MACAULAY WOKE A few hours before dawn but his was a delirious consciousness and he raved about China and the fabled land of milk and honey that lay beyond the mountains. He was not so sick that he didn't realise they had climbed into the mountains and were still with the blacks, who had known the secret path that led over the first ridges. If there was a track up the mountains, there must be a track across the mountains. He said so many times, like a child reciting a rhyme.

Being near Macaulay and being cold, Clancy couldn't sleep but sat, body huddled against his knees, listening to the big man's ramblings but trying to do his own thinking. By sunrise, he had convinced himself that the tribe would keep walking through the mountains and the three whites would follow and thus be shown the way to the west. It would be a grand tour all the way, with plentiful water, because the blacks would know of all the creeks and waterholes, and with food provided, because the men would hunt on the way. They would be led by the hand to Macaulay's green pastures and put on the road to Peking.

Clancy was light-headed, intoxicated by an abundance of good fortune, and had developed a gambler's buoyant expectation of continuing good luck.

But when Nimboola came to them at first light he soon discovered this camp site was as far west as the tribe was going. At first, the chief showed concern for Macaulay. He felt the big man's forehead, examined his wound and stood there, fingers stroking the ornamental scars on his chest while Macaulay waved a weary arm and spoke. 'I'm all right. Just a little tired. Nothing wrong. Jussa little tired. Little tired.' He said it so many times that even a person who didn't speak English would know the man was incoherent.

Frowning, Nimboola called for two young men to join them. They were of the same age, about eighteen Clancy estimated, equally slim and of the same height, maybe five foot seven or eight. They stood silently while their leader spoke, their poses matching: each youth's head cocked slightly to the right, each perched like a waterbird on his left leg with the other leg bent up behind the knee, each clutching a spear in his right hand and grasping his elevated right foot with the other.

Nimboola addressed them, pointing first to the west, then along the rim of the mountains to the south. They understood. He turned to Clancy. Eliza was beside him but his eyes never left Clancy. He did not speak but relied entirely on his hands. He pointed to the west and stabbed several times at the horizon, where only the distant peaks and highest ridges rose above the early morning mists. Then he pointed to Clancy and nodded hopefully.

Clancy didn't move.

Nimboola repeated the gestures, impatience making him talk in abrupt sentences as he moved his hands.

'I think he wants us to go that way,' Eliza said softly.

Clancy stood up, rising clumsily because his muscles were stiff and sore. He pointed to Nimboola, then to the west, then back to the chief. 'Are you coming with us?'

Nimboola touched his chest and shook his head. He swung his arm to the south. He was heading that way. Then he indicated the two youths, turned to face the western horizon and, with his hand, made a slow, stroking gesture.

'Those two are going with us,' Eliza suggested.

'How far?' Clancy asked but couldn't think of a suitable sign. He pointed to the closest peak, then the most distant.

Nimboola raised two fingers.

'Yes, two mountains. I'm glad you can count,' Clancy said with heavy irony.

'He might mean,' she whispered, 'that they're going with us for two days.'

'Or for two miles or two minutes.' He stamped in frustration. 'Why don't these people speak English?'

'I don't think they like us well enough to bother with our language.'

He touched his cap. 'Oh, little miss expert. Knows something about everything. Hey you,' he said, beckoning to Nimboola who did not move, 'what about him?' He touched the reclining Macaulay on the shoulder. 'How are we going to move him, eh?'

Nimboola indicated the young men.

'Oh, I see. They're to carry him.'

'Or help him walk,' Eliza suggested.

Clancy spread both arms, miming a man walking with a helper on either side. Nimboola nodded gravely.

'You could have picked a couple of bigger men. Macaulay's weight will drive these insects into the ground.'

Eliza pulled at Clancy's sleeve. 'I think we should thank him before you make him angry. After all, we're going to have to do whatever he says.'

Nimboola raised a hand. He wasn't finished. Using the tip of his spear, he drew a line in the dirt and indicated he would not dare step over it. Nor would any of the other members of his tribe.

'What does that mean?' Clancy asked.

'I don't know. Maybe we're at the boundary of their land.'

'And they're not allowed to go any further? Or they're frightened to?'

'Possibly. I don't know. But if he's not allowed to go any further, why are those two boys coming with us?'

'Look at them,' Clancy said and they both did. 'They're frightened.'

'Aye, they're leaving,' Macaulay said from the ground when Nimboola had gone to round up the tribe. 'And he doesn't want us along.'

'How are you feeling, old mate?' Clancy said.

'Better. Me head's clear. For a while there I felt like a log that's burning on the inside. Help me up.' He extended a hand and Clancy pulled him to his feet. He held the unloaded musket in his free hand. Nimboola had taken the other two and the remaining gunpowder. 'He's a cunning old bugger,' Macaulay said, his face moving through a range of pained expressions when he tried to walk. 'He was watching me load the guns and he knows we're out of ammunition. He knows I'm not much use to him now. He doesn't need us.'

A woman brought a strip of bark on which were spread a selection of yams and fruit, and laid it on the grass. She hurried away.

Clancy tried a yam, which had been roasted on the coals of the last fire. It had the taste of sweet potato. 'What do you reckon?' he asked, taking a larger bite of the yam. 'Is he going to do us any harm now he doesn't need us?'

'Nimboola? No, he's still friendly.' Macaulay held his side and grimaced. 'We just have to do what he says. And if he says go with these two young lads, that's what we do.'

'That's what I think, too,' Eliza said and Macaulay's thick eyebrows lowered into a scowl. He didn't like women who expressed opinions. They were the ones who nagged and became shrews.

'This thing's about as useful as a bull without balls,' he said,

163

grasping the musket's long barrel with both hands and planting the stock between his feet. 'But it makes a good walking-stick.'

The tribe was already moving, heading into the tall sassafras trees. 'I think they just came here to make new spears,' said Clancy, who felt compelled to show he understood what was happening. 'This must be where the best wood is.'

'Their own little damned factory,' Macaulay said, eyeing the file of men leaving with bundles of spears in their hands or over their shoulders. The men had been busy, crafting spears of different lengths and with different tips; some for fighting, some for hunting game, some for impaling fish.

'So where are they going now?' Eliza asked, feeling abandoned as the women and children, moving as a unit in the middle of the column, entered the tall trees and faded from sight in the maze of shadows.

'Somewhere else,' Macaulay said. 'I don't think they have any home. They just wander around.' He took a few steps, leaning heavily on the musket. The two youths moved towards him but he waved them away. He shuffled to a rise, where he could see the last of the tribe more clearly. Nimboola, travelling with a group of warriors at the back of the procession, turned and, seeing Macaulay, raised a hand.

Macaulay waved. 'Goodbye, you old rascal,' he said, leaning on the gun again. 'You was a useful friend.'

'He saved our lives.' Eliza had joined him. 'But at what fearful cost to our own kind.'

'Oh, you're not one of those, are you?' Macaulay spat on the ground. 'Our own kind, as you call them, want to put a rope around our necks. They're as bloodthirsty as the savages.'

'It was still a terrible thing to do. All those people killed.'

'Because they were killed, you're alive.' Macaulay limped towards Clancy. 'Is she always like this, finding fault with her own good fortune?'

164

'Always.'

'You should have lost her along the way.'

Clancy grinned, glad to have another man mock the woman.

Eliza stood on the rise, wringing her hands. It might have been better to have left with the black women. But they were gone and she was now linked inextricably to these two coarse men.

Macaulay broke wind, shook a leg, sighed with relief and laughed.

Eliza sat on the grass. Tears filled her eyes. She turned away, determined not to let them see her cry. She should have gone back to the river and let the soldiers hang her. But it was too late, even for that.

She felt a light weight on her shoulder. One of the young blacks had touched her with the tip of his spear. He pointed to the west. They were leaving. He was agitated. They must hurry.

They made slow progress, mainly because of Macaulay who moved with difficulty and needed frequent stops, but partly because of the way the young guides operated. One would scout ahead, not so much to find the way, it seemed, but to check that there were no hazards on the way. The other would stay with the group and make sure they were still and silent. When all was clear, the first youth would return and they would move on to the next stopping place. Then the other Aborigine would go ahead. Both youths were nervous. With his poacher's instincts, Clancy recognised their behaviour. They were acting like people who were not supposed to be in this part of the country and feared detection.

From whom? There was no sign of another soul. The land, heavily timbered but easy to walk through, seemed deserted except for an occasional flight of birds, usually white cockatoos that passed overhead at tree-top height in flocks of a hundred or more, diving and wheeling and squawking in raucous challenge to the intruders. There were small birds too, bright finch-sized things which swooped below the canopy of leaves in vast numbers, breaking into streams of colour to avoid the massive tree trunks and making a shrill, chattering noise that swept through the forest like a wave surging towards the shore. All the birds in this strange land made noises. At one of the stops, in the quiet that followed the deafening passage of a flight of these tiny birds, Clancy gazed into the trees and found himself longing for the song of a nightingale. He'd love to hear a bird sing, he thought, not chatter or squawk or cackle.

Their course lay towards a domed mountain. Even from a distance they could see it was covered with trees of prodigious size. Clancy's instinct for marking the trail persisted and, at first, he tried to use his axe on a tree but the blacks stopped him. Too much noise, he assumed. Or might such clear marks be followed?

Very well, if he wasn't allowed to cut his mark on trees, he would remember the way. He had a good memory. He would recall landmarks, count the paces between stops so that he could judge distances. Even build little mounds of stone whenever they rested and wherever he could find stones. He might want to return some day. Or even find the way back if these two lads were doing nothing more than leading them deep into the mountains with the intention of abandoning them. That might have been Nimboola's plan. He didn't know the chief as well as Macaulay did but he wouldn't trust any savage.

With self-protection in mind, he always walked with the axe in his right hand. It fascinated the youths. They'd seen him sharpening the blade at the camp and using it, for no reason other than to display its capabilities, to trim branches from a tree. At the time a number of men had been working away at their spears, laboriously bending over the points, fashioning them into the correct shape with tapered stones that they held

166

in their hands. They had stared at him in awe when he'd hacked off each branch with a few deft strokes. Now these lads furtively glanced at the axe's shining, honed blade. 'Yes, you'd like it, wouldn't you,' he said to himself and gripped the handle even more tightly.

So far the domed mountain was the first clear pointer to the way they must travel. They kept heading towards it. All through the morning and well into the afternoon they walked, moving in short bursts, occasionally stopping longer at one of the resting points to let Macaulay recover. The mountain seemed no closer.

In the evening they came to a wide expanse of bush. It seemed impenetrable but the blacks were unperturbed. They signalled that they would stay here for the night. There was water nearby at a rockhole. Neither of the youths had been hunting or appeared to need food so no one ate.

Macaulay was in great pain. He had thrown away the poultice of bark and leaves. One of the youths went back into the forest and returned with more leaves, which he kneaded in his hands to make a soft and juicy pulp, but Macaulay threw it away. He tried to twist, to look at the wound but couldn't see it. 'Tell me,' he gasped, speaking to Clancy, 'what do you see in there? It's burning like something awful.'

'No maggots yet,' Clancy said, trying to sound cheerful, but the wound looked putrid with pus at the edges and a pinkish liquid seeping out. 'You should let them put those leaves on. They might do some good.'

'I'm not letting them touch me.'

Later, when both Eliza and Clancy were drinking from the rockhole, she said, 'He's going to die, isn't he?'

'How would I know?' There was much bark rotting in the pool and the water had a strange but pleasant taste, like weak tea.

'I've seen people die. They looked like he looks now.'

'Macaulay's too strong to die.'

'I think he will.'

'I wish you wouldn't profess to be an expert on so many things.'

'I don't. I'm not. But I believe what I'm saying. The man's being punished for his sins. It's God's will.'

'He's being punished because he ran into a tree. I wish you'd stop talking as though you were getting letters from this God of yours.'

She bent down to splash her face and rose, head held high so that water ran down her chin. 'Tonight, I will pray for you.'

'If it makes you feel better, go ahead.'

She turned away from him. 'I'd like to wash my feet.'

'Well, wash your feet.'

'A gentleman wouldn't watch.'

He laughed and turned away. He sat on a rock.

'You don't believe in God, do you?' she said as she rolled down one of her torn stockings.

'No,' he answered cheerfully. 'How could anyone, after seeing the things that happen in this world? People in chains, people being whipped and hanged. People starving. Injustice everywhere.' He swung around, but saw only her back. 'Who do you know that's happy?'

'I'm sure there are a lot of happy people.'

'Except you don't know any of them.'

'If people are being punished, it's God's will.'

'Oh I see.' He laughed again. 'And what did you do that was so terrible?'

'How do you mean?'

'Well, look at what happened to you. Thrown into prison. Put on a ship in chains and brought to the ends of the earth. Forced to live in misery and degradation.' He'd heard that expression from Noxious Watts. 'Treated so badly by the guards and everyone else that you ran away. And ended up here.' He waved an arm at the shadowy forest. 'In the land of the black-fellows, never to see a white man again and condemned to eat nothing but lizards and grubs and kangaroos for the rest of your life.' He was starting to express his own worries and stopped. 'So what are you being punished for?'

'God works in mysterious ways,' she said, repeating one of the favourite responses her aunt used when she couldn't answer a question.

'Life is terrible, it's full of suffering and disappointment and people only believe in God and the hereafter because they hope there's something better in store for them after death. No other reason.' He stood up. 'I'm going back to Macaulay.'

'I'll still pray for you,' she said and he laughed.

SEVENTEEN

LIEUTENANT ATKINSON HAD sent an armed soldier with de Lacey to carry food and provisions and attend to his needs, but it was the private with the limp and this perforce slowed them to a pace less than the weary and wounded de Lacey might have managed on his own. De Lacey was furious. It was a further insult, intended to exhaust his patience as well as his body and convey the impression he had not hurried to obey the Governor's summons whereas he had left within the hour, pausing only to bathe, put on his own uniform, drink copiously from a jug of rainwater and eat a peach, before setting off on the long walk.

The soldier was a stout-hearted fellow who struggled on without complaining but his injured leg hampered him so badly he fell behind the lieutenant's modest pace. They stopped only once, for thirty minutes at a small lagoon near the 18-mile mark, where they ate some biscuit, sliced mutton with pickles and a few dried figs. At de Lacey's insistence the soldier removed his boot and soaked his ankle in the cool water.

They reached Parramatta after nightfall.

De Lacey, almost delirious with fatigue, presented himself immediately at the address given him. It was a private house, not the tented accommodation de Lacey had expected. It was a small dwelling with a shingled roof and whitewashed walls that were of rough texture, or so they appeared in the light cast by a single lantern burning near the front door. A guard met him at the garden gate and told him to wait. The crippled private, so lost in pain that he ignored protocol, slumped down against the fence, with his head between his knees, hands barely able to grasp his tall shako to prevent it toppling to the ground.

De Lacey sat on a bench and fell asleep. He was awakened half an hour later by the guard who told him the Governor was busy and would see him in the morning. The private had gone and de Lacey worried that the man might be in trouble; a lieutenant could slump at the Governor's gate but a private was expected to be as stiff as a ramrod until put at ease. He should do something, make some inquiry to ensure the man was getting rest, not punishment, but he was too weary to think of the appropriate action. All he could mumble to the guard was, 'The man who was with me, the chap with the sore leg . . .'

'He's eating, sir.'

'He's a good man. Sore leg.'

'Yes, sir.'

He couldn't say any more. He was too tired. Carrying his plumed hat because the bandage around his head had slipped, de Lacey was shown to a room at the rear of an outbuilding. There, he lay on a couch, aware only of the strong smell of horse dung. He must be behind the stables, he thought, and began to remove his boots but had loosened only one before falling into a deep sleep.

It was ten in the morning before the Governor sent for him. By then de Lacey had bathed and eaten, removed the bloodstained bandage from his head, shaved and dressed his moustache, had a man polish his boots and brush his uniform, and rehearsed the report he would make to Hunter. He was determined to be positive, to emphasise that the men had fought bravely (he would not mention some had run away, in the sure knowledge none of the soldiers involved would contradict him) and he would stress that they had been fighting an enemy who was tenacious and clever, was on familiar territory and enjoyed an overwhelming superiority of numbers. He would also suggest, although not vehemently because he knew the Governor was a stickler for tradition, that a detachment on frontier duty should, perhaps, be dressed differently to soldiers on parade. Red jackets and white pants were not ideal for bush warfare. This lesson, he would point out with some delicacy, should have been learned after the disasters of the American rebellion when brilliantly outfitted troops had marched into the forests and made fine targets for the arrows of the Red Indians who blended with the shadows and were almost impossible to see.

Tragically, it had been a similiar situation with his troops. 'We can't see them but they see us for we stand out as brightly as lanterns in the night.' He would remember that. Lanterns in the night. The Governor might like that phrase.

Brown and green would be better colours. The Governor would not agree to so radical a change of uniform, he was certain of that, but the point was worth making, with as much subtlety as he could muster. He must give the impression he was a clear thinker who had analysed the happenings of that tragic day and could suggest tactics to ensure similar incidents did not recur. A tactical plan was essential because he was certain the natives, emboldened by their success, would strike again.

He would point out that he was the first to have led a punitive expedition following a raid, whereas the officer-in-charge of the detachment on the river had been, it would seem, content to let the natives plunder farms and murder families without effective retaliation. While his expedition had had tragic consequences, valuable lessons had been learned. They should now profit, he would suggest, from the lessons of that dreadful day and, aware of the tactics these hill tribes used, send in a much larger force to wipe out the blacks, once and for all.

Numbers were the key. He'd been hampered by having too few men to do the job. Also, there'd been virtually no intelligence to guide his mission. No one had advised him, he would say in a deliberate slur on Atkinson, that the tribes on the western side of the Hawkesbury were large in number, disciplined, and tactically superior to the miserable species who existed near the settlements. All Atkinson had done was hand him his sword.

These were fierce, resourceful and skilled warriors. Atkinson thought otherwise but he didn't know, being content to let them get away with their murderous forays. Well, maybe he couldn't say that, but Hunter would draw his own conclusions.

It was a farmhouse, with fruit trees at the front and a pigpen at the back near the stables and several sheds made of log and bark and a large area of freshly tilled land, possibly an acre or more, with the soil combed in such even rows that the owner, de Lacey observed, must be obsessed with neatness. Three convicts, unchained and with large, floppy hats to protect them from the fierce sun, were busily planting something. What it was de Lacey had no idea, having no interest in farming although he speculated that it was either cabbage or potato. They grew a lot of that out here, or so he'd heard.

He had no inkling of who owned the place, not being familiar with Parramatta society but, obviously, it was one of Captain Hunter's friends who preferred to see the Governor stay in quarters that offered greater substance and comfort than a tent.

He was led to a room in which sat two men. One was Hunter, the other Colonel Morrison, the officer-in-charge of the New South Wales Corps. Morrison's presence in Parramatta was something de Lacey hadn't expected, which was stupid of him. It was proper that the Colonel should be present. De Lacey would normally have reported to him rather than Hunter but he had been so shocked by the events of the last few days and so hypnotised by the Governor's summons that he hadn't thought logically. He took a deep breath. He should have expected this. He must sharpen his thinking.

They were in a small room that was heavily curtained to keep out the sun although the curtains were not fully drawn, so that a bright shaft of light penetrated the room. He glanced around. The furniture was simple and crudely made. Some convict carpenter had been put to this, he thought, eyeing the sideboard which was made of cedar and entirely devoid of any carving or inlays. There were half a dozen high-backed chairs which, while lacking the slender lines and wonderful grace of the set his mother had bought only three years ago from the furniture-maker Thomas Sheraton, looked as though they might outlast the house. They were stout; that was the kindest description he could give them. The table, he thought, would have suited a country inn. It was at least ten feet long and made from a single slab of cedar, with legs that bore the fine adze marks of the craftsman; so many marks that reflections winked at him from a dozen planes.

Hunter was at the table, on which lay a sheaf of papers beside a crystal inkstand with two quill pens. Without rising, he said, 'Thank you for coming down so quickly, Lieutenant.' He gestured towards a chair.

'No, thank you, sir,' de Lacey said. 'I'm quite content standing.'

'Sit down, please.' Hunter rose and walked slowly around the table and, while de Lacey sat rigidly facing the front, noted the ugly wound on the officer's head and the bruise spreading above his collar. The Colonel was seated against a wall. He stared at de Lacey as if planning his dissection.

Hunter perched himself on the edge of the table. He had

bushy eyebrows, one of which was cocked higher than the other.

'I presume you know why we asked you to come here?'

'Yes, sir.' De Lacey had resolved to give short answers. When asked to expound, he would do so.

'The situation at Mulgrave Place,' the Governor said, using the alternative name for the Hawkesbury settlement, 'has long been of concern to me. They're all ex-convicts, as you know. Mostly thieves.' He sniffed, stood up and walked to his seat. He had the rolling gait of a sailor. 'We started with twenty-two men who were given thirty acres each. Very generous, I would have thought.'

'Yes, sir.' De Lacey wasn't prepared for a briefing and blinked nervously.

'One thing I've learned in my time, lieutenant, is that people disappoint you. More so in this colony than in most places. I don't know why that should be, do you?'

'No, sir.'

'I want you to understand you can speak freely.'

'Thank you, sir.'

Hunter scratched at his chin. 'In the first year, those men who'd been given a liberal grant of land along the river didn't prepare the soil for their crops. Can you believe that? One would have imagined that preparing the soil would have been their first priority. An essential task. No, sir. They spent their time drinking and rioting.'

Hunter paused, allowing time for comment but de Lacey stayed silent. 'That place has been the bane of my life. All the worst characters in the colony, it would seem, have been placed furthest out. I know life is hard for them. They have no ploughs, they sow by hand and turn in the soil by hoe.' He shrugged. 'Well, that's the way it is. Life is not easy for any of us here.'

Time to speak. 'No, sir.'

'A few years ago, what was virtually open warfare began

between the settlers and the natives. We've got precious few men to spare but I sent a detachment of men out to the river to protect our people.' He glanced at Colonel Morrison who tilted his head in acknowledgement. 'And in one day, Lieutenant, you've lost almost half of those men.' He reached forward to pick up the quill and used its feathered tip to touch his nose. 'You might like to tell us what happened.'

Nursing his cap, an occasional twist of his fingers alone betraying his feelings, de Lacey told his story. When he had finished, the Governor called for tea and sat reading some notes. The tea arrived, borne by a convict woman, and was poured.

'In the ten years since this colony was established,' Morrison said, speaking for the first time, 'we've only lost lives in this order of magnitude through pestilence, never in battle.'

'I don't think there's been a battle, has there sir?' de Lacey said and immediately regretted the remark for the Colonel's face went red.

'Skirmishes,' the Governor said. 'There have been skirmishes. We prefer it that way.'

'It was a particularly savage and brutal raid,' de Lacey said. 'I felt it warranted immediate action.'

'You weren't in charge,' the Colonel said.

'Why did you lead the expeditions and not Lieutenant Atkinson?' the Governor asked quickly.

'Lieutenant Atkinson wasn't dressed, sir. Nor did he seem inclined to do anything. However, he was kind enough to lend me his sword.'

In unison, the Colonel and the Governor drank tea.

'I should tell you,' Hunter said before he had lowered his cup, 'that I had your man Anderson in here earlier today.'

De Lacey didn't understand.

'Anderson, the soldier who escorted you. The chappie with

the bad leg.' More tea. 'Tell me, why was a man with such an injury sent on such a long walk?'

'I can't explain that, sir. I didn't choose him.'

'I wanted to speak to him before I saw you because there were a couple of things about this affair that I didn't understand.' He wiped his lips. 'I must say, de Lacey, that when I first heard about this affair I was very angry. All these escapes, you know? I was prepared to make an example of you if you didn't catch these murderous swine.'

De Lacey took a deep breath.

'Well, you didn't of course and terrible things have happened since.' He toyed with the quill. 'But Private Anderson told me some interesting things. He regards you as something of a hero, did you know that?'

'No, sir. I only met him once before.'

'The time you fought the natives, when the raiders were trying to leave town?'

'Yes, sir. I'd been knocked down and he helped me.'

'You had been on your own, I understand, but tried to stop them.'

'It was my duty, sir.'

'The men, I'm told, would follow you anywhere.'

De Lacey smiled ruefully. 'I'm not so sure about that now, sir.'

'Oh I don't know about that. Men can usually judge an officer. Certainly happens in the navy.' He turned to Colonel Morrison. 'I'm sure it's the same on land.'

'I'm sure so, sir.'

'I understand that in the second ambush you charged the enemy who were hidden in the woods.'

'I judged it to be the most effective action.'

'And fought hand-to-hand with some of the natives.'

He nodded.

'You see, Lieutenant,' the Colonel said, leaning forward, 'no

177

one doubts your spirit but the fact is you're going to cause us the most enormous trouble.'

De Lacey, certain that Morrison had never fought anyone in his life, had to hold his temper. 'In what way, sir?' he asked.

'London will want to know why an inexperienced officer, visiting outer areas to report on conditions at various camps and settlements, should have taken command of a detachment of soldiers—not his detachment, but another officer's—and led them into two disastrous ambushes. On the one day. The one day.' He slapped his knee. 'I've never heard of anyone doing that, anywhere. Not even those buffoons who lost the American colonies.' He started to rise, then sat so heavily in the chair that its joints squeaked. 'Why couldn't you have just stayed back at the barracks after that first incident? For God's sake, wasn't it time to stop and think? To analyse the situation? And if you had to go out there again, you could have prepared more thoroughly, taken your time, and not gone rushing off with all those poor blighters into another, bigger trap.'

'The raiding party was still nearby, sir, and we could have caught them.'

'And they caught you.'

'Through treachery, sir, by that convict woman Phillips.'

Hunter lifted a hand to calm the Colonel. 'That was a shameful thing,' he said. 'You're in no doubt it was she?'

'None at all, sir. She was the willing bait in the natives' trap.'

'And the male convicts were firing stolen muskets?'

'I saw one, sir, yes.' There was silence and de Lacey went on. 'If I may, sir, I think there are some worthwhile lessons to be learned from these happenings.'

'You're damned right,' said the Colonel.

De Lacey swung towards him. 'I've been thinking about the methods they used and the way we could benefit from what we now know.'

'What *you* now know?'

'Yes, sir.'

The Colonel snorted. 'You'd be the last person I'd listen to, sir. You've suffered two humiliating defeats within twelve hours of each other, brought disgrace on the name of the Corps and now you tell me you want to lecture us on how to fight these primitive savages?'

The Governor rattled his cup. 'Your commander and I have been discussing the matter, Lieutenant de Lacey. We commend you for your bravery, understand the problems you must have encountered out at the Hawkesbury, and sympathise with your misfortune. Especially the incident with that female convict. Anyone, I dare say, could have been tricked by such a man-oeuvre.' He raised his uneven eyebrows at the Colonel, as if daring him to challenge such a statement. Morrison adjusted his collar. 'But the fact is you're a dashed embarrassment to us.'

All three were silent. The servant came and removed the tea tray.

When she had gone, the Governor said, 'How would you like to do some real fighting?'

'Go after them again?' de Lacey said eagerly.

'Good heavens, no.' Hunter spread his fingers on the table. 'I was thinking of somewhere far away. Europe.' He explained. The war against the French was intensifying. The Royal Navy was blockading the Atlantic and Mediterranean coasts. The British Army and allied units would soon be fighting on Continental Europe. He knew for a fact that the Duke of Wellington was already planning the campaign.

'I have a friend who has connections,' Hunter said. 'Someone with your inclinations . . .'

'Bull-headedness,' interposed the Colonel, without looking up.

'Let's say an officer with your dash might be of interest to someone planning an adventure.'

'You mean leave New South Wales?'

He was surprised. 'There is no question. You must go.'

Despite his vow to show no emotion, de Lacey gasped and leaned back, mouth open, eyes wide. 'Leave the colony?'

They were silent.

'I hadn't thought of doing that.'

'It is scarcely a question of choice,' the Colonel murmured.

'No, there is a choice.' Hunter raised a finger. 'You could resign and go home and no one would ever question you. Or you could allow me to seek a position for you on active duty where you might still serve your country with distinction. And I might say,' Hunter added, turning the quill over and over in his fingers, 'you'd have a great many more opportunities for displaying your daring in Europe, while that dreadful little Corsican is running riot, than you would here.'

The Colonel straightened a sleeve. 'Captain Hunter believes he may be able to arrange a transfer to the Marines. With all the current naval activity, raiding here, raiding there, the marines should be having a merry time. Or if that's not feasible, it should be possible to have you transferred, with the same rank of course, to one of the regiments serving with Wellington.'

'I hadn't considered anything like this.'

'If you resign and elect to stay in the colony, you'll be a figure of ridicule, no matter what the facts . . .' Morrison began.

'You say I must leave the New South Wales Corps?'

'Without question.'

De Lacey's shoulders slumped but only momentarily. 'Forgive me, sir. What are the other choices?'

'As His Excellency says, you could resign and return to England, retire to the family estate, lead the life of a gentleman in London, do whatever you like. Or fight. If it were me, I'd transfer to the Marines. Cut all the links, as it were.'

Hunter put down the pen. 'The Colonel wants you out of the

Corps and I concur. For your own sake, de Lacey, as much as the Corps'. Sorry, I believe you've had a lot of bad luck but that's the way it is.' He stood and walked to the window. 'Now, would you like me to write to my friend, about serving over there?'

'I . . . well, yes, sir.'

'Good. I'm pleased. A good man who's had bad luck needs another chance.' Outside, the trees were shedding leaves as a sudden wind blew and he stared at the sight for several moments. He clasped his hands behind his back. 'We're expecting a ship to call at Port Jackson in a few months' time. It's bound for Bombay. That would be the quickest way home. You should carry my letter with you.' Hunter returned to the table and faced de Lacey. 'I'd like to be going to Europe myself, instead of being stuck out here, worrying about escaping convicts and drunken settlers and blackfellows and the price of wheat.'

De Lacey rose, rolling his cap through his fingers. 'I was wondering, if the ship is not due for some time, whether I might be permitted to return to the Hawkesbury and continue the search for those three convicts.'

'What on earth for?'

'They were responsible for the deaths of many good men. The woman in particular. I'd like to see her pay for her treachery.' He breathed deeply. 'She's the cause of my disgrace.'

'Oh come, come, de Lacey, you're not disgraced.'

'I think that was the term used, Your Excellency.'

'No one is doubting your honour, sir,' the Colonel said.

'I would like to look for them, sir. Catch them. Have them dealt with. Clear up this business, at least, before I'm sent packing.'

'Request denied,' the Colonel said. 'I would like your letter of resignation by tomorrow.'

'You will have it, sir.' De Lacey saluted and left.

*　　　*　　　*

'I feel sorry for the blighter,' Hunter said.

'Damned fool.'

'Perhaps. Do you think we're sending him to his death, Colonel? If I judge him correctly, the man will fight like the very devil to restore his honour. Get himself involved in some damned dangerous affairs.'

'De Lacey himself is damned dangerous.' He stood, preparing to take his leave. 'Mind you, it might all be over by the time the blighter gets over there.'

'I pray so but I think not.' Hunter sighed. 'I'll write a note that ensures de Lacey is involved in the thick of the fighting, wherever that might be.'

'And I hope for his sake that he dies bravely on the field. Couldn't bear to live if I'd done what that man's done.'

Outside, de Lacey walked from the building, his mind in a daze. The wind was strong, a hot summer westerly that whisked leaves from the grass and sent them swirling through the air. He removed his shako because his head hurt, but what did it matter, anyhow, whether he was properly dressed or not? He was being thrown out of the corps, banished from the colony. Casually, he returned the salute from the guard at the gate and sat on the bench where he'd waited the previous night.

Where would he stay? He'd have to find lodgings. Buy clothes. It must be gentleman's apparel but there was so little choice and most of it was rubbish. And people would talk. He'd be ostracised, a pariah in this ghastly place.

But I will endure this injustice with dignity. I will go to Europe. Join Wellington, or whoever will have me. I will fight with distinction. People will talk of my achievements with awe. And when the war is over I will return to New South Wales and if that convict woman Phillips is still alive, I will catch her. With my own hands, I will put the noose around her neck.

EIGHTEEN

T HE TWO NATIVES were astir well before dawn. They insisted on everyone drinking their fill of the tainted but sweet water in the rockhole, making signs to indicate they were in for a dry march, and had the party moving as the first tint of morning stained the sky. As the sun rose, they were skirting the dense brush that had blocked their progress but, after a mile of probing and checking, they found what they were looking for: a place where the undergrowth thinned. There was a way through and, for this part of the journey, neither youth scouted ahead. The party moved in line, following a sinuous and undulating route through the thicket. One of the Aborigines led, being forced to bend for most of the way to avoid the grasp of outstretched branches. Then came Clancy, beckoned into that position by the leader, followed by Eliza and Macaulay. The second youth travelled immediately behind Macaulay, helping him through difficult parts where the big man was required to stoop or step over an obstacle. Every twenty minutes, or after a difficult passage, they would stop to let Macaulay regain his strength which had diminished noticeably during the night. Now, he didn't argue when offered help. He rarely spoke other than to utter an occasional murmur of pain or a soft babble of unintelligible sounds.

After two hours of travel Clancy discovered why he had been

placed behind the leader. His axe was required to clear the way. The scrub became thicker—so crammed with sinewy trunks and twisted branches that he couldn't see Macaulay who was no more than a dozen paces behind him—and for almost a mile he had to hack a path for the others to follow. The youth with him kept indicating the way they should travel. Clancy had no idea. Because of the thick growth that forced him to bend as he hacked at branches, he couldn't see the sun and had lost sight of the domed mountain. But there was a curious change in the attitude of the two youths. Out of sight of each other, they chatted and laughed and were noticeably relaxed. They were no longer concerned about making a noise or frightened of detection. The going might be onerous and slow, but this dense patch of mountain scrub was safe for strangers to travel through, by virtue of its assumed impenetrability.

It was afternoon before they emerged from the scrub. They saw the mountain clearly. It was on their left, a great towering bubble of massed vegetation. Where they stood on a grassy plateau there was only sparse tree cover but above them on the rounded peak the ash and sassafras stood trunk to trunk and were of immense size. Clancy had been counting his steps and estimated the patch of thick brush extended for a total of three miles. Three miles of seemingly impassable scrub, just to the east of the domed mountain. He filed the information away. If ever he came back, he'd need the axe again but he'd left a pathway through a tunnel of mutilated limbs and he'd find his way.

Travel on the plateau was easy but Macaulay was in a bad way so they rested, putting him in the shade cast by some small trees. To the north was a deep valley with its sides lined by precipitous sandstone cliffs. On the far side of the valley a ridge of equal height and similar contours paralleled theirs. Its crest was covered in a mat of vegetation.

'Wild country,' Clancy said, leaning back exhausted after all the chopping. 'Thank God we're on this side of the valley. We'd never move over there.'

'Why do you thank God when you don't believe in him?' Eliza said, still thinking of the previous evening's conversation.

'Just a figure of speech. I could have thanked my father although I don't have much to thank him for or I could have thanked my finches. Yes, they'd be better. Thank Benny and Bess that we're on this side of the valley.'

She sat up straight. 'Who are Benny and Bess?'

'Two of my finches. Birds. I used to keep caged birds.'

'How on earth can you talk about God and your pet birds in the same breath?'

'Easily.' He rolled on his side, away from her. 'I'm tired, Miss Eliza Phillips. That was hard work back there. Please leave me in peace.'

She was silent for a few minutes. She gazed across the valley and at other forested ridges and hazy valleys in the distance. All the way to the horizon and gouged into the mountains like deep scars were walls of speckled sandstone.

'It's very rough country. I've never seen anything like it.'

He didn't answer.

'Have you noticed this ridge here and the one on the other side? It looks like they were joined together once. They're almost the same. One would fit into the other.'

He grunted. 'You say the most stupid things.'

'Look for yourself,' she said sharply, tired of his jibes. 'This bulging bit of cliff near us could fit into that big groove on the other side and that cliff over there . . .' she jabbed her finger towards the far side of the valley. ' . . .the one that sticks out like the tower on a castle, that could fit into the space over here, near us.'

He shook his head. 'God been playing games, has he? Shifting the earth around.'

'I don't know why I bother trying to make conversation.'

'Neither do I.'

'I mean, there are only the two of us and every time I try to say something, you mock me.'

'You deserve it.' He began picking at a blister in his palm, holding his hand high to let her know he found the blister more interesting than she was.

He could be such a pig of a man, she thought, wrestling with her fingers in frustration, and yet he'd given her his coat during the night. Why did he do nice things at night and yet feel compelled to behave so badly in daylight? Was it because he had an audience? Not that the one person who might understand his barbs had given any sign of being impressed. Macaulay was lying flat on his back, mumbling away and being ignored, as people in continual pain often are, and alternatively covering his eyes with his left arm or thrashing the ground with it. She'd seen the wound. It was ghastly, all swollen and dripping poisonous matter and she was sure the reason he was swinging and beating his arm was that it, too, was now aching as the infection spread.

She moved to the nearest tree, choosing a shady patch between its knobbly roots where she couldn't see Clancy or Macaulay, and tried to think of other things. Water. It was a hot day and they'd been making their way through the brush for almost seven hours and she was choking with thirst but too proud to say anything. Everyone must be thirsty, even the blacks. She had faith in the two youths. They would take them to water when there was water. They might be very different to her but they were human. She had to force herself to think that and to convince herself it was true because, since she'd arrived in the colony, people had been telling her that Aborigines weren't human. They were more like wild animals, which meant you didn't have to worry about giving them water because wild animals didn't have the same needs as people and could go without water for long periods.

But it couldn't be true. These boys were nice. Clean, lean and good-looking. They must be thirsty too. She looked at the youths for a long time as they sat together in the shade, talking animatedly and pointing back the way they had come, and decided that people only called Aborigines animals so they could treat them badly without feeling remorse.

As though reading her mind, one of the youths looked her way, cupped his hands, raised them to his mouth and pointed towards the nearest cliff.

'Yes, please,' she said and stood. They all went, Macaulay being supported by the youths.

Five hundred yards from where they'd rested, a trickle of water seeped from a spring in a patch of bright green grass. They drank there, sat for a few minutes and drank again. Then Eliza and Clancy followed the water to the cliff edge, where it became a minute cascade, splashing down a series of stained and polished shelves of rock. One of the youths shouted a warning. His meaning was clear: keep away from the edge. As they drew closer and peered down, they understood. There was a sheer drop of 500 feet to a ledge of broken rock. Some hundreds of feet below that were the first straggling rows of trees, reaching up from the valley floor.

The blacks were anxious to move and once more became agitated. Moving with great caution and having one scout ahead before the whole party moved, they headed for the domed mountain. Climbing almost non-stop, they were halfway up its side an hour before sunset. Travel was pleasantly cool within the peak's towering forest but Macaulay was proving a great handicap. For a while, one of the youths tried carrying him over his shoulders and, while the Aborigine was surprisingly strong, Macaulay made his task impossible by shaking himself free and trying to fight the boy. By now Clancy had the musket so that he carried his axe in one hand, the bag of stolen items over his shoulder and the gun strapped across his back. Macaulay, however, was unaware of this and began a frenzied search for the musket, flailing out with his hands in an attempt to strike the black until, exhausted and off balance, he fell down, slavering at the mouth.

The youths moved to one side to talk.

One returned and, using his hands, addressed Clancy. They were taking them around the hill. He indicated the south. He cupped his hand to his mouth. There was water ahead. He made a pillow of his hands. They would sleep there. And they were to leave Macaulay, who had lapsed into a semi-conscious state in which he occasionally twitched and thrashed the ground with his aching arm.

'No,' said Clancy, shaking his head vigorously.

The young black raised his spear. He jabbed it in the direction of the south, then aimed it at Clancy.

'Don't argue,' Eliza said.

'How can I argue when I don't know what he's saying?'

'I think it's clear. We follow him. Maybe we can come back for Macaulay.'

'Hey,' Clancy called to the black who had begun to walk away. He touched Eliza's shoulder, then his own, indicated the south and nodded. The youth nodded gravely. Then Clancy tapped his chest several times, pointed the other way and gestured towards Macaulay.

The black nodded.

'We've agreed on something,' Clancy said, 'but I'm not sure what it was.' The young man was already off, loping through the trees.

The other Aborigine had disappeared. The track was rough and covered with broken rock. They had to skirt one massive rockfall, where part of a cliff had given way, and push their way through thick growths of palm-like fern, but after only fifteen minutes they found the other youth waiting near a tree of exceptional size. He beckoned to Clancy and led him through a stand of tall ferns to a low embankment where there was a cluster of rocks. Trapped within the rocks was a small pool of clear water. It held no more than a gallon but it would sustain them for the night and, according to the guide who was mimicking drinking and then smiling, it was good. Clancy scooped some in his hand, as was expected of him. It was pure and exceptionally cool.

He was hungry and raised his hand to his mouth and chewed. The young black shook his head.

'No wonder these blighters are so skinny,' he said when Eliza had joined him. They were sitting on the rocks. 'Wouldn't you think they'd go out and spear something?'

'Maybe there's nothing here,' she said.

'No,' he said, shaking his head, 'they're scared. They'd rather go hungry than go hunting in a land where they're not welcome.' He winked and pulled the flour sack between them. 'But have no fear, my child, not while your Uncle Clancy is looking after you.' Furtively, he took a piece of salted pork from the sack and, with his knife, cut it in two. 'Don't let the lads see you,' he whispered, brushing dirt from her piece before handing it to her. 'We're getting low and there's not enough to go around.'

She didn't argue. Hunger was the greatest corrupter of morals, as she knew from observing the way people behaved back in the colony, where most went hungry for much of the time and did illegal, violent, corrupt or depraved acts just to get food, and now here she was, not sharing with the others and relishing the food. It was a most sinful, selfish thing to do. She prayed for God's forgiveness and took another bite. After she'd swallowed the last morsel, and being anxious to forget the episode, she tried to recall what they'd been talking about. Yes. Clancy's theory that the boys were scared. She said, 'Why would they be frightened? There's no one around.'

'Not that we can see.' He wiped his mouth, terminating the meal and sighed, an expression of longing rather than satisfaction, for it had been a small piece of pork. He ran a finger across his lips. 'I'd say this land belongs to another tribe and these lads shouldn't be here. Not that they haven't been here. They know the way, they know where there's water. And they know, right now, they shouldn't be here.'

'Well, if that's true, neither should we.'

He smiled sadly. 'Have you just realised that?'

'Well, what if it's true?'

'Oh, I think it's true all right. It means that they're leading us to a place where strangers aren't welcome.'

'But we're not blackfellows from another tribe. We're white,' she protested.

His eyes blazed with good humour. 'Which makes us even stranger.'

At sunset, Clancy tried to go back for Macaulay, to carry him or help him down or do something rather than leave him alone all night, but the youth who had addressed him blocked his way.

'Not tonight, is that what you're saying?'

The Aborigine shook his head and pointed to the rocks.

'Can I get him tomorrow? Will you go back and carry him down?'

He pointed to the rocks.

'He might be dead in the morning, do you know that?'

Again the rocks. The youth then pulled at Clancy's sleeve, to ensure he was watching, and used his spear to indicate that the path ahead lay down the mountain.

'We go that way tomorrow, after we get the big white fellow?'

With the spear, the young Aborigine indicated another peak, just visible through the trunks of the giant trees. It was about a mile and a half away. He nodded and Clancy, enjoying the tomfoolery, nodded too.

The spear changed direction marginally, being aimed directly at the setting sun.

'And then we go that way. Thank you. I look forward to your company and another long and interesting conversation.' He took the youth's hand and shook it, which astonished him.

All around them were the soaring trunks of stately mountain ash and, during the night, a strong wind blew and the upper limbs of the trees bent and creaked and the wind moaned and sighed as it twisted its way through the forest. Several branches fell, crashing through the lower limbs as they tumbled down to join the mass of debris lining the forest floor.

In the morning, when the rising sun was casting its longest, coolest shadows, they found the two young blackfellows had gone.

NINETEEN

THEY SEARCHED THE area, thinking the guides might be resting among the trees or be quietly searching for food, like the yams, grubs, or birds' eggs the tribe had eaten at the last camp, but there was no sign of them. The youths were gone. They had been abandoned. And then they remembered. At that camp, Nimboola had held up two fingers. Two days. The youths had shown them the way for two days, through terrain that obviously involved them in great risk, and now they were gone. Clancy recalled seeing Nimboola briefing the youngsters; pointing first west and then south. Nimboola indicated he was heading south with the tribe. Therefore, the boys were returning to that camp site and would then head south, along those initial ridges of the Blue Mountains, to rejoin their people.

'They might be with Macaulay,' Eliza suggested and Clancy, who'd had little sleep because of the wind in the trees and whose mind was having trouble engaging coherent thoughts, gave a little wheeze of pleasure. He hadn't thought of that. Of course. They would be with Macaulay, and even now were probably trying to carry his massive bulk down the track to meet them.

Back they went, towards the place where Macaulay had been left, following a path that weaved around the gigantic tree trunks and pushing their way through the clumps of tall ferns that flourished in the perpetual shade. Clancy led, carrying only the axe. About 200 yards along the way, they had to detour down a steep slope to avoid the massive spill of rock. The recent fall had brought down one of the trees, making the area a jumble of sandstone slabs and jagged timber. Aided by the light beams that filtered through the hole in the canopy of leaves above them, they picked their way down the slope and over the last fragments of rock and were climbing again, with Clancy grasping Eliza's hand to pull her after him, when they stopped, aware of noises. Someone was shouting. It was a deep, bull-like roar of a voice. Macaulay. And there were other voices. Angry voices that were high-pitched and firing words in staccato bursts.

'Why is he arguing with them?' Eliza said.

Clancy raised a finger to his lips. 'It's not the lads. It's someone else.'

They climbed back to level ground and, moving cautiously, came to a place where they could see Macaulay through the trees. He was standing with both arms widespread, head back, shouting profanities at the treetops.

Facing him and arranged in a semicircle were four natives. Two were older men with wispy beards and hair drawn back in a bob. The others were younger; lithe, clean-chinned boys of about sixteen. The boys were naked but the men wore belts of plaited hair from which hung stone axes—primitive tools with the handles being merely leather thongs. One held a long, hooked stick in his left hand. All, even the boys, were carrying hunting spears.

One of the older men shouted at Macaulay and shook his spear.

Macaulay lowered his head and squinted at the four, taking time to examine each of them. He shook a fist at the nearest man. 'You give me my bloody gun.' He staggered forward, rolling like a bear. 'Thieves. I'll pull you apart.' Then he grabbed his left arm and wrapped it around his chest and, bent forward as though in intense pain, fell to his knees. He lapsed into gibberish.

The blacks looked at each other. The older of the two men signalled to the boys who stepped back but still held their spears at shoulder-height, ready for throwing.

Now the other man shouted at Macaulay. He was demanding answers and twice he pretended to throw his spear, darting forward and lunging with his arm.

Macaulay was crouched low so that his forehead touched the ground. Slowly, he straightened and stood up. He lifted his arms, gave a bellowing war cry and lurched forward. The man hurled his spear.

It went through Macaulay's left side, just below the ribs. Macaulay, still on his feet, roared in anger and, holding the protruding shaft in both hands, tried to run at the man.

A second spear hit him in the chest. The other man had used his hooked stick to launch the spear and it hit with great force. Macaulay made a whistling noise, staggered back two steps, and fell on his side. He didn't move.

The man who'd thrown the second spear now took his stone axe and advanced on his victim with long, slow steps, like a waterbird delicately moving through the shallows. He stood over Macaulay, arm raised to stove in the white man's skull, but there was no movement in the massive body, no breathing, no sign of life.

The boys came up, talking rapidly. They prodded the body until the older man pushed them away.

With difficulty, the men pulled out the spears, both having to grasp the shaft of the one in the chest to haul its barbs clear of the ribs. They removed Macaulay's torn and bloodstained shirt and tried to take his belt but couldn't undo the buckle. While one man persevered with the belt, the other went searching for tracks and, after a minute, shouted and pointed to the east.

'They've picked up the tracks of our two lads,' Clancy whispered. They were standing immobile among tall ferns.

'What do we do?' Eliza was wide-eyed in horror.

'Nothing. Not yet.'

She grabbed Clancy's arm and stood partly behind him.

'Don't move,' he said, being frightened but feeling remarkably calm. He was experienced in escaping detection and had learned the value of being both still and silent. He felt her take a deep breath. 'And don't talk.'

The man kneeling beside Macaulay's body had grown impatient with the buckle and was now trying to pull the belt free without undoing it. All he succeeded in doing was to drag the body a few inches across the grass.

In disgust, he left to join the others who were already heading east. Walking rapidly, eyes cast to the ground as they followed the fresh tracks, the four hunters disappeared among the trees.

'Thank God for that,' Clancy said and Eliza said nothing.

They hurried back through the ferns and around the fallen rocks to the small pool where Clancy had left the musket and his sack. He hadn't gone near the body, to remove the belt or boots or other valuables or to bury Macaulay, as Eliza had suggested they should do.

'They'll return and if they find fresh footprints, or if the belt's missing, they'll know someone else was here and they'll come looking for us.'

She hadn't argued. Having glimpsed the people who lived in these mountains and witnessed the way they dealt with an uncertain situation, she had resolved to stay close to Clancy and do whatever he said.

She held his hand all the way back to the pool. She was horror-struck and frightened and so was he, but having her hand in his was a good feeling. It made him feel not stronger but less weak, and reminded him of the way Charlotte used to hold his hand when she was a little girl.

He decided to leave the musket. It was heavy, too heavy for him to travel quickly, and useless without powder and lead balls, so he hid it near the pool in a dry shadowy place where spiders nested within the rocks.

'Where do we go?' she whispered but he waved her into silence because he was pondering the same question.

Only now did he realise why the youth had gone to such pains to point out the way across the mountains. The young Aborigine was trying to tell him they were leaving but he hadn't been smart enough to understand. Nor had he been listening intently and he had trouble recalling the instructions. Where to first? Somewhere that was a mile and a half away. He could recall the distance, not the object, so he looked through the trees, first to the west which was wrong because all the peaks and distinctive features were too far away, and then to the south. He saw a hill and remembered. That hill, at the far side of a plateau that had only a light covering of dry eucalypts, was the first landmark. To reach it they would have to descend the domed mountain and cross the plateau. It looked like a relatively simple journey. He nodded to himself, aware that Eliza was staring at him with some curiosity but, thankfully, saying nothing. From the hill they had to travel more to the right, towards the sunset. And from there? He had no idea. They would just keep heading towards the west.

With the sack over his shoulder, axe in hand and Eliza clutching the tail of his coat, he scrambled down the side of the mountain.

The plateau was well grassed with little undergrowth to slow them and they reached the hill after three hours of continuous walking. They found water trickling through a gully and drank and rested for ten minutes, all the time watching to see if they were being followed.

Clancy was now beginning to think as a survivor, not as a fugitive, and realised they needed something to hold water because he had no idea where, in the next few days, they might find a rockhole, creek or river. He rummaged through his bag, spilling the contents on the ground. Scissors, needle, thread, knife, metal mug—that would give them a few mouthfuls on a short journey—hammer, nails and the sharpening stone. He filled the cloth cap with water but it leaked profusely. He'd noticed the women in Nimboola's tribe had carried water in dishes fashioned from bark. The vessels had curled sides and closed ends so that they resembled small boats and were some-how waterproofed. He didn't know how to make one and he dared not use the axe because of the noise it would make, so they drank as much as they could and, with Eliza carrying the mug filled with water and trying desperately not to spill a drop, they walked around the side of the hill and swung towards the west, as the guide had indicated.

They drank the water early on because it kept slopping over the edge of the mug. They walked until sunset when they came to a small watercourse which had cut its way through ridged sandstone and found water in one of the holes. They stayed there the night and ate the last of the pork. They slept side by side, sharing Clancy's outspread jacket and, after midnight, when a cold wind blew across the ridge, curled together for warmth.

Quinton de Lacey delivered his letter of resignation and then got a lift down the Parramatta River aboard a small schooner that was carrying potatoes and turnips to Port Jackson. He found lodgings at The Rocks, near the wharf where Robert Campbell, a Scotsman from Calcutta, was starting business as a general merchant. He preferred to deal with Campbell rather than some of the officers of the New South Wales Corps who were taking control of trade. They, the elite of the colony, had forced up prices to absurd levels and he wouldn't deal with such unscrupulous people. Besides, they would have heard the stories about what happened on the Hawkesbury and he had no desire to provide further material for their bouts of drunken gossip. *Had that fellow de Lacey in the other day . . .* He could imagine the way they would talk. In the short time since his meeting with the Governor and Morrison, he had convinced himself that leaving the Corps was a worthwhile move as it was becoming little more than an assembly of greedy and corrupt rascals.

He found Campbell to be a genial fellow with an instinct for trade sharpened by his years in India. From him, de Lacey bought a tall black hat for two pounds and a pair of shoes for thirteen shillings. Both were English-made and of the finest quality. He also bought a length of suit material woven in the Midlands. He was tempted by some of the samples Campbell had brought from Calcutta, for they were attractive in appearance and much cheaper than the English cloth but he decided against them, recalling how the garb made of Indian cotton worn by some of the convicts was reduced to threadbare rags within a month.

Carrying the roll of cloth under his arm, he was sent by Campbell 200 yards down the road to a tailor named Cedric Watson. De Lacey found Watson working cross-legged on a bench in a dim room at the back of a tiny house with walls of wattle and daub and an undulating floor of compressed dirt. The man was small and hunched, with diminutive spectacles that must have been made for someone else—a rich man's child, de Lacey guessed, for they had gold rims. Watson was from

York, a town de Lacey knew well, and they spent several pleasant minutes reminiscing.

Watson was an educated man and, with some modesty, purported to be the best tailor in the colony, which he may well have been; de Lacey knew of no other. The man was an ex-convict, of course, but, as de Lacey reflected, a tailor was more likely to be transported for fraud or larceny than for making a bad suit. Moving de Lacey to the doorway for the better light, Watson measured him for a three-piece suit which he said would be cut in the latest London style and showed him illustrations from a journal which was less than a year old. He would use real China silk to trim the waistcoat and line the jacket. The suit would be finished in two weeks.

De Lacey went back to his room. He tried on the hat again and stared wistfully at his reflection in a small hand mirror whose silver was so tarnished and crazed it presented the image of a badly weathered portrait in oils. He stared in fascination. He'd like a portrait done some day but in dress uniform. He looked strange, rather drab, in civilian clothes. Never mind, he would soon be back in an officer's uniform and seeing genuine military action, not chasing a mob of naked savages through the bush. The uniforms of the Marines were rather dull, he thought, with that ghastly leather collar. One of the Army regiments would be better, with their plumes and vivid colours. There would be no need for the camouflage of green or brown in Spain because, there, he would be fighting in open fields and against civilised opponents.

He needed to write some letters but had no paper. Damn. In the Corps, he could snap his fingers and someone would bring him whatever he wanted. As a civilian he would have to buy and fetch for himself. So he returned to Campbell, who seemed too busy trying to establish his business to be selling things but was obliging all the same, and purchased a quire of good quality writing paper for six shillings.

He wrote some letters that night. Next morning he thought of buying a horse because he had a long journey to make and was tired of walking great distances over dusty tracks. Besides, he wanted to avoid other people's company and fancied spending the next few weeks in riding to some of the more isolated parts of the settlement. People who'd sailed off the coast said there were good beaches south of the entrance to Port Jackson. He might follow one of the bush tracks to the coast and let the animal gallop over the sand or have its head in a wild charge through the surf.

The only horse for sale was a grey owned by an ex-Marine officer who had retired from the service to take up a 30-acre allotment along the Parramatta River. It was one of eight such grants allotted to Marine officers who, five years earlier, had chosen to stay in the colony rather than sail back to England. The place was called the Field of Mars; an ironic tribute, de Lacey thought, to so-called fighting men who preferred the life of farmers. De Lacey spent the morning trudging up the river to the property. He liked the horse but the officer-turned-farmer, whom de Lacey had met once or twice and held in scorn for his change of profession, wanted 80 pounds for it. De Lacey could buy a good house in England for less than that and set off to walk home. When he reached Brickfield Hill on the outskirts of Sydney Town he had covered, he estimated, a total of fifteen miles. Despite being leg weary, he hurried, with many a backwards glance, for this was an area where the notorious bushranger, the American negro known as Black Caesar, operated. He was much feared by blacks as well as whites and was reputed to have killed the Aboriginal bandit Pemulwy. Once over Brickfield Hill de Lacey continued at a fast pace to negotiate the collection of earthen huts and solitary tents that were scattered through the scrub on the way to Sydney Cove. It was an unsavoury area, with drunkenness and fighting being the favoured social activities. Sydney was known colloquially as 'the camp', an appropriate name for such a scruffy and inconsequential town.

Another American ship was in the harbour. This one had no need for repairs but had arrived on a speculative voyage bearing a cargo of spirits and small quantities of beef, pork and flour which the captain hoped to sell before heading into the southern oceans in search of whales. The ship's sailors roamed the streets and de Lacey, who disliked bawdy drunkenness in anyone but loathed it in sailors because of their peculiarly offensive behaviour when inebriated, stayed in his room and read Homer.

He rested the next day, then walked to the Hawkesbury. He maintained a brisk pace, for he was now almost fully fit, and arrived just before sunset. Rather than go to The Green Hills, he followed the track upriver to the camp where the convicts were building a log granary. He met the sergeant, who greeted him with greater respect than before, having heard the tale of de Lacey's hand-to-hand fight with the natives at the main settlement, but was surprised to see de Lacey in civilian clothes.

'I've asked to be transferred to a regiment in Spain, to help in the fight against Bonaparte,' he said. 'Just waiting for a ship to take me there.' It was his standard response.

He asked to see Noxious Watts.

Watts, wearing a ragged coat over his yellow uniform, was led clanking into the room. He'd been having his supper and was chained to manacles around each ankle with a central link tied to the waist so he could walk. He didn't recognise de Lacey.

'This is Lieutenant de Lacey,' the sergeant barked and Watts cringed, as though expecting a cuff on the ear.

De Lacey stood and faced the convict. 'I interviewed you the night three convicts escaped from here. Macaulay, Fitzgerald and a female, Phillips. You knew them all, I believe.'

'Not the woman.' Watts shook his head vigorously. 'I never saw the woman.'

'I need information. It will be in your interests to tell me what I want to know. That's not a threat but a promise of help.'

Watts didn't speak.

'How long do you have to serve?'

'Five years.'

'Say sir,' the sergeant shouted.

'Five years, sir.' He drawled the words, being as close to insolence as he dared.

The sergeant moved in but de Lacey held up a hand. 'That's all right, sergeant. I'm sure Mr Watts and I understand each other.'

The sergeant made a rumbling sound and Watts knew he was in for a beating when the lieutenant had gone.

'How would you like to be a free man in considerably less than five years?'

Watts shrugged.

'Come, come. I understand you're an educated man. Well read, so I'm told. I'm sure you can answer my question.'

'Well of course I'd like it . . . sir.'

'You tell me all you know, or all you can find out over the next few days about these three convicts, and I'll see to it that your sentence is reduced.'

Watts looked from the sergeant to de Lacey but said nothing.

'I'll be here for the next four days. Each day, you'll come to see me and tell me what you've discovered. Especially about the Phillips woman.'

'I don't get the chance to mix with the women,' Watts said.

'The sergeant will see that you get the opportunity, won't you sergeant?'

The sergeant raised his eyebrows but said, 'Yes, sir. Whatever you want, sir.'

'I want to see them caught. I want to see them hanged. You help me do that, Watts, and I'll see that you're well rewarded.'

Watts glanced at the sergeant before speaking. 'You mean in getting me off early?'

'More than that. I mean a reward. Something that might set you up in a farm or a business of some sort. It depends on the information you gather.'

'Can I ask a question?'

'Sir,' prompted the sergeant.

'Go ahead,' said de Lacey.

'Those three'll be dead by now. Why do you want to know so much about them?'

'Don't be impertinent, Watts,' the sergeant said, tapping his boot on the floor.

'No, no sergeant, it's a perfectly reasonable question.' De Lacey thrust his hands into his pockets. 'I saw the woman and one of the men just recently. They were with a group of tribal Aborigines and were instrumental in leading us into a trap. Many of my men were killed or wounded. Therefore, Watts, I have very good reasons for wanting to see them brought to justice.'

'And all you want me to do is give you some information?'

'Correct information.' The sergeant clapped his hands together.

'But like what?'

'Discover if others knew of their plans and knew what their objectives were,' de Lacey said. 'It would help if we had an idea where they might be heading. If they had colleagues—if others were involved and planned to meet them somewhere. See if you can find out something of their backgrounds. What skills they might possess. Anything. When I was here last I was told you were good at supplying information.'

'He's a real ferret, sir,' said the sergeant.

'What say I see you tomorrow at four?' de Lacey said and Watts was taken from the room.

When the sergeant returned, he said, 'I don't know that you can trust that one, sir.'

'We'll see.' De Lacey was at the window, deep in thought. 'You're probably wondering, like Watts, why I've become so involved in the pursuit of these three people?'

'No, sir.'

'Well, I've sworn on the Bible that I will see them recaptured and hanged. I've made it my personal crusade.'

'Yes, sir.'

'You don't understand, do you, sergeant?'

He looked puzzled. 'Oh, yes, sir.'

'I don't think many would. But I am prepared to follow this crusade for the rest of my life, if need be.'

'Yes, sir. I do understand, sir.'

'I'll be off to Europe soon.'

'To fight in the war, sir. Very commendable, sir.'

'But wars don't last forever and I intend to come back and, if those three are still unaccounted for, I'll resume the search.'

'If I may say so, sir, you're very persistent. Remarkably so.'

'Kind of you to say so, sergeant. Many have said much the same thing. My own mother said persistence was the mark of a truly great person.'

The sergeant left de Lacey staring out of the window. He shook his head in pity. He'd heard the lieutenant had been badly knocked around the head. Now he was as crazy as a loon. He went back to the convicts' quarters to give Watts a few thumps with his stick.

For two days Clancy and Eliza walked to the west, following a line of linked ridges and plateaux that straddled the range of mountains forming a 2,500-mile barrier down the entire eastern coast of the colony of New South Wales. The way they chose had many turns, for it was scored by deep ravines and bounded by valleys that were buttressed by seemingly unscaleable sandstone cliffs but, apart from frequent backtracking to avoid a chasm or retreat from the precipices of a blind spur, it was a relatively simple path, demanding little hard climbing and clear of the thick brush that had slowed them on the second day. While the valleys far below were densely forested, the high ridge they followed, being barren and rocky with a sparse covering of soil, was only lightly timbered and they made good progress. It rained on the first night and there was plentiful water but the only food they found was some fruit which had fallen from a tree and was partly fermented.

On the third day they came to a hill surmounted by a grassy knoll. They climbed it and gazed in awe at the view. They had reached the end of the main range. The mountains tapered down into a lush valley through which a river ran. There were more mountains in the distance but the valley broadened and there were grassy plains and lines of trees where more streams flowed.

Clancy thought of throwing his cap in the air or shouting but was too tired and hungry to do either. Instead, he said, 'I think we've done it,' and, holding Eliza's hand to steady her on the rough slope, began the descent to the river.

Part Two

TWENTY

W ONNGU DIDN'T KNOW his age but he was considered old by the others in the tribe, a wise man who didn't seek or need the counsel of younger persons and so he'd spent the last few days on his own, thinking about his new wife. She was certainly young, about sixteen years; a lithe girl with a winning smile. He looked forward to her but what worried him was the example of old Ngala, who had taken a young wife and then spent all his days following her to make sure she didn't slip away with some of the younger men who smiled at her and scratched their balls when she went by, swinging her hips. Ngala was so persistent in watching her no matter where she went and made such a comical figure that everyone laughed at him, even the children who were too young to know about such things but could recognise absurdity. Wonngu didn't want to be like that but he was inclined to be jealous and he wasn't sure he wouldn't be just as foolish, spending his nights wondering where she was if she wasn't beside him and she couldn't be there all the time when he had two other wives to worry about. Older ones, it was true, but they still demanded his attention. What would the new one be up to when she wasn't needed?

There was another side to it, of course. They said a young wife made an old man young again and he hoped that was true. Warribee, his second wife, had claimed she was looking forward to him having a young wife—Warribee was at least twenty years older than the girl—and she said she was growing restless because Wonngu didn't like having sex any more. A young wife might be just what he needed and then he would become younger in spirit and all the wives would benefit. But Warribee was always joking and making fun of him and he could never be sure when she was serious and when she was joking because she could say outrageous things and keep a straight face.

Worry, worry, worry. He was respected in the tribe as a wise man and could advise other people about what to do with their lives. His pronouncements were made with great clarity. But when it came to his own life, he had difficulty in deciding what he should do in matters where emotions or instincts were involved. Then he became very confused. Well, he'd certainly decided what to do, which was to take the girl as his third wife. He hadn't consciously gone looking for another woman but her father owed him many favours and the simplest way to balance matters was to give him his eldest daughter. But how would he react to suddenly having such a young and comely girl as his woman? Just as important—and he'd only just thought of this—how would she react? What if she didn't like him or respect him? What if she already had some young man? Would he be able to tolerate it if she did have a lover? Or lovers? If she did, would people laugh at him for being so foolish as not to know, so blind as not to see?

Would he be a good lover? He was once, but that had been a long time ago and now he was tired a great deal of the time and preferred to sleep at night.

He was a vain man and he recognised that too. It was normal for a man to be vain, particularly one who was held in such high esteem for his wisdom and logic, but if people laughed at him he would wander off into the bush and sit under a big tree and let himself die. He couldn't stand the thought of being humiliated.

He was trying to rationalise his thinking—put the questions and problems in order and deal with them one by one, as he did when other people came to him with their troubles—when one of the young men came looking for him to tell him about the strange people who had been seen on the banks of the river, about two hours' walk upstream. They were of a different colour and had their bodies covered. One was a woman and the other a man but the man was a poor specimen, unable to catch fish although he had been trying constantly. But he possessed some magical implement that struck sparks and cut down trees and made a great ringing noise.

Wonngu went to see. A diversion like this was good. It would take his mind off the problems caused by his new wife, even though he would probably discover something that was easily explained. Nanbarree, the man who'd seen this mysterious couple, was a notorious storyteller, always boasting about the monstrous animals that had miraculously eluded his hunting spear or boomerang.

Through being cautious, Wonngu had survived long enough for his hair to turn white and so he approached the site with stealth. He had two men with him, Yerrandee and Bidgee Bidgee. They crawled into a bush on a hill about 100 yards from a bend in the river and peered through the leafy covering. What Wonngu saw astonished him.

A man with skin the colour of the palest bark was standing in the middle of the stream, where the water was shin-deep, and he was holding a long spear in his hand. It was a strange spear: too long for fishing and with only a single point, fashioned from the wood itself. Every now and then he would charge down the river, making the water splash around his shoulders and he would shout and throw the spear and then shout again. Then, very much subdued, he would retrieve the floating spear from the current and repeat the whole performance.

It was true: his body was almost entirely covered. Wonngu found it hard to tell from this distance but the man seemed not to be wearing animal skins. Even his feet were covered. Wonngu had seen them when he charged down-river, lifting his knees high to move more rapidly through the water.

'What do you think?' said Yerrandee who was crouching beside him.

'He's a man who's hungry but he doesn't know how to catch fish.'

Yerrandee, who never disagreed with Wonngu, nodded. 'Who is he? Where has he come from?'

Wonngu shook his head. He had learned long ago never to guess. It was too easy to make a fool of yourself.

The third man said, 'There was a woman, too.'

There was no sign of her.

'So what do we do?'

'We watch. He is very entertaining.'

'He'll never catch a fish.'

'He might tread on one.'

Clancy returned to the crude shelter he had made from fallen timber and bark. While only a simple lean-to, it kept the worst of the wind and the rain from them when they slept. It was set back from the river on a grassy flat that gave a commanding view of the country. The river was shallow but wide, with a stony bottom and gravelly banks that past floods had scalloped into ridges. On the bends of the river were slim beaches of white sand. All around were grassy plains and stands of tall trees and, in the distance, rounded hills. It reminded Clancy of Somerset although he couldn't imagine Somerset without farms and fences and winding white roads. He said so.

'And in such a beautiful place we're starving to death,' said

Eliza, who had grown gaunt in the face. It was a statement of fact, not a complaint.

'I'll try again tomorrow,' he said. He'd give everything for a net, or some fish-hooks and line.

'I found some berries,' she said. 'They're very bitter.'

They ate some, neither speaking as they chewed and grimaced and swallowed.

'Tomorrow we'll move,' Clancy said. They'd been there four days.

'Where to? Somewhere where you can run down a kangaroo and hit him with your axe?'

'Up the river. There must be people around.'

'Shame you don't speak Chinese,' she said and immediately regretted her sarcasm. There was no point in humiliating him. Clancy, she knew, had given up thoughts of reaching Peking and had dismissed Macaulay's ramblings about there being a road to China as pure fantasy. They were in the wilds of New South Wales, where no other white man had been, and they were hungry and weak and, almost certainly, were going to starve to death.

They slept badly, both rolling with stomach cramps, and awoke next morning to find an object wrapped in leaves lying near the entrance to their shelter. Clancy removed the top layer of leaves and found two fish.

TWENTY-ONE

O N EACH OF the next five nights food was left on the grassy flat. They saw no one but always there at first light was a gift of food, wrapped in bark or cool leaves. They ate well: mostly fish but some possum, bandicoot and lizard and, always, a supply of yams or berries and fruit. At first they ate the food raw but on the third night they were aroused by the smell of smoke and found a small fire smouldering near the edge of the bank. Clancy had been unable to start a fire. Having no flint, he had tried desperately but unsuccessfully to ignite dry leaves by striking the back of the axe head against a rock and creating sparks. He made a few sparks but none set fire to the leaves. Now, however, they had a fire and they kept it burning, moving the flaming sticks to within the bough shelter where they stored a supply of dry wood, and now they could cook and render more edible some of the morsels being left by their mysterious visitors.

A feeling of contentment, more lethargic than joyous, descended on them. They were safe from the soldiers, they had a plentiful supply of fresh water, they were in a beautiful location and they were being fed. The hot days, the clatter and chirp of insects and the sonorous dronings of cicadas made them drowsy. They slept often. They were still too tired and weak to think of the future.

On the sixth morning they saw three Aboriginal men on the far bank of the river. For some time the men stood there, unmoving, observing the white couple and content to let themselves be observed. Eventually Clancy called out and one man, the oldest of the three with white hair and a wrinkled belly, raised his hand in response. His two companions had spears but the older man was unarmed. It was he who led the others across the shallow river. The two followers, with spears casually angled over their shoulders, stayed at the water's edge but the white-haired man continued until he was on the grassy flat. There he stopped, rubbing one foot against the calf muscle of his other leg, and spread out his hands.

He didn't speak but looked from one to the other, studying their strange garb.

'Are you the good samaritan?' Eliza said. She had put on her bonnet, feeling the need to be properly dressed, and the man cocked his head in curiosity.

'Have you been leaving the food?' Clancy said.

The man was more interested in Eliza and pointed to her, spinning his hand in an obvious request for her to turn around. She did, holding out the tattered remnant of her skirt.

The man laughed.

'That's not being very polite,' she said. She was nervous but not afraid. The man seemed relaxed and showed none of the menace she had seen in the blacks who'd speared Macaulay.

Without waiting to be asked, Clancy spun around too, holding his arms out, clasping the axe in his right hand. The axe fascinated the man.

Clancy signalled for him to join them but he stayed where he was, whereupon Clancy went to their pile of firewood and, with one stroke, chopped a stick in half.

The Aborigine made a whistling noise.

Clancy took off his cap and held it out. The man didn't move.

215

Clancy shook the cap and took a few steps forward. 'Here, it's yours,' he said. He advanced again and the man took a step back.

It was the axe. He feared the axe. Slowly, Clancy bent to put it on the ground and then, hand outstretched and offering the cap, moved towards the man.

When he was close, the man held up his hand and Clancy stopped. 'It's yours,' he said and smiled. 'Go on, take it.'

For the first time, the man spoke. He had a sharp, high voice.

Clancy shook his head but, knowing this man or his friends had saved their lives, kept smiling. If he and Eliza were to survive they would need the help of these people. And, like Eliza, he sensed there was no menace, only an intense curiosity.

Reaching out, he laid the cap on the grass. He then stepped back several paces.

The black man darted forward, displaying surprising agility for an old man, and picked up the cap. He wasn't sure what to do with it. Moving forward slowly, holding both hands in front of him, Clancy went up to the man and placed the cap on his head. He set it at a jaunty angle so that the row of kangaroo teeth that the man had strung through his hair, just above the scalp line, was still visible.

'Very smart,' he said and the man smiled and the two men down by the river cooed in admiration.

And that was how Clancy Fitzgerald met Wonngu, leader of the small tribe who lived along the stream that, years later, white settlers would know as Cox's River.

Quinton de Lacey had long sessions with Noxious Watts who, being both clever and cunning, soon realised the depth of de Lacey's obsession and embellished the information he had gleaned from the other convicts. He was not untruthful or grossly inventive. He merely expanded on the ideas of others and added his own thoughts so it seemed he had managed to gather an enormous amount of intelligence. The more he talked, the more de Lacey seemed pleased and the greater, he realised, was the chance of a pardon or reward or whatever it was the former officer had in mind. He was even given a cup of tea. The sergeant, present at the far end of the room for all the interviews, hated this and Watts enjoyed the tea all the more.

Macaulay was the ringleader of the escapees, Watts was sure, for Macaulay had talked constantly about escape—it was presumed to be mere idle chatter, Watts stressed in case he should be blamed for not passing on the information—but the big man believed in the fantasies spread among the convicts about unchained numbers of their brethren having reached China. Macaulay swore that the road to Peking lay over the mountains. And a land of milk and honey. Milk and honey! This was a land of rum and withered crops, so hot in summer that the birds fell from the sky and lay gasping on the scorched earth. Why would it be any different on the other side of the mountains?

But over the mountains was where they were heading. Which meant they were already dead or would soon perish. The mountains were impenetrable.

De Lacey was disappointed. He had hoped the three escapees might be circling back from the Hawkesbury, plotting either to steal a yacht from the river or some craft from Port Jackson. If they were hiding near town, he could find them during the weeks that he would be in the Colony, waiting for his ship to India.

No, said Watts, by now feeling comfortable enough to offer firm opinions rather than pass on what some uneducated scoundrel had overheard. They were not planning to steal a boat and sail off somewhere, even though Fitzgerald at one stage had been accused of complicity in a plot to steal a yacht and got seven years and fifty lashes for even thinking about it. Neither man could sail a boat. Neither could read a compass. Neither man, as far as he knew, had ever seen a map or ship's chart.

They often digressed to discuss other matters. After the first session, Watts realised de Lacey was lonely and yearned for conversation and so led him on long verbal detours, which both nourished his own intellect and brought more tea. Watts was a cynic and de Lacey, being idealistic, had a dreamer's admiration of someone who held forceful opinions about subjects that were vague shadows in his own mind.

The sergeant, not understanding the conversations, grew restless but Watts no longer feared reprisals. He was de Lacey's man, and therefore under his protection.

Watts delivered a series of character analyses. Macaulay had the strength of an ox and a similar level of intelligence. He might have been the leader in the break-out and would certainly have been the one to murder the guard but he did not possess the intellect to sustain the escape. He would have lapsed into confusion, Watts suggested, and Clancy would then probably have taken over. That's if they weren't already dead—he thought of saying, but refrained because he had deduced that de Lacey wanted them alive and, after the second day, always spoke as though the escapees were alive and flourishing and de Lacey seemed happier.

He described Macaulay in detail and de Lacey was certain that that was the man he'd seen with the musket in the second ambush. Watts was a little more vague in describing Fitzgerald because he looked like a lot of other men.

'He's Irish, isn't he?' said de Lacey and Watts, sensing his interrogator's certainty, agreed even though he didn't know Clancy's origins; he knew only that he'd come from Somerset and told this to de Lacey, but added rapidly that the family had moved from Ireland.

'Can't stand that accent,' de Lacey said and Watts remained silent, even though Clancy spoke like an Englishman.

De Lacey was most interested in the woman.

'She was a quiet type,' Watts said. 'Very religious.'

'Catholic?' Many of the women convicts were followers of Rome.

He didn't know. He hadn't asked. Why would he? Who cared if an escaped woman convict was Catholic, Church of England or Hindu? But he said, 'I believe so,' because de Lacey seemed to take some sort of satisfaction from learning the woman he hated was a Roman Catholic. He'd have been disappointed, even disbelieving, if she were of his faith.

'A good worker, I'm told,' Watts added. 'Never been in any trouble.' People who knew her were surprised, no astounded, to learn she had run away and got herself involved with a bad crew like Macaulay and Fitzgerald.

'Where did she meet them?'

'No one I spoke to ever saw them together.' That was the weak point in his presentation of information. No one could explain why or how the three of them were together.

'She's not very strong,' Watts said, sifting through the dregs of what he'd learned about Eliza Phillips.

'I hope she is. If I don't find her now, I want her to stay alive until I get back.'

'Oh, you'd be a bad enemy to have. So tenacious,' Watts said and de Lacey seemed pleased.

De Lacey might have been out of the New South Wales Corps but he still had influence with Hunter who, admiring his gentlemanly and stoic reaction to the Hawkesbury affair, was pleased to perform a favour. Thus it was that five weeks later, just before the *Acheron*, out of Cape Town and bound for Bombay, sailed into Port Jackson, Thomas Faithful Watts received a pardon from the Governor and a purse of silver from de Lacey.

For the next two weeks Wonngu and his friends came to visit Clancy and Eliza every day. Now they brought the food openly.

Wonngu also brought a fishing spear with several splayed prongs bound to the main shaft, each prong being tipped and barbed with sharp fragments of animal bone. He had one of his companions show Clancy how to fish: where to stand and how to position himself in relation to the sun; how to be still; how to aim, allowing for the refraction of the water when the outline of a fish wavered into sight; how to throw the spear.

After four days Clancy made his first catch, a deep-bellied fish with golden tones on its scales. It was almost a foot long and must have weighed at least a pound. The spear caught it in the tail but he was able to drag it out of the water. Eliza cooked it over their fire. No fish had ever tasted so good.

Several men came to their camp. They wore more clothing than the other wild blacks Eliza and Clancy had seen and they wondered whether this was normal or whether the men were wearing their finery to match the visitors' standards of dress. All the men wore finely woven belts, some made from human hair and others from the softer fur of possums. Some men carried a small woven bag under an arm. What they had in the bags was a mystery: something personal or sacred, Eliza suggested, because they never opened them in their presence. They wore rugs of animal hide which they draped across their bodies like cloaks. The rugs were made from either kangaroo or possum skins. The leather was well cured and soft and sewn together, as Wonngu explained in one laborious session of hand signals, with a bone needle and the sinews from a kangaroo's tail.

Wonngu's own rug, worn like a cloak, had elaborate decorations burned into the underside of the skin.

Every day new men came to see them. All were nervous but their curiosity impelled them into touching Eliza's dress or bonnet. She would stand still while they encircled her, fingers delicately stroking the fabric or—if a man were especially daring—touching her stockings. They laughed a great deal.

From each man's belt hung a crude stone axe. The axes had wooden handles which were bound to the stone by kangaroo sinew and glued by the resin from grass trees. The axes were primarily for food gathering, Wonngu explained, and were used to cut possums out of trees or dig out honey and other delectables.

They all wanted to see Clancy's axe. He demonstrated it, chopping down a few small trees and trimming their branches but, of the Aborigines, only Wonngu was allowed to touch it.

He tried to cut the branch from a tree but struck it at the wrong angle and the axe flew from his hand and everyone laughed.

They saw women, but only on the far side of the river, and always standing behind bushes where they were partly hidden.

It rained heavily one day and when the rain had eased Wonngu came to the camp to indicate that the tribe was leaving. They were striking out to the west. Eliza and Clancy, whose names Wonngu now knew and could pronounce with reasonable clarity, should go with them.

TWENTY-TWO

FOR THE NEXT few months the tribe roamed the valleys and plains to the west of the river. They remained in mountainous country, with every horizon being rimmed by ranges or barred by gaunt cliffs, but they threaded their way through the maze of hills and bluffs, moving slowly, stopping frequently, one week following a narrow creek that rushed from a rocky gorge and the next meandering beside a turgid stream that spread wide on the plains. There was plentiful game and they ate well. At some sites they camped for many days and trapped fish in nets which they made from the cord of bark fibre and strung across shallow channels. At others, where the plains attracted mobs of kangaroos, a party of men would spend all day hunting. They were, Clancy noted, men of extreme patience and great muscular control. They would select their quarry and follow it for hours, waiting for the wind to change or the animal to move before advancing. Even when close but not quite within spear-throwing range, they would stand, usually on one leg and with their arms spread to resemble the outline of a dead bush, and there they would stay, downwind from their target, unmoving for an hour or more while the animal grazed and twitched its ears and occasionally gazed at the strange unmoving shapes. A kangaroo was a prized catch for the meat was good and usually sufficient to feed the whole tribe, who wasted not a piece of the animal—hide, sinew, bone or teeth.

At the end of some days, after hours of patient tracking and stalking, the animal would become agitated and hop clear of the hunters, eluding the spears flung in desperation. When the men were unsuccessful which, in this good season, was about one kangaroo hunt in three, the tribe relied on the women for their food, for the women were the diggers and gatherers, who spent their days getting lizards, grubs, moths, roots, yams, fruit, honey—even the pith from ferns.

While the women worked, they talked. Eliza, who had settled into the routine of travelling and working with the women, as she was expected to do, was amazed at how they enjoyed their work and how they chatted and laughed. She had never known people to like their work but these women did, for it brought them together in harmony for a common purpose. They were the industrious members of the tribe—they worked harder than the men and were proud of that—and their nature was such that they, like children playing games, always had fun performing the daily tasks.

Once, Eliza had feared the blacks but these women were kindly, simple souls. They seemed to like her—they certainly laughed when she tried to speak a few words of their language and apparently said something silly or when she dug for a grub burrowing in the roots of a tree and chose the wrong place. Simple things for them but difficult for her. She laughed, too.

With surprise, she realised these were happy days.

One of the older women had taken for herself the role of Eliza's guardian. Her name was Delbung. She was about forty or forty-five, or so Eliza guessed, for she found it hard to determine the ages of these people. Delbung had several daughters, or so Eliza presumed, for she found it impossible to tell who was related by blood and who was linked by other bonds. All she knew for certain was that a group of about ten girls had attached themselves to this woman and she loved them and they loved her.

Not pleasing for a European to look at with her watery eyes, broad nose and thick lips, Delbung was, nevertheless, a person of considerable compassion and good humour. She had a raspy voice and a cackling laugh but she had a quaint charm, an attribute that Eliza came to appreciate as the weeks passed for, despite having sagging breasts and a big belly, Delbung was a most dignified person, treating others with respect and being liked, it seemed, by all members of the tribe. That certainly wasn't the case with everyone for Eliza soon noticed how people gossiped about each other. Little groups would mutter and stare at some other person with obvious distaste and there always seemed to be some who enjoyed another person's humiliation or misfortune.

Delbung treated Eliza as if she were one of her daughters—a very young daughter who had to be taught everything—and spent hours teaching her words and showing her how to do things their way, from digging over pits and lighting fires to making a coolamon for carrying things. She explained how to use the digging-stick with its bevelled edge for digging up yams and other roots, and told her where to find these things so that the others no longer giggled at her clumsy efforts, and she showed her how to cure and knead the hide of a kangaroo so it became fine, supple leather. She taught her what to eat and what to avoid and what leaves and ground-up roots to eat if you were sick or having your period and what to put on a burn or a cut.

Eliza was a quick learner and Delbung was delighted with her progress and liked to boast about the brightness of her pupil. This embarrassed Eliza for the other women would smile as Delbung ran through the day's achievements and, if they were seated around a fire, would lean forward and tickle her with sticks to make her laugh, to show she was just like them.

Delbung still regarded Eliza as an oddity as, of course, did every other member of the tribe. They had no idea where she was from, why she had joined them, why she looked so different or why she wore such strange garb. By now, Eliza had abandoned the stockings and given her chemise to a young girl who admired it and subsequently gave it to someone else who liked it even more, but she still wore the bonnet when they were out in the sun gathering food and only removed her shoes to wash her feet. No one could recall seeing her naked and there were some who thought the dress was part of her body. Having your body wrinkle into deep folds and billow in the wind, they said, was no more extraordinary than having a face that was as bleached as a dead leaf; although it was true, as some of the women pointed out, that her face was now redder than when she had joined them.

The women thought Eliza to be a person of consummate ugliness with her pale skin, thin nose, tight little lips and eyes that were the colour of the sky. Poor thing, they said when she was not with them, to be like that when everyone else on earth had richly coloured skin, generous features and dark brown eyes.

Delbung accepted that Eliza was not good-looking but she overlooked the disadvantages and recognised the worth inside. She soon grew to love the girl and there were some in the tribe who were jealous.

Because he was a man, although uninitiated in their ways and therefore, theoretically, still a boy, Clancy joined some of the hunts. He was admired for his skill with the curious but lethal weapons he carried: the small axe and the carving knife he'd stolen from the kitchen at The Green Hills. He was of little use on a kangaroo hunt but soon became adept at cutting possums

225

out of trees. His axe was many times more efficient than any of theirs and, even though some of the younger and prouder men spent hours sharpening their blades by grinding them on wet sandstone, no one could strike harder or cut deeper than Clancy.

Clancy had never felt so free. He did not have to steal or live in filth, he was not in chains and he was not required to do what others told him. He was, however, conscious of the need to conform; to do things the way the men in the tribe did them, whether it be during hunting or eating or observing some mystifying ritual (and he soon became aware that these were people bound by strange traditions). He was not permitted to see many ceremonies and would be left with the boys while the men went off to some secret site but, at other times, he was allowed to witness dancing and singing and the banging of sticks and attend what he presumed was the Aboriginal equivalent of a musical evening. On these nights, one person or a group would sing or chant—they sang in flat, nasally voices with a limited range of notes—and the audience would respond. It may have been some kind of church service. He didn't know. He nodded his head when others nodded, clapped his hands when they clapped and kept quiet when he didn't know what to do.

He had no desire to offend anyone through ignorance of their ways and so he always looked to Wonngu for guidance. Wonngu liked this. He was, Clancy realised, the man all others approached for advice. He was their wise man, a role for which Wonngu was well suited and which he relished. He had great patience and devoted hours trying to explain things to Clancy. While they spent little time in formal language lessons, Clancy picked up a few words and phrases and the old man, having a good ear, soon built himself a useful lexicon of basic English. Thus, he and Clancy were able to have a conversation of sorts, with a mixture of words chosen from each other's language and punctuated by signs and expressions.

Wonngu was not concerned with the things Eliza was learning for they were women's work but he told Clancy many stories, often about monstrous animals, birds and serpents that lived long ago. These were difficult for Clancy to understand and so the lectures were slow and sometimes incomprehensible. They seemed important to Wonngu, who often looked at Clancy as if he should know what he was talking about. It was hard to tell what he meant because Wonngu relied primarily on sign language but he looked at Clancy in the most intense way as he told his grotesque tales.

In the evenings, Clancy used to think about the stories, or what he could understand of them. Did Wonngu believe his white visitor was not human but some sort of spirit who was from the time of the gigantic snakes and weird animals that filled his tales? Or was there something else? The old man used to touch Clancy's face and run his finger along a small scar on his cheek and whisper words.

The most important time in the developing relationship between Clancy and Eliza was the period between their crossing of the range and the appearance of Wonngu. In those few days, they'd been entirely on their own. Their quest to find a way over the mountains—the imperative that had sustained them—had been successful but once that journey was done, they were left hungry, lonely and without purpose in a land that offered them little hope of survival. Yet each was dependent on the other and that drew them close, for they shared a bond of suffering and fear. In that brief period they had become entwined in spirit, as only people who believe they are about to die can be.

Now, moving with the tribe, they were thrust into a curious relationship. Dependent on others rather than themselves and with their survival no longer threatened, they found their main interest was not in each other but in the fascinating and sometimes bizarre happenings that occurred around them. They were divided by day, united at night. Being required to conform to the tribe's way meant Eliza worked or travelled with the women and Clancy with the men. But at night they were together, sleeping not with each other but beside each other. And there they talked, each grateful to have someone who understood what the other was saying, after a day of frustrating hand signals and misunderstood words. They felt close. They were the best of friends, linked by shared experience and ethnic similarity in this amiable but alien society.

There was no suggestion of sex. They might sleep beneath a crude shelter that Clancy had fashioned out of branches or simply lie beneath the stars. Eliza, who had endured so much abuse in the colony, liked it this way. She abhorred sex because it was violent and ugly. Clancy didn't force himself on her—in fact, he showed no interest in her physically at all—and for that she was grateful. She was not attracted to any of the Aboriginal men. She liked some but the thought of sleeping with them or having them touch her was repulsive. The sexual promiscuity of the tribe also shocked her. Everyone, it seemed, slept with everyone else. And so many of their rituals were sexually based and disgusting. A young girl had recently had her first period and been subjected to the most appalling indignities, like having her private parts forced open and a stick inserted and blood smeared everywhere and then having to endure a night lying with a host of men. That was the way it was done, Delbung had said. So many of their ceremonies, it seemed to Eliza, involved gore and sex. Even Wonngu, who had recently taken a young girl as his third wife, had been required to let his bride sleep with his brothers and closest friends before she was passed on to him.

No grown man was without a woman and Clancy had the choice of being with Eliza or accepting one or more of the young women Wonngu offered him. Eliza had no choice and she readily joined Clancy as his woman.

*   *   *

There was now time to think about the future. Clancy was happy roaming the valleys and plains but Eliza was becoming progressively more worried and morose. Almost certainly, she would never see another white man. Therefore, she would be forced to continue living with Clancy, which was not a bad thing but no substitute for being married and having a husband. She would remain a spinster all her life. And yet she was living with a man. Living in sin, as her aunt would say. But she was not sinning! What choice did she have? She liked Clancy and he would probably make a good husband, even in white society, but there was no chance of their marrying because there was no minister of religion to marry them. Therefore, she could have no children.

She worried about these things so much she mentioned them to Clancy. He laughed. 'No one's married any of these people. Does that make them sinners?'

She didn't know. Her aunt would have had an answer. 'But they have so many children.'

'You don't have to be married to have children. I thought you might have noticed. It even happens among white people.'

'You're mocking me, just like you used to.'

'No, but this is such a strange conversation. We're a hundred miles from civilisation and if we wanted to have children, we could have a dozen and no one would ever know.'

'God would know.'

He sighed. 'And what would he do, bearing in mind that he leaves these people in peace, to fornicate to their heart's content?'

'Please don't talk about God and fornication in the same breath,' she said and was silent. These were real problems that tormented her and Clancy was turning the conversation into a contest of wit.

'Look,' he said, realising he had hurt her, 'it's people who say you can't have children unless you're married, not God.'

'Oh that's not true.'

'It is, you silly woman. Wonngu and his people haven't heard of God, they haven't been near a church and yet they have children by the score. Why does God allow this? Go on, tell me?'

'He moves in mysterious ways,' she said, and that night could hardly sleep for worrying.

It was well after midnight when he wriggled close to her and said, 'What's the matter?'

'I can't sleep.'

He put his arm around her. He did that sometimes at night when she was breathing heavily and seemingly unaware of his presence. It reminded him of the way he and his sister had slept together when they were little. 'Was it something I said?'

She shook her head. 'I'm just worried. What's going to happen to me? I always wanted to be married and have children. I didn't want much. Just an ordinary life.' She put a hand across his. Her fingers were rough but the sensation was tender. He felt his heart beating faster.

She said, 'If things were different, we might have got married.'

'Not me,' he said but didn't let her go. 'I swore a long time ago I'd never get married.'

'Why not?' She used her spare hand to wipe her eyes.

'Obligation. I don't want that. I want to be a free man.'

'You can still be married and be free.'

'I couldn't.'

They were silent for some time. 'It's cold,' she said and he put both his arms around her. They slept like that.

In the morning they were still together but said nothing. They smiled at each other during the day, as if each had made a small discovery which was too secret to yield. That night they camped in a valley beside a lagoon which was home to ducks and great black and white geese and long-legged waterbirds. The sky was ablaze with stars and a warm breeze sighed as it passed through the valley and the trees rustled and the ducks and geese quacked and honked and a whole chorus of insects chirped and creaked. When they lay down to sleep he immediately put his arms around her and she held his arms tight against her. He felt strange stirrings within him, sensations that were so long dormant they ached in a delicious, teasing, mystifying, urgent way.

He kissed her behind the ear and said, 'I don't love you, Eliza Phillips, I want you to know that. You talk too much and you say the silliest things but you can't help that because you're a woman. And a very good-looking woman. I must admit that. And to be honest, I have to say I admire you. I think you're a very brave and resourceful woman.' He kissed her cheek.

'And I don't love you either, Clancy Fitzgerald. I never could. How could anyone love a man who's so boastful and so sarcastic? Although you've got good points and I'm sure you'd make some woman, maybe not as discerning as I am, a good husband.'

She let him kiss her on the lips. She lifted his hands to put them on her breasts and held them there, pressing tightly.

'Oh, I don't know why I'm letting you do this,' she said.

'And I don't know why I'm doing it.' He kissed her on the lips and she reacted so savagely he was shocked. But only for a moment. Something within him welled up and burst and, locked together, they rolled on the ground, kissing frenziedly and tearing off clothes and making love and crying out until someone nearby giggled. They were quiet for a while, each smiling into the shadow of the other's face, but then they made love several more times, trembling fingers touching warm skin as they explored each other's body, and kissing softly until the sky lightened and the tribe was stirring.

231

She was out with the women all day.

'I have sinned,' she said that night when they were alone again.

'No, you've done something perfectly normal. We both have.'

'We mustn't do it again.'

But once the fires were out and the sky was a miracle of glittering lights, they kissed and she was helpless in his arms.

Each had liked the nomadic life during the balmy days of summer and autumn but with winter setting in and snow capping the highest peaks and with cold winds whistling through the valleys and food becoming harder to find, Eliza became depressed.

'I want somewhere to live,' she said one night while they were sitting together, after a small meal of yams.

'You've got somewhere,' Clancy said. He was using his knife to whittle a hard piece of wood into the shape of a spearhead. 'You're living here.'

'No. I mean I'd like a house.'

He laughed but, on succeeding nights, she mentioned the house again and again. She was tired of moving. She wanted to settle down. 'We could have a farm. Grow our own crops, like wheat and maize. I'm sick of eating lizards and grubs. I long for the taste of bread.'

So did he. The nearest they had to bread was a kind of meal made from the heart of a fern. He missed the crust on a good loaf of fresh bread. How would we grow wheat, he thought, and knew the answer instantly. He'd have to go back to the colony, over the path they'd blazed through the mountains, and steal seeds. Wheat would grow here. The soil was fertile, better than on the other side of the range.

She used a stick to trace patterns in the dirt. 'Do you want to spend the rest of your life living like a blackfellow, getting wet when it rains, sleeping in some different valley every other week?'

He liked this way of life with all the movement and new places to see and the constant hunting for food. There was a wonderful freedom and sense of adventure about the way these people lived.

'I don't mind . . .' he began but let the words trail away. He felt guilty, as if he should automatically prefer the English, civilised way. But he didn't. The English way was to have him in chains or on the end of a rope. He felt at home in this wild and wonderful country with these wild and wonderful people.

In measured tones, she said, 'They're nice and they've been very good to us . . .'

'They saved our damned lives,' he said, slicing off more of the wood than he meant.

'I know.' She lowered her eyes, as if embarrassed by what she had to say. 'But they're so barbaric. If you had a daughter, would you like to see her treated the way they treated that young girl the other day, just because she had her first . . . flow?' She blushed for, as far as she knew, this was a subject no respectable woman ever discussed with a man.

'I didn't see it.'

'Neither did I but it was disgusting.'

'How do you know if you didn't see it?'

'Delbung told me. She tells me everything. I was forbidden to watch and that's another thing. We're never going to be truly accepted by these people. We'll always be outsiders. Do you want to live like that all your life?'

He hadn't thought about it. 'I feel as though I belong,' he said. 'I've never been so well treated by anyone as I have been by these people.'

'But there's a difference. We'd never be one of them. We'd always be outsiders.'

He whittled a little more, concentrating on getting the tip of the spearpoint right. 'Wonngu and his people don't have houses,' he said without looking up. 'They're moving around all the time. If we had a house, we wouldn't see them very often. We'd be on our own.'

'Not on our own.' She clasped her hands and lowered her head. She looked, he thought, angelic. Even beautiful. 'Clancy, I'm going to have a baby.'

Next day, Clancy spoke to Wonngu. He and Eliza, he said, wanted to build a house.

TWENTY-THREE

THEY BUILT THEIR house in a valley surrounded by low hills. It was a secluded place, two days' walk from the river Eliza and Clancy had reached when they descended from the mountains. A stream ran through the valley. Long, thin islands of gravelly stones divided the stream into several braids and there was one place, Wonngu pointed out, that would be excellent for trapping fish. At the far end of the valley the water spread into a swamp which was alive with ducks and geese and a dozen other species of birdlife. Between the house and the stream were several acres of fertile soil that was only lightly timbered and should sustain fine crops of wheat or maize and maybe some potato, onion and cabbage. Even some fruit trees. Eliza liked the thought of a few fruit trees near the house.

The site chosen faced the north, where the low winter sun would give most warmth. Being shielded on three sides by rows of trees, the building was difficult to see from a distance. Wonngu seemed to think this was important. They would be safe if they were hidden, he said. Safe from what? There were no dangerous animals in the country, Clancy was sure, and in all the months they had roamed with the tribe they hadn't seen another soul. Wonngu didn't elaborate but insisted they build on the spot he selected.

In truth, it was a hut rather than a house and it was small, a mere 15 feet long by 10 feet wide, with an earthen floor and a sloping roof of bark strips that were held in place by some of the nails Clancy had brought with him. The walls were made from the thin branches of acacia trees, which grew on the side of a hill nearby. These, being supple, were woven around upright poles cut from young eucalyptus trees. This gave the building the appearance of a basket until the gaps were plastered over with mud. Clancy had helped build such a hut at Rouse Hill, so he had a design in mind and was practised at wattling and daubing. At the front, the roof was carried forward a few feet and supported on stout corner posts to provide a verandah. There were no windows. The hut had a front doorway but no door. The gap was sealed by a mat of woven reeds which hung like a curtain and was weighted with stones to keep it in place.

The hut took ten days to erect. Many of the men and women helped and, while imbued with limited enthusiasm for such repetitive work as digging post holes and plaiting the acacia, they were in awe of the project and constantly stood back and shook their heads and sat in groups and laughed and chattered. They had never constructed a house that was meant to last more than a few months and never seen a building that was as high as a man, let alone one of such size and substance.

With the building finished, Clancy made four items of furniture. Two were stools that he cut from solid stumps. The third was a table made from the boughs of eucalypt trees and trimmed with the axe. The legs and tabletop were bound together by thin strips of animal hide. The other item was a bed, made in the same style as the table but wider and lower. For the bed, some of the Aboriginal women made a mattress out of kangaroo skins, which they stuffed with dried grass. They were greatly intrigued and took turns at lying on it, and giggled because it was all so nonsensical. They'd never heard of anyone needing such things because no one had ever wanted to stay in one place.

Clancy planned to build a kitchen. It had to be a separate building because of the fire hazard, but needed to be no more than a covering for a fireplace, to keep out both wind and rain. He'd also thought about replacing the reed mat with a proper front door but hadn't worked out how to do it. It had to be substantial. He realised his thinking wasn't logical as the wattle and daub walls were thin but he had a fixation about front doors being strong and that meant solid planks, which he had no way of cutting.

The more he thought about the hut and the need to grow crops and the fact that Eliza was going to have a baby, the more he became resolved to return to the colony and get what they needed in the way of seeds, implements and tools. Even baby clothes. He would require someone to travel with him to help carry the load. Eliza couldn't go as she was frequently sick and had to lie down on the kangaroo-skin mattress several times a day.

Seeking someone to travel with him, Clancy spoke to Wonngu and tried to explain that more white people were living on the far side of the mountains and he had to go among them to gather certain items. He would return with gifts. He had in mind stealing some hand mirrors and beads, plus a hatchet or two, and presenting them to Wonngu.

Wonngu was reluctant to let anyone leave on such a hazardous journey. The Aborigines would not return. He was insistent.

Clancy tried to explain that he knew the way and there would be little danger but the old man was unimpressed. It took some time for Clancy to realise that Wonngu thought white men were ghosts—the reincarnation of blackfellows. A journey to the land of the dead was an awful thing for any of his people to contemplate.

'You think I'm a ghost?' Clancy got the word right and tried not to laugh.

237

Maybe not a ghost but a man who'd returned to this world in the guise of a ghost, which was why he was so pale. With conviction and a touching show of affection, Wonngu declared that Clancy was the reincarnation of his uncle, which was why there was such a strong bond between them. He touched Clancy's cheek. His uncle had the same scar.

Uncle? It took Clancy only seconds to realise the advantage he had gained. In this society an uncle would be obeyed, particularly one with the mystical impetus of having been reincarnated, no matter what his colour. And so, from that moment, he spoke to Wonngu with more authority and made the occasional demand. Within two days Wonngu had assigned two of the younger warriors called Berak and Arabanoo to go with Clancy.

Even so, when they were leaving, most of the tribe wailed and wrung their hands in distress, being certain they would never see the young men again.

The mattress was comfortable and Eliza liked to stroke the fine hair on the hide, feeling she was, somehow, caressing a living thing. She would lie on her back staring up at the bark ceiling with one hand on her belly and the other smoothing the kangaroo fur and hoping her baby would get some of the good feelings she had. She had a house, she was pregnant and she had a man she loved. Her love had happened suddenly which, she reflected, made it seem all the more vivid. She wasn't sure how much Clancy loved her—certainly it was not with the intensity she had found herself—but what did the degree of love matter? He was a good, resourceful man and they were free and they had chosen to live in an idyllic place. This was not the life she had dreamed of as a girl, but it was far removed from, and infinitely better than, the hopeless existence she had known as a convict.

Even with Clancy gone, she was happy. He would return with

seeds and farming implements and next year, when she was suckling her new baby, they would have their first crops sprouting in the fields below the house.

Delbung, whom Wonngu had instructed to look after Eliza, used to sit on a stool and smile as Eliza gazed at the ceiling and crooned to her unborn baby. She wondered if the baby would be black or whether it, too, would be pale and therefore be the reincarnation of someone from her tribe or one of the neighbouring groups who roamed these valleys and plains. She had no concept of distance beyond the land she knew, no thought of there being people on earth—real flesh-and-blood people rather than spirits—other than those in the tribes she knew.

She thought of those people who had died in the last year or so. Yemmerrawanie was most likely to be reborn. He had been killed only a few weeks before Eliza and the man with the shining axe had come into their lives. Yemmerrawanie was a good hunter and renowned for his daring but inclined to be foolhardy. He was trying to raid an eagle's nest when he had fallen from a tree. Would he have learned from this experience?

It mightn't be him, of course. It could be Barangaroo but she had been an old woman with a withered leg who had died because she was tired of living. She had simply gone to sleep one night and willed herself not to wake up. Would she be in a hurry to come back so quickly? In any case, Delbung couldn't imagine someone so wizened and crippled as Barangaroo returning as Eliza's baby although it was possible that such a physically ugly person as a white woman would have a baby with a withered leg and not think anything was wrong. Besides, few people would notice the deformity because Eliza could dress the child in a white woman's clothes so that her leg would rarely be seen.

Maybe it would be the youth from the tribe that lived on the other side of the flat-topped mountain. He had been speared in a fight over near the forked river. She didn't know his name;

239

only that Wonngu was worried that his people might be blamed for the death. It was unlikely that such a person would be reborn into this tribe, although she wasn't sure about these things.

Wonngu had said he would return in four weeks. It being almost the end of winter, game was short and so they were hunting up to the north, near the flat-topped mountain where there were kangaroos and wallabies and even emus. Although unable to fly, the big birds were so fast on their legs that they were difficult to catch by any means other than deception. The best hunter of emus in the tribe, because he was both cunning and athletic, was Bidgee Bidgee. He was also a comedian and would entertain the women and children—the men too, if they cared to admit it—for hours by miming the story of a successful emu hunt.

Bidgee Bidgee's technique was to approach slowly, stealthily until he was within a hundred yards of the bird and then stop and stand in the pose of another emu. One hand would be outstretched to resemble the neck and head, one leg would be on the ground, his own head would be bent forward out of sight and the other hand would be at his tail to resemble the emu's crop of feathers. The spear would lean casually against his shoulder.

Now, emus have two fatal flaws. They have poor eyesight and they are impelled by an overwhelming curiosity. Bidgee Bidgee would stand in his emu pose for as long as it took him to attract the attention of his quarry. Almost certainly, the bird would then move closer to investigate the stranger. Some hunters who tried the same technique became impatient or their muscles ached from the difficult stance and they threw their spear too early. Bidgee Bidgee was a patient man and would let the bird get so close he could have stroked its beak. Only then would he uncoil himself with great speed and thrust his spear through the emu's breast. He had been known to trip a bird with the shaft of his spear and then transfix it while it struggled to get up. That was more difficult, of course, but it was a spectacular way of ending the hunt and Bidgee Bidgee was a showman.

Bidgee Bidgee had caught an emu in this way and had entertained the tribe for the next three nights by recounting the deed but neither he nor any other hunter had speared anything since and the people were hungry.

Now they were close to the flat-topped mountain, much closer than Wonngu liked, for the dead youth had not been avenged and, while Wonngu's people had the right to hunt on this land because Caroo, son of Yerranibee, had taken a woman from this tribe as his first wife, the people among these hills were notorious for their bad temper and were more likely to throw spears than sit down and talk.

On their second day in the area a skirmish occurred between three of Wonngu's hunters and some men from the other tribe. Both groups were hunting the same wallabies, which had hopped to the rocky side of a hill. On the hillside, spears were thrown. Wonngu's men weren't certain but they thought one of their spears had wounded one of the other hunters. This was a calamity. The ideal result would have been to score a near miss and make the others jump in fright but an injury demanded revenge.

Wonngu's tribe had to withdraw immediately and, moving through the dark on a night when heavy rain lashed them and lightning was their only guide, they headed towards the enclosed valley where Clancy and Eliza had built their hut.

There, they could hide. Wonngu had no desire to engage the others in a battle. Although his men were brave and skilled with spears and boomerangs, they would be greatly outnumbered by any avenging party for the other tribe was many times larger than theirs. Thus, while they marched along the valleys and through the gorges they knew so well, his men carried their fighting gear: war spears, woomeras, shields, fighting boomerangs, war clubs and stone axes. Although heavily burdened, they travelled non-stop and reached their destination on the morning of the third day.

Clancy found the musket among the rocks. It was dry and, apart from being covered in spider webs, appeared to be exactly as he had left it. He didn't touch the gun, nor show it to the two young men who might have thought it to be some sort of spiritual totem and been reluctant to travel any further. The men were wary of Clancy, even fearful of him, but that was natural, Clancy told himself, because they regarded him as more ghost than human. As boys, they had known Wonngu's uncle and respected him so they did what they were told, but Clancy wasn't sure he could rely on them if they were attacked by the natives who had killed Macaulay or became frightened when they saw other white men.

The young men were extremely nervous while traversing the domed mountain and held their boomerangs as if fearing attack among the shadowy ferns which covered the slopes. He asked if they had been here before. They said no, but they knew of the people who lived in these mountains, and they were fierce warriors.

Macaulay's body was gone. Clancy had expected to find some bones or pieces of clothing but there was nothing. Had the natives returned and dragged the body away? Had wild dogs eaten the remains? If so, who'd taken the bones and who had the belt? He was worried about the belt. It would be useful back at the hut. With the leather, he could fashion hinges for the door he intended making one day.

He didn't tell his companions about Macaulay.

The three of them travelled far more rapidly than Clancy, Eliza and the youths from Nimboola's tribe had managed with the injured Macaulay. Clancy took a few wrong turns but excused himself by saying the country had changed since he was last on earth. The men understood this.

The path he had hacked through the thick brush was still visible although the bushes were partly regrown. He needed his axe in few places and they were through in two and a half hours. Even then he kept moving as quickly as he could, not wanting to risk an encounter with the natives and knowing that to stop was to give his companions time to imagine the ghastly possibilities awaiting them in the land of the dead.

When he reached the site of Nimboola's last camp Clancy realised he didn't know the way down the mountain. He had come up mainly at night, with the painted man. Going down was relatively easy, however, as he could always glimpse the river or the country around it and he marked the track by blazing trees all the way to the bottom of that initial ridge.

Eight days after leaving the hut they were at the Hawkesbury.

TWENTY-FOUR

THE HAWKESBURY SETTLEMENT had been established in 1794 with twenty-two ex-convicts being given grants of land so they might work the rich alluvial flats and, it was hoped, grow the grain and vegetables that the poor, stony soil around Sydney Town produced in only meagre quantities and poor quality. The major crops grown along the river were wheat and maize, the latter being more commonly known as Indian corn, not because it came from India but because it had been originally grown by the so-called 'Indians' of North America.

By late 1798 the number of settlers had risen to more than 600. One of them was Adam Jenkins, who had been farming on the river for two years. A native of Lancashire, he'd been transported for the theft of a bag of carrots and had served his seven years, two of them on a prison hulk at Woolwich before setting sail for Botany Bay, as the colony was still called by those in England most likely to make the seven-month journey to the shores of New South Wales. Jenkins had been assigned 30 acres of land near the river and only a mile from the jetty at The Green Hills. He was unmarried and a model emancipist, not one of the drunken, riotous types Governor Hunter so despised. Jenkins lived in a small wattle and daub farmhouse but planned building something grander; a much larger house made of sandstone. He'd already started cutting some of the blocks. After building, he'd marry. He had a woman in mind, a widow with two children who had a small holding at The Ponds. She had only average looks but was exceptionally industrious and, according to those who had known her former husband, had never been known to nag.

Jenkins planned to improve the quality of his crop and the size of his holding and, with the former target in mind, had procured the highest quality wheat and corn available in the colony for the next planting. It was stored in bags in a small shed at the rear of the farmhouse.

Jenkins knew Clancy Fitzgerald. They had worked together on a road gang soon after Jenkins arrived with the Second Fleet. Jenkins was one of the lucky ones, for two-thirds of the convicts had died on that ghastly voyage from England. Even when the ships anchored in Port Jackson, sailors were still throwing bodies over the side. Jenkins had decided on that day that he was blessed by fate and determined, even then, that he would one day make his fortune in this country.

Jenkins had heard of Clancy's escape. Like most people, he assumed he was dead. He didn't imagine that on this night, when the first warm breeze of the season was blowing along the river and filling the air with the aroma of decaying reeds, his former companion-in-chains was no more than fifty yards away, helping himself to Jenkins's prized stock of wheat and corn.

Clancy and his companions had built a raft, Clancy cutting the timber and the others binding the logs together with reeds. They had waited until sunset to cross the river. They were two miles upstream from the settlement and hid the raft among trees. So far they had seen no white people. Clancy planned making several raids over the next three or four nights and thought it best to leave the young warriors with the raft, to keep them away from any of the settlers. He would bring each night's haul back to the trees. All three could then carry the goods across the mountains.

Finding seed on the first night was an unexpected bonus, for that was the most important prize on his list. There was also an adze in Jenkins's hut and Clancy carried that and the bags of wheat and corn back to the hiding place. It was a heavy load and, while desirous of taking all he needed, he was aware of the dangers of overloading the three of them. They would have to move quickly on the return journey so he intended being selective. He could always come back for more. He'd enjoyed the return trip across the mountains because it was so much easier without Eliza or the crippled Macaulay to slow him. And he now knew the way. He reckoned that, in the future, he could do the journey in six days.

On their second day at the river, his two companions went to a shallow reach and fished with spears. They were seen by whites. They aroused no interest as the settlers were used to seeing natives on the river but the two of them returned wide-eyed and fearful; they had seen their first spirits and felt lucky to have escaped with their lives.

Clancy had to be careful in what he said. As he himself was regarded as a spirit, he couldn't debunk the myth. Nor could he afford to have his companions run off and leave him to haul his loot across the mountains.

'They are my brothers,' he said and they looked puzzled because Wonngu's uncle had only one brother who was still alive, but they said nothing, not doubting him but clearly not understanding his meaning. Spirits, they reasoned, could speak in riddles.

On the second night Clancy visited three farmhouses. From the first he stole a woman's dress and a pair of button-up boots which he hoped would fit Eliza. To his shame, he realised he had no idea of her size but knew for certain that her boots were torn and worn through. At the second house he took a pair of pants for himself, a pair of old boots and a length of rope. At the third farm he found more thread, a box of nails and two hatchets, one of which was old and had a mangled edge to its blade.

He couldn't find any baby's clothes.

Clancy spent much of the third day trying to calm his companions who had seen some settlers—one with red hair—go down the river in a small yacht and were still trembling from the onslaught of unexpected visions. That night he visited several houses, seeking specific items: needles, even more thread, buttons, scissors, another large knife and a baking dish to make bread. He also entered the town to reconnoitre the barracks area and discover where weapons and ammunition were kept. There were several soldiers lolling about, the majority only partly in uniform but thoroughly drunk. He spoke to one of them, a man who stank of rum but could still string words together. They discussed the weather. An old blackfellow was telling them there was going to be 'plenty water', the soldier said. The blackfellow had said they should move the town.

'Cheeky buggers,' the soldier said, and belched. 'They'd say anything to get us out of here.'

'So they could have all the corn to themselves,' Clancy said and the other man laughed and threw his arm around Clancy's shoulder, which was opportune because three other soldiers, in uniform and not intoxicated, were passing at the time.

On the fourth night, feigning drunkenness so as not to be noticed, Clancy again entered the barracks area and made for the arsenal. It was a small shed with a large padlock on the door. Picking locks was not a field in which Clancy regarded himself as an expert, but being a thief who'd specialised in stealing timepieces, he was familiar with intricate machinery and had opened many a watch and put it together again. If a man could fix a watch he could open a lock, Clancy told himself, and proved it by having the padlock open its jaws after only three minutes of prodding and probing.

It was dark inside and he needed a few minutes for his eyes to adjust. He was tempted by a row of muskets but knew he would not get to the road without being challenged if he carried something as big and as obvious as a gun. Instead, he took a small cask of powder and as many balls and wads as he could stuff into the pockets of his coat and pants.

By comparison with the previous night the place was quiet and he had reached the building without seeing anyone. But no sooner had he stepped outside and locked the door than he was challenged. The voice was sober, which worried Clancy.

Immediately, he lapsed into a drunk's roll. 'Where's the piss-house?' he demanded, his voice slurred.

'I said, what are you doing here? What have you got there?'

He could see the man now. He was a young soldier, looking disturbingly erect and sober and carrying a musket which he was now raising. He was fifty yards away.

'Thish?' Clancy raised his unencumbered hand. 'It's a white rabbit for me missus.'

'What are you talking about?'

'She likes rabbits and we ain't seen a one since we got here.'

'There are no rabbits in this country, you fool.' The soldier was closer but Clancy hadn't stopped walking. He was trying to get away from the light cast by a lantern and reach a patch of extreme darkness where trees and bushes grew. 'What's in the other hand, that box you're carrying?'

Clancy transferred the cask of gunpowder to his right hand and raised his left. 'It's another rabbit. This one's black.' He could see the man stop and raise the musket to his shoulder.

'Have you just come from the arsenal?'

Clancy ran. The shot missed and he was among the trees. He could hear men calling out. Someone blew a whistle.

248

He reached a road and heard footsteps. He slowed to a walk.

The man approaching in the gloom was a civilian. 'What's going on?' he asked.

'Some fool saw an animal and started firing.' He put on a purring Somerset accent. 'Bloody fools. Someone's going to get hurt real bad one day.'

'You're right, friend.'

'Oh, I'm right, mark my words. Well, I'll be off.' He was near the settlement's store and turned towards it. He glanced back. A lot of noise was coming from the barracks and the other man was peering into the dark. Clancy slipped behind the building where the dark was intense and listened for a few seconds. Men were shouting. The whistle was blowing.

Within a minute he was out of town and heading along the river for the raft. Passing a farm, a dog began to bark. He started to run but, in the dark, bumped into a man and sent him sprawling. Clancy kept running and the man called for help.

Clancy could hear voices answering. Laden with the cask and with his pockets full of lead, Clancy was soon out of breath. He slowed to a walk, breath rasping, heart pumping. He forced himself to keep going.

After fifteen minutes he was exhausted and his pursuers were closer. He came to the farm he had robbed on the first night and, in desperation, went into the shed. He sat where a sack of corn had been.

He'd been there no more than thirty seconds when the door burst open and Adam Jenkins stood at the entrance, carrying a lantern high above his head.

'Are you the mongrel that took my corn and wheat?'

'No,' Clancy gasped. 'I'm the mongrel that the troopers would like to catch and put back into chains. Then hang.'

Jenkins stepped closer, holding the lantern in front of him. 'Don't I know you?'

Clancy wiped sweat from his face and peered into the light. 'You're not Jenkins, are you?'

'By the living Jesus.' Jenkins put the lantern on the floor. 'I thought you were dead.'

'I will be if you don't help me.'

Jenkins wiped his lips. 'I'm an honest man these days.'

'Be a good friend. It will stand you in better stead when you face your maker. "Were you an honest man, Adam Jenkins?" God will ask, and you will say, "Oh yes, God, but because I told the truth on one occasion, I had a friend of mine hanged." And God will frown, Adam Jenkins, God will not be pleased.'

Jenkins crouched down. 'I'd forgotten how you could talk. Where the devil have you been all these months?'

'Here and there.'

'You'll never get away.'

'I have so far.' He could hear voices which were growing louder by the second. 'I was trying to get down the river to Sydney so I could jump a ship to China or South America.'

A man shouted, 'Anyone home?'

Jenkins rose, frowning. 'Wait here. Don't make a noise.'

He went out and bolted the door. 'Who's there?' he called out.

'Soldiers. We're searching for a man.'

There was, it seemed to Clancy, an inordinately long pause. Then Jenkins said, 'There's no man here. When I heard all the noise, I had a look around.' Another pause, 'But I thought I heard someone running over that way.'

'Thank you,' the soldier said and someone blew a whistle and Clancy heard the crunch of boots on hard soil. One man ran around the shed.

When they had gone Jenkins unbolted the door and came inside. 'I couldn't turn an old friend in.'

'May the Lord forgive you and bless you,' Clancy said.

'Have you eaten?'

'Not for a while.'

'Come inside the house. It's safe now.'

On the way to the house Jenkins said, 'Some filthy mongrel stole all my special grain the other night. I was going to use it to grow me the best crops in the district.'

'They never?'

'Oh they did. Now it's all gone and I don't know what I'm going to do. I worked hard since I came out here, believe me. Now I'm back where I started.'

'Such people deserve to be horsewhipped.'

'I'd do worse than that to them,' Jenkins said and opened the door for Clancy.

TWENTY-FIVE

WHEN THE NOISE of the approaching soldiers reached Berak and Arabanoo they hurriedly launched the raft, on which were loaded all the items delivered by Clancy on the previous nights. They let their craft drift into the middle of the stream where they stayed, lying low and paddling quietly against the current. In the dim light they could see the soldiers sweep past, shouting to each other and crashing through the bushes as though their own noise comforted them in the night.

Every appearance of the pale spirits astounded them. They had seen many pass by, including one lot who came near their hiding place and pointed sticks at the sky and made loud noises that caused birds to fall down. None had shown any sign of having noticed them, even those who had been near when the two men were spearing fish. Maybe they were blind, able to see their own kind but not living beings. The Aborigines were still in awe of these white figures but were no longer filled with the dread that had reduced them to quaking weaklings when they first reached the river.

The noise made by the soldiers continued for a long time. The two men heard them return, following a path much further from the river than before, and when the last faint shout was a memory they paddled the raft back to the bank. There they waited, thinking of the stories they would have to tell when they returned to the tribe but doubting that anyone would believe them.

Clancy stayed in the farmhouse all day. Jenkins was nervous, knowing the penalty for harbouring an escaped convict was the lash and many more years in chains, but he kept saying, more for his own benefit than Clancy's, that it was too dangerous for Clancy to travel by daylight. Someone would see him because the soldiers would still be on the lookout and they'd catch him and then he'd be for the noose. Questions would be asked. Where had he hidden? Had someone given him shelter? They'd search the farms. They'd find something. No, it was better to hide him and let him set off in the dark.

Jenkins went working in the fields for several hours, so no one would notice his absence and grow curious. Clancy slept for a while under Jenkins's bed.

When they talked, they spoke in whispers.

'What's the gunpowder for?'

'I can sell it,' Clancy replied. 'I need money to buy my passage.'

Jenkins shook his head. 'They'll hang you for that.'

'They're going to hang me anyhow.' They both laughed, Jenkins reluctantly.

'I see you've still got your sense of humour.'

'I don't have much else.'

They spoke of Clancy's escape. Clancy professed to know nothing about a female convict. He said Macaulay was crazy and had killed the guard and the soldier. Jenkins was relieved to hear this. It made his decision to hide Clancy easier to justify. He was not protecting a murderer but, rather, keeping from the gallows a man who merely wanted to be free. He understood the feeling. There were times during his convict days when he'd contemplated escape but he had plans to settle and have his own farm and had reasoned that the only way he'd achieve his goals was to behave himself and serve his time. He'd seen many examples of convicts being emancipated and given land. Some were making good. He had been, until someone stole the wheat and corn for his next crop.

He was obsessed by the loss of the grain. The thief must have been one of his neighbours, he said, and the thought greatly upset him. He spent hours trying to decide who it might have been. Clancy listened, making the occasional analytical comment to help Jenkins reach a decision.

That evening Clancy had a meal and left around nine o'clock, when the other farmers were either in bed or in town getting drunk on the rum that officers of the New South Wales Corps were importing.

'God bless you,' he said as he shook Jenkins's hand.

'I don't know how you're going to make it but I wish you well,' Jenkins said, all the time peering into the dark to make sure they weren't observed. 'You won't tell anyone, of course?'

'Of course.'

As he left, Clancy was smiling. Jenkins hadn't noticed the adze was missing. He recalled seeing Jenkins using a spade, which he'd put in the shed. He needed something to turn the soil for his corn and wheat. A spade would be perfect but he couldn't take this one. Jenkins had been kind, probably saved his life, but there was an even more important consideration. The farmer would notice the loss immediately and he'd be in no doubt about who'd taken it. Then he might forget his promise and talk to someone and they might search for him on the other side of the river and find his track.

There was another farm nearby so he went there and found a shovel in a barn.

Laden with the shovel, gunpowder, shot and wads, he reached

the hiding place well before midnight. An incoming tide took the raft up river, which was where he wanted to be and, by dawn, he and the two Aborigines were in heavily timbered hills, following Clancy's axe marks up to the first ridge of the mountain range.

Eliza had trouble sleeping. She was thinking of the voyage out in the convict transport and it was like a dream and she kept dozing off but the nightmare of that voyage continued. She could see again the terrible crowding deep in the holds and hear the moans and coughing and recall the smell of the hot, stale air with its putrid aromas. All around people were dying so that, most mornings, bodies would be taken out and tossed over the side. At least she imagined they were thrown overboard. On the times when she'd been allowed up on deck there was never a sign of a body and there were always people dying so she imagined they had been wrapped in a piece of canvas and hurled into the sea. These could not be Christians running the ship so she couldn't imagine them giving a dead prisoner a Christian burial.

She could see the ship again. She had little idea what it looked like from the outside; her view was from deep in the hull, with beams of light shafting through the openings up high and casting long shadows through the bars of the cells and making a splash of colour when they touched the uniform of a soldier patrolling the corridors. It was worse at night when they hauled up the ladders and the moans of those who would not see the dawn filled the hold. She could see it now, with the flicker of lanterns giving a yellowed softness to the jumble of squalor and misery.

There were several decks with cells running down both sides of the ship. It was a narrow and deep vessel with a flat bottom, built to hold as many bodies as possible rather than sail smoothly or swiftly. The cells had wooden bars which the prisoners used to beat and rattle to get the water bearers' attention when they were croaking with thirst. Each cell held as many as fifty stinking, starving, swearing, suffering people. There was one cell up near the front that was so small and so crowded the men couldn't lie down properly and all night long they used to grumble and cough and cry out when someone put his foot on someone else's face.

The woman next to her had died before they reached Rio. She'd been sick in England and had to be carried on to the ship. The one who took her bed died too, on the way to Africa.

Eliza awoke and found Delbung stroking her forehead and crooning a lullaby. After a while she went back to sleep.

The ship was a square-rigger and she knew what that was, for she'd been on deck and looked up at the mass of swelling sails and thought it looked quite lovely. But now she was down in the cell again and it was dark and people were coughing and cursing and the sea was calm and there was no wind to fill the sails. They were in the tropics and the water was slapping against the hull and the timbers were creaking and the air was hot and foul with the stink of excrement. The sick, lying shoulder to shoulder with the healthy, were constantly wetting their beds and dirtying their clothes. The food was awful because the ship owners were carrying human cargo for profit and operated on such skimpy budgets that there was money to spare only for food of the poorest quality. So what they ate was like pig swill.

She thought of the food and was almost sick and felt Delbung's gentle touch on her hand. She breathed in the cool, clean air and heard the plaintive cry of a duck down at the swamp and then she drifted off again.

The men in the cell next to hers were thieves and proud of it. That's all they seemed to talk about. They boasted of their successes. How they robbed this lady or picked that gentleman's pocket. They regarded themselves as a class apart and seemed to have pride in their craft. The tales were of wondrous pickings and narrow squeaks, of violence and degradation and other people's misfortune, but their stories were the only things that made them laugh. They were a foul lot.

And then her thoughts meandered into fantasy as she slid into a deep, troubled sleep. The men were no longer separated by bars but could come into their cell and they were stepping over the women, picking this one, rejecting that. They were like buyers at a cattle sale. And the crew were among them, just as stinking and foul-mouthed, and grabbing the pretty ones and belting any convict who tried to stop them and taking the women up on deck. One sailor seized her by the hand. He was old and ugly, with a scar across the cheek that started at the mouth and ended in a hole where the ear should have been. He was pinching her as he dragged her up the ladder and he stank of rum and sweat and she was trying to fight him but she seemed to have no power in her arms. When he reached the deck, dragging her after him, there was a loud cheer from sailors lining the rail and Clancy was there, dressed like a gentleman with a fancy velvet coat and cravat and a beautiful white wig.

'Thank you, my man,' said Clancy and took her by the wrist and gave the sailor a silver coin. And he picked her up, so easily he must have been very strong, and was carrying her ever so gently to his cabin when she saw a man rush up behind Clancy with a knife in his hand. The man was black and he raised the knife and she screamed.

She sat up.

Delbung had brought in some burning sticks so they might have light. They were on the earthen floor, near the table. 'Just a dream,' she said and sat on the end of the bed.

'We'd stop at a port,' Eliza said, wide-eyed and staring towards the deep blue of the doorway, where the reed curtain had been pulled aside to let the night breeze stroke the interior

257

of the hut with fingers of cool air. Delbung patted her hand, having no idea what she was saying. 'We'd be there a long time and each night men would come on board. Officers or wealthy gentlemen, I think, and they'd choose who they wanted and take us up on deck. Down to a cabin or, sometimes, off the boat altogether. Some of the girls liked that. It was cool, you see, and the air was fresh, not foul with the smell of sickness and death. I'd fight but it wasn't much use. Some of the men thought that made it more fun.' She shook her head sadly and Delbung shook hers in unison. 'We were treated like whores.'

'Ors,' said Delbung, grappling with the strange word.

Eliza gripped her forehead. 'Forgive me. I've been rambling on.'

Delbung smiled, her broad face crinkling into dark creases. 'When's Clancy coming back?'

'One day, two day. Won't be long.'

'I have a feeling something terrible is going to happen.'

'No,' she said soothingly but was worried. Wonngu had assured her that the man called Clancy was his uncle brought back to life in this strange form. She had no idea what that made Eliza except that she, too, must be some form of spirit. What did the dreams of a spirit woman mean?

Wonngu didn't know. He was not greatly concerned. How would he know what such people dreamed when they lived in some kind of dream world anyhow? And old Delbung couldn't even tell him what the dreams were about. He was worried about the people from the flat-topped mountain because he knew they would never forget or forgive. His main hope was that they wouldn't find his tribe. The valley was well hidden and only someone who knew the area might find the entrance through a narrow gorge.

Wonngu was having trouble with his new wife. One of the

men had told him she had a lover, a young man she'd been sleeping with before her father had given her to Wonngu. They had been seen together in recent times. He was not concerned about her having sex with someone else. He was worried that people were talking and would judge him by his reaction. He had to make sure he looked just, fair and yet firm. A beating might not be enough.

There was one possibility. Her lover had been one of the hunters involved in the spearing of the other tribesman. If he could persuade the flat-tops to have a trial by ordeal, rather than open warfare, Wonngu could assign to the lover the role of defendant. With luck, he might be humiliated, which would mean Wonngu's wife would never want to couple with him again. And there was always the chance in a trial by ordeal that the man would be killed.

They came during the night. Four men found the way into the valley and smelled the smoke from the dying fires and heard a child crying and, eventually, got so close they could see people sleeping near the stream. They returned to the main party.

There were fifty warriors in the group. An hour after dawn they were massed near the stream, shouting insults and threats and banging their war clubs on their shields.

Wonngu went to parley. He had three men with him. There was no point in taking more for any number he could muster would have been overwhelmed. He stopped 200 yards short of the war party and called for the chief to come forth. He sounded bold, which was his intention. He had ordered his men to hide in the bushes so that the others would have no true idea of the force they might face.

A man came forward. He, too, had three companions. He was younger than Wonngu and finely muscled. His beard was plaited into two strands and his hair was curled and knotted so

259

that it followed the outline of his skull. The ornamental scars on his chest were as uniform as a fish's backbone. He was a formidable looking man, thought Wonngu, who had passed the age where fear of death was a factor but his curiosity was that of a young man and he could be honest in judging rivals.

They were ten yards apart.

'Why do you intrude on our grounds?' Wonngu demanded. 'Are you so short of food that you have to come here, to this miserable place?'

'We are not hunting, old man. We seek vengeance.'

The man was blinking a lot, Wonngu observed, which meant he was nervous which could be a good thing or a bad thing. Good if he was easily placated by soothing talk or repelled by bluff. Bad if he was the sort whose nervousness caused him to attack before they had a chance to talk. And, he recalled, these people had a reputation for being impulsive and aggressive.

As though determined to demonstrate that trait, the other man thumped his shield in anger and, in a loud voice, recounted their complaint. Their men had been hunting. They had come upon three strangers who were on their land and hunting their animal. The strangers had started an argument and thrown spears. One of his men had been struck in the leg.

'I'm sorry to hear of the injury,' said Wonngu. 'Was it serious?'

The answer unsettled the other man who had expected Wonngu to dispute the facts. Yes it was serious. The spear had been difficult to remove and the man had lost a great deal of blood. He could not walk.

'Let us not argue about the facts of this matter,' Wonngu said, 'because you will say one thing and I will say another and neither of us, in truth, knows what happened.'

But the other man did want to argue and shook his shield and raised his club and spoke only in a shout. He was, Wonngu decided, determined to impress his own men. Maybe he had not been chief for long.

Wonngu pointed out that his tribe had the right through marriage to hunt near the flat-topped mountain, and that was a law everyone respected. If there had been an argument, well, that was the way of young men, stirred into aggression by the spirit of the hunt. Any dispute should be settled by the men themselves, not used as an excuse to wage warfare in which, he said, gazing around slowly as though he had warriors hidden at every vantage point, there could be extreme loss of life.

They talked some more and the other man's voice gradually subsided. He was not doing well in this discussion and he had no desire to broadcast his foolishness.

'One of our hunting party and one of yours could engage in single combat,' Wonngu suggested with a wily expression that said this would be a very good thing for his side as his champion was unbeatable.

The man frowned so intensely his thick brows engulfed the eyes. But he said no.

Wonngu had expected that. The man was likely to tire of all this talk and throw his spear and then Wonngu's tribe would be slaughtered so he said quickly, 'Well, I am a fair man and there is no disputing the fact that your man was injured. Your hunters could not hit ours with their spears but one of ours hit your man. That is a fact. Therefore, you are aggrieved and I understand that. You may not be correct to feel that way but it is human nature. We do not always act wisely. For many of us, in such circumstances as these, it is not possible to be fair, logical or wise. It's sad but true. I'm sure you've discovered that yourself.'

Wonngu smiled with the benevolence of a saint and the man blinked nervously. He had come here to kill these people, not be insulted by them.

'You are, I presume,' Wonngu went on, raising his voice so that the warriors massed behind their leader would hear, 'a simple man so I will propose a simple solution. We hold a trial by ordeal.'

TWENTY-SIX

WHEN CLANCY ENTERED the valley he saw an amazing scene. On a grassy plain near the gorge that gave access to the valley, two lines of warriors were drawn up. They were facing each other but were standing just out of spear-throwing range. Both sides had daubed themselves with clay and held spears and shields.

He and his two companions moved closer, keeping to the hills where the thick growth of trees and scrub gave them greater protection.

As he drew near the assembled warriors, one side advanced twenty paces, dancing and singing as they moved forward. When they halted they shook their spears and thumped them against their shields and shouted insults. The chanting echoed through the hills and crags, filling the valley with a thousand voices. Then they stopped and the echoes faded and, in an eerie silence, the warriors retreated.

The other side—his tribe, because he recognised some faces behind the clay—now moved forward and did the same thing. They were greatly outnumbered by the others but made up for it by making more noise.

Berak, a lithe young man who had carried the heaviest burden and was glistening with perspiration, moved to his side and whispered, 'They are saying the others threw the spears first and calling them all the bad names they can think of.'

263

Clancy gripped the musket, which he had loaded back at the rockhole. 'Who are they? What's going on?'

'They are the flat-tops. Bad people. A dispute is being settled.'

Clancy and the two heavily encumbered men moved closer, keeping within the shelter of the trees until they found a place to hide their loads. Then they crept to a line of bushes to get a better view.

A number of men from Wonngu's tribe now came forward and ran between the two groups, taunting their rivals. The others threw spears at them.

Berak whispered to Clancy, 'The spears do not have their sharp tips so they will not do any real harm. This is just to let the others get rid of some of their anger.' Berak knew the white man was the reincarnation of Wonngu's uncle but he seemed to have forgotten a great deal and Berak had taken it upon himself to explain things. 'This is the way these matters are settled.'

Several times the men ran across the field, never once being struck, until spears littered the grass. Then they retired behind the line of Wonngu's warriors and one man, armed only with a shield, moved forward. He stood between the two opposing rows, chin jutting defiantly as he faced the other tribe. He called out to them.

'His name is Murremurran and he is being very cheeky,' Berak said. 'He is one of the hunters who threw the spear that injured one of the flat-tops. He says the others threw their spears first but they could not hit a dead kangaroo. This is a very big insult.'

Now the flat-tops began hurling spears at Murremurran, who used his shield to deflect those that came close.

Berak whispered, 'These spears have tips of stone flakes or bone. They would like to kill him.'

For fully three minutes the lone warrior dodged or deflected all the spears hurled his way. Now he stood still and moved his shield so that his legs were exposed.

'In these matters,' Berak said, 'the man usually allows himself to be hit. The side of the leg is a good place. If blood is drawn, everyone is satisfied and they go home.'

A few spears were thrown but struck the ground behind Murremurran. He turned and grabbed the nearest spear and snapped it in half.

Berak moaned. 'Oh, he should not have done that.'

A flurry of spears followed and Murremurran began dodging again without using his shield. One spear, a thin weapon made from reed, struck him in the thigh. He stopped, raised a hand and pulled the spear from his leg. A red patch spread from the wound.

'It's over,' Berak said and sighed with relief.

But another spear was flung and, although it missed, it made Murremurran shout with anger. He picked up the spear and hurled it back. There was a rumble from the flat-tops.

Wonngu emerged from the ranks of his men and, waving both hands, ran to where Murremurran was standing. He grabbed his man by the arm and ordered him to retreat a few paces. Then he faced the others and began to speak rapidly.

'He is saying,' Berak told Clancy, 'that the matter is over. It is silly to fight now when the dispute is settled. Blood has been drawn. Let us all sit down and talk. We will have a feast.'

But another spear was thrown and the leader of the other tribe moved forward a few paces and shook his spear and shouted at Wonngu.

'They are going to fight,' Berak said. 'This is very bad.'

'Don't move from here,' Clancy said and stood up. Gripping the musket in both hands he walked towards the warriors. As he descended the hill, he began to sing. All he could think of was a hymn, one that had been sung on most Sundays at the compulsory church service. He hated it, but knew the words.

All people that on earth do dwell
Sing to the Lord with cheerful voice . . .

In astonishment, the two groups turned towards him. Singing at the top of his voice, he passed the flat-tops, who shuffled away from him, agog at the sight of so strange a figure.

Him serve with mirth, his praise forth tell
Come ye before him and rejoice.

He could hear the buzz of conversation but ignored all but Wonngu.

'Who threw that last spear?' he demanded, speaking in English.

'That one.' Wonngu pointed to the man.

'He has made me angry. Tell them.'

Wonngu translated and went further. 'This man is a ghost and has terrible powers.'

Clancy turned, slowly raised the musket to his shoulder and shot the man. The ball hit the warrior in the chest and flung him backwards. He lay, legs kicking in his death throes, among his massed companions who drew back from him and began to moan and shout in distress.

'He is magic,' Wonngu shouted, believing what he said. 'And you have made him angry.'

Clancy tried to look fierce. To fire again he had to reload and there was no chance of doing that as he'd left everything he needed back in the bush. He had to bluff.

'Go,' he said in Wonngu's dialect. 'Or I will strike you all.'

Wonngu repeated the message to make sure they understood.

Some of his warriors ran forward to join them and they shook their spears.

Hesitantly, the flat-tops retreated, still facing Clancy. But when he began to lift the gun and sing the hymn, they turned and ran. Wonngu's men howled and chortled in glee and chased them until called back.

'Return to the women and children,' Wonngu commanded. 'Those men will not come back.'

He turned to Clancy and his rheumy old eyes were still wide in disbelief at what he had seen. 'What is that?' he said, pointing to the gun.

'My firestick.'

Wonngu dared not get close. 'How does it kill?'

'I point it.' Clancy lifted the musket and Wonngu cringed. 'And it kills.'

'It makes a great noise.'

'It is magic.'

'You came just in time,' Wonngu said.

'It is my way.' He lowered his head, enjoying the role of being superhuman, then gestured towards the hills. 'I have things that need to be carried down. Send some men to get them.'

Eliza had been at the hut, as had many of the women and children who hid in the trees nearby. As a result, she had not seen the trial by ordeal, although she had heard the banging and singing and, finally, the gunshot. She was terrified, thinking soldiers must have entered the valley. Clancy, having first reloaded the musket under the awed gaze of a number of warriors, went to her and held her for a long time, kissing her on the cheek and assuring her he was safe and trying to explain what had happened.

Delbung had gone to find out for herself and returned with her eyes bulging. At the hut she dropped to her hands and knees and crawled to Clancy and touched his feet. 'You save us,' she said. 'My people are happy.'

'She thinks you're a god,' Eliza said.

'They all do,' he said as he gestured for Delbung to get to her feet. 'It's proving very handy.'

'You should tell Wonngu the truth.'

'And spoil everything?' He moved back to see if she was serious. She was frowning. 'Look, what he believes is important to him as well as to us. He's convinced I'm his uncle who's come back to life.'

'Clancy, that's outrageous.'

He leaned forward, a smile curling his lips. 'How do you know?'

She sat on the bed. 'Don't tell me you think you're Wonngu's uncle?'

He spread his hands. 'Who knows?'

'Oh Clancy, this is absurd. You're an escaped convict, an ordinary man, not a ghost or some kind of god.'

'I am to these people and I'm not going to disappoint Wonngu by trying to explain all that. He wouldn't have the slightest idea what I was talking about. Convict? Leg irons? Soldiers? Ships? Do you think he'd understand any of that stuff?'

'You shouldn't pretend to be something you're not.'

'It's been very handy for us.'

'It's been good for your ego.'

He strode to the door. He was angry now. He'd just scored a great triumph and she was arguing with him. 'I've brought back some things. I'm going to fetch them.'

'Why don't you get one of your slaves to do it for you?' she said, but he had gone.

Delbung had been listening. 'Is the spirit unhappy?'

'Oh for heaven's sake Delbung, he's not a spirit.' She said it again, more slowly. 'He's an ordinary man. Do you understand?'

Delbung nodded, but with no enthusiasm. So it was true what some people were saying. The man called Clancy was a supernatural being but the white woman, whom she loved so dearly, was inferior and did not possess the powers of the man. Or, indeed, understand him. Why else would Eliza say the man was not a spirit when he had just performed a miracle, an inexplicable piece of great magic, which had saved the tribe?

Wonngu nodded with contentment at the sight of the two hatchets. It was an amazing gift. Not merely one axe, made from the special stone which did not chip or break, but two. Clancy had brought the sharpening stone and showed Wonngu how to hone the blades to a keen edge, even the one that had been blunted by misuse.

'It is a great gift, Yerranibee.' Never before had he called Clancy by his uncle's name.

'You must always call me Clancy.'

Wonngu smiled and held Clancy's hand. 'Ker-lan-see.'

They had a corroboree that night and Clancy and Eliza sat near the fire and watched the dancing and singing and the re-enactment of Clancy's arrival on the scene.

Eliza had been quiet all evening but said, 'Were you really singing?'

'I wanted them to notice me.' He smiled at some of the elders who had rarely taken their eyes from him. 'I sang a hymn.'

She shook her head. 'I hope because you felt you needed the Lord's help.'

'It was the only song I could think of.'

She lowered her head and clasped her hands as if in prayer.

The performers had now reached the part where Clancy shot the man who'd thrown the last spear. The dancer holding a long, thick stick raised it to his shoulder and made a booming noise and everyone in the audience gasped. The man who was shot then performed an acrobatic leap backwards and rolled on the ground and took a full five minutes to die. The people laughed and clapped and shouted approval. Never had there been so great, so unexpected, a victory.

At the end of the evening Wonngu took Clancy aside and said, 'I'm told your woman is not happy but speaks sharply to you.'

'Women are women,' Clancy said, not knowing what else to say.

The answer seemed to distress Wonngu. 'I had hoped that in the next life women would not talk so much.'

Clancy spread his hands.

Wonngu smiled and leaned towards Clancy so that their shoulders touched. 'I have a gift for you. A small gift, but one that might bring you pleasure.'

Clancy sat back and nodded. He had become good, he thought, at behaving in a superior yet humble way.

'You have seen my daughter Ulla?'

'No.'

'She is a grown woman. Nearly thirteen years. Obedient and hard working. She would never argue. She is yours.'

TWENTY-SEVEN

AS WAS MORE common these days, they were speaking in Wonngu's tongue and the old man was perplexed by Clancy's answer. 'Not now.' What did that mean? How could a girl wait for a husband when she was of marrying age, especially when Ulla had once been promised to old Bangai who—charitable and understanding man that he was—had agreed to sacrifice his own desires and interests to honour the pale spirit.

Clancy wanted to wait? What for? Wonngu mused about the problem for some time and decided it must be to do with the woman Eliza who seemed to have a much greater influence on Clancy than normal women had on their men. This puzzled and worried him. Although later, as he attempted to rationalise the problem, he thought: why should a woman change her personality merely because she had been reborn? She might be wiser, as a man would be, but she could still retain the essential elements of her personality. Just as a good man would be reincarnated as a good man and a wicked man would still be bad, so could a woman be reborn with a sharp tongue if she had been a shrew in real life.

On more earthly matters, Wonngu was worried that Murremurran had emerged from the trial by ordeal with his reputation for bravery enhanced, even if his performance had been too rash for the liking of many of the men. Without doubt, he

271

had endangered the tribe, first by breaking a spear and then by hurling back the one thrown after he had been hit on the leg. Both broke with tradition and were provocative, foolhardy acts. Had Clancy not appeared with his magic firestick, many people would have been killed and, tonight, they would be mourning their dead, not celebrating a great victory. But the way the story was being told, with the usual embroideries to enhance its appeal to those who had not witnessed the scene, Murremurran had stood up to the flat-tops and been prepared to die rather than accept their insults.

A wise woman might regard him as a hot-headed fool but a lovesick girl, no matter to whom she was married, might find him an even more attractive partner for an illicit and sweaty tangle among the trees.

The tribe was camped half a mile from the hut but, late that night, Wonngu went to see Clancy. They walked down to the stream and sat on a sandy spit where the gurgle of water would drown their voices. There they talked.

Wonngu outlined the problems he was experiencing with his new wife. 'What should I do?' he asked. Normally, he sought advice from no one, but Clancy was, by virtue of his rebirth, wiser than he.

'Wait.'

The white man was much given to making brief, enigmatic statements. Wonngu liked this. Clancy's often puzzling remarks made him think. Wait. Yes, there was much wisdom in the suggestion. Better to see what happened in the next day or two.

'You think some women will now find Murremurran more attractive?' Clancy asked and Wonngu nodded, miserable at having given the young man the chance to enhance his appeal.

'Then it's possible one of these women will want him and he may find her more attractive than your wife.'

He had to repeat that several times before Wonngu understood.

272

He agreed. It was possible that Murremurran would be besieged with offers from the more impressionable women in the tribe. All women liked sleeping with a hero. But how would his wife react? If her lover began coupling with every second woman in the tribe would she spurn him or want him all the more?

'Shame you people don't have the pox,' Clancy said and Wonngu looked puzzled.

'Pox.' He touched his crotch. 'Your cock gets sick.'

Wonngu didn't understand. And how could he, Clancy realised, for he had seen no sign of venereal disease in the tribe. It was different on the other side of the mountains. Just as small-pox had wiped out half the blacks around Sydney, sexual diseases were now spreading among them, too.

He tried to explain. After a while, Wonngu began to smile. He couldn't comprehend what Clancy was talking about but he could understand the thought of a man being so sick he couldn't have sex. A plan was forming.

They sat quietly for several minutes, listening to the rush of water and the noise of the ducks nesting in the lagoon. Then Wonngu spoke. He had another problem. 'I have been thinking about Ulla. You said you would wait.' He leaned forward earnestly. 'I don't understand.'

'We white people usually have just one woman.'

'Why is that?'

'It is the way.' It was his version, amended for blackfellows, of Eliza's favourite phrase about inexplicable things being God's will. But the answer seemed to satisfy Wonngu.

'However, that does not mean I refuse the offer. I would like to think about it. I would like to wait.'

'But she is of age.'

'Not for me,' he said and Wonngu sighed as though this explained a great deal. Clancy leaned across and gripped the other man's wrist. 'I need a woman who is older.'

Wonngu frowned. 'I have no daughter who is older and available.'

Clancy raised his hand. 'That's all right. But one thing you must promise me is that you will say nothing about this to Eliza.'

Why not, Wonngu wondered, but said nothing.

'And in the meantime, I will think about it.'

'How long will you wait?'

'When you have lived as long as me, time means very little.'

True. He understood.

'Maybe in a year or two.'

'You do not want her in your house?'

'No.'

'Would you like to sleep with her? I can arrange that.'

At thirteen? Clancy almost laughed but said, 'I should see her first. You will arrange a meeting where Eliza won't see us. She must not know.'

This was all very strange but easily arranged. They would meet tomorrow at a place near the lagoon.

Clancy was in a dilemma and stayed awake, thinking, for most of the night. Wonngu had made the offer in all seriousness. This was possibly the most generous gesture, his daughter the most valuable possession he could give another man. The real significance of the gift was that it meant Clancy was accepted into the tribe. And was being accorded status befitting a person of the highest rank. So he couldn't say no. Wonngu would be offended or severely embarrassed if others found out Clancy had rejected the offer.

But how could he accept? Some of the young black girls were attractive with their slim, firm bodies and flashing smiles, although they seemed to degenerate quickly and he wondered what Ulla might be like at thirty and found himself daydreaming about wandering the plains with a fat black wife in tow. And she was not yet thirteen! That brought him back to reality. He might be a rogue but he was not a lecher or a despoiler of girls. And then he thought about despoiling and remembered what Eliza had said about a young girl who'd had her first period and, as part of the initiation ceremony, had been forced to sleep with a multitude of men. Wonngu had said his daughter was a woman, which meant she must have been through the same initiation, so she was no virgin.

And then, in a rare moment of being concerned about what was lawful and what was not, he recalled that bigamy was a crime. For white people at least. And he thought some more and knew he couldn't be a bigamist if he took a second woman because he wasn't married to the first one. He might be considered greedy or amoral but he wouldn't be a bigamist.

Eliza would never agree to it. He couldn't tell her, or even joke about it. She would think it had, somehow, been his idea and she would be so offended she might take sick and lose the baby. She wasn't well, even now, and news like this could do terrible things to her. Clancy knew little about pregnancy and childbirth except that women got sick and many of them died giving birth so he was already frightened for Eliza. She hadn't been well. She wouldn't say what was wrong with her but she was always pale and weak and he'd seen bloodstains on the mattress.

He couldn't bear the thought of losing her. It wasn't so much that he loved her. He needed her.

What to do? He thought of taking the young girl on as a servant, so at least she'd be in his house and Eliza need never know she was supposed to be his wife, but Ulla, being a female, would talk and so would that leech Delbung and the whole tribe would know that Wonngu's daughter was not sleeping with her supposed husband and then the old fellow would be humiliated, or angry or God knows what.

275

He slept for a while and woke just before dawn, still thinking of the problem, and the more he thought about it the more he was amused by the idea. He didn't know anyone, at least no white man, who'd been given a woman as a gift. If he were to spend the rest of his days in the bush, then why not take another woman? If he lived with Wonngu's people he might as well act like one of them. All the men had several wives. The system seemed to work well. It made sense.

He would talk to Wonngu again. He looked forward to seeing Ulla.

She was an impressive girl but just that: a girl. Long thin arms, thin legs and a body that was not fully developed. The face was attractive with its high, wide cheekbones, full lips and big eyes and she had bathed and been rubbed with animal fat for the meeting, so that her skin glistened. She was afraid of Clancy and didn't smile but Wonngu said she had good teeth and forced her mouth open at one stage so he could see. She could cook and gather food and do all the things a woman was supposed to do.

Clancy had brought along a gift for her; one of the needles he had brought back, plus some thread. Wonngu was impressed and jabbed his finger several times. It was a good gift, he said, because she was adept at sewing with a needle of bone and thread of sinew. With this, she could make him a fine necklace of kangaroo teeth.

Clancy took Wonngu to one side. 'I have to live part of my life as a white man, part as a black man,' he said. 'Therefore, the part I live as a white man I will spend with my white woman and the part I live as a black man I will spend with my black woman.'

Wonngu smiled. This made good sense.

'This will make Ulla very special,' Clancy continued.

'Indeed. There will be no woman like her.'

'But Eliza is not to be told.'

'Agreed.'

'Nor are your people to talk about it.'

Wonngu frowned. 'That will be hard. They will naturally talk about such a thing.'

'They are not to talk to Eliza.'

'The women gossip.'

'Tell them I will be angry. I will point the firestick at them.'

Wonngu gasped but agreed to tell them.

'No other man is to sleep with her.'

'Under pain of death,' Wonngu said.

'And I will visit her when I wish.'

Wonngu coughed discreetly. 'When will that be?'

'When I am ready. Probably not for some time. I will tell you when.'

'It is very unusual,' Wonngu said.

'So am I,' he said and Wonngu didn't know whether to laugh or not, as his uncle had possessed a dry sense of humour, but kept silent.

'Tell her I will give her more gifts,' Clancy said as he was leaving.

Wonngu shook his head. 'Do not spoil her. Women who are given too much become lazy.'

Wonngu went to see the sorcerer, Gogwai, who was on his own near the stream. He was squatting in a patch of dust with his beard almost touching the ground and, at first, Wonngu thought he may have been in a trance and hesitated but Gogwai had heard his step and straightened. He knew who it was without looking around.

'You are worried by that young man,' he said and Wonngu did not know whether Gogwai was reading his mind or had been listening to gossip.

'What do people say about him?'

'Some say he's a fool, some say he's a hero. All say he's your latest wife's lover.'

'He endangered the whole tribe.'

For the first time, Gogwai turned. He gave Wonngu a knowing look. It would have made most men uncomfortable, as if staring into the eyes of a snake, but Wonngu knew Gogwai was well practised in giving such looks. They were meant to unsettle, to make you believe he knew all.

'What do you want me to do?'

'Put a spell on him. I do not want him to be attractive to women. Make him sick, so that his body is continually discharging. No woman can love a man who is covered in shit.'

Gogwai grunted and returned to his original pose. Head low, eyes closed, he made marks on the dust.

That night Gogwai went to the place where old Barangaroo with the withered leg had been buried. It was a journey of several hours. He sat by the grave, talking to her spirit, and then used the leg bone of a kangaroo to dig up her partly decomposed body. With one hour of night left, he cut out her uterus and, for the next two days, dried it in the sun until he was able to grind it into powder. He put the dust in a bag and returned to the tribe, stopping on the way to gather the sap of a particular weed.

Murremurran's wounded leg had been bound with leaves to prevent infection but it was painful, for he had ripped the barbed spear out in a gesture of defiance and torn the flesh badly, and now walked with difficulty. At the evening meal food was brought to him, out of deference to his injury and his new status as folk hero. Gogwai sprinkled some of the powder on Murremurran's meat. He did the same on every second night for the next six nights and spent his days down by the stream, making marks in the dust and chanting a song that had but three notes.

By the end of the week Murremurran was too sick to leave his bed and emitted such a stench that people were reluctant to go near him. Wonngu let it be known that Clancy, the white spirit, was angry with Murremurran and was punishing him for his foolishness.

On the tenth day Gogwai and Wonngu met down by the stream. 'I see trouble,' the sorcerer said without looking up. 'He can be made to die.'

'I do not want that.'

Gogwai made a clicking noise with his tongue and drew marks in the dust.

TWENTY-EIGHT

OVER THE NEXT few weeks Clancy's concern about what to do with Ulla lessened because the tribe went walkabout and she went with them. With summer approaching and game plentiful after early spring rains Wonngu's people headed west once more, their hunters carrying bundles of freshly tipped spears and the whole tribe relishing the prospect of bountiful meat after the lean months of winter. Before departing Wonngu had conferred with Clancy. With some hesitancy he'd asked if Clancy would like him to leave his daughter for a few weeks but Clancy said no, he was in white man's mode and it was good that the tribe was going away. Wonngu took this to mean there were secret things Clancy must do and wondered what they were but probed no further, having noted that Clancy had become more distant and authoritative in recent weeks and having no desire to incur his anger. Clancy had taken to walking between the blacks' camp and his hut with the musket over his shoulder. While the gun had not been used since the affair with the flat-tops, the people remembered vividly what it could do and, while nominally friendly, were fearful of the white man.

Murremurran went too. Although still sick and with his leg not fully healed, there was no question of his staying in the secluded valley. Only those who wanted to die were ever left behind. Murremurran now had a nickname, conceived by Wonngu, spread by a few cohorts and adopted by all with relish. He was known as the man who limps and stinks.

As with most societies, Wonngu's tribe had its quota of mischief-makers and thus eager tongues soon made Murremurran aware of his nickname, which both shamed and angered him, and of the fact that his woes were due to the white man having placed a curse on him. He talked to Berak, who had accompanied Clancy over the mountains, and heard of the strange sights the young man had witnessed near the big river. Murremurran was a cynic with little time for the more fanciful tales of the old folk and wondered if the white spirits were truly the reincarnations of their people. Berak claimed to have seen no one who resembled anyone he had ever known. The pale people spoke in a strange tongue and many of the men looked like women, having no beards. Berak had, in fact, thought they were women until a group who had come near their hiding place dropped their trousers to relieve themselves and, to the astonishment of the two black observers, revealed themselves to be men.

So who was the one called Clancy and was he truly a spirit, the reincarnation of the uncle of that feeble old goat Wonngu? Or was he something else, a different kind of man, but mortal, like ordinary men?

Murremurran resolved to find out and, if possible, take his revenge.

Of the adults, only Delbung stayed at the hut. She was ordered by Wonngu to remain, but it was her wish to be with Eliza. Her two youngest daughters stayed too, to help gather and prepare food and to be cared for, because they were not yet of marrying age although one was already betrothed. The three of them camped near the stream. Only when Eliza was truly sick had Delbung spent the night in the hut and then she had stayed awake, fearing what might happen to her if she fell asleep in such a place. There had been a time when she would have slept outside the hut, under the verandah roof or beside a wall, but since hearing of the magic of the firestick, and sensing that Clancy disliked her, she resolved to sleep in the open, far away from the white man and his house and whatever magic he created within its walls.

Clancy was busy during the first few weeks of the tribe's absence. Using the large axe and Jenkins's adze, he made a door for the hut. He was meticulous, trimming logs into planks until they were flat and smooth to touch. In fact, it took him longer to make the door than it had to build the hut, but he had no help and spent his days in the contentment of enjoyable work, selecting suitable trees from which to cut the planks and then labouring over the trunks with a loving intensity until he had four planks of even size and smoothness and two short cross-pieces and a diagonal brace cut from smaller trees. He made hinges of kangaroo hide and used some of his precious supply of nails to fasten them to the wood.

The door dragged on being opened or closed but was substantial and, when barred with a stout piece of timber that had taken him a day to cut and shape, would withstand a siege. The house might fall down, he thought in a moment of candour, but the door would be intact. He was pleased. It was the best thing he'd ever made.

He spent several more days planting some of his corn and wheat. He used only a small quantity because he had no idea when he should put such crops in the ground. If this crop failed, he would try again. Having no one to ask, he would learn to be a farmer by trial and error. He dug a plot that was 50 yards square and scattered corn in one half and wheat in the other and had Delbung and the girls make containers out of bark and carry water from the stream to water the seed.

After three weeks, however, he became bored. He yearned to be hunting with the men, missed the nightly talks around the fire and longed for the company of old Wonngu. He realised he envied the blacks their free, nomadic life.

He caught fish with nets and went hunting with a long spear the men had made him but always missed the mark, even though he was becoming skilled at tracking and stalking. So he took the musket and, on one memorable day, shot a wallaby.

Delbung skinned and gutted the animal but her hands trembled for she had heard the rumbling echoes of the gunshot.

'He is not a god,' Eliza told Delbung. She had said this many times but Delbung remained unconvinced. 'He is just a man, a normal man with white skin, and I am a normal woman.' Who was going to have, she hoped, a normal baby. She was becoming frightened of the imminent birth, having heard so many stories of suffering and deformity and miscarriage in tales told by the convict women, although Delbung had assured her she had delivered many babies and there would be no problem.

Delbung wondered aloud if the baby would be white or black.

Eliza laughed. 'White. Ours will be a white child.'

Delbung asked the question that had been bothering her for some time. 'Were you born to a black woman or white?'

'White, of course.'

'What was her name?'

'Caroline.'

Delbung knew of no Caroline. She had never heard of such a name. 'And was her mother white?'

'Yes. And her mother and her mother before her.' Eliza then told Delbung of her family and where they had lived.

Delbung sat in front of her, her brow knotted, her broad cheeks compressed into a frown of disbelief.

'We came to New South Wales in a great ship and there are many hundreds of us living on the other side of the mountains.'

Delbung had heard of the great ships. Berak had seen such a thing in the big river, a large canoe with a tall stick and a triangular piece of skin of unimaginable size that filled with air and sent the canoe forward so fast that water hissed around its bows.

'And will they come here?'

'One day,' Eliza said brightly, for she longed for the sight of white faces and the sound of English conversation. 'Someone else will cross the mountains and then the valley will be filled with white people.'

Dead spirits? Ghosts? She liked Eliza but the thought of more white spirits and more firesticks that killed with their sudden noise filled her with dread. Where would her own people go? They could not live among the dead.

'They will bring the word of God,' Eliza said.

Delbung was perplexed. Who was God?

Eliza had Delbung put her hands together, as in prayer, and began to tell her about God.

The tribe returned in midsummer, well fed and happy, for the hunting had been good. Wonngu had added a roll of fat to his midriff and seemed a contented man, for his new wife had been faithful, or so he believed, and when he slept with her she pleased him greatly. He performed like a young man, or so he imagined, and that made him feel good, too.

Ulla had made Clancy a necklace of kangaroo teeth. He spent some time with her—never at night—and taught her some English. To Wonngu he explained that it was essential for him to be able to talk to his new woman in the language of the spirits before they slept together. Wonngu did not believe in conversation as a prelude to intercourse—if a woman didn't know what was on a man's mind she had no right being with him—but spread the reason for Clancy's continued abstinence among his friends. They talked about it for days. Such a decision showed particularly strong resolve, they thought, even for a spirit.

Some were now discussing the question of Clancy's mortality. Would he live forever or would he have to die at the end of his allotted span to make way for some other reborn soul? And if cut, would he bleed? Some swore they'd seen blood on his arms from small scratches but it was hard to tell whether it had been blood or a stain of some sort on his strangely coloured skin.

Murremurran, still weak and smelly because Gogwai continued to administer occasional doses of secret potions, was particularly interested in the latter conversations. He was wondering how the spirit would react to a spear in the back.

'They don't like you any more,' Eliza told Clancy one night. 'Delbung was telling me the men are afraid of you. That's not right. You should stop this silly pretence and explain exactly who you are, where you came from and what we're doing here.'

'I don't want to hurt Wonngu.'

'You mean you don't want him to stop thinking you're his uncle, for heaven's sake, and treating you like some sort of god.'

'I mean if he thinks that's the way it is, then that's all right by me. It's certainly worked to our advantage.'

'Clancy, it's a lie and lying is a sin.'

More and more of their conversations had a religious twist these days. Eliza had even suggested they should build a small church where they could pray on Sundays—not that they had any idea of the days of the week but they could always seek God's forgiveness, she said, if, by mistake, they worshipped on a Thursday.

'There are a lot of other things I'd like to make before I wasted time and precious materials on a church, where only one person would go.'

She was horrified. 'I am teaching Delbung and her daughters about the word of God. It is my hope that, eventually, I might convert the whole tribe.'

'Oh, what have I married,' he said, holding his head in mock dismay. 'A damned missionary.'

'We are not married,' she said icily.

'Then you're a damned whore, Eliza Phillips, which is a lot better than being a damned missionary.' He bowed as he left the hut.

A month before the baby was due Clancy decided to make another trip over the mountains. He would go alone, he said, sensing the reluctance of anyone to travel with him and having no need for any company. Although he would look around the farms for whatever seemed appealing, he wanted to bring back only two things: baby clothes and a Bible. The Bible would be for Eliza, to comfort her and convert whomever would listen. He knew a Bible was the item Eliza would most appreciate, and that was important at this time, to give her courage and reassurance for the birth. But it was more than the idea of such a gift that motivated him. It was the challenge. Clancy liked the idea of stealing a Bible.

Wonngu spoke to him. He understood that Clancy didn't need men to carry heavy items but this, he suggested, would be a perfect opportunity to spend time with Ulla and discover her many attributes. She could gather food and cook for him, was untiring and would do whatever he desired.

'And what do I do with her when I enter the land of the spirits?' Clancy asked, hoping this would frighten him off.

'Protect her.' He gripped Clancy's arm, something he had not done in recent months. 'She will be very useful. Please take her. You will be doing me a great favour.'

People were talking, Clancy assumed, and after much scratching of his beard, agreed.

'I don't want you to go.' Eliza put her arms around him and gripped him tightly. They were in bed and it was late, Clancy having only just returned from his meeting with Wonngu. 'What if the baby comes early? What if something happens to you?' That was the nightmare: Clancy not returning from one of his hunting trips or long expeditions, so that she would be on her own and never know whether he had been killed or injured and had died a lingering, lonely death in some strange place.

He'd mentioned only the baby clothes.

'It's ridiculous to go all that way for baby clothes. We can dress the baby like the blacks do.'

'They leave them naked.'

'I'll have Delbung or her girls make some clothes.'

'What from?'

'Skins. They make beautiful, soft leather.'

'There are some other things I want to get,' he said, thinking rapidly. 'Things for the house, for instance.'

'Like what?'

'A mirror. Wouldn't you like a mirror?'

She'd almost forgotten what a mirror was like. She touched her hair and laughed. 'I don't think I'd dare look in it.'

'You're beautiful,' he said, knowing he was winning. 'And we need yeast to make bread, and salt, and knives and forks. Things like that.'

'Don't do anything dangerous, please. And promise not to break into the army barracks again. I'd be terrified if you did that.'

'I won't be going near the place.'

'I'll pray for you.'

He squeezed her and nibbled her ear. She smelled better than the Aboriginal women.

Eliza stayed awake for a long time. She was thinking about the baby. Wondering what it was. What sort of life it would have. Almost certainly he or she would have to marry a black person which meant their grandchildren would be half-castes. That was a shameful thing in white society. How would the Aborigines react to a white person marrying a black? How would they treat the offspring?

The waterbirds were noisy tonight and she listened to them squabbling and crying out, down at the lagoon. They made such weird noises. There was a time when she would have been frightened by such sounds. Now, she rather enjoyed them for they were a reminder of living things that were timid and beautiful and posed no threat.

She would have to take charge of the child's education. Clancy spent most of his time out of doors and, when he was home, would teach the child there was no such being as God, which would be an appalling state of affairs as it would condemn their child to damnation. No, she would raise their son or daughter as a Christian and tell the child stories from the Bible; at least, those she could remember. She would teach the child to speak good English and to read and write. A thought occurred and she shook Clancy until he was awake.

'I don't want to make your task any more difficult and certainly no more dangerous but do you think you could find a pen and some ink? And paper, too, if that's possible.'

He sat up. 'Where?'

'When you go to the Hawkesbury.'

'What on earth for? Who are you going to write to?'

She took his hand, always doing that when she was about to

make a special request. 'It's for our child. I want to teach it to read and write, but I don't want to be scratching letters in the dust.'

'Can't you wait for it to be born or at least grow up a little?'

'I'd feel happier, Clancy. Please, if you can.'

He made a solemn promise, was kissed on the lips and was soon asleep again.

It was a hot night and the door was partly open so that a sliver of blue showed against the dark wall. She put her hands across her belly. The baby was kicking.

What would happen if Clancy didn't return from this trip? If he were caught by the soldiers, which would mean the gallows, or were speared by those terrible blacks who had killed Macaulay? She and the child would have to spend the rest of their lives living with Wonngu's people. Wonngu was old and probably wouldn't live very much longer. Who would succeed him? Would the new leader be as wise as Wonngu and, more important, would he tolerate a white woman and her child in their community?

Would she be forced to live with a black man? In this tribe women were told who they must live with. Or would she be cast out and made to fend for herself? Would they just go away, hunt elsewhere, and leave her and the baby in the hut? Even take Delbung from her?

And then she thought of what she'd once told Delbung about other whites following them over the mountains. It was inevitable that some day, someone else would find a track across the range and then these fertile valleys and plains would be filled with white people. They would come, just as they had to Port Jackson, with an absolute belief in their right to take whatever land they wanted. What would happen to the tribe? The same that had happened to the Aborigines around Sydney Town, she presumed: they would be dispossessed, moved from their hunting grounds and shot if they attempted to fight. They would catch white man's diseases like smallpox and measles. It would mean the end of them.

Feeling distressed, she got out of bed and walked to the door. The moon was lighting the valley and turning the hills into flowing stripes of blue and violet. There was no breeze and the smoke from the tribe's campfires lingered in the air.

What would happen to her and the child if white settlers came? How could she explain her presence on this side of the range, the hut and all the things Clancy had stolen? They would know she was a runaway convict and someone would soon identify her as Eliza Phillips and she'd be hanged. Her child would be an orphan, and an orphan's life would be as harrowing as a convict's, except it wouldn't be given land after seven years.

She would like to go back over the mountains one day and live among white people once more, as a free and respected woman. Impossible, she knew, but it was her dream.

TWENTY-NINE

ON THE JOURNEY over the mountains Clancy carried a pair of scissors and had Ulla trim his hair and cut off most of his beard, leaving just the moustache and a small pointed Van Dyke to cover the chin. For the plan he had in mind, he needed to appear distinguished or, at least, seem a man of some substance. The girl giggled as she worked, saying she didn't know the face that was emerging.

She was, as Wonngu had said, a clever, hard-working girl. At first she had been nervous and frightened of what he might do or demand of her. On the night of their initial camp, before they reached the mountains, she prepared his food and extinguished the fire and stood, hands clasped in front of her thighs, waiting for him to tell her where to sleep. He pointed to a grassy patch ten yards away. Obediently, she lay down and went to sleep. From then on they slept apart. She was happy with this arrangement, having wondered what the demands of a person with supernatural powers might be, and, as the days passed, became more relaxed; even talkative.

She was expert at tracking and could tell Clancy the names of animals that had crossed their path by the folds in the grass or the imprint of a paw on bare earth—even analysing signs so faint Clancy had trouble in distinguishing any mark. Once, they passed man tracks at a place only a few miles east of where

Macaulay had died, but Ulla said the tracks were several days old. She told him there were six men in the group and they were hunters, either tracking or stalking their prey. How did she know they were hunting? Because they were leaning forward as they walked, and she demonstrated, which meant they were either keeping their heads low to be hidden from the animals or they had their eyes down, following the tracks. She seemed astounded when Clancy asked how she knew they were leaning forward. Was not this the spirit of Yerranibee, her father's uncle and a great hunter in his lifetime? She hesitated, thinking there might be a trap in the question, that he was testing her wit. Slowly, she said, 'Because all the weight is on the front of the foot, as you can see.'

Clancy smiled and so did she, knowing it had been a joke, a wise man teasing the novice.

It rained as they approached the final ridge that led down to the Hawkesbury and, from their vantage point, they could see storm clouds massing over the mountains to the south and south-west. They hurried down the slopes. Clancy's axe marks were still there, although clear only to someone searching for them.

Clancy had been trying to work out the date but all he could be certain of was that it was now 1799 and it was late in the summer, maybe the end of January or even early February. Not knowing the day of the week, let alone the month, had troubled him at first because life as a convict had been so regimented that every day had a different schedule and a man should feel different on a Monday to a Wednesday, or so he'd believed. You ate different food on this day, changed clothes on that, worked here on a Tuesday, there on a Saturday. Sunday was the day he had disliked most of all. It was supposed to be a day of rest but they had been herded off to church, shackled at ankles and wrists, and required to sing hymns and chant prayers that gave thanks to He who had given them this bountiful life.

He didn't know whether to hate God or those who said such stupid, hypocritical things in His name. Either way, he didn't believe. He preferred the Aboriginal way where the people seemed bound to the land and linked with nature itself. They didn't regard themselves as superior beings; just part of some pageant in which the hills and the rivers and other creatures played as great a part as they did. They had some revered beings, or so he thought from a few remarks Wonngu had made, but it was a subject he avoided. They could forgive him for having forgotten the language and their earthly ways in his new life, but, as a spiritual being, he would be expected to know any gods.

No, the more he thought about it, the more he preferred the black people's way of life and the things they believed in. They certainly didn't chain people and force them on their knees to pray and they didn't have parsons who could see someone whipped on a Tuesday or hanged on a Thursday and talk about goodness and compassion on a Sunday.

Clancy hid the musket among trees bordering his path down from the mountains and continued on to the river. To his surprise, he found the raft. It was intact and still hidden among rushes on the western bank. They paddled across in the evening and spent the night in the same leafy hiding place that Clancy and the two warriors had used. Before dawn next day, Clancy put on the clean shirt, trousers, jacket and cap he had carried with him over the mountains and, whistling softly, walked to Adam Jenkins's farm.

Jenkins was astounded to see him and quickly ushered him inside, covering the windows with the hessian drapes he used as curtains to ensure no one could see in.

Clancy told him he had been to Sydney Town and had arranged to be taken on board an American ship due to sail in a week's time. He had come back to the Hawkesbury to avoid arousing suspicion by waiting around the port.

'You're playing a dangerous game,' Jenkins said, shaking his head. He was frightened that someone might see them together. 'Although I have to say, you look different. Even distinguished, with that beard.'

Clancy, much more relaxed than Jenkins, laughed. 'I've been posing as a buyer of grain.'

Jenkins's face set in a grim expression. 'And have you been paying more than Governor Hunter will allow? That man is ruining us. The wretched officers of the New South Wales Corps have a monopoly on trade and they're making a fortune by charging exorbitant prices for everything else and yet the Governor keeps lowering the price of the grain we grow and causing us to starve.'

'Oh, I haven't got around to discussing prices.' Clancy fingered his new beard. 'Tell me, when do you plant your crops?'

Jenkins was still fuming over grain prices and it took him some seconds to absorb the question. 'What the devil do you want to know that for?'

'I was posing as an expert on grains. I want to know if I've said something wrong.' Clancy smiled blithely. 'If I've made a mistake, they'll know I'm a fake and I'll know to keep out of their way when I return to catch the ship.'

Jenkins cleared his throat and spat on the dirt floor, expelling thoughts of Hunter with the phlegm. 'I was going to plant mine in the autumn.'

In a few months. Thank heavens he'd saved some grain. He said, 'Did you ever find out who stole the stuff?'

'I think I know.' Jenkins checked a window, lifting a corner of the hessian to peer out. 'I'm just waiting for his crop to appear.'

'Is he your neighbour?'

'Almost. He has the third farm from here, on the way into town. A real drunkard. His name's Brewster.'

'Don't know the scoundrel.'

'He's a dissolute thief. Oh, we've had some bad types up here. One of the early settlers came up here after his wife drowned in the river near Parramatta. He was never sober and they say his wife, God rest her soul, drank as much as he did. People tell me it was a disgusting sight when the two of them went out. Used to hold each other up or collapse one on top of the other. When she died he sat by her grave, having a sip of rum and then pouring the next on the grave. He was there all day, howling his eyes out.' Jenkins moved from the window and sat heavily on a stool. He scratched his cheek, then cleared his throat. 'Look, I don't want to appear unfriendly, but I really can't afford for you to be found here.'

With a smile, Clancy raised both hands. 'It's no problem. I wasn't going to stay. Just called in. A friendly visit.' He stood. 'I wouldn't mind a little something to eat, if you can spare it, then I must be going.'

'I don't have much, as you can see.' Jenkins looked around him, arms spread wide as if Clancy had been expecting to see food in all quarters of the house.

'Maybe some bread?' He shared Eliza's craving.

'Of course.' Jenkins, who was expecting some extravagant demand, relaxed. 'And something to go with it.' He went to a meat safe hanging from a rafter. It was covered by a net to keep out the flies. 'Have you ever tried kangaroo meat?'

Clancy had to work hard to control his expression. In the last year he'd eaten almost no meat other than kangaroo, except for the occasional lizard or possum. 'Kangaroo?' he said, affecting surprise and interest in the one word. 'I've seen them creatures around of course, but I didn't know white people could eat them.'

'It's not bad,' Jenkins said, extracting a dish laden with a shoulder of meat. Kangaroo was all he had, it being the cheapest meat he could buy and all he could afford. It was sixpence a

295

pound against one and threepence for pork or two shillings a
pound for mutton. 'I eat it a lot,' he added, and cut a slice for
Clancy.

'I'd like to try it.' Clancy smiled and watched Jenkins take out
a loaf of bread and cut two slices. 'This is very good of you.'

'It's the least a man can do.' Jenkins put the food on a plate and
sat opposite Clancy. 'You came out on the first ships, didn't you?'

'Indeed.'

'They say you lot nearly starved.'

'We did.' Clancy was tasting some of the meat which, at least,
was properly cooked, not half raw as the blacks preferred. 'And
we worked hard. We'd start before dawn—at five o'clock, which
is an ungodly hour in winter—and work till the middle of the
day, then start again around two and work until sunset.' He
glanced at Jenkins whose eyes had become glazed. The man was
that worst kind of romantic—one who loved hearing of other's
misfortunes. 'We were put to doing things like digging fields
with a spade or a hoe because there were no animals and no
ploughs, or cutting down trees and digging up stumps or making roads.'

Jenkins gazed up at the thatched roof. 'We worked them
hours, did them things, too.'

'But you were fed. After you came, there was food. We nearly
starved. They kept cutting our rations. Their own, too, I must
say.' Clancy ate a large hunk of bread and lingered over the
crust. 'The first crops they planted failed. The barley rotted,
weevils got in their seed, things like that. And the tools they sent
out on those first ships was rubbish. An axe went blunt on the
first tree, a spade curled its edge if you showed it a piece of hard
earth.' He sighed. 'They didn't care a fig about us, that's what it
was. Do you know, they didn't send no more ships for about two
and a half years after we landed?' He laughed. 'Well, of course
you know. You was on one of the ships.' Another sigh, partly

296

through recalling those days, partly for effect. 'We were in a desperate way.'

Jenkins's face became enlivened. 'I was almost put on the *Guardian*.'

'Were you now?' Clancy had no idea what he was talking about.

'At the last minute they said I wasn't going. Only wanted people with special skills for the new colony, that was the word, so they kept me on the prison hulk for a few more months. Just as well, eh? Damned ship hit an iceberg south of the Cape of Good Hope.'

'Awful. Very lucky.'

'They would have had supplies for you,' he said, but Clancy—who'd slept against the hull on his trip out and had nightmares about the timbers bursting inwards when the ship hit a reef or an island or something—was imagining the pitiful scramble of convicts, anchored by their heavy chains in dark, dank, deep, gushing cells as the *Guardian* went down.

Jenkins said, 'I've heard people say the trouble was that the early bunch of convicts was lazy. They wouldn't work.'

'What would you expect?' Clancy snapped, still thinking of the iceberg. 'We were mainly thieves, pickpockets and highway robbers.' He picked some crumbs from his beard. 'I doubt whether your lot were any better.'

Jenkins shook his head. 'There were some of us who wanted to make something of our lives.'

'And look at you. A fine example.' He was calmer now and reached for the loaf and cut himself another slice. 'And me. I was forced into it. Had a sick father.' He flourished the knife. 'But the majority of them were scum who'd turned to crime because it was easier than work. Who in his right mind would think such people could be brought out here, to a hot hellhole like this, and made to work?'

Jenkins made a grunting noise.

'Laziness is one of the deadly sins,' Clancy said, trying to

297

remember whether there were seven of them or not, 'and it is a characteristic which never leaves the human soul.'

'Amen.'

'But lazy or not, it was a hard life for us all. Some of the marines—we had marines in those days, before they brought out the New South Wales Corps—had no shoes and used to do guard duty in bare feet. Looked ridiculous.'

'I didn't know that.'

'Oh, it's true. Do you know, we were so short of food that a lot of thieving took place. They were very severe on that. A man got three hundred lashes if he was caught stealing food, that's enough to kill a person, but they still kept on trying.' He ate the last of the meat and wondered when he would next taste mutton. 'I've seen a man whipped so bad that his shoulder blades stuck out like pieces of ivory. They hanged a few, too, but people kept stealing food. When you're starving, you do desperate things.'

Jenkins rubbed his hands on his trousers. He was getting nervous again.

'Well, thank you for the food. Now, you wouldn't have some water, to send an old friend on his way?' Clancy pushed his stool from the table. 'A little drink and I think I'll take a stroll through town.'

'Town?' Jenkins hurried to get a jug of rainwater. 'You're crazy.'

'I learned a long time ago that the best way to avoid suspicion was to be cheeky. Walk around in the open. Talk to the police, or in this case, the troops.'

'If they catch you, you'll hang.' He passed Clancy a cup of water.

'Oh, they won't catch me. Cheers.' He drank quickly. 'In any case, no one's still looking, surely.'

'There was a man, I'm told. A lieutenant. Funny name.'

Clancy remembered. 'De Lacey.'

'That's him. You've met him?'

'I once slept in his bed.'

Jenkins walked to the window again. 'I never know when to take you seriously.'

'It's a long story. Surely de Lacey isn't still hunting me?'

'Oh he was. He's very bitter about it all, I'm told. The incident ruined his reputation.'

'How sad. You said he *was*?'

'He resigned from the Corps. Was asked to leave, or so the story goes.'

'And where is he now?'

'Back in England, I think. Preparing to fight the French, or something.' Lowering the curtain, he turned to Clancy. 'They say he's threatened to come back when the war's over and search for you again.'

'Hope he doesn't mind travelling,' Clancy said lightly. 'I'll probably be in America. Nantucket, I would think. Doing a spot of whaling. I've always fancied whaling.'

'You're an amazing man, Clancy Fitzgerald.'

'You don't know the half of the story.' Clancy got up. 'If it's all clear, I'll be on my way.'

It was raining lightly when he left. His plan was to pick a pocket or two in town and amuse himself by buying a few things, just like a real gent. But first, he had something to get.

Holding the peak of his cap to keep the rain from his face, he stopped at the third farm and knocked on the door. No one answered. He tried the handle, which opened easily. He found the family Bible near the fireplace. James and Emily Brewster was written on the flyleaf. He tore out the page and put the Bible under his shirt. Back on the track and on the way into town, he saw a man and a woman working in the fields and waved. They waved back.

The settlement had changed, even in the short time since he'd been there to rob the arsenal. Most buildings were still crude, with walls of wattle and mud and roofs of thatch, but a new one took his eye, partly because it was so roughly built—it had only three sides with the fourth made of bagging—and partly because of what it sold. It was a grog shop.

Out front was a signboard, neatly painted with correct spelling, which was a surprise considering the slipshod quality of the building. It read:

Red Port per bottle 5/-
Cape Wine 3/-
Madeira 4/-
Rum 5/-
Gin 6/-
Porter 2/-
Sydney brewed beer 1/6

Clancy couldn't remember the last drink he'd had and stopped at the front of the building. The weather was getting worse and he hunched his shoulders against the rain while he re-read the sign. A beer would be good. One and sixpence. Where would he get that? He was glancing up and down the street, considering which shops or private buildings would be likely to have loose cash lying around, when he caught sight of a figure within the shop. A man wearing an apron was behind a table made of planks resting on two barrels. On it were bottles and jugs and a line of mugs and cups. He was serving a customer, who already seemed unsteady on his feet, and was filling a tin mug with rum.

Clancy turned hurriedly to cross the street. The man in the apron was Noxious Watts.

Clancy sheltered under a tree on the far side of the road and looked back at the shop. He'd got on all right with old Noxious but the man was a threat. Not only would he recognise Clancy—the trimmed beard wouldn't fool someone with a mind as sharp as his—but he'd turn him in, especially if there was a reward. Noxious was reputed to have been the camp informant. Macaulay had always said so, although he was the man's natural enemy, being big and dull and hairy whereas Noxious was small and clever and bald.

How had he got out so early? He wasn't due for release for a few years and he certainly wouldn't have escaped—Noxious had always condemned the stupidity of those who tried to break-out, mainly because none was ever successful—and, in any case, if he'd escaped from a camp just up the river he wouldn't be selling liquor in this town.

That was another thing. If he had opened a store, even one as ramshackle as this, where had he got the money? So he must have been pardoned and given some money. What for? Who was so important that information about him was worth a pardon and enough cash to start a business?

By nature, Clancy was driven by curiosity but slowed by caution. He thought of going back and facing Noxious. The man would be surprised. No, astonished; so taken aback that he wouldn't be able to speak for a few seconds. Noxious could always pull a weird face when he didn't believe something and he wouldn't believe he was seeing Clancy Fitzgerald. The face alone would be worth the risk. But the rain got heavier and Clancy cooled. Noxious would never tell him how he'd made the step from convict to shopkeeper. Not the truth, anyhow. And a minute after Clancy had left the shop, the soldiers would be after him.

Best to get out of town.

He hurried in the rain, nodding to a few people who were rushing for shelter. He was wet through by the time he reached Ulla. He took out the Bible to make sure it was still dry.

'Big water,' she said.

'I know,' he said, shaking his cap.

'No.' She was greatly agitated. 'River. It come up. Quick.'

'Flood?'

She didn't know the word.

'How would you know if this river was going to flood? You've never been here.'

'It come up. I know.'

He put the Bible in his sack. 'I've still got a few things I want to get. Clothes for the baby. Salt. Yeast. We can't go home yet.'

She was shaking her head vigorously. 'No time to cross.' She pointed to a hill on their side of the river. 'Go there. Quick.'

'Ulla, we'll be seen.'

'Stay here, die.' She turned her head, listening.

'Look, I know what I'm doing.'

'All right for you. Already dead. Not me. I die.' She grabbed his wrist and began to pull him from the shelter of the trees.

He was reluctant to follow but her urgency was compelling. They had almost reached the base of the hill when he heard the sound. He turned. A large wave was surging down the river, bearing a jumble of branches and bushes and uprooted trees. Another wave followed and another. Soon the river had broken its banks and sent curling, foaming tentacles across the land. Now Clancy and the girl ran, and by the time they had reached the top of the hill the trees among which they'd hidden were no more than a swirl in the raging current.

The lower parts of the town were disappearing as the river continued to rise. From this distance Clancy could see buildings shake and crumble and float away in pieces, bobbing and sinking and spinning in the flood.

He sat on the grass, drenched by the rain, stunned by the sights he was witnessing.

'How did you know? Did you hear the water coming?'

Her face was streaming with water and she constantly wiped her brow. 'I know,' she said.

'You saved my life,' he said, but she didn't understand.

THIRTY

BY NIGHTFALL THE river was still rising and swelling across the land. Coastlines were forming on farmlands and grassy paddocks and immediately changing contour; pigpens, sheds and houses were disappearing beneath the flood; the town was a turmoil of deep, raging water which tossed trophies of thatched roof and wooden wall on the crest of its boiling current.

In the fading light, Clancy could see some people perched on top of houses and others taking to boats. Some of those in boats began rescuing people who were stranded, others made straight for the safety of high ground. A few of the farmers whose homes had collapsed in the torrent clung to improvised rafts and drifted with the flood, hoping that providence would guide them to safety. Some, like Clancy and Ulla, had escaped to hillsides and sat huddled in family knots as the water rose and the town and farmlands disappeared.

At night Clancy and the girl sat hushed, listening to the rush of water, the occasional firing of a musket as a signal to someone and the faint cries of women and children. They sat near a fallen tree, felled by some settler but never cleared from the land, not because it offered any protection from the rain, which was easing, but for the comfort of having something of substance nearby to cling to if the water rose further. A few hours before dawn they heard voices on the other side of their hill.

They could distinguish a high-pitched woman's voice, a deep moaning as if someone were either in pain or deeply distressed and the frightened chatter of children. They kept quiet. Not knowing why but convinced it would be wise, Clancy had Ulla dress in his spare pants, shirt and cap so that she resembled a boy.

When the sun rose they found the hill had become an island in an inland sea. The Hawkesbury had risen, Clancy estimated, at least fifty feet. The main current ran at a fierce pace but elsewhere the land was covered by muddy water that curled and swirled and frothed and broke in small waves, tossing debris in its charge to conquer more land. In the area where The Green Hills had been, live pigs and dead poultry were borne on the whirling currents, sharing the river's overflow with waterlogged wheat stacks, bobbing pumpkins and odd pieces of sawn, cleated or nailed timber.

A few houses were visible, some with only a stone chimney showing, others with part of their walls above the water. Near the settlement, those hilltops that were clear of the flood were crowded with survivors.

The rain stopped.

'Let's see who's over the hill,' Clancy said and Ulla, not understanding but determined not to be left alone, followed.

They found five people. A farmer and his wife were sitting down, holding their heads and watching two young children, barely at walking age, paddle in the scum at the waterline. Another man, much older, was lying apart from them with one arm across his eyes. He was moaning softly. The raft that had brought them to the hill was a long, upturned wooden table that had lost one of its legs; they had dragged it on to firm ground.

The farmer jumped up when he heard Clancy's boots squelching on the grass.

'We thought we were alone,' he said, mouth open. 'How did you get here?'

'We ran. Got here before the flood.'

The woman rose and, seeing an Aborigine behind Clancy, grabbed her husband's arm. The children ran from the water with the clockwork motion of toddlers and clutched their mother's legs.

'Do you have any food?' the man said. 'The children are hungry.'

Clancy tapped the sack. 'I have only my Bible.'

'Are you a parson?'

Clancy was tempted. He could read from the Bible, maybe say a prayer and bring the sparkle of an innocuous game into his morning, but he shook his head. 'No,' he said, managing a parson's all-weather smile. 'I'm a visitor. A businessman. The boy helps me.' He gestured towards Ulla and the farmer's wife, obviously nervous in the presence of blacks, peered curiously at her, noting the bright young face, the oversized clothes, the bare feet.

'I'm a farmer. Was,' the man corrected. 'I don't think we have much left.'

'We're ruined,' the woman said, locking her fingers. She had a high voice and rough hands. 'Water came through the house. Took the shed. The walls came down just like that.' She snapped her fingers, frightening one of the children. 'Pigpen, too. I saw the pigs being washed away before me very eyes. We had four of them, too.'

'You're alive, thanks to God,' Clancy said, unable to resist playing just a little of the role.

The older man hadn't moved. He was still moaning.

'Who's your friend?' Clancy asked.

'Lumsden. Grows corn. He can't find his wife, that's why he's upset.'

'He hasn't stopped,' the woman said.

'We bumped into him in the middle of the night. He was hanging on to a long piece of wood. Half drowned he was.'

'Almost pulled us all under,' the woman said. 'The children were on the table, we were in the water, hanging on. He almost turned the whole thing over.'

'We couldn't leave him.'

'We have to think of the children first.'

'But we couldn't leave him, dear.'

Clancy could imagine the shouting and screaming at night when they debated whether to let Lumsden join them or cast him adrift. 'Is he hurt?' he asked.

'Not a scratch,' the woman said.

'He's terribly upset,' the farmer said. 'Poor man thinks his wife is drowned.'

'She was a drunkard. Always gaming and drinking.'

'But we wouldn't wish her dead, dear.'

Clancy swung the sack over his shoulder. 'So what are we going to do?'

The man sat down again. 'I don't know. Wait for the water to go down, I suppose.'

'You could be here a long time. No food, and you wouldn't dare drink the water, not with all the dead animals in it.'

'What can we do?'

'I was thinking. Does that table of yours float well?'

'It held the five of us. It's strong. Made it myself.'

'Why don't the boy and I take it and go for help? We could head for one of the places where there are boats and get them to come and fetch you.'

The man had been hunched. Now he sat upright. 'Would you do that?'

'What about our table?' the woman said.

'I'll leave it where you can find it.' Clancy walked to the table and dragged it a few feet. 'It's heavy.'

'Made from good timber,' the man said.

'How will we find it?' she said.

'Tell me your name and I'll make sure people keep it for you.'

'I'll only have to put another leg on it and it'll be as good as new,' the man said, brightening at the thought of something to do.

'Indeed it will, Mr . . .?'

'Bowen. Samuel Bowen.'

Clancy pushed the upturned table into the water and had Ulla crawl to the front. It floated with her weight but sank to water level when Clancy jumped on.

'We might get a little wet,' Clancy shouted and grabbed two of the table legs to get his balance.

'You take care now,' Bowen's wife called out.

'I'll look after your table, don't worry, ma'am.'

'Oh my wife meant take care of yourselves,' Bowen shouted.

'Of course.' Clancy, settled now, raised a hand and waved. 'Just my little joke.'

Ulla had already begun paddling, heading for a patch of calm water where a floating island of debris and scum had formed. Half a mile beyond was a ridge of land that ran to the east. Some people were standing there.

'Go there,' Clancy ordered and began paddling with both hands.

Ulla, who had remained silent throughout the encounter, glanced back at the family on the hillside. How could it be that ghosts or spirits, or whatever these pale-skinned people were, could be so weak and afraid?

Noxious Watts was holding the cask of rum he had salvaged from the grog shop. Managing to grab only that, he'd got out when the water was up to his waist but he'd seen the building go. It was the first to be lost to the flood, the makeshift walls collapsing within minutes of the initial onslaught of water. As he was scrambling for high ground, he'd turned to see a terrible

308

sight. Mixed with the stream of torn thatch and splintered timber, smashed chairs and broken doors, men holding women in their arms and women holding children above their heads—even a chamber-pot that had been flushed from beneath someone's bed—was a rivulet of jars and casks and bottles, bobbing on the flood that raced through the town. That liquor was his property, his sole asset, the devil's concoction that had been destined to make him heavenly rich.

Watts was now on a ridge to the east of town. With him were two men whom he'd met since opening the grog shop. Both were former convicts. Nilssen was a Swede who'd jumped ship in England, been arrested as a vagabond and thrown on a prison hulk. Kerrigan was an Irishman, transported for sedition. They said he'd begged to be hanged because he couldn't stand the prospect of life in an English colony but the judge, out of spite, had sentenced him to transportation. Both were moderately well-educated men, which is what had attracted Watts, and both hated the English which made Watts sympathetic because he, too, although English, hated most Englishmen.

Despite obvious differences—Nilssen was tall and fair, Kerrigan stocky and dark and each spoke English with accents that occupied opposite ends of the vocal spectrum—the men shared some remarkable similarities. Both had been given land grants on gaining their freedom. Both had failed as farmers and sold their lots for a pittance, Nilssen for ten pounds and Kerrigan for a keg of rum. Both had come to the Hawkesbury to work as hired hands for other landowners. Both—although Kerrigan was the more passionate—despised authority and supported the growing minority who longed for the revolutionary French to invade the colony and throw out the English. And both had become disciples of the demon drink, which is why they were now with Watts.

They were looking at Watts's cask with great interest.

'We don't touch it,' he said. 'This is my future.' And then he had an inspiration. 'Ours. Your future and mine. That's if you want to stick with me. I've got an idea.'

When the flood receded, he explained, there would be easy pickings. If they were quick, there'd be loot to take from abandoned and wrecked buildings. Money, valuables, liquor. They would fossick through the mud, take what was worthwhile and then head for Sydney.

'And do what?' Kerrigan had a surly way of talking.

'Sell what we've got. Make money. Start another grog shop.'

'You start the grog shop,' Nilssen said. Despite his size, he had a light, high-pitched voice. 'What do we do?'

'Work for me. I'll pay you well.' In the distance Watts could see two people attempting to cross a wide stretch of floodwater on what appeared to be an upturned table. He watched them for several seconds, marvelling that they stayed afloat as the table tossed and pitched as they paddled through a large patch of froth and wishing some of his patrons were here so he could take bets on the couple's chances of reaching shore on such an unlikely craft. Five to one, he decided, and with a sigh at the loss of such a golden opportunity to profit from the settlers' insatiable appetite for gambling, turned back to the Swede. 'You can drink to your heart's content every night and smash a few heads, and Kerrigan can start his revolution.'

Kerrigan smiled grimly. He disliked being teased. 'You won't think it's such a silly idea when the French get here and take over.'

'The French are not my favourite people.' Watts had never been to France or met a Frenchman but his opinions were set in the concrete of prejudice. 'Come on. Let's see if we can find someone who'd like to buy some rum. The stuff's going to be in short supply in the next few days.'

'To hell with selling it,' the Swede said, wiping his lips.

'There'll be a sip or two for you but we sell the rest. Get ten times the normal price.' Watts began to walk around the ridge. 'Come on, lads, let's look for customers. If we're going to start making money, there's no better time than now. I always said there's nothing like a good flood to give people a raging thirst.'

With so much heavy rain having fallen, the stream running through the hidden valley had risen and Murremurran had to walk some distance before finding a place where he could cross. Even then, he was up to his waist in water and, many times, had to use the shaft of his spear to steady himself against the flow. He reached the bank about 200 paces from the house where the woman lived. It was a place of many trees and he stood among them, one unmoving shape among the shadows of evening, watching the hut and searching for any movement. Only old Delbung and her two girls should be there. They would be cooking now. He could see smoke rising from the far side of the building. The man known as Clancy was not due back from the land of the spirits for some days, or so people said, but Murremurran needed to be sure.

The woman was due to have her baby soon. The members of the tribe, miles away in a valley where many kangaroos had come to graze on the succulent shoots of grass that followed the rain, were constantly speculating about the baby, wondering who it might be and whether it would be a normal colour or a hideous white.

Some thought it might not even be a human but something else. Who knew what sort of creature such a pair might produce? Even Wonngu admitted he did not know. He'd never heard of spirits having children. He only knew that people were reborn as spirits. In all the stories Wonngu had heard over the years, he'd never been told of ghosts having babies and was as curious as anyone to discover what the woman known as Eliza might produce.

Murremurran had decided the baby would be white. He'd considered the question for many days now—being sick, he had little to do but think—and he'd decided that these were not reborn people who were spirits with supernatural powers but humans of some other race. It was true the man had immense and inexplicable powers but the sorcerer could do magic tricks and yet he was a mortal, just as likely to fall sick or be hurt as anyone else. So it was possible that the white man and his woman were humans of another kind, ugly to behold and able to perform great feats of magic, but humans nonetheless.

Which was why he was here. He would test his theory by cutting the woman to see if she bled. If she bled, she was not a ghost or some kind of god. There were many types of kangaroo and parrot and snake. Why should there not be many types of people? These were merely ones who lived on the far side of the mountains where, according to Berak, there were any number of similar men to Clancy. Women, too, Berak supposed, although he hadn't seen any.

Murremurran heard voices and saw Delbung and one of the girls walk around the hut and enter through the doorway. They were carrying food. He waited and the darkness became intense, for there was neither moon nor stars to light the night. After an hour Delbung and the white woman came to the door. Even with his eyes attuned to the darkness he could distinguish little more than shadows and outlines but there was no doubt one of the figures was the woman called Eliza. Her silhouette was swollen and she stood with her hands touching her belly in the fashion of pregnant women. Her voice was distinct and she was taller than Delbung. The girls must be inside the hut.

He dared not move for, although Delbung's eyes were poor, her hearing was sharp and her instincts even more finely honed and she would note any movement. The two women began to walk down to the stream. He lost sight of them for a while but then heard them talking, and heard the splash of water. One must have thrown a stone.

Quietly, taking great care where he placed each foot, he moved out of the trees and towards them.

Suddenly he was frightened. What if she were a spirit? What would happen if he tried to cut her with the sharp tip of the spear? Would she point and make a great noise that caused him to drop dead? Berak had seen white men point at birds and make a noise like thunder that caused the birds to fall from the sky. Or would she turn him into stone, or a lizard or have him drown in the stream, leaving only his voice to join the rumble of the water for all eternity?

He stopped, bent so far forward that one hand touched the rocks, and talked to himself for some time, coaxing back the daring that had helped him leave the tribe and make the long journey to this place. She might be a spirit or she might be a woman but he had to find out. Otherwise his plan to kill the man called Clancy could not be put into operation and he would live the rest of his life under the white man's curse.

Eliza sat at a place where Delbung had cleared the sand of rocks. The night was dark but cool and the air was crisp after the days of rain. Delbung stood beside her. 'If it's a boy, I will call him John, after my father,' Eliza said and, to ensure the other woman understood, added, 'John. My father.'

'John.' Delbung repeated the strange word. 'It means father?'

'No. It's a very old name. It's the name of one of Jesus' disciples.'

Delbung knew of Jesus. She was surprised that Eliza didn't know if the baby was to be a boy or a girl and that the name wasn't predestined but maybe a woman didn't know about these things. She said, 'And a girl?'

'Caroline. It was my mother's name.' Eliza had hardly known either of her parents but John and Caroline were good names and it was proper that her parents be remembered in this way. Clancy didn't care.

They talked of Aboriginal names. Delbung had called her youngest daughter Carrangorang. Eliza was saying it was a pretty name when Delbung gripped her shoulder and turned sharply.

'Someone there,' she hissed. 'Man.'

Eliza began to rise but Delbung pushed her to the ground and bent to pick up a stone. She was a brave woman, who would have fought to the death to defend Eliza, but Murremurran gave her no chance. He charged her, swinging his club in one hand and holding the spear in the other. With the club, he hit Delbung on the side of the head and, when she fell, used his foot to push her into the stream.

Eliza, on her hands and knees, screamed and tried to back away.

Murremurran jabbed the spear at her, slicing the flesh of her shoulder with its tip. He grabbed her, forced her to the ground and felt for blood. It oozed through his fingers.

'You are woman. Only woman,' he said and ran off, laughing.

THIRTY-ONE

ALFWAY ACROSS THE bay of floodwaters, Clancy was cursing himself for being so rash. A wind had arisen and the table, awash even in smooth water, bucked and dipped and yawed beneath the onslaught of waves. No matter how hard they paddled, progress was slow and their cumbersome craft impossible to steer. A sudden swirl of water sent the table spinning violently and Clancy had visions of being spilled from Sam Bowen's prized slab of wood and drowning in the muddy depths of the Hawkesbury's overflow. After all he'd been through in the last year, it would be ridiculous to die now. His mind teetered between fear and fantasy. He imagined himself at the Pearly Gates, telling St Peter he'd drowned when he fell off a kitchen table, and St Peter sending him to the other place for telling such a silly lie.

A gust of wind raced across the bay, bringing him back to reality with a succession of choppy waves and, abandoning any thought of paddling, he hung on grimly to the table legs. And then Ulla did an extraordinary thing. Without speaking, she began to undress, managing not to upset the table as she removed her trousers and jacket. Leaving only the cap on her head, she slipped over the side in a movement as smooth as an eel's and swam, pulling the platform behind her. There was an immediate improvement. The table floated, it could be steered, and they made progress.

'You're a good girl,' Clancy shouted and she smiled. She had huge, brilliantly white teeth. He turned. In the distance he could see the Bowen family forming a line on the hill. He waved and the farmer waved back. Not Mrs Bowen. She wouldn't wave, Clancy knew, until she was sure her table was safe.

They reached land where a thicket of wattle rose from the flood and they dragged the table into the trees. There, Ulla wiped herself dry with long, supple fingers and dressed. She waited expectantly.

'We'll find someone.' Clancy had been watching her. She was a fascinating mixture of child and adult, with the innocence of a little girl and the embryonic sensuousness of a grown woman. He felt like a voyeur and blushed because she was staring at him intently. 'We'll tell them about the table. Then we'll walk towards Sydney. I think we should get away from here for a while.' She was smiling. 'Do you understand?'

She shook her head.

'Never mind. This place is going to be full of soldiers and officials and all kinds of unpleasant people. And there's a man called Noxious Watts in town and I don't want him to see me.'

She was still smiling but uncomprehending.

'Let's go,' he said and began walking around the shoreline. Clear of the trees, he remembered the Bowens. He could see them, tiny figures on a distant island, and waved. The whole family waved back.

Noxious Watts and his friends found a group of nine men and three women sitting disconsolately on the edge of the flood, not so much regretting their losses as craving a drink. They were perfect targets. When Watts left, with two of the five gallons of rum gone, Nilssen and Kerrigan were carrying a shovel, a gentleman's long black coat, a sack of wheat, a spyglass, a loaf of bread, two women's wedding rings, a silver bracelet, a pair of leather boots, a lace bonnet and assorted trinkets that the settlers had seized in panic in their flight from the flood and given in haste for a taste of rum.

In Watts's pockets jingled a collection of English shillings, Dutch guilders, Spanish dollars and even one gold mohur (worth, he believed, almost two pounds) with a total value, he calculated, exceeding eighteen guineas. Eight of his customers were lying semiconscious on the grass. The other four were still able to sit but, certainly, not to stand. There was no point going through their purses. He'd taken everything of value.

About half a mile around the ridge they came upon another group of men but these had found a dozen of the grog shop's bottles floating in a backwater and were already drunk. Some of the men tried to seize the cask and Watts and his companions were forced to flee. Nilssen fought a rearguard action, using the shovel to flatten two of their pursuers which persuaded the others to give up the chase.

A third group had several children and no interest in rum but a fourth consisted of five men who paid ten pounds for as much as they could drink. Being hungry and weak from their exertions in escaping the flood, they could drink no more than half a gallon between them before collapsing. For Watts, it was a profitable call. Ten pounds for half a gallon was ten times the normal rate.

Kerrigan was all for pressing on and selling the rest of the cask but Watts put them to work, scouring the shores for more of his bottles or kegs. They searched for two hours among the freshly created bays and inlets but found none. The sun was now fierce and by mid-afternoon they were sitting in the shade on a slope overlooking the town. The river had dropped a little and more roofs and shattered wooden frames were visible. Kerrigan and Nilssen drank from the cask and were soon asleep. Watts, who took just one mouthful to clear his mind, was planning their next move. It might not be worth their while waiting for the water level to drop, as that could take days. Better for them to move back to Sydney where they could sell the goods they'd gained by barter and he could do something with his motley collection of coins.

On the way they could do some highway robbery. There might be many people who had salvaged their most valuable possessions and were heading for the coast. They would be tired and confused; easy marks for three resourceful men. It could be a profitable journey.

When Delbung crawled from the stream her first concern was for Eliza. She herself was dazed and bleeding from the ear but she expected to find a corpse, presuming the man had meant to kill the white woman. Instead, she found Eliza sitting on her haunches, dizzy from shock and holding her shoulder and crying out for Delbung, whom she thought was dead. For a while, both women embraced, then explored the other's injury.

Delbung touched Eliza's belly. 'The baby is good,' she said and they sat quietly for some time, holding hands.

'It was Murremurran,' Delbung announced, having recognised the limp and the smell. She thought she understood his motive, for he had told many in the tribe that he blamed the white man for his mysterious and debasing illness. Killing the white man's woman would be a powerful form of revenge. But, according to Eliza, he had not tried to kill her, only wound her. And those strange words he'd shouted while running away. *You are woman. Only woman.* They were words uttered in triumph, as if he'd made a discovery that pleased him greatly. This worried Delbung and, while she tried to stop the bleeding from the spear wound on Eliza's shoulder, she wondered and worried.

What had Murremurran meant? Why had he made such a senseless attack? Why hadn't he stopped to kill them both?

'It is your man that he wants,' she said eventually.

'Clancy? Why?' Eliza moved to the water's edge and began washing blood from her arm. 'He knows Clancy's not here. Everyone knows that.'

'Not now. He will come back.'

'And do what?'

'Try to kill your man.'

Eliza took a deep breath to steady herself. Perhaps it was time to follow Clancy's line. 'But he knows that Clancy is a powerful spirit.'

Delbung joined Eliza at the water's edge and washed globules of blood from her jaw. 'He is crazy, that one. And he tells people your man not a spirit.' She held her ear and, with head bent in pain and worry, added, 'Just as you told me.'

Eliza was silent.

'Is it true?'

Not knowing the clever thing to say but knowing she should not lie, Eliza nodded. 'We are merely people of a different colour.'

But how could she be certain? A spirit, especially a woman spirit, could be born without any knowledge of its past; Wonngu had said so. No one knew for sure. Delbung rocked backwards and forwards on her knees. 'Murremurran was a great warrior and now people laugh at him. He has become very cunning. And filled with hate. Others are fearful of your man. Not Murremurran.'

'But why would he attack us?'

'He attacked you. That was why he came.'

She held her shoulder. 'To do this?'

At that moment, Delbung understood. 'To see if you bleed.'

'Why?'

'Spirits don't bleed. Now he knows you are normal woman. He knows he can kill your man.'

It was almost dawn when Delbung's two daughters reached the valley where the tribe was camped. They went straight to

319

Wonngu and told him of the attack. They passed on Delbung's opinion that Wonngu should send back warriors to protect Eliza and stop Murremurran from attempting to harm Clancy. Normally, Wonngu would have been angry. It was not a woman's place to tell him what to do. On this occasion, however, he was pleased. Murremurran had played into his hands.

He immediately summoned the men. No one had seen Murremurran for a few days. He had told someone he was going to a river to bathe. A few now reported stories they'd heard of Murremurran declaring Clancy was not a spirit and that Wonngu was a fool for believing his uncle had been reborn. They had been too timid to speak before. Now they were bursting to condemn Murremurran. The man was crazy. He could cause dreadful things to happen. The rains might cease, animals disappear from the valleys, the rivers dry up.

'He must die,' Wonngu said and the others agreed. That morning, a hunting party would set off to track him down.

When the meeting was over, Wonngu went looking for the sorcerer. He found Gogwai high on a hill, sitting cross-legged on a flat rock and staring at the sky.

'It would have been simple to have killed him weeks ago,' he said without turning to see who was behind him.

Wonngu was taken aback for a few moments. Then he realised the sorcerer would have seen him climbing the hill. And he would have known that Murremurran had disappeared. It would have been simple for him to guess the reason for Wonngu's visit. Even so, it was an impressive act.

'He has been away for several days,' Wonngu said, short of breath from the climb. 'How will he be, now that he is away from your spell?'

Gogwai frowned. 'My spell is everywhere.'

'But not the medicine you have been putting on his food. Will he get better?'

Gogwai gazed directly at the sun without blinking. 'He will grow stronger.'

'He intends killing the man Ker-lan-see.'

Gogwai blinked. He had no great love for Clancy. People regarded his magic as greater than the sorcerer's. 'How can he kill a spirit?' he whispered.

'He might himself be possessed by spirits. Evil ones.'

Gogwai opened a leather pouch and chewed a leaf. He was silent for several minutes until he began to hum. Wonngu didn't move. He knew Gogwai to be a man of tricks but he also possessed much magic.

The sorcerer spat out the pulpy remains of the leaf. 'He is a great danger,' he said.

'To Ker-lan-see?'

'To many people.'

'He must die.'

'It will be more difficult now.'

'I am sending out a party to hunt him down and kill him. They think it will be easy for the man smells like rotten turds.'

'The hunters may be the quarry,' Gogwai said, mumbling the words because his lips were numbed from the leaf.

'I will warn the men,' Wonngu said and began to descend the hill.

Gogwai laughed. 'You will know what to do next time I suggest you let me kill someone, wise man.'

Wonngu stopped. 'Where has he gone, you who see everything?'

But the sorcerer had closed his eyes and, beating two sticks together, had begun to sing one of his monotonous chants.

Wonngu hurried back because the hunting party was due to leave and he had to warn them to take great care. He would not disclose his theory that Murremurran might be possessed by evil spirits because then no one would set foot outside the camp.

321

However, the men must be made aware their quarry was dangerous and cunning and likely to become more formidable day by day; very different to the man who had been the butt of their jokes for several weeks. He could be strong once more. He might not stink. It was important they knew these things.

He found the camp in turmoil. People were searching the bushes for tracks and, near the fire, a group of women were wailing.

Berak had disappeared.

THIRTY-TWO

AT FIRST, QUINTON de Lacey found life in Calcutta amusing. The city was a sprawling, cacophonous shambles of contrasts with its splendid buildings and rancid rows of hovels, its regal animals and abject humans, its displays of great wealth and hopeless poverty. But, for a curious newcomer, hardened by his time in the Antipodes, the city was—at least in the first weeks after de Lacey arrived from Sydney—a kaleidoscopic delight.

At one moment, Calcutta would thrill the senses with its grandiose buildings, exotic gardens, spicy aromas, richly caparisoned elephants and bejewelled camels and its parades of the privileged in their silken garments, golden bangles and flashing rings. And around the corner would be a jumble of beggars, all bones and rags and burning eyes, and living women with the faces of the dead, and children with their skeletons neatly stencilled on the skin. The air would be filled with layers of smoke so acrid as to sear the nostrils and dense with the chatter of the rabble and the clatter of their way of life. The streets would be awash with urine and slippery with faeces, and always, it seemed to de Lacey, decorated with the bodies of last night's dead, sometimes neatly stacked awaiting collection, at others contorted in the pose of their departure from life.

It was the wealth that impressed him. There were more supremely rich people here, he would swear, than in London.

Some of the men and women he'd seen passing by—walking, being carried by six servants in a gorgeously embroidered palanquin, posing in a horse-drawn carriage or swaying on the back of an elephant—were the most lavishly dressed, most outrageously glittering, most ostentatiously wealthy people he had ever observed. Even the baubles used to decorate an Indian rajah's elephant would pay a European king's ransom.

He'd met a maharajah who, it was rumoured, played polo with a *balti* that was an immense ruby and who rode in a carriage with wheels of solid silver. The latter story was certainly true for de Lacey had seen the carriage in the courtyard of the maharajah's palace. An instant social success in the city, de Lacey had once dined with the maharajah, a man with exquisite manners who, he'd been told, had had his brother murdered ten years earlier. De Lacey's dinner table companion that night, an official with the East India Company, assured him in the most matter-of-fact manner that killing off one's family to avoid challenge was a fine old Indian tradition. Everyone of note did it. Therefore, it was acceptable.

So much about Calcutta was acceptable.

It was a place where an Englishman could enjoy himself. He could relax in the certainty of his superiority and be able to mix with his own kind, which de Lacey found to be a combination that bestowed on him a feeling of remarkable calm after the humiliations he'd suffered in New South Wales. And, while being distanced from the tumultuous throng, he had sufficient curiosity to observe and enjoy the display of all that was odd, grotesque and spectacular that the locals, merely by being themselves and performing their normal routines, offered for his diversion.

But now he was restless.

He'd been too long in the city, too long away from England, too removed from all the excitement of the war against the French.

The ship that was due to take him home had sunk in a storm off Madagascar and he'd have to wait another five weeks before gaining suitable passage on a ship sailing for the Thames. The same vessel that had brought news of the Madagascar disaster carried tidings of Nelson's great victory at the Nile and de Lacey was chafing through inactivity. While the blockade against France was continuing and the frequency of naval engagements accelerating, there were signs that a full-scale land war against Napoleon was imminent. The newspapers in London were rife with speculation. If he didn't get back soon and find a regiment, he could miss out; never have the chance to gain honour under fire and only have that dreadful day in New South Wales as a measure of his ability on the battlefield.

De Lacey had brought with him letters of introduction from the merchant Robert Campbell, who was well remembered in Calcutta. In a society starved of interesting newcomers from strange places, he suffered from no lack of opportunity to become immersed in the social swirl. The women found him attractive and the men interesting. He knew when to talk and when to keep quiet, which was a rare gift in an enclave noted for its garrulous inhabitants.

Having been so recently in New South Wales, de Lacey was often asked to discuss the possibilities of trade and give an opinion on whether the British Government's professed policy of encouraging free settlers was wise. How could a decent man take his wife and children to live in a penal settlement? How savage were the Indians—they used the American term to describe the Aborigines—and how quickly and effectively could they be subdued? What were the prospects for agriculture? Were there jewels to be found, gold to be dug up? Why was the colony so restricted in useable space when it was settled in a land of demonstrably huge dimensions?

Calcutta, it seemed to de Lacey, was a city brimming with

entrepreneurs who would either travel, or send their emissaries, to any corner of the earth where there was the promise of great wealth.

He became the resident authority on Britain's newest and most remote colony. But while his opinion was sought on a variety of topics and his words were consumed with eagerness, not a great deal was known about the man himself. He said little, finding modesty a perfect shield. It was known that Quinton de Lacey was an English gentleman, was well educated, his conversations being sprinkled with Greek and Latin, had volunteered for service in the New South Wales Corps, been wounded in a skirmish with savages, had fought bravely—his hand-to-hand fight with the blacks at The Green Hills, told with suitable modesty, had become a favourite after-dinner tale—and he was admired for the fact that he was on his way to England to join in the forthcoming European campaign.

No one knew of the ambushes.

On an evening when the heat was oppressive and the humidity even worse, de Lacey attended a dinner given by a colonel in the service of the East India Company, which was spreading its tentacles through the subcontinent. The officer, Sir William Featherstone, was drunk before dinner and hopeless afterwards and bombarded de Lacey with questions that circled back on themselves. He wanted to quit India. He'd had a bellyful of mendacious villains whose sole motive in life was profit. A shifty race. No breeding. He thought he might make the move to New South Wales. Make a fortune before the rush set in. Best to be first, what? He didn't say first at what.

Becoming bored, de Lacey headed for the terrace. The house had once belonged to a wealthy Indian merchant and was more lavishly decorated than any villa he'd seen on the Bay of Naples, where de Lacey had been as a young man (and been discontented with his lot ever since). The terrace was covered with finely inlaid marble tiles and bordered by an ornate parapet that held no fewer than twenty statues signifying scenes from the hunt. There were gazelles leaping, an elephant charging, a tiger writhing with a spear through its heart. De Lacey admired a few of the carvings in the light flickering from a dozen lanterns, then headed for a dark corner, waving away a servant who was bearing a silver tray laden with drinks. He wanted to be on his own.

A breeze was drifting across the Hoogli, bringing with it both a measure of coolness and a mixture of odours that varied from the aromatic fragrance of spices to the stench of funeral pyres. He lit his pipe and sat on the parapet. He was above a large pond edged by even more statues—these were of humans, not animals—and by flares that spluttered and hissed as they burned. The pond, at least 100 yards long, was a feature of the gardens that sprawled down the hill towards the river and the bedlam of the city. Noises, made sweet and mysterious by distance, floated to him. He could hear men shouting and, almost hidden by their jollity, the lament of a sitar . . . a goat bleating and dogs barking . . . bells ringing to the sway of animals, a hammer striking metal, someone laughing. The view was hazed by smoke, reminding him of an old oil painting on which the varnish had clouded. The lights from a thousand lamps and scores of fires burned through the darkness. The Hoogli, wide and sluggish at this point, glittered with reflections. He could see boats moving on the water.

'You're on your own, I see.' It was a woman's voice. The face was partly hidden by a fan.

He slipped from the parapet and stood erect. 'Just getting some air, ma'am,' he said, wondering who she was.

Events happened rapidly from that moment on. She lowered the fan to reveal the colonel's wife—a woman more than twenty years younger than her husband. Exotic looking. People said she had Portuguese blood. She needed air. Would he be kind enough to escort her through the gardens? The perfume from the flowers was very refreshing at this time of the year and she was feeling a little faint. The walk would rekindle her energy and spirits.

She held his arm tightly as they descended the steps to the garden. De Lacey could see the shadows cast by servants near the path but none revealed himself. They were discreet; perhaps used to madame taking such walks with strangers. He felt nervous.

She talked constantly. Mainly about the garden. Inconsequential things.

They had been gone no more than five minutes when the colonel came thundering down the path, a servant puffing in his wake.

'So you're the bounder she's been seeing,' he shouted and used his glove to slap de Lacey's face.

The duel was arranged for dawn.

Edwin Rotherby was a young man who'd been present at the colonel's dinner party. He had the easy grace of a man who knew that his pedigree and wealth would gain him immediate entry to the most exclusive circles. Son of Lord something-or-other. A bit of a fop, de Lacey thought. Certainly not a military type by the way he stood with one hand in a pocket, head cocked to one side. He was a listener, rather than a talker, and had large eyes of a brilliant blue that glowed when people said certain things, as if Rotherby were signalling that he knew they were lying or exaggerating but was prepared to keep their secret. De Lacey found him disconcerting and had avoided him. Thus, he was astonished to find Rotherby waiting outside his front door, an hour before dawn.

It was already hot and smoke from the morning fires wafted

through the street. 'Going to be a devil of a day,' Rotherby said. 'That is, for those of us who see it through.'

'Your sense of humour, sir, is a little too keen for my taste.'

'Oh come, come,' Rotherby said, linking his arm through de Lacey's. 'We mustn't get too serious. Life's too short for that.'

De Lacey wrenched his arm free.

'I have come to support you,' Rotherby said, his eyes flashing with that knowing look. 'Act as your second.'

De Lacey was brushing his sleeve. 'That's kind of you sir. I must say, however, I find your good humour a little misplaced on such an occasion.'

'I have often been accused of poor taste.' He bowed extravagantly. 'I apologise.'

They fell into step. 'Why have you come here?' de Lacey asked.

'To be your second. And to say thank you.'

De Lacey raised a finger. 'Then you're the man?'

'I am one of many the good colonel could accuse of having spent time with his lady.'

'Good Lord.'

'Quite understandably, Lady Featherstone is bored with Sir William. He's not only a drunken fool, he's impotent. And at bedtime, loads of money is no substitute for lack of lust.' Rotherby laughed. 'I was one of the last in the line of her paramours, I suspect, which means I could well have been nabbed by Sir William.' He stopped and doffed his hat. 'So thank you, kind sir, for fighting my battle for me.'

'I was not her paramour. I was merely taking her for a walk in the garden.'

'I know.'

'She said she needed the air.'

'I'm sure.'

'I hadn't met her before.'

'More's the pity. She really is a delightful woman. Quite wasted at the moment.'

'So it's a sense of guilt that brings you here?'

'Partly.' They'd reached a corner. 'I have a cab waiting. Would you care to ride with me?'

In the cab de Lacey said, 'I've chosen pistols. That seemed the proper thing to do. I doubt whether the old fellow could lift a sword.'

'I'm told he's rather good. Fenced quite a bit as a young man.' Rotherby used some snuff. 'Surprising, isn't it?'

'And with a pistol?'

Rotherby shrugged. 'He's good at shooting birds.'

'So what do I do?'

'My dear fellow, what do you mean?'

'I mean you'd like me to dispose of Sir William so you can have free and unfettered access to her ladyship.' He held up a hand to stifle Rotherby's protest. 'You have something in mind. What is it?'

Rotherby laughed. 'I was told you were a clever fellow.'

De Lacey waited. They rode through a park where a group of cavalrymen were exercising their horses. They passed close by and the chink of harness was as steady as the beat of a drum.

'Sir William is easily flustered,' Rotherby said, still admiring the horses. 'An outrageous suggestion, a phrase that others might find amusing, could help. You see,' he said, lifting his hand and shaking the ruffles at his wrist, 'his hand trembles when he is agitated.'

De Lacey cocked an eyebrow. 'You know this from personal experience?'

'I have observed it.'

'So I should agitate him?'

'In a gentlemanly fashion. With wit, if the circumstances allow.

330

You see, de Lacey, the colonel is not well liked and there are many who think a public humiliation would do him much good.'

'And a few,' de Lacey said, 'who might welcome his demise.'

'Many would welcome such a conclusion to the duel.' He laughed. 'Oh, I think at heart, de Lacey, you're a bit of a scoundrel.'

'Not as great a scoundrel as you.'

Rotherby slapped his thigh. 'You've picked me in one.'

They rode out of the park and on to a gravelled road that led to a grassy common.

'So I should make a few choice taunts and the old fellow will be so rattled that he'll miss; hit a passing duck, not take my head off.'

'That would be fortuitous. Entertainment and fresh fowl in the one morning.' Suddenly serious, he reached over to tap de Lacey on the knee. 'Have you fought a duel before?'

'Never.'

'But I know the story of what happened in New South Wales.' His eyes blazed. 'So you're a brave man, used to being under fire.'

Under fire. In his story of the fight near the wharf, there was never a mention of shots being fired, except by the soldiers who came too late to help. De Lacey glanced at Rotherby who was looking out of the window.

'Just get him nicely stirred up and you'll be right,' Rotherby said before turning. 'I trust you're a good shot?'

'Good enough to miss if I wish, hit him between the eyes if I don't.'

Rotherby nodded in satisfaction. 'We're almost there. I must say I'm looking forward to some good coffee when this is all over.'

The chosen site was a grassy flat between trees. Secluded, de Lacey noted with satisfaction, for he'd been concerned that natives might be watching. Good enough for a game of cricket, Rotherby thought, and said so. The colonel glared. He was still red-faced from heavy drinking but seemed clear-eyed and his speech was not slurred.

'I am pleased to see you looking so well,' de Lacey said as they selected pistols. 'I had been concerned that you might still be drunk.'

'That is an outrageous thing to say, sir!'

'Not as outrageous as your behaviour last night.'

The colonel's second pushed forward. 'It is not proper to talk at this time.'

'Proper?' said de Lacey, hand on hip in the stance of outrage. 'What Sir William said and did last night was not proper. In fact, it was damned shameful. To defame a good woman who was doing no more than seeking respite from a drunken buffoon . . .'

The colonel raised his pistol and shook it. 'How dare you call me a buffoon.'

'I didn't say from you. I merely said from a drunken buffoon. How strange that you should so readily identify yourself. I must apologise. I hadn't thought you to be so perceptive . . .'

The colonel moved forward but was restrained by his second. 'You are an insulting, degraded cad.'

'What a shame, then, that such a person will perforate that thick skull of yours.'

'I demand satisfaction,' he roared.

De Lacey bowed. 'With pleasure.'

Rotherby took the pistol, checked it and passed it back to de Lacey. 'Nicely done,' he said softly. 'Please be quick. I am yearning for that coffee.'

He felt neither afraid nor nervous, de Lacey noted with pleasure. He did feel a certain amount of anger, for the exchange had been serious in part. The colonel had insulted him last night, casting grave doubts on his moral integrity. Back to back with his opponent, pistol raised to the vertical, he was still not certain whether he meant to kill the man or not. His anger was rising. And as he stepped out the paces, hearing the count and catching a glimpse of Rotherby's anxious face, de Lacey realised that his rage was not entirely directed at Sir William Featherstone. He was seeking to redress the shame and frustration he'd felt ever since being banished from New South Wales.

He reached the mark, turned . . . and hesitated.

The colonel fired. It was an impetuous shot and, if the man's hand shook, de Lacey could see no sign of it. The shot plucked at his sleeve and whistled through the trees.

'Fast, but not accurate,' de Lacey heard himself say and, wondering if the coat could be repaired and marvelling that he could think of so inconsequential a thing at such a time, carefully took aim.

Sir William stood square on to him and jutted out his chin. 'Shoot, you damned villain,' he shouted.

De Lacey moved the pistol fractionally so that its elegantly engraved barrel was pointing first at the colonel's head, then his chest. The chest was the safer shot.

'Will you shoot, sir, and get it over with?'

'I swore to myself long ago that I would never shoot a fool,' de Lacey said and lifted the pistol into the air. He fired. 'And you, sir, are possibly the biggest fool I've encountered.'

He turned and walked to Rotherby. 'Come', he said, 'let's have that coffee.'

'You will be the talk of the town,' Rotherby said as one of his servants poured coffee from a silver pot that was so massive it required two hands to manipulate. 'You were witty, if a little sharp.' He smiled apologetically. 'But you certainly made the old boy look like a fool and, in the end, you behaved impeccably. Spared his life so he'd have to spend the rest of it enduring his humiliation.'

'I thought you might be disappointed.'

'No.' Rotherby waved his cup in a grand gesture. 'An affair is fun but to be vivid, to be fascinating, it must be brief. I realised that this morning. It's time I moved on. Any woman so foolish as to marry someone like Featherstone must be suspect, wouldn't you say?'

'She seemed rather nice.'

'You must come around one night for dinner and I'll entertain you with tales of just how nice she could be.' He offered de Lacey a cigar and lit one himself. 'So what now?'

'I wait for my ship. Go to London. Join a regiment. Go to war.'

Rotherby blew cigar smoke towards the ceiling. He watched the cane fan, operated by a seated coolie, waft the smoke slowly towards the open windows. 'I am aware of what happened in the colony,' he said softly, not looking at de Lacey. 'Those ambushes.'

De Lacey drew heavily on his cigar. 'Who told you?'

'A friend down there who communicates with me. A good man. Very much on your side, I should add.'

'So what did he say?'

'That you'd been extremely unfortunate. But also extremely brave.'

'So now you know.'

'I've told no one.'

'Thank you. However, let me assure you I have no reason to feel ashamed of the events of that day . . .'

'Quite.' Rotherby stood up. 'Of course not. But I understand why you're anxious to move away, get involved in a real war. A matter of personal honour, correct?'

'Of course.'

'Admirable, although there are many people here who would not understand. This city is a hive of merchants and entrepreneurs, de Lacey, where the goal is not honour but riches.'

De Lacey drew on his cigar. He'd begun to like Rotherby but the trend in the conversation puzzled him.

'I owe you a considerable favour,' Rotherby said.

'Nonsense. In your heart, you wanted the man dead.'

'No, no. You've made him out to be as silly as a cuckoo. Much better than a corpse. People tend to get melodramatic about dead bodies but they love laughing at a fool. No,' he said, stopping de Lacey who was about to speak, 'I am in your debt and only hope you will allow me to do something in return.'

De Lacey put down the cigar.

'Have you heard of Lord Thomas Cochrane?'

De Lacey sighed in disappointment. He had been running short of money and was expecting something more substantial than an introduction, an entrée to London society—if that was what Rotherby was about to propose. He shook his head.

'Only a young chap. Younger than you by a few years, I'd say. Very dashing. Highly unorthodox. Something of a genius with things mechanical. Inclined to be contemptuous of authority. Are you sure you've never heard of the fellow?'

'Never.'

'I know him rather well. He's in the navy. Probably run the show one day.' He tapped his cigar on the windowsill. 'Did I hear you telling someone last night that you might join a regiment of the Marines?'

'It's possible.'

Rotherby scratched the tip of his nose. 'Thomas is another Horatio Nelson. Believe me, he will do great things in this war. I thought it might be rather fun if you two got together. I could write to Thomas and have you join him.'

'And do what?'

'Have a merry time. I can guarantee you this, de Lacey. If you fight alongside Lord Thomas Cochrane, you'll either end up in a hero's grave or become so burdened down with medals you won't be able to walk out of your front door.' He sat down again. 'What do you say?'

'I'd like another cup of coffee.'

THIRTY-THREE

FOR TWO DAYS, Murremurran took the captive Berak towards the mountain range. He was careful to conceal their tracks but still followed a meandering path so that anyone who might chance upon their trail would have little idea of their destination. Berak's hands were tied behind his back. Around his neck was looped a rope made of bark fibre, which Murremurran himself had woven to ensure its strength was adequate for the job of restraining a young and hostile warrior.

Murremurran walked behind, the rope in one hand, a spear in the other. When he wanted Berak to turn, he would touch him on the shoulder with the tip of the spear. If he failed to turn, he would jab hard. There had been many turns and many reluctant moments and, thus, the young man's shoulders were raw. He had cuts on the back of the neck, too, where Murremurran had felt the need to impose discipline.

The abduction had been simple. Murremurran had hidden near the place where Berak went to relieve himself and had crept up to hit him on the back of the head with his club. He had then carried the unconscious Berak to a hiding place in the hills where he gagged him, bound his hands and slipped the noose around his neck while waiting for him to stir.

At first Berak struggled but a few jabs with the spear quietened him and he was led away like a tethered animal. For the first two hours they had travelled due west then, taking extreme care to eliminate any sign of their progress, Murremurran had swung in a wide loop through a wooded valley, a rocky gorge and across rough hill country until their general direction was east, towards the mountain range.

At the end of the second day he disclosed his plan.

Having travelled with Clancy over the mountains, Berak must know the secret path the white man had taken. The two of them would follow that path into the mountains until they found a suitable spot where they could hide beside the track. There, they would wait for Clancy to return. Murremurran would then kill the white man.

Berak was horrified. He was tied to a tree but struggled so hard that the branches shook and leaves fell and a nearby horde of cicadas burst into an agitated drone. Murremurran thought Berak might break the rope so he hit him several times with his club. They were not severe blows, merely sufficient to stun the young man and persuade him to sit down and nurse his aching head.

'He is not a god.' Murremurran waved the club, angry that no one else understood that the white man was deceiving them. 'He is not Yerranibee reborn as that old fool Wonngu insists. He is a mortal man.'

Berak didn't look up. 'I have seen him do great magic.'

'He has certain powers. And he is a strange colouring. But he is a normal man. I have seen him piss. I have dug up his turds and they are the same as yours or mine.' He clapped his hands in triumph. 'And I have put a spear in the arm of his woman and she bleeds like any other woman.'

'Why do you want to kill him?'

'Because he has put a curse on me. If I kill him the curse will be lifted.'

Berak lowered his bound wrists and checked the hands for

blood. 'If he has put a curse on you, then he has magical powers. He is not a normal man.'

'He will die like a normal man.' He moved closer, using the club to tap Berak's shoulder. 'Look, it's important to all of us that this man dies. Already he tells old Wonngu what to do. Before long he will be running the whole tribe. Do you want that?'

Berak was silent.

'Think, man, think. You have been to the other side of the big mountains. Did you not see many men like him?'

Of course. He had told the story many times.

'And did they not have the sticks that make thunder and kill?'

He had seen such men point their sticks at birds and the birds had fallen down. That was true.

'Then others will come too. Ker-lan-see will show them the way. They will point their sticks at us. We will either die or be forced to move away from our lands. We will lose everything.'

Berak was silent for some time while Murremurran prepared a small fire.

'What if he truly is a ghost?'

'Then my spear will not kill him.'

'And he will point his stick at you and you will die.'

Murremurran laughed. 'He will not see me.'

'A ghost sees everything.'

Murremurran rose and stood with his hands on his hips. 'You are such a fool, Berak,' he said with good humour. 'But you will see the blood gush from his body. You will hear him squeal. You will know that what I say is true.'

Delbung had not told anyone about the wound to Eliza's shoulder. She had merely said Murremurran had tried to kill the white woman. 'Did he miss?' people asked in wonderment and she had replied that it seemed impossible that Murremurran could miss from such close range but he had. Either that or the spear had bounced from Eliza's skin. The only blood spilled had been hers, from the wound to her head.

The people were amazed. Wonngu was not surprised and strutted through the camp, pleased that the incident had confirmed all he believed. Even so, he ordered two of his strongest warriors to camp near the stream where they could watch the hut in case Murremurran eluded the hunting party and returned.

Delbung allowed no one inside the building. 'She is greatly displeased,' she said, and they understood.

In truth, Delbung's mind was in turmoil. She now knew that her friend was mortal; if not like her, then certainly as vulnerable to injury and death as any other woman. And, because of the shock caused by Murremurran's attack, Eliza had begun to bleed from the place where the baby would come. The bleeding was copious and had started too early, which meant her life was in danger.

By now news of the flood along the Hawkesbury had reached Sydney Town and, although details of the disaster were sketchy, an emergency programme of rescue and repair was under way. Normally, all goods to The Green Hills were carried by water in yachts that sailed out of Port Jackson, north along the coast to the mouth of the Hawkesbury and then upstream to the settlement. But with the river being too swift, swollen and choked with debris for any craft to venture upon its waters, everything needed at the beleaguered settlement went by the inland track through Parramatta and Castle Hill. Walking in the other direction, Clancy and Ulla passed lines of soldiers, sweating in their red and white uniforms as they marched at a forced pace, and gangs of convicts, clanking and shuffling under the twin burdens of heavy chains and cumbersome loads of supplies and equipment. The convicts were escorted by guards, foul-tempered at the best of times, who passed in surly silence, glowering at the prospect of many days of hard work for prisoners and guards alike. Clancy kept well clear of them in case one was a man he had known. He had no time for the guards. Most had been convicts themselves and were a brutal lot, given to drunkenness and coarse language and despised for being excessively harsh in the way they treated their former brethren.

No one was overly curious about the man with the trim beard and mud-stained clothes or his shadowy attendant. A couple of officers stopped to ask Clancy if he had been in the flood and to hear his tale but most tramped on, weary from the long walk and already aware of the proportions of the disaster from conversations with earlier travellers.

Just before sunset Clancy stopped at the bottom of a hill where the trees grew thick and a small creek was running strongly after the rains. He'd seen no other traveller for an hour. Ulla went to find some food, thinking she might catch a possum in the trees. Clancy's plan was to travel towards Parramatta, take a few things he needed from one of the farms there—to replace items lost in the flood, like his precious small axe, and pocket whatever else took his fancy—and then head back for the Hawkesbury. By the time they returned, he hoped, the river would have fallen and they would be able to cross.

Being thirsty, he went to the creek to drink. He heard the clip-clop of a horse's hoofs and turned in surprise, a passing horse being a rarer sight than a falling star.

A man on horseback was coming down the hill.

Both the man and his mount were impressive. The rider was young, maybe no more than thirty, but obviously a gentleman of some wealth and breeding by his clothes and posture. He had on a light-coloured hat of a type Clancy hadn't seen before, with a low crown and an exceptionally wide brim. He wore a creamy jacket of the finest cotton, a bright red neckerchief, twill riding breeches and knee-high, lightly tanned leather boots that glistened in the faint light. The horse was the colour of burnished copper and as big a horse as Clancy had seen. It approached with a high, graceful step and with its neck arched as the rider tightened the reins.

The man stopped about ten yards away and, ignoring Clancy, stood in the saddle to look around him.

The saddle was impressive and, Clancy judged, worth a small fortune. He knew something about saddles, having stolen one from a squire with a renowned stable of horses. That had been a beautiful saddle, so light as to be almost dainty and with elaborate stitching and tooling that made it so distinctive Clancy had been unable to sell the thing. This was a much larger and heavier saddle and, with its leather tassels and rows of silver trimmings, had a foreign look about it. He'd certainly never seen one like it. Saddlebags straddled the horse's rump but these were of plain leather and locally made, Clancy guessed.

Ulla had crept through the trees to watch. She stayed hidden, being frightened, for she had never seen a horse before and was not sure if the man and beast were one animal or two.

The rider sat again and studied Clancy, who was facing him with one hand in his shirt, holding the Bible in place. It was all he'd salvaged from the flood.

'Is this where you're staying the night?' The stranger's voice was friendly, as if they'd already gone through the preliminaries of introduction.

'I thought it a good spot, yes.'

'Indeed. What's it like further on?'

'There's some nice grass.' Clancy remembered a waterhole about a mile away and described it.

'I'd better hurry on while there's still a modicum of light.' The horse began to shuffle sideways and the man steadied it with a pat of his gloved hand.

Clancy was wondering what was in the saddlebags. 'You're welcome to stay here if you wish.'

The man touched the brim of his hat and smiled. 'Very kind of you, sir, but I think I'll move on. My horse is a little nervous. I don't think you'd get much sleep with it around.'

Clancy took his hand from the Bible. 'May I ask what brings you out here?'

'I'm buying land near the river. I've not been in the colony long and thought I should see it for myself.'

'If it's still there,' Clancy said.

The man laughed. 'So I've heard. Which is why I've come to look. Might even be a few more bargains to be had, eh?' The horse was becoming nervous and he tightened the reins, forcing it to take a few steps backwards. 'Cortez isn't used to me,' he shouted as the animal gradually settled and returned to its former place on the track.

'Cortez?'

'My horse. He has Spanish blood. I've only had him off the ship a few days.'

'Lovely animal.'

'Rapid, but a handful, I'm afraid.' He leaned forward to stroke its neck. 'If you'll forgive me saying so, you look as though you've been in the flood yourself.'

'We had to swim for it.'

'Glad you made it. Do you live on the Hawkesbury?'

'I was visiting.'

'Not a good time to be there.'

'No.'

The man bade Clancy good evening, touched his hat and rode off.

In envy, Clancy watched him ride up the hill. That, he said to

343

himself, is the richest man I've met since coming to this country.

He went to the creek and drank.

Ulla was still away when Clancy heard footsteps behind him. He had only half-turned when a man jumped on him. Both fell to the ground. The man was heavy, much larger than Clancy, and his breath stank of rum. They've got me, he thought, fearing the nightmare of recapture had become reality, and pushed himself free just as the other man tried to smash in his head with a piece of wood.

'Finish him off, you fool,' a man shouted and, frightened and shocked though he was, Clancy recognised the voice. It was distinctive: high-pitched, whining. Noxious Watts. So he was being grabbed for the reward.

He rolled into the creek and, rising without losing momentum, charged through the water to the other side.

'Get him, Kerrigan,' Watts shouted.

Only Ulla was near and she was a mere girl but Clancy screamed for help.

A second man rammed him and, even though he failed to grasp Clancy's clothes, the impact drove him back into the creek. The big man was on him again.

'Help!'

'Call all you like, mister,' the big man said in a sing-song voice as he pulled Clancy to his feet. He shook him, as a terrier might tease a rat. He had both Clancy's arms pinned behind his back.

'Let me see what we've got,' Watts said and, for the first time, Clancy could see his old fellow prisoner. He'd been in the trees on the far side of the creek.

'I hope they're paying you well for this,' Clancy said.

'Paying me?' Watts sounded genuinely puzzled and came closer, peering at the captive.

Clancy, struggling anew to free himself, felt the big man tighten his hold to the point where he feared an arm would break and he cried out again. And then he heard a dull crunching sound and the terrible grip eased and the man fell sideways into the water. Ulla was behind him, holding a large rock in her hands.

'Quick,' Clancy said and ran with her for the trees. But Kerrigan was on him and, before he could clear the creek, brought him down with a lunging tackle.

The Irishman sat on him, holding his head underwater until Clancy thought he would drown. When his strength had gone and he could no longer kick his legs or thrash the water with his arms, Kerrigan got off and hauled him to his knees.

Ulla had disappeared. Watts was in the creek, dragging the Swede to the bank. Kerrigan held Clancy in a headlock.

'There was a boy,' Kerrigan said. 'He runned away.'

'Let him go. It's the man I want.'

'Just bash his skull in,' he said, offering Clancy's head, 'and let's be out of here.'

'No, I'm curious. Let me look at him.'

The Irishman thrust Clancy towards Watts.

Free of the headlock, gasping for breath, Clancy managed to stand upright. 'Hello, Noxious,' he said.

Clancy spent ten minutes giving Noxious Watts an entirely imaginary account of what had happened since the escape. He thought he did rather well, considering he had a fierce headache and kept lapsing into uncontrolled coughing—and sometimes, into a deliberate bout of retching when he needed time to consider what to say next. The story he concocted was that he now lived in Sydney Town under an assumed name. He was a wealthy man, being a merchant who imported tea from China. All his wealth was in Sydney, however, and if Watts would let him go, he would arrange to pay him a considerable sum.

It was only when he was nearing the end of his story that he realised Watts wasn't interested in any reward for apprehending an escaped convict. He had no intention of turning him in. He was robbing him.

Clancy burst out laughing. 'I've got nothing, you old goat.'

Nilssen, able to stand again, hit Clancy on the back of the head, causing him to stagger forward. He kept his balance and still smiled.

'You can beat me as much as you like but it's true.' He put his hand inside his shirt and withdrew the Bible. 'This is all I've got on me and I'm prepared to swear on it although, if I remember rightly, it's not a book you're greatly interested in.'

Kerrigan, who had been through Clancy's pockets once, went through them again. He held his fingers aloft. 'All he's got in there is mud.'

'I'm a poor man, Noxious, believe me.'

'What about this tea business?'

'A tale. You know me.'

Watts frowned. He remembered Clancy Fitzgerald's wild stories. 'What about those fancy clothes?'

'I stole them.' He began to remove his jacket. 'You want them?'

Nilssen said, 'Why don't we just kill this liar and be on our way? Take his clothes. They might be worth something.'

'You've had money,' Watts said, eyes narrowing in disbelief. 'Where is it?'

'Oh, Noxious, you never were inclined to believe anything anyone told you.'

'Have you got money somewhere? If you have, we'll let you live if you take us to it. If you haven't, say a quick prayer, if you feel so inclined.'

'Why the devil would you kill an old mate?' He tried to

sound jovial but his voice let him down, croaking on the wrong words. It wasn't Noxious who worried him so much as the other two. Noxious could be persuaded. The others were duller minds who would kill before thinking of alternatives.

'I'd have you killed,' Watts said, careful to have his status understood, 'because you know me. And, dear friend, if I remember you correctly, you're a compulsive talker.'

'Now, Noxious, in the last year or so . . .' Clancy began but he was interrupted by Kerrigan, who shouted, 'Someone coming. A rider.'

The horseman was returning and, despite the dark of evening, he was riding down the hill at a gallop.

'Scoundrels,' he shouted while no more than a dark blur in the night. 'Rascals. Let my friend go.' He was holding something high in one hand; a riding crop possibly. Clancy couldn't tell in the poor light but he felt like cheering for already Kerrigan had started to run. Watts took a few steps back. Only the Swede stood his ground.

The horseman thundered into the group, shouting and whooping as though leading a troop of cavalry. Nilssen tried to grab the reins but the horse shied at the last moment and a lashing hoof struck him on the head. He fell to his knees. Watts stumbled in his haste to get away and tripped over a rock. Clancy stayed where he was. He was not being brave. He was too tired from the near drowning and too shocked by the man's sudden arrival to move.

The rider chased Kerrigan and ran him down, the thoroughbred's massive chest brushing the runner to one side as it galloped past. Arms and legs swinging loose like a rag doll, Kerrigan was flung to the edge of the track and lay there unmoving.

The man wheeled the horse and came back at a slow trot.

'Are you all right, friend?' he called. 'Your boy ran to tell me you needed help.'

'Good lad.'

'Indeed. Tell me you're well.'

'I'm fine.'

'Well, let's teach these thugs a lesson.' He dug in his heels and the horse charged forward.

Nilssen was on his feet. He had a knife.

Clancy shouted a warning but the man was riding hard and leaning to one side, swinging the riding crop as though playing polo. He went straight for Nilssen.

The big man was brave, Clancy gave him that, for he stood his ground and, at the last moment, waved his arms and shouted to frighten the horse.

The animal slid to a halt, reared and dislodged its rider. In an instant, Nilssen was upon him, the knife held high as he leaped.

Clancy ran forward and jumped on Nilssen. He landed with his knees on the Swede's back and grabbed him by the hair and wrenched his head back but the knife arm kept rising and falling and, even in the faint light, Clancy could see the blade darken.

There was a sound like a shot, a faint, muffled sound, and the Swede rolled back, brushing Clancy to one side as he staggered to his feet. He was holding his side.

'I'm shot,' he said, his voice squeaking in surprise. He took his hand from his chest and felt the palm, to confirm there was blood on it. 'The devil's got a gun.'

Watts was already with Kerrigan, helping him to his feet.

'Wait for me,' Nilssen cried and, stumbling and falling and rising again, followed them into the night.

Clancy knelt beside the man, whose breath was as harsh as a leaky bellows. He managed to hold up a small pistol that was little bigger than his hand. 'Only a trinket,' he whispered, 'but effective close up.'

Clancy was feeling the man's side which was sodden with blood.

'Gave him a nasty surprise.'

'You did.' Clancy pulled back the coat for the blood was ruining it. 'Thank you for coming to my aid.'

'Least a man could do.' He made a terrible wheezing sound. 'Where's Cortez?'

Clancy had no idea for the horse had gone but said, 'Just down by the creek.'

'Damned fine animal,' the man said, and died.

THIRTY-FOUR

T HE HORSE RETURNED late that night. It came along the creek, snuffling at the grass and tossing its head at strange smells until it was near the place where Clancy had chosen to bury the body of the stranger. He heard the horse before he saw it, a wide shadow moving through a row of thin tree trunks. He rose slowly, clicking his fingers and making soothing sounds, but the animal stayed where it was, swinging its head from side to side so that the loose reins slapped against the trees, frightening it even more and causing it to stamp and whinny in distress.

Clancy tried to persuade it to come to him but it stayed among the trees, cracking twigs beneath its dithering hoofs and snorting nervously. So, still talking to the horse to stop it from bolting, Clancy got on with the task of burying the dead man.

He removed the stranger's coat, shirt, neckerchief, trousers and boots and laid them in a pile beside the extraordinary hat, and left the body clad in underwear, gloves and silken stockings, the latter being embroidered with the initials WLC. He had never seen embroidered stockings; they were attractive and he was tempted to take them but it was only right that a man should be buried with his feet covered and he fancied the boots more than the stockings. From the man's pockets he took the small pistol, a leather purse and a sheaf of papers and put them in his own bag, to examine in the morning.

Ulla watched but said nothing, fascinated by the sight of a white man who had died, just like normal men did, and puzzled as to whether he had been killed by the big man with the flashing blade or had died through being separated from the four-legged beast.

After a short period of uncertainty, Clancy had realised he had to bury the stranger. He couldn't leave a body on or near the main track to the Hawkesbury, not with all the traffic that would be coming this way in the morning. The body would be found, there would be an immediate search for the assailant and all strangers along the way would be remembered. His own freedom, and therefore his life, would be in jeopardy.

With Ulla's help he had carried the man up the creek, stumbling and tripping in the dark until they reached a place where the rush of water after the rains had caused part of one bank to collapse. He put the body with the knees bent into the chest in a freshly scoured hollow beneath a wall of soft earth.

Digging with his hands, he covered the body with soil and rocks and weeds until it was too deeply buried for any straying dog to pick up the scent of death. The body might be uncovered in the next flood, but by then he would be well away, safely at home in his little house on the far side of the Blue Mountains.

He wondered if he should offer a prayer but immediately dismissed the thought as being hypocritical, for this man deserved to be buried with sincerity and not with a prayer muttered by a non-believer. Therefore, he said, 'Thank you, friend, you were a good man and deserved a better fate, and wherever you're going, I hope they look after you well.'

He sprinkled a handful of soil on the grave and once more turned his attention to the horse.

Hand extended, he whistled a few bars of a melancholy sea shanty he'd heard around Sydney Cove. When the horse lifted its head he whistled softly. After a while the horse came forward, snorting and tossing its head but moving ever closer, as though drawn to the resting place of its dead master.

Clancy had never ridden a horse and never been near something as lively as this Spanish stallion, but he had worked with horses, having been employed by a Somerset farmer to look after a team of Clydesdales when he was nine. His job had been to feed the horses, water them, brush them, keep their hoofs clean and their fetlocks neatly combed, harness them to a wagon or the plough, oil and polish the leather straps and use a broom and a shovel, both of which were larger than he was, to keep the barn clean. He had worked from sun-up to sunset and been paid sixpence a week. The farmer was a good man who fed him a bowl of soup when he finished work—even though, as the man was always reminding the lad, he was not required to—and let him sleep with the horses on some nights, especially if it was raining or thunderstorms were making the animals nervous. If the thunder was bad, Clancy would move down the line of swaying, chafing, towering draughthorses, putting a thin, comforting arm around each great neck and stroking the fine hairs until the animal had calmed. Clancy liked it in the big barn where the horses were kept. He liked the smell of hay, of leather, of manure, of freshly minced earth and the warm, meadowy smell of the horses themselves.

The job had lasted two years, until the day the farmer dropped dead as he was leaving the house. They were, Clancy recalled, the best years of his life. He liked horses and they seemed to like him.

'Here, boy,' he called, softly clicking his fingers.

Ulla was behind him, eyes wide in fright.

'What is it called?' she whispered.

'Horse,' Clancy said and repeated the word slowly to soothe the stallion, which had seen the girl and backed away until one of the saddlebags caught on a branch. 'It's a horse. Good horse.'

And over his shoulder in a whisper, 'Don't talk. Don't move.'

He made the soft cooing noises the Clydesdales used to like. He moved forward a step and, when the horse didn't retreat, moved another two.

He'd been trying to remember its name. 'Cortez,' he said at last and the horse pricked its ears. Clancy clicked his fingers. 'Come here, Cortez. Here, boy.'

He waited. Cortez pawed the ground, then came forward slowly, dragging its hoofs in the carpet of leaves and twigs, letting its head rock up and down. Slowly, Clancy reached forward and took the reins.

'So now we have a horse,' he said, stroking the animal's neck. 'And what the devil are we going to do with you?'

It would be a wonderful surprise for Eliza if he were to return with a horse. Eliza. He hadn't thought of her for a day or two but now he did and wondered when the baby would be born. Neither of them knew much about these things. Women just swelled in the belly for three-quarters of a year and gave birth amid intense screaming by the woman and those attending her, and the baby was either alive or dead and the woman either lived or died. That was the extent of his knowledge on the subject of childbirth.

Still stroking the horse, he turned to Ulla, who had been looking at him most curiously, as if she had uncovered a secret too frightening to be discussed.

'Are you all right?'

She nodded.

'What do you know about babies?' He had to repeat the question.

'They are very small,' she said, wondering why she was being tested in this way.

'I mean, when they are being born.' He did his best to mime the action of childbirth and she giggled, then looked shocked.

'Will you have a baby?'

'No.' He no longer laughed at her strange questions for she thought him to be a god, as did all the tribe, and how could she know what gods were capable of? Soberly, he said, 'Eliza will have a baby.'

She nodded but was still confused by all that had happened. She had seen three white men attack another; she herself had been able to knock down the biggest of the white men by simply hitting him on the head with a rock; her man Clancy, who was capable of performing so many miracles, had been choking and near death in the water, which is why she had run for help; and she had seen the man on the beast called a horse torn from that horse and killed.

'What do I know about . . .' She didn't know the word.

'Birth. The time when the baby is born.'

She shrugged. 'I have seen many babies born.'

'Could you help Eliza when it is her time?'

'Delbung is there.'

'I'd like you to help.'

'Your white woman does not know me. I have been told not to go to the house.'

He frowned. 'If I call for you, will you help her?'

She looked puzzled. Of course. She would do whatever he said. She was his to command.

Ulla had removed her male clothes and was standing in a place where a sliver of moonlight penetrated the trees. She was, Clancy thought, a clever, resourceful girl. Graceful and feminine in her mannerisms, too. He found himself examining her body, softly outlined by the pale light. She would grow into a most interesting woman.

He tied the horse to a tree and after it had tugged at the reins and reared and banged a few branches, he managed to calm it

354

sufficiently to remove the saddle and the two leather bags. He should brush it down, he thought, for it was sweaty and covered in mud but he had no brush and he was too tired to groom it by hand. Instead, he spent several minutes leaning against its flank so it might grow used to his smell and touch. He stroked its finely muscled neck and ran his hand over its rump and the horse grew calm, shivering occasionally and ruffling its mane but content to have this new man touch it.

It was a wonderful animal, surely worth more than a hundred pounds. But where would he sell it? Who would buy it? Only a wealthy man, which almost certainly meant some army officer grown rich through trading, and such a man would be suspicious by nature and ask a barrage of questions that even a person as glib with his answers as Clancy couldn't answer. And there was no point in just letting the horse go free. It would be found and then there would be a search for its owner.

No, he would have to keep it but, if he took it with him, he would have to travel at night, at least as far as the river. Such a distinctive horse might already be known in the colony and to be seen leading it on foot, not riding like an owner would, almost certainly would have soldiers after him within hours.

If only he could ride . . .

Astride the animal, wearing the stranger's lavish clothes, he could pretend he was the owner. He could head towards the river with Ulla walking behind, carrying some of the load like a native boy would do for his master. No one would think a rider in a rich man's clothes and on a fancy horse was an escaped convict. The more he thought about it, the more he liked the idea. It was a daring concept, and that appealed to him, but it was practical, too. On the horse, he could travel without fear of interception back to the river. Many would be curious but no one would be suspicious.

Surely riding was not so hard, if he just let the horse walk at a slow pace? He had seen plenty of people riding horses, even lads, back home in Somerset. But this one was such a highly strung thoroughbred he could imagine a contest of wills in which he was tossed a few times before man or beast proved itself the master.

Worried and uncertain as to what to do, he undressed and draped his clothes across a branch so they might dry. Then he went to the creek and washed blood from the dead man's shirt and coat and put them over another branch. He lay on some grass near the horse and tried to sleep but he was cold and there were ants about and he spent most of the night sitting up, leaning against a tree, shivering and constantly brushing ants from his legs.

In the morning, in a foul temper from lack of sleep and stinging from scores of bites, he went through the dead man's papers. What he found immediately enlivened him.

The man's name was William Lowerdale Clancy. Clancy! Surely this was fate at its most benevolent. He leaned against the horse, which stared at him wide-eyed but didn't flinch. He now had a horse, fine clothes and an identity. If he wished, he could cease to be Clancy Fitzgerald, escaped convict, bound for hanging, and become William Clancy . . . who was what? He read further.

The dead man was from Cape Province. The name Cape Province was familiar but he had to think for a long time to place it. A cape. On the sea. Of course. On the voyage out, they'd stopped at Cape Town on the Cape of Good Hope in Cape Province. So William Clancy was from the southern tip of Africa.

He was an Englishman, twenty-eight years old, who came originally from Dorchester-on-Thames in Berkshire. Near Somerset, country he knew so well. This was getting better and better. If anyone asked him about home, he could describe the land, refer to villages he knew, even talk about the pubs. He thought more and frowned. As long as they asked about England. He would have to invent stories about Africa. Never mind. He would spin some great tales; he would enjoy the challenge.

There was a letter from a sister. He read the letter, written in a fine copperplate. She was, he judged, younger than her brother and, by the tone of the letter, his only living relative. William Clancy, apparently, had been in Africa for some years. He'd made good at something or other. His sister was proud of him and looked forward to seeing him and hearing of his adventures. The letter was comparatively recent, having been written less than a year ago.

Clancy opened the leather purse. There were many coins, mainly Spanish dollars, plus some small gold nuggets, two keys and a silver locket containing a picture of a young woman. The sister, perhaps. She looked rich—as she must have been to have had an artist paint such a portrait—with upswept hair that fell in neat curls, long earrings and a necklace. He went through the bags. There was more clothing, a pair of shoes and two silk handkerchiefs; a groundsheet made of canvas that was stitched at the borders; a tin of snuff, some tobacco and a pipe; ammunition and powder for the pistol; an engraved hunting knife in a leather sheaf; a tomahawk in a pouch of well-oiled chamois leather (he tested the blade and, like the knife, the axe was razor sharp); a cotton wrap with compartments containing a brush to polish the boots, a folding razor with a bone handle and a matching shaving brush, a needle, thread and thimble and a small pocketknife; a pack of biscuits, strips of dried meat of a sort Clancy hadn't seen before, and a silver flask. He opened it and sniffed. Brandy.

He drank a little, ignoring the inquisitive glance of the girl, and read more of the papers. There were legal documents couched in terms he didn't understand and a letter from a banker in Bath. It acknowledged the transfer of 350 pounds into the account of Ruth Clancy. There was also a certificate of mottled parchment, tied with red tape. He unrolled it. The certificate was covered in writing of the sort monks did and had a red wax seal and a coat of arms featuring a pair of prancing horses. The writing was in a language he didn't understand but he guessed it was Spanish as the horse, from what the man had said, must have been bought in Spain. The English words 'the Hon. Wm L Clancy' were in the centre of the certificate. He presumed the document proved William Clancy had bought the horse. But 'the Hon.' What the devil did that mean?

Ulla noted his worried face. 'Something is bad?'

'No.' He rolled up the certificate and thrust it in one of the saddlebags. 'It shows I own the horse.' He touched his chest. 'I am William Clancy, a rich man. From now on, you must call me Mister Clancy.'

'Mister Ker-lan-see?'

'Very good. It is important to say Mister. Do you understand.'

She didn't understand why, but she said Mister and Clancy was pleased so she smiled.

He took the razor and brush to the creek and shaved, then dressed in William Clancy's clothes. The breeches and boots were both a little large but better that than being too tight, he thought, as he bent to wipe mud from the heels of the boots. The boots were made from a fine, supple leather and he vowed to wear them only on this side of the mountains when among white men. Or when he wished to impress Wonngu. The old man would have seen nothing like them. He imagined himself leading the horse as he strutted up and down in front of the tribe, and could already hear the gasps of admiration and astonishment.

The shirt was now free of bloodstains but had knife holes so he thrust it in one of the saddlebags and put on a new shirt that William Clancy had carried in his bundle of spare clothing. The coat was still damp but he put it on, knowing it would soon dry on such a hot day. When he first tried on the hat it came down to his ears but a silk handkerchief stuffed within the inner band made it sit comfortably. He posed for Ulla, who rolled her eyes and made cooing noises.

'Nice?'

'Nice, Mister Ker-lan-see.'

'You're a clever girl.'

He took the heavy saddle to the horse and, only then, wondered how it went on. The Clydesdales had never worn saddles and he'd undone the stallion's straps in the dark, not bothering to think which strap went where.

Sensing his uncertainty, Cortez shied away.

'Oh, we're going to have fun,' he told the horse and slung the saddle across its back. Within an instant, he was on his hands and knees, his thigh numb from a kick.

He got up. The horse's eyes were blazing in anger. Clancy picked up the saddle and waved a finger. 'I'm going to put this thing on you and you're going to stand there, tied to that tree, until I do.'

Horses will always test you, the farmer had said. It doesn't matter how big you are, lad, you've got to show them you're the master.

So he picked up a big stick and waved it near the horse's tethered head but it reared and struck out with its hoofs.

Maybe that's not the way with Spanish horses, he thought, and tried again. Making the soothing noises that had worked so well with the draughthorses, he came forward with an arm outstretched and was lucky to avoid the next kick. 'Oh you're fast with your feet, Cortez, I'll say that for you,' he said and went away to think. He sat beneath a tree, leaning against the saddle.

'The man had this,' Ulla said and produced the saddle cloth.

'Oh,' said Clancy, standing and rubbing his sore thigh. 'I was wondering if you'd found it. Good girl.' He stretched his leg. 'Now, let's do this together and I'll teach you how to put a saddle on a horse.'

Eliza was frightened. Delbung had been making her a tea of leaves and herbs which had stopped the heavy bleeding but she still lost blood intermittently and she was too weak to walk and the baby was moving and she had spasms of intense pain. Her shoulder hurt, too, because the spear wound had become infected and even though Delbung applied leaves and a poultice of finely ground berries taken from a vine that grew down near the lagoon, the cut had turned an ugly purple colour and pus trickled down her arm.

She was going to die. On her own, with only this funny old woman as a witness to her passing and without a minister to say the words that might ensure her entry to the Kingdom of Heaven. And in the proper category of heaven, too, where good Protestants went. What if she were sent to the Catholic part and had to endure the purgatory they talked about, just because she turned up, unexpected and unannounced, and they didn't know what to do with her and thought she was Catholic and not Church of England? She talked to Delbung about this, rambling in a fever, and the old woman gave her tea and held her hand.

She might never see Clancy again. He was late in returning and could well be dead himself or, just as bad, had been caught by the soldiers. Something terrible had happened on the other side of the mountains, she knew, and she would have her baby and die before Clancy returned, if he ever did.

What if the baby lived and she died? Who would look after it? Delbung? One of the younger women?

'If I die,' she said, lifting herself on one elbow, 'who will look after the baby?'

'You will not die.'

'But if I do?'

'We will raise it as one of our own.' Even if it is white, Delbung said to herself.

So the poor mite would be raised as a heathen, never knowing its mother or father and, if it were a girl, would one day be given to some old blackfellow and have half-caste children. She began to weep.

Not knowing what else to do, Delbung wiped her cheeks and persuaded her to drink more tea.

THIRTY-FIVE

AFTER TWO DAYS of climbing, Murremurran stopped at a place where the domed mountain lay on the horizon, its knot of tall timber clearly visible in the afternoon light. The place he chose for the ambush allowed him to hide among trees on a knoll above the track that Clancy would use. Murremurran had scouted the area to make sure Berak was telling the truth and, after an hour of patient searching, found signs that indicated the white man and one other person had passed this way many days ago. He wondered about the other person. Was he with Clancy or following him? Travelling with him, he thought, for the feet were small, almost childlike, whereas someone tracking an intruder would be a hunter, not a child. Berak said he knew of no one accompanying the white man and Murremurran believed him, for Berak's answers so far had been honest. No matter. Even if one were a child, he would kill them both.

He waited, neither speaking nor allowing Berak to utter a noise until the sun had set. Only then was he sure the white man would not be coming that day, for even someone capable of the feats Clancy performed would not travel these mountains at night.

Berak was tied to a tree by the wrists and ankles. Several of the cuts on his shoulders were now covered in scabs and itchy, and

362

he rubbed his back against the rough bark of the tree. 'They say the people who live in these mountains are bad,' he said, while Murremurran busied himself making a small fire. 'If you leave me tied to this tree, I will not be able to help you fight them off.'

'I need no help.'

'But they are notorious. They spear anyone who ventures into their territory, or so the old people say.'

'Good. They will be blamed for the death of the white man.'

Which means, Berak thought, you mean to kill me, too, for if I were alive, I could tell our people the truth. He said, 'I was thinking it was unwise for you to be lighting a fire.'

'It will be so small even the birds in the trees will not notice. And I am hungry.'

Which means you're not going to feed me, he thought. Murremurran had caught a bandicoot that day and Berak had relished the thought of meat, not having eaten since the previous morning, and then only berries.

'This is a terrible thing you are planning to do,' Berak said. 'Ker-lan-see has the power to help our tribe.'

'He has the power to destroy us.'

'He saved your life. Have you forgotten that?'

Murremurran didn't answer but arranged the burning pieces of wood so they would quickly turn to coals.

'If he had not arrived and pointed his magic stick, you would have died and so would many of our people.'

'I wish I had died,' he said, without looking at Berak. 'I wish he and his woman had never come to our land. I would willingly have died rather than have him live among us and bring his white man's poison with him.'

'There is no poison,' Berak said.

'Look what he's done to me.'

'You are getting better. You seem stronger. Why kill him now?'

363

'Because as soon as he returns I will be sick again.'

'So you believe he does make magic?'

'I believe he has the power to make me sick. That is an evil power. When I kill him, I will be rid of the evil.' He tossed the bandicoot on the fire and the pungent aroma of burning fur filled the air.

'Wonngu says he has done much good,' Berak said, his stomach churning with hunger.

'Wonngu is a fool.' Murremurran laughed. 'He cannot even make love with his woman.'

'He is old and that is the way of old people but he is wise.'

Murremurran left the fire and stood in front of Berak. 'I have had a dream, a powerful dream, in which I saw many white men like Ker-lan-see coming into our land. I saw many firesticks. I saw many of our people lying dead. Do you want that?'

'You have been sick and that is a sick man's dream.'

'It is the future.'

'You are sick in the head, Murremurran,' Berak said and expected to be struck but the other man merely laughed.

'I feel sorry for you,' Murremurran said. 'You have helped entice the devil into your lives and he will destroy you all. Only I can save you. Mark my words. One day I will be regarded as a hero.'

Berak was silent for a long time. He watched Murremurran eat and then lie down to sleep and, all the while, his fingers were busy, trying to loosen the knots at his wrists.

It took Clancy and Ulla more than a hour to get the saddle on the horse, with all but one of the straps buckled tightly around its belly. Clancy couldn't see what purpose the final strap served; it was long and not attached to anything, so he put it in one of the saddlebags. He then tried to mount the horse. It was easier than he expected, for Ulla, whose curiosity had overwhelmed her fear of Cortez, held its head and the horse seemed comforted by her presence and stood quietly while Clancy tried to fit his oversized boot in the stirrup and swing himself into the saddle. The leather squeaked and the saddle moved slightly but, once in place, he wasn't going to go through the rigmarole of tying straps again so he sat where he was while Ulla led the horse in a circle through the trees.

The horse felt much larger than it had seemed from the ground. Extremely powerful, too, even when merely walking. It was, however, a good sensation. Sitting high in the silver-studded saddle he had a sense of power and status he had never known, for he was in charge of this awesome beast—or would be as soon as the girl let go—and only the rich rode horses and only the very rich rode a horse like this.

He stopped and got off, almost falling when his boot caught in the stirrup. The horse shuffled in alarm but quietened at Ulla's touch.

Knowing that he'd have to get on the horse in front of others, he then went through the routine of mounting and dismounting until he became reasonably fluent and Cortez grew restless, being anxious to get back on the open road rather than spend the day as a beginner's dummy among the trees. Recalling that the good riders he'd seen in England had always looked relaxed, Clancy began a pantomime of poses, waving to an invisible audience, lifting his hat, nodding to passers-by, muttering courtesies, turning in the saddle to chat to a make-believe companion and holding the reins loosely in one hand and laughing modestly, as though he'd uttered words of contagious wit.

Ulla, dressed in her male clothes, looked on in astonishment. It must be, she thought, that among the trees were people she couldn't see. Ghosts not yet reborn. Mouth agape, she let go the bridle and Cortez immediately moved off at a crisp trot, along the creek towards the road. She followed, grabbing Clancy's bag on the way but, despite running, not being able to keep up.

After many hours of being tied to the tree, Berak managed to free himself and run away. But he was so stiff and numb from being bound, and weak from lack of food, that he could not move quickly and was soon recaptured. Murremurran beat him with the club and dragged him back to the tree. He tied him to the trunk.

'Why don't you kill me now?' Berak gasped through a mouth filled with blood.

'So you can see how I kill the white man, so you will understand that what I have been saying is true.'

'He is not coming, don't you realise that?'

'How do you know?'

'I had a dream, a powerful dream . . .' he began but was stopped when Murremurran thrust a wad of leaves into his mouth.

'You can mock me,' he said, tying a strap of woven bark around Berak's face to keep the wad in place. 'But you will see. I will kill Ker-lan-see first, then I will kill you. I will kill him quickly, but I will kill you slowly, peeling the skin from your limbs, leg by leg and arm by arm, and I will listen to you begging for mercy and saying, again and again, that Murremurran alone knew the white man was a false god who, had he been allowed to live, would have brought ruin to our people. You will say all that before you die.'

Clancy, who had managed to stay in the saddle all the way through the trees, fell when the horse stumbled on rough ground near the road. He landed on soft grass and was quickly to his feet, fearing the horse would bolt but, to his surprise, it stayed where it was, reins dangling on the ground, flicking its tail to brush away flies. It had, Clancy thought, the arrogant stance of a horse used to throwing its rider. Dusting down his clothes, he approached slowly, not demeaning himself by making silly noises but staring it in the eye. Cortez didn't like that and backed away a few steps.

'At least I can outstare you,' Clancy said, feeling some comfort from a small victory, and took the reins. He was standing beside Cortez when Ulla came running out of the trees.

'He is too fast for you,' Clancy said, still breathing heavily from the fall. 'I thought it best if we both walked for a while. I can lead the horse.'

She was grateful. She could never keep up, even when the horse was only trotting.

'Damned fine animal,' Clancy said, recalling the owner's last words.

Eliza was in labour. Delbung wanted her to move outside the hut and be on the grass, where women gave birth, but Eliza stayed on the bed. 'That is where white women have their children,' she said during a time when the pain was not intense and Delbung wondered if, perhaps, white women lost their blood before they gave birth. Otherwise, why would they not lie on the grass rather than stain such a fine rug? She was excited, feeling she was about to witness a miraculous happening and was bursting with curiosity to see what emerged.

'It would be good if it was black,' she said wistfully, at a time when Eliza was gripping her hand as the pain returned.

'It will be my colour,' Eliza managed to say.

Delbung shook her head sadly. 'I have been praying to your God, like you showed me.'

'For what?'

'For the baby to be normal.'

'It will be normal.' She was grunting now.

'But black.'

Eliza groaned. 'It will be pink.'

Delbung straightened. 'What is pink?'

'Red.'

The black woman covered her mouth in horror.

Eliza was in labour for twenty-three hours. She was exhausted when the baby was delivered. It was a girl, a healthy girl with a hint of red in her hair and, just as Eliza had said, pink skin.

Wonngu was informed of the birth and spent much time on his own, wondering what this meant. The baby was red, both in its skin and hair. Was this a portent of evil times? Many of the women believed so, reasoning that a baby born the colour of blood was a symbol for pain and suffering, and were already gathered near the stream, wailing in fear of events to come.

Wonngu had never seen a red child, nor ever heard of one. He would wait for Clancy's return, to have him explain the meaning of such a birth. It could be a good sign, the mark of an exceptional spirit. He forced himself to be calm and think in a reasoned fashion.

Even in an optimistic mood, he was worried about Clancy, who had been away longer than expected. Could he have decided not to return, or had some misfortune befallen him? Thinking of all the possibilities, his mind turned to Murremurran, who had not been found despite the hunting party having searched the area for days. Murremurran hated Clancy and blamed him for his illness. Could there be a link between Clancy's absence and the fact that Murremurran had eluded the hunters? Why had he taken Berak?

One of the hunting party was back in the camp, having hurt his knee in a fall, and Wonngu called for him, to explain precisely where they had searched for Murremurran. No, they had not gone into the big mountains. They had found no trail leading there.

Wonngu thought about that for some time and then summoned Arabanoo, the young man who had travelled with Clancy and Berak on that initial journey over the mountains.

Could he find the track they had used?

He thought so.

Could he show Wonngu and a party of warriors the way?

At this, Arabanoo grew nervous and began tapping his knee in agitation. Everyone knew the mountains were inhabited by a savage and merciless tribe and he was afraid to venture into their territory without the protection of Clancy and his magic fire-stick.

'We will be too strong for these savages,' Wonngu said, in as calm a voice as he could muster. 'But we must go there, for I believe that is where we will find Murremurran.'

'Why don't we just let him go?' Arabanoo said, voicing a common feeling. 'Berak must be dead by now. Murremurran is sick. Why don't we let him waste away rather than put more men at risk?'

'Because of my friend Clancy,' Wonngu said and, without explaining further, rose to prepare himself for the journey.

THIRTY-SIX

THERE WERE TIMES on the journey back to the Hawkesbury when Clancy thought of staying on the eastern side of the river, of riding back towards Sydney and playing the part of William Clancy, gentleman, adventurer and wealthy horse fancier from Cape Province. It was the role that tempted him. He would make such a fine William Clancy. Better, more colourful, more engaging than the original. The letter from sister Ruth had said William must tell her of his adventures. His adventures. What wonderful tales he could spin about life in Africa. He'd been to Africa, although he wasn't let off the ship, of course, but he'd been on deck for an hour of exercise and he'd seen the big table-topped mountain and the black people, bigger and stronger than the Aborigines of New South Wales, carrying all the supplies on board. But he'd heard people talk about Africa, particularly one-legged Charlie Simms who used to drink in the pub at Bridgwater when Clancy was only a lad and had had a job there for a few weeks, helping in the cellar and cleaning out the stables. Old Charlie had been a sailor. Many times he'd sailed to Africa, or so he said, and had been to the Cape of Good Hope and even to an African island with the wonderful name of Zanzibar.

Charlie Simms spoke of Hottentots—what wonderful images he floated before young Clancy's dreamy eyes—and of giant negroes with spears and shields made of animal hide and with feathers around their ankles and, if the other drinkers gave him a tot or two of rum, he'd get up on his one leg and hop around, like the big blackfellows danced, and everyone would roar with laughter. When he talked about the island of Zanzibar, he told stories of Sultans and Arabs and slaves and the men in the pub would listen for hours and buy him more drinks and leave their scraps for him to eat. He was a generous old fellow and sometimes gave Clancy a few bones that still had meat on them.

Clancy would tell better stories than old Charlie Simms or the recently deceased William Lowerdale Clancy. He'd recount enthralling accounts of the life of a gentleman adventurer in Africa: of how he fought the Hottentots, explored the hinterland with twenty slaves to carry his guns, shot fierce lions, did his bit to build the Empire. What fun it would be to play the part of a gentleman of substance in such a rough, young, gullible town as Sydney. He'd have people lapping up his words, admiring his clothes, plying him with food and drink, ogling his horse.

But there were problems. What if he encountered someone who knew the real William Clancy? What if men recognised the horse, even if not the rider? Surely people would already be talking about Cortez, there being so few horses in the colony and probably none that matched this magnificent animal? They'd know that one man had ridden it out of town but another had brought it back.

He might get away with the deception for a few days, a week perhaps. Then he'd be found out, questioned, arrested and hanged.

He laughed. It would have been fun. Zanzibar. He shouted the word and Ulla looked at him, not understanding but smiling when he smiled. She was always reluctant to offend and anxious to please, which was good in a female.

371

He should get back over the mountains. In his heart he wanted to get back, to be with Eliza, to be there when the baby was born. It was true that he hadn't thought about her much—there hadn't been much time, he mumbled aloud, defensively answering the barbs of some ghostly accuser—but now that he thought about her, he truly missed her and was worried about her.

But no more than that. He now realised, with great clarity and for the first time since they had been living together like man and wife, that, much as he had grown to like Eliza, enjoyed her company, relished the lovemaking and liked to spend some time with her, his real love was for the unconstrained, adventurous, nomadic life he could have with the tribe.

He didn't want to spend all his life with her in the hut. He was a man who could never settle down.

The rain had gone and the days were hot and almost insufferably humid as the sun drew back the moisture given so lavishly to the land. Insects hummed and throbbed and cicadas chirped, so that every step was to nature's drumbeat. Trees that had been bent and withered now stood straight and wore the bright green fuzz of sprouting leaves. The paddocks were alive with birds fossicking for delicacies left by the deluge and the air was filled with their chatter. To their left, a grassy hill was whitened by a flock of grazing cockatoos, to their right a marsh lay ringed by a pink and grey boundary of galahs and ahead, a stand of trees was ablaze with the crimson flashes of resting rosellas, as thick and bright as an abundance of ripe fruit.

Several times Clancy and Ulla met people coming from the flood. They were impressed by Clancy's dress and were deferential to him, and all admired the horse although none dared approach it. They talked of the devastation at the settlement, of the ruined lives and the acres of sour mud where once houses and farms had been. But they said what Clancy hoped to hear: the river level was dropping.

Clancy rode occasionally, hoping to become accustomed to the horse and improve his skill in the saddle, but after only an hour of joggling and jarring and battering his buttocks, he would dismount and walk, to ease the pain and get his cramped leg muscles working again. Why did people choose to ride when horses were such rough, contrary animals? Cortez could not be persuaded to travel at anything less than a trot, which not only shook Clancy from teeth to toes but caused Ulla to drop far behind.

He fell only once but, luckily, it happened out of sight of the girl. So, for most of the journey they walked, with Clancy leading the horse and whistling, for he had a feeling of supreme contentment, while Ulla followed behind with Clancy's bag slung over her shoulder.

She was still in awe of the horse although no longer afraid of it. She had never seen such a large animal and spent hours admiring its graceful step, yet wondered how it could be that a creature with such a thick, muscular rump—greater than any she had seen on any creature—should have such slender legs. It had a tail like finely shredded bark and such strange, hard feet. She would study their curved imprints in the dust and think how easy it would be for a hunting party to track such a quarry. She was fascinated by its droppings, which Cortez, eating much grass on the way, deposited with great frequency and which she, travelling near its tail, was well placed to observe.

'They are so big,' she would squeal, comparing them to the pellet-like droppings of the largest animal she knew, the plains kangaroo. Sometimes, she would take a stick and prod the deposit but this made Clancy angry.

'You must not do that,' he would say. 'It is not good.'

This astonished her, for animals were tracked by their

droppings and everyone studied them, to discover how fresh was the trail and to estimate the size of the beast. Examining droppings—animal or human—was one of the first things she could recall doing as a little girl.

She asked a question that had been worrying her. 'Can you eat it?'

He stopped. 'The manure?'

'The horse.'

People ate horse, he knew, but he had to be careful what he said. Cortez had enough meat on him to feed the tribe for several days and he knew they regarded animals, not as beasts of burden or as pets, but as objects to be eaten.

'No,' he said. 'The spirit of the horse would make men go crazy.'

She seemed to think this was a logical answer and nodded sagely. She said, 'Are there any more like this animal?'

He hesitated. He didn't like lying to this girl and said, 'I haven't seen any.' In recent times, he thought.

'Could there be others?'

'Anything is possible.'

She was carrying a long, thin stick and began to tap Cortez on the rump. It made the horse do a nervous, shuffling dance and she enjoyed that until, testing the limits of tolerance, she hit too hard and the horse kicked and she had to jump out of the way.

'He's troubled by the flies,' Clancy said without turning.

'Flies are bad,' she said and, being a girl only thirteen years of age, tapped Cortez on the rump once more.

They came to the Hawkesbury two days later, well upstream from The Green Hills and not far from the site where Clancy and Eliza had first waded across the river. Ulla made a crude raft from flood debris, then undressed, packing her clothes in

Clancy's wheat sack. He took off the boots and coat but wore the hat, being reluctant to destroy its shape by squeezing it into the bag. They launched the raft at a place where the river was wide but the current slower. While Ulla stood at the front, pushing with a pole to propel them forwards and counter the sideways drift of the current, Clancy sat at the back, holding the reins to pull the horse after them and marvelling at the way Cortez immediately and naturally began to swim once they reached deep water. The horse was not afraid of water; a little timid at first, perhaps, but certainly used to swimming. Clancy wondered if he might have ridden across. That would have been a wonderful experience, even in bare feet. He resolved that, when he became more expert in the saddle, he would ride Cortez across a river somewhere on the far side of the mountains. Now that was an exciting prospect: galloping into a stream, water splashing high, man and animal crossing at unbelievable speed. He would do it for Wonngu. The old man would be impressed.

Near the far bank the raft was rammed by a floating log and began to fall apart but by then they were in shallow water and thus were able to jump clear and wade ashore. Concerned that someone might have seen them, Clancy pressed on immediately. By nightfall they were near the beginning of his track across the Blue Mountains.

Delbung washed the baby constantly, carrying water from the stream in a bark coolamon to bathe it but it remained pink—a little lighter perhaps than when she had been born and certainly less wrinkled, which had given the impression that the skin was striped—but the hair was red. There was no doubt. It was a red baby.

'Isn't she beautiful?' Eliza would say every time the baby was washed and dried and handed to her. She was weak but happy and ravenously hungry and longed for bread or beef; anything other than the delicacies Delbung had been feeding her which were fat grubs and a type of small lizard that she grilled on a stick and had an oily, salty taste.

On this morning, when the sun was hot and the drone of blowflies filled the hut, Eliza sat on the edge of the bed, trying to feed the baby, fanning her cherubic face to keep the flies away. Little milk was coming and Delbung appeared at the doorway with a short, fat woman who was feeding a newborn baby herself. She had pendulous breasts, one of which Delbung lifted to show Eliza.

'This woman got plenty milk. Be good for baby.' And maybe turn it black, she thought. She'd seen a lot of light-coloured babies (although never white nor red) that turned the correct shade with only a few weeks of good feeding.

'I'll feed her myself,' Eliza said, looking in horror at the woman who stood there, smiling helpfully as Delbung displayed first one, then the other of her well-filled breasts. They were not the same size, Eliza noted and turned her head.

'Thank her but kindly take her away.'

'Baby hungry.'

'I will feed my baby.'

Delbung took the woman outside.

'It is true,' the woman said. 'The baby has hair the colour of fire.'

'It is so ugly.' Delbung shook her head sadly.

'Maybe it will die,' the other woman said hopefully.

'Where did you get such lovely hair?' Eliza said, gently stroking the baby's head. Who in her family had red hair? Not her aunt, nor her mother. She knew little about her grandparents. Her aunt never mentioned her father's side of the family at all, as though there was some disgrace there. Maybe that's where the red hair was. People who did disgraceful things often had red hair although Meg, the convict woman who'd been such a good friend, had flaming red hair and she was nice. Outrageous in some ways and wicked in others, but good at heart.

Red hair could be on Clancy's side. He had the colouring, with his fair skin and an inclination to sunburn, which gave him a ruddy complexion. She wondered how he would react on seeing his daughter and spent several minutes, eyes closed, imagining his arrival.

He would stride through the door with a spring in his step, anxious to tell her about his adventures on the far side of the mountains . . . he wouldn't see the baby at first . . . just Eliza sitting on the edge of the bed, her hair neatly parted with the comb of fishbone that Delbung had made and her face freshly washed and shining with love. And then, when he was halfway across the floor, he would come to a stop, his jaw would drop and he would stammer . . .

'Eliza, what is it? What has happened?'

'It's a baby, silly.' She would hold out their daughter. 'It's a girl, a beautiful girl.'

And he would have tears in his eyes and he'd probably drop to his knees to give thanks . . . no, not Clancy . . . he would stagger a little and then rush to her side, grasp her by the hands and tell her how much he loved her and kiss her so much she would laugh and finally have to tell him to stop it. Then he would stand back and, in a moment of total silence, she would hand him their child . . . his daughter.

She touched the nose, the ears, the perfect lips. 'You are such a lovely baby.' The girl slept. She spoke to it for a long time, smoothing a sticky spot on one eyelash, using her fingernail to scrape a flake of dried skin from the scalp. The baby made a whimpering sound and seemed about to cry but settled back to sleep in her mother's arms.

She wasn't drinking enough and Eliza felt bad, guilty that she didn't have the bountiful, fountain-like breasts of that terrible woman Delbung had brought for her inspection. But she was trying and, God willing, she would soon produce enough milk and the baby would suck hard, and then things would be wonderful.

She lay back with the baby in one arm and fell asleep.

Delbung entered the room, took the baby and carried it outside. The squat woman with the large breasts was waiting.

'Here,' she said, handing the girl to the other woman. 'Give it a proper drink.'

It was many years since Wonngu had led a hunting party, let alone one whose purpose was to kill human quarry, but he marched at a resolute pace, knowing the others would be watching him keenly. He did not intend to take charge of the attack when they found Murremurran. He was wise enough to know his days as a fighter were over, but he was still the one to plan the most effective strategy and prevent some of the hotheads from rushing into a trap that the wily Murremurran might lay for them. Much as he disliked Murremurran, he had respect for his cunning. The man knew he would be followed. And, if the potion that the sorcerer had given him was truly wearing off, he would have regained much of his formidable strength and fighting prowess.

It was around noon on the second day of their journey that Arabanoo found the trail. He had brought the others to the place where he and Berak entered the mountains with Clancy. Now the men waited while he scouted the area, conscious that he was being tested in front of the tribe's finest warriors. The first sign he found was a fractured branch on a small shrub. It was about thirty paces up the climb. The sap had dried at the break although the tip of the branch was still supple, so the branch had been damaged for only a few days. He examined the angle of the break. It had, he thought, been deliberately snapped, which meant Berak had done it.

There was no other sign nearby but he went further up the hill and found faint marks where weeds had been crushed at the base of a large rock. Someone had slipped, he deduced, and landed heavily. He crouched down to touch the weeds and the earth around them.

Wonngu had come up behind him. 'Not a kangaroo or wombat?'

'No. All other marks have been brushed away.' He smoothed the dirt with his fingers. 'It is too even. And animals do not brush the ground behind them.'

Wonngu turned and took a deep breath. So Murremurran was following Clancy's track, which meant Berak was alive but being forced to show him the way. What was Murremurran's plan? Did he intend to go to the place where the white spirits lived? Or was he heading into the mountains, to wait for Clancy's return?

Clancy was already late and a terrible fear filled him. Supposing Murremurran had done some harm to this man who was his friend, his spirit relative and who had brought such good fortune to the tribe?

He was inclined to move quickly in case Murremurran had not yet intercepted Clancy but if Murremurran was setting a trap for the white man, they themselves could blunder into it. For several minutes he sat on the ground and covered his face while the men, anxious to get on with the hunt now they had found the trail, gathered in small groups and whispered to each other, waiting for their leader to decide what they should do.

Wonngu stood, conscious that he moved stiffly these days and hoping the men would not take it as a sign of frailty. It was important that they thought him strong, so they would do exactly as he said. He raised his spear high in the air.

'I believe Berak is still alive,' he announced. 'I believe Murremurran is setting a trap for Ker-lan-see. We must stop him. We must try to rescue Berak and we must save Ker-lan-see from the evil that Murremurran is planning. But we must not rush blindly on, or we will fall into Murremurran's trap.' There were murmurings of agreement.

'I believe he will set his trap not here, where he might expect to find a hunting party searching for him, but deep in the mountains, where none of us but Berak and Arabanoo have ever been.' There were more murmurs and nervous glances at the densely forested ridges that towered above them.

Wonngu then ordered Arabanoo to go on ahead, following the trail with two warriors. Another two would follow behind, far enough back to be out of sight. Then another two. Then would come the whole of the hunting party.

'We must assume that Murremurran is now well and strong again. Therefore he will be a formidable and cunning opponent. Take care. Be prepared for any trick.'

Arabanoo was trembling with fear and Wonngu went up to him and touched his shoulder. 'Yours is a great responsibility. Only you know the way. Therefore, the lives of Berak and Ker-lan-see are in your hands. Be careful. Be brave. Be quick.'

With his spear he pointed to two older warriors. Both were lean, finely muscled men and skilled hunters. 'Go with Arabanoo.'

The three left, bent in poses of extreme caution as they began to climb Clancy's track.

THIRTY-SEVEN

AFTER RETRIEVING HIS musket, Clancy sought a different way to scale the first ridge in the mountain range. The initial part of his crossing was too steep for the horse and so loose-surfaced that the animal might fall and break a leg. Surveying, testing, often retreating, the climb took a day. However, once over the ridge and able to rejoin the original route, the going was surprisingly simple. The big Spanish thoroughbred moved easily through timbered country and there were no hills too steep for it to climb, no descent too intimidating, even when horse and new master were forced to slither down slopes in a cascade of loose stones and chopped dirt.

Only when they came to the wide patch of scrub that guarded the way to the rounded mountain did Clancy have to take out the dead man's tomahawk and cut a higher and wider path than he or Ulla needed. This task, exhausting in the stifling heat, took almost two days and they spent a night among the tangle of menacing branches, with neither sleeping and Cortez fretting from the lack of water.

By now the girl was able to lead the horse—and the horse was willing to let her do so—and thus, while Clancy chopped a path, Ulla guided Cortez through the tunnel in the scrub. The animal found the girl's presence soothing. No longer did she tease it with a stick but would stroke it behind the ear and utter a symphony of soft ululation whenever there was a pause in a place of sinister shadows or the thud of the axe caused it to quiver in distress.

At the start of the climb Clancy had removed his long coat because of the heat. He'd also taken off the wide-brimmed hat, which was becoming his most prized possession, to prevent it being plucked from his head by a succession of grasping branches. Now he removed his shirt, too, and when they emerged from the barrier, the hides of humans and animal alike were striated with scratches. But a few scratches were nothing for Clancy because he was proud to have got through with his horse. His horse. The ordeal in the scrub had made him even more possessive of this magnificent creature. William Lowerdale Clancy would never have got Cortez up the mountains, let alone through such an obstacle.

He was proud also of the quality of his other acquisitions, boasting to an uncomprehending Ulla that, while the saddle-bags bore the marks of many jagged encounters, none was ripped, so strong was the leather. Such quality reflected on the taste of the owner, he told her, the inference being that he was talking about the present owner, not the departed WLC. He fingered the elaborate saddle, removing a twig that was caught on the pommel, fitted the hat at a jaunty angle and folded the coat with great care, putting it in the saddlebag that now had the musket thrust under its flap.

She was pleased to see him so content.

'I feel like riding,' he announced when the sun was still an hour from the end of its day's journey, but suggested—so that she wouldn't be left behind—that Ulla should walk in front and lead the horse with the extra leather strap, whose purpose he still hadn't guessed.

'Tomorrow, I will ride the horse again,' he said and she wondered when she would have sufficient courage to ask him if she, too, could get on the horse's back. There would be room for both, with him in the saddle and her on the rump. In that way, she could put her arms around his waist.

It was the next morning. Murremurran heard a sound. A strange noise, like sticks being broken underfoot. Not by a human but by an animal—and a large, heavy animal at that, and one that was indiscreet in the way it covered the ground. He was intrigued, never having heard a sound like it. Now came a regular noise, a kind of clicking or clopping. What on earth was it?

Then he heard a laugh. A girl's laugh, surely?

Berak was tied to the tree and sat in his own filth. Still dazed from the beating and close to exhaustion from lack of food, he lifted his head.

'What is it?' Murremurran hissed but Berak could do no more than moan.

'Quiet.' Murremurran could hear other sounds. Eyes darting up and down the track, confused by an onslaught of alarms after days of silence, he had heard a voice but it came from the other direction. It was a man's voice, muted but calling out to someone. He thrust his hand over Berak's mouth, then bound the young man's jaw with the bark strap. He picked up the two fighting spears, thrust the stone club into his belt and crept towards the outer line in the thicket of trees.

The clip-clop sound grew stronger, the laughter more intense.

And from the other direction came a shout, then others, but the sounds were a long way away. He crouched, confused and frightened.

From out of the scrub, and with the morning sun still so low as to dazzle his eyes, came a bizarre creature. A huge brown animal, with four legs and with hair covering its neck and tail, was prancing towards him and on its back, or joined to it, were two people. One was a white man, the other black. No, the black person was a girl who was holding on to the man and squealing with delight as the animal moved in an amazing way, dancing first to one side, then the other. He looked again at the man, whose face was in shade, partly hidden by an enormous hat.

He raised a hand to shield his eyes from the sun.

Clancy.

And he wasn't carrying his firestick.

Confused by the strange and fierce looking animal but emboldened by Clancy's lack of a gun, Murremurran stood clear of the trees and raised a spear.

'Ker-lan-see!'

Clancy stopped and looked up.

'You are not a god, not a ghost. You die.' Murremurran threw the spear.

He threw hard and straight. The spear struck Clancy in the chest. He reeled under the impact and fell from the horse. Then he stood and, with both hands, pulled the spear out. He threw it on the ground.

'Want to try again?' he shouted, holding both arms out and facing Murremurran on the rise above him. Laughing, he went to a saddlebag and withdrew the musket.

Murremurran dropped his other spear and ran away.

Ulla slid from the horse's rump. Cortez galloped down the track.

Suddenly sweating, legs shaking, Clancy slumped to the ground. He put his hand on the Bible inside his shirt and felt the jagged hole in its wooden cover.

Arabanoo ran back down the track, knowing his two companions were dead and ducking as another spear whistled past. Then another, which rattled in the branches of a tree above him. In desperation he called out to the two men who were supposed to be following close behind. Where were they, and could they hold back the war party that had attacked them?

384

Another spear flew past him. It stuck in the ground and in swerving to avoid it, he tripped. Scrambling to his feet, he saw a man hiding behind a tree. It was Bulladerry, his father's friend, a fabled hunter who could put a spear through a kangaroo's chest at fifty paces. The man's eyes were fixed on the pursuing blacks, right arm poised to throw one of his spears. From the other side of the narrow track a hand reached out to pull Arabanoo behind a tree. It was another of the tribe, a younger man who could hurl a spear even further than Bulladerry. These were the men Wonngu had sent as a follow-up party.

'There are many of them,' Arabanoo gasped. 'Mountain people. They've killed . . .'

Before he could finish, the young man pushed him aside and darted into the open. Grunting with exertion, stretching his legs until he was almost kneeling, twisting his body in a frantic burst of energy and swinging his shoulder to put maximum thrust into the throw, he launched his spear with lustful savagery. He was back behind the tree before Arabanoo heard the cry that meant the weapon had found its target.

Bulladerry hurled his spear too, using a woomera to put venom into the throw and there was another scream of pain, then shouts of confusion.

'Come,' said Bulladerry and ran down the track, with Arabanoo and the younger man racing after him.

'They were waiting for us,' Arabanoo gasped as he ran. They came to a stand of tall eucalypts, where Bulladerry signalled for them to stop and stand absolutely still among the massive trunks.

'Where are they?' Arabanoo asked, peeking from behind a tree whose bark hung in strips. 'What are they doing?'

'Trying to decide how many of us there are.'

'I counted twenty of them. There may be more.'

A stone landed at Bulladerry's feet and he spun around.

Behind them, crouched low as he made his way through the speckled shadows, was a warrior from Wonngu's main group. Others followed, moving silently through the trees. Arabanoo counted. Twelve men.

Wonngu joined them, bent forward with one hand touching the grass, covering the ground like a crab.

'Is it Murremurran?'

Arabanoo shook his head. 'We ran into a war party.' He was still perplexed and pointed to the east. 'They were going the other way. They were not after us. We thought we were safe but one of their men, travelling far behind the others, saw us.'

'Where are your companions?'

'Dead. We had no chance.'

Wonngu shook his head. 'We have no cause to fight these people.'

Bulladerry, a second spear ready in his hand, said, 'It is too late for talk,' and then stepped out to make his throw because six men, painted for combat, had begun to rush down the track.

A shower of spears from the front rank of Wonngu's men met them and the three survivors stopped, stared momentarily at their writhing comrades, and ducked for shelter. A great howling came from the bush.

'They are angry,' Bulladerry said.

'There are more than twenty of them,' Wonngu said and looked around for a better place to defend than this open grove.

They heard the whistle of spears that had been tossed high, more in anger than in hope, and hurriedly sought shelter as the missiles thudded and twanged against the trees.

Wonngu pointed to Bulladerry and Arabanoo. 'You watch, the rest of you hide. Stay out of sight.'

Another lethal shower fell.

'They're coming,' Arabanoo shouted, and Wonngu, not quite settled behind a stout eucalypt, glanced around the trunk. Ten men were coming down the path, not running, but advancing steadily. The leading two carried shields of bark.

'Let them come closer,' he said.

More men followed the first group.

'Eighteen,' Wonngu said and thought again about retreat.

He heard shouts from those still in hiding behind the advancing ranks of the war party. 'Quick, throw,' he commanded, wondering what was causing all the noise, and as the spears were launched, he heard the sound of timber snapping and a strange drumming as if the earth was shaking. As one man, the eighteen mountain warriors stopped and looked behind them.

Two fell to the spears.

Through the bush burst Cortez.

Nostrils flaring, mouth flecked with foam, the horse bolted through the back row of tribesmen, scattering bodies with its flashing hoofs and great battering ram of a chest. When it reached the front line, it stopped, rearing high, thrashing with its front legs and whinnying like a demon.

The warriors ran.

The horse dashed forward but saw Wonngu's men and circled in terror, rearing on its hind legs, tossing its head to whip bushes with the loose reins, scything the air with its fearsome hoofs.

The fleeing mountain warriors were out of sight, somewhere beyond the far bushes, when a shot rang out. Its echoes tore through an eerie silence which was followed by a loud wailing, a sound that gathered strength like the surge of an ocean wave. And then came the crunch of dead leaves and breaking sticks as the mountain men began running wildly, indiscriminately, through the bush.

Wonngu's men stayed within the trees, fascinated by the noises, seeing no sign of their enemies but fearfully watching the horse buck and lash out with its legs.

'What is this demon?' Bulladerry was pulling his hair,

convinced the doors of Hell had opened to release this monster.

'Not a demon.' Wonngu moved clear of the trees to get a better view. He knew what the gunshot meant and spread his arms to calm his men. 'This,' he announced, 'is Ker-lan-see's work. It is a miracle.'

Numb with shock, feeling horribly vulnerable, Clancy stood in the open, holding the smoking musket and wondering where the devil all the warriors had gone. One moment they were charging him, screaming and shaking their weapons and then, with only one shot—which had hit one of the leading men in the leg, he thought—they had all turned and gone running blindly through the bush.

He began the agonisingly slow process of reloading, glancing about him in case the blacks attacked again and cursing his fingers which shook so badly he kept spilling gunpowder. If only the horse had stayed, he could get the tomahawk and defend himself. He rammed down the wad, dropped in an iron ball. He vowed that next time he went across the mountains, he'd get another musket. Maybe two. He could teach Ulla how to reload so that when he fired he would always have another gun ready. This was too slow. The blacks would be out of the bushes and upon him long before he was ready to fire again.

Down with the final wad which he tamped in place. He dropped the ramrod on the ground, wiped his face and cocked the musket ready for firing.

Wheezing for breath, he looked around him. He could hear noises, but they seemed to be of people running away.

Where the devil was the horse? He called its name then lifted his face to the sky and, in desperation, roared out, 'Cortez. Come here you big brown bastard. Cor-tez!'

To his astonishment, the horse appeared. It hobbled through a patch of tall grass at the end of the track, with one front leg tangled in the reins.

'Where did you come from?' He laughed but the horse swished its tail and stamped a back foot. There was no sign of recognition. Its eyes were ablaze with fear.

Clancy moved a few steps towards it, clicking his fingers, making the noises the draughthorses liked, all the while scanning the countryside for some sign of the blacks. Cortez backed away.

'What have they done to you, boy, eh?' A few more clicks of the fingers. Some soft whistling. Another glance at the bush. The sound of men running through the scrub was fading.

The horse tried to run and, with one leg caught, almost fell.

'Don't do that or you'll hurt yourself.' He moved closer. It lifted its head in a sudden movement that dragged the front leg off the ground.

Clancy stood still, leaning on the musket. 'If you want me to fix it, I will,' he said. 'But you've got to come to me.' He waited. The horse didn't move.

'Well, just this time, I'll come to you.'

Slowly, whistling all the time, Clancy advanced, stopping every now and then when Cortez seemed agitated.

It occurred to him then that the horse must have seen the blacks, may even have been attacked by them. He searched its flanks for signs of injury. There were no spears projecting from its hide, no new cuts.

'They didn't hurt you, did they?' he said, cooing the words as he moved ever closer until he could reach out and touch it. 'Well now, are you all right?' He stroked its neck and, in the same action, caught hold of the reins. He patted it again. 'Thought I'd lost you,' he said, and bent to free the animal's leg.

At that moment, Wonngu appeared through the long grass.

'Is it yours?' Wonngu called out. 'And did you send this monster to save us?'

Clancy took a deep breath. 'Yes.'

Wonngu fell on his knees.

THIRTY-EIGHT

THEY WERE ABOUT to leave the area, all in the group being anxious to depart before the inevitable return of the mountain men. According to Wonngu, the others must soon regain their courage, or at least have their curiosity sufficiently rekindled to come back for a secretive look at the strange beast and, perhaps, to count the enemy. The members of the war party would immediately realise they outnumbered the intruders and would fling a few spears from the safety of the dense bush edging the track. A massacre could follow, even allowing for the presence of the demoniac animal and Clancy's firestick. Urging his men to hurry, Wonngu had them gather their fallen weapons, plus the bodies of the two men who had escorted Arabanoo. But at the moment of departure Ulla arrived with Berak.

Still in shock from the appearance of the animal that Clancy now led by the nose, Wonngu had been concentrating on the need to retreat. He had forgotten about Ulla. So had Clancy.

She was half-carrying Berak and dragged him, legs trailing in the dust, into the middle of the group. There, with her father's sense of the theatrical, she laid him on the ground. His arrival caused further consternation because of the tale he now told.

Rising on one arm, he said he had seen Murremurran try to kill the white man. He had heard Murremurran vow that the

390

white man was a normal human, not a ghost or a supernatural being. He had seen Murremurran's spear pierce the white man's body. But there had been no blood, no injury, even though with his own eyes he had seen Clancy have difficulty in removing the spear, so deeply was it embedded in his side.

And he had seen Clancy throw down the spear and laughingly challenge Murremurran to hurl another one.

A murmur of admiration spread through the men, for they loved tales of daring and heroic challenge.

Murremurran had run away, with the look of a madman in his eyes.

There was a rumble of laughter. The noise stirred Wonngu into action. Time for talk later. They must move or risk being slaughtered like unwary kangaroos gathered at a waterhole.

Someone carried Berak. He wanted to continue talking but was incoherent. Wonngu walked beside him, giving him an occasional sip of water and patting him on the shoulder, to make sure he understood he was back with his tribe.

Ulla said nothing. She had seen the Bible but didn't know what it meant. Had it saved her man's life? Was it something Clancy had put there, knowing he would be attacked and knowing the precise place where the spear would hit? Would its absence have made any difference?

He could bleed. She had seen him scratched and bleeding when they were in the scrub. She had seen him overwhelmed by the three white men. She had seen the man with the horse killed and he had bled profusely.

There were questions about white men too difficult for her to contemplate, let alone answer. One day she might ask her father what everything meant. She would not speak to him now. He was euphoric, rejoicing in their humiliating victory over these mountain people, marvelling at the miracle of the horse and the firing of the gun and, now, at the story of Clancy's impregnability. It justified all he had been saying about the white man. No, it was certainly not the right time to mention the Bible or to cast doubts on her father's strongest beliefs.

As they hurried back down the track, forbidden to talk for fear of attracting the war party, she found herself thinking what a shame it was that Murremurran had appeared on that morning. She and Clancy had been having a wild, wonderful ride on Cortez, with the animal trotting through the bush, flattening scrub and travelling at an unbelievable pace, and they had both been laughing with the joy of a special moment.

She liked being with Clancy. She wondered when he would take her as his full-time woman, and sleep with her and let her have his babies.

They travelled through the night, with two of the best trackers leading the way and Bulladerry and his friend, who had proved themselves in combat that morning, forming the rearguard to ensure the tribe was not followed in its flight from the mountains.

Clancy walked with the horse in the middle of the line. No one dared come near him until, just before dawn, Wonngu approached as they were crossing a wide stretch of grass where Clancy had stopped to let the horse graze.

'What do you call your animal?'

'Horse.' Cortez was a private name, one that only he and possibly Ulla would use, when training the animal.

'Orse?'

'Ker-lan-see's orse.' He liked the longer title.

So did Wonngu, who repeated the name several times, peeking shyly at the horse in the faint light. 'Very good.'

He mimicked the horse kicking and rearing. 'Good fighter,' he added, hoping Clancy might add some details to explain its extraordinary behaviour, but when he stayed silent Wonngu gave such a good imitation of its frantic whinny that Cortez was startled and Clancy had to tighten his grip on the leather strap.

'Where he come from?'

'Same place as me.' Clancy could see the answer puzzled the old man.

'Same mother?'

'No.' He shook his head without a hint of a smile. 'Same place. Over the mountains and far away. Over the big water.'

'What big water?'

Clancy spread his arms wide. 'Over the mountains there is much big water. We call it "the sea". On it are ships. Boats.' Wonngu was not following. 'Big canoes.'

'Ah. Did Ker-lan-see's orse come in big canoe?'

'Yes.'

Clancy tried to imagine the picture Wonngu was forming in his mind.

Wonngu pulled at his grey beard. 'What does a red baby mean?'

It was Clancy's turn to be puzzled. 'How do you mean?'

'Good thing or bad thing?'

'Well, I've never seen a red baby.' He gripped Wonngu by the wrist. 'Has Eliza had a baby?'

'Yes,' he said, not thinking it strange that he hadn't mentioned it during the previous day or through the night. Men's women were always having babies.

'And it's red?'

'Red skin, red hair.'

Clancy put back his head and laughed. 'The devil it has. Red hair, you say?'

'And red skin.'

'I think you mean pink.' He pulled Wonngu closer. 'What is it?'

Wonngu had forgotten and had to ask one of his men. 'A girl. Your woman has had a red girl. We have never seen such a thing.'

393

'Is she beautiful?'

Wonngu covered his mouth before answering. How could he tell the truth?

'She is an amazing sight.'

Clancy couldn't stop laughing. 'And Eliza. Is she well?'

She must be extremely distressed, Wonngu thought, but said, 'Yes. Delbung says she is well.' The horse flicked its tail and Wonngu jumped clear. When the horse was grazing once more, he said, 'You must tell me, Ker-lan-see. What is the meaning of red baby? Is it good sign, an omen of good times, or is it bad sign?'

'Your people are worried?'

'Yes. The women cry and make terrible noises ever since baby was born.'

'Tell them not to worry. A red baby is wonderful. The best omen you could wish for.'

He repeated that several times until he was sure Wonngu understood, then watched as the old man dashed among his men, shouting the good news. And despite being near exhaustion from the forced march, they rattled their spears and clapped their hands against their legs.

Ulla had been travelling with Berak. She walked up to Clancy.

'Eliza has had a baby girl.' He grinned. 'According to your father, a red girl.'

He was laughing and Ulla covered her mouth. The poor man. The sooner he had normal children, the better.

It was only a tiny ball that had been fired into Nilssen's side but the man was near death for several days. Around the time that a surgeon dug the metal from the Swede's ribs, an officer of the New South Wales Corps came to see Noxious Watts.

The story he'd heard was that Watts and his two friends had been attacked by bushrangers on the road from The Green

Hills. Several attacks had been reported in that region.

Watts had to be careful. He and Kerrigan had robbed two individual travellers before they'd reached Parramatta and he'd been avoiding the soldiers. But here was his chance.

He described how he and his companions had been attacked while they slept on the side of the road. There were several men. Three, he thought. And a black boy.

'So they have a gun?'

'Some sort of hand gun. We couldn't see. It was dark.'

'Did you recognise any of the men?'

Watts sighed. No self-respecting ex-convict would incriminate a former mate.

'Come, come, Watts. They damned near killed your friend.'

'I thought he was dead,' Watts answered, his eyes glazed by dreamy recollections.

'Who?'

'The same man who murdered the guard and that poor soldier up on the river a year or so ago. Clancy Fitzgerald.'

It was many years since Captain John Hunter had lost the *Sirius* in a storm off Norfolk Island but, despite that disaster, the Governor of New South Wales still yearned to be back at sea. He felt comfortable in its rolling vastness but, increasingly, was finding the land to be reefed with hazards. He'd now been Governor for four years and there was no doubt that people were conspiring against him, people who were more concerned with their own mercenary interests than the future of His Majesty's newest and most remote colony. He heard talk accusing him of incompetence and of countenancing graft and corruption. The instigator, he was sure, was that wretch John Macarthur, who was complaining to all who would listen that Hunter was running the colony to suit the voracious appetites for profit of the officers of the New South Wales Corps and making life impossible for the free settlers and traders. Which meant, Hunter believed, that Macarthur wasn't making enough money himself. One day the man would go further than merely talk, he feared, for Macarthur had powerful friends in London and would run to them with his tales and there could be some back home who might believe his scurrilous charges.

Hunter had been a loyal servant of the Crown, always done his duty, never been concerned with personal gain and, while he'd sometimes been accused of being stodgy and unadventurous, he had always been an industrious and fair man who had tried to steer the fledgling colony on a course that would see it become a useful outpost of the Empire. Certainly more than a mere repository for England's unwanted convicts.

Curse the convicts. Along with Mr Macarthur and his kind, they were the bane of his life. If they weren't being rebellious and lazy, or wasting their leisure hours in gaming and in drinking themselves into a stupor, they were causing him to worry about their well-being, for he was a man of extreme compassion; he would admit to that charge. Take the latest news. The Reverend Samuel Marsden, in his role as magistrate, had sentenced an Irish convict to 1,000 lashes. Undoubtedly the man deserved punishment and had displayed the insolence which was a hallmark of the race, but 1,000 strokes of the whip? No man could endure such punishment, not with Marsden supervising the whipping to ensure each stroke was delivered with venom. If the convict was as stubborn as most of the Irish, he would allow himself to be beaten into unconsciousness, with a few curses and cries of protest but certainly no call for mercy. He might endure 100 to 150 strokes. Then, unconscious and with his back raw, he would be dragged away until he had recovered sufficiently to be hauled back to the whipping post some days later, when the count would resume. This time, he might last for fifty to seventy-five lashes, by which time his body would spray the earth with blood and his brain would be addled by pain. He would still not beg for mercy. The whole process could take a month or more, until the wretch died.

It was a waste of time and all that would happen would be that the man would become a martyr, and an Irish martyr was the last thing the colony needed.

Hunter was handed a note and the messenger, aware of its contents, was astonished when the Governor laughed.

'I'll be damned,' he said and turned to the soldier. 'And the woman was there, too?'

'The man Watts thinks there might have been a woman in the background, yes, sir.'

Hunter rolled the paper and used it to scratch his nose. 'I must write to de Lacey,' he said, his mouth still crinkled in a smile. 'I think that poor man might be inclined to forget the French and come back here to resume his crusade.'

Later that day Hunter forgot about John Macarthur, Samuel Marsden and Clancy Fitzgerald. The whaler *Rebecca* reached Port Jackson with the much delayed news of Horatio Nelson's great victory over the French fleet at the Nile.

Hunter ordered that all artillery be fired in a salute to Nelson's triumph. There was much revelry and rejoicing in the streets of Sydney Town. The battle may have been fought half a world away but the result was felt keenly in the colony, for every defeat of Napoleon's forces meant there was less likelihood of the French bothering to attack such a distant target as New South Wales, a prize ready to be taken by even the most modest force the French could muster.

When the celebrations were over and the last drunks had crawled back to their huts, the Governor found the note about Clancy Fitzgerald and the Phillips woman and wrote a letter to

Quinton de Lacey, care of his mother in England. It was the only address he had.

He wondered vaguely what de Lacey was up to.

De Lacey was at sea, bound for Cape Town, Rio de Janeiro and London. With him was Edwin Rotherby, who had been forced to flee Calcutta at the last moment due to threats from several gentlemen who felt his absence would have a most beneficial effect on their individual marriages.

THIRTY-NINE

WONNGU SENT A runner ahead to warn the tribe that the party was returning. The messenger brought a lively tale, suitably embellished to ensure a grand welcome. Wonngu's party had ventured into unknown territory and fought off an attack by the legendary wild men of the mountains. Berak was safe, Murremurran had run away and was reputed to be crazy and Clancy had joined them at a critical time in the battle, bringing with him an amazing animal that breathed fire and slew men with its flailing legs. Naturally, all the tribe gathered by the stream to witness the arrival of the triumphant procession.

Delbung told Eliza.

'He has brought an animal?' Eliza asked.

'A huge monster that kills men with its feet.' Delbung demonstrated, swinging her hands in the clawing motion she had seen the messenger use. 'It struck men down all around it. Only Ker-lan-see can touch it, and with him, it is tame. No one else may go near it. The monster and Ker-lan-see's miraculous arrival saved our men from certain death for the others were in a war party and greatly outnumbered our people.'

Eliza was more interested in the animal. 'How many legs does this monster have?'

'Many. And they are very long.'

'And it is big?'

'No one has ever seen such a large animal.'

Thrilled that Clancy was safely returned but brimming with curiosity, Eliza prepared for the party's arrival. She washed her face in the stream and combed her hair. She had been wearing a covering of kangaroo hide but put on her convict garb of shift, dress and bonnet—all mended and threadbare in places but scrubbed clean for this occasion. She wrapped the baby in a rug of possum skin that Delbung's daughter had made and was standing in the doorway with the baby in her arms when the men entered the valley.

At first, there were the birds. A flock of white cockatoos rose in the air, as ragged as scraps of paper tossed high in a strong wind. Then small birds, darting in many directions and emitting the shrill screech of a thousand tin whistles as they flew. They were the tiny green and blue birds that the tribe considered such a delicacy and tried to trap in nets strung from the trees; they kept low, as they always did when confronting danger, and regrouped to fly along the stream in wild, brilliant splashes of colour. Then came the dust, for there had been no rain for many days and the feet of the marching men soon caused a yellow haze to rise at the entrance to the valley. And there was the noise, as the tribe rushed to greet the returning men, shouting as they ran.

They came down the stream, with Wonngu strutting at the head of the procession and raising his spears to acknowledge the cries of the tribe. Berak was behind him, the prized trophy of the hunt. There was a gap in the centre of the line and it took Eliza some time to see Clancy because the women and children had formed a ring around him. But she could see a horse.

She laughed, and Delbung glanced at her in surprise.

'Is it not a most amazing animal?'

'It is indeed,' Eliza said and shook her head. Why would

Clancy steal a horse when there were so many useful things they needed? And what on earth was he wearing?

She didn't see Ulla, who had slipped out of her man's clothing and quickly merged with the others in the tribe.

As the men drew nearer and the noise increased, Eliza felt shy, insecure. What if Clancy didn't like the baby? What if he'd seen other women, dressed in fine clothes and wearing bracelets and rings and other things to make them pretty, while he'd been on the other side of the mountains? Maybe that's why he was so late. He'd been with another woman. She felt ashamed of her worn clothes, her rough hands, her windburnt cheeks.

Clancy broke away from the procession and, with Wonngu and the others standing deferentially near the stream, led the horse up to the hut.

'And what have you got there, Clancy Fitzgerald?' she said, blinking nervously.

'And what have you got there, Eliza Fitzgerald?' He'd never called her that. It meant he considered them to be man and wife.

'A baby,' she said, trying not to cry. 'Our baby.' Passing the baby to the hovering Delbung, she ran forward and flung her arms around him.

'I love you, Clancy. I've been so worried about you.'

He stroked her cheek. 'Are you all right? I mean, after the baby.'

She pushed him away. 'You'll be wanting to see it. It's a girl. We have a daughter, Clancy.'

'Oh, I know all about it. First, I've got a present for you.'

'Don't you want to see her?'

'Your present first.'

She laughed. 'I don't want a horse.'

He withdrew the Bible from inside his shirt. 'I brought you a Bible.'

She gasped and took the Bible. She felt the damaged cover. 'It's got a hole in it.'

'A man tried to put a spear through me. It got stuck in the book.'

She pressed the book to her chest.

'That devil Murremurran. He tried to kill me.'

'And the Bible saved you?'

'You can see for yourself. The spear got stuck in the wooden cover.'

'God was protecting you. I shall treasure this Bible all the more.'

He let go the reins, allowing Cortez to nibble a patch of lush grass, and gripped her by the shoulders. 'Now, is it true the baby's got red hair?'

'Lovely red hair.'

He swept her off her feet and carried her to where Delbung was waiting. The black woman's eyes were on the horse.

'Is it true it kills men?' she whispered. She rarely spoke to Clancy.

'True. But only if I tell it.'

'Oh, Clancy,' Eliza said, pulling back the possum skin cover so Clancy could see his daughter, 'don't tease her. Horses don't kill.'

'This one does,' he said and took the baby in his arms.

The horse was tied to a sapling near the stream where it was surrounded by most of the tribe who kept well back but surged with noise whenever the horse snuffled or flicked its tail. Eliza and Clancy were alone in the hut.

'I'd like to call her Caroline,' she said.

'Weren't you thinking of another name?' He'd forgotten.

'It was my mother's name.'

He was nursing the baby. 'Fine. Caroline Fitzgerald it is then. Caroline Eliza Fitzgerald.'

She touched his hand. 'You'll give her your name?'

'Of course. I haven't got much else to give the little mite.'

He walked to the door to make sure the horse was all right.

'Would you ever consider getting married?'

He smiled. 'I'll ask Wonngu, if you like. I'm sure he'd do it.'

'Oh Clancy, I'm serious.'

'So am I. There are dozens of people married in this tribe. They're just as much married as white couples are.'

'How can you say such a thing? Especially after you gave me a Bible, the holy book that saved your life which is a sure sign that God is protecting you. Us,' she added rapidly.

'Next time I go over the mountains, I'll bring back a parson. Would you be happy then?'

'Please don't joke.' She went to him and took his hand. 'I'd like to go back to Sydney Town one day. Bring up our daughter in a civilised society. Let her mix with white children. Maybe marry a nice man.'

'And you'd like us to get married.'

'Wouldn't you?'

He sat on the bed. 'How would you like to be married to William Clancy, wealthy gentleman adventurer from Cape Province?'

And he told her the story of his meeting with William Clancy and how he had gained a horse and some fine clothes, and a sheaf of papers that had belonged to a free citizen.

'We could use them one day,' he said as they sat at the table and ate a meal that Delbung's daughter had cooked over the coals. 'But it's far too early now. People would recognise us.'

'You've been back several times and they haven't recognised you,' she pointed out. The papers seemed like a gift from God.

'Noxious Watts did. There'd be others.' He chewed on a fatty piece of gristle that had once been part of a lizard's tail. 'Besides, we could scarely play the part of wealthy new arrivals when we've got nothing.'

She sat still for a long time, neither talking nor eating. 'It seems like such a good opportunity,' she said eventually.

'It will be, love, it will be.' He reached out to pat her hand. 'One day, but not now.'

'And what will change in the future? Are you suddenly going to become rich, out here, living with the blackfellows, so that we can return to civilisation and you can play the role of William Clancy to the hilt?'

'Who knows?' he said and, eyes afire with thoughts of impossible happenings, licked the grease from his fingers.

She slept little that night. The baby was restless and cried frequently and a strong wind blew through the valley, causing the trees to moan and sigh, but it was more than the baby or the wind that kept her awake. She was thinking of life on the other side of the mountains. Of her wearing pretty dresses and having bonnets trimmed with lace. Of possessing boots made of finely grained, supple leather and cotton gloves that were a dazzling white. She might even have a pair of silk gloves, like the wife of the lieutenant at Rose Hill, who used to keep them in a special drawer packed with dried lavender that she'd brought with her from England. They were beautiful gloves, too good to wear in such a rough and sweaty place as New South Wales, but the lieutenant's wife used to open the drawer when she thought no one was watching, and take out the gloves and smell them and hold them to the light and make little gurgling noises, just like a child with a favourite toy.

If they lived in Sydney, Caroline could wear dresses made of silk, not crude coverings of possum skin, and they'd have a perambulator with big wheels and silk ribbons and, after church on Sunday mornings, they'd take their daughter walking through the park. Eliza wasn't sure which park but she knew there must be a park in a big town like Sydney and it would be near the church, for there was always a graveyard and a park near a church and the park would have lovely gardens with real English flowers and proper trees that had masses of dark green leaves and were shaped like trees should be, and weren't always dropping their leaves or shedding their bark.

She cried a lot during the night.

This was an impossible dream. Finding the dead man's papers had been fate dealing its cruellest hand. Clancy was right. Playing the role of a rich man and his family required riches and no man on earth was less likely to become rich than Clancy. Their daughter was condemned to a life among the blackfellows. They might be kind, as indeed they had been with her, but the thought that repelled her was of Caroline reaching the age of sixteen or seventeen and being taken by some old man as his wife. That would happen, she knew, if they stayed here. Her daughter would become the possession of a wrinkled old heathen and her daughter's children would be coloured.

They could, of course, just cross the mountains and mix with the other white folk and pretend they were free settlers. Clancy would spin a believable story that might trick the authorities. There must be many emancipated convicts in the colony these days so two more would not be perceived as being oddities. But they would have no papers and Clancy, clever man that he was, was no forger. They'd be found out and hanged.

What would become of Caroline? Would they hang the baby too, or would she be sent to some orphanage? Did they have such a thing in Sydney, or even a poorhouse? Probably not. It was such a small, primitive place and yet it tempted her as if it were paradise on earth.

Not that Clancy, deep in his heart, wanted to go back. He seemed strangely contented leading the life of a blackfellow.

Much of his contentment was vanity; she was aware of that. Only this evening, instead of being with her and talking with her and loving her, as she had longed for him to do, he had gone down to the stream and spent hours talking with Wonngu and some of the elders and regaling them with stories of the horse and the magical way he had intervened in the battle and saved the tribe—once again.

He loved being free to do as he wished but, even more, he loved being a hero. Only on this side of the mountains could he lead such a life.

Wonngu had discovered that his new wife had been unfaithful while he was away but he was in a surprisingly jovial mood. People would have laughed at him and called him a useless old dodderer if she had gone off with some other man while he was in the camp but she had chosen to be adulterous while he was away leading a hunting party whose exploits would become legendary. For generations to come, the tribe would tell, in song and dance, the tale of Wonngu's great victory over the mountain men and of the wonders of Ker-lan-see's horse. He was a hero. The stupid girl had chosen to have sex with some nondescript youth who wasn't even fit to join the hunting party. Now people would despise and ridicule her.

'My new woman has had a lover,' he told Clancy, when the other men had drifted back to their women. His rheumy eyes were bright with the need to tell more.

'She must be a fool.' Clancy knew his words would please the old man.

'I should not have allowed myself to be talked into taking her.' Wonngu tapped the ground several times with a stick and then tossed the stick into the stream and watched the ripples float slowly with the current. 'Never mind. There's more than one berry on the bush.'

'So what will you do?'

Wonngu slapped at an ant that had strayed on to his thigh. 'Cut her.'

'Cut her?' Clancy drew a finger across his throat.

Wonngu laughed. 'No, no, no. On one of her beautiful, round buttocks. I will make a small, straight cut and fill it with ash so that it heals in a hard, high ridge. And then every time some lover fondles her arse, he will know she is a woman who has slept with many men.'

Clancy thought that a strange punishment because all the women in the tribe, as far as he knew, had slept with many men, but he nodded as though this was a wise decision. 'You think she will be unfaithful again?'

'Oh, she cannot help herself. Some women are like that.'

They talked for another hour until the cool wind had Wonngu shivering and rubbing his leathery skin to keep warm. Raising both hands in farewell, he waded into the stream, drank some water, urinated on the far bank and then headed for the place where the tribe was camped.

Despite the wind, Clancy chose to sleep outside. He could hear no noise from the hut so assumed Eliza and the baby were asleep. He found a place where the grass was soft and where he could lie on his back with his head cradled in his arms and gaze up at the stars and the scudding clouds.

He might go back to Sydney in a few years' time. Preferably when there was a new governor, who had never heard of Clancy Fitzgerald, and a batch of new soldiers had arrived to join the New South Wales Corps. If he were shaven and dressed in William Clancy's clothes, even the old convicts who had known him mightn't recognise him. They would think him long dead.

It could work. He could pretend he had been robbed, which would account for the lack of any money or possessions. He might have to go back to the colony to steal some clothes for

Eliza or the baby but that could be done. He might get away with it.

Having money was the key to the plan.

Would he take the horse? Probably not. The horse was such a distinctive animal that many would recognise it and associate it with the stranger he was attempting to impersonate. No, he'd have to leave Cortez on this side of the mountains. Which meant he would want to travel back to this valley from time to time, to be with the horse again, for it was his most prized possession and the thought of abandoning it was anathema.

So if he went to Sydney, he'd like to be free to return, as and when he wished, to be with the horse, to ride it, to feel the sense of power he gained when astride its massive back. He'd like to see Wonngu, too, who was the wisest and purest man he had known; even Ulla, who would soon be a woman.

That would be a perfect way to spend the years: part of the time with white people, pretending to be William Clancy, enjoying the luxuries of civilisation, playing a wonderful game of deception, of posing and pretending—which, he reflected, was what life with his own kind was mostly about—and part of the time with the blackfellows. He preferred the Aboriginal way. All that truly mattered was survival. Certainly, they surrounded themselves with complex rituals and believed in strange things but their life was simple. They lived from day to day, concerned only about food, shelter and companionship, didn't impose their will on others and were not cruel to each other; certainly, no one was ever put in chains or whipped or locked away from their fellows.

A double life. That would be good.

It would need time.

Part Three

FORTY

ON THE VOYAGE to England Edwin Rotherby spent so much time talking about his friend Lord Thomas Cochrane that de Lacey felt he knew the man rather well. Cochrane was the heir to the Earldom of Dundonald in the Scottish lowlands. The Dundonalds had once been a rich and powerful family but centuries of fighting the English, in flesh and spirit, had seen the erosion of their estates and the loss of much of their wealth.

Lord Thomas might have been the future tenth Earl of Dundonald and been raised in a castle, but he was born to an impoverished family. His mother died when he was young. His father, after a brief and, according to Rotherby, chaotic career in the army and the navy, turned to science and spent most of his time in his laboratory where young Thomas gained much of his education.

Cochrane never went to school. He had several tutors but, essentially, his learning was acquired at his father's elbow. The result was that he was inventive, adventurous and rebellious.

'He's wonderful,' Rotherby said. 'Whereas his father drifts along in a dream world, inventing things but doing nothing with them, Thomas knows exactly what he wants. Treads on a few toes. Has an immense aura of authority about him, yet has absolutely no respect for authority.'

When Rotherby had last seen him, Cochrane was working on a few inventions. One involved the use of mathematics to determine the lines of a ship's hull, so that it would create minimum resistance in the water. He waited for de Lacey to express surprise, or at least admiration, but obviously the concept was beyond his friend because all de Lacey could say was, 'Mathematics?'

'Yes, he does his sums and . . .' Rotherby waved his hands, drawing the lines of a hull '. . . comes up with these shapes.'

Cochrane was also working on a scheme to use smoke or poison gas in warfare. 'A few of the old toads in the War Department are shocked,' Rotherby said, eyes twinkling. 'They say it would be ungentlemanly. They don't mind a man having his head lopped off by a sabre or having his guts shot out by a cannonball but they can't stomach the idea of his being blinded by smoke. Still, Thomas is pressing on. Last time I saw him he was trying to work out how to lob the smoke or gas into the enemy lines, not your own. He'll get it right some day.'

Cochrane's father, the Earl, may have been a dreamer but he had powerful connections. Anxious to see his son in the army, he had Cochrane commissioned into the Horse Guards before he was ten. An uncle, a distinguished admiral, had also placed Cochrane's name on the rolls of his various flagships as a cabin boy. As a result, when Cochrane chose to join the navy as a 17-year-old midshipman, he already had seven years seniority in service.

Within five years he was court-martialled for insubordination but, being the son of an earl proved a powerful defence, and he'd been let off with a reprimand.

'What's he been doing in recent times?' de Lacey asked.

'Either fighting the French or fighting the British Admiralty.'

Lord Thomas Cochrane happened to be in London when their ship berthed and they met him only a few days later. He was a tall man with a long nose and a lean, angular body that seemed to be all elbows and jutting knees.

What de Lacey hadn't expected was his lordship's youth. Cochrane was no more than twenty-five.

They met at Cochrane's club. It was a gloomy place, with velvet drapes and dark paintings of admirals with cracked faces. The attendants neither smiled nor spoke and moved across the wooden floors in reptilian silence. Cochrane wanted to hear about Rotherby's exploits in Calcutta. He'd heard rumours. 'Juicy ones, I trust,' Rotherby said and proceeded to elaborate, making the stories of his various affairs even more colourful than the versions de Lacey had heard on the ship.

Two scotches later, Cochrane asked, 'And you, Mr de Lacey, what brings you from distant New South Wales?' He had the soft burr of a lowlands Scot.

Rotherby, still charged with the spirit of story-telling, answered for him. 'He wants to do some serious fighting.'

'Goodness me. Is there any other sort?'

Rotherby giggled, as he tended to do when he'd drunk too much and talked too much. 'Quinton broke a longstanding tradition by pursuing some Aborigines who had crept into a village and murdered a few white settlers. He fought a few of them hand-to-hand, and on his own I should add, and then chased them across the Hawkesford River.'

'Hawkesbury,' de Lacey said softly, not wanting to interrupt Rotherby's narrative but feeling the need for accuracy.

Cochrane wagged a long finger at de Lacey. 'Edwin said you broke some sort of tradition. I don't understand.'

'No one had bothered about the raids in the past. They'd just let the blacks go. They'd never followed them across the river.'

'And you did. What happened?'

413

'He got ambushed.' Rotherby clapped his hands. 'Twice in the one day. Fought very bravely. More hand-to-hand combat. Overwhelming odds. All that.'

Cochrane seemed amused. 'And you want to get involved in more serious fighting?'

'Not a term I would have used myself, m'lord. But after what subsequently happened in New South Wales, I feel it's a question of honour.'

'And what happened in New South Wales?'

'Frankly, m'lord, I was an embarrassment to them. I was asked to leave.'

'To resign from the New South Wales Corps?'

'Yes m'lord.'

'Who did that?'

'Captain Hunter, the Governor.'

Cochrane made a small, grunting noise. 'He himself is being asked to leave, or so I hear. Something about allowing the army officers to monopolise trade.'

'The officers are more interested in profit than in fighting. These natives needed to be taught a lesson or else the raids would have gone on forever.'

'And have the raids stopped?'

De Lacey chewed his lip. 'I don't know. I left.'

'For India, where we met up,' Rotherby said quickly.

'But there were no more raids in the months while I was waiting for a ship.'

Cochrane peered through his whisky glass at the amber light from a wall lantern. He had lopsided eyebrows 'I'm not sure I understand. Do you want to see action over here?'

'Yes. As a means of redeeming myself.'

'Surely no one doubts your courage?'

'Men were killed. I was blamed for that.' He leaned forward earnestly. 'You see, the blacks of New South Wales are perceived as a miserable lot, hardly worth fighting or worrying about. The truth is that those still living in a wild state, the sort I was up against, are a formidable lot on their own ground.'

'Like the Indians of America.'

'Exactly. Although,' he felt compelled to add, 'possibly less well-armed but certainly equally cunning, very skilled with their weapons, and brave.'

Cochrane put down the glass and stared at the ceiling. 'I've just been given command of a ship. A sloop called the *Speedy*, which is neither fast nor well-armed. However, I intend giving the enemy hell. There could be some hand-to-hand combat, which seems to be your speciality.' He gave a quick smile. 'You're very welcome to join me.'

'I'd be honoured.' De Lacey spread his hands helplessly. 'But what as? What would my role be?'

'Oh, we'd soon work something out. Probably make you a marine. I understand you were a lieutenant. You'd have the same rank. Would you be happy with that?'

'I'd be delighted, sir.'

Cochrane turned to Rotherby who raised both hands. 'No invitations for me, please, Thomas. I may be adept at many things but I am no fighting man.'

Cochrane reached down and lifted a bag on to the table. From it, he extracted a quantity of small cannonballs. 'That, my dear Lieutenant de Lacey, is all I am able to muster in one broadside. Pitiful, isn't it? We will be a minnow fighting sharks. In fact, I'm off to the Admiralty this afternoon, to show someone this paltry lot and see if we can do something about getting decent guns put aboard. Or better still, another ship.'

Rotherby said, 'They will nod their heads and pull their whiskers and do nothing.'

'I believe you're right, Edwin.' He rolled a cannonball across the table to de Lacey. 'Not much, is it? Especially when the

French and the Spaniards have got such big ships with big guns. Still interested in joining me?'

'Indeed,' de Lacey said, examining the lead ball, which fitted in his clasped hand.

'I think we'll have some fun.'

'I'll drink to that,' Rotherby said, aiming his glass at first Cochrane, then de Lacey. 'May you two have some fun.'

FORTY-ONE

THE *SPEEDY* WAS small, a little tub, as Cochrane liked to call her, with a single mast and a paltry row of guns on the upper deck, but Cochrane was an audacious leader and for the next year he and his crew played havoc with shipping around the Spanish coast. In that time they captured nearly thirty enemy vessels. Most were merchantmen, bound for French or Spanish ports, but in the booty was a goodly mix of small men-of-war and this gave de Lacey considerably more experience in hand-to-hand combat, because Cochrane's favourite tactic, inspired by the fact that he was usually out-gunned, was to pull alongside the enemy and storm the decks. Cochrane was always at the front of any assault, leading by inspiration, apparently immune to fear and exempt from injury. The men of the *Speedy* would follow him anywhere. They'd become devoted to de Lacey, too. He usually led the alternative charge, taking his smaller band of men over the side of the enemy vessel in a different place to Cochrane's group so that, even when the *Speedy*'s crew was outnumbered—which was most of the time—the ferocity of the dual attack and the blood-thirsty cries that de Lacey's men shouted, convinced the enemy they were being attacked by a superior force and caused a rapid surrender.

'My own primitive warrior,' Cochrane called de Lacey, who

was held in awe by his men for his daring and skill with the sword. Fighting with an almost desperate fearlessness, he took more risks than his captain, prompting Cochrane to wonder if de Lacey might welcome death as a means of expunging the shame of New South Wales. A better swordsman than Cochrane but more reckless, de Lacey now bore several scars, one a six-inch jagged tear, still pink from recent healing, that ran from cheekbone to throat.

At the end of the year the two men enjoyed the friendship known only to those who have shared the constant threat of death and the heady surges of success in combat.

By now Cochrane was aware that his feats had made him well known to the Spaniards and the French, who had ships out hunting for him. He also knew that unrelenting audacity guaranteed a short life and, as there was a real risk of being lured into a trap, decided to temper his daring with a dose of cunning. He had the *Speedy* refitted in Malta. He'd seen a Danish brig, the *Clomer*, which was similar in size and shape to his sloop and so had the *Speedy* repainted to resemble the Danish vessel. To further the deception, he took aboard a Danish quartermaster and dressed him in a Danish uniform.

The test came off the south-east coast of Spain, when he sighted what appeared to be a merchantman and closed to within gun range. At this point, the other vessel opened her ports and rolled out her guns. She was no merchantman but a Spanish frigate, far too powerful and fast for the *Speedy*.

There was no question of trying to flee. They'd be blown out of the water. Cochrane hove to and a boat was sent from the Spanish ship to investigate.

A quarantine flag was raised. Out came the Danish quartermaster. When the boat was within range, the Dane shouted that they were two days out of Tangiers in Morocco where the plague was rampant.

'The plague?' the Spanish officer repeated and a shudder went through the men at the oars.

'It's a terrible thing.'

The Spaniard agreed, wished him good luck and ordered his men to row hard, back to the frigate.

There were those aboard the *Speedy* who didn't like this deception. They were fighting men, used to accepting an unequal challenge. Because of the number of ships they had taken, they were also wealthy by the standard of sailors and didn't like sailing away from any potential prize.

Cochrane heard the talk and when, a few weeks later, they sighted a Spanish frigate, there was no question of bringing out the Danish quartermaster or lofting a quarantine flag. He set full sail and attacked.

'Wise, old boy?' de Lacey asked. He was on the bridge with Cochrane. The frigate was still little more than a blur on the horizon and, with luck, they could turn and be out of sight before the Spaniards realised the identity of the other ship.

'I have a few tricks up my sleeve.' Cochrane had been examining the frigate through a telescope and passed it to de Lacey. 'You've fought the blacks once or twice. How would you like to be on their side for a change?'

The frigate was clearly visible now as the *Speedy*, mainsail filled, jib taut and rigging crackling under the stiff breeze, bore down on her. De Lacey was nervous. The frigate was a formidable warship, four times larger than their vessel. She was well capable of sinking them before they got within range. 'On the blacks' side? I have no idea what you're talking about.'

'I want you to take your men and have them paint their faces and arms black.' The young Scottish nobleman's burr thickened, as it did when he was excited by the prospect of battle.

'Black?'

419

'And when we come alongside, I'll take the rest of the men and attack over the stern. I want you to come over the bow. I'll go first. You come after me. Give me about twenty seconds.'

'With the men painted like blackfellows . . .'

'Exactly. And no uniforms. I want you to look like savages. Stay out of sight until you're ready. Be quick. We haven't much time.'

When they were within gun range, Cochrane shouted two orders. The first was to come about. The second was to hoist the American flag.

The Spanish vessel hadn't fired and Cochrane could see the master studying them through his own telescope, trying to determine who the devil they were. A sharp gust of wind hit them and he ordered the attack to be resumed. He also hoisted the French colours.

Cochrane could now see the name of the vessel: *Gamo*. He could also detect frantic activity on the larger ship as the Spaniards realised this was no friendly vessel approaching under full sail. The frigate got in only one broadside, which whistled through the rigging and tore the mainsail, before the *Speedy* was alongside.

They came in so hard that Cochrane fell to his knees. The rigging of the *Speedy* became entangled in the masts and spars of the larger vessel so that the two ships, although wrenched apart momentarily by the surge of waves, slammed back together to be caught in a web of fallen shrouds. Amid the sounds of groaning hulls and splitting timber, the decks were showered with canvas, pulleys, and writhing lengths of line. The Spaniards fired again but the British vessel was so much smaller that the shots passed well clear of her decks. But the *Speedy*'s guns, raised to maximum elevation, caused terrible destruction along the *Gamo*'s mid-deck. The first broadside killed the frigate's captain and boatswain.

With the vessels locked together, Cochrane led his men through the rubble and smoke over the *Gamo*'s stern. Even by his standards the assault was an enormous risk because the frigate carried five times more men and he was attacking with only half his crew.

Swords drawn, the Spaniards met Cochrane's party amidships.

At first Cochrane thought they might be overwhelmed, so great were the numbers opposing them but, at that moment de Lacey, having scaled the bow, brought his group of 'savages' up behind the Spaniards. They attacked with bloodcurdling war cries.

The Spaniards turned and stared in disbelief at the bizarre figures, with black faces and hair frizzed and dusty with charcoal, that were appearing through the white smoke of the bow guns.

Only the night before de Lacey had dreamed of his own death. It had been in combat, a battle against hopeless odds and, in his dream, he had seen people weeping over his body. Part of the way through the funeral, the dream had ended when a midshipman came to wake him, but he recalled the wonderful things the mourners were saying about him. He had died a hero and the shame of that day on the Hawkesbury was forgotten.

If he were to die, this would be a glorious way to go. In fancy dress, thumbing his nose at the enemy and facing overwhelming odds.

With a wild shriek, he swung his sword above his head and charged at the Spanish line. A sailor, barefooted and with his long hair covered by a red and yellow bandanna, faced him but was soon on his knees, holding the remains of his right arm. De Lacey singled out an officer, resplendent in boots, domed hat and long coat. He expected a fight but the man's eyes were wide with shock and, almost immediately, he dropped his sword.

The next person encountered by de Lacey, still yelling battle cries and lusting for death, was Cochrane. The captain had been sprayed by another man's blood and was wiping his eyes.

They stood back to back and looked for opponents but all had surrendered. Cochrane spun around and embraced de Lacey.

'Quinton, my black wonder, we've won, we've won.'

The Spanish colours were lowered and the surviving crew locked below decks. They had captured 263 men and a fine fighting ship.

In fourteen months, Lord Thomas Cochrane captured thirty-three vessels, carrying a total of 128 guns and 533 men. But, inevitably, his luck ran out. The amazing voyage of the *Speedy* came to an end one night with the capture of a merchantman. The ship was too large for Cochrane to put aboard a prize crew so he set fire to it. Unhappily for him, the vessel was loaded with barrels of oil and the leaping flames attracted three French battleships which had been cruising over the horizon.

The crew of the sloop fought gallantly but, this time, the odds were insurmountable and after a fierce fight Cochrane was forced to surrender.

The men were taken to a French prison. Within weeks, Cochrane had been exchanged for a French captain. De Lacey, whose left leg had been badly wounded by a dagger thrust, remained a prisoner of war.

FORTY-TWO

FIVE YEARS PASSED. While de Lacey remained a prisoner of the French, Eliza and Clancy continued to live in their hut in the secluded valley. Caroline grew into a sturdy child who, in a white community, would have been regarded as exceptionally pretty but there were those women in the tribe who were repelled by her red hair, narrow nose and thin lips, her strange blue eyes and pale skin. She was, however, a favourite with some of the tribe who gave her the special attention that people in civilised societies might reserve for a precocious dwarf or some other appealing oddity.

There were no more children, for Clancy and Eliza seldom slept together. Clancy went hunting often, always taking the musket but rarely using it because he was running short of shot and powder. He had become reasonably proficient with a spear, although not to the standard of the best hunters, and usually adopted the role of a patrician observer, to applaud a good hunt and praise the successful men around the fire that night. Sometimes he rode the horse but, generally, Cortez was an embarrassment, frightening the game long before the hunters were within throwing distance. He preferred to ride on his own, favouring a small valley about five miles away. It had a few rock-holes where the horse could drink, was covered in abundant grass and had a flat field where he could let Cortez have his head and, standing clear of the saddle, whirl an imaginary sword above his head and imagine he was taking part in a cavalry charge. He had built a stockyard and stable for the horse. He'd also extended the verandah and built a new, larger kitchen where Delbung and her one remaining unmarried daughter could cook their meals undisturbed by the weather.

He was seeing more of Ulla, who had grown into a shapely woman. She still lived with her father and his wives, which puzzled everyone in the tribe except Wonngu who had learned never to be surprised by anything Clancy did. He was, however, pleased with Ulla's news. She was three months pregnant.

Ulla had known how a baby was created. It came primarily through the introduction of a spirit into a woman's body, although intercourse with the man was necessary. Her tribe believed that the man contributed the bones of the child and the woman its blood and flesh. They also believed that a man should sleep with the woman for six successive nights, so that the build-up of semen would arrest the menstrual flow. The spirit came from the man but the woman had to eat the right food and avoid certain others, and her milk had to flow internally at this time, to nourish the foetus.

All this was known to everyone.

Two things had worried Ulla. The first was what sort of spirit would enter her from a man who already was a spirit, and a white one at that? Would she be able to receive it? Would it leave her body? Would its entry into her body kill her?

The second worry was more practical. How was she to persuade Clancy to sleep with her for six successive nights, and ejaculate on each of those nights to ensure the birth process might begin? She had slept with him occasionally. Never on successive nights, let alone for almost a week.

She had seen her father who took her to the sorcerer, Gogwai.

He had been sitting cross-legged on the side of a hill, drawing marks in the dust.

'If the baby is born dead,' he began ominously, 'you are to eat its flesh so that the spirit remains within you, awaiting rebirth. You should then become pregnant again as soon as possible.'

She would know the right time to become pregnant. She would see the spirit of the child from a distance in a fire, or in an unusual shoal of fish or mob of kangaroos. The sign would be clear and she would recognise it.

'What if the spirit refuses to remain in Ulla's body?' asked Wonngu, who was beginning to share his daughter's shame at her having been married for so long without producing a child. He understood Clancy's reasons, or so he told himself, but many in the tribe were saying the white man found Ulla unattractive.

'If the spirit enters the girl's body,' Gogwai said, staring at his latest drawing, 'it will remain there. Ker-lan-see is the reborn Yerranibee and your uncle will wish for a child to be born.'

Gogwai had then issued a set of orders to be followed at the birth. If Clancy were away, Ulla was to go to the creek near the hut. She was to be accompanied by her mother and several women. They were to light a fire, then dig a hole in the soft ground near the creek. The afterbirth was to be buried in the hole. The umbilical cord was to be cut with a sharp flint and then wrapped loosely around the child's throat; this would prevent it from crying. The women were to use cold ashes from the fire to stain the body of the baby black, in case it were born white.

'How do I make him sleep with me?' Ulla had asked mournfully, returning to her main reason for consulting the sorcerer.

Gogwai would make a special, long string with a feather at each end. He would have one end of the string hidden in one of Clancy's possessions, possibly a bag. The string would stretch across the creek to where Ulla was camped. She was to hold the second feather. As soon as Clancy touched the bag, he would feel an irresistible urge to be with her.

Clancy had come to her on the third and fifth nights and they slept together. Those were the only times they had intercourse but, miraculously, the spirit had entered her, even though she had seen none of the signs Gogwai had forecast. The baby was now due in the time of six full moons.

For all of those five years, Clancy had known it was still not the right time to cross the mountains and assume the role of free settlers in the colony. The people of Sydney might have forgotten them but they would be forced to play the part of impoverished immigrants, which hardly fitted the image of William Clancy Esquire, a free settler from Southern Africa who, by his clothes and his papers, was a wealthy man. Clancy had thought of a dozen excuses to explain their poverty—they'd been robbed, they'd been shipwrecked and so on—but each circumstance would have stirred a dozen questions and, inevitably, they would have been found out.

But, in February of 1804, something happened which changed their lives.

Wonngu, who now walked with a limp from arthritis of the hip, came to see Clancy. He had come from the tribe's summer camp, a day's journey away, to report that two of his young men, while hunting emu further to the west, had heard of another white man living on this side of the mountains. The hunters had gone to see him. The man was old, with a white beard and with smoke coming from a stick in his mouth, and he lived in a hut which was much smaller than Clancy's. And he was sick; so sick that he could scarcely move from his bed.

Despite his great curiosity, Wonngu couldn't walk all the way to the place where the white man lived but escorted Clancy back to the summer camp. On the way, he said his youngest wife, who had grown very fat (although she still had the thin legs he favoured) now bore eleven scars on her buttocks. He thought it a great joke. He was no longer interested in sex and cautioned Clancy that this was inevitable with age. Clancy agreed, which Wonngu expected for Clancy himself had once been an old man.

From the camp he sent the two young hunters with Clancy to meet the white man.

Heading west, they travelled through open country, crossing rolling, grassy plains for a day and a half until they came to a wide river which flowed to the north-west. This was another tribe's territory but they were friendly and, in fact, the sister of one of the young men had married a warrior from the other tribe, so they moved without fear, but being careful not to kill any large animals for they had not sought permission to do so. The understanding was that they could feed themselves but not take animals for the tribe.

They camped by the river on the second night, feasting on a meal of fish which the young men caught in a net they carried. On the following morning they struck off to the north, but regained the river next day. After following its course for two hours, the river swung to the west. Their path was to the north across well timbered, hilly country where the slopes were covered in rocks. They made slower progress now, climbing several of the hills and following the occasional meandering way of a stream. There was much game in the hills, and the young men cast eager but frustrated eyes at the occasional furry kangaroo they saw emerging from the sanctuary of rocks or pairs of emus scudding across a valley.

On the fifth day they came to the site. A mass of low hills, all rounded and rocky and bristling with scrub, surrounded a narrow stream that had dried over summer into a chain of waterholes. Near one waterhole stood a crude building, no more than a lean-to that was five feet high by eight feet wide. It was made of bark lashed to a couple of sturdy branches. Inside was a cot covered with layers of dried grass. On the cot was a man with a long white beard and a face as weathered as the grass. His clothes were the tattered remains of convict garb. His pants had been torn away at the knees and his exposed legs were lumpy with scars. Around his feet were wrapped animal skins, bound at the ankles. A sling made from knotted strips of material—probably from the old man's pants—hung from the end of the cot.

A small fire smouldered in a corner of the hut.

Clancy left the others and approached. He had the musket under his arm.

'And who would you be?' he said.

The man seemed to be sleeping. Or dead. Clancy prodded him with the barrel of the gun.

'Are you awake, old man?'

The man opened one eye. 'By the Jesus, I've been caught.'

Clancy laughed. 'No. We're both convicts, friend.'

The man rubbed his eyes. 'Have they found the way over?'

'No. There's just you and me.'

The man tried to sit up but the effort was too great and Clancy had to help him.

'How long since you've eaten?' Clancy asked.

The man scratched his skull, disturbing a mat of scabs and long white hair. 'Don't remember.'

'We've got some fish. Why don't you have something to eat.'

His name was James Wilkes. He was from Lincolnshire and he'd been a tinsmith. He didn't know his age. He was, however, certain he was dying. He had consumption and coughed frequently, each time shaking the cot and causing dry grass to flutter to the ground.

428

'Not much of a house,' he said. 'I've had other things to do.' He gave Clancy a conspiratorial wink. I've got a secret, he was saying, and if you're a good man, I'll let you in on it—but not yet.

Clancy waited until the old man had eaten some fish. Then Wilkes started to talk.

He had been here for a year. He'd escaped about two and a half or three years earlier. He wasn't sure of the month or even the year when he'd got away, except it had been cold and there was a lot of rain at the time. Yet he was sure he had been at this site for twelve months. There was something special about the place.

'There was four of us made the break. We was working in a gang west of Prospect when we made off. We had nothing but the slops we was wearing. It was raining so hard I don't think the guards bothered looking for us.'

He seemed to lose interest and rummaged beneath the cot until he found a pipe. He got up and staggered to the fire and lit it.

'I've forgotten what tobacco's like,' Clancy said.

'So have I,' Wilkes said and broke into a cackling laugh. 'I've found a weed that burns tolerably well. Tastes terrible but a man's got to have something.' He sat on the cot again and, between puffs, resumed his story.

They had gone south from Prospect. One of his companions had given up after three days and returned. The others continued to follow the ranges to the south for another two weeks, living off berries and once catching a small animal like a rat, which they ate raw. They thought of going back, but doubted they could survive the return journey so resolved to find a way through the mountains at that point. There was a creek running from the range and they followed it to a gorge, which they climbed. The going was extremely rough and the third man died.

Wilkes and his surviving companion, an Irishman named O'Callaghan, found their way down to a stream that flowed to the west. They'd hunted with a sling—Wilkes had been good with a sling as a boy—and they lived off birds and small animals.

The stream became a river and they'd come to flatter country. They'd turned north and meandered through valleys and across plains. O'Callaghan had broken his ankle while crossing a rocky hillside and been compelled to walk with a stick. Game was scarce and they'd been reduced to eating lizards and grubs, even a snake which Wilkes had killed with a rock.

About eighteen months ago they'd been attacked by a small band of Aborigines. O'Callaghan, slowed by his injured ankle, had been speared in the leg but Wilkes had driven them off with a few well placed rocks from his sling.

O'Callaghan's wound had turned poisonous and he'd died after three weeks. Wilkes had been on his own ever since.

'The winters here are cruel,' he said and coughed violently. 'Snow and frost everywhere. The waterholes freeze over.'

'Why have you stayed here?' Clancy asked.

Wilkes delved into the beard to scratch his chin. 'What's your name?'

'Clancy Fitzgerald.'

'Irish?'

'My father was, but I was born in England.'

'That makes you Irish.' He paused. 'O'Callaghan was a good man. Never complained, even when he was dying.' He drew deeply on the pipe and coughed again. The cough seemed to sharpen his mind. 'What are you doing here?'

'I've been over here for six years.'

'Longer than me?'

'By a few years.'

Wilkes grunted. 'I was beginning to think I was the first. Took a sort of pride in it.'

'There may have been others before either of us. Who knows?'

'You haven't found the road to China?' Wilkes winked and laughed cynically. 'Load of bilge, all that talk. There's nothing here except bush and blackfellows.'

'I've been living with the blackfellows.' Clancy nodded towards the two young hunters, whom Wilkes seemed not to have noticed. They were standing as though on the hunt: each was on one leg with the other tucked behind the knee and their gaze was fixed on the old man.

'Why are they staring at me like that?'

'It's just the way they are,' Clancy said. 'They're friendly.'

'Do you trust them?'

'Yes.'

He made a series of grumbling noises and then looked up. 'Are you a good man, Clancy Fitzgerald?'

'I'm probably as good a man as you are, James Wilkes.'

'And I'm a bit of a villain. But who isn't, eh?' The old man winked and then busied himself emptying the pipe. 'Can you read and write?'

'Yes.'

'I never could so maybe you're better than me.'

'Who knows?'

'I've got a son back home. He's called James too. Don't know what he does. He'd be a man now. I want you to make me a promise, Clancy Fitzgerald.'

'What is it?'

'If you ever get back to the other side of these accursed mountains, I want you to write to me son and tell him what happened to me.'

'James Wilkes, Lincolnshire. Of course.'

'Bamforth, Lincolnshire,' Wilkes said, noting the flippancy in Clancy's voice. 'I want your solemn promise. I want you to write

431

to me son and tell him his father died a rich man.' Wilkes extended his arm and they shook hands.

'Give me your solemn promise,' he said without releasing his grip.

'You have my solemn promise,' Clancy said. 'And I'll say you were a rich man, if that's what you want.'

'But it's true. I am a rich man.' He pulled hard on Clancy's arm. 'Here, help me up. I want to show you something.'

At Wilkes's insistence, the two Aborigines stayed where they were. They squatted on the ground, still clutching their spears, fishing nets and other travelling gear. 'Don't move until I get back,' Clancy told them, anxious to be seen as the one in authority, not this other white man.

With Wilkes holding his arm for support, Clancy was led up from the creek to a small cliff face, encrusted with so many dark rocks that it looked like a giant fruit pudding. The old man stopped where several bushes grew at the base of the cliff.

'We have to crawl,' he said and dropped to his knees. Clancy followed. Behind the bushes was a small cave, hip-high and about four feet wide.

'You wait,' Wilkes said and crawled through the opening. Clancy could hear him laughing, then coughing while he still tried to laugh.

He emerged a minute later holding a bag fashioned from a bandicoot's hide. He laid it on the ground and opened it. It contained about two handfuls of nuggets and yellow dust.

'What is it?' Clancy asked.

Wilkes slapped his leg in delight. 'Gold, you fool.'

Clancy was silent while the old man observed him, as a hawk might watch its prey. Eventually, he said, 'I've never seen gold before. Not like that, anyhow.'

'Not many people have.'

'And you found all that here?'

The old man had wrapped his arms around his chest. 'Not just this lot. The cave's full of the stuff.'

'You found it in the cave?'

'No. I keep it there. I found it all over the place. In the creek. In the hills. I've tripped over the damned stuff.' Carefully, he wrapped the skin around the gold. 'That's why I want you to write to my boy and tell him I was a rich man. You seen it for yourself. You know I'm telling the truth.'

'How much more is there inside?'

'Ten, twenty times that much. Not that it'll do me any good. I'm not long for this world.'

Clancy's eyes were roaming from the old man to the cave. 'Could I look inside?'

'Not yet. You know where it is. That's enough. Here.' He thrust the bundle into Clancy's hands. It was surprisingly heavy. 'Take it. You can have the lot when I'm dead. All you got to do is write to my boy.'

'And tell him you were a rich man.'

'He'll be very proud of his father.'

Wilkes sat on the ground, eyes closed, head nodding. 'Where'd you get the gun?' he asked softly.

'I stole it.'

'When you broke out?'

'No, I went back and got it.'

The eyes opened. 'You've been back?'

'A few times.'

'Must be a different crossing to mine.' He shook his head. 'I couldn't face that track through the gorge again, even if I was fit. Couldn't find it for that matter. Don't know where it is. Don't know where I am now, come to think of it.' He laughed mournfully. 'You're not going to shoot me, are you?'

'Why would I shoot you?'

'Because of the gold. Some men would. They couldn't wait for me to die decently. They'd put a bullet through me head and take the lot and be off.'

Clancy had stuffed the gold inside his shirt. 'We'll get some more food inside your belly. The trouble with you is that you're starving.'

'A kind thought,' he said, painfully leading the way out through the bushes. 'But I'm dying and it's not from lack of food.'

Back at the hut, Wilkes soon fell asleep. Clancy squatted on the ground and opened the bandicoot skin. He let his fingers riffle through the gold. He had no idea what it was worth so tried to estimate how many gold rings a jeweller could make from it but soon gave up: there was so much. And Old Wilkes reckoned there was more in the cave.

And it was all his.

All the old man expected was for him to write a letter. Well, he'd do it. It would be easy to take the gold and go but he'd write the letter, a wonderful flowing letter full of pleasant lies that would make the son weep with pride at the wonderful, glorious success his father had enjoyed at the far end of the world.

Supposing the son wanted some of the gold?

He'd have to be careful what he said. Not mention gold. Just say his dad had become rich. Maybe as a farmer—a free, respected, wealthy farmer. That would be safer.

He let the gold run through his fingers. There were many small nuggets and he put them in his hand and jiggled them like dice.

This was so hard to comprehend. He was suddenly rich. Stupendously rich.

He signalled to the older of the two blacks and showed him the gold.

'Have you ever seen stones like this before?'

The man shook his head. There was no interest in his eyes.

'Do you know what it's called?'

'No.'

'If you see any, tell me.'

The man nodded.

'It might be in the water, or lying on the ground. Tomorrow, I want you to look for it.'

The man seemed puzzled by such a request but agreed.

'Now, I want you to go out and get more food for the old man. He's sick and needs food.'

'We can't hunt.'

'No one will miss a lizard or two. Something small. Meat, to make him strong.'

The two loped off, leaving Clancy to try to comprehend the magnitude of the day's discovery.

FORTY-THREE

CLANCY AND THE two hunters spent the night by the creek. At dawn—a bright, crisp flush of light fanfared by a chorus of chirps and squawks, flute-like whistles and guttural warbles from hundreds of birds that came to drink at the water-holes and peck at the grassy hillsides—Clancy was tempted to go to the cave and see what was inside. Wilkes need never know. But it was a matter of honour that he did what the old man wanted and so he vowed not to go until he was asked, or the old man died. The latter seemed imminent, for Wilkes had had a bad night, coughing and spluttering and groaning in pain until the sun rose, which seemed to soothe him, as though it were testimony to the amazing fact that he was still alive.

The two Aborigines went walking down the creek and returned an hour later with their hands full of pebbles. They gave them to Clancy. Most were pale stones but he found six which seemed to be gold. He compared them to the gold wrapped in the bandicoot skin. Yes, gold.

'Where did you find these?' he asked, making sure the men knew he was pleased.

'In the water,' the elder man replied. He had a wispy beard and hair so tightly plaited that his skull rippled with tiny corrugations. He pointed down the creek. 'Three pools from here. We saw a big stone caught in the earth of the bank. It was the same colour as the stones you showed us, but larger, so we left it.'

'Get it, please.'

They were gone for half an hour. When they returned they produced a nugget, dimpled and dirty, that was the size of Clancy's palm. He whistled.

'Does this please you?'

'You have done very well.'

The man would normally be reluctant to speak to Clancy in any but the most formal way, but his curiosity overwhelmed his normal caution. 'Why do you want stones, Ker-lan-see?'

Clancy hesitated before answering. A ghost or superhuman should not appear greedy. 'These are special to me and to me alone,' he said. 'With them I can make magic.'

'What do they do?'

'Nothing for you or for any other man. But if I have them and I wish to make magic, they help me do amazing things.'

The men looked at each other.

'Do you want more?' the younger man asked.

Clancy shook his head. Only he and Wilkes knew of the gold. There'd be plenty of time to return and get more. He'd bring Cortez next time and use the animal as a packhorse and fill the saddlebags.

'I have enough to do the things I want to do.'

The older man frowned. 'Will they be terrible things?'

'No. They will be good things.'

Good things indeed. Now that he had gold, he could do wonderful things.

All night he'd been planning what to do. He would stay with Wilkes until he died, to hold his hand or do whatever the old fellow wanted, and he would bury him where the wild dogs couldn't get to the body. He wouldn't mark the grave, however. He didn't want someone else coming along and finding a white

437

man's grave and wondering what there was in these hills that had brought him here, and start fossicking around.

He would have to tell Eliza about the gold but he wouldn't tell her where it had come from. It was important that no other white person knew of the find. The blacks didn't matter. They had no idea of its value.

So he would come back with the horse and bury a cache of the stuff near the hut. Then, he'd cross the mountains with Ulla, go to Sydney Town and try to sell some of the gold. It would have to be a small amount, so as not to raise suspicion, and he needed to know its value. He also needed to find an agent who would be prepared to take a continuous supply of gold. Then he would buy clothes for Eliza, the baby and himself. Maybe get a packhorse or a mule to carry gear; he knew from the trip with Cortez that a horse could make the journey over the mountains but he wanted a sturdy load-carrier, not a thoroughbred. He would take time to look around Sydney Town and see how it had developed in all the years since he had been there. They would need somewhere to live. A fine house, perhaps. There was much to do on that first journey.

Later, he would return to Sydney with Eliza and the girl and they would become Mr and Mrs William Clancy and family. For each day of their lives, he and Eliza would have to take care with everything they did or said. But he was excited. He was rich and he could play the role of his life.

Wilkes died that afternoon. Clancy held his hand until the last rattling wheeze left the old man's lips. The two hunters stood well back, naturally respectful but also fearful, never having seen a white man die and wondering what might happen.

'We bury him,' Clancy said and chose a site well clear of the creek where the ground was softer. He carried the body there. Using sticks, the other two scooped out a trench in which

Clancy laid Wilkes's frail body. He put the pipe on the old man's chest and they filled the grave with earth and loose rock.

The two Aborigines, who were now grasping their spears and standing one-legged, looked at Clancy in expectation of more for, in their culture, the burial of an old man was an affair soaked with ritual. So Clancy clasped his hands and closed his eyes.

'Bless you, James Wilkes, tinsmith, from Lincolnshire.' He was silent, trying to think of what to say next. 'May you rest in peace. God have mercy on your soul.' He needed to say something personal. People did that at funerals, except when the dead person had been hanged. 'I will always remember what you've done for me and I promise you, most solemnly, that I will write to your son in Bamforth, Lincolnshire, and tell him you died a rich man. Amen.'

He raised his hand. He wasn't going to cross himself like a Catholic but he felt he should make some gesture. He signalled to the two Aborigines to do the same and all three men held their hands high.

'Amen,' he shouted and the word echoed through the lonely hills.

'Right, that'll do.' He pointed to the creek. 'You two wait for me down there. I've got something else to do.'

At the cave, he took the musket from his shoulder and laid it under the bushes. Then, quivering with excitement, he crawled through the opening.

It took several seconds for his eyes to adjust to the faint light. The cave kinked to the left but all he could see around the entrance was a floor littered with small stones. He examined several but they were merely normal stones. He crawled around the bend.

Lining the wall of the cave was a series of bundles made from animal skins. He took the first and crawled back to the better light near the cave's mouth. He untied the bundle and spread the skin on the floor. It was filled with gold, mainly small nuggets although there were some fine grains. The second bag had much the same. The third held only two nuggets but they were large, each being the size of the first joint of his thumb. He put them in his pocket.

He counted the bundles. Fourteen. The old boy had got all this with his hands? He'd come back with a spade, an axe, a dish, whatever was needed. He'd let Ulla in on the secret, although not tell her of the worth of what he was seeking. Not that she'd have any concept of money. Just let her think he needed the yellow stones because of his magic. She'd be handy as a cook and a worker and she had amazing eyesight, much better than his.

He sat on the stony floor, wondering what to do. He was tempted to carry as many of the bags as possible back to the hut now, but that was absurd. He'd leave it here until he had the horse to carry such a heavy load.

What if someone came? For several minutes, he imagined some stranger chancing upon the cave and going off with all the gold and, for the first time in his life, experienced the anguish of a rich man worrying about his wealth.

As far as he knew, there was now only one white man living on this side of the mountains and that man was Clancy Fitzgerald, who would be back in little more than a week, to clear the cave and see what else he could find along the creek.

And so, with one pocket carrying two golden nuggets, the bandicoot-skin bag under his shirt and his head swimming with fanciful ideas, Clancy Fitzgerald set off on the five-day journey back to the hut.

At first Eliza refused to believe it was gold. 'Of course it is,' he said and bit on a piece, as he'd once seen a fellow thief do to a ring. Why, he had no idea, but it seemed to be the right thing to do with gold.

'And where would a man like you be finding gold?' She filled her hand with grains of the yellow metal and let them trickle from one palm to the other.

He told her about Wilkes, although he didn't tell her the dead man's name. The less she knew the better.

'Did you say a prayer for the poor man?'

'I did. A handsome prayer. You'd have been proud of me.'

She was examining some nuggets. The pieces seemed too small to be valuable. 'What religion was he?' she asked without taking her eyes from the gold.

'What's it matter?'

'A great deal. You had no right burying him and saying a prayer if he was a Roman Catholic.'

'You mean I should have kept him alive and brought him back to find a priest?'

'You say the most ridiculous things, Clancy.'

'It's a habit I got from my wife.'

She looked at him with solemn eyes. 'You called me your wife.'

'You're now Mrs William Clancy, Eliza Clancy, wife of William Clancy, gentleman adventurer from . . .' He'd forgotten.

'From Cape Province in Africa.' She gripped his hand. 'Oh Clancy, there's so much we've got to remember, so much to learn, so much to be careful about.'

'We'll get by.'

'But you're good at that sort of thing. I'm not.'

'Then don't talk too much.'

She checked the baby, who was sleeping on the bed. 'I want to take Delbung with me.'

He'd begun gathering the gold and stopped. 'Are you mad, woman? We've just come from Africa and you want us to turn up with an Aboriginal helper!'

441

'People might think she's from Africa. They're black there, too.'

'But different. I've seen them.'

'I need her. I've come to depend on her.'

'You'll have to leave her. Anyhow, she wouldn't leave the tribe.'

'Caroline will miss her. And who'll do the work?'

He finished wrapping the gold. 'Mrs Clancy, you're now a rich lady and able to afford a dozen housemaids if you want them.'

'Is the gold really worth that much? How much is it worth? There's no point in thinking we're rich if we're not.'

'That's one reason I have to go to Sydney. To find out what it's worth and to buy a few things.' He told her he planned an exploratory trip on his own. 'You just work out what you want me to buy you. Clothes and those sorts of things so we can arrive in style. But first,' he added quickly, when he could see her brow furrowing in worry, 'I've got to return with the horse and bring back some more of the gold.'

'I wish you'd spend more time at home.'

'If I stayed at home, we wouldn't be rich,' he said and, picking her up, danced across the earthen floor.

He took Cortez and Ulla, who rode on the back and walked whenever Clancy walked as he led the horse through the rough hills. She was excited about riding to a strange place and being alone with Clancy but showed little interest in the fact that he was looking for yellow stones. Gogwai, the sorcerer, had special stones too, although his, she had been told by one of the women who claimed to know these things, were special because of their shape, not their colour.

Clancy seemed cheerful and affectionate but she didn't tell him she was pregnant. She would wait a few months.

He showed her the cave. He had decided she was the only

442

other person he would entrust with the information. 'I want you to remember this spot,' he told her. 'I want you to come back here every now and then and search along the creek for more of these yellow stones. You are to put them in this cave. You may bring someone with you to accompany you on the journey but no one else must see the cave.'

She nodded.

'I want you to come with me over the mountains again. To where the white men live. Will you do that for me?'

'When?'

'As soon as we get back.'

She nodded happily.

They entered the cave. The other skins held smaller amounts of gold although one had a single nugget that was the weight, he estimated, of two musket balls. They rewrapped the bundles and carried them outside where they put them in the saddlebags.

Clancy carried one bag down to the creek but had Ulla stay at the cave to remove all footprints from the dirt outside. When she returned, staggering under the load of the second saddlebag, he had demolished Wilkes's hut and was busily scattering the timber along the creek bank.

'I don't want anyone to know that a white man lived here,' he said. 'It is our secret.'

'Yes,' she said, not understanding but watching in fascination as he threw pieces of wood to the other side of the creek, up the bank, wherever he could.

'It would make a good fire,' she said.

'I don't want any big fire.'

When the last of Wilkes's bed had been thrown away, Clancy used a short rope of kangaroo hide to hobble Cortez so the horse might graze on nearby grass.

He looked immensely pleased with himself. 'Now,' he said, stretching his back, 'we're going to look for more gold.'

'What is gold?' she said and he regretted the slip of the tongue. He mustn't use the word.

'I mean, we are going to see if we can find more yellow stones.'

'You need more?'

'I need to see where they are.'

'I have never seen stones like this anywhere before. They are rather dull.'

'They are. Not pretty at all. But special to me.'

They searched for an hour without finding a trace of gold, but four waterholes downstream from the site of the old man's hut Ulla saw glints of colour in the bottom of the pool and, wading in, came back with one hand filled with river gravel. She had Clancy open his hands and poured the gravel slowly from her hand to his.

'There,' she said, plucking a sliver of yellow from his palm, then several more.

'They are so small,' she said.

But his thoughts were larger. 'We need to dig up the bottom. We need to bring a shovel and a bucket. Maybe a big tin dish to spread the stuff out on, so we can see what we've got.' He cursed himself for not bringing the shovel and the baking dish. He could have used both.

She was concerned that he seemed angry. 'There's more down there. Do you want me to get it?'

He laughed, realising avarice was turning him into a fool. 'No, some other time. A man mustn't get greedy.' He slipped the pieces of gold in his shirt pocket. 'Let's see what else is up here.'

They walked along the creek for another twenty minutes but saw no more. Maybe, he thought, Wilkes had got all there was to be found. Then Ulla glanced at a gravelly cliff face and tugged at his sleeve.

'Up there!'

Using a stick, they dug away part of the vertical bank. Ulla was immediately on her hands and knees, digging in the pile of gravel as though she were after witchetty grubs.

'Here,' she said, and handed Clancy a thin, flat piece the size of his fingernail. 'And here.' The second nugget was shorter but rounder. 'Ah.' She burrowed frantically, then held up her hand. 'This is what I saw.'

It was a nugget shaped like a boomerang and as long as her middle finger. She rubbed it against her leg to brush away the dirt.

'Are you pleased, Ker-lan-see?'

'Very pleased,' he said and she smiled. Now would be a good time to tell him she was having his baby, she thought, but some men reacted strangely to such news and so she kept quiet.

He was thinking. With the shovel, he could dig away the entire cliff. And other cliffs. Explore other creek beds. The area was a veritable treasure chest of riches.

'So what will we do now?'

He was dreaming and she had to repeat the question.

As black as coal, she was covered with beads of sweat and little else: only a necklace of kangaroo teeth, a belt woven from human hair and a short, ragged skirt made from the finest possum skin. She was a glistening black goddess and the effect on him, already reeling from the discovery of so much gold, was electrifying.

He said, 'I was thinking of going for a ride. A fast, hard ride. Would you like to come?'

Ulla had vaulted on to the back of the horse before Clancy was fully mounted. She threw her arms around him and, even through his shirt, he could feel her wet skin and firm, slippery breasts pressed against his back.

The going was rough at first and he let the horse pick its way through the rocks. When they came to a grassy flat that stretched from one bend in the creek to the next, Cortez began to gallop, a wild, frightening, rough ride that became swifter by the moment. Clancy, holding on for life, wondered what had got into the horse before he realised that Ulla, screaming in delight, was slapping its rump, urging it to go faster.

They came to more rocks and the horse slowed and stumbled. Clancy pulled hard on the reins. When the horse stopped, he slid from the saddle. She fell on top of him, giggling and pulling at his shirt.

'You're an animal,' he yelled, laughing and protesting but she had the shirt from him in seconds.

'I am a snake.' Rolling, wriggling, laughing, she wrapped her legs around him and slid her body across his ribs and around his back, entwining herself in his arms, legs and torso.

She stood up, undid her belt and let the simple skirt fall to the grass. He faced her. 'I feel overdressed,' he said in English and she did not understand the words but knew the intent when he removed his belt and let his trousers slither to his boots. She bent to remove the boots and, with a laugh, threw them far away in opposite directions.

'You cheeky possum,' he said, shaking his pants clear as he chased her. She ran to the nearest pool. It was deep and the water was clear and she dived in, fishlike in the way she cleaved the water and darted this way, then that, under its surface.

He jumped in.

She'd moved to the shallows and turned, waiting.

'What is cheeky?' she asked.

'This is.' He grabbed her by the buttocks and pulled her hard against him. She pulled too, locking him into her and he was surprised at her strength. Less secure in his footing, he was tipped on his side and, laughing, she rolled on top of him.

They were now on a short, smooth beach and she rolled him along the sand, half in, half out of the water but with her legs locked around his hips, pulling him deep inside her, content to lie totally immersed when he was on top but careful to lift his head so he could breathe when she was dominant.

'Are you a fish?' he tried to say before being spun into the water.

'I am woman. Best woman you'll ever know. Better than white woman.'

They came to the end of the sand and she lay beneath him, writhing, squeezing, sucking him into her until he burst and she held him tight, no longer moving, frozen for several minutes in her own recollection of ecstasy.

On the horse on the way back, with his clothes draped across Cortez's neck, he made her sit in front of him and then on him and, with his arms around her and his lips kissing her ears, she could not imagine a lovemaking so intense, so rhythmical, so profound. It was a pure, screaming-for-joy, never-ending rapture. The horse, jogging slowly back to their camp, drove them to their peak at the same instant. Then she twisted, without losing her balance, and rode the rest of the way holding him and kissing him and loving her man with an intensity, she was sure, that was deeper than any woman could have known.

FORTY-FOUR

GOVERNOR HUNTER HAD been gone from the colony for almost four years, a victim, as he had feared, of John Macarthur's poisonous prowess with the pen and the influence of Macarthur's friends in London. His replacement was a fellow naval officer, Captain Philip Gidley King. Both had served on board the *Sirius* when the First Fleet sailed for Botany Bay. Not having been in the colony for some years, King was untainted by Macarthur's slurs about corruption in the New South Wales Corps and had the further advantage of being twenty-one years Hunter's junior. Running such a remote and unruly place as New South Wales, some of the Whitehall decision-makers believed, was too much for an old man.

It was King's name that Clancy heard when he stayed the night in a tavern at The Green Hills. It puzzled him. He thought the others were talking about the monarch in unflattering terms until one man added the word 'Governor'. He was tempted to ask many questions but played the role of listener and spoke only when he was brought directly into the conversation, which was a rare occurrence, for the men gathered for a game of cards showed little interest in a visitor who'd come to the river to look at land. They didn't ask where he was from, which was the one story Clancy had rehearsed. They assumed he was from Sydney Town. There was nowhere else.

Clancy had poor luck with his cards—he was also severely out of practice—and lost a few shillings. The others were content, everyone liking a loser in such circumstances.

Clancy had brought only a modest quantity of gold, which he had stitched into various parts of his clothing. He was paying for his accommodation and meals with the money he'd stolen on his last visit. It was such a quaint feeling to be able to pay for things.

Ulla had allowed Clancy to cut her hair and was dressed in a cap and man's clothes. She was sleeping in the stables.

He had thought at first of following past practices and sleeping out but it would be ridiculous for a man posing as a free and wealthy immigrant to be found hiding in a clump of bushes, so he walked into town and demanded a bed for the night. Ulla stood dutifully behind, carrying his bags. He had shaved that morning, leaving only a well-trimmed moustache, and wore one of William Clancy's outfits. The wide-brimmed hat he had left behind, it being so distinctive as to jog memories. But he did need a hat. People would stare at a gentleman who went hatless and he had resolved to buy one in the morning.

The town had been rebuilt although, he was surprised to note, it was on the same site. The blacks, so despised by the whites, would not have made such a mistake, although, he had to admit, it was a mistake they couldn't make as they didn't build houses. But they would never have wasted their energy on constructing something that was certain to be washed away or at least inundated at some time in the future.

With the game over and the last drink downed, he went outside and stood in the street, longing for the sweet air of the bush but tasting the acrid fumes of household fires.

'Pleasant enough night.' One of the players had joined him.

'Dashed good.'

'I didn't catch your name in there.'

'William Clancy.'

'You said you were buying land?'

'Having a look.' He thought of adding 'old boy' but decided the man beside him was low class; probably an emancipist who had some business in town. His hands lacked the roughness of a farmer.

'A few people are selling up,' the man said.

'So I hear.'

'Hunter ruined a lot of good men.'

'So I believe.'

'Ridiculous prices for their crops, he set.'

'Absolutely.'

The man brought out a pipe and flourished a tobacco pouch. 'Care to join me?'

'Not tonight, thank you.'

The man lit his pipe and drew deeply. 'Up from Sydney Town?'

'Just arrived, actually.' He was doing well with his speech, he thought, recalling the way an upper-class officer had talked.

'So you're new to the colony, eh?'

'Quite new.'

'I thought as much.'

'That's very keen of you, sir.'

'I can tell.'

Clancy patted his vest and smiled. 'Is it the clothes?'

'Oh no. There's something about you.'

'Goodness me, I'll have to be careful.'

The other man's lips smiled around the pipe stem. 'No, it's the way you bear yourself, the way you talk. Obviously, a very distinguished gentleman.'

'That's kind of you, sir.'

'May I ask where you're from?'

'Cape Province.'

'Ah.' His face was blank.

'Africa.'

'Goodness me.' He sucked noisily on the pipe. 'Africa.'

'Family had land there.'

The man frowned. 'Aren't there dangerous animals there?'

'Not if you're a good shot, sir.'

'I see.' Then he really saw and laughed. He belched and the air was sickly with rum fumes. He apologised and said he must be off. He had a shop to open in the morning. He sold men's wear.

'I need a hat. Mine blew away today. Dashed thing landed in the mud. Had to leave it.'

'Well, please, I mightn't be able to sell you land but I can certainly sell you a hat.'

'I'll call around in the morning. And what is your name, sir?'

'Perkins.' They shook hands.

Perkins headed away from the river. He was drunk and staggered slightly.

Clancy slapped his hands together. A very distinguished gentleman. He was going to enjoy his new life.

Perkins had hats that ranged in price from fifteen shillings to two pounds, five shillings. He started to apologise for the prices, complaining about transportation costs as everything had to be brought up the river but Clancy quickly silenced him by choosing the most expensive hat, a handsome black piece with a high crown and a rolled brim.

Unable to resist, he then displayed a handful of Spanish dollars, explaining that dollars had been the currency of the last port he'd visited.

'Perfectly all right,' Perkins said and produced a list showing the value of currencies available in the colony. The Spanish dollar, he said, was worth five shillings and sixpence and then

451

showed Clancy the list to verify his honesty. 'It's a change to see real money,' he said, adding that most transactions involved promissory notes which were generally expressed in bushels of wheat.

'Have you seen one of these?' Clancy handed him his most valuable coin, the gold mohur.

'Never.' Perkins held it up to the light. 'Gold.'

'Yes. A gold mohur.'

Perkins checked his list. 'My God, they've even got it here. It's worth one pound, seventeen shillings and sixpence. Where's it come from, sir?'

'Africa,' Clancy said but immediately chided himself. He had no idea where the coin originated. He'd have to be careful with his glib answers or one day he'd encounter someone who would know he was lying.

'What's gold worth?' Clancy asked casually.

'Oh, I wouldn't know, sir.' Perkins laughed. 'Not too many people flash gold around here.'

And nor will I until I get to Sydney, Clancy thought, and bade Perkins goodbye. Ulla was waiting outside. She smiled at the sight of him in his new hat.

'You look funny,' she said.

'No, I look distinguished.' Setting the hat at a jaunty angle, he set off to walk to Sydney.

It was a wet day when Clancy and Ulla arrived in Sydney Town. Heavy rain had fallen in the morning and the sky was bruised with the roiling menace of blue-black thunderclouds. They hurried to find shelter before the next downpour. Climbing Brickfield Hill, they passed two gangs of convicts who were struggling in deep mud to haul carts laden with bricks. Surprisingly, they were the first gangs they had seen since leaving the river and Clancy turned his head away, as if in conversation with his black servant, rather than risk being recognised.

He would have to learn to look a convict in the eye. No one would recognise him. And most of the men he knew would be pardoned by now, for seven years was the average term.

He passed two soldiers. More composed, he nodded as a gentleman would. They saluted as soldiers should.

Clancy remembered Sydney Cove as little more than a tent settlement spread around an inlet where there was safe anchorage for ships and a supply of fresh water from the Tank Stream. How it had changed! Now there were substantial buildings of stone and rows of cottages made of brick and plaster with roofs of thatch or shingle. Trading houses and boatbuilders flourished at the northern end of High Street, and from the street—still only a cart track—narrow lanes dipped down to the water's edge which was lined with wooden wharves and launching ramps.

Several ships were at anchor and the town was filled with roistering sailors. He was no longer used to crowds and he found himself intimidated by so many people and so much noise. Men were shouting as if already drunk, harlots were beckoning from every other doorway and he could hear the shrill cry of a harridan berating some man. Dogs were barking, hawkers calling out to passers-by as they tried to sell their goods, waifs were running through the streets and alleys, begging, laughing, fighting. He came to a row of caged parrots hanging from the front of a wooden building. Someone blew a whistle and the birds began squawking and screaming as the shop owner, a whistle in one hand, leaped out at Clancy.

'From South America, sir,' he shouted, to be heard above the clamour. 'Make wonderful pets. You can carry them around.' He had one on his shoulder although, Clancy noticed, a chain ran from the bird's leg to the man's belt. The parrot had buried its enormous beak in its owner's hair as it sought some morsel in the man's scalp.

The man blocked Clancy's path. 'Only fifteen shillings.'

'Robbery,' Clancy said and wished he had some means of pushing the fellow out of his way. He regretted the lack of the musket, which had been across his shoulder for so many years he now felt naked without it. He had the pistol, but he could scarcely shoot the man. He vowed to buy a walking-stick. A man should have something in his hand when he went walking.

A carriage passed and splashed mud over both men. The carriage stopped and a man in a top hat and frockcoat emerged.

'My dear fellow, are you all right?' he said and signalled to his driver to wipe mud from Clancy's clothes.

'I'm quite all right, sir. Not your fault. Just these damned roads.'

'Fourteen shillings,' said the man with the parrot.

The stranger had a walking-stick and raised it. 'Be off with you. Leave this gentleman alone.'

'A pox on you both.' The man with the parrot retreated into his shop.

'Cheeky fellow. I don't know what the place is coming to.' He gripped Clancy's sleeve. 'I had asked the driver to go slow but you know what these fellows are like.'

'Damned difficult to find a good man,' Clancy said, wishing the driver would leave the mud alone as he was merely spreading it across his trousers.

'I wish there were something I could do.'

'There is,' Clancy said. 'I'm a stranger and I need lodgings for the night. Is there somewhere you can recommend?'

The man pulled at the whiskers lining his jaw. 'There's an inn just up the road. It's respectable, which is all I can vouch for. Still that's something, eh?' He handed Clancy his visiting card. Lieutenant Kedron Jamieson. It gave an address. 'Why don't you call on me some time. Maybe we could have a drink.'

I must get cards done, Clancy thought and introduced himself. Yes. He'd be pleased to call on the lieutenant. Maybe later in the week?

Clancy booked in at an inn bearing the sign The Pig and Pheasant. Once more Ulla, who was well disguised in cap, scarf, high-necked shirt, jacket, pants and boots, stayed in the stables. The owner was reluctant to allow a black person on the premises but a Spanish dollar in his hand soon melted his principles.

For the next two days Clancy walked around town familiarising himself with streets and buildings, asking questions, listening to conversations. He was particularly interested in learning what ships had arrived recently. One, the *Isabella*, was loading cargo at a wharf. She was a three-masted square-rigger that, according to a sailor, had been there a week, having sailed from the Thames and called at Rio and Cape Town.

Clancy went on board and asked to see the master. His name was Wonson. No, the captain said, he was not returning to England as his visitor had heard, but was setting sail in two days' time for Lima, on the west coast of South America. But yes, he would be coming back to Sydney and yes, he might be sailing for London then. That gave Clancy the opportunity to inspect one of the cabins and, by the time he had left the ship, he could describe the cabin, the vessel and the captain, plus the voyage they had endured in rough weather from Cape Town to Port Jackson.

Back at the inn, he remarked to the proprietor that he had been forced to return to his ship, searching for something he must have misplaced on the voyage out. There was no sign of it, of course.

'Valuable piece, too. Been in the family for years,' Clancy said without saying what he had lost.

'Can't trust no one on the ships,' the man mumbled but

would from that day swear to anyone who asked that William Clancy Esquire had arrived from Cape Town on board the *Isabella*.

Of all the houses he saw, the one that most fascinated Clancy was a brick mansion not far from the inn. It stood on the corner of High Street and the bridged road that crossed the Tank Stream near the harbour. The house was two storeys high with an imposing balcony and was set in gardens filled with flowers and fruit trees. The original owner, a Lieutenant Kent of the New South Wales Corps, was reputed to have spent the incredible sum of 300 pounds on the gardens alone.

What interested Clancy, however, was that the house had been bought by Governor King for use as an orphanage. He had paid 1,539 pounds, seventeen shillings and threepence for it. And he was using it to house unwanted children! According to gossip, the Governor's wife had persuaded him to make this extravagant, extraordinary purchase. She was, people said, a woman of missionary zeal who was concerned about the homeless waifs roaming Sydney's streets. There were estimated to be more than 1,000 of them, primarily the illegitimate offspring of soldiers and convict women.

Clancy had mixed thoughts while gazing at the house. One was that Caroline might end up here, if he and Eliza were caught and sent to the gallows. The other was that such a home had cost around 1,500 pounds. How much gold did he have? What sort of house could he buy with it? A modest stone cottage or a mansion like this?

He went to the address on Lieutenant Jamieson's card and observed his house from a distance. The residence was in Mulgrave Street, only a short walk south of the old Government House. Obviously, officers in the New South Wales Corps were a privileged lot, he decided, for it was a two-storeyed home made of sandstone, with four pillars at the front, a double-width front door of ornately carved wood surmounted by an arch of stained glass and a semicircular driveway for carriages. It had a modest garden—nothing like that in the Kent mansion—but was impressive, nonetheless.

Those who were sent to the colony in chains were leading lives as miserable as man could devise but those who came in officers' uniforms were making for themselves immense sums of money and all they had to fight for, he assumed, was a share of the profits.

Lieutenant Kedron Jamieson must be one of those officers who had gained control of all trade in the colony. He could well be interested in buying a little gold.

He was. That morning Clancy had bought a pouch of the finest leather and from it poured gold fragments on to the scales that Jamieson produced. He was watching Jamieson, not the weights he used. The man was licking his lips.

'I had thought of going to a bank,' Clancy said, apologising for the inconvenience he was causing.

The lieutenant laughed. 'Not possible yet, sir, not yet. Maybe one day some adventurous soul will start a bank.' He was removing the smallest weight, trying to achieve balance.

Clancy had brought less than half the gold he'd carried with him but Jamieson immediately offered him two hundred pounds.

'I will take all you can give me, sir,' he said, rubbing his hands in such a way that Clancy knew he could get a better price elsewhere. Later. For now, he was happy to have two hundred English pounds in his pocket and the knowledge gained by rapid calculation—for he was good with sums—that he could undoubtedly afford to buy the best house in all of Sydney and still have a fortune left over.

Jamieson had had no trouble accepting Clancy's story that the gold was from Cape Province. With the grace of one wealthy man dealing with another, the lieutenant didn't press for any details as to where the mine might be or how much he had brought with him, but he clearly understood there was much more to come. All he did was caution Clancy against showing the gold to anyone else.

'The town is full of thieves and letting people know you carried gold would be like dangling meat in front of a pack of starving dogs. Just be careful, sir.' He gave a wink. 'Just you and me. No one else should know.'

During the next two days Clancy bought many clothes for Eliza and the child and, for himself, several shirts, a coat, two pairs of trousers plus a stout pair of walking boots. He bought Ulla a pair of boots too, for the ones she was wearing were not a good fit, and a necklace of colourful glass beads which she stared at for hours, preferring to admire its flashing colours rather than wear it under her shirt.

He bought only the best quality clothing, introducing himself to several traders and letting it be known that he was looking at property along the river but might decide to settle in town. They were a talkative lot, happy to discuss the housing situation and suggest areas where he might find property suitable for a man of his station.

From a pawnshop he purchased a wooden chest such as he'd seen people take on board ships, and a large leather case. The case was in good condition although the leather was scuffed from use and impressed as having belonged to a well-travelled man, which was precisely the effect he wanted. From a stables in the southern end of High Street he bought a packhorse and, from a shop nearby, a pair of canvas pannier bags with thick leather straps.

He stabled the horse at the back of The Pig and Pheasant and asked the owner if he could leave the chest there until he returned in a few weeks' time with his family, who were staying in the country. The man was delighted to oblige.

Clancy had slightly more than forty pounds left and sent a messenger to advise Lieutenant Jamieson he proposed calling in the morning. Would his visit be convenient?

Jamieson was pleased to see him. Clancy began by saying he was embarrassed to discover there was no bank in the colony because he had a considerable amount of gold with him and, if he chose to settle in the colony, would bring more.

Jamieson had the smile of a cat that has seen a mouse trapped in the corner.

'I was wondering,' Clancy said hesitantly, 'if you could exchange some more gold or, at least, advise me where I should go. I'd like to set up some sort of regular arrangement. At a fair price, of course.'

'There are any number of traders in town who will take your gold, Mr Clancy.' They were drinking tea from the finest china. The rims of the cups were, Clancy noted, lined in gold. Jamieson sipped from his cup. He frowned. 'I can't guarantee that many of them will give you a fair price, however. This place is a nest of rogues, as you must have discovered. And also, as I mentioned the other day, it would be unwise in the extreme to let people know you're carrying gold. Most unwise.'

'I appreciate the warning, lieutenant.' Clancy drank more tea. 'By the way, I assume our discussions are entirely between ourselves. Gentleman to gentleman.'

'My dear fellow, of course.'

Clancy realised he'd let his accent slip and, instead of talking like an educated man from the Somerset region, he was mimicking the lieutenant's voice, which was more Midlands. He'd have to be careful. He needed practice.

'I'm not unused to dealing with ruffians,' he said. 'Shot a few in my time. We had trouble with the savages when we first started the mine. Difficult area.'

'And where was it, if I may ask?'

'Well inland. About twelve days' hard march. Do you know Africa, lieutenant?'

'Afraid not.'

Clancy smiled. 'Been there a few years. Worked very hard as you can see.' He held out his hands. 'And what I've got, I've earned. Wouldn't want to lose it or be cheated by some scoundrel.'

'That's what I'm saying, Mr Clancy. A gentleman in your position has to be careful.'

Clancy pushed his cup to the middle of the table, leaned back in his chair and stuck his thumbs in his belt. In his role as William Clancy, explorer, goldminer and shooter of savages, he could afford a few rough mannerisms. Mustn't be too much of a dandy. 'So what do you say, lieutenant? Are you able to help me out? At least, with this lot?'

'Why certainly, sir. I am a man of some substance.' He rose and went to a window, drawing the curtain to reveal a view of several ships moored in the harbour. 'One of the ships over there is the brigantine *Eleanor* out of Boston. The one with two masts. Came in with a cargo of salted meat, flour, tobacco, rum. I bought the lot.'

And you'll sell it for five times the price, Clancy thought, but said, with wide-eyed innocence, 'I thought you were in the army?'

Jamieson stayed at the window but turned, so that he was framed by a view of shingled roofs, masts and on the far side of the harbour the blur of bushland. 'There's no war here, Mr Clancy.'

Clancy stared blankly.

'There's nothing for a soldier to do.'

'Oh, I see. You do a little business on the side.'

'Not a little. Quite a lot, actually. Be damned boring, otherwise.'

'You know,' Clancy said pleasantly, 'I think we're alike, really. I went to Africa not so much to make money but because I was bored.'

'And you found a goldmine.' Jamieson laughed.

'Possibly we've each found our own goldmine, eh?'

'Well said.' Jamieson went to get his scales. He stopped at the door. 'Have you brought much today?'

'Just a little. There are a few things I must buy before I set off for the country.'

Jamieson's eyebrows rose sharply. 'You're going to the country?'

'I'm looking at land, out along the river.'

'If I might offer a word of advice, I'd be wary of land out there. Prices for produce have been most erratic. Not a good investment, I'd suggest.'

'And what is?'

'I've found trading to be interesting.'

'I know very little about trading.'

'And I know a lot.'

Jamieson was smiling and Clancy said, 'What are you suggesting, sir?'

'Nothing really. It was just that the thought occurred that we possibly should talk about some sort of joint venture . . .'

'Of what kind?'

Jamieson moved back into the room. 'These days there are ships coming every week. Many are on speculative voyages, where the ship's master brings a cargo and sees what he can sell. Gold is the most welcome of all currencies and with a reasonable supply, we might be able to do more, buy more, sell more than anyone else.'

'And make more money,' Clancy suggested.

'Oh, I'm sure we could do that.' Jamieson went to get his scales.

Two days later Clancy and Ulla set off to cross the mountains once more. He had the packhorse in tow with the leather suitcase strapped to its rump and the panniers filled with gifts for Wonngu and others in the tribe. Stitched into his clothing was currency worth 210 pounds. The wooden chest, packed with many of the clothes he'd bought, was stored at the inn. He was feeling remarkably pleased. Not once had he been challenged, no one had recognised him and, as far as he knew, not once had his story been doubted. And he had a business partner, well accepted by Sydney society, who was hypnotised by the prospect of abundant gold.

Part Four

FORTY-FIVE

CLANCY RODE FROM his house on the hill and turned down the narrow track that curved through the stand of wattle. It was one of the few places close to town where the trees were abundant, wattle being in demand for building the walls of the huts and cottages that were now to be found standing in rows, a full mile and a half from Sydney Cove. The trees were in bloom and he guided the gelding through the puffy ranks of golden blossom. He stopped beside one tree and, bending down, peeled some gum that had oozed from the trunk. He liked the sweet, syrupy taste and often stopped here, on one of his rides along the southern shores of the harbour, to fill a cheek with a glob of wattle gum and chew while he rode.

Rather than take the longer but easier track, he followed the zigzagging path that scratched its way down the sandstone slopes to Woolloomooloo Bay.

He had arranged to meet Larsen, the boatbuilder, but Larsen was late. There were many people in the area, some having come by horse and even carriage, and this puzzled Clancy because normally the bay was a quiet place but a man told him this was to be the site of a fight between rival groups of Aborigines. Even at this stage of the afternoon there was much betting on the outcome. One of the groups was already there, four men with long spears and woomeras who, the man said, had come all the way from Jervis Bay, far to the south. They were arousing much interest, being unusually hard-faced with long beards that were plaited in several strands and were, by common agreement, uglier and fiercer looking than the local blacks. They were naked but for belts of animal skin and squatted on the grass, tall spears rising from their knees like bulrushes in a swamp. They sat alone, neither talking nor smiling as they waited for the fight to start. Some of the white onlookers were already wagering they would win, even though their opponents, who were local men and renowned for their skill with the spear, had not arrived.

Such battles had become a common part of the Sydney social scene. Most had been fought around Brickfield Hill but, these days, any flat area away from houses, where people could gather and get a good view of the contest, was likely to be used.

Some were duels between two men, others full-scale battles between rival tribes. Some were to settle differences, others merely a matter of pride. A fight normally finished when a man on one side was wounded but many ended in death. A favourite from some years back, a man with the extraordinary name of Gome-boak, was still remembered and talked about whenever a new champion appeared and people were tempted to make comparisons. Gome-boak, a small man of exceptional build and strength, had come from somewhere down south, travelling to Sydney purely to challenge others and demonstrate his prowess. He defended himself with a body-length shield and struck with spears of exceptional size. In the years of his reign he hadn't killed anyone, winning his bouts by wounding the other man or forcing him to concede defeat, thereby gaining the respect of his rivals and never creating enemies among tribal survivors who might feel honour-bound to seek revenge.

His career ended when he met a man whose ethics and aim were not as finely tuned as his.

No one was sure why the blacks did this, wounding and

killing each other for the entertainment of the whites. Some people, tiring of these macabre spectacles and likening them to Roman gladiatorial contests, speculated that it was the Aborigines' way of gaining respect from the strange new arrivals, of displaying their own skill and bravery and, perhaps, adapting to the white man's culture, it being obvious that the whites enjoyed blood sports.

Clancy wondered what his old friend Wonngu would make of all this. Wonngu normally deplored fighting and would do what he could to avoid any confrontation, whether it be between two males in his own group or a clash between tribes. Could he comprehend a situation where black people, once the undisputed masters of their own territory, were prepared to kill each other for the amusement of these interlopers?

A shout interrupted his reverie. He thought at first the rival group of natives might have arrived but it was merely two men, both poorly dressed and uncouth in manner, arguing over a wager and the crowd, anxious to see some early blood, were trying to provoke them into a bout of fisticuffs. But someone laughed and one of the men walked away and there was much back slapping and noisy banter.

Clancy was mounted on Prince, a six-year-old bay gelding he'd purchased the previous year from Henry Hawkins, an emancipist who'd built up a good business as a carriage-maker and kept a few horses for sale. Clancy had paid 110 pounds for the gelding. It was not in the same class as Cortez but was fast and had a good nature and was specially good on kangaroo hunts. He often went shooting, there being a plentiful supply of kangaroos in the hills edging the harbour.

Not caring for the boisterous nature of the crowd, Clancy rode to the east, covering half a mile or so as he looked for kangaroos, in case he came this way tomorrow for a little sport, but the noise of the gathering must have driven all animals away, for the hills were deserted. Further to the south, where the bush was dense, smoke rose in several places. The Aborigines must have been burning off the bush, which was a habit of theirs, thought to be caused by their need to promote a fresh growth of grass, to attract more game.

On seeing a sail, Clancy returned to Woolloomooloo Bay, reaching the agreed place just as Larsen beached his yacht. The man was breathless and gushing apologies.

It was the flood, he said, which was the standard excuse used these days by anyone who was late in delivering goods, inefficient in service, or about to raise prices to astronomical levels. Some said this flood of 1806 was worse than the one of 1799. Certainly, the Hawkesbury settlements had been levelled again, crops destroyed and farmers ruined. Once more Sydney was short of staples like wheat, maize and cabbage, while grain and vegetable prices had risen to absurd levels. A bushel of wheat now cost from seventy to eighty shillings and a two-pound loaf of bread could be as much as five shillings—at a time when a man might earn only seventeen shillings for such gruelling work as felling an acre of timber.

Not that such things were of great concern to Clancy. He was one of the wealthiest men in the colony.

Clancy wanted Larsen to build him a boat. He already owned a vessel, a two-masted brigantine of 105 tons that he'd purchased from an American the previous year. The American, a hard-drinking, garrulous fellow named Ballantine, had sailed her around the Horn but grounded the ship on a reef near the Friendly Islands. He just managed to reach Sydney, with canvas and pitch plugging some of the holes torn in the hull. Some people, with a knowing wink, suggested Ballantine had sound reasons for not returning to his home port of Boston, which was why the man was so desperate to sell the vessel. Clancy, who found he had a knack for hard bargaining, had offered Ballantine half the price he wanted and ended up buying the brig for only 875 pounds. Some old hands on the waterfront said he paid too much but these were men who couldn't afford to buy an oar for a humble rowing boat.

Clancy was happy. It was a good-looking vessel and perfect for his needs. He spent another 425 pounds having it repaired and refitted. She was now back in the South Seas, with a young captain who swore he knew where to get vast quantities of sandalwood.

Larsen had done the repair work on the brig's hull. She was now named *Caroline*. Eliza had liked that, although it was the only thing about the deal she had liked, having been extremely critical of Clancy's decision to get involved in the shipping business.

What did he know about shipping?

Nothing, he would respond—and the discussions went on for days—except there was more money to be made owning a ship than in buying its cargo. He'd soon discovered that the number of independent captains who sailed to Sydney on speculative voyages was diminishing and those who still sold their goods to the highest bidder were becoming increasingly avaricious.

He needed to have his own business, he argued, because one day the supply of gold would run out or someone would stumble upon his creek and that would be that.

But ships? He was not a sailor.

Which was why he'd engaged young Thomas Murchison to run his ship and find the sandalwood.

What did he know about sandalwood?

It was worth as much as gold, that's what he knew.

And what if Murchison decided to sail away to some other country and keep the sandalwood and keep the ship?

Clancy gave up at that point.

But Eliza did like the name *Caroline*.

The brig was on her first voyage since the refit. If she were wrecked on some cannibal island Clancy would lose a lot of money—and an enthusiastic young captain—but if she returned with her holds filled with sandalwood, he'd make a fortune—much more than he'd paid for the vessel. He'd already spoken to a buyer who was prepared to purchase all he could supply and would then pay the cost of having it shipped to China, where sandalwood was highly valued for its delicate aroma.

Larsen had begun with a yard near Dawes Point, where he had repaired Clancy's brigantine. Subsequently he had started a boatbuilding business on the Hawkesbury, to make small craft for the river trade. Previously there had been a ban on private boatbuilding in the colony, both to protect the monopoly of the East India Company and to minimise the risk of convicts seizing a vessel and sailing to China, still the preferred destination of all escapees. The ban had been lifted after Hunter left, and a small boatbuilding industry was now flourishing on the Hawkesbury. Or had been until the flood. Larsen had lost everything. All he had left was the fifteen tonner he'd arrived in.

But, he was quick to add, he was starting again. What was it Mr Clancy wanted?

Clancy told him he needed something large enough to bring coal down from Port Dalrymple and do a little sealing in southern waters. And yet small enough to navigate the Hawkesbury, to transport grain to the Sydney market once the farms along the river were re-established. It would need to be a versatile little vessel.

About 40 tons, Larsen suggested, the cogs in his mind whirring under the powerful impetus of imagined profit. He could have it finished in six months.

So soon? Clancy was pleased but surprised.

Larsen had already begun rebuilding on the river. That's where he'd been, why he was delayed today. Trouble getting deliveries of the necessary timber.

They agreed on a price and a delivery date.

Clancy could make a handsome profit from a small craft. There was money to be made in seals; he knew that from talking to all the Americans who were in these waters. There was also a need for more shipping to haul coal down from the new fields on the Hunter River and, because some vessels had been lost in the floods, there would be a shortage of suitable shipping to bring produce from the Hawkesbury settlements once the farms were producing crops once more.

However, his main reason for wanting his own small vessel was not to do with carrying sealskins, coal or wheat, but gold.

Every six months or so, he'd gone back over the mountains to get more gold. Even though he had made more than 16,000 pounds from the lot he'd brought when he and Eliza came to settle in Sydney, there always seemed to be a need for more. But beyond that, he was driven by the fear that someone, some day, would cross the mountains and stumble upon his creek. He could make no claim of prior ownership to the gold. It would be lost. Therefore, he needed to get what he could, while he could.

Every time he returned Ulla showed him another pile of gold she had found and buried in the cache near the old hut. He and Ulla, carrying their infant son, would then take Cortez, with the shovels and picks Clancy had brought from Sydney, and camp out on the creek for a couple of weeks and get what they could. There still seemed to be a plentiful supply. They were currently working on a gravelly cliff face near one of the waterholes upstream from where Clancy had found old Wilkes.

While they dug, the boy played.

Their son was big for a two-year-old. More Aboriginal than white, he had finer nostrils and thinner lips than were common among the boys of the tribe, and heavily-muscled legs. He was very bright, Ulla said. She had called him Wileemarin. Clancy liked the name and called the boy Willy.

Clancy's linking his desire for gold with his need for a boat centred on the curiosity of Sydney folk. He was a prominent citizen and people were speculating about where he went on his long trips away from home. He said he had a property near the river but he knew it was only a matter of time before someone put together his absences and his never-ending supply of riches and deduced that he was getting his gold locally. Inevitably, they would follow him.

On his first journeys he had taken the packhorse but that was too dangerous, the horse leaving too clear a trail for others to follow.

Hence the boat. With a craft that made regular ocean voyages, the problem would disappear. He could board the boat, pretending he was off sealing or travelling to some distant port. In China perhaps, where he already did business. The master of the boat, who could sail it solo if need be, would take him up the river to a place near The Green Hills. There, Clancy would don bush clothes, disembark on the western bank and arrange for the man to pick him up in six weeks' time.

The master would be well paid to keep quiet. He would wonder where Clancy was heading, of course, but Clancy would say he had property along the river, and hint there was another woman and the man, being a sailor, would understand.

Eliza liked living the life of a rich lady, and especially enjoyed being able to dress Caroline in fine clothes and to employ a maid, a cook and a nanny to take Caroline walking or playing on The Common. Even so, her first year in Sydney had been filled with apprehension. People seemed to accept Clancy for what he claimed to be and asked him few questions. These they reserved for her. How long had she lived in Africa? What was life like there? Were the black Africans as big and fierce as people said? Where was the goldmine? (There had been no chance of keeping secret the fact that they had gold.) Why had they come to New South Wales? Was it true her husband had worked side-by-side with black labourers at the bottom of a mine shaft? Had he killed savages in hand-to-hand combat? All of Clancy's wild tales seemed to be brought to her for elaboration. People weren't doubting the stories. They wanted more, the meek and vulnerable wife's version of amazing events. This she found hard to do, not being blessed with Clancy's vivid imagination and not being sure what stories he had told.

So in those early months, she and Clancy would spend hours together, sitting on the terrace of their newly built sandstone mansion, running through the stories they would tell others, inventing their own family history, questioning each other, practising responses. Clancy made a point of meeting someone from each ship that had come from Cape Town and asking a few questions over a drink or two in a tavern. He was a subtle questioner and a good listener. He would then tell Eliza all he'd learned. Eventually, they felt they knew what Cape Town looked like, having learned the name of a few streets, taverns and trading houses and discovered that the Dutch lived there, as well as the English.

They should go to Cape Town one day, Clancy decided. They could go in the *Caroline.* Maybe take a shipment of sandalwood or some other commodity that would sell well. A two weeks stay in Cape Town would make them as familiar with the place and its people as they need be.

Eliza had hated the voyage out from England, having been sick for much of the time and surrounded by dying prisoners and no, she didn't want to go.

Well, he'd go. It was important that they knew something about the town where they were supposed to have lived and been married.

They were arguing a lot these days.

According to their story, she was English and had gone to Africa to stay with an aunt after her father had died. Her maiden name was Richardson; that was easy to remember, Richardson having been the name of her real aunt. The aunt had died when she was nineteen. She had met William Clancy soon afterwards, when he returned to Cape Town from his place up in the bush, a few hundred miles to the north of the coast. He was a dashing figure. They had fallen in love and been married within three months of their first meeting.

They had been married in St John's Church, Cape Town. Clancy had never heard of the church, of course, but the man who forged their marriage certificate vowed that he'd spent six months in Cape Town and had seen such a church. It was on a hill overlooking the bay. He described it. Yes, it was Church of England, he was certain, and that was important to Eliza who could tolerate a poor forgery but not the wrong religion. There were Dutch churches nearby, the forger had said, which made Clancy think the man might have known what he was talking about. Whatever the truth about St John's, the certificate looked impressive, as did Caroline's birth papers.

Clancy had thought of getting the forger to do some more work—other papers in another name could be handy if he ever had to leave the colony in a hurry—but only a week after finishing the job, the man had been killed beneath the hoofs of a runaway horse which, on reflection, wasn't a bad thing. Now there was no one to know their papers weren't genuine.

People accepted Eliza because she was rich but it was always made clear—or so she felt—that the respect befitting their superior status in society was accorded her husband, not her. People were polite, but behaved as if she were from another, cruder stratum. Clancy got away with the deception because he was such a natural actor and slipped easily into the role of a gentleman adventurer, a man of breeding who had become fabulously rich through taking the most appalling risks in Black Africa. He was much admired, and the rough edges were accepted as being the inevitable result of living a hard, dangerous life.

She worked hard on her speech, for that was the flimsiest part of the charade. She engaged a music teacher, Mr Sinclair, who not only gave her lessons on the spinet Clancy had bought as a surprise gift—for their wedding anniversary, he said, without so much as a wink—but taught her singing and worked long hours on her enunciation. He slowed her speech, rounded her vowels and taught her how to finish words properly and not swallow the endings in her eagerness to get on with the next sentence.

'A lady,' he said pointedly, as if guessing the truth, 'is never in a hurry to say anything. You must let people wait to hear what you have to say, and be sure they understand you and admire the cultured method of delivery.' He was a former convict who spoke in a deep voice roughened, she guessed, by the passage of much grog. He rolled his r's like a foreigner and seemed unable to speak without making extravagant gestures with his hands. People said he had been an actor.

More and more, Eliza was devoting her life to her daughter. She was determined that Caroline would have all the opportunities she had missed. She must be accepted in the best circles, mix with the children of privileged parents, and one day marry a man who was both wealthy and cultured. To do that, her mother had to be accepted as being what she pretended to be.

Her life was pretence. It was the cross she would have to bear until death.

Clancy was enjoying his role in Sydney society but his frequent absences worried Eliza. Other men's wives were always asking her where he went, there being so few places where anyone could go. 'People are saying he has a goldmine on the Hawkesbury, upriver from the settlement, where the country is totally unexplored,' one woman said, not pausing for breath in her anxiety to deliver a question that had bothered her for weeks. Eliza had laughed, as if the thought was meant to be humorous.

She was aware that Clancy went back over the mountains for more reasons than mere gold. He enjoyed life with the blacks. It was an astounding thought. How could any white man, particularly one who had suddenly gained such wealth and reached an exalted station in life, want to live with naked savages? The thought also frightened her for she envisaged the day when he mightn't return, having decided to spend his remaining years hunting kangaroos, wandering the plains and valleys with the tribe, living and enjoying the lie of being a reincarnated super-being.

In the last months of 1806, while snow was falling in the mountains of the Alpes Maritimes and icy winds swept across the ruffled waters of the Mediterranean, Quinton de Lacey escaped from the prison that had held him for the past six years. He had escaped twice before and been recaptured. This time, however, he made his way to the coast where he was accepted as a fisherman. He looked the part with his long hair, ragged beard and scarred face. He limped from the knife wound to his leg, and he spoke the language of the coast, having picked up the patois of the south during the grim years of his incarceration.

He joined a trawler heading for fishing grounds off the north coast of Africa. De Lacey was wondering how he could either persuade or force the captain to land him at some friendly port when the fishing boat, while within sight of the shambles of mud brick and minarets that was Carthage, was stopped by a large Arab vessel. It was a slaver, travelling from the Ivory Coast and bound for Turkey. It had been a poor voyage for the slavers, who had space in their holds and were aware of a sultan with a preference for white slaves. The French vessel was unarmed, except for a few small guns, and was quickly overrun.

Once more, de Lacey found himself in chains. A few days later, while sailing east along the African coast, the Arabs were intercepted by a British warship bound for Malta. De Lacey could hear the British shouting their challenges to the Arabs, and, being fearful that the warship would go away, called out in English. It cost him two lashes across the face. Another Arab with a curved sword was preparing to remove his head when a British officer appeared at the entrance to the hold and shot the man dead.

Within a week de Lacey was on the dock at Valetta. Within two months he was back in London.

De Lacey retained the beard, trimmed to follow the contour of his chin, for it covered much of the scar across his face. Women, he discovered, adored him and he had several affairs.

Edwin Rotherby was amused. He was beginning to think, he confessed, that de Lacey could show no interest in women and knew he was not the other way inclined. The long stint with the French, he said, had done the man good. Rotherby had been busy in London, having had an affair or two but, as always, with other men's wives; or, even worse, their mistresses.

'There are women who are both attractive and yet unattached,' de Lacey had pointed out.

Rotherby, who found unattached women resistible, had been compelled to fight a duel only a few days before de Lacey's unexpected arrival and produced his jacket with a burn mark left by the passing ball. He'd missed with his shot and everyone seemed satisfied except the woman, who believed the things Rotherby had said, and expected the two of them to run away somewhere.

'I was thinking I might run away somewhere on my own,' Rotherby said. 'Possibly New South Wales.'

Rotherby had heard the colony was flourishing from no less a source than his acquaintance, William Bligh, who was the new Governor of the colony. Bligh, triumphantly acquitted at the *Bounty* mutiny court martial, was anxious to have free settlers migrate to the colony and had promised inducements to entice the right type.

'Surely he couldn't have meant you,' de Lacey said, his English wit having been restored after the years of French suppression.

De Lacey now had money from the prize fund Lord Thomas Cochrane had established from the *Speedy*'s fourteen months of raiding. De Lacey's share was worth several thousand pounds, more than enough for him to live like a gentleman and start some kind of enterprise in Sydney Town.

Cochrane was in Britain, busily planning a series of raids on the Spanish coast—his little wars or *guerillas* as he called them. A resistance movement had sprung up in Spain and his idea was to support them by staging a series of lightning attacks from the sea, on towns and roads all along the Spanish coast. Napoleon, he had estimated, would be compelled to station several hundred thousand of his troops along the coast, thereby scattering his forces and making him more vulnerable in the campaign being planned by Wellington.

De Lacey was tempted to join him again. He had been promoted to the rank of captain and was held in high esteem by people of influence, the generous Cochrane having spread many stories of his valour and daring. But the leg troubled him and would make him more of a liability than an asset in a raid.

And so he declined Cochrane's invitation. He resigned from the Marines and decided to accompany Rotherby to New South Wales. He would go back as a hero. Make his fortune. And find out what the devil had happened to that woman convict.

FORTY-SIX

LARSEN TOOK EIGHT months to build Clancy's 40-tonner. It was a sloop, broad of beam and with a shallow draught. People said it would roll in rough seas, as most colliers did, but should be perfect for the river trade, particularly as the Hawkesbury had silted up in places after the last flood. Clancy called her *Empress of China* and some snickered, thinking it too grand a name for such a stout workhorse, but it implanted in people's minds the thought that William Clancy would be trading with China, even sailing there in this vessel, and that was Clancy's purpose.

On her first voyage, the *Empress* brought coal from the Hunter River. Clancy boarded her for the next voyage. Eliza knew of his destination but he told others he was sailing to Captain Cook's Possession Island, at the northern tip of New South Wales, to investigate rumours that the shallow waters around there were filled with *bêche-de-mer* and other delicacies much fancied by the Chinese. People regarded him with envy, not for the voyage but for the money he'd make. William Clancy, rich beyond most people's dreams, was continually discovering ways to make himself even richer. *Bêche-de-mer?* Few knew what he was talking about but none doubted there was money in harvesting this exotic delicacy.

Of the *Caroline* and Captain Murchison, there was no sign.

'You're a fool, Clancy Fitzgerald,' Eliza said as Clancy prepared to leave. 'I told you this would happen. The man's taken your ship and your cargo and disappeared.'

'I don't mind you calling me a fool,' he said, wagging a finger, 'but you mustn't call me Clancy Fitzgerald or we'll both swing on a rope, with you calling me names and me wondering how I ever got myself involved with a silly woman like yourself.'

Leaving Eliza clutching Caroline to her knees, Clancy had stalked from the house, dressed for the town but carrying a large bag with all the gear he'd need for his journey.

As the sloop's skipper, Clancy had engaged a dour Scot named Andrew Craddock who took with him a couple of Malay deckhands who could also dive and, fortuitously, spoke no English. Craddock's instructions were to drop Clancy near The Green Hills, then leave the river and sail north along the coast into tropical waters. At a suitable location, he was to let the Malays dive for *bêche-de-mer,* trochus, mother-of-pearl and whatever else they might find. Craddock was to be back at the Hawkesbury in six weeks' time, seven at the latest. If he came back with a cargo, there'd be a handsome bonus.

Craddock was an experienced sailor in eastern waters, having been mate on a merchantman that traded between India, Java and China. He also said he was familiar with river navigation, having been 500 miles up the Yellow River. Or so he claimed. Clancy had learned to distrust most things sailors told him, for they were in his class as inventors of fanciful tales but, whatever the truth about Craddock's past, he had one priceless asset—he was the quietest man Clancy had met. He appeared to have no friends, drank alone and rarely spoke to anyone.

The Hawkesbury's banks had been ravaged by the flood and Clancy was dropped off on a sandbar a mile before the settlement. He carried a knapsack containing salted pork, salted fish, onions, bread, biscuits, a flask of brandy, a hunting knife, small axe, flint and length of cord, two pistols and a quantity of powder and balls, some for the pistols and some for his musket which he'd hidden, wrapped in an oilskin, in a cave on the early part of the climb. He also had a spare shirt and a canvas cape, to sleep on and keep him dry when it rained.

The load was heavy and he wished he'd brought the pack-horse. Maybe he could leave it with someone on the river—perhaps Adam Jenkins, although that would be dangerous, as Jenkins knew his real identity. He walked along the river bank looking for Jenkins's farm but there was no sign of the house, only a jumble of posts and broken timber. It must have been washed away in the flood.

He'd find someone else, hire space on his farm to keep the horse. Walking was too hard.

He dismissed the thought after ten minutes. The farmer would grow curious, follow him, and discover his secret crossing.

He'd have to walk.

He drank some brandy, loaded both pistols and stuck them through his belt.

On the third day, having passed through the barrier of tangled scrub, Clancy was approaching the domed mountain where he intended to stop for the night. He was threading his way through a stand of trees whose leaves rustled in the light breeze when he was confronted by a group of blacks. There were six of them. All were armed with hunting spears, throwing-sticks and clubs.

Clancy had been thinking of other things and their sudden appearance shocked him. They were only twenty yards away, dusty shapes in a region of wavering shadows.

One of them shouted at him and banged his spear against a club.

Clancy raised his hand in greeting.

The man rattled his spear.

'I am the ghost of Yerranibee,' Clancy said in the language of Wonngu's tribe but they didn't understand. The musket was over his shoulder. He dared not remove it for they were looking at him intently and jiggling their spears. They spread out, forming an arc in front of him.

Slowly, Clancy took a pistol from his belt.

'I can do magic,' he said but no one moved.

A second man shouted at him, then a third.

The blacks began talking to each other, growing more excited by the second. One spread his legs and prepared to throw his spear.

'No,' Clancy shouted, pointing the pistol at him but the man drew back his arm.

Clancy shot him. The ball struck him in the middle of the chest, the impact throwing him on his back with his arms and legs spread wide.

While the blacks looked at their fallen comrade in astonishment, Clancy slipped the musket from his shoulder and cocked it.

One man darted to his fallen friend, grabbed his lifeless hand and shook it. He made a mournful, wailing noise, like a dog howling.

They should run away, Clancy was telling himself, but none had moved. He had hoped they might have been among the men who attacked Wonngu's party all those years ago and knew of the deadly abilities of a gun but they were probably too young. They had never seen a white man. Nor were they frightened; shocked, of course, but that was a different thing.

With the musket at his hip, he walked slowly forward.

'I am the ghost of Yerranibee. I can do magic.' A man at the end of the arc grabbed his club and lunged forward. Clancy spun around, not having time to aim, and fired. The shot hit the man in the shoulder, spinning him around. He fell down, got up, then fell down again. He sat on the ground, howling in pain.

The echo of the shot rumbled through the hills.

There was a gap in the line and Clancy walked through, swinging the musket from side to side to keep them clear. They were staring at him in horror, but not moving. Beyond the gap, he turned and, holding the musket in his left hand, took out the second pistol. He had one shot left.

'Go,' he screamed and shook the empty musket.

Two ran but two stayed, one on either side of him. Breathing heavily, Clancy raised the pistol and pointed it at the nearer man's head. The man had his spear raised but he was trembling.

Clancy lifted the useless gun, which was the more imposing of his weapons, and walked slowly towards him. He counted his steps. 'One, two, three.'

They were so close Clancy could smell the man's sweat.

'Bang,' he shouted and lunged forward. The man ran. So did his companion.

Clancy watched them disappear in thick bush, then turned and bolted for the mountain. He ran until dark, when he reached the waterhole where he had once hidden the musket. There he sat with his back to the rocks and reloaded both weapons. He also withdrew the hunting knife and spent the night with the guns and the knife laid in front of him, not sleeping, listening for sounds and longing for daylight so he could continue his journey to friendly territory.

The Irishman Kerrigan had been to The Green Hills, meeting with some of the other Irish who had settled along the river. He brought them the message he had been spreading in Sydney. He'd had a letter from a friend. The French were reputed to have a fleet in the Pacific. They would surely land in Sydney, where the English force was relatively small. They would be counting on the Irish to stage an uprising, to attack from the rear while the French bombarded the English soldiers from the harbour.

Could he rely on them to help? They would need arms and should begin gathering what they could. If not guns, then axes and reaping hooks and whatever they could find.

The French would help them drive the English out and they could then start their own republic. The French would leave a garrison of troops, arrange regular supplies, give them money.

Kerrigan got little support. Most of the settlers were content.

He was still angry when he returned to Sydney. 'They are fools,' he told Noxious Watts when they were talking in the storeroom of Watts's shop at the slovenly end of High Street. 'They've forgotten all the things the English did to us.'

'People are like that.' Watts had little time for the republican cause. He was making plenty of money.

Kerrigan was silent for a long time, tapping the table, shuffling his boots but not speaking. He stood up. 'By the way, I'm sure I saw that man again.'

Watts was adding up some figures. 'Which one?'

'The one where Nilssen almost got killed.'

Watts pushed away the figures.

'The one we thought we saw in town? All dressed up like a toff? Fitzgerald?'

'That one.' Watts waited, eyebrows lofty, anxious for more and Kerrigan said, 'He was at the river. I was having a meeting with a few men under a tree on the river bank and I saw this fellow walking on his own on the other side.'

'And it was the same man?'

'I'd swear it.'

'Dressed in fancy clothes?'

'No. But he was striding out, like he knew where to go. Had a pack on his back.'

'They say that man comes from Africa. They say he's got gold.' Watts sat at the table, scratching his chin and thinking.

Lieutenant Kedron Jamieson knew Clancy was away, not on one of his regular journeys to his property in the hinterland but sailing in his new sloop. Off to get *bêche-de-mer*. That amused him because Clancy was making so much money from his other enterprises that he saw no need for him to branch out into some new industry. But the man had a golden touch. He'd probably make a fortune from *bêche-de-mer*.

Jamieson still acted as Clancy's banker for the gold, or some of it. He was aware that, in the last year, Clancy had found another source in town. A jeweller, he believed. His theory was that the cunning Clancy had purchased the jewellery business so that he was trading with himself, fixing his own rate for the precious metal and ensuring the shop had a steady supply of gold. He knew for a fact that the man who ran the business, an old, bent Jew who had worked at the craft in London before being transported, had a small foundry at the back of the premises.

Jamieson had heard the rumours. Clancy had found gold in the colony, people were saying, and he laughed at those who said it to his face and told them he had proof that the gold was of the type that came from southern Africa. He had no idea whether that was true or not but it stopped the talk. Still, he wondered. He kept a check of ships arriving from Cape Town and there had been occasions when there had been no ships from Africa but Clancy had presented him with more gold for exchange. It was not proof, of course. Clancy might well have had the gold under lock and key in his house. But he wondered. Gold in New South Wales. Now there was a thought. The place would boom, settlers would pour in and he could double—no quadruple—his fortune.

Jamieson entertained lavishly. He was famed for his dances

and had his own orchestra of seven players. That coming week-end, he was holding a reception in his house. Normally he would invite William and Eliza Clancy but it was awkward with Clancy away. A woman was rarely invited on her own. She was a good-looking woman, which made him all the more hesitant in case people started talking, hinting at some affair, as they were inclined to do in this town of swirling rumours. But to the devil with such people. He would invite her. He was sure she would find his guest of honour most interesting.

Captain Quinton de Lacey, a hero of the war against Napoleon and a daring associate of the fabled Lord Thomas Cochrane, had just arrived in the colony. He would have the most extraordinary tales to tell.

FORTY-SEVEN

WONNGU KNEW CLANCY was returning. He had received no word, seen no sign to suggest the white man was coming. He simply knew. It was the way things were. It was the way one tribe advised another that they wished a meeting to discuss an important matter. The message was sent by the mind, and they met.

Normally, he would rejoice at the prospect of Clancy's return, for Clancy was good to him and always carried gifts. More important, he brought good fortune to the people and his deeds were already enshrined in tribal lore. This time, however, Wonngu was filled with apprehension. It was because of the horse.

By Clancy's decree, only Ulla was allowed to touch the animal. It was kept in the valley where it could roam free with plentiful food and water and find shelter, if it wished, in the stables Clancy had built. No matter where the tribe wandered, Wonngu always left two men to guard the entrance to the valley to make sure the horse stayed there and was safe.

But the young man Gerung Gerunga, son of Moilow who was one of Wonngu's most trusted men, had taken it upon himself to ride the animal. He was known to be daring but Wonngu couldn't imagine any one of his people being so disobedient and foolhardy as to mount something as sacred or fearsome as Clancy's horse, and then ride it up and down the valley, as

Gerung Gerunga had done. The young man had been thrown several times but, being as stubborn as an old wombat, had climbed back on the animal and, with his hands gripping the mane and his knees locked around its sides, had tried again.

Eventually, astonishingly, the animal surrendered and Gerung Gerunga rode all the way to the lagoon, scattering birds and shouting and waving an arm in triumph. Until the animal had trodden in a hole and thrown Gerung Gerunga into a patch of rushes by the water's edge. Much worse, the horse had hurt its leg. Flicking its head and whinnying pitifully, it had hobbled back to the stables.

Wonngu had been told this by Gerung Gerunga's companion, who swore he had tried to stop the youth but had been brushed aside. Wonngu had been to see the horse. Its leg was swollen and the animal let it hang limp.

Wonngu had immediately banished Gerung Gerunga from the tribe. He had left amid much wailing and wringing of hands, for not only was he popular but the people were fearful of Clancy's wrath.

Clancy knew. Wonngu was sure of this because he sensed that Clancy was extremely upset about something. He could feel the agitation; either fear or anger.

Despite the pain in his hip, Wonngu decided to go out and meet Clancy, to talk to him before he entered the camp so that his temper might settle by the time he reached the people. He did not want him pointing his thunderstick at those he believed had betrayed his trust.

He took two men, Berak and Arabanoo, whom Clancy liked, and Ulla, who carried the boy Wileemarin on her hip.

Clancy had had a nightmare of a journey since encountering the mountain men. He believed he had been followed, having seen bushes moving in the distance when there was no wind and heard the soft crackling of feet on fallen leaves, but he had seen no one.

He was overjoyed to meet Wonngu and embraced the old man, who wept on his shoulder in a confusion of happiness and trepidation.

'The wild people of the hills attacked me,' Clancy said, anxious to appear calm but still trembling from the shock of the encounter.

'But you are not hurt.' It was not a question but a statement of certainty.

Clancy had been carrying the musket in his hand and put it down, resting it against his knees. 'The mountains are becoming a dangerous place.'

Wonngu agreed. He would never again venture there.

Clancy's legs felt weak and he sat down. Wonngu joined him and, after sharing some food and drinking water that Ulla brought from a nearby rockhole, told him about the horse.

Clancy made strange sucking noises, like a man who has run to the point of exhaustion. He held his head in both hands. 'Is the leg broken?'

'I don't know. I cannot touch the horse, as you know, but it hangs like this.' He let his arm swing loosely.

Clancy knew enough about horses to know what happened to those that broke a leg.

'I may have to shoot it,' he announced solemnly.

Wonngu was astonished. He had hoped Clancy might touch the leg and effect some miraculous cure.

'It is our way.'

'The horse did wrong?' Wonngu suggested.

'No, but when it breaks a leg, we shoot it. It cannot be fixed.'

Barangaroo had broken her leg and lived for years. She could still walk, right until the day she had died.

It was different with horses.

Wonngu had not thought of this. He had anticipated Clancy's anger but not such an extreme reaction as killing his wonderful animal.

'Will you eat it?'

'No.' His face became flushed and Wonngu was frightened. Clancy raised his hand, then lowered it to cover his eyes. When he spoke, his voice was firm but controlled. Wonngu clasped his hands, waiting.

From a distance, Wileemarin cried and Wonngu could hear Ulla trying to quieten the boy. Still he waited for Clancy to speak.

Without looking up, the white man raised a finger. 'Neither will you eat it. No one will eat it. Your people will bury it.'

Bury the horse? Waste that meat? When his people were hungry, this having been a lean season . . .

'You will bury the horse,' Clancy repeated.

So that was to be their punishment. He would sacrifice the animal but forbid them to taste its meat. He glanced at Clancy, who was still covering his face, and admired the strength of a man who could do such a terrible thing.

On the way back to the camp Clancy spoke to no one other than Wileemarin. He often carried the boy, whispering to him, the only one who could not understand his words, confessing his fear.

He had to go back over the mountains, and he was frightened.

At Clancy's bidding Wonngu ordered six men to dig a big hole near the stables. Clancy then sent them away and led Cortez, hobbling and snuffling, to the edge. He patted its sleek neck, then shot it with his pistol. He filled in the hole himself and sat by the grave all that afternoon and night. He was still there in the morning. Wonngu, hiding among bushes on the far side of the stream, watched him. Clancy had the big gun across his lap. He would point it at anyone who came near.

The distance was too great for Wonngu to see but Clancy's face was stained with tears. He was crying because he was overwhelmed by confusion, by feelings of loss and shame and fear.

The fear had come first but it had merely been the gateway to other sensations. His mind was a jumble of thoughts.

He had loved the horse more than anything he had ever possessed. It had given him a sense of power and freedom. And it had known him as an ordinary man, not some sort of god. Riding it, frightened by its pace, thrilled by its power, had been moments of truth, which were the rarest things in his life.

He hadn't meant to kill anyone. He had been acting as Yerranibee, long dead uncle of Wonngu, white ghost and superhuman, when he shot the two men in the mountains. He wasn't brave. He was playing a role. When it was all over, when reality had rushed back to seize his mind, he'd been so frightened he couldn't sleep, had been in such turmoil that he'd imagined pursuit in every stir of the wind, every click and whir of an insect.

Now Wonngu thought he was punishing the tribe by shooting the horse and thus displaying a terrible kind of strength.

He was too weak to tell the old man the truth.

He was tiring of the game of deception that was his life.

On this side of the mountains he acted as some kind of god, disseminating false wisdom, striking fear by the simplest of gestures, using his worldliness to deceive the innocent. On the other side of the mountains he played the role of a rich man, an educated man, a brave man. Everything he did was pretence.

He couldn't blame the boy for taking the horse and riding it. It was the sort of thing he'd have done himself, as a wild, rebellious youth. He was worse than the lad. He was a thief and a liar. Gerung Gerunga was merely a wild boy, filled with curiosity, imbued with daring.

On the second day after shooting the horse he went looking for Wonngu. He told him he had forgiven the boy. He was to be brought back into the tribe.

That night there was rejoicing in the camp.

Eliza was nervous and at first reluctant to attend the reception on her own. It was not proper, she knew. And with Clancy gone she would be exposed to questioning by some of the sharpest minds in the colony. But Jamieson insisted and sent a carriage to take her to the house.

There were forty guests. It was a hot night and the lanterns on the terrace wore haloes of insects, buzzing and slapping the glass in their suicidal insistence to reach the flame.

The orchestra played. The members were all men on Jamieson's staff. Some were servants, some gardeners, one was his boatman. The lieutenant had bought the instruments, insisted they learn, and hired the man who gave Eliza music lessons to teach them. They were rather crude, said some who had pretensions to a cultural upbringing back home. The condescending described Jamieson's orchestra as being very colonial. That was another derogatory term, said pleasantly but meant to hurt.

But everyone danced when they played quadrilles.

'I cannot dance,' she told Jamieson who thought she meant because of propriety. So while most were whirling to the music of Jamieson's homespun orchestra, the host introduced her to his guest of honour who, needing a stick to walk, was standing well clear of the dancers, beside the punchbowl.

The name meant nothing to her. Clancy might have mentioned it but she had forgotten.

She found Captain Quinton de Lacey to be an extraordinarily attractive man. He was in dress uniform. His beard was neatly trimmed but the tip of the scar showed. She knew how he had gained such a disfigurement, Jamieson having told her something of the captain's exploits in the Mediterranean. It was, she thought, a mark of distinction. He spoke well, with the voice modulation her coach would admire. Unlike many men in this bombastic society, he encouraged her to talk and seemed genuine in his interest. The more they talked, the more she marvelled that this erudite, modest and quietly spoken man could have performed the marvellous feats that Jamieson had described. There was not a hint of crudity about him, unlike Clancy, and he was a genuine hero, unlike Clancy. Yet he had a vulnerable look about him. He would be kind, she decided, and considerate to his wife.

He was the sort of gentleman she hoped Caroline might meet some day. She judged all men by that criterion.

Jamieson had not told her de Lacey had been in the colony many years before.

She was shocked when he mentioned it. No one ever came back to Sydney. Not voluntarily. She said, 'When was that?'

He waved his hand. 'Last century,' he said, as if it were in the unimaginable past. He poured her some punch. The orchestra had stopped playing but they were still talking and de Lacey escorted her to the terrace. There was a cool breeze blowing and she was able to lower her fan.

Others were watching them.

Rotherby was holding court, entrancing a circle of listeners with his account of the latest happenings in London society, and glancing nervously at the terrace where de Lacey was dominating the attention of the most intriguing woman at the party. Before they had come to the reception, Rotherby had drilled his friend on their *modus operandi* for the night. He would scout the field to see which were the most interesting and desirable of the married women. De Lacey should concentrate on the single ladies. He was, Rotherby had been telling him, the marrying sort and now might be a good time for him to choose a wife.

And here he was was, chatting to a woman whom Rotherby knew to be the wife of possibly the richest man in the colony.

He should be the one out on the terrace, sipping punch and delivering witticisms, not de Lacey.

Eliza was more than nervous. She was frightened. The people staring at them tonight, not bothering to hide their disapproving looks, would be talking about them tomorrow. The scandalous Mrs Clancy. It was shocking enough that she had attended on her own. Now she was flirting with the handsome war hero.

Much of it was envy, she knew, but envy was the most powerful impetus to rumour. And people who gossiped about her, and enjoyed the experience, might feel compelled to search for more to say.

De Lacey frightened her, too. He was so intellectual, so worldly, so superior to her in every way that she felt each question hid a trap that would leave her caught in her own deceit. Although, she had to admit, he seemed to enjoy her company and was remarkably attentive when she made some bumbling attempt at conversation.

He mentioned Africa in one of his stories and she would have sworn her heart stopped. He said Carthage, but she had no idea where that was. Only that it was imperative to change the subject before he moved around the coast to Cape Town. So she kept asking him about his experiences with Lord Thomas Cochrane and, when there were no more questions to ask, she was silent.

He was silent too, gazing at the ships on the harbour and the spangled reflections from their lanterns.

She was sure he was bored.

Intriguing was the word de Lacey would have used for the woman he knew as Mrs Eliza Clancy. She was attractive, dignified and cultured; all admirable traits but no more than he would expect in a woman. More fascinating was the fact that she seemed to enjoy the occasional silence, as did he, and such a habit would have deemed her unusual in most circles but made her a positive rarity in this vulgar and boisterous community. When she spoke, she talked slowly and measured her words, as though each was valuable. This, too, he admired, although he couldn't place the accent; somewhere to the west of London, he thought. Oxford, Bath?

Beyond these qualities, however, was one that had him truly fascinated: she was mysterious. The enigmatic glances, the unexpected silences, the eyes that smouldered behind layers of distant secrets; all made her delightful, distinctive yet puzzling.

He saw Rotherby looking at him and frowning. He raised his glass and Rotherby looked away, the frown even heavier.

'You are not going to get your hands on this one,' he thought.

Other men might not appreciate her qualities but de Lacey had special tastes in women. He would certainly not have admitted it—was probably not aware of it—but he preferred women with many of the characteristics of his mother. Good looks were important but not paramount. He liked a woman who possessed the natural dignity that came with good breeding, was honourable, intelligent and had strength of character. If there was a touch of the mysterious, an exciting uncertainty about her, so much the better.

There was a strength in the way Eliza Clancy looked at a man, a dignity in her sparse conversation that he admired. She asked him nothing about life in London and, being bored with the vacuous nature of London society, he was grateful for that.

She was by no means the best-looking woman there. There were several who were pretty but would have been mortified at so modest a description. They were young, no more than eighteen and seemed to be in some kind of competition to see which of them could hide more of her face with her fan. They chattered like squirrels and, presumably, had a similar level of intelligence.

There was one stunning creature, older by ten years, who always had two or three men around her. Italian, he'd been told. From some aristocratic family in the north of that country. She was the wife of a recently arrived major who was many years her senior. She had dark, flashing eyes and glossy black hair that must have required an hour with a hairbrush and comb every night. She seemed to relish the attention men gave her, melted them with a smile, drew them towards her with a glance. He wondered why Rotherby was ignoring her.

Sydney had neither an abundance of free women nor a prevalence of beauty. It was a hard place for women and those who had lived there for some years reflected the hardships. Their skin was roughened by climate and labour, their faces prematurely lined, their mouths set in firm strokes of disillusion.

Eliza Clancy bore some of the signs of colonial life. The one of which she was most conscious was the condition of her hands. The skin had a hardness that would never disappear, even though the roughness and cracked seams had gone, due to her constant application of the exotic oils Clancy imported from India, and to the fact that she no longer had to do manual work.

De Lacey thought only that there was a firmness, almost a manliness about her handshake. He didn't mind. He couldn't tolerate limp, unused hands, whether male or female. And of course, this woman had lived in Africa where life must have been harsh, no matter how great the Clancys' wealth. She would have shared the rigours of bush life with her husband who, people said, had worked in his own mine, digging out the gold himself because he could trust no other man.

He had been looking forward to meeting William Clancy, who seemed to be the most interesting man in the colony. Now, having met his wife, he had mixed feelings. Strange, irrational feelings that bordered on jealousy.

FORTY-EIGHT

ALTHOUGH THE SIGHT of a sail off the coast was more common than in the early days, when an approaching ship might mean the difference between starvation and survival, there were still times when the arrival of a vessel caused excitement and brought hundreds of curious onlookers to the foreshores of the harbour. So it was when the *Caroline* returned. As she breached the mile-wide gap between the headlands that formed the entrance to Port Jackson, Captain Murchison fired the small cannon in the bow of the brigantine. He'd had it fitted in case of trouble with savages but now he used it to reveal his own unrestrainable excitement. He fired it several times as he sailed the six miles down the main fork of the harbour towards Sydney Cove and could be seen at the wheel, waving his cap to the spectators who lined vantage points along the way.

In a community nurtured on talk and sustained by rumour, everyone knew about the *Caroline*. She'd been sailed here as a near-wreck, bought by the adventurous William Clancy and turned into the most handsome vessel in the colony. She'd been off to the South Seas, to a place called Feejee where the men were reputed to be fierce, huge in size and voracious in their appetite for human flesh. She'd been away much longer than expected and many were wagering that the elegant

Caroline had either been raided by savages or caught on a reef where she was gradually disintegrating under the gnawing insistence of the tides. An inevitable consequence was that young Tom Murchison and his crew had added a few rolls of fat to the bellies of cannibals on some obscure island in the South Seas.

But here was Murchison, firing his cannon and waving madly.

Jamieson went to fetch Eliza. 'Your ship is back.'

'The *Empress*?' She was astonished. Clancy wasn't due back for several weeks.

'Your brigantine, not the little yacht,' he said with the supercilious expression she so disliked. 'The captain's firing his cannon. Everyone's getting very excited. Shall we go and see what it's all about?'

She didn't trust Jamieson. Neither did Clancy, she believed, although he would never admit it because it would be a confession of his having misjudged another man's character, and that was something he would never do.

'I'd go and fetch your parasol, if I were you,' Jamieson said. 'It's very hot today.'

'I'm perfectly all right as I am, thank you, lieutenant.' With a defiant tug at the strings of her bonnet, she climbed into his gig.

Jamieson flicked the reins and the mare broke into a canter. She had to admit Jamieson had better horses than Clancy. At least in Sydney; he'd be astonished if Clancy produced a stallion of the calibre of Cortez. However, she knew Jamieson envied Clancy his ship; she'd heard talk that he wanted to buy it. He probably hoped the *Caroline* had come back with empty holds so that Clancy would be in the mood to sell.

'Hold your bonnet, now. There's a strong breeze blowing and the mare's quite fast.'

Jamieson treated her like a simple girl; that's what upset her. So did Clancy, come to think of it.

De Lacey had been out walking and heard the noise. Someone told him it was Clancy's brig returning from a trip to the cannibal islands, so he walked down to the cove. He saw Eliza arrive with Lieutenant Jamieson and his heart beat faster. He had been wondering how he might see her again and now fate had delivered her to him.

Although . . . if this were her husband's ship, it meant Clancy was returning home. He'd heard he had gone sailing somewhere. De Lacey thought of withdrawing before Eliza saw him but had the good fortune to speak to a man who was fishing from a jetty.

'No, Mr Clancy's on his new boat, the *Empress of China*. Saw him leave meself. Won't be back yet for a while I'm told.' He wanted to say more but de Lacey was off towards Jamieson's carriage.

She saw him approaching and smiled.

'Captain de Lacey. What an unexpected pleasure.'

'The pleasure is all mine, ma'am.' He'd always spoken this way but now he hated such talk. It was so stilted, so formal, so meaningless. He wanted to say other things, to articulate the blood-red, turbulent thoughts that were rushing through his head.

'A truly beautiful day,' he said.

She agreed.

Only then did he greet Jamieson, who was tying the mare to a rail. Jamieson had seen them together at his reception, heard the talk. He had no desire to spare either from further gossip so he said, 'How fortunate. I have business to discuss with Captain Murchison. If you would be so kind, Captain?'

He kissed Eliza on the gloved hand, then offered it to de Lacey.

Without speaking, de Lacey took Eliza by the arm.

Jamieson hurried towards a wharf, which was the closest point to where the brig was mooring in the cove. Already, a boat was rattling from the davits.

'I had thought him to be more of a gentleman,' de Lacey said and Eliza covered her mouth to hide the smile. 'Although, I must say I am pleased at this unexpected opportunity to see you again.'

She blushed. Her heart was beating faster. She looked around to see if people were watching but all eyes were on the brig and its exuberant captain, who was in the boat and giving one final wave to the crowd.

'He seems extremely excited,' he said. 'Do you know why?'

'I presume he was successful in his quest for sandalwood.'

'Ahh. A valuable cargo indeed.'

'He said he knew a secret place. My husband promised him a bonus if he filled the holds.'

'He seems to have done better than that.' De Lacey could see large canvas bales lashed to the deck. He could also see Jamieson standing at the end of the wharf and signalling the boat to come to him.

'I have to say that man worries me.'

She said nothing.

'Is he involved with your husband in his business enterprises?'

'Some. Not this.'

'And yet he's greeting the captain.' De Lacey looked around them. 'Does your husband have a manager or agent? Someone to whom the captain can report?'

She was flustered. Clancy told her little about his business dealings. 'Not that I am aware of,' she said.

'What is your captain's name?'

'Murchison.'

'Then I think Captain Murchison should report to you. It is

only proper that you, as wife of the owner, should be the first to hear the exciting news . . . whatever it may be.' He led her to the wharf.

Jamieson was not pleased to see Eliza approach. 'I should like to hear the captain's news,' she said, in as firm a voice as she dared. De Lacey was impressed and Jamieson gave a cursory nod.

'I thought it proper,' the lieutenant said, ignoring de Lacey, 'that I, as business confidant of Mr Clancy, should apprise myself of the news. Perhaps unravel some of the complex issues that may be involved. Explain them to you.'

He glanced at de Lacey, who was looking at the crowd lining the shore, but had the beginnings of a smile teasing his lips.

'Thank you for your concern, lieutenant,' she said, 'but I am anxious to hear the news myself being, as it were, Mr Clancy's constant partner. In all matters,' she added after a significant pause. 'And I am quite capable of unravelling complex information.'

Jamieson bowed. 'If you would prefer me to withdraw . . .'

'Please stay.' She felt wonderful. So strong. It was the first time she had spoken to anyone like this. It was so easy.

It was three weeks since Murchison had left the river mouth where he had anchored in the islands, but his eyes were still ablaze with excitement. He had formed an alliance with a local chief. The chief had provided the men who had harvested the sandalwood from the forests near his village. All he required in return were certain items of trade. Murchison had taken things like axes, knives, pots, kettles and a few shiny gewgaws, such as beads and mirrors.

'They have no understanding of the value of this substance,' Murchison said. 'They value most the things that might be useful in battle, for they seem to be constantly at war with their

503

neighbours. I was thinking to take a few muskets next time . . .'

'I think you should discuss that with my husband,' Eliza said, recalling the impact a solitary gun had had on the tribes west of the mountains. 'It may not be wise. If they are happy with simple things, why not take them simple things?'

'I am anticipating competition,' Murchison said, glancing nervously at the crowd lining the cove. 'He who has the best gifts gets the most sandalwood.'

'Perhaps. I will discuss it with my husband and then he will talk to you.' How brazen of her. Clancy never discussed business with her, never listened to her ideas, but she liked the deferential way Murchison touched his cap. People, she was realising, would not take you seriously unless you acted the part.

Even from the wharf they could smell the aromatic oils given off by the cargo.

'I have never seen such sandalwood,' Murchison said, holding his sleeve to his nose, for the scent had permeated his clothing. 'It's like a vine,' he added, for Eliza's benefit. Despite her display of authority he still felt the masculine compulsion to treat her as an inferior being. She frowned and Jamieson, who had never seen sandalwood in his life, nodded knowingly.

'It grows on all these trees, like some sort of blight. Wraps itself around the trunk of the host tree.'

'And kills it eventually,' de Lacey interposed and Murchison, who wasn't sure who the captain was or why he was there, stammered an agreement.

'But there are many miles of the stuff. Enough to fill . . .' Murchsion waved a hand. 'Fifty ships. Maybe a hundred.'

'So we must keep the location of your river a secret,' de Lacey said and Eliza agreed.

'You must tell no one. I want you to write the location and seal it in an envelope, which you will hand to me. The only person I expect you to discuss the site with is my husband, who is due back in Sydney in a few weeks.' She looked at Jamieson who had removed all expression from his face.

'Very wise,' he said softly.

Jamieson had excused himself, claiming urgent business elsewhere and Eliza and de Lacey were strolling back to her house. While crossing the bridge over the Tank Stream they stopped to admire the view across the marshes to the harbour, where the *Caroline* was riding at anchor. There were many people out walking, so there was little risk of their being accused of doing anything improper.

'You knew Jamieson intended to ask the captain where he'd got the sandalwood,' she said.

'I thought it likely.' De Lacey stroked his moustache. She had been most impressive in the way she'd kept Jamieson on his side of the fence. This was an aspect of her character he hadn't expected. 'And he would have had a chartered vessel on its way within the week. Long before your husband returned. Jamieson could have ordered the master to sail with the load directly to Batavia or Shanghai. Your husband need never have known.'

What should she say? You have been most helpful. You have been too kind. There were so many platitudes that the rich used and she hated them all, because they were the sauces that flavoured the conversations of the insincere. So she said nothing and felt embarrassed.

They resumed walking, she feeling inept, he admiring her for the silences. They came to a rough patch in the pathway and he stumbled.

'I'm so sorry,' she said, stopping until he had regained his balance.

'Perfectly all right. The leg gives me little trouble, not much pain, except I can't recover quickly from a trip or a stumble.' He laughed. 'As you just observed. I used to be quite nimble. A fair dancer, if I may be permitted to boast.'

'I don't dance.'

'I noticed. It was a shame the other night, although I admired your sense of propriety.'

Her brow was damp with perspiration and she patted it with a lace handkerchief. This was not a subject for which she'd rehearsed a lie. 'It was not propriety, captain. I can't dance.'

He stopped. 'How can it be?'

'Very easy. I have never learned.'

He was regarding her with the strangest expression.

What to say? She groped for the truth. 'I was raised by an aunt.'

'Ah,' said de Lacey, raising a hand to stop her. 'A churchgoing type. Forever concerned about the evils of modern society. Music, dancing, laughing. I know the type. Am I correct?'

She smiled and he felt as if his joints had loosened.

'My mother was not dissimilar. Although I was taught to dance.'

She brushed something from her glove. 'And became most expert at it, I'm sure.'

He lifted the stick and walked a few steps, to show he was not dependent on it. 'In fact, the other night I was thinking of asking you to dance. Of putting away the jolly old cane and hopping out on the floor. Would have made a fool of myself, of course, but there must have been something in the night air that made me think of foolish things.'

'I would have been delighted to accept. Except . . .'

'. . . You don't know how to dance.' He thumped the stick's brass ferrule on the ground. 'I may not be able to dance very well these days, but I could certainly show you. Would you permit me?'

She thought he meant there and then, and looked around her, blushing wildly.

'Not now, fair lady.' Although he would have. He would do

anything, no matter how outrageous, with this woman. She drew from deep within him feelings that he thought he had forever repressed in his quest to represent the ultimate in an English gentleman. Today, however, he was feeling very Neapolitan.

'With your permission, of course, I was wondering if I might call on you one afternoon, and perhaps show you a few steps. A lady of your class cannot learn in public. The lessons must be private.'

'I don't know what to say.'

'I think "yes" would be the appropriate answer.' He swung his stick. 'Do you have someone who could supply music?'

'I have a music teacher.'

'Excellent. Could he be available tomorrow afternoon?'

'I . . . I could send a message.'

'Tomorrow afternoon, then.'

'Captain de Lacey, this is most unusual.'

'You compel me to do unusual things.'

'My husband is away.'

'On his return, he will be delighted to discover you can dance.' And he wished that William Clancy might be delayed for several more weeks on his voyage to the north. He even found himself daydreaming of a shipwreck.

He walked her to the front gate of her house. It was an impressive building with its eight deep windows, wide balcony and arched entranceway. People had told him it was lavishly furnished inside; far superior to the new Government House.

All the way to the front door, her eyes had clouded in doubt and several times he sensed she was about to speak. But she remained silent. Not once did she say no.

He was swinging his cane as he left.

Rotherby's face twisted between admiration and envy. 'You're getting into deep water, old boy, and you may not know how to get out.'

De Lacey poured himself a sherry.

'Married women are very special game. I am experienced in the hunt. You are not. You are an absolute tyro.'

'We'll see.'

'We'll see,' Rotherby mimicked. 'How many duels do you want to fight? How many cities are you prepared to leave in a hurry?'

'None. I rather like it here.'

Rotherby fell on to a sofa and spread his arms wide. 'You're not in love, are you?'

'Of course not.'

'Love is the ultimate sickness, the disease for which there is no cure.'

'I'm not in love, Edwin. I scarcely know the lady.'

'It is not necessary to know someone intimately to love someone deeply.' He shook his head. 'My dear Quinton, you are so innocent. You can face a dozen Spaniards and cut them down, one by one, but one flutter of a lady's eyelashes will disarm you.'

'Talking of fluttering eyelashes,' de Lacey said, anxious to speak of something else, 'how is it you paid no attention to that gorgeous looking Italian woman the other night? Surely you saw her? She was quite ravishing.'

'And surrounded by men. I am never one of the mob.'

'You didn't find her attractive?'

'Most. But I can bide my time.' He winked. 'I know where she lives. I know something of her movements. In fact, I'm planning a chance meeting.'

'I am relieved,' de Lacey said with heavy irony. 'I had thought either your eyesight or your instincts were failing you.'

'I was also thinking,' Rotherby said, as if his friend hadn't spoken, 'that perhaps I should be the one giving Mrs Clancy the dancing lessons.'

'Don't you go near her.' The voice was serious.

'Oh, ho, ho,' he rumbled, eyes sparkling. 'Let me remind you, Quinton, that you are the one who has trespassed on another's territory. We had agreed that the married ones were mine, the single ladies yours.'

'That was a ludicrous arrangement.'

'You say that with hindsight. Before you fell in love.'

De Lacey went to the door. 'Edwin, you do talk nonsense.'

'It's my most charming habit.'

'But I want your word that you will leave Mrs Clancy alone.'

Rotherby raised an eyebrow. 'There are many names on my list before the name Eliza Clancy comes up.'

'I want your word, Edwin.'

'Of course.' He rose, to do some trifling thing.

De Lacey left feeling ruffled, as if his most secret thoughts, which even he had never fully examined, had been exposed.

De Lacey had already been to the authorities to see what reports there were on the escaped convicts Macaulay, Fitzgerald and Phillips. He'd thought about them many times in the French prison. It was one of the things that had kept him going; an illogical thing, he knew, but his hatred for them, his fanatical desire to see them punished, had been the spark that had kept him alive on many grim occasions. Whenever he was weak from illness or recovering from a beating after an attempted escape, he would conjure up the image of the Phillips woman on that distant hill, beckoning him and his men into the trap, and his hatred would strengthen him.

Logic told him they should have died in the bush years ago. The records, however, contained a report that Fitzgerald had been sighted near Castle Hill. The woman was seen too, although there was no sign of Macaulay. That was only a few years ago, about the time when he was sailing with Cochrane.

Fitzgerald had become a highwayman, or a bushranger as the

locals were now calling such people. He'd held up some travellers on their way from the river to Port Jackson. De Lacey read the name of the person reporting the incident and was surprised. It was Thomas Faithful Watts, the man who had given him much information about Fitzgerald and the others many years ago, the former convict for whom de Lacey had sought a pardon.

It was, he thought, an amazing coincidence.

Watts now ran a grog shop at the southern end of High Street.

The shop was made of wattle and daub, with a roof of bag and pitch and a front made from stitched pieces of canvas. Although the sun was still up, it was dark inside and a lantern glowed on a table. The air was thick with the sickly smell of cheap rum, tar and the pungent fumes from a coal fire. Watts, who lived in a lean-to behind the building, came from the storeroom when he heard de Lacey asking for him. There was another man in the shop—Irish by his accent—but he moved to the back room with the barrels and bottles of grog while Watts spoke to the captain.

Watts had heard de Lacey was back. Surely he wasn't still looking for the three convicts?

'Just a point of interest,' de Lacey said, holding a handkerchief near his nose. 'They're not really of concern to me any more but I was curious and checked the records the other day. I was surprised to see, Mr Watts, that you saw them only a few years ago.'

Watts was wondering how he could make more money from this man. 'Alive and well,' he said.

'And what were they doing?'

'Robbing me.' He laughed.

'All three of them?'

'Fitzgerald was the ringleader.' He was searching de Lacey's face for clues, for a flash of interest when he mentioned a name.

'The big fellow, what was his name . . . ?'

'Macaulay, sir.'

'That's right. Was he there?'

'To tell you the truth, sir, I didn't see him. It was dark, but there were several of them in the gang.' There was no suggestion in de Lacey's face that he had a particular interest in Macaulay. That left the woman.

'And the female?' The eyes had enlarged.

'In the background, sir.'

'You saw her?'

'Oh yes.'

De Lacey gripped his stick with both hands. 'So they're quite possibly still alive?'

'I've heard nothing to the contrary, sir.'

De Lacey read the labels on a few bottles. Such cheap rubbish. He turned his back on Watts, to become a silhouette in the light slicing the gap in the canvas.

'You'd hear a lot of rumour here, I imagine?'

'Oh yes, sir. People talk a lot when they drink.'

'And you've heard nothing more about Fitzgerald and the others?'

'Not a thing.'

De Lacey turned, using his stick to tap a few bottles that were lining a shelf. 'I want you to promise me something.'

'If I may be of service, sir.'

De Lacey disliked this man but he'd learned that if you wanted to trap scum, you had to use scum.

'I'll be in town for a while. If you hear anything about them, anything at all, I want you to contact me.' He handed Watts his card. 'Send a messenger. I'll come to your place. Don't come to mine.'

'Oh I won't, sir. I wouldn't think of it, sir.' What a conceited ass this de Lacey was. He may have gone to better schools, being from the privileged, pampered class, but Watts doubted if he were as well read. He liked to boast that he'd read every book in the colony. 'I wouldn't want to embarrass you, sir.'

De Lacey fiddled with his purse. He handed Watts five pounds. 'I'll pay for every bit of information you receive.'

Watts had bent himself into the pose of servility.

'Tell me,' said de Lacey as he held back the canvas flap, allowing the late afternoon light to flood the shop, 'what did they look like?'

'How do you mean, sir? Fitzgerald looked hearty, as though he was eating well, if that's what you mean, sir.'

'Don't be an imbecile, Watts. I want to know what they look like. A description. I have no idea of their appearance, except in the most basic of terms.'

Watts remembered Macaulay well and described him in detail. He had no intention of describing Fitzgerald to the captain because he had his own plan for dealing with Mr Fitzgerald. Therefore, he invented a description that was sufficiently bland to guarantee the two men could pass in the street with no more than a nod of greeting. He knew nothing of the woman so let his imagination run free. The captain seemed to have bitter feelings about her, so he painted an ugly picture.

He thought there might be more money forthcoming but de Lacey merely touched the brim of his hat as he left.

Kerrigan emerged from the storeroom. 'Don't you hate them type?' he said. 'So smart. So superior. Never done a day's work in their lives but behave as if they're our masters by divine right.'

'I've heard some interesting tales about Captain de Lacey,' Watts said but Kerrigan was in no mood to pay heed.

'They're the enemy and they'll be the first to go when we take over.'

'I hope you're good with the sword,' Watts said.

It was even darker in the storeroom and Watts went there to think. Despite what he'd said, he hadn't seen the woman Phillips

512

on that night when the stranger on the horse had interrupted their work and Nilssen had got himself shot. He thought he'd seen a black boy with Fitzgerald; that was all.

The woman may or may not be alive. Obviously, it was in his interests to let de Lacey think she was. He might have to arrange for someone to 'see' her, to keep the captain busy and the money rolling in.

De Lacey was a queer one. There'd been rumours about him from the old days, although he'd forgotten what the stories said. He'd have to make some inquiries about the captain. And keep him away from Clancy Fitzgerald because Fitzgerald, with all his gold, was his.

De Lacey was in a state of torment. He must do something, anything, to take his mind off Eliza Clancy. She was another man's wife and it was shameful for him to be contemplating being with her while the husband was away. Dancing lessons indeed! He just wanted to touch her hand, hold her in his arms, smell her perfume, listen to her voice, look at her, be with her.

He was worse than Rotherby. At least Edwin was flippant about his affairs and never allowed himself to become emotionally entangled. Edwin's affairs were pure lust, conquest and ego. As Edwin liked to say in defence of his excesses, these were primitive feelings, which were natural to all men and which he, being more blessed (or cursed) than most, was unable to control.

With de Lacey, it was different. He was propelled by that most dangerous of qualities in a paramour, sincerity.

Certainly there was lust. Only last night he'd had the most erotic dream about her and feared that if they were together he might not be able to control himself. But it was not ego or the male imperative for conquest that drove him on. It was love. Blind, stupid, destructive love. It was hopeless for him to think there might be some future for the two of them and he knew, with absolute clarity, that if he continued with the affair, only shame and tragedy would follow.

He needed a powerful diversion, which is why he had gone to see Watts.

Deliberately, he had disinterred the hellish thoughts about the three convicts that had tormented him for years. There was a time, on returning to England from the French prison, that he thought he could forget them and bury the memories. The shame of the Hawkesbury incidents was forgotten. He was known as a hero from the Napoleonic wars.

But now there was Eliza Clancy.

A few weeks away from Sydney Cove might be a good thing. He would devote his time to searching for the three. Even if he were to discover nothing more than the fact that they were dead, it would be a good thing.

On the way back to the house where he and Rotherby were staying, de Lacey passed the gaol and saw the familiar line of shadows on the gallows. There were six of them. They'd been strung up that morning and were left on the rope, as was the custom, as a warning to others. The warning didn't seem to work, he thought, as the gaol always had a row of lifeless bodies turning in the breeze.

The public liked hangings. Particularly the children, who threw things at the hapless victims and cheered those who danced and spluttered for the longest time.

Well, by God, he'd give them a show. If he caught Macaulay, Fitzgerald and the Phillips woman, he'd see that their bodies dangled for a week before they were buried in the pit reserved for murderers.

FORTY-NINE

WITH THUNDER ROLLING through the hills, Clancy and Ulla worked rapidly to build a shelter before the rain came. He used his axe to cut timber and strip bark. She formed the poles and the bark into the simple semi-dome of a wurlie whose wall protected the west, where the darkest clouds spilled from the horizon.

Only Clancy, Ulla and Wileemarin had come to the secret place. Clancy had thought of bringing other men to help carry gear and bring back the gold, but he was fearful of discovery and trusted no one.

When the rain came, it beat down so heavily they had to shout to be heard. Wileemarin began to cry. Clancy took him in his arms and the boy immediately became quiet and played with Clancy's finger.

'I thought this time you might not come back,' Ulla said.

'I told you I'd always come back.'

'But your time is longer than ours.'

He was in no mood to play god games. 'I am back,' he said.

'And you will be leaving soon.'

'In a few weeks, Ulla.' She had never questioned him before or hinted at dissatisfaction. 'I will be with you all that time and then I have to go back.'

'Ker-lan-see, my husband . . .' This was new. 'I would like to be with you all the time. To go with you when you cross the mountains.'

'That is not possible.' He handed the boy to her. 'You are my wife when I live here. When I am with the white people, I live with a white woman.'

'Eliza.'

'Yes. You know her. You've always known about her.'

She gripped his hand, as though he had misunderstood and she wished to make herself clear. 'I do not mind that you have another woman. Every man does that. It is just that I would like to be with you. To sleep with you. Just sometimes.'

He shook his head. 'It is not possible. Now, please stop. I do not want to talk about this again.'

She brushed strands of hair from Wileemarin's forehead. 'I know you are not a god, Ker-lan-see. No one else knows. I will not tell anyone, unless you wish it.' She looked at him hopefully.

'What are you talking about?'

'I have seen all the white people who live on the far side of the great mountains. I realise they are human, just like us. As are you. I have seen you bleed when hurt. I have seen you perform wondrous feats but they are not miracles, as others believe. They are things white men can do. I know you have fear. You were frightened after your last journey across the mountains.'

He frowned and she gripped his hand.

'These are normal things. I like you better as a normal man, even if you have white skin and do many strange things. And as you are a normal man, I should live with you as a normal woman would.'

She had rehearsed the words, he was sure, and now she sat back with the boy in her lap, staring ahead, not daring to look in his eyes.

'Ulla,' he said, matching her pose, 'I am normal only by the standards of white people.'

'I want to live with you. People have been saying I should take

516

another man.' She risked a brief glance to see if he were angry but he was staring at the rain sweeping through the gully.

'Another man?'

'They say it is not right. I could have many more children.'

He had taken to smoking cigars and, for the first time since being with Ulla, reached in his bag for one. She stared in fascination as he lit the cigar, drew deeply and blew a cloud of smoke into the storm.

He was eating fire? Had she said too much?

He removed the cigar and held it between two fingers. 'Maybe you could come with me in a little while.'

'How little?'

He was puffing on the cigar again and didn't speak.

'I want to go with you now. With our son. I want to live with you.'

'That's impossible. You know that.'

'You have built a house for your white woman.' He had described it to her, even told her where it was in Sydney, with such precision she was sure she could find it. 'You could build a house for me. Only a small house.' She lifted her hand to touch the roof of the wurlie. 'No bigger than this.'

He laughed and she wondered what she'd said that was amusing.

'Wileemarin and I need only a very small house. Or no house at all. We can live among the trees.'

'Ulla, stop.' He waved the cigar at her and she recoiled, thinking she might catch fire. 'I am not taking you now. It is impossible. I might take you at some time in the future. That's all there is to the matter. Do not speak about it again or I will become very angry.'

She shuffled a little to one side, to be further away from him. No matter. She knew what she would do.

They stayed there for another two weeks, working along the creek and among the hills. Sometimes they found specks of gold in the water but their best yield came from the embankment where Clancy had already begun to dig. Along one desiccated ridge he found so much gold it reminded him, he said, of picking plums from a pudding. That meant nothing to Ulla but she was pleased that the discovery of these dull stones still brought him pleasure.

Clancy bemoaned the lack of better equipment, for he was sure he was missing gold due to the haphazard way that he searched. He had read a story about gold in a London journal. The article had been accompanied by illustrations of men using chutes and sluices and long, cradle-like devices that they appeared to rock or move backwards and forwards. What their purpose was, he couldn't work out—not from the drawings and the few words that accompanied them.

What he needed was the help of an expert prospector. Neither equipment nor advice was possible until someone else—with government blessing—found a way over the mountains and white settlers moved into these hills. Then he, as William Clancy, prosperous goldminer from southern Africa, could discover this creek, bring in whatever equipment he needed, employ the most experienced people. And, he hoped, keep on making a fortune.

Until then he was reduced to digging out gravelly embankments or sifting through river stones with no one more expert than Ulla at his side.

Always, he was driven by the thought that, one day, someone would follow him or stumble on his find.

In those two weeks he gave no more thought to what Ulla had said during the storm. He enjoyed having her with him. She did whatever he asked, never complained or argued and, without bidding, would hunt for or gather the food they needed. She also prepared the fire, cooked the food and helped him with the digging.

She looked after the baby, of course, but Clancy liked Willy and made time each afternoon to play with him. The boy's favourite game was throwing sticks. They would sit on the ground facing each other and throw sticks from one to the other. The lad had a good eye.

He was learning the language of the tribe but Clancy taught him one word of English. By the time they were ready to leave the creek, with their sacks heavily laden with gold and the equipment they used to dig for it, Wileemarin could say, 'Daddy.'

Ulla was also pregnant again.

Wonngu wondered whether Clancy would return in good humour or still be troubled by the loss of his horse. He showed him the undisturbed grave. He himself had stationed guards there for the first week to ensure no one was tempted to dig for the meat.

'The matter of the horse is past,' Clancy said. 'I am not angry with your people.'

Yet something was troubling the white man.

He had a great deal to carry, for the yellow stones were inordinately heavy for their size. 'Shall I send two men with you to carry the load?'

Clancy spent the night thinking about Wonngu's proposal. It wasn't the load that concerned him, for he was leaving all the digging gear and taking only the gold, his weapons and some food with him. He was frightened of the mountain men. He sensed they would be waiting for him.

Despite his years in the bush he did not have the nose or the tracking instincts of an Aboriginal hunter. A couple of good men might keep him from blundering into a trap.

The escorts need not go all the way. Possibly through the stand of thick brush or to the last ridge. Wherever he would feel safe and where Wonngu's men would not be seen by any whites.

He, William Clancy, shipowner, who was now allegedly returning from a voyage to Possession Island, mustn't be seen coming out of the mountains with a couple of naked, wild-eyed, tribal blacks.

Yes, he would take two men, he told Wonngu, and the old man was pleased. He needed to make a grand gesture such as this—a willing sacrifice, as it were—to compensate for the terrible wrong a member of the tribe had done.

Wonngu told Berak and Arabanoo to go. Neither was pleased and their womenfolk spent the night wailing and slashing themselves, but both men smiled dutifully when they reported to Clancy in the morning.

Ulla had already left the camp. Carrying white man's clothes, some food and one of Clancy's hunting knives in a shoulder bag and with her son in her arms, she was hiding near the track when Clancy and the others passed the next day. She gave them an hour's start, then followed.

Noxious Watts sent a messenger to the address on de Lacey's card. The man had a slow trip, for news had reached Sydney of Nelson's great victory at Trafalgar and there were drunken mobs in the streets, dancing and singing, falling and entangling themselves in the legs of anyone in a hurry.

'It is great news, Mr Watts,' de Lacey said when he eventually reached the shop.

'Oh wonderful news,' Watts said, aware that Kerrigan was in the storeroom in a mood of murderous frustration. He was both drunk and bleeding from the hands, having beaten the walls in his anger. The defeat would mean, he had said with the perception of a naval strategist, that the French would recall their ships from the Pacific area to bolster the remains of the main fleet.

'But a tragedy to have lost such a man as Nelson.' De Lacey

dabbed his nose with his handkerchief. The stench was appalling.

'And yet, sir, what a good way to go. As a hero. Killed in the moment of his greatest triumph.' Watts closed one eye, as if peering at de Lacey through a telescope. He had been asking about the captain, had heard the old stories and thought he understood why the man had fought with such savagery against the Spaniards and French. 'Death with honour,' he said and the closed eye winked.

'Great honour, sir.' De Lacey tapped the floor. 'I believe you have news for me.'

Watts had concocted a story about a woman, resembling the convict Phillips, who had been seen near one of the settlements on the river. His source was not certain if it was Phillips but thought so. The man's wife knew her well, having served with her in the old days. Watts thought he should travel up to the Hawkesbury to check.

'Did your friend see either of the men?'

'There was a report of a man of exceptional size being seen near one of the farms.'

De Lacey touched the scar on his cheek. 'Strange that they should still be in that area, where they are known.'

'Oh, it's a long time ago, sir. The people have changed. It's a big place now. Very different to what it was in your day.'

'And when would you be going?'

'Straight away, sir.'

'And you'd need some money, I presume?'

'Oh yes, sir. I'd take a few men with me, just in case.'

De Lacey walked to the entrance and stood with his back to Watts. 'Perhaps I should go up there myself. I need to get away from Sydney for a spell.'

This was not in Watts's plan. 'Begging your pardon, sir,' he said, ambling up to de Lacey's side, 'that mightn't be a good idea. The characters I want to see and talk to might be

521

frightened off by the sight of a gentleman such as yourself.'

'Frightened?'

'They're a disreputable lot. They'll only talk to their own kind.'

De Lacey raised an eyebrow. 'But they'll talk to you?'

'I'm one of them, sir.'

There was a commotion in the street outside, where two dogs were fighting. De Lacey used his cane to lift the canvas flap for a better view. When one dog retreated, yelping and bloodied, he turned back to Watts and examined first him, then the store. 'You know, Watts, when I sought your pardon, I had hoped that you might do something better with your life than this.'

'Well this is what I am, sir.'

De Lacey faced him. 'And what are you?'

'A humble man, sir, who knows his place.'

De Lacey had little time for cant or pretence and he suspected he was being given a display of both. Never mind. The man was good at gathering information. Impatient to be out of this place, he tapped the ground several times. 'You'll let me know immediately you have some news?'

'Straight away, sir.'

He gave Watts 20 pounds. 'That's a great deal of money. I expect good value in return.'

'I'll be most assiduous, sir.'

Assiduous? Where on earth had a rogue like Watts learned to use a word like that? How much of the man was real and how much a facade, erected to deceive? And if deception was the man's game, what was his purpose?

Perhaps he should go to the river after all and engage someone disreputable to observe Watts.

When de Lacey had gone, Kerrigan emerged from the storeroom. His hands were bandaged in dirty rags. 'I'd like to cut his throat,' he said. 'Him and all like him.'

'Well, you'll have to wait a while, you will. We're off to the river.'

Watts meant to ask many questions: not about the woman but about the man who now called himself William Clancy. According to gossip around the waterfront, the wealthy Mr Clancy was on his new boat, sailing up north somewhere. And yet Kerrigan had seen him at the Hawkesbury, hiking along the far bank and dressed for the bush.

Eliza had been thinking about de Lacey and feeling ashamed of her thoughts. She was looking forward to his coming and yet it was sinful. Even with Mr Sinclair present, to play the spinet and act as a kind of chaperon, it was a disgraceful thing she was doing. What if people passing by in the street should hear? What if someone should see them through the windows? What if they heard laughter, a man's voice? She should have told him he was impertinent for suggesting dancing lessons. She should have been firm. He would have respected her more. There would have been no risk of further gossip.

But she wanted him to come, wanted to have him take her hand, put his arm around her waist, let his body touch hers, if only lightly . . .

She was disgusted with her life. Everything was pretence. Even her sense of sinning was false. She was acting like a married lady, which she was not. She was living in sin with a man she didn't love, had borne him a child out of wedlock, was pretending that she was married and rich and respectable.

She was rich. Nothing else.

She tried to think logically about the situation but, as usual, became terribly confused.

Because she and Clancy had lied so well, people never doubted they were married and yet, it was only because people assumed she was a married woman that there was a problem with her seeing Captain de Lacey. If she were a single woman which, in fact, she was, she could see whomever she liked. People might still gossip but seeing the captain would not be immoral or shameful.

It would be the sort of thing a person in love would do.

Love?

She hadn't thought of that and the word shocked her. It was ridiculous of her even to think of such a thing. She hardly knew the man. He was attractive, certainly, and brave, courteous and cultured; all the things a woman might desire in a man. It was true she felt a strange warmth spreading within her when she was with him. She had no idea what it was, although she knew it made her cheeks flush. It was a new sensation. Very pleasant, in a disturbing kind of way.

There was a time, when she and Clancy had first crossed the mountains and were living with Wonngu's tribe, that she'd imagined she was in love with Clancy but she soon realised her feeling was a mixture of gratitude and dependence.

She could not love a man who seemed to have no warm feelings for her, rarely expressed concern, mocked her constantly, appeared to enjoy the company of others more than hers and was away from home for long periods of time. Unnecessarily long periods, she thought. Mrs Piper, the wife of one of the officers, had suggested that Mr Clancy must have another woman tucked away somewhere. Mrs Piper had laughed when she said it. It was a joke. One worldly woman talking to another. But it was meant to provoke a response; a flicker of the eyes, a flushed cheek, and the woman had watched her with the cold eyes of a hawk.

'Oh, my husband is far too busy to have another woman on his books, Mrs Piper,' she had replied, and Mrs Piper had laughed as though that was an exceedingly witty response.

But she wondered.

He was due soon. Mr Sinclair arrived half an hour early and asked if she would like to hear some music or recite a poem he had asked her to learn but she declined, had the maid bring him tea, and went to her dressing-room to be alone.

The problem was of her making and it had no solution. She had become enmeshed in a web of lies. There was no way out. She could never tell the truth. She and Clancy were joined forever by their necessity to deceive.

And yet she . . . she forced herself to modify her thoughts . . . she liked the man. Exceedingly. She had never felt this way about any other man. Maybe he felt the same about her. He was kind to her. She'd noticed him smiling at her when he thought she wasn't looking. He didn't treat her as a nincompoop, as Jamieson did, nor was he forever making fun of her, as Clancy did. He enjoyed listening to her, didn't seem to mind when she had nothing to say.

She felt good when he was near her.

She went to her Bible and opened it but did not read. She found herself wondering about the scar down his cheek and the wound to his leg and wishing she might have been with him years ago, to hold his hand and help ease the pain. She thought about the French prison—he never spoke of that although Jamieson had told her—and wished she had known him then, so that he could have thought of her and she of him for all those long years, and each could have eased the loneliness being suffered by the other.

The maid came. He had arrived and was in the drawing room.

FIFTY

THE CURTAINS WERE drawn, as was Eliza's habit. Not only did she like passers-by to see a rich display of curtains, she and Clancy having paid 200 pounds for the sumptuous drapes, festooned with fringes, that hung in the eight windows facing the street, but after the years of living in the hut with its invading shafts of sunlight, swirling dust and fat, droning blowflies, she preferred to be in a cool and darkened room. It gave her a sense of security, privacy and quiet.

She stood in the doorway for several seconds, letting her eyes adjust to the faint light. The western wall glinted with golden shapes from the gilded frames of the four oil paintings. The crystal vases imported from Venice twinkled faint reflections. The surface of the intricately carved rosewood table shone like a mirror. The backs of the chairs were arched shadows.

She liked this room and spent much time here, learning poetry, reading books and the latest magazines from London, or practising her writing.

Sinclair was sitting near the spinet, an unmoving presence in the darkest part of the room. The silver tea service was on a small table beside his chair.

Captain de Lacey was standing near the window. Leaning on his stick, he was admiring a painting of a hunt. The riders' red jackets blazed in the gloom.

She cleared her throat and he turned immediately.

'My dear lady,' he said, advancing to take her outstretched hand. 'I have taken the liberty of bringing some music.' He removed several sheets of paper from a slim leather case and gave them to Sinclair, who seemed startled to see him, as if the musician had persuaded himself that no one else was in the room.

De Lacey put his stick and the case on a chair and moved to the clearest part of the floor, between the windows and the rosewood table.

'I thought we might start with some basic steps,' he said, spreading his arms and opening his hands, waiting for her.

'I thought you might like some tea,' she said, flustered by his rapid start, nervous at the thought of being in his arms.

'Not yet, thank you. I thought we should begin.'

The years in the bush had left her slim and firm and she had a tiny waist, the most prized feature any lady could desire. She was wearing a dress of pink silk with a high waist and a neckline cut to hint at the breasts and enhance the display of a necklace of diamonds and sapphires. She possessed larger, more valuable necklaces including one enormous piece made in Sydney from Clancy's gold, but this was the afternoon, not the evening, there were just two of them—already, she was discounting the shadowy Sinclair—and she wished to seem appealing, not brazen.

She thought he might compliment her on her appearance but he said, 'Where the couple dance as a pair, not as part of some group as in a quadrille, we start thus. The man leads.' She let his hands guide hers. Her raised right hand in his left. Her left on his shoulder. 'Very good,' he said, like the most detached tutor, and put his right arm around her waist, placing his hand in the small of her back.

He was strong, with lean shoulder muscles; she could feel them ripple through the padding of his coat.

Sinclair began to play.

They stopped after twenty minutes. Realising his leg was bothering him, she said, 'I am quite exhausted. I never knew dancing could be so vigorous.' She glanced towards Sinclair, for approval of her speech, but he was looking the other way.

'And I can scarcely believe that you have never danced before. You take to it as naturally as a bird to flight.' He led her towards some chairs near the window, away from Sinclair. 'You are the epitome of grace.'

Epitome. She'd never heard the word before. It must be complimentary. Had she carried a fan, she would have fluttered it. As it was, she blushed and said nothing.

They sat beneath the scene from the hunt. The horses' necks, she thought, had never seemed so long, so elegant, so unnaturally curved, as if striving to hear what was to be said.

De Lacey signalled to Sinclair by tapping the armrest. The old man turned, his eyes wide and blind, like an owl disturbed in its nest. 'Maestro,' de Lacey said, 'a little music, please. Handel perhaps?'

Sinclair nodded and began to play.

'When just a lad, my father saw Mr Handel play in London,' de Lacey said. 'The King was present. It was quite an occasion.'

She had no idea what to say. The only music she had heard was in taverns. Bawdy stuff that inspired drunken men to stagger about, spilling their ale and pinching girls on the knickers.

'I hope you don't mind Handel,' he said. 'He is a favourite of mine.'

'I am delighted with the choice.'

He leaned closer. 'I felt a little music might be appropriate, while we talked.'

Talk was the thing she most feared. His questions. She would find it hard to lie to this man, so she began speaking more rapidly than Mr Sinclair would have wished. 'I am sorry to have caused you pain,' she said. 'Your leg . . . I have been very selfish, enjoying myself while you have endured pain most nobly.'

'Not at all.'

'But you must tell me,' she said, not letting him take the initiative, 'how your leg was injured. I am told it is a most romantic story.'

'Not very romantic, I'm afraid. A villainous looking Corsican who had been knocked to the deck put a dagger through my leg. I was busily fighting another man.' He touched the back of his thigh. 'He hit me there.'

She put her hand to her mouth.

'The wound was jagged. It took some time to heal.'

What to say next, without seeming indelicate or unladylike? 'And is it true you spent all those years imprisoned in a castle?'

'In a chateau, yes. I refused to give my word that I would not attempt to escape so they flung me into a dungeon that was dark and damp and filled with rats. When I have a nightmare now, I hear the scurrying of rats.' He smiled, wondering why she was talking so, and surmising she was as nervous as he.

She forgot about indelicacy. She was intrigued. 'Yet you escaped?'

'They were foolish enough to put me to work in the fields. I got away.'

'And sailed home to England.'

'After a time.' He laughed softly. 'I joined a fishing boat that was bound for the African coast.'

She remembered. He had mentioned Carthage at Lieutenant Jamieson's reception. She'd looked it up. Carthage was on the Mediterranean coast of North Africa, the city from which Hannibal had launched his attack on Rome.

'And . . .?'

'We were intercepted by pirates. Slavers, actually, bound for Turkey where the slave market flourishes.'

'They were going to sell you as a slave?'

'That was their hope. I was one of a potpourri of lithe Guinean savages and swarthy French fishermen jammed in the hold. I tried to convince my captors I was a Mozarab in the hope that they might spare me and put me ashore.'

He smiled as though the recollection were amusing and she tilted her head in inquiry. 'Mozarab?' That was a word she could safely challenge.

'A Christian owing allegiance to the King of the Moors. Such men are allowed to retain their faith and move freely in the world of the Muhammadans. However . . .' He spread his hands.

'They didn't believe you?'

'They preferred to think of the sum I might fetch at the slave market. Eventually,' he said, tiring of the story, 'we were rescued by a British warship.' He waved a hand. 'And here I am.'

Sinclair was playing a new tune, more melodic, it seemed to Eliza, than the Handel.

'Herr Mozart,' de Lacey said, lifting his head as a dog might to detect a scent. 'A Viennese, I believe. I heard some pieces of his while in London. Most amusing.'

'I like it,' she said and they listened for a while. 'Yes, I like it.'

He took her hand and she could scarcely breathe.

'My dear lady.' He could not call her by her husband's name. Eyes lowered, voice soft, he said, 'Eliza.'

She was shocked. Not offended but frightened as to what he might say next. Or how she might react. She felt hot and, with her free hand, touched her temple.

He had the look of one who was about to unleash a torrent of words but all he said was, 'I've been troubled over the last few days,' before pausing to clear his throat.

Sinclair seemed to be playing more vigorously.

De Lacey's hand now rested lightly on hers. 'Most troubled. Scarcely able to sleep, in fact.'

'I was worried when first I saw you. You looked so tired.' Dear God, why couldn't she tell him what she felt? How she admired him, how he excited her, how she wished to spend more time with him. How her life with Clancy was a sham, in every way.

He'd been raised to control all feelings, to present the facade of the perfect English gentleman, impervious to emotion, and yet a delicious and pure feeling, scandalous in its implications, was welling within him. His months with Lord Thomas Cochrane had transformed him into an impulsive, daring man who acted first, then thought of the consequences. His years in the French prison had made him cherish the present, be suspicious of the future.

He was no longer content to wait.

Honour, he now realised, was a form of madness. He'd killed men who were too honourable to run away. Known men who had loved a woman but lost her because of a warped sense of doing what was correct, whether she had been beneath their class or committed to another. They were dismal companions, whose lives had foundered on the rock of honour.

He was tempted to lean across, touch her cheeks with his fingers and kiss her.

But it was too soon. She would fly away like a startled bird.

'There was a time,' he began, 'when I was guided by the conventions of society, no matter how crass the convention or the society.' He hesitated and she smiled demurely.

Amused or agreeing? He wasn't sure.

She didn't understand.

'We are raised to disguise our true feelings, to be silent when we should speak, to be still when we should act. I used to believe that was the proper way to be. In other words, I was a fool.'

She had no idea what to say. He became nervous, fearing he had offended her.

'I . . . I may have to go away for a few days.' He lowered his voice. 'If I stay, I'm not sure what I might do.'

'I don't understand, Captain.'

He leaned closer. 'I have never met a woman who so captivated me.'

She knew what she should do: be offended, reprimand him, ask him to leave. She lowered her eyes.

'Have I offended you?'

'You've surprised me.'

He squeezed her hand and she turned to make sure Sinclair was not looking.

'I know it is impossible. But while I'm prepared to do nothing, I'm not prepared to say nothing. My feelings are too strong, too sure for that. I know I'm being foolish, extremely so. But I'm being honest.'

'We've known each other a very short time.' She could not bring herself to say she was a married woman. It was trite and it was not true.

He felt some unseen barrier had been passed. He took a deep breath and the air felt good. He leaned back in the chair.

'I am going to the river,' he said, his voice light once more. 'Possibly for a few days.'

She adjusted her necklace. 'And what takes you there, Captain?' It was as though the previous minutes had not happened.

'I feel the need to be out of town for a while.' He left his hand on the armrest, with his fingers outstretched so they touched her tips. 'It's also something of a vendetta. A piece of personal foolishness.'

Sinclair had stopped playing.

'More Mozart, please,' de Lacey asked. 'Mrs Clancy enjoys Mozart.'

'I only know the one piece,' Sinclair said without taking his eyes from the spinet.

'Then play it again, there's a good fellow.'

'Please, Mr Sinclair,' she said. 'It was most enjoyable.'

They listened to the music for some time, content to enjoy the other's pleasure. Each wore the mask of a sophisticate, sharing the guilt, enjoying their secret.

She said, 'You used the word vendetta?'

He picked up the cane. 'Oh it's an unpleasant affair. I feel ashamed to confess. An old matter. I took it up again to get my mind off other things.' He risked a knowing look. 'You see, I heard that someone I've long wanted to catch was seen recently at the Hawkesbury.'

'To catch? Captain, that is an extraordinary thing to say.'

He twisted the cane in his hand. 'It's an extraordinary story. It goes back to the time when I was first in the colony. Three convicts escaped.'

Eliza stiffened and de Lacey, noticing, patted the armrest. 'I'm sorry to mention such matters.'

'Why a vendetta?' she said in a small voice.

'Possibly the wrong word, as there's no family feud, but I was involved in two incidents which did my career a great deal of harm. At that time,' he added hastily.

'I don't understand. Three convicts, two incidents, your career?'

'The convicts murdered two men in their escape. Later, while I was leading a troop of soldiers on the far bank of the river, one of the convicts deliberately led me into a trap. Several of my men were killed. Look,' he added quickly, tapping the cane on the floor, 'this is all very messy. The point is I'm going up to the river to see if I can find the woman, or any of her companions.'

'Woman?'

'Yes. She was the willing decoy for a group of blacks who ambushed my men.'

'Decoy?' She was having difficulty in controlling her voice.

Sinclair had finished the Mozart piece and the room was quiet. Behind them, the horses with the elongated necks were straining to hear.

'Someone purports to have seen her near The Green Hills. It's probably all nonsense and I'll be back, tired and bad-tempered, in a few days' time.'

'What were the names of these convicts?' she managed to ask.

He seemed surprised. 'I doubt that you'd know them. This all happened before you came to New South Wales.'

She was waiting.

'Macaulay and Fitzgerald. Those are the men. The woman was called Phillips. It's the woman I particularly want to see apprehended, because of the deaths she caused.'

'And what will happen if you find her?'

'Oh, she'll hang. I swore that I'd send her to the gallows when I was here all those years ago.'

The air seemed to have grown abrasive.

'And even though this happened so long ago, you still want to see her hanged?'

'Of course. It was a despicable thing she did. A treacherous act.' He stood. 'You mentioned tea. Is it still possible?'

She was different after that and, as he left, de Lacey knew he'd said too much. Her eyes were distant, her breath short, her hand at her throat as she bade him goodbye.

He was a fool to have talked about the convicts. He'd been judged a brute. Not a man impelled by a sense of justice but a fanatic driven by the lust for revenge. This cursed mission of his, that had tormented him for years, might now cost him the woman whom, at this instant, he knew he loved.

High on the ridge in the mountains a hundred cockatoos burst from the trees above them, their rasping cries of alarm making Clancy wince. The sound would travel across the peaks and valleys and anyone in the area would know something had disturbed the birds. He couldn't see Arabanoo, who was up ahead scouting the way, but Berak was close behind and he was already nervous, suspecting they were being followed. He'd had that feeling for two days.

They'd seen no one.

Clancy was carrying the gold and the guns. Berak had the rest of the load. Both the blacks were carrying hunting spears, with their clubs and stone axes suspended from belts made of possum skin.

At sunset they reached the barrier of scrub and camped at its entrance. Berak and Arabanoo were to take turns in standing guard. Clancy would rest sitting up, with his back against a low bush whose gnarled limbs supported his shoulders. He had his musket across his lap and both loaded pistols in his belt.

He chewed some dried meat and waited for the night.

Ulla had found the going difficult with the child. Wileemarin was at the worst age for travelling through rough country: too small to walk except for short distances, too large to be carried all the way. She had him on her back, riding in a loop formed by one of Clancy's old leather belts that he'd used with the horse. The belt was around her neck and the buckle, which she found attractive, was at her throat but it hampered her breathing and, to make things worse, the boy was restless. He was a good boy, making no noise, but he could not stop wriggling and as a result she was choking for breath and near exhaustion by the end of the day.

Clancy and his two companions had been setting a fast pace, which made her task even harder. They left few marks. Berak, whom she'd glimpsed once or twice in the distance, was attempting to eliminate their footprints where the track was soft or dusty but the pace was too fast for him to be thorough.

In the faint light of dusk she came to a sandy patch and saw marks. She stopped. Four men had passed.

He had grown lean and strong in the years since being banished. He had taken two women from the tribe near the flat-topped mountain and lived as an outlaw, shunned by all, hunting on his own, surviving on his wits. He was a little crazy, and knew it, and had spent all those years longing to meet the white man again so that he might try once more to kill him.

On the night of the full moon he'd been near the river where the big mountains began when he saw three men approaching. One was white. The other two he knew and despised. And so, leaving his women at the river and armed with his fighting weapons, Murremurran had followed Clancy and his two companions into the mountains.

At dusk on this evening, he had seen them stop at the edge of the thick scrub. He would kill the two black men first. This was a perfect place because they could not run into the brush. One he would spear tonight. Possibly Arabanoo, because Berak was more inclined to panic and might run away, thinking they were being attacked by the mountain people. He could let Berak go or kill him on the spot. He would then track the white man for another day or two and wait until he fell asleep.

He would not risk using a spear again. He would beat out his brains with the club. Smash the skull until the bone was in splinters.

Murremurran retreated a little to rest for an hour or two. He planned to attack just as the moon was rising. He found a grassy patch on a rise and sat down with his back to a slab of fallen rock. He would take three spears; he fingered their shafts with loving strokes. He listened, straining to hear any sounds from the camp, but they were quiet, as usual, having rarely spoken on the entire journey.

He heard a noise behind him. It was faint but out of place. Not the sound of the wind in the trees or of possums scampering along branches, or birds disputing a nest. It was a human noise.

Taking the spears he crept back along the track.

It was a baby crying.

The noise stopped. There was a gurgling sound, then childish chatter. Then more crying.

Being compelled to hunt on his own, Murremurran had developed exceptional skills. He had the hearing of the most nervous kangaroo, possessed the wiliness of the most cunning dingo, moved with the silence of the faintest breeze. His eyes were deteriorating but the other senses compensated.

He took ten minutes to cover a hundred paces, scanning the bush constantly, listening for other sounds. He came to a small clearing. In its centre, clearly visible in the dim light, was a child. It was sitting and playing with a long belt made of thick leather.

Crouched low, one spear held ready in his right hand, he stayed unmoving for a full five minutes. There was no one else. Just the child.

What was a child doing here? And how did it come to have a fine piece of leather, something he himself would treasure? Straining his eyes, he saw the glint of the buckle.

This was the white man's belt.

Murremurran was contemplating whether to go forward or circle the clearing when the metal blade of a hunting knife, honed to extreme sharpness, slid between his fifth and sixth ribs. The thrust was made with great dexterity. He, who had heard no sound, now made no noise other than the soft hiss of escaping breath.

He was dead before he hit the ground.

Ulla rushed to pick up Wileemarin and put her hand over his mouth to stop him crying. She took him down the track, away from Clancy's camp, until Wileemarin was quiet. With the child back in the leather belt, she returned to Murremurran and dragged the body into thick bush far off the track.

She spent half an hour erasing all marks at the clearing, then cleaned Clancy's knife and put it back in the pack. Only then did she hide with her son in the bush. He slept briefly, then awoke, hungry. She fed him the remains of a lizard cooked the previous night. They would drink in the morning, licking dew from the undersides of leaves.

Her hand shook. She had killed animals, never a man.

FIFTY-ONE

FOR SEVERAL HOURS Eliza stayed in her bedroom, lying on her pillow until it was saturated with tears. When she felt more composed, she stood at the window to gaze through a chink in the curtains at the long shadows striping the street, now milling with bands of noisy children and vendors who pulled carts, rang bells and kicked at dogs that pissed on their wheels.

She turned away. Why did fate reserve its meanest, most diabolical tricks for her?

She loved this man. Even though it was a hopeless love, she might have been able to spend time with him. Discreetly or publicly, it wouldn't have mattered. It would merely have been another pretence in her life of deceit, but made enjoyable because she was sharing the secret game with him. It would be enough to be with him or near him, to enjoy his conversation, his presence, his secret glances and be thrilled to know he held her in high regard. High regard. She was even thinking in the stilted way that people—the best bred, the richest, the most educated, the most boring—talked and wrote in their letters to each other. She meant love. Wonderful, fiery, strengthening, hopeless love.

He'd hinted at love but how could she dare think his feelings were as deep for her as hers were for him?

Clancy led such a dangerous life, with his frequent crossings of the mountains and his encounters with hostile natives, that it was possible something would happen to him one day, and then she and the captain . . . She stopped, horrified that she could think such dreadful things. But it was true. Everything changed with time. She would have waited, contented if de Lacey were near.

And now she must leave.

He was a man of intelligence and perseverance. If he had set his mind on discovering what had happened to the three convicts who'd escaped in 1798, somehow, inevitably, he would find out.

It wasn't fair. She hadn't killed anyone. Neither had Clancy. That wouldn't matter. They'd both hang. And the avenger, the instrument of justice—the only one in the colony who seemed to retain any interest in the matter—was the man she loved.

He already hated her, as Eliza Phillips, for something she hadn't done. Now he would be shocked by her deception, hate her even more for the way she'd tricked him, made a fool of him. He would send her to the gallows with a tear perhaps, but without hesitation.

Clancy was always urging her to think logically and so, after sundown, when a servant had fed Caroline and put her to bed and when the vendors had left the streets and the homeless children were lighting their fires in the fingers of bushland reaching through the town, she sat down with a sheet of paper and wrote out the things she should do.

She should pack. Be ready to leave the house with little warning. She would have to do the packing herself. The servants must not be aware of what was happening.

So urgent did the need for packing seem that she got up and began the job immediately. She packed two bags: one for herself and one for Caroline. She would pack for Clancy when he returned, although she had little idea when that might be. He'd said he'd be away for six or seven weeks. That meant he might be home in three days or ten, although one could never be sure with Clancy.

The first things she put in her bag were her best items of jewellery. They consisted of rings and bracelets and necklaces; even a tiara made from Clancy's gold and with gems imported from India. The collection was worth, Clancy had once assured her, more than 6,000 pounds, enough for them to start a new life somewhere. She also took a few nuggets from the cache of gold they kept in a safe beneath the floor. Clancy could carry the rest of the gold.

With both bags packed, she sat down again with the quill and sheet of paper and made notes.

She would not cross the mountains again. It was unthinkable. She could not bear to return to that primitive way of living. She would not force Caroline to grow up in such a degraded society, be given to a black man, have half-caste children.

They would take one of the vessels and sail somewhere. Somewhere civilised, where Caroline could gain an education and where white people lived. She would ensure Caroline had the opportunity to marry a white man. Preferably one who spoke English and was a Protestant.

Perhaps they should leave as soon as Clancy returned. They could tell people they were returning temporarily to Cape Town. Sailing to China. Any story would do. If there was time, they should sell the house and its trove of treasures . . . no, they couldn't do that because de Lacey would return long before they could dispose of anything, and he, like most Sydney citizens, would wonder at their flight. She must not do anything to make de Lacey suspicious.

She let her eyes roam the page. The quill's feather tip touched her cheek. The candle was burning low.

Outside, someone was shouting and she was momentarily frightened, imagining the police at her door. But it was just men arguing, a common sound.

They should say they were sailing away for a few months. On business. Clancy was always doing business. No one would doubt the story.

They could take the *Caroline* and sell the sandalwood in Shanghai. That would mean more money for them. They could stay in Shanghai. She'd read there was an English community there.

And yet she hated the idea of leaving so much, abandoning all they had built and acquired.

Then a thought occurred to her. She was presuming they had to flee. What if Captain de Lacey were to leave? To go suddenly, before he had a chance to make further investigations?

She put down the pen and sat at the table until the candle guttered and the flame expired with a hiss.

She should see him before he left for the river. Tonight. She would confess her love for him, point out the futility of the affair, and ask him, as a gentleman, to leave the colony.

He would go, of course. His sense of duty would impel him to do the gentlemanly thing.

She would lose him. But after today's revelation, the affair was ended irrevocably and in this way she would be guaranteeing her daughter's future.

She knew de Lacey's address. He was staying with Edwin Rotherby, a man of breeding and wealth but lax morality. He was regarded as being sinfully flirtatious and many women were already gossiping about him; some, she thought, out of spite for his having neglected them. Rotherby might be in the house. It couldn't be helped. A man who corrupted ladies had one virtue: he should be silent about a fellow sinner's private affairs.

She had the stable boy drive her there in the gig. He was a quiet lad, part Javanese, who was devoted to the horses but had no friends among the staff. She had urgent business to discuss, she said, and asked him to wait. He led the mare down the street to where it might graze on ample grass.

De Lacey answered the door. He was astonished to see her and took her quickly into the drawing room. No, Mr Rotherby was not at home. He was visiting friends.

'My dear lady, I hope it is not bad news that has brought you here,' he said, taking her bonnet and scarf.

'No. And today, you called me Eliza.'

He stood, open-mouthed for a few moments, then offered her a chair.

'E-li-za.' He stretched the word to impossible limits.

She closed her eyes. She prayed she could say the things that must be said, succeed in doing this terrible thing, persuade him to leave her.

The room was brightly lit with no fewer than five candles on the main table. The air had the tang of cigar smoke. A glass of port, half drunk, stood on a shelf above the fireplace.

Sitting opposite her, he leaned forward anxiously. 'I feel I should apologise for some of the things I said today. In particular, the affair of the convicts. That was tasteless on my part and I sensed my words upset you.'

She shook her head. 'I thought it time to speak frankly.'

'Please.' He spread his hands. 'By the way, did you come on your own?'

'There's a boy outside. He's waiting down the road with the gig.'

'There's no one else in the house. Edwin won't be returning for many hours. You may say what you wish.' He rested his chin on his clasped hands. And waited.

She'd rehearsed the opening lines but now the words were reluctant to emerge. The house was quiet. She could hear a faint ticking.

'Is that a clock?' She hadn't meant to start like this.

'Yes,' he said brightly. 'Edwin brought one with him from London. That makes us something of a rarity in the colony, I understand.'

'Clocks are rare.'

'There is one in town now, I see.'

'Yes.'

The sound of the clock seemed more distinct.

He said, 'Would it help if I were to start?'

'That would depend on what you were to say, captain.'

'To begin with, may I ask you to call me Quinton?'

This was developing into a game of nervous parries and thrusts. With a burst of resolve, she said, 'I know it's irregular, highly improper of me to visit you tonight, while we're alone like this. However, I've been thinking of what you said this afternoon. You said I captivated you. I think that was the word?'

'It was.' His eyes never left her so that she was forced to look elsewhere, at the five small flames arranged in an arch on the table and with each candle sitting in an overflow of hardened wax. Obviously, the men either had no help in the house or the servant was lazy.

'Captivated was the word,' he said, to end the embarrassing silence. 'You have captivated me. Entranced me. Caused me to think of no one else, of nothing else.'

'It is not merely improper, Quinton.' She let her eyes return to him for an instant. 'It is impossible.'

'I know.'

'You also talked about society's conventions.'

'I did.'

'And of how you had been brought up to disguise your true feelings, to show no emotion.'

'As all English gentlemen are.' She didn't react to this snippet of self-deprecation and was silent once more. She was so stiff. He felt the need to help her relax. 'I admire the Neapolitans. Have you been to the Bay of Naples?'

She shook her head. She felt a mad desire to admit she'd never heard of the place, had no idea who Neapolitans were, but she remained silent. This was not the time to chisel a crack in the Clancy family facade.

'The people there have a most open way. Quite remarkable. Not to everyone's taste, but increasingly to mine. They display their emotions. You never doubt their true feelings.'

'They sound . . . honest.'

'Yes. Florid, but you know exactly how they feel. Today,' he said, leaning back in the chair and drumming his fingers on the armrests, 'I felt positively Neapolitan.'

'Then I like the Neapolitans.'

He laughed gently. She held back a smile.

'I've been thinking about what you said. And about how I feel. I, too, was brought up strictly. Was told what I should and should not do. Who I should and should not like.'

He sat quietly, nodding with her words.

'It is all very wrong.'

'Quite.'

'And yet, there are limits. Some we cannot transgress.'

He frowned. 'True.'

'What I want to say first,' she said, pausing to take a deep breath, 'is that I share your feelings.'

He reached for her hand. 'Eliza.'

She held her hand clear. 'I do not have a happy marriage.' The voice within her wanted to scream: I am not even married and therefore I am available. For you, if you would have me. It is only stupid convention that prevents us from being together—that and the fact that I am the woman you want to send to the gallows.

'I am sorry.' He leaned closer.

'My husband is often away. We have not been close for some years. He prefers a more adventurous life to the existence he finds here.'

'I hear he has done some quite remarkable things.'

And the most remarkable, she thought, he dare not tell you about.

'He is rich, I hear.' His voice had a poor suitor's hint of apology.

'He found gold.'

'I admire self-made men.'

'Everything Clancy has become, he has achieved through his own efforts.' She had said Clancy, not Mr Clancy or William. He seemed not to have noticed. 'I admire him in many ways. I do not love him. Is that a terrible thing for a woman to say?'

'It strikes me as being remarkably frank and honest. I perceived those qualities in you from the outset.' Oh God, he was sounding like a communication from the Colonial Secretary. 'I mean,' he said, grabbing her hand and holding it firmly, 'I knew you were like that. Right from the first time we spoke.'

'Quinton, you know so little about me.'

'I know what I need to know.'

'I admire you so much. You are everything . . .' She began to cry.

He removed a handkerchief from his cuff and dabbed her eyes. Now he took her other hand.

'I know it sounds absurd, Quinton, but I love you. We've known each other only a few days, met only a few times and yet I'm sure.'

'As I am.' He leaned forward to kiss her. Her lips were warm,

546

soft, and wonderfully enticing. He'd kissed many women but they were hard, cold or bought. Never had he known such a sensual feeling. A flow of hot, erotic desire coursed through him and he drew back.

'What is it?'

'It's me. I don't know what's happening to me.'

She felt flushed and desire had made her moist between the legs and that was something she'd never experienced. She, who had been taken by force and learned to despise men and hate sexual contact, wanted this man. She kissed him, with a passion that was close to savagery.

'Oh God,' he mumbled and she feared she had gone too far, but his fingers were already undoing the buttons at the back of her bodice.

'Quinton, there's something I must say.' Her voice was soft and remote, as if someone in the far corner of the room were speaking.

'Don't tell me no, please, or I will die.'

He'd picked her up and was carrying her to the chaise longue.

'Quinton'. Her voice was no more than a murmur.

'I know you say it's hopeless, but there must be hope when we feel the way we do.' He lowered her to the chair. 'You do love me?'

'Oh yes.' She had a sensuous woman's fear of bright light and asked him to snuff some of the candles.

When he had done so, he removed his jacket. She had taken off the dress.

'I have so much light because I have poor eyes,' he said.

'I will guide you.'

She had experienced brutality when she was a plaything of the soldiers. There'd been tender moments with Clancy. Never had she known anything like this.

He was strong but held her tenderly; he was passionate and yet gentle in the way he caressed her and teased her nipples and traced wandering patterns across her hips and diminutive waist and burrowed in the fur; he was caring when he stroked her hair and touched her cheeks and kissed her lips, the tip of his tongue following the line from bow to full bottom lip, but dominating in the way he made love.

She was drawn to him, against him, under him and when he was deep inside her and their bodies flowed as a single wave, she engulfed him, legs encircling his buttocks, hands pulling him to her.

When he thrust, her roaming fingers could feel the scar on the back of his thigh and she ached for him.

They sang cries of joy.

When they were spent, he lay with her, breathing heavily, as a man who has nearly drowned comes back to life. He kissed her again, softly this time, and stood. He would like a cigar but that would be appalling so, not knowing what to do, he sat on the corner of the table.

'Oh God,' he said.

'Are you all right?'

'I thought I was dying. I might have, for I think I've just been to heaven.'

He took several deep breaths and returned to the chaise longue and sat with her legs across his lap.

'Eliza, I love you more than ever and I would give anything or do anything to ensure that we could spend the rest of our lives together.'

She pulled her silk slip across her chest and over her hips. 'I've made things even more diffficult for us.'

'How?'

She wanted him to stay, so that they could make love, over

and over again during stolen moments. And there'd be many chances, because Clancy was away so often. But the spectre of Eliza Phillips was hovering, with her prison boots swinging from the shadows of the ceiling.

She had to say it.

'It would be impossible for us to live together in this town, feeling as we do.'

God, he wanted a cigar. 'Why?' he asked with the disarming cheeriness of a casual lover.

'My husband will be back. This is a town riddled by rumour. There would be scandal.'

'Not necessarily.'

'I couldn't control myself, hide my feelings for you. I would look at you and melt with desire, say foolish things, betray myself with every glance and people would know.'

'Let them know.'

'Quinton, that's not possible.'

He stood and began to dress. 'Now is a bad time to be discussing such things. Immediately after lovemaking is the worst time to be discussing an emotional subject.'

'It's what I came to tell you.'

He was buttoning up his fly. 'Well, why didn't you just tell me and leave?'

Dear God in heaven, she'd forgotten how men could be after sex. They were different. Immediately. But he was right. This was not a good time to be talking of such a thing. But it had to be said.

'Dear Quinton, I love you more than I thought I could love anyone, and what I did just then was because I was overwhelmed by my desire for you. And I would do it again, whenever you asked me . . .'

'Then why are you asking me to leave?'

'Because next week, next month or next year, the world

around us will talk and life will be impossible. You will destroy my reputation, which is important to me.'

'Always is, with a woman.'

'This is terribly hard for me. Please don't make it worse.'

He sat facing her and scratched at his beard. 'I'm sorry. You're right. Forgive me.'

'You do understand what I'm saying?'

'Of course. Before you came, I had been thinking I should talk to your husband.'

'No. Please.'

'Is he not a reasonable man?'

She shook her head.

'Would you consider leaving him?'

She shook her head again but less forcefully.

'Is it the child?'

Her eyes widened. 'Partly. Yes, very much so. I have to consider her. Her future. And, if you'll forgive the word, her reputation. I do not want her growing up as the daughter of a woman who created scandal by running off with another man.' She sat up, pulling the slip tightly around her shoulders. 'Oh Quinton, please say you understand.'

'I may never agree.' He nodded to himself. 'But yes, I think I understand.'

'You will go away?'

'Being a man of honour, I have no choice, do I?' He went to the window and pulled back a corner of the curtain. 'Damned quiet outside.'

'When will you go?'

He released the curtain and turned slowly. 'Should I go tonight? Would you give me a few minutes to dress and pack?'

'Quinton, please.'

'Sorry. Dashed bad form.' He walked towards the hallway. 'I was planning to sail up the Hawkesbury tomorrow, as I think I told you. Let me do that. When I come back, I promise you I'll go.' He opened the door. 'I'll leave while you dress. Mustn't forget to do the things a gentleman should do.'

She wept for a full five minutes before she was able to begin dressing.

FIFTY-TWO

EDWIN ROTHERBY WAS late rising next morning and was surprised to find his friend packed and ready to leave. De Lacey explained that he'd arranged to travel up the Hawkesbury on the *Raven,* a 14-tonner that had been built on the river three years earlier and was heading back to The Green Hills in the hope of picking up a load of produce. The captain had agreed to take him.

'You're going sailing with a lot of cabbages?' Rotherby asked.

'Only on the way back.'

'Quinton, your behaviour never ceases to amaze me.' He tapped his forehead in distress. 'Will you be away in two days' time?'

'I'll still be up the river.'

'Good God, man, but the Governor is having a soiree. I've been asked to go and I'm sure he would have liked your company.'

'The invitation arrived yesterday.'

'And you're not going?'

'I will send him my apology.'

Rotherby paused in front of a mirror to search for wrinkles and other signs of decay in the ruthless morning light. 'Are you mad, dear boy?' he said, fingers stretching the sagging pouches under his eyes. 'Bligh has not been here that long, has already accumulated a formidable list of enemies and I, as a former acquaintance, am expected to bolster his side. In other words, he needs friends. The poor chap hasn't had that good a time of it ever since that damned mutiny in the South Seas.'

'You cheer him up.'

'And what will you say when you return from your little escapade? That you had a prior engagement with some cabbages?'

'When I come back, Edwin, I will tell him I am about to leave the colony.'

Rotherby sat down. 'What on earth for?'

'My business, Edwin.'

'It's that damned woman, isn't it? Good heavens, man, if she's pregnant, there's no problem. The woman's married. Her husband will probably be delighted to have sired another child. No one will suspect her of any misdemeanour.'

'She is not pregnant.' He hadn't thought of that and tried to dismiss the possibility.

'So it is Mrs Clancy. Now tell me, what have you done or what has she done that is making you leave New South Wales when your shadow has scarcely had time to attach itself to the soil?'

'It's something I have no wish to discuss.'

'People will ask me.'

'Use one of your excuses.'

He put on a dressing-gown and stood near de Lacey.

'I have run because of many husbands but I have never run because of a woman.'

'Your choice of words is unfortunate.'

'Have you met the woman's husband?'

'You know he's away.'

'Well then, wait until he comes back. The man might be a monster and it might be your duty to take this poor woman

553

from him.' With a theatrical gesture, he cupped a hand around his ear, to provide easy access to a denial.

De Lacey sighed. 'I have to leave. I will be back, however.'

'Quinton, in all my years of being involved with other men's wives . . .'

He was heading for the front door. 'Edwin, I do not want to hear about your various conquests, defeats and flights.'

Rotherby raised a finger. 'Never a defeat.'

'I only want you to promise me you'll stay away from Mrs Clancy. I don't want you visiting her and asking her questions. I want you to leave the lady alone.'

Rotherby searched for his pipe. 'It is an error of judgment not to attend Captain Bligh's function. Newcomers simply do not refuse invitations from the Governor.'

'I am passing through.'

'What the devil are you going to the river for, anyhow?' He had the pipe and waved it triumphantly. 'It's those convicts, isn't it?' He ran after de Lacey and caught him by the arm. 'Quinton, dear Quinton, do not go racing off now to search for ghosts from eight years ago. You will do no more than open up the whole sorry mess, get people talking again. Listen to me, friend, no good will come from this.'

De Lacey was at the door and took Rotherby's hand from his arm. 'I know what I'm doing, Edwin. You'd do me a great favour by telling people I've been called there on urgent business.'

'Which is what?'

'Looking for the convicts. They've been seen.'

Rotherby grasped his forehead. 'I don't understand this. You're going up the Hawkesbury because those convicts have allegedly turned up after all these years in the wilderness, and somehow, Mrs Clancy is involved.'

'Mrs Clancy is not involved and kindly do not mention her name to anyone in connection with my journey.'

'Well, how the devil is she involved?'

De Lacey put down his small case. He was taking a few clothes, cigars and some liquor. 'I need to get away for a while.'

'The husband's coming home, is that the problem?'

'Good Lord, Edwin, can't you think of anything else?'

'Your every word and gesture implicates her in some way. I'd like to know why she's causing you to go off on this improbable, hopeless chase after three convicts, who probably died many years ago . . .'

'They've been seen.'

'Piffle. Have you been flashing your money?'

'What do you mean?'

'If you've told anyone that you're looking for these people and will pay for information . . .' He left an eyebrow hovering. 'Quinton, there are people in this town who will tell you anything, identify anyone, if they can make money.'

De Lacey's lips were dry and he wiped his mouth.

Rotherby continued in a low voice. 'So that's the excuse. You're continuing your quest for the three villains. Cheers for you. Now, where does Mrs Clancy fit into all this? After all, you're not just sailing up the river. You're planning to leave the colony for good.'

'For good, yes, Edwin. That's an appropriate term to use. I'm going for good.' De Lacey moved down the steps.

'I shall look forward to a more extensive conversation when you return,' Rotherby called after him but de Lacey was hurrying away towards the harbour.

Who the devil was this Clancy woman? Perhaps he should find out more about her.

For the next two days Rotherby inquired about Eliza Clancy. She and her husband had arrived in somewhat mysterious circumstances a few years ago. They were from Cape Town. It was said he had discovered gold there. It was known he was immensely wealthy.

William Clancy was in town several weeks before anyone saw his wife, according to one source. How was that? No one knew. Clancy had said he was buying property in the country. Possibly she was there.

Someone recalled the couple had arrived on board the *Isabella*. Rotherby examined shipping records but their names were not on any lists. The *Isabella* had been lost on a voyage to Peru, so there was no chance of checking her records.

Why had they come here, to join a fledgling community that was largely peopled by convicts and emancipists? Why had they not stayed in Africa or gone home to England? No one knew.

What was Eliza Clancy's background? She was a woman of mystery. Not very interesting, it was true. Dull, some thought. William Clancy was different. He talked a great deal about his past and was full of colourful stories.

There was something very strange about the Clancys. They were figures without substance. No one had known of them before they arrived in Sydney. Clancy's stories about their past were based entirely on what he alone told people. By contrast, she was a mouse, almost a recluse who avoided conversation. Her sole interest seemed to be in her daughter.

She was a good-looking woman, well-dressed and inclined to wear lavish jewellery; Rotherby himself had noted that.

But how would she have attracted de Lacey? Why would he leave the colony because of her?

The latter was the easiest question to answer. Quinton was such a starchy fellow, so impossibly steeped in tradition, that he would do the right thing even if it were stupid. Rotherby guessed she had either asked him to leave, or he had decided he must go because he felt he was becoming fond of her. And she was a married woman.

The fool.

He smelled pretence. He would not have his friend sacrifice himself for a woman who was not what she claimed.

Eliza Clancy was not at the Governor's soiree, of course, which gave Rotherby the chance to talk to more people about her, but he learned nothing new. He did, however, hear rumours that Clancy's gold was not from Africa but had been found locally. Someone said he had been seen at the river many times and spent his weeks there in unexplored territory, digging for gold, not working a farm.

Bligh himself was worried about the stories. 'The last thing we want,' he told Rotherby, 'is someone finding gold here. We'll have an influx of desperadoes from China, India, California and other unsavoury places, and there'll be no holding the convicts. They'll all be off and away because there won't be any soldiers to guard them. They'll be out looking for gold, too. The place will become chaotic.' He intended speaking to Clancy when he returned from his sea trip up north.

Rotherby thought Bligh had become even more pompous than he remembered. He tolerated no one's opinion but his own. He had some friends but many enemies, mainly among the ranks of the powerful officers of the New South Wales Corps.

Rotherby sensed that here, in one of His Majesty's most remote and troublesome colonies, revolt was in the air. Not from the convicts or the Irish element, but from those who perceived themselves as being the real rulers of the land.

It might be amusing to wait and see what happened. There was always more money to be made, more fun to be had, when the corrupt were in charge. He must persuade de Lacey to stay.

Berak and Arabanoo accompanied Clancy all the way to the last ridge in the mountain range. From there they could see the great river and, far in the distance, the smoke that rose in thin columns from the fires of Sydney to join the haze shimmering above the coastal plain. Even the Pacific was visible but the stain of blue rimming the horizon meant nothing to the young men. Having no understanding of the sea, they could not recognise it as anything more than a line of the palest colour.

Clancy gave them each a gift. To Berak, he presented a pair of trousers with an old belt. He gave Arabanoo a shirt with metal buttons and two deep pockets. They put them on. Arabanoo looked covetously at Berak's belt.

They waved goodbye and Clancy began the long descent, laden with his guns, the gold, clothing, remnants of food and other small items.

The two Aborigines watched him for some time. They were about to return when they became aware of a figure behind them, standing on higher ground. It was Ulla. She was carrying the boy, Clancy's son Wileemarin.

Berak was immediately angry, having been entrusted with the task of guarding their rear and not having known they were being followed—by a woman!

She came forward. 'I am going with Clancy,' she said. 'I will live with him in the place where the white people live.'

'I knew someone was behind us,' Berak said.

'That is true,' Arabanoo said and showed his great teeth in a smile. 'But you did not know it was only Ulla.'

'Murremurran was behind you. He intended to kill you.' She told them the story.

When she had finished, Berak asked, 'How do we know this is true?' He was still angry.

'You can go back and see the body for yourself. I'll tell you where I hid it.'

Berak had always known that Ulla was regarded as being a superior young woman, the best in the tribe and a fine catch for any man until Wonngu had given his daughter to the white man. Perhaps Clancy had bestowed some of his magic upon her.

He regarded her with awe. Murremurran had been a great hunter.

'You saved our lives,' Arabanoo said.

'I killed him because he meant harm to Ker-lan-see.'

'So what will you do?'

'Follow my husband. And you will come with me.'

Both men shook their heads. Frightened as they were of the mountain warriors, they were more fearful of the white people.

'Where did you get those clothes?' she asked.

'From Ker-lan-see,' Arabanoo said. He looked once more at Berak's leather belt and she saw the envy.

'I can get you a belt. Ker-lan-see has many. I can get you both whatever you need.' She pointed to the other man. 'Berak, what do you want?'

He shrugged and thought. 'A hat. With a feather through the band.'

'I promise to get you a hat. To get you both whatever you want. But I need you to come with me.'

'Why?' Berak asked.

'Because I will need you with me, to help Ker-lan-see.'

Her man would need help, she knew, because her mouth was bitter with the taste of impending trouble.

Noxious Watts had travelled to the river by pony and cart, a combination he used to haul grog from the wharves to his shop. Kerrigan was with him. So was the Swede, Nilssen, whom they'd found in a drunken stupor in a brothel at the lower end of High Street. The rough ride in the cart had shaken him awake in a series of vomiting spasms and a day of temperance and boredom at The Green Hills had turned his mood into one of lethal hostility. He was eager for violence and ready to bash anyone on

Watts's order. Anyone who looked at him, for that matter.

While Nilssen lay in the cart, snoring and farting and occasionally scanning the street for someone to fight, Watts and Kerrigan had been asking questions.

Watts didn't bother asking about the woman. He was interested only in Clancy Fitzgerald and in determining whether he was, in fact, the man who now purported to be William Clancy.

He'd been thinking about it on the journey out in the cart and it seemed far-fetched. William Clancy was a rich man, married, respected and a pillar of Sydney society. Hardly an escaped convict, he'd decided and thus, since reaching the river, he'd spent much of his time thinking of ways to extort money from de Lacey.

And then, in the afternoon, he met a farmer who reacted to the description of Fitzgerald. He'd met such a man once on a hill during the great flood of '99. The man had sailed for help on a table—this man's table—with a black boy.

That would have been around the time that he'd attempted to waylay Fitzgerald, Watts calculated, and while he was interested he was hardly excited. He knew, to his cost, that Fitzgerald was at the river around that time.

And then the farmer said he'd seen the same man again—several times, in fact. The farmer now had a property right on the river. It was the furthest from the settlement. Either he or his wife had seen the man crossing the river by raft, which was most unusual, and heading into wild country on the other side. Not often. Perhaps no more than once or twice a year. But they'd wondered if it were the same man they'd met because they'd never got their table back and would like to know where it was.

Later, another man, who spent most of his time in Sydney, said he thought he'd seen William Clancy up here at least once. He'd been dressed in rough clothes and had come into town to buy something.

'People say he's found gold up here. I've heard the rumours meself.' The man laughed. 'Poppycock. The only gold you'd find up here is what you brought in yerself.'

'How do you mean?'

'I done some prospecting. Around here is not gold country.'

Watts and Kerrigan walked upstream for a few miles but saw nothing. Then they went back through the settlement and followed the river downstream for a mile or two. They found a sloop, large for the river, anchored near the far bank. It was the *Empress of China*.

The *Raven* had been delayed a day in leaving Sydney and was only now approaching The Green Hills. De Lacey saw the *Empress* moored among some trees. 'Who owns that?' he asked the skipper, recalling some talk about the vessel but forgetting the owner's name.

'New boat. Built up here. Good job. Done for Mr William Clancy.' The captain had a wiry grey beard which he pressed constantly, as if crushing lice. 'Strange that she's here. Heard she was up north.'

'After *bêche-de-mer*,' de Lacey said, filling in the story.

'Couldn't have done well. Must be after a load of vegetables or something.' He became agitated, imagining how much would be left for him after the 40-tonner's holds were filled.

'Do you know this Mr Clancy?'

'Seen him a few times.'

'What's he look like?'

The skipper pointed to a figure walking on the far bank. 'Like that gentleman there. That's Mr Clancy.'

At this point the river bank was endowed with rows of old eucalypts whose bulbous trunks were matched by thick, bent branches that hung low across the water. Although the channel was deep, the *Raven's* captain was reluctant to move in close for fear of snagging the mast, but he was persuaded to send a dinghy for Clancy.

De Lacey had called his name and seemed friendly, and Clancy had no choice but to respond.

'Forgive me,' de Lacey said as he helped Clancy on board, 'but you are William Clancy?'

'I am and what is there to forgive you for?' He'd left the musket in its usual hiding place and had stowed the pistols in one of his bags but was conscious of the gold he carried. As the weight might excite interest, he lowered the bag gently to the yacht's deck.

'For interrupting you. You must be busy.' He held out his hand. 'I'm Quinton de Lacey.'

Clancy remembered the name and was so shocked he almost dropped the second bag, with the pistols. He hadn't recognised the bearded face, which wasn't surprising as he'd seen the man only once. He did, however, recall sleeping in de Lacey's bed. He almost said, *You're back*, but restrained himself in time.

'I've only been in the colony for a few weeks. I must say I've been looking forward to meeting you. And here we are.' This was not going well, de Lacey thought. He sounded like a pretentious fool. But he wanted to see the man, judge whether William Clancy was worthy of Eliza and decide once and for all what he should do.

'Looking forward to meeting me? Whatever for?'

'Oh,' said de Lacey, trying to think of his original, pre-Eliza reasons. 'I've heard so much about the exploits of Mr William Clancy that I was hoping for the chance to meet you.'

'Ah. Well, as you said, here we are.' Clancy had learned the value of letting someone he either feared or mistrusted make the running in any conversation. Particularly if they seemed unsure of themselves. Whatever was the man doing back in New South

562

Wales? He had one thought, recalling what he'd been told about de Lacey, but dismissed it; no one would pursue so radical a cause for so many years, surely.

'I'm proving a poor host,' de Lacey said. 'I have with me whisky, gin, sherry. You look hot, as though you've been working hard. May I offer you a drink.'

He asked for whisky.

'The crystal is hardly up to your standards,' de Lacey said when he produced two metal mugs and began filling them.

My standards? Has de Lacey been in my house? And then he thought, don't be silly now. Stay calm. This man doesn't know who you are. He's just a talkative old goose. Might be interested in my gold, like most of the others.

The skipper interrupted to ask Clancy if he had bought all the vegetables and produce available from the farms.

'Why no,' he answered, wondering what the man was talking about. He was about to deny they were buying anything and give the man a sharp rebuke for his cheekiness, but had the wit to slow down and say, 'I'm sure you'll find enough to fill the holds.'

This worried the man, who was anxious to get into town to start a little dealing himself. He bent over de Lacey and said, 'I'll leave as soon as the captain's ready.'

Captain? Was de Lacey reduced to captaining the smallest commercial craft on the Hawkesbury? There were so many questions he'd like to ask.

'He'd heard you had sailed for the far north in search of *bêche-de-mer*,' de Lacey said when the man had gone back to the wheel. 'Immediately we saw your vessel, he assumed you'd had a poor run and had come here in search of a load of . . . whatever.'

Clancy nodded. He was enjoying seeing this man run out of words.

Their conversation was innocuous. De Lacey asked about

Africa; he hadn't been there, which was good news, although he had been along the north coast, which didn't matter a damn.

He asked about goldmining and Clancy told a few of the tales he'd spread around town. But without any flourishes. This was bland Clancy, not interested in prolonging the conversation.

De Lacey said he was surprised at the size of Sydney Town. It was much larger than he'd expected. This gave Clancy the chance to ask if he'd been here before and then discover why the devil he'd come back, but he didn't. He asked few questions. It gave him the high ground in this conversation. De Lacey was interested in him. He wasn't interested in de Lacey.

Whisky finished, he refused another, agreed that their next meeting would be pleasant, and was taken ashore.

Clancy felt contented. The man who had reputedly devoted his life to the search for Clancy Fitzgerald had just given him a whisky and seemed as dangerous as a toothless dog.

De Lacey was pleased but disturbed. William Clancy was below him in class, education and conversation. What on earth was a woman like Eliza Clancy doing married to an amiable but rough person like this? Was it just his money that had attracted her?

He would see her when he got back, speak to her again, have her agree that he should change his undertaking to leave the colony. But he must see her before her husband returned. Calculating the amount of money he had with him, he went to speak to the captain, to persuade him to forsake his cabbages and return immediately to Sydney.

The *Empress of China* was moored within the embrace of the knotted branches of a eucalypt. Clancy walked along one branch and jumped on board. No one was in sight.

'Craddock, where the devil are you?' he called out and went below.

Noxious Watts was seated at the end of the cabin. Kerrigan and Nilssen were on either side of him. Watts was holding a pistol.

'Do come in,' he said.

FIFTY-THREE

THE *EMPRESS* WAS new but the cabin had the stink of an old boat. Confined in that small space and as tangible as the three men facing Clancy was the stomach-wrenching smell of wet boots, drenched canvas and damp coaldust, of sweaty clothes and unwashed skin, of prawnheads and rotten fish, cooking fat and aromatic spices, belched grog and pipe smoke, fresh varnish and stale vomit.

The sick was still on Nilssen's shirt. He came forward to bar the steps.

'And who are you?' Clancy said, facing Watts. His heart was racing but his voice was tolerably under control. He had that knack; his legs could be quivering but his mouth would be firm.

The gold was in the bag on his back, the pistols at the bottom of the bag in his left hand. All were soon gone, Nilssen grabbing the bags so violently that Clancy staggered a few paces. The Swede put the bags on the table.

'I'm trying to decide,' Watts said, rising and walking slowly around Clancy.

'You don't know who you are?'

'I'm trying to decide about you.'

Clancy hadn't been sure which role to play, but now determined to be William Clancy. 'What are you doing on my boat and where the devil is Captain Craddock?'

566

Kerrigan was about to open one of the bags. 'He and his slant-eyed mates are nicely trussed up down below. They wasn't at all pleased to see us. They'd prefer to sleep for a while, I'd be thinking.'

'I repeat,' Clancy said, trying to sound enraged rather than terrified, 'who are you, sir?'

'The voice is different. But the name Clancy. Now that's a clue.' Watts came closer to touch Clancy's beard, then returned to the chair. 'Older, of course.' He spun around when he thought he heard a noise. 'Nilssen, up top. Quick. Have a look around.'

The big Swede had drawn his knife and took the stairs three at a time.

'He'd like to have someone to stick that thing in,' Watts said with a smile. He went back to his seat.

Kerrigan had pulled a cloth sack from the bag and opened it. He dug in, lifted his hand and let gold trickle through his palm.

'Look what we've got here,' he said. 'Enough to make me rich. I can buy me own bloody guns.'

'Hand it over,' Watts said, eyes bulging at the sight.

The Irishman, in no mood for orders, shook his head. 'Do you know how much gold is in here?'

'I said hand it over.'

Clancy shuffled to one side of the cabin.

Kerrigan was thinking only of the gold and of Watts, who was now pointing the pistol at him. 'Nilssen,' he shouted, 'come on down here and see what I got.'

'Show it to him and he'll take the lot, you fool,' Watts said.

Kerrigan was backing up the steps, holding the sack of gold in front of him as a shield.

'Nilssen, come quick.' He was at the top of the steps and looked around. There was no sign of the Swede. 'The bugger's gone,' he said.

'What do you mean, gone?' Watts was halfway up the steps.

'Disappeared. Vanished. He just ain't here.'

In the cabin, Clancy dashed for the second bag. He took out a pistol and, racing up the stairs, used the barrel to jab Watts in the back.

'Drop your gun, laddie,' he said.

Watts half turned. 'Where'd you get that?'

'No questions. Just drop your gun or I'll put such a big hole in your head that you'll be forever catching cold.'

Watts dropped the pistol and came down the steps. The curious, crouching form of Kerrigan filled the upper entrance.

'You too.'

The Irishman came down the steps slowly, one hand holding the gold, the other opening and clenching in its longing for a weapon.

Clancy made them both sit on the floor.

'You're Fitzgerald, aren't you?' Watts said as he watched Clancy put the gold in its bag.

'I don't know who you are, sir,' Clancy said, 'but I'm going to get the police and if you follow me up those steps, I will shoot.'

He meant to go slowly, to be ready to fire if either man showed his head above deck but once in the fresh air he bolted for the nearest limb of the giant eucalypt and scrambled for the shore. Only when he was on the bank and running did he remember Craddock and the two crew members.

He stopped, but a shot whistled through the trees. He turned and fired but already he was too far away to be accurate and his shot went wide. He had nothing more. The second pistol, all the powder and balls were in the other bag. He ran again.

From the boat came a cry. It was not a warning or a shout of anger or anything Clancy might have expected, but the sort of noise a man makes with his last breath, when shock and fear and violent muscular contraction combine to produce an ugly farewell.

Kerrigan was staggering backwards across the deck with a long spear through his middle. He fell over the side and was soon swept away in the current, to join the log-like form of Nilssen, floating fifty yards downstream with only the thin shaft of a hunting spear to suggest there was something special about that piece of river debris.

Watts fired a shot. Not at Clancy but into the bushes nearer the boat. He began reloading the pistol.

'Who's there?' Clancy shouted, first in English, then in the language of Wonngu's tribe.

To his astonishment, Ulla answered. 'Over here.'

He ran through bushes, keeping low in case Watts was ready to fire again. She was standing beside a gnarled gum. The boy was behind the tree, wide-eyed, fingers in his mouth.

'What are you doing here?'

'I knew you would need help.'

'Who's with you?'

'Berak and Arabanoo. Berak killed the first man, Arabanoo . . .'

'Never mind. I don't want you getting hurt. Or the boy. Keep him away from that gun. The man is very bad.'

Clancy heard the thud of a spear hitting wood. Watts fired again.

'Tell them to let that man go. Hide. Make sure you're safe. But when the bad man goes, I want you to send Berak into the boat to release three men. They are friends of mine. They will take the boat back to Sydney. Do you understand?'

'Yes. What will you do?'

'I don't know.' He thrust the empty pistol into his belt. 'Probably go to Sydney. I will walk. I cannot stay here.'

She seemed puzzled. 'Why don't you kill the bad man?'

How could he explain that his gun was useless, that he was frightened and his thoughts were so scrambled he only wanted to run? He needed to get to Sydney. There, he could have a ruffian like Watts silenced, deal with the dithering de Lacey. Still speaking her language, he said, 'Someone will have heard the noise of the guns and come here and then there will be trouble. I mustn't be seen. Nor should they find you here.' That was certain. Once one of the speared bodies was discovered, there'd be a hunt for Aborigines and spear-carrying tribals like Berak and Arabanoo would be shot on sight. Ulla too, and probably the boy. The limits of a blackfellow hunt were not defined by reason or compassion.

He kissed Ulla. 'Go home. I will come to see you one day. Just go home before it's too late, and get the boy out of danger.'

'You are my man, Ker-lan-see, and I love you, as a good woman should.'

'And I love you as a good man should.' He said the words as a trite chant but spent a precious five seconds looking at her, and it was as if he'd never seen her clearly before. She was good-looking, loyal and brave, regal in her stance and perfectly at home among the trees and bushes and lush grass along the river bank. Maybe he did love her.

'Now do as I tell you,' he said and ran away.

Clancy had been gone for ten minutes before Noxious Watts emerged from the cabin. He had two pistols; his own and Clancy's second, smaller weapon. As instructed, the two black men stayed hidden. Watts looked around, then took the dinghy and, staying in the middle of the wide stream, rowed up to the settlement.

Aided by a flourish of coins, de Lacey had persuaded the captain to set sail for Sydney that evening. First, he wanted to spend an hour or two at The Green Hills, trying to find Watts and discover what he'd learned about the Phillips woman.

The *Raven* was moored at the settlement's jetty when Noxious Watts arrived in the dinghy.

De Lacey was beginning to think this was the place where fortuitous happenings occurred naturally. Hands on hips, he said, 'What on earth are you doing in that boat, Watts?'

Watts was still shaken by his encounter with Clancy and the hidden blacks but he was never a man to be cowed. He shielded his eyes to get a better view of de Lacey. 'And what are you doing up here, captain? I asked you not to come.'

'You did. And I decided to ignore your advice, Watts.'

'Well, you're a fool, sir.' Watts was in no mood for tact. He needed to catch Clancy before he hid the gold somewhere. But de Lacey was money, too, if on a lesser scale. He modified his tone. 'If you don't mind me saying so.'

'I do mind,' de Lacey thundered. 'You're an impertinent ass, Watts. I'm quite aware that you're leading me on, spinning stories so that you can extract as much money from me as possible.'

'Oh am I now?' He got out of the dinghy in a rush, letting it float free from the jetty.

'Here, you're losing that boat,' the skipper of the *Raven* shouted.

'Damn the boat. I'm on the trail of someone who can tell me exactly where your Miss Phillips is, Captain de Lacey, and I can't spare a moment.'

'You're what?'

'I've found one of them. Now, if you'll only let me be on my way, I'll catch him for you.'

De Lacey turned to see who it was that Watts was chasing.

'You won't see him. I'm a few minutes behind.' Watts brushed past de Lacey. 'Will you be in Sydney?'

'In the morning.'

'I'll contact you in a day or two. Have a lot of money ready.' He left, half running, half walking, to get to his pony and cart.

571

He didn't know where Clancy had gone but was gambling on him making a run for the coast.

Rotherby had sent a note to Eliza Clancy's house. It read simply: *I know who you are. I think we should talk. Rotherby.* He reasoned that if she were the woman she purported to be she'd ignore the note. But some hours later she sent back an answer: *Be here at six.*

She might have a horsewhip waiting for him but he decided the risk was worthwhile.

First, he saw Jamieson, whose house was not far from the Clancys and who, only the previous night, had asked him to drop in for a drink. It was an inebriate's invitation but Rotherby meant to keep the lieutenant to it; he was the only man who seemed close to William Clancy and, as a friend, might know something about Clancy's wife.

Jamieson was already well on the way to being drunk. He must have suffered recent criticism, either for his wealth or his ethics, because immediately he launched into a rambling defence.

'I'm a good man, Mr Rotherby, in an evil town. There are those whose sole motive is greed. There are others whose sole ambition is intoxication. One depends on the other.' He paused, to make sure he'd got his words right.

'Indeed.' Rotherby was drinking little of Jamieson's fine whisky, but his host was doing his best to empty a crystal decanter that had begun the afternoon coloured to its neck.

'There are those who say we have an unfair monopoly of trade, which is utter piffle. Pure balderdash. Agree?'

Rotherby raised his glass.

'Can you imagine what would happen if some people in this town were in charge of trade?'

'A horrifying thought.'

'It is not the desire for material gain which motivates us Mr Rotherby.'

He was pausing a lot and Rotherby said, 'No?'

'I have no need to soil my hands in trade.'

'I'm sure.' Rotherby gestured towards a glass display case filled with ornate silverware. 'You're obviously a man of both distinction and fine taste.'

'Thank you, sir. But can you imagine what would happen to the weak—that is, to the majority—if we were not acting to protect them against those whose sole motive is greed?'

'Whereas?' A silence would have been more discreet but Rotherby couldn't resist.

'Whereas, sir, the officers who have decided to indulge in these commercial transactions are guided by one thing. A gentleman's code of honour.'

He raised his glass. 'I drink to you, then, sir.'

They drank.

'And yet there are some traders who are not officers,' Rotherby said, in an indifferent voice. 'What's the gentleman's name . . . friend of yours, I believe . . . Clancy?'

'Ah yes. I've had some dealings with the fellow. Helped him quite a bit. A real novice, you know.' Jamieson was in the mood to say disparaging things about both Clancy and his wife. He was annoyed that the man had a shipload of sandalwood riding in the harbour and would undoubtedly make a fortune from it, and he was angry with the woman for thwarting his plans to find the source and make himself an even greater fortune.

It irked him that an inferior like Clancy could make more money than he.

For ten minutes he talked about Clancy. Good fellow. Adventurous. Self-made. Needed quite a bit of tuition in trade and such matters. Not worldly. A little rough on the edges but a man had to be, to do what he'd done in Africa, eh?

'I hear tell his wife is a very different proposition.' It was a dangerous thing to say, for a sober Jamieson might have shut tight or been offended by Rotherby's lack of discretion. But Jamieson was neither sober nor inclined to spare Eliza Clancy.

Yes,' he said after a pause long enough for him to think of her insulting performance when the *Caroline* arrived. 'Strange woman.'

He was waiting for Rotherby's help in unbuttoning his thoughts.

'So I've heard.'

'Have you now?' Another drink. 'Can't say I'm surprised. The woman does not know her place.'

'I've heard that too.'

He seemed pleased. Silence was the best magnet now and Rotherby busied himself filling both glasses.

Jamieson gave a little cough, as if to test that he was awake. 'Class, breeding, always shows through, don't you think?'

'Indisputable, sir.'

'I say, that's rather a large glass you've given me,' he said, his eyes swelling in approval of the brimming whisky glass.

'I've heard it said,' Rotherby prompted, 'that she's unnaturally quiet.'

'Oh, she can speak up when she has a mind to it. The instincts of a fishwife, I'd say. But, no, that's true. Put her among people and she behaves like a clam. Get nothing from her. There are times I'd swear the woman was frightened of something.'

'Really?'

'I've seen her look to her husband for guidance. Do you know how it is? Someone asks her something and she looks at Mr Clancy as if to say, "what should I tell this person?". Very odd.'

'Why would that be?'

'Something in her past, dear boy. The woman's frightened of something. Fears discovery.'

574

'You're most perceptive, lieutenant.'

'Oh, I've had years of dealing with bounders, liars, all that sort. Soon get to tell one.'

'So what do you think it is?'

'Think what is, old boy?'

'The trouble with her. The reason she behaves the way she does.'

Jamieson leaned forward and spoke in a raspy, conspiratorial voice. 'On one occasion, I heard her talking to one of her female servants. Didn't mean to eavesdrop. Couldn't help hearing. She used expressions that only a convict would know.'

'Convict? You're saying Eliza Clancy was a convict?'

'Perhaps.' The eyes darted deep into Rotherby's, to make sure he'd done the damage. He was rewarded with the glaze of shock. 'Plenty of them around,' he added hastily, benevolently. 'Nothing wrong with that, of course.' Jamieson kept talking about the number of convicts and ex-convicts and free settlers in the colony, but Rotherby was no longer listening.

Eliza Clancy might well be a former prisoner, which could explain a great deal about her behaviour. But if that were true, who was William Clancy, the prosperous, adventurous and mysterious gentleman who was alleged to have married her in Cape Province?

Rotherby had stayed longer than he'd meant at Jamieson's and was two minutes late at the Clancy house. There was no horsewhip. No line of burly servants to beat him and throw him back on the street. He was shown into the drawing room.

He sat near the row of oil paintings. She sat on the other side of the room.

She didn't speak.

He'd expected a flurry of words, indignation, accusations about his own morality, but she damned well did nothing. Just looked at him until he wriggled uncomfortably and said, 'I want to say from the outset I don't wish to cause you any harm. I'm more concerned about my friend.'

Even then she didn't speak.

He knew that people, like nature, abhorred a vacuum, and few could tolerate silence. Tempted sufficiently, they would rush in to fill the emptiness. Gush. Say things they meant to keep to themselves. He knew. So, it seemed, did she.

He said, 'I presume you know whom I'm talking about?'

She had a silver bell beside her chair and touched its handle. 'There are men in the house, Mr Rotherby. If I ring this bell they will come to my aid.'

My God, he thought, she thinks I might try to seduce her. He felt like laughing. 'You are quite safe,' he said. 'Neither violence nor seduction are on my mind.'

'What is?'

'The wellbeing of my friend. I have no desire to see him leave the colony.'

So Quinton had talked. She was astounded. She had assumed all they had said was private. How much had he told this rogue? Had he described everything? Had they shared a hearty laugh at his description of her wantonness?

She had resolved to be calm, to let him talk. But it was time to speak.

'If I have a weakness, Mr Rotherby, it is curiosity. Which is why, when I received your cryptic and puzzling note, I decided to see you, rather than have you horsewhipped out of town.' There was no malice in her words. Almost no emotion.

A blowfly had entered the room and was buzzing near the window. For the first time, Eliza seemed unsettled.

'I have no idea what your note was referring to,' she said, 'but I am puzzled. And I should warn you, a frivolous explanation will force me to ring this bell.'

He smiled. She was talking. It was time to play the one card he had.

'Do you remember Molly Brewer?' It was an entirely fictitious name but it had, he thought, an authentic ring.

'No. I've never heard of such a person.'

'She remembers you. From the convict days, Mrs Clancy.'

She lowered her head and her hands began to fight each other.

'I do not know anyone called Molly Brewer.'

'As I said at the outset, I am not here to cause you harm. My interests are purely those of Captain de Lacey.'

'I am . . .' She was forced to look down at the rug to regain her composure. 'I have no idea what you're talking about or what you want.'

'Are you after money?' he said, with a sharpness meant to prod her into rashness.

'Me?' Her flattened hand covered her breast. 'I thought you were the extortionist. I thought it likely, knowing of your reputation.'

'I have never been in need of money, dear lady. Unlike you. I was thinking that past habits linger and that possibly, you had been tempted.'

Insults exchanged, they sat like fighters out of breath, watching each other, waiting for the first move.

Eventually, he said, 'I know about your husband, too.'

'And you will tell Captain de Lacey. You cannot even let that poor man be free of the horrors that have followed him for all these years.'

What was this? He sat stunned, trying to absorb the implications of what she had said.

'I am only concerned that you leave the captain alone and, for whatever reason, do not force him to leave.' He stood. 'I think it's time I left.'

She didn't speak. He found his own way out and, mind whirling with outrageous theories, walked back to the house.

FIFTY-FOUR

THE MAID ELIZA most trusted was a Welsh woman named Emily Waters. Eliza summoned her and told her to take Caroline to a nearby guesthouse for the night. She was to wear ordinary clothes, dress Caroline similarly, and pretend the child was her own. Under no circumstances was she to reveal the girl's true identity. Emily was astonished but too conscious of her position to question her mistress's orders.

If she did not hear from Eliza by midday, she was to take Caroline to Sydney Cove and seek Captain Murchison. She was to hand him a sealed envelope, which Eliza then entrusted to her care. She also gave Emily the case she had packed for Caroline. In it, but out of sight under clothing, was a small leather pouch filled with gold dust.

'You may have to take a sea voyage with my daughter,' Eliza said. 'Captain Murchison will know what to do.'

'Are you coming too, ma'am?'

'Possibly not.'

Eliza kissed the sleepy Caroline goodbye and sought the Javanese stable-hand. She told him to sleep in the hallway near the front door. If he heard anyone outside, or if the bell was rung, he was not to open the door but to come and wake her. She would be spending the night in the stable loft.

He wondered if the captain were visiting the house during the night, but dared not ask the question.

'If anyone comes, whether you know them or not, wake me before you do anything else,' she repeated. 'And be as quiet as a mouse.'

A simple lad, he thought that amusing. His sleep was disturbed by mice.

She took with her the packed case and a long dark hooded coat. She thought she would be awake all night but she fell asleep soon after entering the loft. She had bad dreams.

Clancy and Quinton were in a tavern. Both were drunk and laughing and slapping each other on the shoulders. Clancy spoke with the broad accent of someone from Lancashire. 'Fook her again,' he was saying and de Lacey was laughing and saying, 'No, dear boy, it's your turn.' She was serving ale, great jugs of frothing swill, and she had to step over entwined, heaving, grunting couples to get to the table where the two men, the one who pretended to be her husband and the one who pretended to be her lover, were seated.

'You're too early, loove,' Clancy boomed. 'We haven't decided.'

De Lacey bent over in a paroxysm of laughter. As she stopped, uncertain of what to do, he leaped at her and grabbed her arm in a cruel hold. 'Got you,' he shouted and beckoned to another table, where sat a large, fat man wearing the hood of the hangman.

'I told you you talked too much,' Clancy said . . .

She thought she felt someone shaking her and woke with a start but it was merely one of the horses moving in its stall below. She could hear rustling in the hay. It was mice.

She dreamed of her aunt and the millrace where her sister drowned and she saw her sister again, screaming for help and

579

waving her arm, and it was Caroline, not her sister and she made a yelping noise and woke again.

She dreamed of Catholic priests, tall thin men in black robes who had no faces and she watched them walk past, a long procession of terrifying figures, until one stopped and smiled at her. He had a face but his skin was coal black and he had a broad nose. One front tooth was missing. 'I will marry you and Clancy,' he said 'and then you can pretend you are single.'

'We have a child.'

'No,' he said, 'we have the child' and she could hear Caroline screaming but she couldn't see her.

She sat up and the horses moved, shuffling like wheat in a breeze.

If they hanged her, it would put an end to all these dreams and the terror she'd known for the past years. Captain Murchison seemed a good man. He was only young. Perhaps he would marry Caroline one day and they could live together in the English enclave in Shanghai. He was Presbyterian. That was all right . . .

Clancy had intended to walk through the night, knowing that if he kept his pace up he could be in Sydney by dawn. But it was a dark night and he stumbled many times on the rough track and even lost his way once, finding himself in a paddock infested by lank weeds that scratched at his knees. With nothing to guide him but the black of trees against the malevolent grey of the sky, he spent ten minutes groping across the paddock until he regained the rutted line that would take him through Castle Hill and Parramatta. He lasted until midnight, when exhaustion overtook him and he was forced to rest. He got well off the track and crawled under some bushes.

He was worried about Ulla. Watts had a gun and, no matter how proficient Berak and Arabanoo were with their spears, he would have an advantage. Clancy had no idea what other weapons Watts might have brought or found on board the *Empress*. He tried to think what guns Craddock had carried. He would certainly have a musket or two to defend the crew against natives when they landed for water or food somewhere along the northern coast, and Watts might well have found them.

He was close to sleep but the vision of Noxious Watts firing a musket at Ulla kept him awake.

And yet he must have slept, for he found himself sitting up and shouting 'For God's sake, run' and, for several minutes, quivered with fear as he waited for some voice from the night to challenge him.

Clancy had begun to feel that he was two men. There was the outside one, the shell that he showed the world. The inventor of tales, the wonderfully adept improviser, the man who could be brave, confront wild savages, shoot people, be revered as a god. The pretender, the liar.

There was another Clancy and he was appearing more often these days. He was the inner man, mortal, frightened, weary of all the posturing and pretence, anxious to live a quiet, genuine life.

Impossible, of course. He had gone too far, built too great a false edifice, told too many lies.

It was the second man who was thinking about Ulla, who was worried for her safety, ashamed of the fact that he had left her and run away.

The characters began arguing.

He had left Ulla because he must keep ahead of Watts. Watts was after his gold. Watts could denounce him. Watts could bring down everything he had so painstakingly created and present both Eliza and himself to the hangman. He had to reach Sydney before Noxious Watts.

Why? the other character asked, and for a moment the

turmoil in his head eased because the first man didn't know what to say.

Then the answers came. The action of running away was instinctive but correct.

He would be safe in Sydney. He was William Clancy Esquire. Watts was a rogue, a dealer in cheap grog, a known informer, a man whose word could be bought for a few pennies.

There was a thought. He'd been thinking he might have to engage some ruffian to dispose of Watts but he could merely pay the man off. Give him a few pounds a week to keep quiet. Even buy his business and pay Watts a handsome salary. That way, Watts would never denounce him. He could even make a profit.

But the idea of giving Watts money was repulsive.

What a shame Arabanoo hadn't put his spear through Watts, rather than the Irishman.

Why hadn't he shot Watts on the steps?

Because then, said his defender, you would have had nothing left to deal with the Irishman. He had a knife. He'd have killed you. How were you to know that Ulla and the two warriors were in the bushes on the bank?

How could he know? How could he have done otherwise? He was damned lucky to be alive.

He had to get to Sydney.

Somewhere, thoughts and dreams melded and he found himself talking to Tench again. He'd liked the Captain. A better man than most of the marines who'd come out with Phillip in the First Fleet. Most of the marines thought they were to be the defenders of a new colony but found themselves cast in the roles of prison guards and, feeling downgraded, made the convicts pay for their frustration.

Not Watkin Tench. He'd taken a few prisoners with him, including the young Clancy Fitzgerald, when he went searching for a way across the mountains. They didn't find the way but they were good days. He treated the men fairly, Tench.

He was saying, 'So you've found the way. Good for you, Fitzgerald. In a hundred years' time, when there are free settlers living in this land, people will talk about you and make you something of a hero.'

'No one else knows.'

'You must tell people. I'm writing a book. Do you want me to put it in my book?'

Then the dream got muddled. The old farmer with the draughthorses was there and so was Macaulay and they began arguing about the book and the horses were restless and their harness began jingling and Clancy was a boy again and had to grab the Clydesdales and quieten them. The men were still arguing and Tench was trying to talk above them. The shouting was painful. Clancy awoke with the sharp end of a branch caught in his back.

He got up and started walking again.

He thought of the boy. The sight of him hiding behind the tree had touched him, made him frightened for the boy's safety. That was his son. Big eyes, strong features, more like his mother than his father, but his son. He'd never truly thought of him in that way. He was Ulla's boy, the result of a casual union, one of a squad of youngsters who ran along the creek and followed their mothers when the tribe went hunting. He enjoyed playing with the boy. He liked the touch of those delicate little fingers gripping his hand, felt a certain affection touching that sleek, dark skin or running his hand through the boy's mop of curls and he liked to hear Wonngu's people tell him what a good, strong, bright boy he was. But it wasn't until the moment when he knew his son was in danger and saw him helpless behind the tree that he had a feeling of attachment.

His boy. He might never see him again.

What would happen if he were caught, never able to return across the mountains?

Ulla would probably be handed on to some other man and Wileemarin would be raised to know another father. He would grow up, take a black woman, maybe two or three, and Clancy's seed would be spread among the people who lived on the far side of the mountains.

He could never raise a son with a name like Wileemarin in civilised society. Will, perhaps. Not that it mattered for no one would ever accept a coloured lad as his son. Wonngu's people had no trouble coping with a boy who was half white, half black but Sydney would never recognise him as William Clancy's heir. He might be tolerated as a servant. A coachboy perhaps, to be dressed up like a black doll.

Just as he'd never thought of Wileemarin as his son, so had he never regarded Ulla as his wife although, in truth, she was just as much his wife as Eliza.

He was confused. He liked both women although he found it easier to live with Ulla than with Eliza. Except for that one pathetic speech begging him to let her accompany him to Sydney, Ulla had never made any demands. By contrast, Eliza was being increasingly critical and more demanding; insisting that he spend more time in Sydney, read more, speak better, go to church every Sunday. Pretend to be a man that he was not.

He told her he was doing enough pretending. There were some things he could not alter. Why was she complaining? They were rich. She had all any woman could desire.

The simple truth was that she was behaving like a white wife.

Now might be a good time to go to Cape Province. Sail away for a few months. He had the *Empress* and the *Caroline* and he could go where he wished. China, perhaps.

But what to do about Noxious Watts?

*   *   *

584

Watts had trouble in catching his pony. It had broken away from its tether and was a mile away, grazing in a paddock but still attached to the cart. As a result, he was two hours late leaving The Green Hills. At about one in the morning he passed the place where Clancy was sleeping and around five, when a hint of dawn first defined the ruffles in the clouds filling the night sky, he decided that no man on foot could have gone so far and stopped where a dense thicket provided a hiding place for the pony and cart. With both pistols in his belt, he sat beside a clump of bushes overlooking the track and waited.

Ulla was feeling sick. It was the new baby and several times she stopped to retch although Wileemarin, exhausted from all the bumping and jogging, remained asleep on her back. Once she stopped at a creek to drink and wash her hips and legs, where the boy had wet himself in his sleep.

Clancy was still ahead of her. With the sky lightening, she now caught an occasional glimpse of him but mainly she sensed that he was ahead. She'd stopped when he'd stopped during the night, although she hadn't slept. She'd heard a horse pass and had stayed hidden, holding her hand over Wileemarin's mouth for he was restless at the time. Neither Berak nor Arabanoo would come with her. They had done as she asked and released the three men on the boat, then left the river and headed for Clancy's crossing. She had promised Berak his hat and Arabanoo his belt although she was not certain if she would ever see them or any of her people again. She was Clancy's woman, committed to him and she would go wherever he went.

No one came during the night. Eliza had had nightmares about falling from a great height and hurting herself so she could not go and claim her daughter, and in the dream she had seen a sailing ship leaving the harbour and she was lying on a hard floor, unable to move or make a noise.

Over the water, she could hear Caroline crying for her mother until the sound faded and the ship disappeared from view.

When she woke, therefore, the first thing she did was send the Javanese boy to the guesthouse to fetch Emily Waters.

She was to stay with the girl in the stables, she instructed. Food and water had already been placed there. If someone came, she was to hide in the loft.

'Is there trouble, ma'am?' Emily asked.

'If I am taken away,' she replied, not looking at the maid and finding it hard to express her thoughts, 'you are to wait until the callers have gone and then take Caroline to the cove and find Captain Murchison. You will give him the letter.'

Ulla thought of calling out to warn Clancy because she could see the man hiding in the bushes, but she was too far away. All she could do was move off the track so that she wouldn't be seen, and approach through the trees.

She saw the man—the same man who had been on the boat—jump out with a gun in his hand. She saw him make Clancy turn and saw him hit Clancy on the head with the gun. He then went into a thicket and emerged with a small horse and cart, piled Clancy and a bag into the back, looked in the bag for some time, and then drove off.

She began to jog and Wileemarin cried but it didn't matter. No one would hear the boy's cry, and the horse was drawing away from her.

FIFTY-FIVE

CLANCY HAD THE smell of rum in his nostrils when he first stirred, because the boards of the cart were impregnated with the stuff. Rum and sweat. Not just his own, either, although there was plenty of that, but there was a strange sour, sweaty smell and it was in the cloth pressed tight against his face. The sort of smell a man makes when he runs until the sweat pours from him because he's frightened and the fright adds its own peculiar stench. Repulsive, like fear itself.

The back of his skull hurt and his body ached from shaking up and down on wooden planks and there was a constant gravelly rattling noise, a kind of a swishing sound with a tinkling, clanking, wheezing and the clip-clop of hoofs. Hoofs?

A horse?

He knew it was a horse. His mind was clearing. He was in a cart. On his face, jammed against the back of someone. He moved his head to get away from the stench.

'Oh, you're awake, are yez?' Noxious Watts slowed the pony to a halt.

He got out quickly and led the pony off the track. With one hand holding his pistol, he used the other to sling the reins over a branch.

'Out' he said.

Clancy's legs scraped and slithered on the floor of the cart but didn't move him an inch. They seemed detached, belonging to someone else. 'Can't move,' he said in a slur.

'Move, you bugger.' Watts grabbed him by the ankles and hauled him out, so that he landed chest first on the dirt. The fall hurt, but it shocked him into a kind of alertness. He lay there, wondering whether to feign unconsciousness, pretend he'd broken his leg, make a bolt for it or try to talk his way out of it. Watts kicked him in the ribs.

'You and me are going to have a little talk. You're going to tell me where you're finding all that gold. Do that and I might not put a bullet through your skull.'

That cleared things a little. He now knew he could run and not be shot. In the legs, maybe, although that was a difficult shot, but not in the body or the head. The man would not risk killing him, not until Noxious had discovered what he wanted to know.

His legs still felt remote, strange. He wiggled his toes.

'If it's gold you're after, we can do a deal, Mr . . .'

'Oh come come, Clancy. When you talk like that I know for sure you're Clancy Fitzgerald. He was always full of the sort of blarney you're goin' on with.'

'I'll be anyone you like, if it makes you happy. But we can do a deal. What do you want? The gold?'

Watts laughed softly. 'Not just the piddling amount you've got in that bag, me lad, but the mine. I want to know where it is.'

'And I suppose if I said Africa, you'd be less than reasonable?'

'I know it's on the other side of the river.'

Clancy was testing his legs. They felt good. He sat up, moving with an exaggerated display of stiffness. The morning flies had found them and were tickling his skin and burrowing into every orifice. He slapped his face. 'Damned flies. They're not as bad as this in Africa.'

He thought Watts was going to hit him with the pistol.

'Will you stop talking about Africa? Why would you be carrying a bag of gold with you out here if you'd found the stuff in damned Africa? Now, don't test my patience, man.'

'Look,' Clancy said, rising to one knee and extending a hand, as though preparing to negotiate.

'No tricks,' Watts said, backing away and raising the pistol.

'It's an amazing thing,' Clancy said, holding his head and taking a few dizzy steps, 'but I think we've stopped quite close to where the place is.'

'You're not saying there's a goldmine near this track?'

'No but the gold I found when I was in Africa is buried near here. I came back from Cape Province with quite a haul. Far too much to leave in Sydney. There are too many thieves around there. So I buried it out here.' He was pleased with that. A remarkably believable thing for a man to say, particularly one with a splitting headache and a fear burning within that would scorch the devil himself.

He took a few steps, then ran. He weaved as he went, in case Watts did shoot, but his legs weren't as good as he thought. Too wobbly. He went at the knee on a rough part of the track, recovered, then crashed on his side. When he rolled on to his back, Watts was above him with the barrel of the gun pointing between his eyes. The man's hand was shaking. Whether through nerves or anger, it was a bad sign.

'It's in a cave,' Clancy said, determined to have the last word. 'I've got a black boy guarding it. You might have seen him last time we met out here.'

At that point, the pony bolted.

Having crushed some berries that she knew had a mildly narcotic effect and fed the juice to Wileemarin, Ulla had left the sleeping child in a safe place and crept up to the cart. She had taken the bag and loosened the reins. She knew what a slap on the rump would do to a horse. Now she backed into the bushes as quietly as she could, hoping the man with the gun would follow the bouncing cart, not come back to see what had caused the pony to bolt.

She had taken off Clancy's old trousers for they were light in colour and too easily seen. She wore only his long brown shirt that came to her knees and had drawn it around her waist with a belt of plaited hair. She lay in the shadow of the bushes and watched.

'The gold,' Watts shouted as the pony and cart disappeared down the road. He began to run after them but he took no more than a few steps before spinning around to make sure Clancy had not got away. 'Up,' he shouted, waving the pistol frantically and jumping up and down in frustration. 'Get up, get up. Run. In front of me.'

And so the two men ran down the road, Clancy jogging and holding his head and going as slowly as seemed reasonable and Watts shouting at him and waving the pistol. The pony stopped once on the crest of a rise and began nibbling a patch of grass at the side of the track but then Watts shouted and the pony took fright and cantered across a rough paddock, so that the cart bounced and shook and rarely had its two wheels on the ground at the same time.

'Can you see the bag?' Watts shouted and, in truth, Clancy couldn't but he didn't answer for he was short of breath and if the bag had fallen out, that was a good thing and he wasn't going to help Noxious Watts find it.

What he was hoping for was that Watts would mistakenly fire the pistol—pointing up in the air, of course—as he ran over the rough ground. Then he could turn and either fight it out, and he had no doubt he could beat Watts in a fair fight, or just run away.

What he did not want was to run into a squad of soldiers; but as they jogged over a hill they came to a small camp being struck for the morning. There were a few soldiers lazing around a fire, muskets stacked in interlocking tripods, but already dressed in their red coats and white pants and tall shakos. Some guards, sombrely dressed and looking unhappy with the prospect of facing another day, were supervising about twenty convicts who were pulling down the tents and packing gear.

One soldier, crimson arms waving, stopped the pony and held it by the reins.

Clancy kept running, already being within twenty yards of the group, but Watts stopped and let the pistol dangle.

Three soldiers took their muskets. Another stepped forward, a tin drinking mug still in his hand. 'What have we got here?' he said.

'Thank God,' Clancy said. 'This man has assaulted and robbed me. You saw him chasing me over the hill.'

'Whose horse is this?' A runaway horse, it seemed, was of more interest than two running men. He had not yet seen Watts's pistol.

'Mine.' Watts came forward. He'd thrust the pistol through his belt. His mind was racing. He was not going to get Clancy to tell him where the mine was or where this mythical store in a cave might be. Not now. He still had a chance of walking back along the route taken by the pony and finding the missing bag of gold. So he said, being temporarily impelled by vindictiveness rather than greed, 'And this man, sir, is an escaped convict, wanted for murder.'

'Nonsense,' Clancy said, spreading his legs and thrusting his thumbs into his belt. 'This man had me as his prisoner until a little while ago. It was only when the pony bolted that I was able to get free. He has beaten me, threatened my life and stolen my belongings.'

'And who are you?' the soldier asked

'William Clancy, merchant, shipowner and respectable citizen.' He pointed at Watts. 'And this villain is known, with good reason, as Noxious Watts. He runs a sly-grog shop in Sydney and is a known criminal.'

'I'm a free man,' Watts protested, ' and an honest one. I want this man arrested.'

One of the guards stepped forward. A small man, as toughened and twisted as a dead branch, he walked up to Clancy, then Watts.

Clancy saw him and his heart chilled.

'That's Noxious Watts all right,' the guard said. He returned to Clancy. 'And this is another man I served with. His name's Clancy Fitzgerald. He and a big bastard by the name of Macaulay are wanted for murdering two soldiers.'

The soldier had no great liking for the guards. Many were former convicts and renowned for their cruelty towards those who were still in chains. 'And who are you?'

'The name's Ned Corcoran. Back in '98 I was in the same gang as these two and that brute Macaulay.'

'But this gentleman says he's William Clancy. I've heard of William Clancy. Everyone has.'

'He's Clancy Fitzgerald.' Corcoran moved closer to Clancy. 'Your pal Macaulay almost broke my arm to get on the end of the line so's you two could escape. I never forgot. I swore I'd get me own back and now I will.'

They took both Clancy and Noxious Watts to Parramatta. After more questioning, Watts was released. He immediately got in the cart and whipped the pony into a trot, to meet de Lacey and give him the news.

Later, a manacled Clancy was marched under guard to Sydney Town.

FIFTY-SIX

T HE *RAVEN* REACHED Sydney that morning. The captain had done well. Pleading the need to wait for a turn in the tide and using some of de Lacey's cash to hire extra labourers at the jetty, he'd managed to load one ton of cabbages and two of potatoes before setting off down the river. He'd anchored overnight near the wide sweep where the Hawkesbury met the Macdonald River. Early in the morning, with a strong wind whipping spume from the crests of curling waves, they'd followed the white sails of the larger *Empress of China* down the coast and had moored in Sydney Cove by eleven o'clock.

Rotherby was waiting. He'd had time to refine his theories into alarming worries.

'I assume your voyage was fruitless,' he began. 'And please, Quinton, don't say "No but there were plenty of cabbages" because I've been worried about you, dear boy—in fact, worrying *for* you—and I could not bear one of your droll responses.'

'Not fruitless. I met William Clancy.'

'On the river?' Rotherby sat down in disorder, one surprised limb getting in the way of another.

'At the settlement. The poor chap had had no luck in his quest for *bêche-de-mer* and was calling in to see what produce he might pick up. Gather some crumbs, as it were.'

'You talked to him?'

'Dull fellow. Quite a disappointment, after all I'd heard.'

Rotherby had regained his poise. 'You told him your name?'

'What an extraordinary question. Of course.'

'And he wasn't surprised?'

'My dear fellow, why would he be?'

'My dear fellow, you were possibly looking for him many years ago and he would be well aware of the fact.'

De Lacey was silent. He lit a cigar, frowning. 'I don't follow you, Edwin.'

'I have reason to believe,' Rotherby continued, 'that William Clancy is, in fact, Clancy Fitzgerald, the fellow you've been obsessed with for all these years.'

'Impossible.'

He took one of de Lacey's cigars. 'Hear me out. While you were away, I went to see the Clancy woman.'

'How dare you call her that and how dare you do that. I expressly forbade . . .'

'Quinton,' he said, lighting the cigar and expelling the first smoke with a flourish that filled one corner of the ceiling with a swirl of grey, 'the situation was desperate. Your life, your career was on the brink of ruin.'

'Nonsense.'

He ignored the interjection. 'Before seeing her, I was told certain things.' He recounted his conversation with Jamieson.

De Lacey walked to a window and wrenched the curtains apart. 'A convict woman? You base such an assumption merely on the fact that a drunkard like Jamieson alleges to have heard a piece of slang.' He spun around. 'What if she did use such an expression, as a means of better communicating with her servants?'

'Quinton, she did not deny that she had been a convict.' He waved the cigar like a wand. 'What do I care if the woman's an emancipist? No business of mine. Good luck to her. But then I thought, if she were a convict, what do we make of the story William Clancy tells about their meeting in Cape Province? And all the other stories about their purported past in Africa.'

De Lacey sat down. 'I don't care if she was a convict.'

'Good for you.' Rotherby sat beside his friend. 'But I took a gamble. Believe me, my sole purpose was to get to the truth, to protect you from scandal or from doing something foolish.'

De Lacey had lost his anger. His eyes wandered towards Rotherby, tripping over details in an aimless journey.

'I said to her, "I know about your husband as well".' He drummed a tattoo on his knee. 'Up to that point she had been well under control. Had me rattled, in fact. She was even-tempered, aggressive when appropriate, absolutely unruffled. But the remark about her husband seemed to be her undoing. She said the most remarkable thing. She said that I, of course, would tell you. That I could not even let poor Captain de Lacey be free of the horrors that had obsessed him for all these years.'

'Obsessed me?'

'Those were her words. She was, of course, referring to your search for the three convicts.'

De Lacey turned away. 'I don't understand.'

'Quinton, you have to face the very real possibility that Eliza Clancy is the woman you've been hunting, Eliza Phillips.'

Ulla had seen The Green Hills at the time of the flood but never a town like Parramatta. She followed a long, narrow track that had been smoothed for easy walking and it had houses on either side although the buildings were set a long way back. On one side all the houses were in a line and looked the same. They were all larger than Clancy's hut in the valley. They had high-pitched roofs and stone structures at the side that were almost as high as the roofs and were shaped like hollow tree trunks and emitted smoke so that the street was wreathed in fumes, for there was no wind and the smoke hung low. The people seemed obsessed with bringing an artificial orderliness to the land, because the ground around the houses had been dug up into furrows, as neat as rows of the finest curled hair, and there were rows of green plants, all in squares, all the same size, all the same colour. Trees had been cut down and some of the larger buildings at one end of the long track had high wooden fences.

It was an alien landscape.

On her side of the mountains, people lived with the land. Like the animals who shared the country with them, they took what they needed and moved on. They didn't dig up the ground, except to get lizards or grubs. They didn't build houses because they never stayed in one place and they didn't plant strange bushes in neat little rows, or dig trenches or make long straight tracks to walk on, or build fences or light fires that were hidden within stones where no one could use them.

The fires mystified her.

People were used to seeing Aborigines lounging around town and the sight of a woman wearing an old shirt and carrying a child and a couple of bags excited no interest. She sat under a tree near the building in Parramatta where they had taken Clancy, saw the other man drive off in his pony and cart and was there when four soldiers brought Clancy out and marched him off to the east. His wrists were chained together. So were his ankles, although the central part of the chain was hooked to his belt so he could walk more easily.

They were moving slowly, and thus she was able to let Wileemarin walk for some of the way. She had food in the bag and gave him some dried meat and berries she'd gathered on the way from the river.

It was mid-afternoon when they reached Sydney Town. She followed them to the gaol, a stone building erected near the upper end of High Street seven years earlier. She could see the bodies of four men hanging from the gallows beyond the wall. Several blacks were squatting in the shadows outside. She joined them.

She tried talking to the other Aborigines but no one understood her. After a while she walked around the walls, calling softly in her own language. At the third wall, whose shadowed stones were already dripping sad curls of moss, she was answered. It was Clancy's voice. She moved to a barred window. It was too high for her to see inside.

'Ulla, go home,' he whispered. 'It's too dangerous for you.'

'I will stay with you. What are they doing to you, husband of mine?'

'They intend to kill me.'

Inside the cell, a thought struck Clancy and, in a rattle of chains, he struggled to his feet. He moved as close to the window as he dared. 'Ulla, love of my life,' he said, still speaking in the dialect of Wonngu's people, 'I want you to do something for me.'

'Of course,' she answered.

'Go to Eliza. You know Eliza?'

'Yes,'

'I've told you about the house many times. Can you find it?'

'I can see it. It is on a hill, with other houses?'

'Yes near the corner.'

'I see it. It is the biggest house, with many eyes.'

'Good girl. Go there straight away. Tell Eliza she must run away. They know who we are. They will come for her and hang her. Do you understand?'

'What is hang?'

'It doesn't matter. Just remember the word. Can you tell her that?'

'Yes.'

'Repeat the message to me.'

She did and she was word perfect.

A guard came to the door of the cell. 'Who are you talking to?'

'Just singing an old Irish song,' Clancy said. 'Do you know Gaelic by any chance?'

'Stop this nonsense.'

Clancy sang, 'Go now, Ulla. Tell Eliza. Then come back and talk to me again. Be careful.'

'I said stop that noise,' the guard snarled.

'At a guess, I'd say you're not Irish.'

'And thank God for that because I'll be alive tomorrow and you'll be dancing on the rope. Save your songs for then.'

The pony had gone lame crossing a creek and Noxious Watts walked the last six miles to Sydney. Limping from sore feet, he'd taken the pony to the stables behind his shop, unhitched it from the cart, had a stiff rum and then gone to the house where de Lacey was staying. The captain, still numbed from his conversation with Rotherby, was incensed at the sight of Watts who, by now, was as ruffled as a rag doll that a cat might have played with.

'I told you never to come here,' de Lacey said and stepped back, for the man smelled of horse dung and rum and sweat.

'And I said I'd come if I had news.' Watts was exhausted from his efforts. So much of his energy had been devoted to reaching the captain before someone else brought him the news (and possibly claimed a reward) that his thoughts on tactics were inchoate.

He blurted out, 'I got him.'

'You've got whom?'

'Fitzgerald. Clancy Fitzgerald.'

'What do you mean you've got him?'

Rotherby joined de Lacey at the front door. 'Who is this scallywag?'

'A ruffian who is trying to extort money from me. Thomas Watts.'

Watts straightened his coat and did up two buttons. 'When I last saw you,' he said, ignoring Rotherby, 'I was in pursuit of Fitzgerald. I waylaid him on the road to Parramatta. By cunning and sheer physical strength, I overpowered the villain.'

Rotherby leaned forward. 'Was the man sick?'

'Edwin, please.' De Lacey moved out on to the step.

'He should by now be in prison in this town. If you wish to see him, I suggest you hurry because already they are talking of execution.' Watts had one leg on a step and leaned forward. 'By the way, he had been living in this town for some years under the assumed name of William Clancy.'

De Lacey said, 'You caught William Clancy?'

'Indeed. In *propria persona*.'

Rotherby laughed. 'A pretentious scallywag.'

'What are you talking about?' de Lacey said.

'I have proved that Fitzgerald and William Clancy are one and the same person.'

'Nonsense.'

'Don't you nonsense me.' Watts waved a hand at the building's facade. 'Just because you live in a fancy house.' He immediately regretted his rashness, but he was tired beyond caution.

De Lacey's eyes narrowed. 'I'll ignore your impertinence, Mr Watts, if you'll tell me what you're talking about.'

'The man known as William Clancy, but who is in reality Clancy Fitzgerald, is now in the gaol here, less than ten minutes' walk from your house . . . your very nice house.'

'I met William Clancy on the river only yesterday. He, like I, has this morning sailed down from the Hawkesbury. We followed his vessel into the harbour.'

'That cannot be possible.'

'Oh, I tell you, it is.'

'You promised to pay me money if I found the convicts and I have.'

De Lacey momentarily re-entered the house and emerged with a riding crop. He raised it threateningly. 'Will you be off? I want no more of your tales.'

'That's Clancy Fitzgerald I caught which means the woman he's been living with must be . . .'

De Lacey struck him on the shoulder and, lashing out with a fusillade of blows, forced Watts on to the street.

'You promised to pay,' Watts shouted before running away.

'Quite a good show, old boy,' Rotherby said from the top of the steps. 'But he's merely saying what I've been suggesting.' He raised a hand in mock defence. 'Why don't I go down to the jolly old gaol and see who's there? You wait here. I'll be back soon.'

Ulla came to the Clancy house and, not knowing how to attract anyone's attention, threw stones against the door. After a while, the Javanese boy came to a window. 'Go away,' he said.

'Eliza.' She had forgotten most of her English. 'Eliza and Ker-lan-see.'

A few minutes later, the front door lock rattled, the hinges creaked and Eliza peered through the narrow opening.

'What do you want?'

In her own language, Ulla said, 'I am Ulla, daughter of Wonngu and wife of Ker-lan-see, my father's reborn uncle.' It was a formal introduction, a statement of tribal belief.

Eliza had not spoken the language for some time and didn't understand all that Ulla had said. She had to stop to think of the words to use. 'I don't know you. And my husband is not your father's reborn uncle.'

'But I am Ulla, daughter of Wonngu and wife of Ker-lan-see.'

'And I am Clancy's wife, not you.'

'You are his white wife, I am his normal wife.'

'You are not his wife.' She had begun speaking loudly and checked herself. She looked up and down the street. It was important that no one, not even the Javanese boy, heard her conversing in an Aboriginal tongue. She opened the door a fraction more. 'Come inside,' she said.

The Javanese boy was hovering nearby. Eliza ordered him to the end of the hall, to make sure no one interrupted or overheard.

A sickening feeling was swelling within Eliza. 'You have a baby. Whose is that?'

'Mine.' Ulla smiled shyly. 'It is a boy. He is Ker-lan-see's son. We call him Wileemarin.'

'Clancy's son?' she said weakly.

Ulla nodded and said, 'I have come from Ker-lan-see. He has a message for you. He says you must go. He says . . .'

'Just a minute. Where is Clancy?'

'In the house where the walls are thick and the windows have sticks across them.'

'I don't know what you are talking about.'

'I followed him there.' Ulla put down the bag with the gold and used her free hand to draw pictures in the air. 'He was taken there by men with red coats and high hats with a feather on the top and long thundersticks, like Ker-lan-see first brought to our camp.'

'Soldiers? He's been caught by the soldiers?'

'He said they knew who you were. You are to run away or they will . . .' she paused to think of the word and to stop Wileemarin fidgeting on her back, '. . . they will hang you.'

Eliza took her into the drawing room. She sat down. Ulla squatted on a rug and put the boy on the floor but he was frightened and stayed clinging to his mother's arm.

'How long have you been married to . . .' Eliza couldn't say 'my husband'. 'To Clancy?'

601

'Long time.'

'How old were you?'

'Almost thirteen.'

'Oh my God.' Eliza had visions of Clancy indulging in wild orgies with a child.

'And he lives with you when he goes to the other side of the mountains?'

'Yes. We get the yellow stones together.'

Eliza studied Ulla for some time. She was a pretty girl— woman—although her face was already lined by strain and weariness.

'You're only a child,' she said.

Ulla misunderstood and said, 'No, there will be another one.'

They sat silently, facing each other.

'So,' Eliza said at last, 'Clancy is in gaol and he told you I am to run away.'

'Yes. He said it was important. He said they will kill him but you are to run away, while there is time.' Ulla held Wileemarin in both arms. 'Why are the white men going to kill Ker-lan-see?'

'Because white men are cruel.'

'We would not kill such a man.'

'No.' Eliza felt very old. She nodded to herself several times. 'Have you eaten?'

Ulla shrugged. 'When we could.'

'I will send you to the kitchen. They will give you food and milk for the boy.'

'Thank you.'

'Then you must go. The soldiers mustn't find you here. You will go out the back door. Someone will show you the way.'

She rang for the maid who tried, with little success, to appear unsurprised at either the sight or the request.

When Ulla had gone, Eliza began to cry.

FIFTY-SEVEN

ROTHERBY WALKED OVER the bridge that crossed the Tank Stream and proceeded along High Street to the gaol. With his tall silk hat, long black coat, ankles protected from the mud by tailored spatterdashes and his silver-tipped cane, he was undoubtedly the best-dressed visitor to the gaol that day. The gaoler, a tall man with a face unmarked by any hint of feeling, unravelled himself from a wooden chair and regarded Rotherby with astonishment.

'Are you aware that Captain de Lacey of His Majesty's Marines has been seeking a man by the name of Clancy Fitzgerald for the past eight years?'

The guard might have asked who the devil Rotherby was but was overawed by his appearance and his question. He said, 'Who's Captain de Lacey?'

'Oh dear, oh dear.' Rotherby turned in a circle, examining the area. He used the tip of his cane to touch a stain on the gaoler's jacket. 'A hero of the European war, a confidant of Lord Thomas Cochrane, future Earl of Dundonald and a man who dares tell Governor Bligh to wait at his convenience.' He moved the cane from one hand to the other. 'Now answer my question.'

'No, I didn't know.'

Rotherby was using the cane as a Neapolitan might use his

hands. He let the handle touch his chin. 'Then I hope for your sake you really do have Fitzgerald here. I'm told the man you have detained is in reality William Clancy, Esquire.'

'So he says. But we got two witnesses that says he's Fitzgerald.'

'And who might they be?

'A gentleman called Corcoran and a gentleman called Watts.'

Rotherby roared with laughter. 'I don't know Corcoran but Watts is a rogue. No man in his right mind would listen to him.' He leaned forward and winked. 'How much did he pay you, eh?'

'He didn't pay nothing. Fitzgerald was just delivered to me.'

'But I've no doubt that, for the right sum, you'd do what you were asked?' The man's eyes narrowed and Rotherby knew he'd discovered an area worthy of development.

He used the cane to brush some rubbish out of his way. 'If the man you're holding is William Clancy, you'll probably be on the end of the rope, not your prisoner.'

The gaoler gripped his hands tightly. 'I just do what I'm told.'

'Then clean the place up. When Captain de Lacey comes down here and finds you're running a pigsty, he'll have your head.'

'Why's he coming here?'

'I told you. He has been leading the search for Fitzgerald for all these years. Fitzgerald should have been delivered into his custody, not yours.' He turned to leave. 'There'll be hell to pay for this, mark my words.'

Eliza had already sent a note to Captain Murchison asking him to have the *Caroline* ready to sail at a moment's notice. His ultimate destination would be Shanghai, where the sandalwood would be sold. He was to tell no one of her plans; she understood that Lieutenant Jamieson was planning a rival operation.

Murchison sent a reply that he could leave two hours after

sunset, when wind and tide should be most suitable for sailing down the harbour. Now, Eliza sent the maid Emily with Caroline to board the brigantine and wait for her. She would go later, suitably disguised in shawl and long coat, and board soon after dusk.

She took the remaining gold from the safe beneath the floor and put it in her case and went to the drawing room, where she would hear anyone approaching the house.

She sat in the semi-darkness, thought of playing the spinet, and even touched some keys to let the sound of a few discordant notes expire in the far corners of the room.

She could never think of this room without thinking of de Lacey. She wanted to see him before she left. It was irrational, dangerous, but she yearned to be with him, to touch his hand, to say goodbye.

That was impossible, for it was de Lacey who would hang her. She would send a note instead and have it delivered in the morning. She went to the desk and began writing.

Clancy had decided he was going to die. Since being captured he'd met no one with a glimmering of sympathy—nor intelligence, which was just as damning—and being back in chains, locked in a filthy cell and without hope of reprieve, he was resigned to hanging. He'd go cheerfully. Turn on a good show for his final performance. Play the part of William Clancy to the end and leave people puzzled.

So this was the end. Never mind. He could have been caught on the first day and strung up to the nearest tree. He'd had eight good years. Remarkable years. He was, he reflected, probably the first white man to have lived with the blacks. He understood them better than anyone else. Liked them, too. He'd have been happier if he'd been born a blackfellow.

And he'd had a couple of entertaining years playing the role of the richest man in Sydney, enjoying himself and fooling everyone which, for him, were the two most important things in life.

It had been worthwhile.

Ulla was back on the other side of the wall.

'You saw her?' He whispered because there would be no hope of tricking the guard again with a tale about Gaelic songs.

He caught her soft, sibilant 'yes'.

'And what did she do?'

'She gave me food.'

'But is she going to run away?'

Not knowing, Ulla didn't answer.

De Lacey had been busy, using his quill and finest paper to write a few documents and letters. When Rotherby told him what he had seen, he dressed in his uniform and went with his friend to the gaol.

'Bring him to me,' he demanded of the gaoler.

'He stinks, sir.'

'So do you. Now bring him here.'

Rotherby noted the location of Clancy's cell and went outside. He'd seen people waiting by the walls of the prison and went to the outside of Clancy's cell. A black woman was sitting there. She had a child and two bags.

He was in the mood to act on impulse. He knelt beside her. She seemed frightened and squirmed away. 'Clancy?' he said.

She had enormous eyes. 'Ker-lan-see.' She touched her chest, then laid a hand on Wileemarin's curls.

He pointed to her and said 'Clancy's woman?'

She nodded.

'And Clancy's boy.'

'Son.' She knew that word.

Thoughts tumbled in Rotherby's head. The long absences. The inexplicable, never-ending supply of gold. Why Clancy had been inland, up the river, not up the coast. This woman was the key to so much.

'What's in the bag?'

She didn't understand.

He touched the smaller bag.

'Yellow stones,' she said innocently.

'Let me see.'

The gold meant nothing to her and she let him look.

He almost whistled but stopped in time. He kept two small nuggets and admired them.

'Yellow stones. Clancy?'

She nodded and closed the bag and, feeling she had done something wrong, clutched it tightly in her lap.

'I give these,' he said slowly, touching his breast as he spoke, 'to Clancy.'

She nodded. 'My man.'

'Yes, your man.'

When he returned inside, Rotherby found Clancy seated at a bench. He was covered in mud and grime and was chained hand and foot.

'You wretch,' de Lacey addressed the gaoler. 'This is my friend Mr William Clancy. I can personally vouch for him.'

'I've been told to hold him. A magistrate's coming some time and they're going to hang him.'

'No they're jolly well not. Unlock him now.'

'I can't do that, sir.'

De Lacey withdrew his sword.

'Oh dear,' said Rotherby, moving in to take the gaoler by the arm. 'I've seen him take off a man's head with a single blow. It's quite a feat. Pretty to watch. Depending where your point of view is, of course.'

The gaoler tried to shake himself free but Rotherby had a remarkably strong grip.

'Captain de Lacey is empowered to take Clancy Fitzgerald into his personal custody,' he said in a soft, winning voice. 'So if you really have Fitzgerald, you must hand him over straight away. He will sign for him and absolve you from all blame. However, if the man is really William Clancy, as the captain insists, you should hand him over anyhow. You don't really have a choice.'

'I was told to hold him.'

'By Captain de Lacey?'

'No, of course not.'

'No need for impertinence.' Rotherby delved into his pocket and produced a nugget. 'I was going through Mr Clancy's things and I found this. He has a goldmine, you know.'

'I heard talk,' the man mumbled. Rotherby let the nugget fall into the gaoler's hand.

'Can you keep a secret?' By now, he had produced the second, slightly larger nugget.

'He has a mine twenty-seven miles upstream from The Green Hills. Ever been there?'

'No.'

'Twenty-seven miles. On the western bank of the river. It's near a large gum tree that's bent over, like a hook. I'm told you can't miss it.'

'Why are you telling me this?'

'Well, if you give me your keys, I won't tell anyone else about the gold until tomorrow morning. There's a lot of gold there. In half a day, you'll be rich.'

The man reached for the nugget. Rotherby clenched his fist. 'The keys, first.'

The gaoler produced the keys, unlocked the manacles at Clancy's wrists and ankles, accepted the second nugget and ran from the building.

'Is there any truth in what you've been saying, Edwin?' de Lacey asked as he replaced the sword in its scabbard.

'Let's take Mr William Clancy home and find out.'

De Lacey turned to Clancy. 'People will be watching, Mr Clancy. When we get outside it's important that you walk upright and proud, like a free man.'

'There's a woman outside,' Clancy said, his voice croaking because he'd been without water all day.

'I know about her,' Rotherby said. 'I'll bring her along.'

At de Lacey's house, Clancy bathed and drank tea and had a quick meal of bread and mutton. Ulla and Wileemarin were in the stables. Only Rotherby joined the two men. He sat quietly in a corner of the room.

'I think it's time for some truthful answers,' de Lacey said.

'First I should thank you for getting me out of there,' Clancy said. 'But I'm puzzled. You have committed an unlawful act. You have placed yourself in jeopardy.'

'I have my reasons.' They were now drinking sherry and de Lacey eyed Clancy over the rim of his glass. 'Now please, no games. Are you Clancy Fitzgerald?'

'Yes.' Clancy had resolved to tell de Lacey the truth about himself but he would lie to spare Eliza. 'And I know who you are. May I ask a question?'

De Lacey was sipping his sherry and nodded.

'Are you doing all this so you can take me back with you to England, have me hanged there, to sort of clear your own conscience or whatever it is that's been driving you all these years?'

'Not at all.'

'Then what are you going to do with me?'

'It depends on what you tell me.'

Clancy leaned back in the chair, crossed his knees and began to talk. His eyes never left de Lacey.

'Macaulay and me planned to escape,' he said, lapsing into the rough voice of Clancy Fitzgerald. 'I didn't think we could

609

make it but we got off the chain and I went down to the river while the big fellow went into the camp to get the keys to get rid of these.' He shook his wrists, as if they were still encumbered by metal bands. 'Macaulay was very strong but not clever and so he murders a guard he didn't fancy. Meantime, I'm down by the river where it's shallow and I find this girl there.'

'What girl?'

'I don't know her name. I never did know her name. She'd had a hard time with the guards and just come down to bathe herself. You know, have a wash. Nothing more.'

'And you didn't know her name?'

'Never did find out. She was just a slip of a girl. Had a hard life. Nothing ever went right for her. You know the sort. This place's full of them.'

'Go on.'

'Well, Macaulay comes storming down to the crossing and half the army's after him and the girl panics and comes with us across the river. Macaulay and me gets separated. I ran into him later. He told me he'd killed a soldier. The man was a brute. Mind you, he had plenty of cause to kill someone. We'd been given a hard time and him most of all, being the biggest and stupidest.'

'So you had nothing to do with either murder.'

'Nothing.' He didn't seem to care whether he was believed or not and he didn't care, being convinced he would ultimately meet the hangman.

'What happened to the girl?'

'She died. No food. She didn't last long. She was weak to start with.'

'And Macaulay?'

'Speared by the blacks.'

'Why weren't you speared by them?'

'I wasn't with him. He'd hurt his leg and was dragging behind me. We were moving down the river and he must have run into this war party. Anyhow, he got himself killed.'

'And you didn't?'

'No.'

'Where have you been all these years, Mr Clancy?'

Mr Clancy. Was there a hint of respect in the question?

'I met another mob of blacks. Friendly. The woman outside is the daughter of the chief. Her name's Ulla.'

'And when did you come back to civilisation?'

This was the tricky part.

'I don't want you to be trying to drag Eliza into all this. You can hang me if you like but you should leave her alone. She had nothing to do with this.'

De Lacey refilled his glass. 'I merely asked when you came back to town.'

'I stole some money, got on a ship bound for Cape Town. Got off there. That's where I met Eliza. Her name's Eliza Richardson, by the way.'

'So she's not a convict?'

Clancy bristled with indignation. 'Who told you that?'

'Never mind.' De Lacey glanced towards Rotherby's corner. 'Go on.'

'What else is there?'

'The gold. How did you acquire so much wealth?'

'There's gold in Africa.'

'You're not telling me you found all that gold in Africa.'

Clancy smiled. 'Have you ever heard of anyone finding gold in this God-forsaken land? You're lucky to find grass, let alone gold.'

'Back to the woman, whose name, incidentally, was Eliza Phillips.'

'Eliza?' Clancy seemed amused.

'The Phillips woman led me into an ambush. Many men died.'

Clancy nodded to himself. 'She told me about that. She was on a hill or something?'

'I saw her waving. I took my men up the hill. The savages were hiding in the forest.'

'She told me she was going to give herself up. She didn't know the blacks was there.'

De Lacey spent a long time examining the sherry bottle. 'So she didn't know?'

'No. She was done in. Ready to give herself up.'

'Why didn't the blacks kill her?'

'They had their hands full with the soldiers, I suppose. I don't know.'

De Lacey rose, took the sherry bottle and refilled Clancy's glass.

Magistrate Henry Shawcroft had been relishing the prospect of handling such a *cause célèbre* as the trial and subsequent execution of so scurrilous a hoaxer as the man who had played the role of William Clancy. The hanging, he thought, should attract at least a thousand people, some even to the elevated area of The Rocks where they would gain a view of the miscreant dangling and dancing on the rope. He would order only one hanging that day, so special would be the occasion. However, Shawcroft arrived at the prison late that afternoon to discover both prisoner and gaoler gone. Others reported having seen the gaoler run from the building. Later, Clancy left in the company of two distinguished looking gentlemen. The magistrate immediately ordered soldiers be sent to the Clancy house.

Eliza had just finished her note to de Lacey when she heard the tramp of boots on the path outside. She ran to the back of the house, found a maid and instructed her to answer the door in one minute's time. She was to say the mistress had been out all day and the master was still not back from his voyage to the north.

Clutching her case beneath the shawl, Eliza left through the stable gates. She didn't know where to go. To head for the waterfront would almost certainly result in her being seen by the soldiers. She couldn't bear the thought of confessing to Lieutenant Jamieson. Instinct, rather than intellect, took her to de Lacey's house. She entered through the back and, in the stable area, saw the black woman, Ulla, sitting in the shade of a peppercorn tree.

They went into the stables and talked.

Rotherby, checking to ensure the Aboriginal woman had not gone walkabout—a habit of certain blacks, he had been told—heard them talking. He stayed outside for several minutes before entering the stables.

'My dear lady,' he said, venturing surprise at seeing Eliza, 'what on earth are you doing here?'

'There are soldiers at my house. I believe they have come to arrest me.'

The stench in the stables was awful and Rotherby raised a perfumed handkerchief to his nose. 'Thank God you came here. It is probably the one safe place in all of Sydney Town. Although for how long, I cannot guarantee.'

Eliza touched Ulla's arm. 'The lady has been telling me that Mr Clancy is here. I believe the captain has taken him from the prison and brought him to his house. I don't understand.'

Rotherby took Eliza by the arm. 'Come, I think it is time you saw the captain.'

FIFTY-EIGHT

ELIZA HAD EXPECTED to find Clancy in chains; in a cellar perhaps or in some dingy room, with his face clouded by an expression befitting a man whose freedom had ended and whose life was limited to hours. Instead, she found him in one of the front rooms—on the chaise longue of all chairs—laughing as if he'd told one of his jokes (for he had a special way of laughing at his own wit) and drinking sherry. De Lacey rose as soon as she entered and took her hand.

'How propitious that you should call.'

'It was more necessity,' she said, her face flushed at seeing de Lacey and Clancy together. 'The soldiers are at the house. I left by the rear entrance.'

Clancy raised an eyebrow. 'You've met?'

'Once before,' she said.

Rotherby came forward and took de Lacey aside. 'She believes they have come to arrest her,' he said and then continued in a whisper. 'I found her in your stables, with the black woman who is attached to Mr Clancy. And Quinton,' he added in an even lower voice, 'she and the Aboriginal woman were talking in another language. She was fluent. I think you will draw the same conclusion that I have.'

'An Aboriginal dialect?'

'Hardly French, Quinton.' He was about to withdraw to his corner but turned sharply and took de Lacey by the arm. 'The satisfaction of the hunt is in the hunt, not in the capture. You have the chance to go two ways, Quinton. Back into the past and continue this life of torment you have chosen for yourself, or you can go forward, forget the sorry happenings of all those years ago and think only of the future.' He left and sat at the far end of the room.

Eliza sat near Clancy. There was room on the chaise longue but she avoided it.

'Some amazing things have happened,' Clancy said brightly. 'I've told the captain everything. How I really am Clancy Fitzgerald. How the two who escaped with me, Macaulay and the woman, whatever her name was, both died within a couple of days of the escape.'

De Lacey let him talk.

'The woman died?' she said, not being able to stop herself.

'I never told you that, did I? There was a woman involved when we crossed the river. Poor thing died of hunger. Macaulay got a spear through his gut. I got away and spent a year or two living with the blacks. You know about that.'

'Yes,' she said, thinking of Ulla.

'The captain knows your name is Eliza Richardson, that we met in Cape Province, and all that stuff.'

She lowered her eyes. 'And what is he going to do?'

De Lacey came forward. 'Actually, I'm in rather a ticklish situation. I couldn't let them hang Clancy. It seems I'm the only one still interested in the case and from what Clancy tells me, it was Macaulay I wanted, not him or the woman.'

'No.' She was about to say more until she caught the warning flare in Clancy's eyes.

'You're not implicated, of course,' de Lacey said and, at the far end of the room, Rotherby let his lips curl in a smile. 'The one they'll be after is me. I told the man at the prison that your husband was definitely William Clancy and Edwin somehow persuaded the fellow to unlock the chains and let him go. When the fuss really starts, the one they'll be looking for is me.'

'You?' she said.

'Clancy has kindly done a couple of things for me.' He produced a scroll. 'At my suggestion, he has signed this paper giving full ownership of the *Caroline* and her cargo to you.' He handed her the paper.

'But why?'

Clancy stood up. 'I think you should go away, at least till the fuss dies down. You know what these people are like. They're inclined to hang someone first and then get around to discussing the wisdom of it at leisure. So you've got to go. Tonight.'

'By coincidence, the ship is ready to sail,' she said.

'Wonderful. Get on it. And remember, it's yours. You'll be needing some money. Sell the sandalwood. Keep the ship or sell it. It's yours.'

'And what about you, Clancy?' She glanced, not at Clancy but at de Lacey.

'I was thinking I might go back over the mountains.'

'I met your . . . your woman.'

'She's a nice girl. Wonngu's daughter.' And then he added rapidly. 'Wonngu was the name of the chief of the tribe I lived with for a while.'

'Oh I see,' she said and Rotherby, enjoying the performance, touched the tip of his nose.

'Did you say "over the mountains", Mr Clancy?' Rotherby said.

'I found a way.'

'How remarkable.'

'I'm a bit of a blackfellow at heart. Which is why I'm going back.

I was tiring of life in town. All the money, all the trimmings, all the worries of the rich.' Clancy laughed. 'So you see,' de Lacey said, 'Clancy and I have agreed we each need to get out of town, fast.'

'And I, the expert at rapid departures, will probably stay put,' Rotherby said.

No one suggested that Clancy and Eliza should go together.

'Where's the girl? Caroline,' Clancy added, as if the name had escaped him for a moment.

'She's safe.'

'She'll go with you?'

'Of course.'

'I've written a letter to Edwin,' de Lacey said, temporarily losing sight of his friend in the shadows.

An eyebrow raised in surprise, Rotherby came forward. 'To what do I owe this honour?'

'Officially, you'll discover the letter tomorrow,' de Lacey said, passing it to Rotherby. 'It explains how I've departed for South America with my good friend, William Clancy. I say in the letter that I'm convinced of his innocence but doubtful of his receiving a fair hearing in this town. You know the sort of stuff. It is quite an eloquent letter. People might even think the whole notion rather romantic.'

'Quinton, you'd never met Clancy prior to this afternoon. People know that.'

'Not met him in this country. In the letter, I point out that we'd met in Africa.' He laughed, amused by his own inventiveness. 'There is, by happy coincidence, a vessel leaving in the morning for Valparaiso so please don't spread the news until that ship is well clear of Port Jackson.'

Clancy had gone outside to speak to Ulla. Rotherby, so adept at being a shadow, had disappeared. Eliza and de Lacey were alone.

'You asked me once to leave,' he said. 'Now I must seek your help in leaving.'

'But you're sailing for Chile.'

'My letter says that. In truth, I had hoped I might go in the opposite direction. Seek an enormous favour and sail with you to China.'

She caught her breath.

'There are things I don't understand,' she said, not daring to meet his eyes.

'There are things we need never discuss.'

'I can never repay you.'

'Oh, but you can.'

'It will be a very long voyage, or so I am told.'

'Exceptionally.'

Clancy returned.

'Are there any further things you need?' de Lacey asked Eliza.

'No. I have all that's necessary.'

'And I have nothing,' Clancy said, 'which is enough.'

De Lacey said, 'Well, I must get a few things together. If the soldiers are already at your house, they'll be here within the hour. I'll be back within five minutes.' He left them alone.

'Well,' said Clancy. 'Who'd have thought . . .'

'You have acted most honourably,' she said. 'Thank you.'

'You're a good woman, Eliza. Far better than I deserved.' He walked slowly down the room, touching the back of a chair, admiring a painting. 'Do you like that man?'

She covered her eyes. 'How can you ask that?'

'Because I could sense a certain feeling between you two. Did you see him while I was away? Is that what's happened?'

'Once or twice. And nothing's happened.'

'Such a shame he's off to South America.'

'Yes.' She felt bad at the deception but she was never as accomplished a liar as Clancy Fitzgerald, even in intimate moments.

618

'You will look after Caroline? After all, she's part mine.'

'A pity you didn't feel that way about her more often,' she said.

'Well, that's life, and that's the way I am.'

'I know that to be true,' she said.

The soldiers came at sunset, as the party was making its way past the peppercorn tree. As they crossed the stretch of bushland at the back of the house they could hear the blows on the front door and Rotherby's voice, strident in his demands to know what the racket was about.

Clancy had brought with him some ash from the fireplace and now proceeded to blacken his face and hands. He removed his boots and socks and did the same to his feet.

'The first thing to do,' he said to de Lacey, who was watching in fascination but listening for the sounds of pursuit, 'is to get away from this area. Do you mind if a couple of blacks follow you? Your servants, perhaps?'

'You'd better carry the bags,' de Lacey said and Clancy muffled a laugh. He stuffed his muddied jacket into Ulla's bag and his boots in the bag with the gold. And only then did he notice she had the gold.

'You do miraculous things,' he said and she smiled.

'There's gold here,' he said as they hurried off, de Lacey and Eliza leading, Clancy and Ulla following, burdened with the bags and the child. 'I think we should share it. A third to Eliza, a third to you, de Lacey, and a third to me.' It seemed natural not to include Ulla in the division. 'I have gold,' Eliza said.

'I have no need. You might,' de Lacey said.

They came to High Street and were immediately challenged by a squad of soldiers.

'We're looking for a Mr William Clancy,' the leader said.

'I believe he lives over that way.' De Lacey pointed.

'We've been told to search everyone heading towards the port.' De Lacey pulled back his cloak to reveal his captain's insignia. 'Oh, beg your pardon, sir. I didn't know, sir.'

'If we see him, we'll call out. I know the gentleman by sight.'

'Thank you, sir.'

When they were out of earshot, Clancy said, 'A dangerous thing, wearing your uniform, wouldn't you say.'

'I thought the risk worth taking. And I am not going to leave town scurrying like a rat, but in style.'

'Give me the rat every time,' Clancy said, wiping his blackened cheeks.

Near Sydney Cove, they separated. Clancy and de Lacey shook hands, Clancy kissed Eliza goodbye. It was a kiss on the cheek, a cool brother temporarily farewelling his sister.

'We might meet again,' he whispered when de Lacey had taken a few steps to ensure the way was clear. 'Down by a river, perhaps.'

'You're a good man, Clancy Fitzgerald.'

'Indeed I am. Take care of our girl, won't you?'

De Lacey had returned.

'You've got a long wait, captain, if your ship doesn't sail until the morning.'

'Things are organised. And what about you, Clancy? You've got a long and hazardous walk ahead of you.'

'I'd better be getting used to it. My days of riding fine horses are past, I'm afraid.' He reached for de Lacey's hand and drew him closer. 'You know, don't you, you crafty bugger.'

'I'm sure I don't know what you're talking about.'

'Just look after her, that's all I ask. She deserves better than me.'

With his arm around Ulla, he watched them walk towards the wharf where the boat from the *Caroline* would be waiting.

'What will we do?' Ulla asked in her own tongue. There was no suggestion of anxiety; just curiosity.

'We'll take it easy to start with,' he said and when de Lacey and Eliza were out of sight, led her towards the waterfront. He'd noticed the *Empress of China* anchored at her usual moorings.

Captain Andrew Craddock was delighted to be offered half the gold. And, even more, to be given the *Empress*. 'I wrote something out back there,' Clancy explained, passing him a sheet of paper. 'It's a bill of sale. She's yours, legally. Now give me back the gold. That's the price.'

He laughed at the look of reluctance on the Scotsman's face. 'Just joking, Craddock. Testing your sense of humour. Both the boat and the gold are yours. All I ask is that if I ever need a lift somewhere, you'll take me and my family wherever I ask.'

'Oh you've got my word for that, sir.'

They led the *Caroline* down the harbour, for the *Empress* was easier to get under way and more nimble in enclosed waters. But once through the heads and travelling north towards Broken Bay and the mouth of the Hawkesbury, the larger brigantine began to overhaul them as it crowded on sail.

It was now night but the sky was ablaze with stars. Clancy was alone on the bow. In the starlight he could see the brig's sails glistening silver to match the shivering caps of the Pacific's swell.

The *Caroline* drew close and, just as Craddock was about to swing to port and enter the river mouth, Clancy caught a glimpse of Eliza, standing alone by the rail.

'Now that's a lovely sight,' he said and briefly closed his eyes, enshrining the vision to memory. When he opened his eyes again, he raised a hand and, in the faint light, imagined he saw her wave back.

On the far side of the mountains, where the night wind blew through the valley and the possums rattled the eucalypt branches, old Delbung woke from a deep sleep and began to wail. She knew, she told her daughters, that she would never see Eliza and her strangely coloured baby again.

On the same night Wonngu had a dream and in the morning his heart was filled with joy for he knew Clancy was coming home.

HISTORICAL NOTE

THIS BOOK CONTAINS a mixture of fictitious and real characters. Governor Hunter, of course, is real as are George Bass, the surgeon turned navigator-explorer, and such major characters as the other governors of New South Wales. Morrison, the colonel in charge of the NSW Corps, is fictitious. The real CO of the Corps as of January 1798 was Col. Francis Grose, who left that year to join the British army in Ireland. There were nine lieutenants, but none named de Lacey!

The first settlement on the Hawkesbury was at Windsor in 1794. Until Macquarie's time, the settlement was known as The Green Hills—the name used in the book. An alternative name was Mulgrave Place. The town was built on the banks of the Hawkesbury, but was devastated by the flood in 1799 and inundated by several more floods in the early 1800s. Governor Macquarie later moved the town inland to higher ground. It is therefore accurate to say that Clancy Fitzgerald could see buildings from the river. Early drawings show large stone buildings right down to the river bank.

It is also worth remembering that the Hawkesbury has changed course considerably since the last years of the eighteenth century, due to the frequency of floods and consequent erosion of the banks. (There were ten major floods between 1799 and 1819.) In the Windsor region, the river now flows 500 yards south of its original course. The word 'Deerubin' used in Chapter 5 was the Aboriginal name for the Hawkesbury.

The flood referred to at the end of Chapter 29 was real. At the time of our story, the sources of the Hawkesbury were unexplored and, thus, the settlers had no knowledge of the swollen streams that fed the river. In February and March of 1799, major floods swept the Hawkesbury. In the first, the one Clancy and Ulla witnessed, the river rose in just a few hours to a height 50 feet above its usual level. The town was badly damaged (the store being among the buildings washed away) and crops destroyed so that Sydney nearly starved.

In 1802, the noted ornithologist, George Caley, referred to the kookaburra as the Laughing Jackass or the Hawkesbury Clock—the name given the bird by the settlers along the river. He made the point that there were virtually no clocks in the region. Thus, the settlers were dependent on the kookaburra to rouse them in the morning.

In Chapter 4, Clancy and Eliza are carried back by the tide from a sloop moored at The Green Hills. These days, the river is tidal only to Wiseman's Ferry—certainly not to Windsor. But 200 years ago, it was tidal all the way to the Grose River junction, well upstream from Windsor.

The route Clancy and Eliza took over the Blue Mountains is virtually that taken in 1822 by Archibald Bell jnr (the Kurrajong to Lithgow road now known as Bell's Line of Road). He travelled from Richmond Hill, where he lived, to the Cox's River, taking with him a baggage horse and encountering the conditions described in our narrative. The domed mountain referred to is Mount Tomah, readily seen from today's highway.

In Chapter 22, there is reference to Wonngu's tribe camping beside a lagoon where there were large black and white geese. These are magpie geese which, these days, are only found in the far north but in the time of our story, were spread through the whole of the continent.

In Chapter 26, the hymn that Clancy sings is Psalm 100—known as 'old 100th' and written by William Kethe, who died in 1594.

The gold that the old convict, James Wilkes, had discovered and passed on to Clancy was found in what is now known as the Sofala–Hill End area, north of Bathurst.

The High Street of Clancy's return to Sydney is today's George Street. It did not acquire its modern name until 1810 when the name was changed to honour the king, the part-mad, half-blind George III. Sydney was a different town, geographically, to today. The waters of the harbour extended all the way to modern Bridge Street, so named because of a bridge over the Tank Stream. Circular Quay, which required a great deal of land filling in its construction, was not started until 1839.

Lord Thomas Cochrane, featured in Chapters 40 and 41, is a real character, if outlandish in his behaviour and achievements. The actions referred to in the book are true—his time in charge of the *Speedy*, the black-face incident when he and his crew overwhelmed the crew of the Spanish frigate *Gamo* and the *Speedy*'s capture by the French warships. True also are the later references to Cochrane's 'little wars' or guerillas, which compelled Napoleon to tie up many hundreds of thousands of his troops to guard the Spanish coast. In many ways, Cochrane was a more colourful and more enterprising commander than Horatio Nelson but Nelson was a hero of the establishment whereas Cochrane was a thorn in the side of the admiralty, constantly criticising the lords and their bumbling ways, and was denied the good 'PR' that Nelson got.

E. G.
Sydney, 1995

Evan Green
Dust and Glory

The world's toughest car race. Twenty-one days and ten
thousand miles of searing heat and rock-hard desert
tracks; of driving rain, flooded rivers and icy mountain
trails. Twenty-one days of blowouts and breakdowns; of
subterfuge and sabotage. Ten thousand miles of dust
and glory.

Driving at breakneck speed over Australia's roughest
roads and through the most appalling conditions
imaginable, six competitors break free from the pack
and fight for the lead, gradually finding themselves
entangled in a web of deceit, betrayal and danger:

Jack Davey, the radio star, whose tragic secret threatens
the lives of those closest to him;
Kit Armstrong, Davey's co-driver, determined to beat the
ex-lover she believes has betrayed her;
Harley Alexander, the idealistic young reporter who
uncovers underwork sabotage attempts . . . and becomes
their next target;
Gelignite Jack Murray, the legendary Redex winner,
larrikin and cult hero, who must fight to clear the name
of a mate;
JJ Chesterfield, the ace American driver who is forced to
cheat in the race by a Mafia boss who is holding his
daughter hostage;
Carey Roberts, a Mafia strongman sent to Australia to
make sure Chesterfield wins, who realises, too late, that
his own life depends on the outcome of the race.

Dust and Glory is bestselling author Evan Green's
stirring account of the most gruelling race of them all, a
hair-raising, careering ride that accelerates to a gripping
and unforgettable finish.

Evan Green
Bet Your Life

'You say you could drive into the outback and hide from
the police for a week?'
'Yes,' Kelly nodded vigorously. 'Guaranteed.'
'Bet you couldn't.'
Kelly leaned forward and took his partner's hand. 'You're
on.'

A partner who frames him for murder.
A beautiful wife who double-crosses him.
An innocent bet that could cost him his life . . .

From the best-selling author of *Alice to Nowhere* comes
a blistering action adventure of betrayal and survival. A
compelling thriller about a man and a woman who will
stop at nothing to get what they want . . . and the man
trapped between them.

Evan Green
On Borrowed Time

Who the hell was he? An angel of mercy, impervious to cyclones and shotguns, too holy to debase himself with a woman, or a grade one certifiable looney?

Stephen Malek isn't sure himself.

He's just been sacked from his job as a hack journalist on business tycoon Alex Pascoe's newspaper the *Star*. Believes, due to illness, he has only a year to live. Has diminishing sexual powers. An overprotective Polish mother. A money-grabbing ex-wife. And has basically been a prolific failure for forty-three years.

However, he's about to embark on the most exhilarating month of his life . . .

On Borrowed Time is the action-packed adventure of an ordinary man suddenly thrust into the limelight as a heroic cyclone survivor, a negotiator in San Francisco street crime and the central player in the fight against an international terrorist organisation.